Jack and the Lad

The Barrow Boys of Barking

Book 1

By

Mickey Mayhew

To Ruby, much merriment, Mickey Mayhew!

Text copyright © 2013 Michael J Mayhew

All Rights Reserved

For Wolvie

Prologue

A fair few years ago

'Tell me the Minty Hardcore story again,' Jamie said. 'I'm not tired yet.'. He propped himself up onto his elbows and waited; further down the duvet Pellow's ears pricked up at the mere mention of the name. The dog shuffled over to the far right hand corner, where the covers had been tugged down to conceal various old shoe boxes stuffed under the bed. Uncle Phil was almost at the door, wanting to go back downstairs and watch the rest of the Benny Hill Show; he would cry tears of laughter at the closing sketch, when they played 'Yakety Sax' and the nurses pursued Benny around the park with the film speeded up. But Jamie knew how to pout petulantly, and if this basic button pushing failed, then a simple slam down with all of his fingers on Uncle Phil's emotional keyboard would do the trick. Uncle Phil gave in graciously, smoothing out a space for himself on the blue and purple of the West Ham United duvet cover. 'I want *that* story,' Jamie said, 'you know, the Minty Hardcore story.'

'Minty Hardcore...' Uncle Phil said slowly, and Jamie nodded, punctuating his point. Jamie liked the Minty Hardcore story most of all, even more than the stories about the Hammers; stories into which Uncle Phil would often insinuate himself, jokes about manager John Lyall calling on him to play because Julian Dicks had been taken ill, something like that. Once he'd even said John Lyall had called on him to play when the entire team had been ill, and Uncle Phil had won the game against Arsenal single-handedly. Now, even Jamie, with his tendency to cleave to Uncle Phil in all things, didn't believe that, although the way Uncle Phil told it you would have thought it was true. Not even Uncle Phil could play as well as Julian Dicks. Stories like these made all of Jamie's mates want an uncle like Uncle Phil, who could tell tall tales and make them sound like they'd actually happened. He wasn't like most boys' uncles, half-bladdered in the Barking Dog on a Sunday afternoon and reading someone else's newspaper, a pint in one hand and the other busily scratching the fluff out of their belly button; on a Sunday afternoon Uncle Phil would be giving an impromptu performance of the latest Whitney Houston power ballad, smack in the middle of Station Parade, wailing slightly off tone but still loud enough to cause curtains to twitch and cars to sound their horns, before an enraptured audience of local youngsters.

'Minty Hardcore...' Uncle Phil said again, pursing his lips. He seemed to run the idea of Minty Hardcore around on his tongue like it was something good to taste. He began, 'I don't even know what her real name was. No one does, to this day. All that matters was that she was here, in Barking, all the way from wherever it was she came from, with her girlfriends in tow, for one final night of fun before they were presented as debutantes proper…'

'What's a debutante…?' Jamie asked.

Uncle Phil raised an eyebrow. 'A debutante? A high society girl, my son; dead posh, dead classy. Not East London or Essex at all, although don't tell your Aunt Rose I said so. Or any of your other aunts for that matter. Now, your Uncle Rupert, he once told me that Minty Hardcore originally came from a farm somewhere in the Forest of Dean, and that she was never a deb at all: there's many a myth surrounding Minty Hardcore.'

'Uncle Rupert was dotty, though, wasn't he? In the end, I mean?' Jamie shifted a little.

'Kind of,' Uncle Phil nodded, 'and don't think I never noticed you and your brother asking him who the prime minister was and laughing your socks off when he told you it was Gladstone!'

Jamie grinned. 'That was Jack's idea.'

'Which means it was probably yours, mister!' he jostled Jamie playfully.

'I swear! I don't even know who Gladstone is!'

'Yeah, well…' Uncle Phil eyed him with playful suspicion. 'Anyway, where was I?'

'Minty Hardcore?'

'Right, Minty Hardcore; well there she was, she and her girlfriends, and they were out for a good time on the night before their presentation. Now I'm not sure what a good time in Barking meant two hundred years ago, but I bet the Blockbuster video store wasn't there, don't you?'

'Or the KFC!' Jamie piped up.

'Exactly. Well apparently they arrived on the last night of the Barking Fair; the stalls and sideshows had been cleared away, and our ancestor Jaden Woodfield and his brother were centre stage and slogging the life out of each other, bare-knuckle style, for a baying crowd…'

'Do I look like him?' Jamie asked. 'Jaden, I mean.'

'Well,' Uncle Phil made a frame of his fingertips, superimposing it over the boy's face, clicking his tongue to take a pretend Polaroid picture of pale blue eyes and choppy blond hair startlingly stiffened by handfuls of gel from the 99p shop. 'Hard to say. He was fair too, apparently, and very tall with it. Maybe you'll be as tall one day. Now Minty Hardcore, she saw him lay his brother out and was overcome by the sheer bravado of it all, and it's said that they fell madly in love on the spot; those who saw the fight said it thrilled her no end, that she got dirty dabbing his cuts with the hem of her gown. As the crowds clear away it was said that he and Minty went off to consummate things…'

'…have it off, you mean?'

'Exactly, this taking place in the tavern that would become the Barking Dog. Now she, being a bit of a naughty girl, began the performance by pulling his trousers down and biting him as hard as she could on the bum; apparently she said, "That's thanks for the thighs that'll thrill me so

5

thoroughly!".' And Uncle Phil stopped the story then, slipping his fingers under his shirt and hoisting it up so that the lower part of his back, with the lightly blurred lip print, was exposed. 'And there it is, to this day, passed down to me,' and he added with a grin, 'we're all of us Woodfields daubed with her desire.'

'Mine looks like that too,' Jamie peered under his pyjamas. 'But Jack's is like, crystal clear! It's like one of Uncle Eddie's tattoos, it's so clear.'

'Be thankful yours is blurred.'

'Why?'

'Just be thankful, Jamie Woodfield. But I digress.'

'And what does that mean? 'Digress'?'

'I'm rambling,' Uncle Phil sniffed, stuffing his shirt back in his trousers. 'Anyway, at that point her father and his friends stormed in and caught them in a state of undress, and he was furious, absolutely livid, I tell you! He grabbed her and he bellowed, "If you like these roughnecks so much you can bloody well stay here with them, permanently!' and she of course was delighted, because she didn't much fancy any of the toffs she was due to be paired off with. He sent her to the nunnery - what's now St. Margaret's - just over the road from your Aunt Delia's place. The nuns took her in and there she stayed, only Jaden went after her and made one hell of a ruck, but they wouldn't let her go. There she was, in tears, all dressed up in a nun's habit, and lo and behold one of the wittier sisters had christened her 'Minty Hardcore'. 'Minty Hardcore' went to her window every night where Jaden would be waiting underneath, and they'd coo sweet nothings to each other, but that was all they could ever do. Eventually she'd get upset and frustrated and run inside, and cry into her pillow. She told that pillow everything. It became her only confidant in that place. Those nuns were so mean to her, I tell you, mean and nasty in the way that plain people often are to the beauties of this world, although the plain people, well they'd deny that was ever the case. They picked on her constantly, trying to shoo Jaden away every night, although he constantly came back; they'd cross themselves when they heard him shouting up to her window, and her replies so enthusiastic also! - "I love you, Minty Hardcore!!" he'd shout, and she'd holler back, "'I love you too, Jaden Woodfield! Oh so very much!!". Sometimes she'd call to the nuns in the adjoining windows and say, "Come and look at my Jaden! See how handsome he is!!' and when they heard such talk, well the nuns would cross themselves and go off to say Hail Mary's for the damned, debauched soul of Minty Hardcore.'

'Uncle Eddie says that's why they're called 'nuns',' Jamie said, "coz they don't get nun; you know, 'nun',' and he framed the word with little quotation marks made by his fingers.

'That may be true,' Uncle Phil cocked his head. 'Now, as word got around, other men came to see this beauty in bondage, but Jaden would beat them all back, declaring, "Who's the Daddy?? Who's the Daddy?!?" and Minty Hardcore would cry out, "Oh but you are, Jaden Woodfield!!"

However, time went on and Jaden didn't come to the abbey as often as he had. He stopped trying to do things to impress her. The fact was, he'd found a nice girl and had a baby, and he sort of forgot all about Minty Hardcore.'

'Why couldn't she escape?'

'Her father had washed his hands of her, and on a generous stipend to the abbess there she was to stay, until the day she died. She had sisters who could be presented to high society in her stead, so he didn't need her anymore.'

Jamie kissed his lips. 'That sucks.'

'Don't it just.' Uncle Phil sniffed. He laid back, hands behind his head. 'She grew older, no more the daisy fresh girl, upset to see Jaden married but happy that he was happy, and happy too when he had a son. This son got married and had children of his own, long after Jaden himself had passed away. Now apparently Jaden's son wasn't much to look at, but Minty Hardcore kept an eye on him, and on his children in turn. I think she thought they – Jaden's grandkids - were a bit more of a chip off the old block than his son turned out to be, you know? She was very taken by Jake, the elder by five minutes, as he grew up...'

Jamie glanced over at him. 'Like Jack's my elder by five minutes?'

'That's right, but the youngest one – his name escapes me - well she wasn't much bothered by him, and he died of croup when he was only five.'

'What's croup?'

'Kind of like the flu,' Uncle Phil said, 'but a bit more vintage. But before that happened, well they were orphaned in a tragic accident when they were toddlers, and the nuns had to take them in, as was the custom in those days.'

'I like this bit the best,' Jamie propped himself up a little more. 'Tell it like you always do, with the voices and everything.'

Uncle Phil nodded, closing his eyes. 'One day, when Jaden's grandson Jake was all grown up, one of the nuns, a particularly nasty one called, rather ironically, Sister Loveday, well she came to Minty Hardcore's door and said, "Have you heard, Minty Hardcore? The grandson of your beloved Jaden Woodfield is doing a star turn at the Barking Fair tonight, and after that it's rumoured he will take his act into London proper, and never will Essex see his like again! They say he can walk a stretch of hot coals without even flinching, and wrestle wild beasts to the ground with his bare hands!! They say the sweat of such exertions mats the hair to his chest!" and to this Minty's eyes widened.'

'Do you look like Jake, Uncle Phil?' Jamie asked. Pellow's ears flicked up at this, and he sidled along the bed and nestled himself under Jamie's arm.

'Well I don't know, little fella...' Uncle Phil made a steeple of his hands, his long fingers barely touching at the tips; an ample arch. 'It was all a very long time ago. Jake was darker than his grandfather, from all accounts; I think your cousin Casey is supposed to look a bit like him.' He went on,

'Now Minty was absolutely frantic. She paced up and down the length of her drab little dorm, clutching her pillow to her chest, whispering to it, her voice becoming so frantic that all the other nuns came to the door of the cell to watch, and to laugh, pointing their fingers with their horrible, dry nails arching accusingly at her.' "Jaden," she was whispering, over and over and over, and "Jake" too. Anyway, the nuns went to sleep at six, and…'

'Six!!' Jamie gasped. 'We're just watching 'The Simpsons' then!!'

'Well, this was how nuns lived, little fella. Now, Minty Hardcore waited until there was silence throughout the abbey and then she got up and went to the door, and began to pick the lock, because you see, they locked her in, daily; they'd locked her in from the time she'd first arrived there, as a girl of fifteen. And here she was, now almost eighty five years old. They put a chastity belt on her sometimes too, but the less said about that the better; awful things, chastity belts.'

'Eighty five…' Jamie's eyes widened, 'even older than Aunt Queenie!'

Uncle Phil nodded, 'Even older than Aunt Queenie. Now, Minty Hardcore picked the lock, and out into the corridor she stepped, her precious pillow tucked under her arm, feet bare so as not to make any noise. She could hear the other nuns snoring in their cells on their own pillows, but their pillows weren't special, like Minty's was.'

'Why was it special?'

Uncle Phil seemed to be searching for the words but seemed unable to expand on the saucy sentiments that were causing a faint upward curl of his lips. 'It was just a pillow, at the end of the day; worn and stuffed with horsehair, stitched at one end, a head-shaped dip near the right side. And it was the most precious thing in the world to her, her only confidant all those long, lonely years. Rumour has it she whispered all the love she had for Jaden into its thread and its seams. Legend has it that the pillow heard how frustrated she was, and echoes those lusty lamentations back to whoever now lays their head on it.' And he seemed distracted, as if remembering, that upward curl of his lips threatening to erupt into an out and out smile. 'When you're older some pretty girl will tell you all about it, you little heartbreaker,' and he ruffled his hair. 'Now; Minty crept along the corridors, down the steps, and was at the main door when lo and behold, she heard a voice boom out behind her, "Don't you take another step Minty Hardcore, you crafty little whore, you!!" and who else was it but the Mother Superior, flanked by that awful Sister Loveday, and on the other side of her sour old Sister Harkett, a woman who could've curdled McDonald's milkshake just by looking at it. Minty Hardcore was cornered, her back to the door, the nuns advancing on her, their sticks in their hands, rhythmically slapping them against their palms as they closed in on her. "You have a whore inside of you, Sister Minty," the Mother Superior said, "a crafty little whore that craves fine, virile young men, men such as Jake Woodfield, and you nothing more than the aged whore lover of his grandfather!!"

"They say a fount has sprung where he waited for her," Sister Harkett sneered, over the Mother Superior's shoulder, "a fount that baptises all the boys bathed therein with unholy endowments; this sickening spring erupting from the longings your Jaden left there for you each and every night!" and they crossed themselves at the mere mention of it, one and all.

And the Mother Superior said, "Well Minty Hardcore, we are going to do what we should have done a long time ago, what your father begged me to do when he put you into our care; we are going to beat that whore out of you. And you'll thank us for it!".' Uncle Phil shifted a little, 'Now, tomorrow night I'll tell you if Minty made it out of there or not, and if she got to see Jake doing his final turn at the Barking Fair, and most importantly of all, if she managed to pass her precious pillow to him.'

'Why would she want to give him her pillow?!' Jamie gazed at him as though he were quite mad.

Uncle Phil kissed Pellow's wet nose and then ruffled Jamie's choppy crop a final time. He went to the door, his thumb hovering above the light switch. 'Go to sleep, Jamie Woodfield. Put your head on your own sweet pillow and go to sleep. We've got a game tomorrow, remember.' And with that he snapped the light off and closed the door; from behind it came the whispered, 'Love you millions.'

It was two forty five in the morning when Jamie woke up, the snow coming down heavily on Station Parade, collecting on his windowsill. The faulty light on the Barking Underground sign meant that the 'B' would flash off and on and make strange shapes on his walls and his ceiling. This made the snow look like it was moving.

He'd been dreaming of something scary, not quite a nightmare but bad enough that he'd woken up with a start; some horrible harridan trying to drag him into the fridge or something, and Uncle Phil sleeping right through his awful screams as he'd raked his nails on the new linoleum in a final bid to free himself. Anyway, he'd woken with a start and was just settling back down onto the pillow when he'd heard Uncle Phil's bedroom door open, a pause, and then the sound of it closing, followed by footsteps padding down the stairs.

He slipped out from under the duvet and demurely opened his door, catching sight of Uncle Phil's unkempt brown hair disappearing down the staircase and into the kitchen, the beam of a torch lighting his way. Jamie heard him pad down the second flight of stairs to the front door, open it, step out, and then close it purposefully behind him. Jamie patted the sleeping Pellow and then crept along the landing and down the first flight of stairs into the kitchen, peering through the curtains. He could just see Uncle Phil as a blue blob in his pyjamas running across the road, past Donna's newsagents, past the jewellers, before careering to a halt by the KFC. A woman was waiting for him there, a woman who obviously wasn't his Rose, waiting for him with folded arms. She had wavy blond hair, big elaborate finger curls all around her face, and skin that looked like paper, wonderfully white and unblemished. Her large, dark eyes took in the sight of Uncle Phil with delight, a faint smirk forming on her lips. Those lips were like a big smear of red that curled and pouted as Uncle Phil came closer to her, shining the torch in her face. She wore a big fur coat, kind of pastel pink, matching the dress underneath. On her head sat a big, round sun bonnet, to Jamie's mind a wonderfully weird thing to wear on such a cold winter's night. It was kind of mean to think it, but she was prettier than Aunt Rose, but Aunt Rose was all soft and warm and all smiles, and despite her sun bonnet Jamie knew this woman was as cold and brittle as the snow beneath her feet.

His eyes still full of sleep as he opened the front door, Jamie thought maybe it might have been his best friend Adam's mum; she had wavy blond hair, and was always throwing herself at Uncle Phil, bending over and dropping things in front of him so you could see her pastel pink bra. When she wasn't doing that she was asking him to come and take a look at her tumble-dryer when her husband was at work and there was nothing really wrong with it anyway; a lot of Jamie's friends' mums fancied Uncle Phil, but Aunt Rose would laugh about it, saying light-heartedly that she only wished they would take him off her hands for a while. Uncle Phil had big brown eyes that all the ladies loved, and he was tall too, and Aunt Rose had told Jamie that being tall when you were a man was like having a magic key that opened the lock to many of life's problems. However, she'd added, if you were a woman and you were tall then unless you were very pretty that key was in fact a bit rusted and bent, like if Uri Geller had gotten hold of it. This lady over by the KFC had to crane her neck as she looked up at Uncle Phil, putting her fingers, the nails of which were painted that same shocking red as her lips, lightly against his chest.

Jamie strained to hear what they were saying, but someone somewhere was playing music. The Bull pub down the end of East Street was always open at the oddest hours, Jamie knew because Uncle Phil had played cards in there at three in the morning for a birthday present for him once, a games console, complete with all the 'Sonic the Hedgehog' games. The woman was gesticulating now instead of speaking, fingers first to herself and then to Uncle Phil, then up at the flat, and then all around in a broad, theatrical sweep of her arm that took in the whole of Station Parade from the Barking Dog pub at one end to the Blockbuster video store right down the other. All the while Uncle Phil was shaking his head and generally providing what appeared to be a resounding negative to everything she seemed to be suggesting. Finally he turned on his heel, all too abruptly for Jamie, who was caught out, ducking behind a waste paper bin as fast as he could but clearly given up by the purple and blue of his West Ham pyjamas.

'Little fella?!' Uncle Phil's eyebrows did that funny jiggle thing, one going up higher than the other, then down again as the other did the same. He took Jamie by the wrist and led him back towards the flat, pausing only to cast a glance over his shoulder at the woman. She hadn't moved, staring at Jamie with a vaguely disinterested look on her face.

'Who's that?' Jamie asked, forgetting for a moment to whisper. 'What does she want?'

'That,' said Uncle Phil as he opened the front door, bustling him inside, 'is Minty Hardcore. And when you're older, if you know what's good for you, you'll steer clear of her. Well clear.'

Jamie turned and gazed at the woman, wondering why she wasn't dressed like a nun and on top of that how she could be so young still. For a moment he thought about running over there and asking how Uncle Phil knew her, how she'd managed to escape that awful Mother Superior. She seemed to register his curiosity and chuckled. 'Perhaps I'll tell you one day, my pet,' she said, 'although if the truth were told I'd rather regale your brother, Jack.' And she shivered theatrically, the way most of the girls at St. Margaret's did whenever Jack walked past. 'What a barrow boy he'll be,' she sighed, her hand across her brow. And then she turned on her heel, throwing back her head and chuckling, slipping away into the snow, the laughter soft and syrupy, reminding Jamie of cereal bowls with silver spoons thick with sugar stuck in them. He felt a delicious shiver then, like fine fingernails being trailed up and down his spine.

Chapter 1

Saturday 24th December 2005

There was a fight going on at the coffee stand on the opposite platform, as Jamie waited for the Westbound District line train; two men were pushing each other backwards and forwards in that strange way that seemed to be the precursor to proper fisticuffs, a crowd of onlookers engorging the space around them, some cheering, a few taking pictures on their mobiles, and one or two slightly more responsible citizens maybe actually thinking about calling the police. It was a lot like the pitch-side brawl he and Uncle Phil had been bellowing at in the privacy of the sickroom, some twenty minutes previous, before mum had barged in and grabbed the remote from the top of the DVD player, hitting the 'off' switch with a single, carefully varnished nail; 'Bev!!' Uncle Phil had slapped his brow in disbelief. 'There was no need, sweetheart!'

She'd rolled her eyes at him before turning her gaze on Jamie, who'd been waiting for Uncle Phil to assert himself and switch the thing back on. 'Go and get your brother home for Christmas,' she said, tossing him his hoodie and then removing a fiver from inside her purse. She folded it over not once but twice, waiting until he'd disengaged himself from the somewhat garbled garment before tucking it into his back jeans pocket, patting it there in much the same way she did with the milkman when she paid him, but without the usual punctuating pinch. 'Go and get him and bring him home for Christmas; just him mind you, none of those fancy friends of his. And if he needs any more persuading, give him this.' And off she'd gone into the kitchen in a whirl of lemon-blond hair and market stall scent, returning seconds later with a brown envelope, worn at all corners from repeated handling.

'Mum, he doesn't even like me,' Jamie had said, turning the envelope over in his hands.

'No, he doesn't,' she said, clasping her hands to his face in that way she had, that she usually conferred on all his cousins. 'He loves you.'

'Yeah, but he doesn't like me, does he?' and he'd been about to add, 'and I don't like him much either,' but she'd made a little noise and then gone back to the kitchen. He'd followed her, watching as she turned the beef stew up a bit on the hob, flicking the kettle on almost as an afterthought. 'You're not exactly his biggest fan either,' she'd said, pulling the wooden spoon out of the stew and waving it at him. And she'd caught the guilty grin on his face, one that he'd rapidly wiped away simply by thinking of Uncle Phil in the next room, as sick as a parrot.

Jamie had cleared his throat and said, 'I mean, he doesn't even call me his 'baby brother' anymore.'

'He hasn't called you that since you turned sixteen; you're all grown up now.'

'Yeah, but he didn't stop on account of how old we were, did he?'

Mum made another little noise, and then a kind of cluck, chucking a dismissive gesture into the mix. 'Everyone wants to see Jack, so just you go and get him.'

'Fine,' he'd sighed.

'And the fiver's for my cigarettes, so don't get any ideas about buying one of those nasty 'lad mags' or anything with it!' and then, as he was almost out the door, 'there's a sale on in the Pound Shop, so get me some of those roll-on underarm deodorants, the ones that smell like a wet forest.'

And that was that. Jamie was jerked out of himself as the District Line train finally pulled into the station, just about the same time that the first punches were finally thrown on the other platform. He squeezed the brown envelope between finger and thumb, held it up to scrutinise its content; judging from the jangle there was a key of some sort inside, possibly several. He boarded the train, vetoing sitting near a girl he found rather fit, on the grounds that it was in poor taste to be eyeing totty up when his Uncle Phil wasn't well. He slumped back in the seat and slid the envelope into his pocket as the train rumbled out of Barking and began the brief journey to East Ham, a slight step away from everything he knew, but actually the first of seventeen or so increasingly dissimilar and unsettling stops that would eventually deposit him on his brother's doorstep, or near enough.

Despite being Christmas Eve the train was somewhat sparsely populated, or maybe that was because it was Christmas Eve; he'd never strayed far from the family's safe confines on this particular night. He took advantage of the relative isolation to scrutinise his appearance in the glass window opposite, framed nicely in backdrop by the approaching dusk; there was something humbling about putting oneself forward as the subject of scrutiny for a twin brother who hasn't seen you in a while, a twin brother whom everyone else had always deferred to quite openly as being 'the superior model', in every way, shape or form. Jamie's stubble was growing a treat, and it hardened his overly boyish face into something a little more edgy, the buzz cut punctuating the point. He still had that vaguely wounded, mistrustful expression; he just couldn't help it. He wondered if Jack had kept the same hairstyle also, so that from a discreet distance they could pass for the near-identical twins they actually were. Jamie had pale blue eyes whereas Jack had ice blue eyes; Jamie's eyebrows met in the centre and had to be tweezed into some semblance of normality by their cousin Marie, but Jack had perfectly arched eyebrows, thick and black, hooded, so that those eyes appeared deep-set and even more intense; and on and on it went, as Jamie found himself comparing this and that and falling flat almost every time, and that was just the physical. The biggest word Jamie knew was the word for the type of twins he and Jack were; 'dizygotic' twins, which meant that they weren't identical even though they'd been fertilised together. That was better, in his humble opinion, than being the sort that were carbon copies of each other; had they been blessed equally in both departments he wouldn't have been able to fall back on the rumour that Jack got all the brains as well as all the looks, thus freeing him up to spend the greater part of his time 'dossing', as he was wont to do. That's how it lay with their looks, and it was pretty much the same with anything social. Here he was visiting his brother, who was doubtless enjoying a prolonged Christmas break from the London School of Economics where he was studying psychotherapy and sociology combined, but for Jamie selling sun faded second-hand paperbacks on a stall on the Ripple Road would continue right over the festive season, barring the big-day itself; there would always be some poor old codger by himself who wanted something to read on Christmas Eve, mum had said only the other day.

The train pulled into East Ham and a group of men in Hammers tops and stonewashed jeans boarded his carriage, laughing loudly and carrying bags of shopping with tubes of brightly coloured wrapping paper sticking out the tops. His own present for Jack, a bottle of genuine Calvin Klein 'Obsession', deftly shoplifted, hastily wrapped and stuffed in his inside jacket pocket, seemed like the sweetener to a blow, given the news he was going to have to deliver after he handed it over. He stretched his legs out and wondered suddenly if there was the possibility that he might be marooned in the West End if the trains gave up early. ''scuse me mates,' he called out to the four men. 'Any idea what time the line packs up tonight?'

The four men took this enquiry as an invitation to pick up their bags and join him, inadvertently sparing the fit girl from their lecherous intents, a fact of which he was rather proud when his brain actually caught the connection. They spent the journey from East Ham to Mile End sharing their cans of cheap ale with him, and talking about what presents they'd brought their 'birds', and before that what they were going to give their 'birds' before they actually gave them the present; the innuendo was so badly delivered Jamie didn't get it until he'd switched to the Central Line and was pulling into Bethnal Green. This was where Aunt Amanda lived, seventy odd – very odd - years old and still refusing to tow the line by living in Barking proper, like the rest of the family. For a moment he considered hopping off for a chat, a cup of tea and a slice of her homemade chocolate button cake, but then one thing would lead to another and he'd end up spending the night on the couch and it would be Christmas day and he wouldn't have brought Jack home and mum would want to kill him, as she so frequently did; mum issued more death threats than those radicals with the tea towels on their heads.

The real change came when the train pulled into Liverpool Street, any last vestiges of Essex and the East End giving way to a tsunami of suits, broadsheets folded under one arm and their leather briefcases under the other, a grim look on their faces as they contemplated things that seemed a world away from Jamie's own personal sphere of birds, booze, and second-hand books. Part of him – no, make that a lot of him - wanted to be on the Ripple Road right now, near the band-stand, listening to the carol singers as the other market traders packed up their stalls and headed up to the Barking Dog for a Christmas drink. Maybe after he'd have gone to midnight mass with mum, Uncle Heath, Uncle Brian and Aunt Betty, but then again Uncle Heath always got drunk on Christmas Eve, his misery mounting as the night wore on and everyone else's spirits soared; poor Uncle Heath lamenting the departure of his wife, Jamie's Aunt Sophie, as though it had happened only last week and not some seven years previous as was actually the case.

The train pulled out of Bank and into St Paul's, and he almost dozed off. The group of guys had given him a whole can of Stella as a goodbye gift. He'd downed it then and there as the girl sitting further up the carriage found herself flanked by two rather portly city gents, stealing almost as many glances at her cleavage as he probably was, although he was more of a leg man himself, if the truth be told. He dozed a little again and would've missed his stop if someone hadn't got their walking stick stuck in the door at Holborn. The old lady to whom it belonged banged angrily on the driver's window with it after the fact, much to the merriment of the passengers, some of whom even went so far as to give her a round of applause. As the announcement for the imminent arrival at Tottenham Court Road came over the tannoy, Jamie checked the present and the brown envelope were still in his pocket and readied himself by the door. He turned and stole one final glance at the girl, but she broke it off and turned to study her own reflection in the window opposite.

He'd forgotten her by the time he'd bounded up the escalators, swiping his ticket through the machine and then taking the right hand stairway up and out, which left him at the top of New Oxford Street, directly opposite Burtons and with Centre Point just behind, looming over him like some disapproving figure of West End pomposity. A blast of icy wind rattled through the crossroads and Jamie blew into his hands; an unusually cold December, Aunt Amanda had said some four months ago, locating an especially lucid picture of a snow-blanketed capital in her crystal ball after she'd polished it with some Pledge and then wiped it clean with the back of her sleeve. He fished the directions out of his pocket and unfolded them, scampering behind the bus-shelter as they were blown out of shape by another gust of wind. The bar his brother had pinpointed was somewhere down Charing Cross Road, something called 'Salsa'; the ink was smudged and it might well have been 'Saucy', which got his hopes up that it might have been a strip joint or something. It made him think of the time he and Jack had wandered into a rather ominous looking building off the Shoreditch Road when they were bunking school with several of their cousins, Hayden and Nick, and they'd been greeted by a woman with the biggest pair of bazookas they'd ever seen, dancing around on a stage in purple tassels with something by Culture Club in the background. The manager had thought them quite amusing, with their eyes agog and their jaws on the floor, until someone twigged that they might be Woodfields, helped in part by Nick's rather vocal cautions about Aunt Amanda living just around the corner. At that point they'd been abruptly ejaculated from the premises. Jack had always maintained that he'd developed his desire for large-breasted women as a result of being denied the opportunity to ogle at his leisure on that sunny afternoon; Jack was a budding psychoanalyst, so he was probably right. As for Hayden Woodfield, well he'd gone back a week later and done the windows of the place in, but that was Hayden for you.

The Salsa bar was located directly adjacent to the bottom of Old Compton Street, the façade decked out in a hue of puke orange, big green wreaths signifying the season, and posters proclaiming tickets still available for the big New Year's Eve bash. The bouncers wore those Santa hats with the flashing knobs on the ends of the tassels, which they doffed as he passed. There was no entrance fee at this time of evening, so Jamie slipped down the steps and into the cavernous interior, where the music was booming so loud he could actually feel his bones rattling. He couldn't see Jack anywhere and didn't have the slightest idea what any of his posh university mates looked like; it was at least a year since his first graduation, and the only person Jamie remembered or had even liked was Frank, the Mancunian with the cheekbones and the tendency to make large, expressive gestures with his hands whenever he spoke, kind of like a queer might; cousin Bobby was a queer, everyone said so, and he was always putting his hand over his mouth whenever he was shocked, or throwing his hands up in the air whenever he dropped something and going, 'Oh my gawd!'.

The staircase split at the bottom, the left culminating in a fenced-off dining area, whilst the right yielded the bar and a modest dancefloor. He was jostled from the side by one of the most exotic looking girls he'd ever seen in his life, all strawberry blond hair and cat-like eyes sidling past him with a tray of drinks; she seemed to do a double-take over her shoulder a couple of feet after she'd passed, a vaguely puzzled expression flitting across her face. She didn't look much like the sort of girl Jack went for; he tended to prefer bottle blonds with pretty, if uninteresting faces and average, unthreatening personalities; if pressed on the matter he'd say he wanted to "...fuck two-thirds of Atomic Kitten", and that would be that. The big breasts however, were an essential.

'Jamie!!' he heard his name called before he saw Jack, and then a second time before he was able to discern its location. Jack was sprawled out on a great big leather couch to one side of the busy dancefloor, flanked on his left by a dark haired young lad with large, unblinking eyes – not Frank - and to his right by one of the aforementioned bottle blond types with the big breasts, running her hands up and down Jack's arm and squeezing his bicep at regular intervals; in-between her admiring clutches Jack would give his arm a playful flex, and the comically large muscle would bulge upwards obligingly. To the right of her that exotic looking girl with the cat-like eyes was busy making herself comfortable, eyeing Jamie ever more suspiciously as he moved in. Jamie was pleased to see Jack hadn't abandoned the crop hairstyle after all, about the only thing they did share these days. He looked considerably well groomed, clearly using a costlier pedigree of product than those found on the shelves at the Vicarage Fields shopping centre's ASDA at home. In fact it merely confirmed everything Jamie had mulled over in his mind on the journey here, and beholding his brother framed between two of the fittest girls in the club merely punctuated the point. In fact the details positively dug at him; Jack always seemed taller, his limbs and especially his legs marginally longer than Jamie's; his nose was straighter, prouder, and his profile pretty much perfect, whereas side-on Jamie's nose was revealed as being a somewhat stubby, boyish affair. Jack had a lantern-jaw, verified amid much cooing by cousin Jessica, who'd ran her fingernail up and down the length of it whilst Jack had rolled his eyes and pretended he didn't love all the adulation. That jaw supported a wide and generous mouth, with a smile like a set of piano keys. He was beautiful, put blatantly, although 'beautiful' wasn't a word Jamie bandied about that often, and certainly not where boys were concerned; 'hunky' was another, more popular byword for Jack Woodfield. Moving in closer Jamie took in the t-shirt tight around a near perfect set of pecs, the material suffering the same strain that the sleeves around the biceps were enduring. He was mind-bogglingly buffed, if the truth be told. 'Take a seat, J,' Jack commanded, patting the spot next to him. 'Guys, this here's my twin brother Jamie you've all heard so much about; Jamie, these are…'

'Jack, I got something I need to say, private like,' Jamie licked his lips uncertainly, nodding in recognition of the strangers but wary of them at the same time, as wary as they appeared to be of him. 'Family business…'

There were swings in the little park behind St Giles Church, the kind with those stretched rubber seats that rather moulded themselves to your arse but made actually leaning backwards to relax rather difficult. Their feet scraped backwards and forwards on the safety conscious rubber surfacing as they sat there, Jack gratefully toking on the joint his brother had produced from inside the folds of his Fila hoodie. 'I got you this,' Jamie said eventually, handing over the modest present of the Calvin Klein scent from another pocket. 'Open it now if you ain't gonna come back to Barking tonight. It's your favourite.'

Jack shook the present, and he grinned at the sloshing sound that followed. 'Obsession?'

Jamie sniffed, and gazed off, a little embarrassed, 'Uh huh. I reckon you ought to come back tonight though, seeing as how…' and it began to rain at that moment, a fine mist. Jack's eyebrows did that funny little jig, the way Uncle Phil's eyebrows often did, one raised and the other lowered, kind of quizzical; Jamie had tried to animate his own eyebrows thus on many occasions but had ended up pulling expressions that made him look vaguely, in his own words, 'like a spakker'.

'...seeing as how what?' Jack asked.

Jamie found the envelope, shielding it from the rain with his sleeve. 'Mum says you should have this; Uncle Phil didn't want you to have it but he's like...well he was too weak to put up much of a fight.'

Jack took it and held it up to the light of the moon, his breath wafting over the four corners like dry ice; the light from above, helped by exposure to the rain, had turned the thin paper all but transparent, illuminating what indeed turned out to be two keys inside. 'What are they for?' he asked. 'There's a bit of paper in there as well, isn't there?'

Jamie shrugged. 'Don't ask me, I'm just the messenger.'

Jack let loose one of his big, cheesy grins; on this occasion it looked less like a piano and more like he was gargling on one of those Apple Mac keyboards, glimpses of functional and radiant white that cousin Jessica had christened his 'big, sexy canines.' 'Are these the keys to the family fortune?' he asked, and as he said that his eyebrows went up like a sort of sigh, because they both knew that the Woodfield family, as bloated as it was, didn't actually have two pennies to rub together.

'It was Uncle Phil's,' Jamie explained, wincing as he found himself referring to him in the past tense. 'It *is* Uncle Phil's....only now they're yours 'coz, well...you're next, I guess.' And he sniffed. 'He's sick you know, Uncle Phil is; real sick.'

'What's real sick?'

Jamie felt his eyes well up, and wiped them with the back of his sleeve. 'They reckon he won't see the New Year, Jack.' And then, as if to punctuate the point, 'he's all shagged out.'

Chapter 2

Saturday 24th December 2005

Jamie's brother shared a basement flat off the top end of Islington's Upper Street, just around the corner from Highbury Fields and a stone's throw from the lush veneers and curling iron fences of Barnsbury; former home of the prime minister, mum would say whenever anyone mentioned Jack in relation to where he lived. Unfortunately St. Clements Street seemed little more than an afterthought to the wealth and suburban splendour of Barnsbury proper, the abundance of fly-tipping at the far end only punctuating the point. Right now the abandoned contents amounted to several half-dismantled refrigerators, a tyre, a clothes-horse, and a motorbike. It wasn't quite what Jamie had been expecting, after years of listening to stories that Jack was going to have a penthouse flat in Mayfair, that and a swank office job on Cheapside or Cannon Street, with an Armani suit and a corporate clutch-bag.

Jack led him down a flight of rather blocky stone steps covered in dead leaves and congealed chewing gum, into a little nook housing the battered black front door and the electric meter, the plastic covering of which was cracked and swung to and fro whenever there was a gust of wind. A branch from what Jack would later tell him was the Rowan tree hung at the top of the door, held there by a single rusted nail. 'We haven't cleaned up in a while,' he warned him, a slight grin on his face, 'so don't expect great things.'

'You should stay over with Uncle Heath sometime,' Jamie pointed out. 'I bet this is nothing in comparison. It's a party when he does the hoovering.'

'Mate, it's a fucking rave when we do it,' Jack winked, and slid the key into the lock. There seemed a method to this, as he slid it back out again and then jerked it first one way and then the other before the door itself actually gave.

The flat was rather dingy and dank, any daylight coming into the box-shaped sitting room obscured by the wall and the shrubs outside. The hallway by which they entered was the worst, almost oppressively gloomy, leading also to the bathroom on the left and the bedroom at the end. The sitting room led on through to the rather spacious kitchen, which clearly benefited from the open windows and glass door at the back of the property, where a building site seemed to have been all but abandoned. 'It's quite central when you think about it,' Jack said, slinging his Stone Island trench-coat, with the brown envelope still inside, down onto the nearest of two sofas, this one a soft fabric tangerine affair, and the other a jarring black leather beast that could have sat four or five at least. 'I can be in the West End in ten minutes,' he said. 'And Islington's trendy, you know;

Upper Street has more bars and restaurants than any…well then any other main thoroughfare that I can think of. More than any of the tat on offer down East Street, anyway.'

'How long does it take to get from here to Essex?' Jamie asked.

'Dunno,' he shrugged, making for the kitchen. 'Not tried that way yet, can't say its high on my list of things to do. You tend to drive away from Essex, not towards it, you know?'

Jamie sat himself down on the big leather beast facing the TV; Jack's sofa, as it turned out. He slung his feet up on the coffee table in a touch of disdain for the supposed swankiness of it all. 'Can I have something to drink?' he called out.

'Tea?' Jack hollered back, 'Or something a little stronger?'

'Is that the line you usually feed to that girl you were with? Not the blond, I mean, the other one? The Kate O'Mara clone.'

'Dorothy?' Jack called round from where the kettle was coming to a slow boil. 'She's great isn't she; really exotic looking. I feel a bit sorry for her, she gets hassled every time she walks down the street, and she's really brainy too, you know?' and Jamie could almost see him nodding, verifying the fact for himself. 'Really brainy; she's in my class, and she's always up on her feet declaring this opinion or that, or deriding it, more often than not. She's got a kid too.'

'So are you and her…'

Jack stuck his head around the door, 'Early days, J. A girl like that is worth taking your time over. How's your Tiffany, by the way?'

'We're fine.' Jamie slumped back against the sofa and took in for the first time the rather tame efforts at Christmas decorations; the artificial tree, around three feet high, balanced precariously on top of the TV, and the occasional spray of threadbare tinsel linking one wall to the next. It all seemed very sparse compared to their mum's own outpouring of festive merriment and merchandise. A shelf some way above the TV housed a collection of DVDs and the odd video or two, but it was hard to tell what belonged to Jack and what to his flatmate. Jack abhorred science fiction, or anything in the fantasy vein, instead opting for hard-boiled dramas and the occasional 'cheesy war film'; his movie of the moment, so he'd told Jamie on the way back, was 'Jarhead'. In the other corner near the window a selection of soft toys lay largely neglected and swamped by old Pizza Hut boxes. The bookcase to the left contained row upon row of Jack's university texts, titles so convoluted to Jamie's mind that he couldn't even tell where the title itself ended and the author's name began. Jack abhorred literary fiction in much the same way he did anything vaguely fantastical in the cinematic vein, and so he guessed that the remaining books, collections of ghost stories and Clive Barker novels must have belonged to his flatmate as well. There were some pictures on the opposing edges of the bookshelves; their mum, a kind of haze over the camera giving the shot a slightly ethereal quality, all soft colours and her big, doe eyes; one of their cousin Jessica, always a cut above the other mascara splattered birds who worked in the Vicarage Fields shopping centre, petite and pretty in a strapless dress, the message in black marker like the signature of some b-movie starlet or other, 'To my darling Jack, oceans of love always, 'jess'. Just down from that there was a picture of Jack and Hayden in Universal Studios in LA from several years back, the last big family outing; Jack was on the left, sun-bronzed, blond, and muscular, a big, cheesy grin on his face, his arm around his self-confessed favourite cousin. Hayden was roughly the same size as Jack but beefier, his face a little rounder, eyelids bruised, lips a natural pout that he hated; '…a cherub chock full of piss and vinegar', is what Uncle Phil had called him once. And that jarred Jamie, made him remember. 'Uncle Phil would love to see you,' he said suddenly, almost to himself.

'How bad is it?' Jack asked, returning with a tray and setting it down on the coffee table, slumping himself on the tangerine sofa. 'Oh hey, it's gone midnight by the way; Merry Christmas.' And they clinked their battered green mugs together in unison, and then Jack added, 'You'll have to crash here tonight unless you're willing to fork out for a minicab; travel's a bummer on Christmas Eve.'

Jamie shrugged. He wanted to talk about Uncle Phil, not about what time the 'Tubes gave up. 'Like I said, they don't think he'll see the New Year. He went down real sudden, and he's been bedridden ever since. I've never known him to be like this. Uncle Phil was always so full of life. He's not even that old, you know.'

'Forty two,' Jack said under his breath.

'He's gone all gaunt and drawn,' Jamie went on. 'And his hair's suddenly gone grey at the temples, and his sideburns have gone grey as well. Mum says she can't even bear to look at him like this, that she has to turn away every time she takes the tray into him; once she looked away so much she spilled the tea over him and scalded his chest and everything, and she felt even worse then than she did to begin with.'

'I'll come back with you,' Jack said suddenly, 'and I'll stay for Christmas dinner, veg out for a bit, but I'm coming back here in the evening. You know I can't stand the big family get-togethers. A wake would be even worse. Plus with Hayden being 'away' and all…' 'away' being Jack's polite way of saying this his favourite cousin was banged up along with his twin brother Nick for GBH, something Nick had had nothing to do with and Hayden, along with his trusty custom-made Linder 9465 blade, had had everything to do with, late one night outside Legends on the London Road; Nick had refused to grass on the sight of his brother carving a rictus grin onto the face of one of his assailants, and on account of that he'd gone down as well; 'Nick's the salt of the earth, so he is,' that's what Uncle Phil said about Nick. He wouldn't even waste his breath on Hayden though, and for Uncle Phil, who loved everyone and could charm the Eskimos into buying ice cubes, well that was really saying something. 'Still,' Jack said, glancing at his pictures, 'Jessica'll be there, so yeah, I'm in.'

Jamie seemed so relieved by this he was almost willing to participate in some gentle Woodfield-baiting himself. 'And they don't come much bigger than our get-togethers,' he winked. 'I'm sure there'll be another cousin or two we didn't even know existed coming through the front door expecting a free meal and a paper hat.'

They laughed a little, and then the silence settled, like a shroud. Jamie didn't know what to talk to his brother about; this was the longest they'd been alone in a room together for six or seven years at least, and whilst for him things had remained relatively the same, for Jack they couldn't have been more different. Jack had grown up and left Barking, gone to university in that six or seven years, and made new friends. Jamie found himself peering at him out of the corner of his eye, and familiarising himself with all the other details he'd missed or forgotten, such as the fact that Jack's accent still swung between Barking born and bred and something now slightly more cultivated; the fact that Jack had thick dark blond hair on his meaty forearms, from the hand right up to the elbow, and Jamie had none; 'a man's arms,' Jessica had cooed. There were countless other glaring and even some more subtle points of masculinity, of the kind of almost 'super' masculinity that Jack evinced, that galled Jamie by virtue of the fact that he himself didn't possess them; enormous upper legs and rock solid thighs, shoulders so broad you could perch a pretty girl on either side, and a nice thick neck whereas Jamie was always perturbed by what he considered his 'pencil neck'.

'How is everyone?' Jack said suddenly, breaking the silence with such a start that Jamie almost jumped.

'Fine,' he said. 'I mean, apart from the obvious.'

'And you?'

Jamie shrugged, 'Same as always. There's fuck all to do in Barking, as usual.'

Jack laughed. 'Tell me about it.' and then, 'heard from Nick lately?'

'Yeah, he wrote to Aunt Delia, and Uncle Phil read it out to me; he says Hayden loves it in prison, that he's thinking of doing someone over so he can stay longer; he threw hot water with sugar in it in some old guy's face the other week, 'coz he said he was 'pretty'.'

'I wouldn't put too much stock in what Nick says,' Jack laughed softly. 'He's a bit apt to exaggerate; it's the actor in him.' Nick had always wanted to be an actor, had even had a bit part in 'The Bill', but that was about it. Jack reached forward, and with a set of the longest, meatiest fingers Jamie had ever seen in his life, he gripped Jamie's forearm and squeezed it. 'I'm glad you're here, J,' he said. 'It's great to see you.'

Jamie sniffed, and tried to sound casual. 'Yeah well, I was the only one who could be bothered to…'

There was the sound of a key in the lock, that special way of opening it, and the dark haired lad who'd been sprawling with them in the Salsa Bar popped his head around the door, took in the situation, and smiled accordingly. He was a little bulkier than Jamie had first registered, his eyes large and faintly doe-like; in fact there seemed to be a strange mixture of the manly and boyish about him that congealed into something slightly unsettling. Jack tipped his cup towards him. 'J,' he said, 'this is David, my flatmate, best mate, and so on and so forth; Davey boy, this is my twin brother Jamie.' He seemed about to add something else, but thought better of it.

'Pleased to meet you,' David seemed to glance uneasily from one to the other, then back to Jack. 'Enough water in the kettle for me, is there?'

'Should be,' Jack nodded and tapped his fingers on the arm of the sofa. 'Jamie's gonna crash here tonight, then I'm heading up to Barking to pay my respects to our Uncle Phil. What time is your dad coming to pick you up tomorrow?'

'Unspeakably early,' David smiled, broadening the grin as he threw it to Jamie, who didn't take it up. 'Roads should be clear so he'll be up here in no time. You can take my car if you want.'

'Cheers matey,' Jack nodded. He caught the look of uncertainty that flitted across Jamie's face and kicked out at him playfully. 'Don't worry, J, no more shenanigans on the Whitechapel Road, I promise. I only got three points on my license for that, and it was all down to my 'bruddah' anyway,' and he nodded to the LA picture. That was what Jack and Hayden called each other; 'bruddahs'. The incident on the Whitechapel Road had been Hayden's fault as well, when he'd pointed out a busty blond sashaying along on the opposite side of the road, slapping Jack on the back and saying something like, "You'd give her one, wouldn't you, mate?!"; Jack had been so enthralled he'd mounted the kerb and pronged the car against a lamppost that turned out to be a heritage piece, all gaslight fittings and such, real 'Jack the Ripper' imagery. He'd had to pay two hundred pounds on top of the initial fine just to get it fixed.

'I wouldn't get in a car with him,' David winked.

They spent the rest of the early hours watching 'Carry On Camping' on BBC1, something Jamie found hilarious and the perfect antidote to his sombre mood, but Jack and David didn't seem to share his enthusiasm, or his tendency to slap the arm of the leather sofa in fits of hysteria at the seaside humour, in much the same way that Uncle Phil always did; Uncle Phil adored the Carry Ons.

They called it a night at around three in the morning, but not before Jack did twenty minutes with his dumbbells while he watched the BBC 24 hour news service, sat on the edge of his sofa with the sweat forming in neat little rivulets on his forehead. Jamie made do with a spare quilt slung over his big brother's sofa and tucked in at the ends. Twice during the night

David walked through for a glass of water, and twice around six am he got up and went to piss it all out, igniting a din each time by turning on the bathroom light, which in turn began heating the rusty old gas boiler. Jamie dreamt of Uncle Phil, and in the dream he was well again, and telling him tall tales of Minty Hardcore and the nuns of Barking Abbey.

Early on in the morning Jack came in dressed just in his briefs, dropping down to the floor and performing a series of one-handed press-ups that left Jamie breathless, peering as he was out of the corner of his eye whilst pretending to be fast asleep still. And there it was for all the world to see, just above Jack's bubble-butt, a clear lip print that anyone else would have thought was a tattoo, red and pouting; 'thanks for the thighs that thrilled me so thoroughly'. That was Minty Hardcore's kiss, '…daubed with her desire,' so Uncle Phil had once said. Only the Daddy had a kiss as clear as that; Uncle Phil was the Daddy, but not for much longer.

Chapter 3

Sunday 25th December 2005

The song 'Tarzan Boy' had been remixed sometime during 1993 when it was used in the soundtrack to 'Teenage Mutant Ninja Turtles III', but the rather disconcerting thing was that the purported re-jigging sounded almost exactly like the version that accompanied the original promotional video, in which a rather drawn Jimmy McShane had energetically made the most of a pulsating back-drop that alternated between cartoon frames sporting psychedelic jungle backdrops and something a whole lot more indecipherable besides. It was this rather modest reinterpretation of one of Jamie's favourite songs – Uncle Phil had sung it to him as a toddler - that was drifting lazily out of the car radio as they drove along the Mile End Road and towards Essex proper.

Jamie knew full well that Jack found such a visit a bone of contention, but for once his priorities were being overlooked in favour of Jamie's; Jamie was understandably not in his right mind, wandering around the flat only an hour or so ago in a kind of daze, sometimes doing things he'd fully expect to find himself doing, like rolling a joint and then smoking it wistfully, and then doing things he wouldn't expect to find himself doing at all, like checking his hair in the little round mirror that hung on the airing cupboard in the kitchen, or maybe sobbing quietly to himself in the sitting room, gnashing his teeth together and grinding the heel of his Reebok trainer into the coarse blue carpet.

The drive took them well over an hour even though the traffic was relatively light and the way clearly signposted. They'd pulled over on the Mile End Road and asked a policeman for directions and he'd put them on the right track when they'd been in danger of veering off towards Stratford East, and the burgeoning developments for the 2012 Olympic Games. Jack kept on trying to cheer him up by pointing out the few fit birds on the street, and flirting with a pair of girls in the car adjacent at the traffic lights near the Blind Beggar pub on Whitechapel Road, but Jamie just wasn't in the mood. Passing through Stratford proper, they skirted around Docklands for a bit and finally pulled into Barking around three in the afternoon, settling in a dingy corner in the car park on the London Road. It smelt of petrol and rubber and Sinitta's 'So Macho' was streaming out of a car nearby, although it was hard to pinpoint the exact location; maybe it was all acoustics. Someone had pissed in the only spot available to park in, and Jack made great play of tutting and shaking his head. He turned the engine off and the silence that followed was so...well, so loud, was the only way Jamie could describe it, left him shifting uncomfortably in his seat, as though the whole world outside were waiting for them to speak. Jack was wearing his Stone Island jacket again, a pair of jeans and some trainers, dressing 'Essex' just for him, he imagined. Jack gazed at him and said, 'You okay, J?'

Jamie nodded. 'Yeah.'

'You don't look it.'

He swallowed. 'Uncle Phil's not gonna get better, that's what the doctors say. They say it's like…like AIDS, what he's got; like he's wasting away, only it isn't AIDS. They don't know what it is.'

Jack reached over, and put his arm around the back of the passenger seat. 'I'm here for you, mate,' he said.

Jamie looked at him, and then said, 'I don't want you. I want Uncle Phil.' And what a pleasure it was, to see the hurt expression on his big brother's face.

They left the car park in silence, walking up towards the bandstand at the top of East Street in a kind of daze. 'Mum'll be chuffed to see me,' Jack was saying, adopting a more casual swagger than usual, suddenly asserting himself to the fore of their little twosome. 'I bet she cries; mum always cries when she hasn't seen me for a little bit.'

'It's about Uncle Phil today,' Jamie reminded him. 'But yeah, they'll all be happy to see you, they always are. Don't expect your typical Woodfield Christmas though.' They passed under the window of Aunt Queenie's flat on Linton Road and called out up to the open window, but there was no reply; Aunt Queenie was usually passed out by around two in the afternoon, Christmas or not, the consequences of downing several spoons of rum with her daily medications. They reached the Murphy Estate, and their mum's flat on the first floor a few minutes later; Slade was streaming out of a battered radio on the windowsill and clashing with Paul McCartney's 'Simply having a wonderful Christmas time' from the flat directly above. 'My life'll be shit once Uncle Phil's gone,' Jamie said, fumbling for his key. 'He shouldn't have had to come here just 'coz he was sick; why couldn't he have stayed in his own flat, just me and him, the way it's always been?'

Jack took out his roll-ups and lit one. 'Your life won't be shit, J. People die all the time. I'm still here, you know.'

Jamie gazed at him just as he had in the car park, as though he were mad, as though everything he'd ever said were nothing more than the ramshackle ramblings of your average lunatic. 'Don't go thinking that we're friends now or anything,' he heard himself saying. 'Just 'coz I had to come get you, I mean.'

The roll-up flopped rather forlornly out of the corner of Jack's mouth. 'I'm kind of putting that last statement down to all the stress you've been under,' he said.

Jamie shrugged. 'I couldn't care less if you're here or not, it's just everyone else thinks the sun shines out of your arse, and all.'

Jack shook his head, and straightened. 'So it's still like that, is it?'

'Uh huh.'

'And last night, at my place? When you were almost human, I mean.'

He shrugged again. 'Aunt Amanda reckons I'm in some kind of premature shock, on account of Uncle Phil and all. She says I might do or say some crazy things.'

Jack nodded. 'That's what I figured, so like I said, I'll let it slide.'

Jamie shrugged. 'Do what you like.' He grinned suddenly and said, 'Yeah, I been doing some crazy things since Uncle Phil got sick, like nicking that scent I got you.'

'Mate...' Jack reached out. 'You're hurting...'

'Fuck off,' Jamie said quietly. 'I don't want you, or your stupid hugs.'

'You're hurting, J.'

'Since when do you care?'

Jack's face was a picture of spurned affection. 'You know I care. I'm always asking mum how you are, what you're...'

'Yeah, well I don't care.' Jamie turned and shoved his key into the lock, giving the door a shove. He stood back, giving Jack all the room he needed to make his grand comeback. Their mum's place was quite fancy, as far as council flats went; a main hallway offered a large living room complete with plasma TV screen on one side, overlooked by a kitchen with a service hatch and all mod cons, and on the other two bedrooms – one of them acting as the sickroom – and the bathroom and kitchen. The colours were primary, pastel pinks and creams, the bathroom benefiting from a rather icy blue touch. Her beautician's table was tucked away in one corner, along with all its accoutrements, various lotions and potions, towels and trays full of dyes and 'deep sea cleansing masks'. Cousin Jessica was halfway up a ladder in the hallway, giving the hanging tinsel above the kitchen door a twist to make it hang even, and polishing the stainless steel 'Merry Essex-mas' signs with a dirty rag and a bottle of 'Pledge'. She was a year younger than either of them, although most people mistook her for around seventeen; shockingly beautiful, but in what one of her classmates had once referred to as '...such a cheap way'. With Jessica it was all bouncy blond hair, lots of make-up, usually pastel pink, big breasts, short skirts, and hoop earrings, again pastel pinks, although she carried it off without being too offensively tarty, simply by virtue of having the biggest, brownest, drowsiest doe eyes imaginable, eyes capable of erasing the possibility of any further remarks on her pedigree simply by widening, and then holding the intended victim in their unblinking childlike gaze. Jessica was something of a minor celebrity in the extended family, although for what could be considered all the wrong reasons; she'd got as far as the final five girls auditioning for pop group 'S Club 7' but she'd only been fourteen or so at the time, and they'd caught her out despite her buxom assets, and given the job to Rachel Stevens instead; she'd sold her "slut Rachel stole my star" to the Barking and Dagenham Post for five hundred pounds, which had helped pay for a little holiday she and Jack had taken, the less said of which the better. Following that there'd been the soft porn photos, the wet t-shirt contest in Brighton when she was fifteen, and the biggest accolade of all, when she became the youngest ever page three girl from Essex in the SUN, aged just fifteen and three hundred and sixty four days. None of this would have been quite so bad if it were not for the fact that her father was the well-respected Father Brian Woodfield, of St. Margaret's, just around the corner on the Broadway. For reasons that Jamie couldn't quite fathom Jack found her escapades highly amusing, and would erupt into peals of helpless laughter when informed of her latest doings. Jack was also fiercely protective of Jessica and would drop everything at a moment's notice to race over if she needed him. Jamie wondered if he still held that power over Jack, and whether or not to put it to the test someday.

Catching sight of the pair of them from the sheen she'd been so lovingly cultivating, Jessica jumped down off the ladder and made for Jack with open arms, her voice a veritable shriek of delight. 'Jack!!!! Oceans of love, Jack!!'

Jamie managed a weak smile, and shoved his hands in his pockets whilst she showered Jack with hugs and kisses and funny, squealing little girl noises. She jumped into his arms and he picked her up and spun her around, once, twice, three times, and once more for luck. They were close in a way he and Jack would never be, and their back-story could fill volumes. He sniffed and glanced around, up, down, anywhere really. 'Is mum around?' he asked eventually.

'In the sickroom,' Jessica said, her arms around Jack's neck and her legs locked around his waist, their eyes fastened. 'No one's coming until this evening, she wants to have the dinner late because Uncle Phil always seems to perk up when it gets dark, but he's made her promise to prop him up on his pillow for the Queen's speech. It's not exactly your typical Woodfield Christmas, is it?' and all this said without even a sideways glance at Jamie.

'Just what I was saying to Jack…' Jamie nodded.

'J's still ducking and diving,' Jack said, disengaging himself from Jessica and adopting the stance of a boxer, throwing out the odd play punch, something Jamie only reluctantly responded to.

Jessica waved her duster in the direction of the kitchen. 'Tea? still like it strong and sweet?'

'Don't we have some tipple?' Jack dropped the stance and wandered past her, doing a quick circuit of the sitting room, taking in the decorations and picking up the presents under the tree, checking which ones had his name on the label. 'I mean, it *is* Christmas.'

'Yeah but the family doesn't exactly have much to celebrate,' she opened the sideboard and pulled out a bottle of vodka, ASDA's own brand, 'this plus a bit of lemonade okay for you?'

'Guess it'll have to be, kid.'

Jessica poured three glasses and gazed curiously at him. 'So, have you got a girl on the go at present? Or is that a stupid question?'

'Yeah, something like that.' Jack nodded. 'I'm between ports, if you know what I mean; I've finished fucking Fiona and I'm contemplating doing Dorothy,' he winked.

'You're a slut,' she said.

'Yeah but 'jess,' he took the glass from her and winked. 'You know you're the only girl for me, for real.'

'Well I haven't been faithful to you,' she pouted playfully. 'In fact I've been a perfect whore.'

Jack grinned. 'Kid, I wouldn't have it any other way.'

The sudden thought came to Jamie that Jack's visit was the most exciting thing that had happened to them in a long time, and especially to Jessica, who when she wasn't doing the soft porn and the Page 3 spent her days filing her nails on the front desk of a dreary hair salon in the Vicarage Fields shopping centre. Jack seemed not only to know this, but was beginning to luxuriate in the idea. Jack said, 'I have to get back sometime this evening. I can't really leave my flatmate there alone.'

'You're not even staying the night?!' she squealed, 'Jack!! You can't do that to me!'

'I have coursework...' he sighed.

'Fine then,' she folded her arms and turned on her heel. 'If you don't want to see my 'Parisian schoolgirl' outfit again then that's your call.'

Mum emerged from the sickroom ten minutes later and after kisses and promises of further visits from her 'big, blond angel' had been ensured, she disappeared into the kitchen to finish cooking the dinner. She didn't even mention that Jack hadn't bought presents for anyone; if anyone did mention it then she'd probably just say he had enough to deal with paying his university fees, and that would be that. Between the four of them they polished off an early Christmas dinner of turkey, roast potatoes, sweetcorn and piping hot gravy, portions of chocolate chip ice-cream and all. It was the kind of gratuitous indulgence only allowed in times of deep personal crisis. Jack let out an indiscreet burp and loosened his belt, rubbing his swollen belly in some appreciation.

'I'll go in and see Uncle Phil in a sec,' he nodded, sucking out the last of his cola through a double set of straws. Jamie sat and played with the bits of turkey leg left on his plate, watching Jack as he left the table and went to the window, glancing out at the veneer of the Vicarage Fields, then to the left where he'd just noticed the first flakes of snow beginning to fall. Someone had scrawled 'Minty Hardcore lives!' in bright blue spray and a faintly Italic scrawl on the side of the At Barking pub. Jack rubbed his belly a second time and slipped his fingers in-between the gaps of the buttons on his shirt to massage the skin suitably. A text came through on his mobile, a better make than the one Jamie currently possessed, he noted, and after reading it he suddenly decided, 'I'm not in any great rush to leave after all; David's in Bournemouth for a few days at least. Reckon I could kip on the sofa or something, mum?'

'Sweetheart, you can kip anywhere you'd like,' mum popped her head through the service hatch from the kitchen. 'Your Aunt Rachel has room to spare and she'd love to see you.'

'Is Tracy there?'

'I think so.'

'I'll pass then,' he sighed.

'Aunt Delia would put you up in a shot,' mum said after a moment's thought. 'And you know Clay would be made up if you stayed there. Or there's your Aunt Hannah…'

Experiencing something of a reality check, Jamie stopped listening to the many names being touted as possible places for Jack to lay his head for the next few days and suddenly remembered that Uncle Phil was dying in the next room, dying whilst he was admiring his brother's mobile phone and his longer legs, his larger feet, and everything else that seemed so exceptional in Jack and so very average in himself. He gazed down at his plate where a lone slice of turkey waited to be impaled on the end of his fork, but Jessica reached over and swiped it away with a nod and a wink. Several possible scenarios flashed across his mind, the most comforting of which was to pretend that this simply wasn't happening, that Uncle Phil was hale and hearty, but he'd never really been very good at that. If Jack didn't go in and see him in the next few seconds then he'd go in there himself.

Mum leant over him and cleared up the rest of the dinner things. 'Do you want to talk to Uncle Phil too?' she asked, tapping her fingers on the table to Take That's 'back for good'. Jamie nodded. He couldn't remember a Christmas when he hadn't been sat next to Uncle Phil, laughing and joking at his seaside-style humour, when Uncle Phil hadn't adored him and loved him and paid him the kind of near-constant attention that only Uncle Phil ever did, showering him with an abundance of trinkets and oddities that he was urged to keep despite their apparent uselessness. He began to seriously consider how on earth he was going to cope with this.

'I'll go in with Jack,' he said, pushing back his chair and leaving the table. 'The rest of the family will be here soon; we'll be swamped.'

'Is your Tiffany coming?' Jessica asked.

'Nah…' Jamie thrust his hands in the pockets of his hoodie and strode over to the Christmas tree. 'She didn't think it was appropriate, what with Uncle Phil and all…'

'Oh nonsense,' mum sighed, piling up the plates and taking them through into the kitchen. 'She's practically family, your Tiffany is. You text her right now and tell her to get on over here.'

'Mum…' Jamie stuck his head through the service hatch. 'She might be with her own family, you know? It isn't everyone's idea of a merry Christmas to be gathered around someone's deathbed. She's not good with death, 'tiff is. She went to pieces when her uncle died, remember?'

'Perhaps you're right,' she opened the oven to check on the pudding. 'Maybe she can come tomorrow when we need help eating all the left-overs.

There'll be more than usual this year, what with Hayden and Nick being…away. Jamie, did you give your brother that envelope?'

'I did, mum.'

'I'll go in and see Uncle Phil now then,' Jack called out, making a bee-line for the bedroom, Jamie coming in close behind him. The door was ajar and there was a funny smell coming from within, the smell of something awful. Uncle Phil's eyes were shut and he looked like he was dozing. His striped blue pyjamas were buttoned neatly up to his chin and not tight enough around his thin neck. Jack sat on one side of the bed and Jamie on the other, and when this didn't wake him they knew straight away that he was dead. His hands were clasped to his chest, in much the same vein that the figures of certain sorts of knights on tombstones clasped their swords to their chests, only Uncle Phil had no sword, just his West Ham scarf and season ticket, the former wrapped around the latter, the ends blowing in the breeze coming from the open window nearby. Jack swallowed and got up, moved around to Jamie's side of the bed, and put his hand on his shoulder. 'J…mate, I am so sorry…'

'Get mum,' Jamie said.

Jack knelt down behind him, and wrapped both arms around his shoulders. 'J…I am so, so sorry.'

'I told you I don't want your stupid hugs!' Jamie pushed him away. 'Now get mum!!'

Jack nodded, swallowed again, and got up. He paused at the door, and turned and said, 'Mate, I am here for you, you know. And I'll keep saying it.'

Jamie made a little derisive noise, and shook his head. He reached out and took Uncle Phil's hand, already cold, and clutched it to his face. Then he turned and glared at Jack. 'Don't you understand?!?' he said, the tears erupting in his eyes. 'I hate you!! I fucking hate you!!'

Chapter 4

Sunday 1st January 2006

Although he hated the idea of breaking down in public, Jamie began to cry quietly as he pulled up outside Aunt Amanda's nineteenth century terraced house on Vallance Road, tooting the car horn repeatedly in an attempt to drown out his sobs. Aunt Amanda double locked her front door and then paused a moment, inhaling the crisp winter air with a sigh. 'Statuesque' was the word of choice for Aunt Amanda, with her long legs, her sturdy shoulders, and her magnificent rouged cheekbones, all topped off by a wonderfully gin soaked voice that Jamie had seen subdue even the most volatile of situations with its undulating rhythms. She climbed into the passenger seat, or attempted to at least, the wide brim of her hat preventing such normal maneuvers, eventually forcing her to toss it onto the back seat and then smooth her crumpled skirts out before giving him the nod, and they pulled away. 'How are you feeling, darling?' she asked, squeezing his shoulder, the many rings on her fingers clanking like old tin.

'Like shit,' Jamie sniffed and wiped his nose with the back of his hand. 'I can't believe we're burying my uncle when he was just forty-fucking two.'

'Well that's the tragedy of the people who make us laugh, you see.' Aunt Amanda reached into her fake Louis Vuitton handbag and pulled a handkerchief out, dabbing the corners of his eyes for him as they turned onto the Bethnal Green Road. 'There's always been this awful case of premature deaths with the Carry On films too, you know; so many of them died before their time, just like your Uncle Phil. He loved those films.'

'I know, Aunt 'mandy; he used to watch one every Friday night when he got in from the pub.'

'Poor Patsy Rowlands for instance,' she went on. 'She died not long ago, and she was only seventy-one. That's no age these days, is it? not for a woman. It's only Babs Windsor and dear old Jim Dale left now.'

'Are you trying to take my mind off it?' Jamie asked, hitting the indicator.

Aunt Amanda put her hand on his. 'Of course, darling.'

'So...what about June Whitfield then?'

She removed her hand and fished around in her handbag, locating and then clicking open her compact. 'June Whitfield doesn't count.'

'Uncle Richard rung to say he'd be late,' Jamie made the turning into the Roman Road and hit the accelerator. 'The trains in Brighton are up the creek for some reason.'

'Unavoidably delayed, hopefully,' she closed the compact. 'I really don't want someone of his social calibre as a witness to my weeping. The memorial service is at four pm sharp, and I don't intend for him to perform some slapstick routine that might make ideal fodder for the morning papers, with the church door slamming so loud that everyone turns around to see what the matter is, and him tripping over his shoe-laces or something.'

'Uncle Richard loved Uncle Phil too, Aunt 'mandy.'

'Everyone loved your Uncle Phil, darling. He was just that sort of man. But your Uncle Richard is a silly old queen.'

'Do I look ok?' Jamie asked her when they reached the next set of traffic lights. 'I know the trousers don't match and all, but I don't own a whole suit. I own bits of a suit, but not an entire one whole and complete, you know? I wanted to borrow one of Jack's but he wouldn't let me; he said I didn't know how to wear an Armani.'

'What an arsehole your brother is, darling.'

'Yeah, he is that,' Jamie nodded, considering whether he should improve Jack's stock by admitting that he'd offered him the Armani unconditionally, but that Jamie himself had been afraid he wouldn't be able to 'wear' it. They spent the rest of the journey, though into Stratford, into East Ham and finally arriving in Barking around 3pm in complete silence. Jamie didn't even put the radio on, and Aunt Amanda seemed to be content to gaze the familiar sights as they flashed past on either side of them. As they were entering the car park on the London Road she said suddenly, 'Did I tell you I took your Uncle Phil to meet Patsy Rowlands once?'

'I don't think so...' Jamie put the car in reverse. 'I know he's met Babs Windsor a few times, and he met Hattie Jacques before she died too. The only thing Uncle Phil loved more than the Carry Ons was West Ham.'

'They were filming 'Carry on Loving',' Aunt Amanda smiled fondly. 'We went up to Windsor to see them on location, you know. And well, we waited outside for Hattie and Patsy, I mean, and when we saw Patsy your Uncle Phil ran up to her and he hugged her so tight that he accidentally broke the pin of the brooch she was wearing and it stabbed her left bosom. There was blood and everything.'

They left the car and set off on foot to make the short journey to St. Margaret's. The church was built on the site of the old Barking Abbey, founded in 666AD, with only the old curfew tower still standing of the original structure. Jamie's Uncle Brian was the vicar, and he lived in the rooms above with his wife Betty, and cousins Jessica and Bobby. Jamie didn't like Uncle Brian much; it was quite strange that it was his wife, Jamie's Aunt Betty, who was Jack's favorite aunt, was the one the family simply adored, and not the blood son, who was something of a tyrant and a religious fanatic; 'the Pope' was the favorite nickname for him. Awful stories abounded of the way Uncle Brian had brought his three children up – older Cousin Casey now lived over the side of Barking with his wife and kid – that he'd made Jessica's life a living hell, prohibiting her from wearing any make-up, and even demanding that his wife sellotape their daughter's breasts down when she hit puberty and it became clear that Jessica was going to be quite a busty little thing.

Seven or eight black limousines were lined up outside St. Margaret's, plus numerous other cars; various Woodfields were standing around smoking, chatting, occasionally crying, and being comforted by the numerous family friends who made up the rest of the congregation. There were countless floral tributes, the largest of which said simply 'The Daddy' in West Ham colours; Jamie's own contribution, which said 'Uncle Phil forever' was relegated to a position just behind the aforementioned.

The crematorium itself was packed to capacity, those members of the family and their friends who couldn't get inside listening to the service on speakers stacked in piles of two and three, hastily arranged by Clay Woodfield and his twin brother Springer. Jamie sat in the front row with his mum to one side, and Uncle Heath on the other. Jack was sat to the right of Uncle Heath, next to Aunt Amanda, wearing the Armani that had been offered to Jamie only days earlier, and wearing it probably a whole lot better than Jamie ever could anyway, thus validating the refusal, in his mind at least. Uncle Brian stood to take the service, looking older than many of them remembered, and still a little yellowed from the kidney problems that had blighted him for most of his life. 'I bet 'the Pope' is loving this,' Jack whispered, nudging Jamie's foot and nodding up at him. 'He always thought Uncle Phil was a 'sinner', didn't he?!'

'You hush up now, Jack Woodfield,' Aunt Amanda leant over and all but scowled in his direction, just as the organ began to play. Following the welcome, sentences and introduction they sang 'Morning has broken'; Jack had a rather beautiful singing voice, slightly high but soulful; he'd been in the choir at St Margaret's up until the age of eleven and could've continued longer despite his voice breaking with rather hilarious consequences at a Christmas nativity when he was ensconced in the role of 'singing narrator' to a rather bizarre, politically correct nativity play. Jamie on the other hand couldn't sing at all, and was content merely to mouth the words and take comfort in glancing at others who did the same, squeezing Aunt Amanda's hand now and then; each squeeze was returned two-fold, and at one point she turned and looked at him and Jamie saw that her eyes were bloodshot and welling up with tears, so reddened in fact that they looked like they were about to haemorrhage. Uncle Heath got up to read 'All is well', a piece that Jamie had heard once before, at his Aunt Sophie's funeral, and one that seemed to become ever more morbid each time he heard it. Jack seemed to echo this thought, leaning over and nudging Jamie's shoe with his own. 'Who wrote that awful bit?' he whispered.

'Henry Scott Holland,' their Aunt Rachel leant in from the pew behind, so close they could smell the cheap perfume she was wearing from the East Street market. 'It's a classic funeral reassurance.'

'I hate that bit,' Jack went on. "'...I am waiting for you', I mean God, how veiled a threat is that?!'

Their mum was due to give a reading but broke down before she'd even uttered the words, '...my brother.' Before anyone could intervene their

Aunt Delia took the speech from her in what could only be described as a blur of bangles and hoop earrings, and handed it to Jamie. 'You were closest to him, even though we all loved him,' she said. 'You read it, Jamie dear.'

Jamie disengaged himself from the pew and walked slowly to the podium, opening the speech; the rustling of the paper was like a thunderclap in the hushed silence. He saw the expectant faces looking up at him, enraptured. His girlfriend Tiffany, strawberry blond and exquisite in a way that screamed Belgravia and not Barking, seemed to be chewing her lip in anticipation, ready to move from her seat next to Aunt Betty to be with him. Jamie gazed down at the speech, which was several pages long and full of corrections, sentences crossed out and amendments made and referred to in the makeshift margins by little love hearts in the midst of the text. It might as well have been written in Arabic. 'Um…' he looked up, then down at the speech again. 'I just want to…that is, this speech says…' and his eyes went first bloodshot, then swelled with tears. 'I can't read it, okay?' he threw the paper down on the ground. 'I can't fucking well read.'

As various members of the family gasped, whispered, digested the news and showed their sympathy Jack all but clambered over Aunt Amanda and retrieved the speech, his Gucci loafers ringing off the cold stone floor. He mounted the podium and adjusted his tie.

'Go on, Jack,' Clay Woodfield said.

'You the man, Jack!' Daniel Woodfield punched the air with his fist.

Jack cleared his throat for effect; he winked at Jessica Woodfield, nestled against her Aunt Rachel. 'What my brother is trying to say,' he said, 'is that Uncle Phil's death has left a hole in our family's life that might never be filled. And this is what mum says, ok mum?'

Mum nodded, mouthing the words, 'I love you,' at him. Jamie was helped back into his seat by Tiffany, who was whispering something in his ear and stroking his buzz-cut gently.

'He was my big brother,' Jack said, scanning the speech intently and reading it essentially verbatim, 'As much as Heath was, but more. And to me, and to all those who knew him, he was magic, pure and simple.' Members of the family smiled at this, laughed and nodded; Uncle Heath, every inch the quintessential Essex man, didn't seem to mind in the least being referred to in what Jamie thought was a slightly demeaning sense; he was nodding and squeezing the hand of his little daughter Debbie, whilst on his right her twin brother Daniel chewed his lip uncertainly. Great-Aunt Amanda smiled knowingly as the speech continued; 'He was a father to my boys, to Jack and to Jamie when their real father…well let's not go there, shall we. He was the husband I needed to help me carry the groceries home, the boyfriend whose shoulder I cried on when my real boyfriends let me down, or didn't want to know because I had two little lads already. He had the biggest brown eyes I'd ever seen,' and here again Jack paused so that a ripple of laughter could pass through the chapel, and heads could nod knowingly, and faces smile fondly. 'He looked like a deer caught in the headlights.' Again came a ripple of well-meaning laughter, and someone else crying, somewhere near the back. He went on, 'He was tall and handsome, and a real cheeky chappie. He was generous and kind-hearted, and he never had a bad word to say about anyone. I know they say that all the time about people who've died, but with Phil it was the truth. He looked after the family. He was the Daddy. I'll never forget him, and I'll never be the same without him. None of us will. I love you Phil.'

Daniel Woodfield thrust his fist in the air. 'Who's the Daddy!' he shouted. Others followed suit, and soon the church echoed to the question, or the declaration.

Mum came up onto the podium and kissed Jack on both cheeks, then turned and kissed the coffin. Jack looked like he was going to do the same but then thought better of it; Jamie looked like he wanted to as well, but was unable to squeeze back out of the pew. 'If I never see you again' by Wet Wet Wet began to play as the doors to the incinerator opened and the coffin began to trundle towards them. Uncle Heath moved out of his pew and took mum by the shoulders as she began to cry, and somewhere near the back little Meggan Woodfield said, 'Come back Uncle Phil,' and this set several more of the women to crying.

*

'It was a lovely service,' Aunt Amanda said, grinding the bottom of her heel into the light snow. 'Lovely words, Beverly.'

'Thanks,' mum blew her nose and buried her head against Heath's shoulder. 'I feel sick. The cold's making me feel sick. Where are my sweethearts? Where's my Jack, my big, blond angel?!'

Jamie was close by, talking to Tiffany, her arms around his neck and wiping at his tears with her thumbs. Jack was surrounded by a throng of family and close friends, so many in fact that only his Gucci loafers accentuating him up to almost six feet four inches actually picked him out of the sea of ornate hats and buffed hair-dos. At the head of them stood Uncle Eddie, bladdered already and declaring Phil's good nature to all those passing the bottom of East Street, his throaty gurgle erupting into good-natured bouts of laughter every couple of seconds or so. Jessica Woodfield clung tight to Jack's arm and occasionally he'd bend down and whisper something in her ear, or smooth her hair back and kiss her forehead.

'I'll want to talk to Jamie,' Aunt Amanda said matter-of-factly, nodding to him. 'Not now of course, he's far too upset for that. But when he's better tell him to come and see me at my house, and to come alone. In fact, you make sure he comes alone.'

'Don't you want to see Jack?' mum asked, dabbing at her eyes.

'No, just Jamie.'

'But Jack's…'

'...just Jamie.' She said firmly. 'Now I'd like someone to call me a taxi please. I don't think he's in any fit state to drive me back.'

'I can,' he said, breaking away from Tiffany a moment. 'I just need a sec to...'

'You'll do nothing of the sort, darling,' she put her hands on his shoulders and then on his neck, and the cold of all of her ten rings almost made him jump.

'I'll drive you, mum,' Uncle Heath said. 'I'll go get my car.'

'You do that,' she nodded, removing her hat and ruffling her rather alarming red hair out, sending an explosion of it tumbling down her back. She looked at Jamie, who was now wringing his hands in exasperation as he tried to explain something to Tiffany. Little Luke Woodfield was tugging at his trouser leg and asking him to lift him, which he did eventually. 'He's such a handsome young man,' she said, 'even more than his uncle.'

'Jack's the real looker,' mum smiled for the first time today. 'They say he could have been a model if he wasn't so much into his academia. He's my big, blond angel.'

'He does have a certain aesthetic...appeal,' she nodded. 'But I find Jamie here to be more wholesome; unlike his brother, Jamie isn't a crashing great slut with an ego the size of the Blackpool Tower.'

'Oh Jack is very handsome,' Aunt Delia said, joining them and fanning herself theatrically. 'Why, if I was twenty years younger...'

'Don't you mean forty years younger?' Aunt Amanda raised an eyebrow, and then threw her a cheeky wink.

'They say he looks like Jeramiah Woodfield,' mum's eyes all but glazed over. 'Have you ever seen a picture of him, mum? He looked like a Forties film star, he did.'

'Of course I've seen a picture of him,' Aunt Amanda sighed. 'But I think Jamie's...'

'How tall is Jack, Bev?' Aunt Hannah asked, sidling over with a cigarette between her rather thin lips.

'Oh six two, maybe six three; six four in those shoes, that's for sure.'

'Taller than Phil then,' Aunt Rachel nodded.

'Broader than Phil too,' Uncle Heath had to admit.

Aunt Amanda took her cigarette holder out of her purse, stuck a cigarette in it, and lit up. She said, 'It's not just looks that matter...'

'But my Jack has looks *and* brains,' mum nodded. 'He's at the LSE, and it doesn't get much better than that, does it Delia?'

'No it doesn't, dear,' Aunt Delia nodded.

Does Jack actually have a steady girlfriend yet, or is it still just anything in a skirt?!' Aunt Amanda sighed, blowing the smoke out in concentric circles.

'There is someone...' mum was frowning at her. 'Her name is Fiona, I think. Or was it Dorothy?!'

'I bet he's got the girls falling all over him,' Aunt Rachel sighed. 'I mean, look at that big, square jaw; oh, and just look at the way Jessica gazes up at him. They're two peas in a pod, Jack and Jessica.'

'And those arms of his...' Aunt Delia nodded.

Aunt Amanda gazed at Jamie. 'Are you alright, darling?'

He nodded, sniffed. 'Guess so.'

Mum took her camera out of her purse and snapped a shot of Jack unawares. 'That'll go next to Phil in the special album.' she said.

'That's right,' Aunt Delia said. 'It's all down to Jack now.'

Uncle Heath smiled, and cleared his throat. 'Who's the Daddy?' he said.

Someone else took up the question, and then someone else, and before long almost everyone was chanting it, and they were all looking at Jack, and Jack was smiling graciously and trying not to look like he wanted to turn and leg it onto the passing no.238 bus; 'Who's the Daddy!!' they chanted; 'Who's the Daddy?!?'

Aunt Amanda slid her arm around Jamie's shoulder and kissed the top of his crop.

Chapter 5

Friday 6th January 2006

The soft drizzle that had been falling as Jamie left Bethnal Green Underground station had become a hard rain by the time he was knocking on the door of Aunt Amanda's house on Vallance Road, pulling his hoodie up over his head and glancing this way and that. It was such an oddity, this house, the only original edifice this side of the soot stained Liverpool Street viaduct that had survived the renovations of the mid-Sixties, it stood in defiance alongside newer, more modern two-up/two-downs just a few feet away, it's red brick facade chipped and faded, the doorstep almost a breezeblock, flanked on both sides by drowsing potted plants. This was the house his mum had grown up in, Uncle Phil and Uncle Heath too. He couldn't imagine it, the four of them cramped into the little square rooms, using the outside toilet, and the bath barely big enough for Pellow, that time he and Uncle Phil had taken him for a walk in Weaver's Fields; the rain had made a mud bath of the pitch that the little golden retriever had rolled around in for ages. He stood back from the door and waited, pulling his hoodie up a little tighter and gazing from left to right, back towards Bethnal Green Road and then the other way, past the aforementioned viaduct, all the way up towards the Whitechapel Road. Aunt Amanda was in her dressing gown when she opened the door, her dark red hair still wet from where it had been washed. 'Darling!' she declared, grabbing him by the shoulder and forcing him through the door, looking from left to right before she closed it. 'You came.'

'I had to get Aunt Queenie's shopping for her,' he followed her into the long wooden hallway. 'And when I took it to her flat she said she wanted 'Daddies' ketchup, and I'd got her ASDA's own brand, so I had to go back and change it. She like, insisted!' he pulled his hoodie down. 'Are you ok, Aunt 'manda?'

'Bearing up,' she led him through into the kitchen, closing the back door. Maybe she hadn't washed her hair at all, he thought, but had instead been standing out in the rain, all sombre like. 'When you're as old as I am death isn't the shock it must be at your age. I've probably buried more Woodfields than you've been to West Ham matches, my darling.'

Jamie pulled up a chair at the table by the window; the curtains were open and the rain ran down the pane and mesmerised him the way it often had as a child, wherein he'd often become completely entranced by droplets racing each other to reach the bottom. 'Yeah, but Uncle Phil…' he said. 'He wasn't just any old Woodfield, was he?'

'I know.' She seemed to pause as she put the kettle on, and to become momentarily lost in thought. 'I know.'

He wanted to stay sat at the kitchen table, where he and Uncle Phil had soaped Pellow down so many times, in summer, when the back door would be open to let in a draught, and the noise of the other kids still playing on Weaver's Fields had drifted through the house like music. But Aunt Amanda shooed him through to the sitting room, following on with the teas and a tray of assorted biscuits leftover from Christmas, the bog standard present she'd received from Uncle Heath for the last decade or so. 'I don't like the winter evenings,' Jamie said. 'This time of year is always the worst, 'coz Christmas is over and summer seems like a lifetime away.'

'I know,' she said, completing the hat-trick of affirmations. Aunt Amanda knew a lot of stuff, sometimes more than Uncle Phil, it seemed. Whenever Uncle Phil had been on one his rants she'd roll her eyes to heaven and then put her hand on his shoulder and purr in that sultry voice of hers, 'Pipe down, darling.'

'What did you want to see me about?' Jamie asked, sipping his tea. He always drank his tea piping hot, and people teased him about it, calling him 'iron gullet'. He set the cup down on the sideboard and made for the comfiest chair, the one that had been Uncle Heath's favourite as a child, and was still pretty much moulded to that body shape, so that you kind of fell into it rather than actually sitting on it.

Aunt Amanda made a steeple of her hands, her many ornate rings flashing as they caught the light from above. 'Darling, I am about to put to you perhaps the most important proposition you may ever receive.'

'Wow.' He sat back, his hands behind his head. He could imagine Uncle Phil cracking a joke about some of the propositions he received from the girls down the East Street market on a Saturday afternoon, but said nothing. Anyway, Aunt Amanda appeared to have read his mind because she grinned and then shook her head. There was the sense that they could idle away the rest of the evening reminiscing about Uncle Phil, but there were other, more immediate matters to be addressed.

'Now,' she went on, dunking a digestive into her tea. 'You've always known that your brother is the…ah, how shall we say it, the favourite?'

Jamie pursed his lips, shrugged. He saw Jack for a second as everyone else seemed to see him, as the sunshine breaking through the clouds after a storm. 'Everyone loves Jack. Hayden said to me once that I was just his afterbirth.'

Aunt Amanda rolled her eyes. 'Everyone loves you too, you just don't realise it. True, you've had your…moments, shall we say, but that's all in the past now. You've grown up a lot since your brother went off to university.'

'Everyone wants him to come back,' Jamie said. 'That's all anyone ever says; "When is Jack coming back?", like I'd be the last to know!!'

She smiled. 'Jack isn't all that, believe me. Your brother can be vain, shallow, and empty-headed; a lot like I was at his age, as a matter of fact. And don't even get me started on Hayden Woodfield. Funny, but I seem to recall he's been sent down for a year for GBH, whereas you, well, lo and behold here you are in front of me, hale and hearty and with little more than a caution for daubing West Ham slogans on the upstairs back seats of the no. 238 bus. Hayden Woodfield on the other hand, is a nasty little piece of shit.'

'Aunt Amanda!!' his jaw nearly hit the floor. 'Aunt Delia would go ballistic if she heard you speaking like that!'

'We never discuss Hayden,' Aunt Amanda folded her arms. 'She knows my feelings on the subject, and so we steer well clear. You see, it's often the way with twins; Hayden is a complete arsehole…'

'…Aunt Amanda!'

'…but Nick is to die for, and your closest cousin to boot. I had such high hopes that he might marry that dear little Gwendolyn girl, but thanks to his brother it just wasn't to be, was it. And so it is with you and Jack, one way or another. Oh don't be so fey, darling,' she waved a hand dismissively. 'And regarding Jack, well he can flash that megawatt smile all he wants, flex his big arms and give the whole 'Jack the lad' thing, if you'll pardon the pun, but believe me, I've seen it done before, and with far more style.'

'He's going to be a psychoanalyst,' Jamie said. 'How is that empty-headed?'

She made a sound that seemed to him a lot like she had just kissed her lips; Aunt Amanda had always been pretty quick when came to the latest cussing trends, and was kissing her lips in annoyance at the post being late before most of the black girls at Eastbury secondary school had even started doing it. She said, 'He knows all the terms and nothing about the actual human condition; oh, I admit he is rather sharp when it comes to…'

'…whereas I'm thick as shit.'

'Darling…'

He shrugged, ran his finger over the table. 'Everyone knows now, after the tit I made of myself at Uncle Phil's funeral. I can't read; I can't even write my own name. That's a real crock, considering I sell second-hand books for a living.'

'People will always want cheap books, darling.'

'That's what mum says.' He gazed at her, and found thought of Uncle Phil rather easily usurping any lengthy conversation about Jack. 'Me and Uncle Phil, we were gonna do things, you know? He was gonna take me to New York, and stuff. Now it's all shot to fuck.'

'Well we're just going to change all that,' Aunt Amanda said matter-of-factly. 'I know a place, where I have a few favours owed to me, by some very nice people indeed. It's a secretarial college in the main, but they have a special section where they teach people to read and write. I'd like you to go there. And then…'

'…and then what?'

She made sure she had his full attention before she went on. '…and then I'd like you to go to university, like your brother. I think what Jack wants is a nice flat in Notting Hill Gate or somewhere similar, and a nice job psychoanalysing big city types in Cheapside or Cannon Street, wearing a Saville Row suit and carrying a Louis Vuitton briefcase, don't you? Lord knows he's said so enough times; a nice, normal life, slightly affluent, but nothing too ostentatious. I don't think he wants to be hanging around Barking wearing fake Filas and being 'the Daddy', do you?'

'But Jack is the Daddy now,' Jamie said. 'Everyone knows that. The Daddy's the biggest, butchest one of all, and that ain't me, is it? Everyone thinks I look about fifteen still.'

Aunt Amanda made a steeple of her hands. 'If Jack were to be the Daddy, he'd end up the same way as Phil, most likely in half the time; Jack may have the muscles, and the brains too, but he's kidding himself on the savvy. She'd shag him to death in a second.'

'Who would?'

Aunt Amanda ignored the question, fixing him with a steely glare. 'You're not a slut, like your brother is. You're shy with girls, and when you have one, as with Tiffany, well you're strictly a one-girl guy. She won't get you half as easily as she might him.'

'Who won't?!'

Aunt Amanda was regarding him. 'No, you're not like Jack at all, Jamie Woodfield. Wouldn't you like to be the favourite? The one everyone looks up to, the one everyone goes to with their problems? Wouldn't you like to be…' and here she paused for emphasis, and for effect '…the Daddy?'

'Jack's not a slut,' Jamie said, scratching his head. 'Boys can't be sluts. He's…he's a stud! He's been with tons of girls! Like, maybe hundreds!'

'Jamie,' she exhaled slowly. 'I just asked you if you wanted to be the Daddy.'

'Yeah but…' and then it dawned on him. 'You what?!'

'That's right,' she nodded, 'you, Jamie Woodfield; the Daddy.'

'Me?!?'

'You.'

'But…Jack's gonna be the Daddy.'

She kissed her lips for certain this time. 'Not if I say so. Jack is going to have a wonderful career as a psychoanalyst; as I said, the last thing Jack wants is to be wandering up and down Station Parade beating his chest and wiping the noses of all your cousins. You, you can be the big man, the head of the family.'

'Me?' he allowed himself a moment's luxuriant fantasy, imagining himself holding court in Uncle Phil's flat on Station Parade, of dolling out advice and money to an endless stream of cousins, of being called upon in the early hours to sort out domestic disputes, of having to face down local tough and bullies, and of being hoisted aloft by his many fans at the end of the day, as they carried him up to the Barking Dog, where a pint of Stella and a packet of roasted peanuts awaited.

'You,' Aunt Amanda nodded. 'It's what you've always wanted, isn't it? To be like your Uncle Phil? And to have all the attention that Jack had, knowing that he was next?'

Jamie swallowed. 'Well yeah...but I'm not...I don't know if I can, Aunt Amanda.'

'Don't you want to get the person who murdered your Uncle Phil? Don't you want to make sure she doesn't murder Jack as well?'

'She?'

Aunt Amanda made a steeple of her hands, and nodded. 'Minty Hardcore; when she barrels in on things, shouting the odds, saying you're not as tall as Jack, not as handsome as Jack...arms not as big as Jack's...thighs not as sturdy as Jack's...that you're too boyish to be the Daddy...' Her eyes narrowed, and she leant forward in her chair. 'And that's when I'll get her. And I'll get rid of her the same way she got rid of your Uncle Phil, when he tried to stand up to her, when he got in her way.'

Jamie swallowed hard, that luxuriant fantasy dissolving rather rapidly. 'Minty Hardcore?!'

'Minty Hardcore.'

'But...she's just a fairy tale,' he said. 'Uncle Phil used to tell me, when I was little...'

'No,' Aunt Amanda shook her head, and outside the rain began to batter at the window panes, as if to punctuate her point. 'She was no fairy tale. She was a whore; a crafty little whore who as good as murdered him.'

Chapter 6

Monday 16th January 2006

They were murder on Jamie's feet, these cast-off Gucci loafers of Jack's. They were just one of many casualties of the clear-out he'd conducted during his pre-London School of Economics induction, leaving them at their mum's flat for him like Jamie was supposed to be grateful or something. They weren't even in tip top condition; the tips were scuffed when Jack had locked himself out of the Islington flat and taken his frustration out on the adjoining wall, Jamie knew that was the real reason for offloading them. Jack's feet were bigger by a good inch or so and the resulting slack meant that the backs scraped Jamie's calf something rotten. Still, they looked the business, them, a pair of trousers and a matching shirt from the East Street market. All this was topped off by his Firetrap navy blue jacket, something Tiffany had gotten him for his birthday in the Selfridges summer sale, when she'd been flush from a modelling job involving standing around dressed as a Fifties good time girl along with several other similarly suited women, waving placards and directing tourists toward the wonders of Carnaby Street.

He carried the piece of paper with the address of the Sight & Sound secretarial college on it in his hand but had to ask directions as he couldn't actually read it himself, something Aunt Amanda in all her matriarchal wisdom seemed to have overlooked. He soon found himself standing in the foyer of the Charing Cross Road college, waiting to be buzzed up to see someone called Monique, exchanging pleasantries with the doorman, a genial and totally chilled out black guy called Don.

Monique was a soft featured, almost sultry mixed race woman in her early twenties who put Jamie entirely at ease with her wicked sense of humour and totally offbeat attitude. She lived in Leytonstone and shopped in Barking '…when she could be bothered', and had even had coffee at Morelli's coffee counter; when he'd asked her if she knew Tiffany, who served there six days week in-between waiting for modelling gigs to turn up, she'd looked rather blank and said, no, but that she promised she'd look out for her next time she was there.

Jamie was one of seven 'youngsters' in the group she would be chairing who couldn't read, but one of only two who couldn't actually write their own name on top of this initial 'indignity'. In fact she showed him how to write his name on the spot, whilst they were still in reception, holding his hand with the pen to steady his grip and then holding it up and beaming, reading it out to him; 'Jamie Woodfield.'

He was one of only two boys, the other being a rather large and spotty Greek with wiry hair, called Omiros. There were five girls, none of them really his type but one, a brunette called Louise, made a beeline for him and kept trying to catch his eye throughout the lesson; she was kind of cute but she looked about twelve. They were all in different stages of difficulty and he and Omiros were in the bottom end of the class as far as literacy skills went. During the next few months they would also be taught job interview skills and how to type, and when Monique went around the group asking what their ambitions were Jamie volunteered and stood up in front of everyone, saying that he would like to go to university in the autumn and do a degree, even though he didn't have any qualifications; he told them his brother was at the London School of Economics, and that he wanted to be '…just like him.' Monique reassured him with one of her wicked smiles that there were ways around the problem of not having any actual qualifications, and that some sort of certificate that the college would provide could help him on his way to actual academia.

By the end of the first day he could write his own name fairly confidently, and was by way of demonstration asked to demonstrate the fact on the cover of his progress manual. He made a mess of it, and ended up with 'Jaime Woodfield' instead, but no one really got on his case about it at this early stage. He was given a basic starter book to take home, and any fears that it might have been one of the 'Jamie's first book' type thing were allayed when he was presented with a rather bland white folder with various words and characters therein emblazoned in neon orange, in no particular order and telling no particular story, simply to be copied out on the adjoining pages in the spaces provided.

He went for a McDonalds down the bottom of Oxford Street with Louise and her large friend Maggie, and asked them over a Big Mac and Fries what they thought of the class. 'We don't like Omiros,' Louise told him. 'But we love you.' That said, she still took enough of his side order of McNuggets to piss him off and put the kibosh on the idea of asking her to lunch solo style.

*

'That place is going to give you airs and graces,' mum said as she laid the table. 'Why it isn't good enough for you to be selling books on the stall anymore I don't know. You make enough on it and it gets you out there instead of sitting on your bum all day. People will always need books, you know.'

'Mum, I'm almost twenty five…I want to make something of myself.' Jamie was flicking through the copy of OK! he'd found down the back of the sofa. 'What's for tea anyway? Five minutes after a McDonalds and I'm like, famished all over again.'

'Fish fingers, beans, and mashed potatoes.'

He leant back and directed his voice in her general direction. 'The lady there reckons I could make university in September. It wouldn't be as posh as the one Jack goes to but still, she thinks there's a chance. She lives in

Leytonstone, you know; she said she shops in the Vicarage Fields sometimes.'

She peered through the service hatch at him, frowning. 'Does that mean you'll be moving to the West End as well, and coming home once every six months like your brother does?'

'No, I can commute if it goes well.' He chucked the magazine aside and made a beeline for the remote control; seconds later the plasma TV screen flared into life. 'Aunt Amanda wants me to stay in Barking anyway. She says we've got stuff to do, and that I need to keep a cool head if we're gonna do it right. She says it doesn't matter I'm not as tall as Jack, or I don't got hair on my chest.'

Mum rolled her eyes, and slammed the oven door perhaps a little too hard than was actually necessary. 'Aunt Amanda wants this, Aunt Amanda wants that…you'd think she was your bloody mother and not me!'

'She said it's what Uncle Phil would have wanted,' he chewed on his bottom lip and for a moment wanted to pick the magazine up and hurl it across the room, in much the same way as he'd actually lost his rag at Aunt Amanda's house when she'd told him what had happened to Uncle Phil; then he'd upturned the nearest chair with his foot and punched the wall by the window so hard she had been convinced that one of his knuckles was fractured. 'We got to go and get her now!!' he'd shouted, meaning Minty Hardcore. 'Fuck it, just point me at her!'

Aunt Amanda had knelt down in front of him and taken his knuckles in her hand, kissing the one that had struck the wall and massaging the redness until it died down a little. 'It doesn't work like that, my darling,' she'd whispered. 'If it was easy as that we wouldn't be having this conversation now. Think of it…think of it as a game of chess, if you like; a game of chess, and the person we're playing against is ever so clever, as clever as me, even.'

'I can't play chess,' Jamie had muttered. 'Uncle Phil said it was boring; football was better.'

Mum marched in from the kitchen, rupturing the reminiscence. 'Well she never mentioned it to me,' she said. 'Then again, she never tells me anything anyway. She lives in her own little world, that woman does. I tell you, you think I'm difficult, you want to try growing up in that house!'

'Yeah,' Jamie nodded. 'She never tells you anything 'coz he can never get a word in edgeways 'coz you're always going on about how great Jack is, how he's 'the big, blond angel' and everything.'

'Your brother will do this family proud,' she waved her serving fork at him. 'I think he's the first Woodfield to get a degree, let alone a Masters! He might even do a PHD next, and become a proper psychoanalyst.' And here her eyes glazed over, and Jamie wondered whether she was envisioning some future graduation ceremony, herself at the front in a posh new hat, dabbing her tears away with a frilly handkerchief. 'Can you imagine that?'

she said, 'my son, the psychoanalyst. It brings tears to my eyes. It makes it all worthwhile.'

As for Jamie's eyes, they were busy rolling in his sockets. 'Mum, he doesn't give a toss. He's also the first son to leave Essex.'

'That's not true,' she waved the fork a little more threateningly. 'Gary Woodfield was away for three years in First World War, and your Great-Uncle Alexander was too; I think your Uncle Rupert was away in the Second World War, but I always get the dates mixed up....'

'Jack's not gone to war; he's gone to the London School of Economics.'

'And you should be proud of him.'

Jamie kissed his lips quietly. 'I am mum, but he just...he's not bothered about the family. Jack's different. It isn't necessarily a bad thing, I think he just wants his own life. He wants to have a job down Cannon Street.'

She marched back into the kitchen and plucked the fish fingers out of the oven. 'He'll steer the family just like your Uncle Phil did. He's the Daddy now, and the sooner he gets of his backside and realises it, the better we'll all be.'

'He won't. He's not interested. He only comes back to see Jessica.'

'He will.'

'He won't.'

She stuck her head out of the service hatch and took careful aim with the serving fork. 'Do you want these fish fingers or not?!'

'Yeah yeah,' he sighed. He flicked channels again, and then found himself saying suddenly, 'Mum, why is Jack the Daddy now, and not me?'

She breezed through a moment later with his tray, replete with a cup of cola, a bottle of ketchup, and the salt shaker, and set it down on his lap. 'What was that?'

'I said why is Jack the Daddy now and not me. Uncle Phil liked me more.'

She gazed at him, frowning. 'Why do you ask?'

'Just wondering,' he said, emptying the ketchup all over the side of his plate.

'Jack's older.'

'By about twenty minutes.'

'A lot can happen in twenty minutes,' she said, bustling back into the kitchen. 'Some of the best sex I've ever had in my life lasted twenty minutes, or less, usually!'

'Oh mum!!'

'Well you did ask, sweetheart!'

Jamie stuffed half a fish finger into his mouth, chewed, swallowed, and said, 'It's not just 'coz he's older though, is it? I mean...'

Mum sat down with her own dinner and switched onto Channel Five. 'Don't you worry about it, sweetheart,' she said. 'Just eat your dinner.'

'It's 'coz he's tall, isn't it?' Jamie said. 'Uncle Phil was taller than Uncle Heath, and that's why he was the Daddy and not Uncle Heath, isn't it?'

'You're talking about things you know nothing about, sweetheart…'

'And it's 'coz he's better looking than me, isn't it? Everyone says I look like a kid still, but Jack, well Jack looks like a proper man, doesn't he?'

Mum sighed. 'I'm trying to watch 'Home & Away'!'

'Jack's got big arms; she likes big arms, doesn't she?'

'Sweetheart…'

'I bet she like his big cock too!'

'Jamie!' she snapped, 'enough out of you now, mister.'

'And it's 'coz of this, isn't it?' and he put his tray to one side and lifted his shirt up, turning so she could see the blurry lip print just above his buttocks. 'Mine's a bit faint, but Jack's is like, so clear people think it's a tattoo or something.'

'It's just a birthmark.'

'So how come Uncle Phil had it. All the boys in our family have one, even if it's just a pimple. Aunt Amanda says it means '…thanks for the thighs that thrilled me so thoroughly'!'

Mum sighed, and threw down her knife and fork. 'I'm going to eat in the kitchen if you don't clam up!'

Jamie kissed his lips.

Chapter 7

Monday 23rd January 2006

    Although it was about the most interesting place to visit in Barking – according to online guides and people who had tired of the Mall in Dagenham - the veneer of the Vicarage Fields shopping centre still made Jamie kiss his lips every time he regarded it for anything more than a moment. This idea of 'interesting' wasn't exactly the most sincere selling point either; it was interesting only if you parked your taste at the front doors and hoped that someone hadn't nicked it on the way back out. That's how he saw it, anyway. If pushed he could admit there was something urbanely charming about the piped pop music and the cut-price stores, the hairdressers with the framed photo of David Beckham – 'that prissy poof', Uncle Phil called him - circa 1998 thanking them for services rendered, the ASDA where cousin Laquisha worked, and the rather odd fact that if you entered on street level on Station Parade you'd end up on the first floor but if you entered on street level on the Ripple Road then you'd actually wind up in the basement. It was also the place where his long-term girlfriend Tiffany worked, a world away from her old local in Holland Park, the Kings Mall, but then again, she'd assured him that they didn't have a signed picture of thanks from David Beckham in there, and somehow she found that slightly more thrilling than the fact that she could get Gucci in the Kings Mall. Gucci was so overrated anyway; that was what she'd told him, and herself, by the looks of it, when she'd put everything she had with that name on it on eBay.
    Tiffany worked on Morelli's coffee counter in the basement/ground floor on the Vicarage Fields, directly in front of the aforementioned ASDA, spending eight hours a day – give or take lunch and toilet breaks - pouring hot chocolates and lattes, spooning lumps of cream onto piping hot doughnuts, and grinning inanely at customers from under the rusty red cap she was forced to wear over her strawberry blond hair. Hers was the classic example of the mundane job being simply a means to an end, and not looking pissed off about just how mundane it usually was, was a testament to her generally upbeat character, that and the fact a talent scout for a modelling agency had approached her there several years previous, and she'd had a couple of teen magazine photoshoots as a result, vindicating at least some of the hours of slog and drudgery. Lately though the offers from the girls magazines and the hand-cream advertisers were starting to dry up even though her skin wasn't. For the life of him Jamie couldn't imagine why she wasn't on the cover of every top notch fashion magazine going; to him Tiffany was the most beautiful girl he'd ever seen in his entire life, and that had everything to do with the fact that she wasn't Essex born and bred, that

she had more class in one of her carefully painted fingernails than most of the other girls he knew had in the entire contents of their trackie bottoms.

Every lunchtime at around two or three Jamie would come in with his books from Sight & Sound under his arm, plus a novel they'd decided to work on together to improve his reading skills, and that was her cue to take a late lunch, pull that wretched cap off, and shake her hair loose. They'd pull up a chair somewhere discreet and spread the book out, pinning the pages down with the metal pronged things normally used to rest the larger coffee pots on. The novel they'd chosen was a battered paperback copy of L. Frank Baum's 'The Wizard of Oz', although neither of them could remember whose choice it had been, but had decided to stick with it out of some slightly amused mutual consent, case in point;

'When does the Wicked Witch appear?' Jamie asked, sniffing. 'This Dorothy is getting on my nerves.'

'Isn't Jack's girlfriend called Dorothy?' Tiffany had one finger on the text, the other playing with his fingers, entwining them together into something like a cat's cradle. 'Or did you say her name was Fiona?'

'I think it was Dorothy...' he squinted at the text. 'He never said she was his girlfriend exactly...'

'Is she pretty?'

He shrugged. 'Exotic; that's what someone said, his flatmate I think. Tell you the truth I thought he'd shacked up him with him when I first got to the flat!'

'Jack's not gay,' she laughed, brushing her hair out of her eyes. 'He's about as gay as you are, which is,' and here she slid her hand under the table and fleetingly along the top of his thigh, '...not very much at all, really.'

Jamie said, 'Mum thinks the West End turns people gay. She said Aunt Hannah knew a woman whose son went to live there and he was as tough as Uncle Heath, but when he came back to visit two years later he was having a sex change, and he wanted everyone to call him 'Marsha'; they were on 'Trisha' and everything. Hey,' he glanced up at her. 'You seem kind of convinced about him anyway.'

'That's because I turned him down about ten minutes before I met you, my first day on the coffee counter here, when I spilt the hot chocolate all down his top and he over-egged it by taking it off on purpose to show me his pecs.'

'He came on to you first?!' he gasped, loud enough for those close by to twig, and then to listen, if the mood took them.

'Uh huh,' She was amused by his indignation. 'But I didn't even have to consider it; Jack doesn't float my boat, he's far too full of himself, and ok, that's attractive, but only to a point. And you hadn't met me then, so it doesn't count and you can't take it as some sort of slight; you were still in Top Man, I think, trying on Lonsdale trainers or something.'

Jamie digested this, then followed her finger back to the text and began to read, slowly but surely. After a moment he said, 'You don't think I'm dyslexic, do you?'

'No. Why?'

'No reason. One of the girls in class said it might be that, that her mum thought she was dyslexic but she wasn't, she'd just rather go out and get bladdered than read a book.'

'Sounds like most people I know.'

'Mum says some people were readers and I'm just not one of them. She says I'm far happier kicking a ball around with Uncle Phil and Nick, just regular stuff.'

'I bet she didn't say that recently,' Tiffany said.

'Well no...'

'I know, baby,' she squeezed his hand reassuringly.

For Jamie the subject of Uncle Phil was only broached if he raised it first, and then strictly on the understanding that sufficient time was allowed for him to reminisce and look like he was about to cry, until the Essex boy within reasserted himself and he became calm again. As if sensing this might be her train of thought, Jamie sniffed and said, 'Uncle Phil's ashes came back this morning.'

'Oh baby...' she closed the book, after placing their mark in it, and clasped his hands, quite ready and willing to wipe those tears if they came.

Jamie went on, 'They're in this skinny metal container, it looks like something you put hot chocolate in, but mum's going to put them in some sort of urn. Uncle Phil told me he wanted them put in a West Ham mug, or something similar with a screw-on lid, but he never stip...'

'...stipulated?'

'...yeah, never said so in his will so no one except me knows, and I'm thinking I might just swipe them and do it anyway.'

'I think your mum might notice.'

'Nah; Uncle Phil said once that someone he knew had wanted their ashes scattered at Upton Park but their wife didn't want it, so one night his brother switched the ashes for turmeric or something, and she kept the turmeric in an urn on the mantelpiece and his ashes got scattered at Upton Park after all.'

*

Life began to smooth out a little bit for Jamie as the visceral memory of Uncle Phil's death gradually faded into something slightly more dreamlike. Instead of him feeling like he couldn't go on and wanted to end everything he now felt like he couldn't go on and wanted to end everything but was willing to see what tomorrow was like just in case he felt a bit better. Everything of routine that he'd put off doing for fear of reigniting painful memories ended up being done, one way or another, everything except going into the Barking Dog for a drink without Uncle Phil. There were still mornings when he didn't want to get up, when he opened his second-hand book stall later than usual, when he was sat by the fire nursing a cup of tea and just staring into space, watching hour after hour of dull as dishwater daytime TV, and once or twice when he didn't even go out at all, and to hell with the money he lost on the pitch. All of these things were surmountable, but the Barking Dog was the family local; it was the pub they went into before and after matches, usually with Uncle Phil and several cousins, and where they knew almost everyone; Jamie's Uncle Eddie could be found propping up the bar almost seven days a week, three hundred and sixty five days a year, pontificating about nothing and everything, to anyone willing to listen and buy him his next pint.

The bar was run by the Wetherspoons chain, thus affording prospective punters the promise of getting completely plastered on a relatively modest budget; often the stallholders on the Ripple Road outlasted the football fans whether it'd been a win for West Ham or not, downing pints until it was closing time and sometimes even hanging around for the occasional lock-in, but that didn't happen very often these days. The décor was a little hard to describe, but Aunt Amanda had once nailed it as set out by '…someone with a modicum of taste, but only a modicum, mind you.' She'd concluded that '…it was kind of like the bastard child of a trendy wine-bar and a traditional family pub that you'd normally find tucked away on some quiet country lane in the Lake District.' Tiffany had found that hilarious, and Jamie had mustered a smile after she'd broken it down into something more palatable for him. Tiffany adored Amanda and her snappy one-liners, and seemed to take great comfort from the fact that it was indeed possible to inject a certain amount of chic into one's every day appearance, as she swirled in from Bethnal Green in a haze of fiery red silks and matching handbag.

Jamie's best mate Adam worked behind the bar in the Barking Dog; he was a year older than Jamie, darker, and slightly more aggressive looking, although Jamie could match it if he furrowed his brow and thought of something really nasty, like kissing a bloke or something, or being civil to Jack, which in Jamie's book was probably worse than the first thing. Cousin Michael was the actual bar manager; a year younger than Jamie, but with the same blond colouring, only slightly more Neanderthal looking, with squinty eyes and enormous hands, hands almost as big as Jack's, in fact.

Adam was on his break and mopping tables when Jamie and Tiffany wandered in, around dinner time, 'The Wizard of Oz' clutched tightly under Jamie's right arm, his left around her waist as he escorted them to their favorite nook, just over the left side of the bar proper. Jamie had made them both aware that tonight was his first time back post-Uncle Phil, and as a result all talk of anything of that orientation was on the back-burner, that is, unless he himself instigated it. The first round was on the house, and five minutes after they'd sat down they were approached by several stall holders wishing to express their delight on seeing Jamie out at last, and then how sorry they were about Phil; Tiffany squeezed his hand under the table as they said the name over and over again, and he ended up squeezing so hard back she that she was forced to yelp in pain in order to get her hand back.

She was trying to take his mind off these constant commiserations by glancing up at the portraits of various historical locales that adorned the walls above most of the cubicles on either side of the bar and comparing them to how they actually looked in the present day. There was a black and white shot of the Ripple Road circa nineteen sixty-seven, around the time maybe Uncle Phil was just a toddler. The picture showed that the market that ran down East Street from the bandstand had been around for decades, not to mention the bandstand itself, although judging by the hues afforded by the faded photograph it was painted a lot less garishly then than now. The shot existed in that kind of way that reinforced a certain slant they both had of thinking about pre-1970s TV; that the entire world had existed in monochrome up until this point, and any forays into colour, up until that time in the main confined to Hollywood films, were some sort of anomalistic wishful thinking.

'I'm gonna have that pic taken down if you don't stop gawping at it,' Adam said as he leant over the table and pulled the empties away. 'And speaking of getting on with things, you gonna come to the game next Saturday, mate?'

'I guess…' Jamie downed the last of his pint. 'I guess I should get back into the swing of things, but Uncle Phil not being there…it's like I've lost a limb or something; feels weird, like I shouldn't be doing what I used to do now that he's not around.'

'Not what he would have wanted,' Adam checked his watch; five more minutes of break to go, but on a chilly Monday evening the bar was hardly busy. 'Not if I knew your Uncle Phil; he'd be disgusted you were moping at all. That geezer was wired, man.'

'He was like, the most alive person I ever met,' Jamie sniffed, glancing at Tiffany for confirmation. 'One more for the road, babe?'

'One more for the road,' Adam gave the nod to a rather lardy barmaid who hurried over with their refills, bludged a cigarette off him, and then was on her way. 'Tell me about this course thing you're on. Oh, your cousin Daniel was in here the other day again, trying to blag it with a fake ID; can't you sort him out?!'

'Daniel's okay,' Jamie leant back. 'It isn't really my place to have a word…'

'Ok, I'll have a word with him then.' Adam lit up, squeezed himself in next to Jamie, and exhaled. 'You know this ain't easy for me either, Jamie. The whole fucking bar was gutted when they heard about Phil, and there isn't a day that goes by when I don't have to stand there washing out glasses and listening to what a great geezer he was. It's the constant 'was' bit, you know?'

Jamie nodded. 'I can't even say 'was' yet. And his ashes came back today too.' And under the table he squeezed Tiffany's hand again; in response she ticked his palm with her finger and then slipped her shoes off, swinging her legs up onto his lap.

'So anyway, where is this place you're learning to be a brain-box at?' Adam asked again.

'It's up the West End,' Jamie said. 'I thought it was like a spaz thing but it's like a general vocation course but they sideline in teaching people to read and write better. The woman in charge, Monique, is like, so your sort! Mate, you'd die for her!!'

'I love half-caste birds,' Adam beamed. 'Is she like Halle Berry?'

'The way you should say it now is 'mixed race',' Jamie supped from his new pint. 'I said 'half-caste' once and it's only 'coz I reckon I'm her favorite that she let it slide. She's got more hair than Halle Berry though.'

'I might get my hair shorn like that,' Tiffany said. 'What do you think?'

'Sweet,' Adam glanced at her and nodded absent-mindedly. 'And the plan after this is what, Jamie?'

'To go to university in Sept; Monique thinks South Bank is a good bet; Aunt Amanda wants me to do sociology; basically what Jack did. She reckons I can use his old notes.'

'Not heard from his royal highness then?'

Jamie shook his head. 'Not since about a week after the funeral, and that was only a text; even mum was a little bit pissed off at that.'

'He's a cunt,' Adam said, after a moment's careful consideration. There was no censorship between them, and Tiffany knew better than to butt in when it came to their more heartfelt opinions. 'Your twin brother is an absolute cunt,' he went on. 'I've never met a bloke as into himself as he is; I've told you before I'd mark him as queer if it wasn't for the fact that he's shagged just about every decent looking bird in Barking, and half the ones in Dagenham too.'

'I said that too, to 'tiff earlier today,' Jamie's face brightened. 'He's got a flatmate who's queer, leastways I think he is, but then she goes and tells me Jack tries to cop off with her before I did! Ain't that right, babe?!' and here he turned and gave her hand a cursory squeeze.

Tiffany nodded. 'Just because Jack has a gay friend - if he is gay - it doesn't make him a queer. Nor does wanting to wear something a bit better than Burberry, you know.'

'Oy oy mate!!' Adam slapped the table with his hand. 'Reckon she's sweet on Jack, do we?'

Tiffany rolled her eyes. 'And I'll tell you exactly what Jamie said when that old paranoia flared its head again this lunchtime; I don't 'do' Jack; he's just too arrogant. He thinks you're a bunch of chavs, you do know that, don't you? He thinks he's *way* superior, and I find that a whole lot of a turn-off.' She sipped her rum and coke, and then something seemed to dawn on her, and her big green eyes widened. 'Do you think he thinks I'm a chav too?'

'How can you be a chav?!' Jamie gazed at her as though she were unhinged. 'You're posh!! You're not even from here!'

She shrugged. 'Not that there's anything wrong with being a chav, of course…'

Adam grinned and winked at Jamie. 'Your Tiffany's just one 'a them posh West End birds who enjoys a bit of East End rough!'

'Hey!!' she laughed. 'I do not like a bit of rough!!'

'Aunt Amanda wants me to take his place, you know,' Jamie said suddenly, changing the conversation with all the subtlety of a smack in the gob. 'Uncle Phil's place, I mean.'

Adam looked up. 'Take over what…the whole family shtick?'

'Yeah; the whole kit and caboodle,' he nodded. His brow furrowed and for a moment he looked as brooding as his buddy. 'I'm scared, mate; scared that I can't do it and…scared that maybe I can.'

*

Stuck above the Carphone Warehouse on the Ripple Road, Uncle Phil's flat was a rather bright and airy affair, a vast contrast to Jack's gloomy Islington basement pad, and therefore the one thing Jamie could feel some sort of superiority about. The curtains and the carpets were all done out in Uncle Phil's favourite hues of West Ham purple and navy blue, the kind that seem to absorb the sunlight and then glow as a result rather than the more oppressive end of the spectrum.

The staircase up from street level gave on to a spacious sitting room on the right and on the left a kitchen with all mod-cons; no one asked where Uncle Phil had got the money from, and even Jamie was none the wiser. A huge oak dining table was the centrepiece of the kitchen, its bottom end obscured in shadow by the second staircase that led up to the two bedrooms and the bathroom. Uncle Phil's curving art deco metal bed was neatly made and looked just like it was waiting for him to come back to it; Uncle Phil would often collapse backwards onto his bed still fully clothed and fall asleep like that, trainers sticking up towards the ceiling like radars. Jamie wandered through into the kitchen, also spotless; mum had obviously been here with one of her dusters and given the place a thorough once-over. He thought maybe she'd done it before Uncle Phil had died, like some sort of therapy, that if she cleaned the place up then somehow it made her feel like he was going to come back and live there again.

This was the flat where Jamie had lived almost his entire life; his first memories were of this flat, of watching the football results on a Saturday afternoon, then 'Doctor Who', and then either 'Jim'll Fix It' or 'the Generation Game', all this whilst eating takeaways that were in all honesty probably a little too spicy for his pre-pubescent stomach; this was the flat he'd returned to after school each day, with his dinner cooked and on the table, lovingly prepared by whichever girl Uncle Phil was seeing at the time. He'd never called them 'aunts', because he had enough of those already. And this was the flat where he'd told her he'd seen many weird and wonderful things over the years, things such as the kitchen cupboard that you could climb into and then find yourself coming out of the Morelli's doughnut stove in the Vicarage Fields on the other side; the framed photos of various West Ham players and 'Carry On' stars from over the years who winked and grinned at you whenever you looked at them, but returned to their former more stoic pose when you stole your gaze away; and the lightbulbs whose luminescence changed to match your mood, and sometimes brightened in response to a particularly dark moment. With Uncle Phil gone the photos were just photos now, and the lightbulbs were a constant one hundred-watt hue.

There was still food and drink in the cupboards; one of Uncle Phil's six-packs of lager, baked beans, sugar, all the essentials, and yet he'd always been a bit like a beanpole, especially at 6'2 in his bare feet.

Jamie went into the sitting room and checked the electricity worked by flicking the plasma TV on, relieved to see that they hadn't been cut off. He sat on the sofa, staring at the indent in the cushion where Uncle Phil would park himself before throwing his long legs up onto the coffee table, lager in one hand and the remote control in the other. A couple of moments later their dog Pellow would follow suit, resting his chin on Uncle Phil's leg and gazing disinterestedly at the TV screen, but even Pellow was gone now.

Pellow had been knocked down by a Royal Mail van when Jamie was fourteen and they'd buried him in Aunt Rachel's garden on the Ripple Road because they didn't have one of their own.

The doorbell rang, then there was the sound of a key fiddling in the lock and a couple of seconds later Mum popped her head around the door. 'I thought I'd find you here, sweetheart.'

'I was just coming back,' Jamie got up and followed her into the kitchen, where Tiffany was busying herself making tea and wiping down the surfaces with a dishcloth. 'I was having a look around the place. I've been thinking.'

'I've got his ashes here,' mum said, offering forth the battered West Ham mug that Uncle Phil had drunk his tea from since he was a teenager. 'I thought they'd be better in here than some poncey old urn after all.'

Jamie gazed at the mug, and felt Tiffany watching as he gingerly lifted his hand out and took them, gazing down inside as though he expected to see Uncle Phil in there, shrunken somehow and gazing back up at him. 'I've been thinking, mum,' he said again. 'I reckon I might move back in here.'

Tiffany started, made a little sound; this was news to her, obviously. For months she'd been trying to persuade him to move in with her into her flat on the London Road, but it had been kind of futile when Uncle Phil was still alive, even when they'd moved him from here to the flat on the Murphy Estate. 'What?' mum looked aghast. 'Alone?'

'Yeah,' Jamie nodded.

'You mean, by yourself?!'

'Uh huh.'

'Without anyone else?!'

'That's what I meant, mum.'

'Not even with Tiffany here?' and she gave her a cursory nod.

'No.' he found himself unable to meet her gaze. 'I need some time to myself; Aunt Amanda thinks it's a great idea. In fact she's willing to sub me...'

'I thought she'd be behind this,' mum sighed, setting the mug on the coffee table. 'What has got into her lately? Bad enough she subs Jack so that he's become accustomed to living his West End lifestyle, but you...'

'What's got into you, you mean?' Jamie glared at her. 'She brought you up, mum, but you talk about her like...well like you don't even like her anymore. She's my gran, as good as.'

'It's not that,' she sighed again. 'She just...well like you said my sweetheart, she brought me up and I know she can be a bit...eccentric. I just don't want her filling your head with all sorts of nonsense. I'd have had a more normal upbringing if I'd been raised in a hippy convent sometimes, I swear to you.'

Jamie chose to ignore this last remark. 'What, filling my head with silly ideas like how I could go to university, you mean?'

'No. You know what I mean.'

'No mum I don't,' Jamie thrust his hands into the pockets of his hoodie. 'Why don't you tell us?'

'She had some strange ideas,' mum seemed to be staring into the past as she gazed around the kitchen. 'I know my sweetheart, because I grew up in that house with your Phil and Heath when our own mum died. Now I never said I wasn't grateful, but still...'

'You think she's a crank or something; a witch.'

'Oh Jamie!!'

'Yes you do. Just like you always thought Uncle Phil was something like that, even though you loved him to bits. You'd much rather I'd lived with you, or with Uncle Heath. Well I'm going to carry on living here.'

'But you'll get lonely,' Tiffany said, 'there's something missing without him here, Jamie.' and a moment later his mum voiced exactly the same concern.

'How can I get lonely?' he said. 'You're only over the road!' and found himself almost throwing up his hands in exasperation. 'Uncle Heath is just around the corner, and Casey, not to mention Aunt Delia and Uncle Brian, Aunt Rachel...'

'Friday nights are the worst,' mum said. 'You can get so lonely on a Friday night; lord knows I do. It's been so lovely having you with me but I suppose that's going to stop, and now with Phil gone...well I'm just going to decline into an old spinster, aren't I?'

'I thought Clay had moved in, to help with Uncle Phil and all?' Jamie plonked himself on one of the stools by the sink and rested his chin in his hands. 'Anyway, I'll be fine; like I said, money isn't going to be a worry 'coz Aunt Amanda's going to pay most of the bills.'

Mum made a little noise. 'She wants you locked up here for some sinister reason, no doubt.'

'Not sinister!' he laughed. 'I think she thinks Jack's...well, he's not up to the job.'

'Sweetheart,' mum sighed. 'Let me tell you something. You may think I'm dead set on Jack being the Daddy just because he's the elder – by all of twenty minutes, I find myself reminding you - and because he's a high achiever and all, but let me tell you, it's nothing to crave; nothing at all. In fact it's a heck of a responsibility; a <u>heck</u> of a responsibility.'

He made a little derisive noise. 'How so?'

Mum sat down, her own tea cupped in her hands. 'Whoever the Daddy is, whoever leads the family finances and sorts all our stuff out, they have to be on tap to the family twenty four hours a day, seven days a week, like your Uncle Phil was. Got a problem with noisy neighbours? Go and see the Daddy; got a problem with a bloke hassling your wife? Go and see the Daddy, and so on, and so forth.'

'Well...'

'...and you want that to be you, do you? You be glad you don't have to, that's all I can say. If I had my way it would be someone else entirely, Nick or someone, but no one else has...well, no one else has what Jack was born with, as you said so yourself the other day. Don't think I want it to be either of you, but it's tradition, you know? And who am I to go against tradition?'

'What was Jack born with again, mum?'

Mum sighed, and made a face. 'Let's not go into all that again.'

After a moment Jamie said, 'Uncle Phil made it look so easy.'

'That's because he was a star, my sweetheart,' mum sighed, cocking her head to one side as one of a million memories doubtless flooded her mind. 'Do you really think you can pull it off with as much style as he did?!'

Chapter 8

Monday 30th January 2006

Uncle Phil had had style, that and a kind of cheeky chappie way about him that made the declaration of impending excitement, adventures just around the corner, even more exciting than if someone rather dull had announced a far grander fact, and even if Uncle Phil's idea of adventures were usually only what he could afford on what he made from the second-hand record store anyway. He would come bounding into Jamie's bedroom and clap his hands together, twice or three times, thrusting the curtains apart and drenching the room in some early morning sunshine, and then turn and stand there, illuminated in the glow from the window like some kind of gangly angel, a big toothy grin on his face and mischief in his big brown eyes; 'What's it to be today?!' he'd say. Just shy of his thirteenth birthday, Jamie had been awoken one morning by the gust of cold air that accompanied his door being thrust open as Uncle Phil marched into the room in just such a fashion, neatly bypassing the bed and drawing the curtains, West Ham style, hooking them up at either end. 'Up and at 'em, little fella,' he'd declared, thrusting his hands deep into his jeans pockets, 'we're going on an adventure!'

'Don't wanna go on an adventure,' had been the reply, with the quilt - again, West Ham style - rapidly engulfing him. Pellow's ears had pricked up but he remained where he was, just to the right of Jamie's head and with one paw seemingly shielding his eyes. Jamie slid his arm out and ruffled the dog's ears. 'We wanna stay in bed,' he said. 'Nip over the road and take Jack.'

'I don't do Jack,' Uncle Phil's voice floated down on him, kind of a cultured cockney. 'He's not interested, and after a couple of years of trying quite frankly neither am I. So get up, get yourself some toast or cereal, brush your teeth and stick your hair up, 'coz we're heading into London! Your Aunt Rose is out for the day so we're free to do whatever it is we want.'

'What for?' this piqued the interest a little, and Jamie peered over the top of his duvet.

'Oh I don't know...' Uncle Phil began taking great steps, strides even, that carried him back and forth the length of the room at least five times in as many seconds. 'I thought we'd have a slap-up meal, visit the video stores, and then...maybe then I'd take you to see a game?' and as he said that he turned and fixed Jamie with a wicked glint in his eyes, and this itself was all the prompting Jamie needed.

They left the flat with their slices of toast still in one hand and their cups of tea in the other, and as they walked up Station Parade to the Underground Uncle Phil did that wonderful thing where he tucked the empty cups in his pocket and then they'd be back on the shelf in the kitchen when they arrived home later that night, all washed and dried as well. He brought them a pair of one-day Travelcards on the Underground concourse, winking and flirting with the girl behind the Perspex window just like he always did; she as ever was extremely responsive, even craning her head around to catch one last lingering glimpse of him as they moved away. Uncle Phil took the steps down to the platform three at a time, and whilst they were waiting for the train he produced a packet of chewy sweets from his pocket and offered them to Jamie, and then another to the rather stern looking businesswoman waiting nearby, who melted rather quickly and even kept on smiling at him when one of the sweets got stuck in her teeth and had to be gouged out with one of her freshly manicured nails. 'Gonna be a nice day by the looks of it, missus,' Uncle Phil had said, squinting as the first rays of sun broke through the clouds, giving her a nod and a cheery wink.

They'd boarded the train and Uncle Phil had sat as he always did, with his legs wide apart and his toes tapping to a tune that only he seemed able to hear. As they passed through East Ham and Upton Park Jamie began to notice little things, odd things; things such as the fact that the newly modernised cabins had reverted to their rather tatty wooden interiors, and by the time they reached Mile End the kind of clothes people were wearing were drastically altering from the hoodies and Hammer-pants of the early Nineties. Now it was more a case of Seventies sideburns and the odd pair of flares, and the black guys he saw were sporting what he honestly thought were joke afro wigs. Uncle Phil had registered Jamie's burgeoning astonishment with one of his trademark toothy grins, beaming from ear to ear and once again giving the flirt to two girls who sat opposite, both of them sporting the biggest beehive 'dos Jamie had ever seen. Everyone was carrying little Union Jack flags, or wearing it as a badge on their lapel or their hat. Everyone seemed upbeat, no, make that positively exuberant and as the train suddenly seemed to veer wildly off the District Line the crowds boarded and soon there was barely even any standing room. 'Uncle Phil?' Jamie leant forward.

'Little fella?'

'We're not on the District Line anymore...'

Uncle Phil winked. 'We're not even in 1994 anymore...' he saw a little old lady hankering after his seat and sprang to his feet. 'Here ya go, love,' he said. 'Park your bum there.'

'Oh you are kind,' she sighed.

'Tha's alright, love,' Uncle Phil nodded.

When they disembarked the crowds were so fierce that Jamie had to hang off the back of Uncle Phil's trenchcoat in order to prevent himself from being swept away. Uncle Phil seemed as ever utterly unperturbed, hands thrust deep in his pockets and whistling 'Penny Lane' as they strode up towards the twin towers of Wembley Stadium. The noise was incredible, with the cheering and the chanting forming a kind of rumble that left an echo in the eardrums. 'Uncle Phil...' Jamie tugged at his sleeve. 'Is this...'

'What's the date on your Travelcard, little fella?'

'30th July 1994...'

'Rewind a bit; too modern, the Travelcard is.' Uncle Phil led him through the turnstiles and produced what should have been a kosher football ticket but was in fact a page torn from the Barking and Dagenham phonebook. The man who clipped the tickets seemed entirely satisfied by this and handed it back with the standard tear in the middle to show that it had been checked and found suitable. They had to fight to get to their seats and everything they said from then on had to be shouted in order to make themselves heard. 'See him?' Uncle Phil nodded down and to the left. 'Alf Ramsey. If we're lucky I'll get you his autograph afterwards. I can't see the Queen though; was the Queen here?'

'Sorted!!' Jamie slapped his brow in disbelief. 'World Cup '66?'

He nodded. 'Better than a Hammers match?'

'Any day!!'

'Good stuff,' he nodded, suddenly producing a bag of boiled sweets from one of his pockets. 'I tell you, little fella, if ever I happen to kark it unexpectedly, well you just tell your Aunt Amanda that this is where I want my ashes scattered, ok?'

Jamie nodded, just as the opening whistle blew. 'I want my ashes scattered here too!' he said.

*

Jamie gazed down into the battered West Ham mug and imagined once again Uncle Phil gazing back up at him; Uncle Phil pulling another one of his amazing tricks and shrinking to the size where he could fit inside just such a mug as easily as he might have clambered into the little bath at Vallance Road or something. The ashes were a kind of metallic grey colour, and they moved around like cocoa powder when he shook the mug. He turned and gazed at Aunt Amanda, her hair blowing out behind her and looking like flames, like the side of her head was on fire, in fact. 'Are you ready?' she said to him. Beyond them the expanse of the Upton Park football ground looked strange against the setting of a winter sun; the grass looked blue rather than green, and the blue and purple of the stands looked black; black and a kind of navy blue, and he couldn't hardly see the words at all. He knew the layout of this pitch off by heart; he'd been here with Uncle Phil, with Uncle Heath, Uncle Eddie, and countless cousins more times than he could remember. Only a real crisis had ever forced them to a miss a home game, or even an away one. He wanted to tell Aunt Amanda how it felt, to be sat up in those seats with his strip on, his scarf when the weather was cold, sandwiched in-between Uncle Phil and Uncle Eddie, shouting as loud as he could and not feeling the slightest bit self-conscious, because that's what everyone else was doing too; shouting and yelling, jubilantly one minute and in something like rage the next. It was the fluidity of a football match that so excited him, that it could go any which way, right up until the very last minute.

Jamie glanced at her again. 'I don't think I can do it, Aunt 'manda.'

'We only have a limited time here, darling,' she wrapped her arm around his shoulder and squeezed. 'Come on now; you know it's what he would have wanted.'

He nodded; someone nearby was playing 'The power of love' by Frankie Goes to Hollywood, Uncle Phil's favourite song for dancing with Aunt Rose, and for throwing a cheeky wink at Jamie as he serenaded her around the bar of the Barking Dog; it was the song Uncle Phil had sung to him when he'd come down with a bad case of scarlet fever, his face a mess of scabs and blisters, his temperature high, his tongue swollen and red like a strawberry. Mum had come in with a cold flannel and spread it across his forehead, then gone to buy some ice lollies that he might eat, to bring his temperature down. Uncle Phil had pulled up a chair and sat with him for four whole days, only moving to get iced water, and to change his blankets when the fever caused him to sweat uncontrollably. 'The power of love' had been high in the charts at the time and was on the radio every five minutes. Uncle Phil had sung it to him over and over in fact, changing the words and making Jamie giggle; 'I'll protect you from Minty Hardcore, keep the vampires from your door…'

Jamie sniffed and looked up at Aunt Amanda; her eyes were full of tears but she nodded firmly when she caught his gaze. He lifted the mug up and shook the ashes out. The wind caught them and scattered them far and wide, and soon Jamie couldn't see them at all, they'd spread that far out over the pitch. He let his chin fall onto the top of his chest, so that she wouldn't see the tears streaming from his eyes, but she knew he was crying. 'Don't, darling,' she said, and swept him up in a swirl of red. 'It's done now,' she whispered in his ear. 'It's done. He'll be happy here. He loved it here, you know he did.'

Jamie nodded, drew back, and wiped his eyes with the back of his hand. 'We're gonna get her, aren't we? Minty Hardcore, I mean? Get her and make her pay for what she did to him?'

Aunt Amanda nodded, guiding him away, back towards the exit and the stewards who'd known Phil, who'd made this private visit possible. 'Yes we are, my darling,' she said. 'It begins now.'

Chapter 9

Monday 13th February 2006

'Begin please, Jack,' Susie Orbach said, and sat down behind her desk.

Jack took a deep breath and cleared his throat. He was aware of the eyes of the entire class on him, but he only made contact with one of them in return, the pouty little brunette with the big chest directly opposite, throwing her a sly wink and making her blush. Beside him Dorothy caught the wink and kicked his foot. 'Ah,' he nodded, 'identities. Well according to Freud, every aspect of our identities springs from our sexual desires.'

'Would you agree?' Susie raised an eyebrow.

He could feel himself breaking out into one of his biggest, cheesiest grins, and the class grinned along with him. 'In my case?' he said, 'or generally?'

'In your case,' she was the one throwing the wink now, 'go on, Jack.'

'Well, it depends how I perceive myself,' he said, 'and how I'm perceived by others.'

'Very cute,' she said.

He was the one blushing now, a rarity indeed. 'Okay well, how much do I define myself by my sexual desires? Well there's a lot of pressure put on me from outside sources; I'm from the East End, I've got an East End accent...'

'...you're trying very well to mask it.'

'Thanks. But still, it's there, and there's a certain perception that goes with it, you know? I'm perceived as being a bit thick, a bit slow...'

'...and yet here you are, doing an MSc at the London School of Economics.'

'Well exactly, but it's the identity I'm coded with, being a young man, and with the loaded words 'East End' or 'Essex man' tagged on top. I'm supposed to be a bit of rough, and...'

'Oh I'm sure you are, Jack.'

'Thanks,' he bowed his head, trying to figure out exactly how to stop beaming. It was quite easy, really; he just thought about being the Daddy, and that wiped the smile right off his face. 'In my family there's an awful lot of expectation in regards to men and *that* kind of identity. They're very much a traditional East End/Essex family, and the males are very much expected to fall in line with that, you know?'

'And you don't want to?'

He shrugged; outside the rain began to fall a little harder, to make itself a little more audible against the window-panes. 'It didn't go down too well when I left to go to university. My family's kind of close-knit in a way that would do your head in. We're expected to stay in Barking, you know? I had to fight my way here.'

'But would you say you remain an East End man in a West End world, or are you trying to adapt the identity that had been coded on you?'

He glanced down at Dorothy and she tried not to smile; she knew how much he loved being the centre of attention, only when it suited him, of course. 'I'm kind of veering towards a 'metrosexual' experience,' he said. 'You know, buying into better brands and the lifestyles they purport to offer; I've got a gay best friend, which is like, so unheard of where I come from. And just this, you know?' and here he spread his arms to encompass the entire room. 'We're very working class, my family. They run market stalls and sell doormats, second-hand books…'

Susie Orbach made some notes. 'You shuddered when you said 'second-hand books'.'

'Ah,' he gazed down at the desk, at his Muji plain brown notebook, his Muji metallic blue pen; his copy of Renata Salecl's '(Per)versions of love and hate', and his half-finished bottle of Evian. 'That would be Jamie.'

'Jamie?'

'My twin brother; my baby brother.'

'Really?' she shifted a little. 'That's very illuminating. Of course the research on twins is huge; have you read Endre Peto?'

Jack shook his head. 'If anything I've avoided the subject.'

'You're not close, you and…Jamie?'

Jack frowned, and sifted around in his mind a little, well aware of the eyes of the class still fixed on him; the pouty little brunette with the big chest seemed transfixed, and beside him Dorothy was rapidly writing something in a shorthand he'd never seen before. 'Not really, no.' he said finally. 'Jamie went to live with our Uncle Phil when he was about four, only up the road but it might as well have been miles away; we're products of a single-parent family, you see, but the extended family is enormous, so there was always someone on hand to help our mum.'

'Never mind your mum' Susie leant forward, intrigued. 'You shuddered at the thought of second-hand books just then, and I'm guessing in relation to Jamie; why was that?'

'Not so much the thought of Jamie…' Jack met her gaze and puffed his chest out a little; it always worked in the past. 'Jamie sells second-hand books on the same market half our uncles and aunts work on. He sells second-hand books, he hangs on the no.238 bus and writes WHUFC slogan on the backs of seats with a permanent marker, he goes to football; and that's his life.'

'So in that respect he very much conformed to the traditional identity coded onto him.'

He shrugged. 'I think he's too slow to have thought about it either way; he takes everything at face value, you know? J just…'is'.'

'You call him 'J', though,' she said. 'That indicates some level of affection, or at the very least familiarity.'

The rain came harder still now, and the window-panes rattled slightly. Susie got up and switched the lights on. Jack cleared his throat again. 'We never really fought; we did our own thing, more like. The only thing we ever really agreed on was this girl...'

'Ah, it was a girl!!' she laughed, and the class laughed with her. 'It all becomes clear now! It's always about a girl, isn't it?'

Jack laughed sheepishly. 'Maybe.' And he said suddenly, 'or maybe that was just the straw that broke the camel's back. If anything it was our sixteenth birthday; that's where it all went pear-shaped.'

'Are you comfortable continuing?' she asked. 'Because I must say, this is fascinating.' He nodded and she made a few notes. 'What was her name, this girl?'

'Tiffany.'

Susie nodded. 'Lovely name. Greek, I think; 'Revelation of God'. Tell me, did she have a heavenly body?'

Jack laughed out loud, deep and throaty. 'Well...'

'I'll take it from that lovely little boy grin that she did, then,' Susie smiled. 'Did Tiffany have anything to do with your decision to leave Barking behind?'

'Kind of. Like I said, what happened with her was like the last straw. When we met...'

'...this is therapy at its most revelatory,' Susie quickly informed the class, 'although normally he'd be sitting down.'

'...when we met I dated her before Jamie did, but I think I turned her off a bit with my...'

'...with your?'

'Naked ambition?'

'I see...' he could feel her eyes running up and down him; she was the kind of woman he might've had a crush on when he was at school himself, all open-necked blouse, shoulder-length brown hair and kitten heels despite the fact she must've been fifty, give or take a year. 'So Tiffany opted for Jamie because he more conformed to the coded identity?'

'I guess.' Jack frowned, and stared at a point in the middle of the floor. 'Are we talking physically or emotionally here?'

'You tell me.'

'Well, emotionally yeah. But physically? Reckon I'm the better bet, if I do say so myself.' And here he tried to make light of it by flexing his bicep theatrically, but Susie was playing with her pen and studying his expression intently. 'She told me so, as it happens,' he went on.

'She did?'

'Uh huh. The day she 'stepped out' with J we had a final...'fling', and she basically said it was me physically, but J emotionally; she said I was...' and here he fought with his own self-perception. 'She said I was up my own arse.'

The class laughed, but only after he'd laughed himself, a kind of 'stupid girl, what did she know', type laugh. Susie made some more notes. 'You have good Body-Ego image, Jack?'

'I work out, yeah.'

'I can see that. But that's not what I asked.'

'…well, I don't go without…'

'Oh come on,' she said. 'You swagger in here in your tight t-shirt, showing your big arms off; you're over six feet and blond, and you have what most of us would call 'classical good looks'. If you tell me you don't have good Body-Ego image then you're lying.'

'Well thanks…'

'Don't mention it. And Tiffany was right, you know.'

'She was?!'

'Only kidding. But it galls you, doesn't it? That you perceive yourself as better looking than Jamie, far more well-educated…'

'…I think he's got like, one GCSE.'

'…and yet still Tiffany chose him.'

He nodded. 'Yup.'

'Do you love Jamie?'

Jack bowed his head, and swallowed. He struggled for a minute, and the rain lashed the window panes suddenly. 'Yeah,' he said. 'I do. I hate the little shit, but I love him to bits too, you know?'

'Do you really love him unconditionally? Don't hold back now, Jack.'

'Yeah,' he nodded. 'I do. I'd go to hell and back for that boy.'

'That's very interesting.' Susie made some final notes, as the rain outside seemed to change direction suddenly, and to hit the window panes in a veritable torrent. 'What does Jamie think?'

Jack bowed his head. He inhaled, and his nostrils flared briefly. 'He hates me, absolutely.' His chest rose, and he let out a world-weary sigh. 'It's practically irretrievable, I'd say. We only spoke recently because a close relative passed away. He was courteous enough, but I think he didn't even know what day it was, to tell you the truth. As soon as he was lucid he…well, like I said, it's irretrievable.'

Susie nodded. 'That was very brave of you, Jack,' she said. 'And take it from a much older women that few things are as irretrievable as they may seem when they're you're age.'

He smiled weakly. 'Thanks.'

She nodded. 'You can sit down now, but first,' and here she turned to the rest of the class, 'a round of applause for Jack please.'

'You arrogant prick,' Dorothy whispered under the adulation, kicking his foot again.

He mouthed her a gentle kiss, and then, as the class gradually dissolved out the door, made a beeline for the pouty little brunette with the big chest.

They found David in the library, up on the second floor, near the section devoted to journals and articles. His head was buried in several collections of material regarding media documentation and representation of so-called 'paranormal' activity. 'Looks like a load of old bollocks, if you ask me,' Jack said, leaning over his shoulder and running his eyes up and down the screen. He enjoyed flirting with David this way, placing one hand either side of his own and demonstrating just how much bigger, and hairier his own hands were. Sometimes it was more fun to flirt with David and his gay friends than with girls, because it only stroked his ego even more to know that he could probably get any man he wanted as well as any female; females sometimes just took a bit longer, that was his experience, although not so much on a Friday or Saturday night, when he was wearing one of his figure-hugging Versace t-shirts. He leant in a little further on either side of the desk so that David was essentially encapsulated inside of his presence, then tapped out something on the keyboard and hit 'enter'. A few seconds later his search results flooded the screen, and there, about a fifth of the way down, was his own family name, and next to it a reference to a Fortean Times article written in 1980; next to that there was the catalogue number for an out of print book on 'the haunted London ghost walk'. 'Reckon you can add to that little list, matey?' he peered down at David and raised his eyebrow.

David swallowed and hit the 'back' button, returning to the previous screen. 'I don't see why not, do you?'

'Why not indeed?' Jack stepped back and rubbed his hands together. 'I fancy a spot of lunch; how about you two?'

'You should have seen him in class just now,' Dorothy slung her handbag on the desk and sat herself on the edge, crossing her legs. 'The teacher was all over him like egg on toast; 'you're so handsome Jack; you've got such big biceps, Jack', and I'm like, my god woman, a little decorum please, you're a seasoned professional!'

'Hey, I happen to think she's a fantastic teacher,' Jack folded his arms. 'I thought you did too.'

'Oh I do,' Dorothy nodded. 'I just can't get my head around her informal teaching style. When we have Renata we can't get a word in edgeways, but with Susie it's always so…interactive.'

'I bet he loved it.' David gazed up at Jack lovingly.

'She fancied me,' Jack said simply. 'You can't deny it.'

'Not everyone fancies you,' Dorothy rolled her eyes. 'I don't.'

'Yeah, but I'm working on you,' Jack sat next to her and squeezed her hand. 'I love a challenge now and then; modern girls are so easy, you know? You're a bit like something from the Fifties!'

She shook her head. 'You are so bad, Jack Woodfield.'

'Yeah, but you love me, don't you?!'

They left the library a little over an hour later, after books had been returned and new texts taken out, and in Jack's case several fines for overdue items begrudgingly paid. Stopping off in the student union shop he perused the selection of Valentines cards available, selecting one with a huge red heart against a white background and purchasing it, stuffing it hastily into his rucksack, too late to stop the others from catching on, however. 'Just the one?' Dorothy folded her arms. 'I thought you had more women waiting than a gynaecologist.'

'It's for Tiffany, I bet' David cut in, beaming, 'he wuvs her! Yes he does, he weally weally wuvs her!'

'Tiffany's the one that got away,' Dorothy nodded knowingly. 'That's all it is; his ego has been slighted and until he can get an answer straight from her mouth as to why she forsook his big biceps over Jamie's more modest assets he'll be forever tormented, isn't that right, dear, dear Jack?'

'I admit I may have been a little...arrogant in the past,' he conceded. 'But I'd just got my acceptance to university through; I was like, on a chemical high! But I guess she prefers safe little Jamie and his West Ham DVDS...'

'He's not bitter really,' Dorothy lolled an arm around David's shoulder and they laughed easily. 'In class he positively gushed about Jamie, for seven seconds at least. I think all the girls who didn't want to fuck at him at that point wanted to marry him, at the very least.'

'I think it's sweet,' David said. 'Look at his little puppy dog expression; we've hit gold, you know; we've found the Essex man who shows his emotions!'

'Bite me, you big queen,' Jack jostled him playfully. 'I'll drop this off there tomorrow though, kind of inconspicuous like. If my mum corners me I'll be there for days. Plus I'm sure J has a wonderful day planned for 'tiff; a Subway ham and cheese meal for two, and then a quick grope around the back of the Bull. Ah, romance.'

*

The pizza arrived at the Islington flat late, and they ended up with cheesy wraps instead of chicken wings, but Jack was in a good mood and he tipped the delivery boy anyway. 'Meat Feast is good,' Dorothy nodded, setting out the plates before them and giving the ketchup bottle a rather overenthusiastic shake, 'although my waist will be moaning in the morning.'

'Tuck in guys,' Jack took the bottle from her and sprayed it all over the side of his plate; he couldn't eat anything without ample amounts of ketchup. For some reason that probably pertained to the class earlier today he called that the same went for Jamie, although on the rare occasions when someone had tried to point it out as a quaint little way of fastening the two of them together in 'twin-dom', either one or the other would usually regard the 'interloper' as though they were quite mad. Jack added quickly, 'Here's to the impending Easter break!'

'No, to Valentine's Day,' David said. 'To love!'

'Not so much of a break when you've got coursework,' Dorothy sighed. 'What do you have to do?'

He shrugged, cutting off his own slice and gouging the onions out with the tip of his knife. 'Not too much since I'm part-time. Got to type up everything Jack's told me about his funky family so far though, get my dissertation into shape; Fortean Times won't let me submit it as an in-house piece until it's in a more saleable form. They're talking about a good two-thirds of an issue though, cover and all. I'll get a cover credit, which is quite something. There might even be a book in the works. How's the relational psychotherapy going?'

Dorothy waited until she'd finished chewing. 'That's all fine and dandy. However, Jack and I have to finish up that presentation on postcolonial attitudes to sexuality for next week in our 'gender and contemporary society' unit, and then we're done for Easter. I've had Fanon up to here, I can tell you.'

'Postcolonial attitudes to sexuality?' David laughed, 'sounds fun. Is it all recriminations and the like?'

'It bores me shitless,' Jack sat back, swigging on a glass of cola. 'Last term was far more interesting; it's only the fact we have the same teacher makes me stick at it. I think she fancies me, you know. I also think she's a lesbian, but hey, I've broken down that barrier a few times too, so what the hey.'

David cleared his throat, cut off the next three slices and shelled them out. 'Jack and I were thinking of doing Europe this summer, D. You want to come? You could bring your little one with you.'

'What would your family say about that, Jack?' Dorothy raised an eyebrow dubiously, 'you running off to Europe without them?'

'I can pretty much do what I like,' he stretched his arms over his head in an all-powerful kind of way. 'As long as I pretend I'm interested in fake Filas and the like. It's kind of a family tradition; I was gonna try and explain it to Susie but I thought she might've tried to get me sectioned, you know?; one boy in the family is given the duty of steering the family fortunes, looking after the family finances, stuff like that; kind of like in-house wet-nursing, really. She'd balk at the patriarchy of the whole thing.'

'Who's the Daddy?!?' Dorothy giggled, but there was something else in her voice, somewhere between derision and dread.

Jack smiled. 'I mean, we don't have much money but we do have a certain status in the community. My family owned half of Barking back in the day. Now of course I realise that it's a shit-hole, but that's not the point. Property is property, even in a shit-hole.'

'I like the whole guardian angel angle,' David prompted. 'It's a bit homo-erotic, isn't it?! I mean, you just happen to be this big, strong handsome guy, and there they go and charge you with protecting everyone else…'

'Yeah kind of,' he nodded, his mouth half full. 'And on top of that, conforming to that 'butch' ideal is supposed to bring us good luck, good fortune, that kind of thing. I suspect however that it's all a pile of crock 'coz all my cousins are still wearing those fake Filas and fake Fred Perry, and they're still in council houses and doing dead-end shit jobs, either that or they have no jobs to begin with. Running a stall on the East Street market is about as good as it gets in my family. Still, I wonder what they'd say if they knew I was…'

'…knew you were what?'

'…selling family secrets to Fortean Times to finance my way through LSE…it's kind of cuntish, isn't it?!'

'Look,' Dorothy took her plate into the kitchen, returning moments later to pick up the pizza packing. 'I'm sure your family's lovely, but they do have some silly ideas about things, if you don't mind me saying. So you're making a break; you're not the first and you won't be the last. And in regards to Europe in the summer, yes I'm up for it, as long as you don't mind me bringing the little one along.'

'We can be mummy and daddy,' Jack beamed. 'And Davey boy here can be his 'funny uncle!''

*

David did the washing up while Jack smoked a roll-up by the back door, gazing up at the stars. It was a clear, chilly night, the rain having long ago cleared away. His breath, mixed in with the smoke, made little clouds that drifted up the back stone stairway and beyond, into the overgrown little garden beyond. 'Are you really going to give that Valentine card to Tiffany?' David asked, quite out of the blue.

'Hhhmmm?' Jack half turned, frowning. 'What?'

'That Valentines card; are you really going to give it to Tiffany?'

'Well…yeah,' he said. 'Why?'

'Don't you think that might be creating a little?'

'Mate, I haven't signed it,' Jack said. 'That's the point. At least she'll get one off me; J just marks his with an 'X', I know 'coz that's how he sends his Christmas and Birthday cards, heck, everything with J is just a big 'X'.'

'I wondered who that card was from last year,' David smiled softly. 'Poor bugger. Maybe if you weren't so busy fucking everything with the biggest cup size you might have been able to spare him five minutes to teach him how to sign his name properly.'

'Oh don't you start as well,' he sighed. 'My Aunt Amanda rang me just the other week, as it happens, and asked if I wouldn't mind doing just that, and I'm like, 'to fuck with it!'; I'm trying to do a Masters here, you know! What the fuck do people think I am?!'

David turned, drying his hands on the towel that hung over the bin. 'They think you're 'the Daddy', don't they?'

Jack flicked the roll-up out into the darkness. It landed somewhere on one of the steps and burnt briefly, then went out. Wolvie, their pretty little black and white cat with the smudge on his nose appeared out of nowhere and went and sniffed at it, then wrinkled his face up as the last gasp of smoke erupted all over him. Jack laughed and then turned and fixed David with his steeliest gaze. 'Fuck that, mate,' he said. 'Being the Daddy, I mean.'

Chapter 10

Tuesday 14th February 2006

The night Jamie and Tiffany had come out as a couple, at the party mum and Uncle Phil had thrown for them, Jack had taken Tiffany to one side in Uncle Phil's flat – somewhere he didn't particularly like to go – and, underneath the balloons and the banners, had promised her that if she went with him and not Jamie, that he could '…take her away from this shit hole.'

'Which shit hole are you referring to?' she'd said, rather coldly. 'You can't be magnanimous about where you come from, can you? Rather you have to downplay it at the best of times and positively deride it at the worst.'

'Barking…Essex!' he'd thrown his hands up in the air almost in disbelief. 'Okay, that's where I come from!!'

'And there's nothing wrong with it,' she'd replied. 'I like it here. I like your family. They're good people, Jack.'

He'd sighed, rolled his eyes. 'You've been approached for modelling contracts, do you really want to stay here with these chavs for the rest of your life?! You're better than this, 'tiff.'

'These chavs?!' she'd gasped, shaking her head in disbelief. 'Jack, to which 'chavs' are you referring?'

'Listen to me,' he'd braced himself against the wall behind her, leaning in closer and not caring who saw them. 'I'm getting out of here, you know this. I've got my degree and my flat in Islington is in the pipeline, and now I've been accepted to the London School of Economics to do my Masters. I'm going to live in that flat in Islington, and you could come with me. You could do a course in something or other, I know you did gender at college, I could help you with that; you could do it degree level, do some modelling on the side, we could have a damn good life, the way I see it. You don't belong here anymore than I do; heck, moreso! You're from Holland Park, for fuck's sake! You could change you name to 'Persephone' or something!'

She'd fingered the lapels of his Stone Island jacket in amusement. 'Funny…you can take the boy out of Barking but you can't take Barking out of the boy.'

'I like it,' he'd shrugged. 'Mum got me it. I wear it as a statement of irony.'

'Well,' she buttoned it up for him, 'you go off to the London School of Economics and I hope you have a really nice time there; be as ironic as you like. Who knows, maybe your brother could go there too if you'd just help him along a little, instead of just thinking of yourself all the time, and of how much better you are than everyone else.'

Jack had wet his lips. 'Not my fault J never put in the study hours, is it?' And he'd made a great theatrical sweep with both arms. 'You'll go nowhere with him, 'tiff. You'll end up pushing a second-hand pram around that dreary shopping centre on a Saturday afternoon with all the other young hags, Hackney face-lifts and all. I know your mum; she'll have kittens if you end up like that.'

She'd shifted defensively. 'I might go back to college...'

'...and there's also the one glaring fact,' he'd said. 'You fancy me a lot more than you do him. You like a bit of rough, 'tiff; I know you.'

She had disengaged herself rather rapidly at that point, swallowing hard. 'If you'll excuse me, I have some ASDA pizza slices to serve to the guests, and some ASDA's own brand Lambrusco to wash it all down...'

Jack had watched her go, puffing the air out of his cheeks and then laughing to himself, shaking his head in disbelief. That was almost four years ago, and almost four years on from that simple but significant exchange Tiffany still lived with her best friend Elisha in a modest two-bedroom flat on the London Road, adjacent to the car park and right around the corner from the Murphy Estate where Jack had grown up. Her flat was also directly above the Legends nightclub; sound-proofing was almost non-existent and as a result they'd ended up paying the bare minimum in rent, and didn't tell the landlord that a pair of earplugs and a heavy rug effectively put paid to any unwanted nocturnal noise. The girls had done the flat up as best they could, having the awful lime-green carpet pulled up and replaced with wooden tiling and the aforementioned rug, something Jack had done for them on a couple of rainy Sunday afternoons last spring.

That block of flats, just behind the Murphy Estate, were about the first thing that sprung into view on this rainy Tuesday evening as the tube pulled towards Barking. It ground to a halt, disgorging its usual array of commuters, and Jack himself, in jeans and a white t-shirt under that Stone Island jacket, and holding a great big bunch of pink oeillets. He hurried up the steps and made a sharp right, almost jogging down Station Parade and onto East Street, eager to avoid any chance encounters with aunts or uncles, or any of his countless cousins. He arrived at St. Margaret's almost soaked to the skin, shaking himself off like some big, shaggy dog before he rang the buzzer. A moment later his Aunt Betty's voice crackled over the intercom. 'Hello?'

'Aunt Betty?' he sniffed. 'It's Jack! Is Jessica there?'

'Oh Jack!!' she gasped. 'Yes she is; come on up.' And she'd buzzed him in. He readied himself for what he considered to be the rather rank odour of the flats above St. Margaret's. It hadn't changed, even though he hadn't set foot in there in maybe a year. It was sort of musty, like stale, wet wood mixed with old brickwork that ran up from the foundations of the church, and wafted down from the Curfew Tower, the only remaining part of Barking Abbey. Minty Hardcore had run up the steps to the Curfew Tower and flung herself off it, so the fairy tales that Uncle Phil had told them as kids said. Jack smiled as he remembered this, smirking at how melodramatic

Uncle Phil had made it all sound, his big brown eyes widened for effect as the cousins had clustered around to hear it told, Jamie closest of all, each and every one of them spellbound. Only Jack had hung back, sitting there shaking his head, sometimes saying, 'What utter cack!' - he'd never liked fairy tales, not even as a kid.

The stale smell grew worse as he walked into the living room. Religious artefacts, horrible cheap plaster statues and rosaries draped over almost every picture jumped out at him, offending his sensibilities on levels he hadn't even cultivated the last time he'd been here. The picture only brightened when his beloved Aunt Betty stuck her head around the kitchen door, her squinty brown eyes widening in delight. 'Jack!!' she laughed. She had such a cheery, though slightly hoarse voice. She'd been a chain-smoker until she'd married Uncle Brian, and he'd kicked that out her although he hadn't managed to do down her indomitable spirit, miserable old bastard that he was. As though sensing his stream of thought Aunt Betty said, 'Your Uncle's not here right now, Jack; Bobby's at work at the KFC, but Jessica's in her room, chatting to her friends on her mobile. They're having one of those clever three-way conversations, please don't ask me how it works because I just don't know; these new-fangled modern contraptions...'

'Hiya Aunt Betty,' he beamed. He picked her up and spun her around, kissing her on both cheeks before settling her back down. 'You look well.'

'Oh Jack,' she laughed. 'You always knew how to make an old woman blush!'

'What old woman?!' he glanced around in mock concern. 'Where?!'

'Oh Jack!!'

'Any chance of a cuppa, Aunt Betty?' he said.

'Of course, dear; and a slice of lemon drizzle cake?'

'Please,' he wielded the flowers and waved them at her. 'I'll go see 'jess now then.'

'You do that, dear,' she said. She took the flowers and looked them over, and then sort of shrugged before passing them back. 'I'll be along in a moment.'

He went and pressed his ear to Jessica's door and listened, smiling as her light, cheery voice drifted into his ears, laughing and joking. He gently opened it and sidled slowly into the room; he wanted to surprise her. That room was in fact little more than a cell, in more ways than one. She'd made the best of its cramped conditions and the fact that the wall on one side was the awful cold brick of the Curfew Tower, pinning up numerous posters of her favourite pop stars and the like, and scattering her pink cuddly toys all over the place. Jessica loved pink; she was just so girly that way, a sexy little stereotype that make his inner sociologist squirm in a marvellous mixture of delight and despair. Right now his little pink girl was spread-eagled on her front on her pink duvet, in her pink panties and her pink t-shirt with its red sequinned love-heart, legs bent at the knees and her feet curling one around the other, her ankle bracelet with the pink love heart slipping up and down the silky smooth flesh first slow and then suddenly, depending on how she moved. A pink hair grip kept her tumbling blond tresses in place, and both sets of nails were the same shade of pink. It was so soft and warm, and the sheer defiance of it against the awful dreariness of this place made him smile. Here was his other half, spiritually, although he'd left her behind all those years ago when he'd made his escape. He'd left her to fend for herself, and that thought had to be banished straight away, lest it consume him. He rustled the paper at the bottom of the bunch of flowers and she glanced up. Her big liquid eyes widened, and she said to whoever it was she was talking to, 'There's a man in my room!' and she'd smiled up at him, breaking his heart with its brilliance. 'Oh he's very tall,' she said. 'And he's blond…he's all soaked through, and his t-shirt's clinging to his chest…great big chest, yeah…oh of course he's got big arms. Big blue eyes, too. Yeah, I'm going now!!' and she quickly turned her little pink phone with its sliding screen off and secreted it under her pillow. 'Jack!!' she gasped, leaping into his arms, 'oceans of love, Jack!!'

'Hey there, baby girl,' he kissed the end of her nose, lifting her as though she weighed nothing, letting her lock her legs around his waist. 'Thought I'd drop in and surprise you, seeing as it's Valentines and all…' and holding her steadily with one hand he'd waved the pink oeillets under her little button nose. 'For you.'

'Oh, they're lovely!!' she sniffed them, closing her eyes and savouring the fragrance. When she opened them she looked every inch the guilty girl. 'I'm being shockingly unfaithful to you again,' she said. 'Darren Richardson's taking me out for a meal, and then he'll probably want to shove his beastly little cock up me when we get back to his place!'

He raised an eyebrow. 'He treating you right?'

She made a face. 'I guess.'

'He doesn't, I'll come and kick his head in.'

She ran her finger over his lips. 'Promise?'

He kissed it, and nodded. 'Promise.' And then he'd narrowed his eyes, and gently with his free hand brushed the loose hairs back over her ears. 'Anyone hurts you, I'll fucking kill them. You're my little girl.'

Jessica rested her head against his shoulder, and closed her eyes. 'My big, strong Jack,' she whispered.

Aunt Betty came through the door at that moment, using the tray to open it, the tray with tea and lemon drizzle cake, biscuits and a pair of apples on it. 'Here you go,' she said, settling it on the bedside drawer. 'Jack, will you be staying for tea?'

Jessica looked at him, still in his arms, legs still locked around his waist. 'Say yes.'

'I can't, kid,' he shook his head. 'I just wanted to pop in and see Tiffany, really. How is she?'

'Oh, awful business,' Aunt Betty said, shaking her head. 'They say if it hadn't been for that nun, well then the no.238 would have mown her down, right there on the London Road!'

Jack nodded, swallowed. It was pretty much the same story mum had told him on the phone earlier today; Tiffany had been to ASDA to get some cake mix for something she was putting together for Jamie, a congratulatory cake on beginning his Sight & Sound course, and the bag had split as she crossed the London Road and headed for her flat. She'd chased the items all over and not heard the no.238 as it bore down on her, too fast to stop, beeping frantically, and then from out of nowhere, so said those who'd seen it, a nun had shoved her out of the way of the bus. Tiffany had fallen badly and hit her head, but at least she was alive. The nun was nowhere to be seen, when passers-by had rushed to thank her. 'It was a proper nun though,' Aunt Betty went on. 'My friend Nadine saw it all, and she said there was no mistaking it; a semi-enclosed habit, black tunic and scapular, white guimpe, coif and bandeau, all topped off with a rectangular black veil. Oh, I do love nun's outfits,' she sighed, clasping her hands together in some sort of mock prayer pose. 'I wanted to be one when I was younger. I think that's what attracted your father to me in the first place!' and she burst into one of her riffs of high pitched, slightly braying laughter, jostling Jessica's shoulder.

'Thanks for the lemon drizzle cake, Aunt Betty,' Jack settled Jessica back down on her bed, and picked up his tea.

'You just call me if you want any more,' she said, going out the door.

'Will do!'

Jessica shifted up against the brick wall but Jack shook his head, and before she could ask why he'd lifted her bodily, depositing her against the soft pink pillows, taking the chilly side of the chamber for himself. He wrapped his arm around her shoulder, kissed her forehead, and then took a hearty swig from his cup. 'This is nice,' he said, listening to the rain hammering against the window pane. 'I've missed this.' He looked down at her. 'I've missed you, kid.'

She nodded, and sniffed, jostling his chest with her little fist. 'You abandoned me, you big beast.'

'Don't say that,' he said. 'You know I didn't.'

'I cried for days when you went off to university,' she said, 'leaving me to fend for myself in this shit-hole.'

He changed the subject quickly. 'How's 'the Pope' been treating you?' he asked.

'Same as always'. She rested her head against his chest and closed her eyes. 'Whenever I go out, all made-up, he shakes his head and sometimes he even starts to say a Hail Mary. Mum calls him a silly old duffer, but...'

'He's a cunt,' Jack said, eyes narrowed.

'Yeah, he is that. But he is my dad.'

'That's no excuse, 'jess.'

'He loves me.'

He looked down at her. 'So do I.'

Jessica gazed up at him with those eyes. 'Do you really?'

He nodded, giving her arm a little squeeze. 'You know I do.'

She smiled. 'I love you too,' she said, and closed her eyes again.

'I love the way you defy him,' he said. 'How you defy the whole fucking system. Don't ever let him beat it out of you, kid. Don't let him lock you up in a tower, and leave you to rot.'

'Don't worry,' she said. 'I won't.'

They sat in silence for a long while, just listening to the rain as it continued to hammer down on the window, the wind whipping up out of nowhere and causing the branches of the trees outside to scratch and claw against the panes. She was dozing lightly when he reached over to eat his slice of lemon drizzle cake. He smiled down at her and felt the most warming, unconditional love he'd ever felt for another human being perhaps in his entire life. He'd always wanted to protect Jessica, from as far back as he could remember. He could've sat here with her all night, wrapped her up in his arms and never let her go.

But when the digital clock on the dresser ticked past eight he gently kissed her little nose again, and whispered in her ear, 'Kid? I got to go. I've got to see Tiffany, and then head on back to Islington.'

'Okay,' she gazed up at him. 'I better go and make myself nice for Darren Richardson then.'

'You're perfect as you are,' he said. He ran his thumb lightly down one rosy cheek. 'You're beautiful.'

'I'll be a whore the moment I step out that bedroom door,' she said, 'once dad catches sight of me.'

'Fuck him,' Jack curled his lip contemptuously. 'Just fuck him.'

*

The kitchen surfaces in Tiffany's flat were made of some sort of substance that shone like alabaster, and on which household spills simply trickled away. Such a surface looked like it came in extremely useful when baking a 'well done Jamie' cake, following the recipe from a DVD she had to keep pausing and unpausing as she set the oven to the correct temperature, baked the thing, let it set, and then began the pain-staking process of shaping the words in blue and purple West Ham style icing. 'Does it look ok?' she'd asked him, flicking the kettle on.

'It looks great,' Jack nodded, pulling up a stool and watching her work. 'Are you sure you're okay? That's a nasty bump on the side of your head…'

'It looks worse than it is,' Tiffany waved a hand dismissively. 'It's funny you should show up here tonight actually, Jack,' and she left the cake and set about showing him the final stage of her little surprise for Jamie, namely a collage of old photographs of the two of them together from various holidays, trips and just generally larking about. In the shoebox of abandoned extras under her bed she explained how she'd come across a picture of Jack at the top, and sat down on the edge of the bed and stared at it for a little bit. It wasn't a posed shot; he was talking to someone just next to the person taking the picture, smiling broadly; his hair was newly cropped and it added a sharpness to his already angular face that made it almost painfully vivid. 'You are a handsome bugger, aren't you?!' Tiffany waved the photo at him. 'And you've always known it.'

Jack peered at the picture, and smiled. 'I can't believe you kept that.'

'I'm not the vindictive kind,' she said, sugaring his cup.

'Did you keep the letters I used to write you too?'

'No,' she said, colouring slightly. 'I burnt them in a symbolic pyre inside Morelli's stove on the night that I finally decided it was Jamie that she wanted to be with.'

'Oh.'

'Oh don't give me that little boy lost look,' she said, adding some milk and then pouring the hot water into the cup. 'If it's any consolation my girlfriends were smacking their brows in veritable disbelief at my decision. I told them you were a player, that you had so many girls on the go that it was almost obscene, but they still called me crazy.'

'So Jamie was taking you to the cinema in Dagenham and wooing you by singing underneath her bedroom window on the Salisbury Road finally won out, huh?' Jack took the tea gratefully.

Tiffany rubbed the slight gash on the side of her head, then nodded, pulling up the stool opposite him, the kitchen unit itself the divider. 'I was initially impressed by your easy way with words, your decidedly un-Essex opinions on things, and your tendency to actually listen to me when I talked. You were a bit of a curiosity, as well as being,' and here she seemed to struggle to find the right words, 'as my girlfriends would say, "…a fucking gorgeous hunk of a man".'

Jack smiled. 'Give me their numbers sometime, will you?!'

'Oh get you,' she sighed. 'But yes, it was Jamie's cheeky grin and that child-like attitude to life that charmed me finally, his tendency to come bounding up to Morelli's with a bunch of flowers in his hand, and me knowing full well Uncle Phil had subbed him the money for.' She stuck her finger out and tested the icing on the cake, re-doing the 'J' in Jamie because she insisted it looked a little odd, and then when she stepped back and viewed the thing as a whole she was quite pleased with her work. While she was engrossed Jack discreetly slipped the Valentine card he'd brought her under the microwave, so just the corner stuck out. There was the risk Jamie might find it, but then again it wasn't signed, and Jamie couldn't read anyway. When he looked up he saw Tiffany examining her reflection in the glass of the kitchen window, pouting her lips one minute and then jutting her jaw out the next. 'You know,' she said, 'that nun, the one who saved me; she said the strangest thing to me, as we were lying there, in the middle of the road.'

'Yeah?'

'She said, "There's a little bit of me in an awful lot of you naughty, modern girls.".'

'Yeah?' he raised an eyebrow. 'What the fuck's that supposed to have meant?!'

Tiffany turned. There was something in her eye, a glint or something, and her mouth was turned up at one corner in a smile. 'I don't know,' she said, and she yawned suddenly, and stretched her arms high over her head, pulling her white t-shirt to the limit, forcing the shape of her nipples against it. 'She was gone by the time I'd properly come 'round,' she said.

Jack glanced at the clock on the wall. 'What time's Jamie getting here?'

'Why'd you ask?'

'Just…I better clear off before he does,' he said. 'You know what he's like.'

'I think it's such a shame,' Tiffany said, walking around to his side of the unit. 'I thought maybe Phil's death would have mellowed him, but where you're concerned he can still be such a childish little brat.'

Jack smiled weakly. 'I tried my best, 'tiff. He just doesn't want to know.'

'Well at least one of the brothers is an adult,' she said, her hand on his shoulder. 'At least one of you is a man.'

He looked up at her; they were eye-level, him still on the stool. You couldn't hide the fact she wasn't Essex, and it was shameful of him to compare her to the girls around here, but her breeding stuck out a mile. Her little delicate upturned nose, he wanted to kiss it the way he always wanted to kiss Jessica's nose. Tiffany's beauty was a little more on the haughty side, slightly harder. But she was a beautiful person too, on the inside. She never once bemoaned the fact she'd gone from West to East and from money to nothing, and she treated everyone around her with respect. She was well liked…no, even loved by the Woodfield family. 'You're a special girl, Tiffany Grieve,' he said, his hand on her face, his thumb gently on her cheek the way it had been on Jessica's only an hour or so ago. 'Jamie's a lucky lad.'

'You're taller than Jamie,' she said suddenly, 'isn't that funny, you being twins and all.'

'Non-identical,' he said. 'Dizygotic, if you want the exact terminology.'

'You're so much broader too,' she said, her eyes running over his shoulders with complete license. 'Jamie's very boyish, and not just in his personality.'

'I work out.'

'No, you were born this way, Jack,' she said. She ran her fingers up and down the thick, curly blond hair on his arms. 'You're so hairy too. A girl could go wild, having arms like that wrapped around her.' And she turned, and faced away from him. 'Hold me,' she said, 'just for a moment. I want to know what it's like to be held in those, big strong arms.'

Jack swallowed. 'I should go,' he said.

She peered at him over her shoulder. 'Do you want to?'

'No.'

'Then hold me.'

He did as he was told, and she let out a little sigh. He found himself nestling his chin against her shoulder, smelling the sweet fragrance she wearing, patchouli, if he wasn't mistaken, and letting her rusty red tresses tickle the end of his nose. 'You're beautiful,' he whispered.

She ran her fingers up and down the hair on his forearms again, into it, and scratched at the skin with her nails. 'Take me to bed,' she said, peering at him over her shoulder.

Chapter 11

Tuesday 14th February 2006

Jack unlocked the door to the flat as quietly as he could, wincing every time the key caused a bolt to shift with any amount of noise, pushing it open gingerly and checking that the light was out in the bedroom before he went inside. He closed the door behind him and walked into the living room, turning on only one of the small tableside lamps that David's mother had given as a flat-warming present. Then he threw his Stone Island jacket down on the couch nearest the TV, and slid his Fred Perry t-shirt up over his head. He pivoted on his heel and examined his back in big mirror directly opposite the door to the hall, and let out an audible gasp at what he saw there; his entire back was covered in scratches and even the occasional bite mark, rakings that ran in threes and fours up and down his spine and over his well-developed Trapezius and his near-perfect Rhomboids. Further down he caught sight of the thing he always made such an effort to cover up at the gym, or when he went topless during the summer months; the near perfect lip print in the small of his back, a great big smacker of a kiss, in all honesty.

'Jack?' it was David, framed in the doorway directly behind him, in a casual t-shirt and briefs, eyes bleary with sleep. 'What time is it?'

Jack glanced at his watch. 'Eleven thirty.'

'Thanks.' As his vision cleared he caught sight of the scratches and the bites. 'Shit. What happened to you?'

Jack felt like cracking a joke; 'I fell in a bush' seemed a good one, with great double entendre, but all of a sudden he had a painful twinge from an as-yet unveiled bite on his groin, and had to steady himself against the wall. 'I fell over a wall,' he said instead, 'with a bush on the other side.'

'You went to Barking...' David scratched his head. 'Oh god, did you have a fight with your brother?'

'What do you think J is, some kind of mad scratching girly poof?!' he snapped, and then caught David's face as it fell. 'Sorry mate. I'm in agony here. Have we got anything to put on these?'

'It'd help if you told me how you came by them.' David said, to which Jack coloured a little, no, make that a lot. 'Oh Jack...' David's big eyes widened. 'You didn't...'

He nodded. 'Yeah, I did.'

'Your own brother's girlfriend?!'

Jack was about to say, well it isn't the first time, and to cite the example of Nadine Leukes when they were seventeen, but Jamie hadn't been that keen on her anyway; she'd had short stubby legs, and Jamie loved long legs as much as Jack adored big tits. 'Look,' he said, shifting onto what they considered to be David's sofa, the one directly opposite the window, with considerable difficulty. 'I don't exactly feel that great about it myself, but if it's any consolation to your sensibilities, she came on to me; ravenously, I might add.'

David shook his head, and then went into the kitchen. Jack heard the sound of the cupboard under the sink being opened, and then the sounds of David rifling through their assorted pills, in the main large collections of hang-over cures, all powerful packets of Nurofen and the like. He heard the sound of Wolvie scratching on the back door and of David letting him in, and then the sound of the kettle being filled up, and two cups being prepared. A moment later David popped his head around the door, waving a tube of cream in his hand. 'This is for insect bites but I think it might be just as good for...well, for girly passion scratches. Hang on and I'll finish making the tea, then we can get them sorted out.' Jack sniffed, hunching forward when he found the fabric of the sofa irritated the marks too much. He reached forward and flicked the TV on, hopping from channel to channel and finally settling for something about pole dancers on Channel Five. David brought the teas in and set them down on the bookcase. 'Move forward,' he said. 'So I can get in behind you.'

'Don't you go getting any funny ideas while you're there.'

David rolled his eyes. 'Jack, you've just all but told me you've screwed that poor girl into next week; I don't really think questions about your sexuality are in any doubt, do you?'

'Well no, but still...'

'...and besides, I'm passive; I'm in totally the wrong position.'

Jack sniffed. 'Well that's alright then.'

David emptied in a little of the cream onto his finger and began to dab at the nastiest of the scratches with it. Jack winced, but then cleared his throat and made great play of flexing his arms impressively and gritting his teeth together and not making a sound every time the cold stuff made contact, and then began to sting. 'This must have been some session,' David said, a few minutes later.

'Mate, she was like a wild animal,' Jack lowered his eyes, noticing some of Wolvie's fur snagged on the edge of the rug under the table and kicking it free. 'I think I've got friction burns too, you know, down there, I mean.'

'I hope you used protection.'

'Well...'

'Oh Jack.'

''tiff isn't a crafty little whore or anything,' he waved a hand dismissively, and then started as some of that cream hit another tender bit. 'I think apart from J she's only ever had one other bloke. She's not an Essex girl, you know, I mean, not by birth, much less attitude. She's from Holland Park.'

'What the hell is she doing in Barking then?!'

'Parents split up, mum didn't do so well out of it, and they had relatives there. Shit, huh?'

'Jack, I think some of these scratches might need looking at; they're pretty deep.'

Jack turned the sound up a little on the TV. 'She might be on the pill anyway,' he said.

'It's not babies I was worried about, although that is something to take into consideration.'

'What then?'

'Well, you're such a man whore yourself, and all...'

Jack scowled, and turned slightly. 'Are you trying to say I might have given her something?!'

'How many girls have you slept with since...well, since the New Year?'

Jack shrugged, and then went to counting. 'Not many. Five, maybe six.'

'Christ Jack,' David shook his head. 'It's only February. Were you safe with them?'

'Mate,' Jack pivoted a little more. 'You being ginger and all, shouldn't this conversation be going the other way?!'

'What the hell is 'ginger' when it's at home?!'

'Cockney!' he sighed, shaking his head and turning back to the pole dancer. 'You know, 'ginger beer; queer', that sort of thing. My Uncle Heath uses it all the time.'

'Charming.'

'Oh mate!!' Jack shook his head. 'It's just banter, you and me. You know I don't have a problem with it.'

'I thought psychoanalysis was kind of intolerant though?'

'Used to be, but I tell you, its cock mad too; Freud was obsessed with it; 'phallocentric', they call it. You'd love it. This Willhelm Reich, he had this idea that the cock was like, the centre of the universe, and that fucking some bird was akin to releasing energy, you know? I myself buy into that particular avenue of thought.'

David finished applying the cream and sat back. 'That feel better?'

Jack nodded. 'Thanks mate.' He reached over and squeezed his hand. 'You're alright, you know, for a ginger.'

David climbed off the couch and took the cream back into the kitchen. He'd put a dressing gown on top of the t-shirt when he returned. 'Did Tiffany say anything, you know...after the fact?'

Jack was mesmerised by one of the dancers on the screen, the one with the obvious implants. 'Huh?' he turned and frowned. 'What was that?'

'Did Tiffany say anything after the fact?'

'She has great tits, you know.'

David followed his gaze. 'They look false to me.'

'No, I mean 'tiff. I spent almost four years looking for a girl with a chest like that. It's all that matters in life, trust me. I've been through more big chests than a fucking pirate looking for treasure.'

'And now that you've had it?' David finished off his tea. 'Jack, did she say anything after the fact??'

'Like what? If you want titillation then yeah, she did rub my chest and say, "Oh god Jack, oh god…" like, several times.'

'I meant did she say anything of substance? It was a one-off, right? I mean, you've had her now, so no one need be any the wiser.'

He thought about it for a minute, and then switched the TV off. 'She wants out, that's what she told me.'

'Out?'

'Out of her relationship with J. She wants to go back to college; she used to do gender stuff too, you know. I could teach her stuff. Heck, she'd pass with flying colours if I…'

'Jack, she's Jamie's girlfriend.'

'I could take her away from all that chav shite…like I said I could, almost four years ago.'

'Jack!!' David slapped him on the shoulder, inadvertently causing one of the scratches to flare up. 'She's Jamie's girlfriend.'

Jack bowed his head. He exhaled, long and slow, then inhaled, letting his shoulders rise and fall. He stood up finally, and turned around. 'Yeah, you're right,' he said. 'She is. It was a one-off.' And with that he turned and made for the hall, and the bedroom beyond it.

Chapter 12

Friday 24th March 2006

The boxing gloves were smelly and the insides were a little sweaty from the last person to use them. Jamie slipped them on and had Aunt Amanda tie the little string bits around his wrists, and he banged them together. 'How do they feel, darling?' she asked.

'Kind of weird,' he said, glancing up at the ring, where his soon-to-be sparring partner was donning his own pair of gloves and receiving a pep talk from their boss. 'Do I really have to do this?'

She nodded. 'You have to learn to handle yourself.'

'I can handle myself,' he sniffed indignantly.

'Can you fight?'

He nodded. 'Uncle Phil taught me how to throw a punch.'

'Darling, your Uncle Phil only ever used his fists as a last resort.'

'Then why do I got to do this?'

'Because he still knew how to use them, if needs be.'

'Jack can't box,' Jamie said.

'No, but Jack's pushing six foot four in a good pair of shoes, and he's built like a brick shithouse,' she said. 'Never mind that it's all gym-honed and just to look good in a tight t-shirt.'

'And Hayden taught him how to fight anyway.'

'I don't ever want you fighting like your cousin Hayden,' she fixed him with a steely gaze. 'There's a reason he's in prison, you know. Hayden Woodfield is a dirty fighter.'

'Yeah, but he's never lost a fight, has he?'

'Well, no…'

Jamie sniffed. 'I'd be terrified to get into a fight with him.'

She sighed, and slowly raised herself. The West Ham Boys Amateur Boxing Club was relatively quiet this Friday afternoon, and Aunt Amanda had secured the friendly sparring match by way of calling in an old favour that the owner, a big, hairy guy called Bob owed her. Jamie never knew how Aunt Amanda knew all these people, or what she could possibly have done for them to make them so indebted to her. There seemed nothing she couldn't achieve, if she put her mind to it.

Bob gave the nod and she ushered Jamie up into the ring, and then clambered through the ropes herself, and sat him down on the stool facing his opponent, an Asian boy with spiky black hair and a thin, almost cruel mouth. 'Keep moving,' she said, glancing at the boy, then back at Jamie. 'That's how your Uncle Alexander used to fight, and unlike your Uncle Phil he used his fists first and foremost. Keep moving, keep dancing, dart from left to right, make it impossible for him to lay a finger on you.'

Jamie gazed down at his arms, rather spindly but firm, and as often bothered him when he saw Jack, totally hairless. He'd asked Uncle Phil once why he didn't have hardly any body hair and barely any beard, and Aunt Rose had laughed and said it was because he was blond, and often blond men didn't. But Jack was blond, he'd point out, and Jack was shaving when he was fourteen, and he had big, hairy arms and hair on his belly when he was fifteen; Jack had a hairy chest by the time he was seventeen, and people thought he was about twenty five, and he could get into clubs and buy cigarettes and everything. Mum had told him he was silly to worry about such things, but he'd hit back that she didn't know what it was like to be a boy, and that he knew girls worried about having big boobs and stuff, and that this was no different for a boy. The trouble with the Woodfield men was that they were all so…what was the phrase Aunt Amanda used? 'hyper-masculine', that was it. Jamie didn't know exactly what it meant but it sounded pretty much about being tough and being tall, and having a big square jaw and big, hairy hands. Jamie came pretty low on the tier system for such things; even the reviled cousin Hayden, with his pouty lips and clear, smooth skin, had Jack's big, hairy arms and the solid, manly swagger that Jamie couldn't seem to perfect for love nor money.

Bob's shout for the match to begin broke him out of his revelry and Aunt Amanda whispered something that sounded a lot like 'good luck' in his ear and then almost pushed him bodily into the centre of the ring. The boy - Zavid – danced as nimbly as Aunt Amanda suggested he ought to do, and then suddenly threw a series of punches so quick and so devastating that Jamie found himself slumped down on the canvas and gazing up at the ceiling, watching the overhead fan spinning hypnotically. 'Get up, darling!!' he heard Aunt Amanda yell. 'For God's sake, get up!!'

He spat, and tasted just the faintest metallic tinge of blood. He thought of Minty Hardcore, although he had no real idea what he was supposed to be thinking of, since Aunt Amanda had refused to tell him, and a sudden surge of indignant fury surged through him. He was on his feet and swinging his arms almost like propellers, and he landed several punches but this Zavid just laughed them off and danced around to the left and hit him on the side of the face, although not as hard as before. 'Come on, Jamie lad!!' Bob shouted. 'You can do better than this! You're a Woodfield, for Christ's sake!!'

'Jamie, you're doing so well!' Aunt Amanda cried, somewhere to his left. 'Think of all you've achieved recently!'

This was true; he thought briefly of the fact that he'd passed his initial reading and writing tests at Sight & Sound and could now author complete sentences, and read entire paragraphs of 'The Wizard of Oz' unaided; in essence he was free to leave the college if he wanted, but had decided to stay on under the mutual insistence of both Aunt Amanda and Monique to do advanced reading and writing, and also to learn basic office skills, with an emphasis on typing, something that would come in useful if he did indeed go on to some form of higher education. He had done that, so why couldn't he do this?!? He couldn't do this, so he reasoned as another flurry of punches rained down on him, because Uncle Phil had always been around to take care of any trouble he'd ever encountered. Uncle Phil had always stood between him and strife of any kind. That, and because as much as he hated to acknowledge the fact, Jack had always looked out for him too, usually when they were at school, places where Uncle Phil wasn't around, even though Jamie had told him to 'butt out', or 'go to hell' whenever he'd tried to help.

He glanced over at Aunt Amanda, her flaming red hair artfully tossed over one shoulder, her ruby red lips mouthing encouragement that he couldn't quite decipher. He swung blindly in an attempt to impress her, but hit only empty air, and then tasted more blood as Zavid hit him full in the face.

'Darling,' Aunt Amanda kissed him on both cheeks, and much to his embarrassment, once on the forehead, where the biggest of his burgeoning collection of bruises was just beginning to show, 'still adorable despite such a poor initial showing.'

'He was experienced,' Jamie sniffed, following her up the escalator. 'I reckon I should've been up against a beginner, like me.'

She waved a hand dismissively. 'Where are you taking me for lunch today?'

'Um…' he patted his pockets. 'I'm a little strapped for cash, especially now that Clay's doing the book stall instead of me. I'm skint.'

'Darling, don't be silly,' she threaded her arm through his and led him out of Leicester Square Underground, over the road, and up the steps into the nearby Garfunkel's. 'It's on me, as always. You can take your old aunt out to the Ritz once you've passed your degree.'

'Aunt Amanda!!'

'And why shouldn't you?!' she sat herself down at a window table, bypassing the 'please wait to be seated' sign completely. 'You're doing fine by all accounts.'

'I don't even have a university place yet,' Jamie threw his coat onto the seat beside him. 'And term wouldn't start until the end of September anyway.'

'Plenty of time to get you in somewhere,' she scanned the menu. 'Obviously we need to think modest, but where would you like to study, Essex or here, in the West End?'

He picked up a knife and examined his reflection in it; one of his eyes was going to be sporting a terrific shiner come the morning. 'I don't know. What do you think?'

'I think it's entirely up to you, darling.'

'Well I don't really know universities, and I certainly couldn't get into the London School of Economics with Jack…'

'…and we wouldn't want you to,' she tapped the side of her nose knowingly. The waitress sidled up to them. 'I'll have a mineral water,' Amanda nodded, 'sparkling. Jamie?'

'Pepsi.'

Amanda nodded. 'We'll order our meals in a moment.' She waited until the waitress had receded before resting her chin on her hands and fixing him with a loving look. 'You don't think I was too harsh, do you, darling?'

Jamie shrugged. 'I'm fine. I have been in fights before, you know.'

'Really?'

'Really.' He nodded. 'One time this boy had a go at me when Jack and Hayden were bunking off somewhere, and Michael had the flu, and I can't remember where Clay and Springer were, but…

She raised a carefully pencilled eyebrow. 'Jamie…'

He shifted uncomfortably. 'Well anyway. It's hard, that's all, everything you've told me these past few weeks. And Tiffany's been a little distant since she had that knock on the head. You don't think she thinks I'm changing too much, do you? I'm trying to think in a Daddy mindset, and all…'

'I thought you said she was helping you,' she leant back as their drinks were served, and they ordered their meals. 'You said she was all for it.'

'I guess she's just got a new modelling contract or something. She used to read with me every night to start with but now it's only when she can fit me in. I'm thinking she's suddenly realised exactly how dumb I really am. What if that knock on the head brought her to her senses?!?'

'You're both young,' Aunt Amanda took out her cigarettes, slipped one into the engraved holder Uncle Phil had given her for her sixtieth birthday, and lit up. A moment later the waitress sidled over and informed her that they were in a no smoking restaurant. Aunt Amanda batted her eyes, and something strange happened, like a distortion in the air like the heat wave on a hot road, and she purred, 'You really haven't noticed me smoking, my dear; in fact, no one here has.'

Jamie watched the waitress rather absent-mindedly toddle off, and grinned. 'I love it when you do that. It's like what Obi-Wan Kenobi did in 'Star Wars' when the Stormtroopers stopped Luke Skywalker's Landspeeder!'

'Doing those sorts of things is how I'm going to get rid of her,' she rested her spare hand on his. 'You're the bait, and I'm the trap.'

Jamie laughed uneasily, scratching his baby stubble. 'So I got to get her to want me more than she'll want Jack?!'

'Darling, you're a Woodfield male,' she said it as though it were a universal truth, as obvious as red London buses and rain in June. 'That places you head and shoulders above most of the other men I know. And she'll want you – at least I hope she will - because Jack doesn't believe in her. Jack is very modern that way, and sickeningly cynical about such things. Now let's see…' she cast her eyes around the restaurant, and seemed to settle on something a few moments later. 'I'm going to show you just what I mean. I'm going to make the salt and pepper shakers dance.'

'What?!' he laughed.

'You heard me. Don't worry, no one will notice…much. I'll make them dance. I'll make them do the Conga.'

Jamie lowered his eyelids and glanced around. 'Real magic?'

She nodded. 'Real magic.' And she made a little steeple of her hands. 'And you're going to help me.'

'I am?'

'You are, but never you mind how. Let's just say that today's little display has left me all charged up.'

'Uncle Phil could do it,' Jamie said. 'He could do all kind of weird stuff. I bet I couldn't do it. I'm not like him.'

'Oh but you are like your Uncle Phil, darling,' she smiled. 'You've just never really grasped your wand firm enough, is all.'

Jamie licked his lips and sat back. He didn't know whether to close his eyes in case he got scared or keep them open but he was conscious of people maybe watching, so he kept them open. A tingle rose on the back of his neck, a lovely shiver that travelled into his head and up and down his spine, and when he looked up the salt and pepper shakers were doing the Conga along the tables, backwards and forwards and from side to side, in and out, little metal arms grasping their partners front and back. 'Wonderful,' said Aunt Amanda, with a smile.

Chapter 13

Tuesday 28th March 2006

'Wonderful', was how Dorothy referred to her apartment, the converted attic in an old red-brick building in Queens Park that dated back maybe a hundred and fifty years or so, neatly hidden down a leafy side street just off the main thoroughfare of the Salisbury Road. Unlike most girls her age she wasn't renting but actually buying, managing the mortgage with the help of her parents, both respected psychoanalysts, and part-time work as a trainee relational psychotherapist that she could fit in between her rather demanding MSc on the aforementioned subject. She was extremely house-proud, she'd warned Jack and David on the short walk from the Underground, and the place was always spotless, sometimes clinically so. She didn't have a TV, something the two of them found rather shocking, and it took David especially several moments to contemplate exactly what life might be without one, before he dismissed the idea with a shudder and bent forward to examine an 'arty' black and white shot of Dorothy aged six, all strawberry blond curls and prominent beauty spot, perched on her mother's lap. Her mother was an attractive woman with a slightly large mouth and high cheekbones, with the same the exotic, almost heathen looks that Dorothy sported, complete with the upturned, slightly feline eyes. 'She's pretty isn't she?' David said to Jack. 'I mean, the both of them are.'

'Your mum's pretty, D' Jack nodded, straightening up and moving to the next picture, a family shot, 'you an only child then?'

'Uh huh,' she was in the kitchen, preparing cups of tea. 'Mum wanted me to have a little sister or something but dad was against it. Kids were too much of a distraction, as far as he was concerned.'

'He's a psychotherapist too, right?' Jack asked.

'Certainly is. He's written a few books, worked with some well-known names. My mum's into all the gender side of it; they met at the same place. My mum did her Masters with our Susie Orbach, you know.'

'Okay,' he moved back from the mantelpiece and stuffed his hands in his pockets, then saw a shot of a little boy, perhaps three or four, all big brown eyes gazing wistfully out at the camera from under a shock of dark blond hair. 'And this is your little one?'

Dorothy paused, pouring the milk into the cups, and then glanced over her shoulder. 'That's my Justin. He's at nursery at the moment.'

'He looks a little cutie.'

'Oh he can be a little monster too, believe me,' she said. 'But don't ask me about the dad; let's just say he's out of the picture. I'm off men; the two of you, you're a radical experiment.'

'Ouch,' Jack accepted the tea gratefully when it came, and sat down beside her on the couch, David next to him. 'Sounds like you have a few…issues.'

'Kind of,' she tilted her head to one side. 'Let's just say my dad thinks being a single mum is something to be ashamed of; he tells everyone he meets that Justin's father was killed.'

'That's terrible,' David said.

'Fuck that.' Jack rolled his eyes. 'Well you don't want to become all bitter and twisted about it.' he reached into his rucksack and pulled out a handful of rather lightweight textbooks. 'So, where do you want to start?'

Dorothy looked at him. 'Do you think I am?'

'Do I think you are what?'

'Bitter and twisted?'

'Hell no,' Jack laughed. 'I love you, girly. We wouldn't hang around with you if you were. It's kind of refreshing to have someone outside the family, I mean a girl, who I actually haven't…'

'Dated?'

'Yeah, that sounds about right.'

Dorothy smiled to herself. Jack had never met a girl like her, looks-wise. It was like he'd said to Jamie on Christmas Eve, he felt sorry for her that she elicited so many comments on her exotic appearance as she walked down the street. He garnered just as many for his broad shoulders, big arms, and ice blue eyes, but it was different for a girl. A lot of the time Dorothy walked with her head bowed and her arms folded. She gave of the impression of being aloof, or distant, although remarkably enough it had been her who had initiated their friendship in the first place, making a point of sitting next to him in their opening gender & society classes, and offering him spearmint gum, turning and raising her eyebrows as the teacher made suggestions she thought were faintly ridiculous, and the like. He'd been fully expecting her to hit on him at any moment, and when after a fortnight it hadn't come he'd decided to take the matter into his own hands. They'd been standing in the student registration area, waiting for David to finish completing a form for a grant he was applying for, and she'd been leaning up against the wall and he'd moved a little closer, then put his arm above her. She'd stared at him and then her lips had curled up slowly, into a smile. That was the signal, he'd thought, and moved in slowly; apart from the one member of staff and David there was no one else around to see them. And then he'd felt her hand on his chest and heard a little giggle. When he'd opened his eyes she'd been shaking her head. 'What?!?' he'd said, slightly offended. He could quite honestly say he'd never been rebuffed by a girl before, and certainly not with a giggle to punctuate the point.

'Nothing,' she'd said. 'You're exactly like…' and then she'd shaken her head, and stood on the tips of her heels and planted a delicate, decidedly platonic kiss on his lips. 'You are a big cheeseball, Jack Woodfield. But I love you.' And she'd turned and walked purposefully over to David, and lolled an arm around his shoulder.

Dorothy pulled him back to the present, saying, 'I've been thinking about emailing Susie or Renata about some revision classes before the exam in June. What do you think?'

'I think I want to get the gender essay out of the way first,' he said. 'Then maybe when we're all done, you, me, and Davey boy here can go away for the summer, like we said the other day; go around Europe or something. I want to go to Rome, and crick my neck gazing up at the Sistine Chapel. Bring the sprog, if you want.'

'Aren't you supposed to do that in a gap year?'

'I didn't do a gap year,' Jack began making notes in the margins of the top textbook in the pile. 'I went straight from college to university to my masters, no break whatsoever. Oh, well I did do work experience in an office down Old Street.'

She was looking at him, smiling. 'Why the urgency?'

Jack sat back and made himself comfortable; there was something about the flat that was indeed too clinical, and therefore a little cold; kind of like Dorothy herself, although with her there were moments at least when the sensible, somewhat formal façade faded a little. He couldn't imagine spending hours here either studying or whatever else she had in mind. 'If you lived in Barking you'd understand,' he said. 'I couldn't get out of there quick enough.'

She laughed, and David laughed a little as well. 'Is it that bad?'

He finished marking the book and went on to the next one. 'Worse, if you come from my crazy family.'

'And are they really so bad?'

Jack paused to consider before his answer. 'Yes and no. You come from such a tiny family that it's hard to explain. Like Davey boy here.'

'Whoever said I came from a tiny family?' the corners of her mouth turned up in a wicked grin. 'Maybe my family's as big as yours, and twice as crazy.'

'Well your immediate family...'

'...is rather minimal, yes. But perhaps I have a massive 'alternative' family; a veritable fraternity of psychoanalysts...'

'Well mine isn't minimal, either the immediate family or the extended one. We breed like rabbits.'

'Your family's rather famous, aren't they?' she sipped her own tea. 'In Essex, I mean. They go back a long way. Everyone knows the Woodfields. Even I've heard of some of them; wasn't Jeramiah Woodfield a friend of Aleister Crowley?'

'He certainly was,' David sat forward, suddenly animated. 'Apparently he taught Crowley all he knew, and then Crowley disowned him when it turned out that Jeramiah's...familiar was only interested in him, and not in Crowley. Of course you can read all this in my dissertation, wherein I'll...'

'…we're mentioned in a few books, yeah,' Jack cut in. 'Everyone knows the Woodfields; you got that right. '

'You sound almost ashamed,' she said, jostling him playfully.

'It's just that name…just saying it, you don't know the connotations that come with that name, 'Woodfield'. It isn't a name like other people's family names, it's a connotation all of itself; it's like 'Kray', or something. You have to really push yourself unless you want to end up just another one of them.'

Dorothy pursed her lips. 'Well your brother seemed nice enough when I met him, happy enough just to be 'one of them'.'

'Jamie?' Jack raised an eyebrow. 'Yeah he's ok, in a clueless kind of way.'

'That's not too charitable. You know I clocked him the moment he came into the Salsa Bar, that time on Christmas Eve; I could tell me was your twin straight away, although you're a bit taller, and quite a bit broader.'

'And a whole lot hunkier,' David said with a wry grin.

'Jamie is everything I don't want to be,' Jack said, giving a theatrical little shudder. 'Stuck selling second-hand paperbacks on a shitty stall on East Street for the rest of his life, his entire weekend revolving around some football match or other; and that's just the tip of the iceberg. You know he can't even read?! Or write?! Can you imagine if I'd said that in the impromptu session the other day?!'

'There are worse crimes.'

'Yeah he's harmless I guess; whenever I get demotivated I just think of Jamie and it fires me up again. God, poor Tiffany.'

Dorothy turned, and gazed out of the window. 'He seemed so sad, on Christmas Eve.'

Jack made a face. 'Yeah, I think I told you, our Uncle Phil was ill. He died on Christmas Day. He was J's hero.'

'You said…' she turned back, and downed her tea in one. 'They were very close, weren't they?'

'Yeah, like father and son,' Jack sat back. 'Our real dad scarpered not long after we were born. Mum won't even tell us his name. I had about ten different dads when I was growing up. She loves blokes, my mum.'

'Wow. That's frank of you; Susie would either applaud that or get you on the couch straight away.'

'Whatever.' He seemed lost in thought, then realised she was waiting for an answer. 'Sorry.'

'S'ok. So you and Uncle Phil weren't so close then?'

'Nah. I did my own thing when I was little, but Jamie hung on his every word. You would have thought he was God or something. Jamie even went to live with him when he was about four, I told you. Not that I blame him, 'coz it was more fun than being stuck with a single mum in a block of smelly flats overlooking the Underground, which is so fucking noisy I can't begin to tell you. I'm more close to my cousin Hayden, only he's…away. And there's Jessica too; she's kind of like my sister, only…'

Dorothy brushed these offerings aside and straight went back to the meat of their conversation. 'What did your Uncle Phil die of?'

Jack sniffed. 'Um…kind of an inherited genetic thing. It strikes down a lot of the men in our family. They kind of get…shagged out.'

Dorothy's eyes widened in what seemed to him to be genuine concern. 'Not you, I hope.'

'Oh no,' Jack smiled to himself. 'Let's just say that I've taken the most preventative step possible…'

'What's that?'

'I left.'

Chapter 14

Friday 31st March 2006

'I left in a right old hurry,' Jamie said to Aunt Amanda, hoping for some massive show of sympathy. 'They really like me you know, Louise and Maggie and all them. They think I'm cute.' His Friday afternoon meetings with Aunt Amanda were becoming something of a regular occurrence, forcing some half-baked apology or other to be issued to the aforementioned as he darted out of Sight & Sound and off down the Charing Cross Road, a vision in Reebok t-shirt and trainers, weaving expertly in and out of the passing peoples. This week the West End had been vetoed in favour of a more traditional Woodfield locale, namely the Roman Road, Bethnal Green end. The weather was mild for the time of year, but a fine drizzle prompted Aunt Amanda to pop up her black umbrella and pull Jamie to her, snuggling him inside her large fake fur as she led him past rows of council flats and off licenses, ignoring his previous comment entirely as her eyes drank in the surroundings. Just before the Sceptre Road turn-off, she paused and nodded to a doorway that now seemed to lead to nothing more than a set of flats above a newsagent/grocers. 'This used to be a nightclub,' she said, moistening her lips. 'And today is the first time I've been able to stand here and look at it, without wanting to balk, anyway.'

Jamie sniffed, and gave her left hand a cursory squeeze. It didn't look like much of anything now, but he knew that a family connection of one sort or another was coming. 'Back in the Sixties?' he ventured, 'or the Fifties? Is it to do with Uncle Phil?'

'Late Fifties, early Sixties,' she nodded. 'My twin brother died here; your Great-Uncle Ben.' And then she'd turned and gazed down at him, smiling. 'Not everything I'm going to tell you will be about Phil, Jamie. But in order to understand what happened to Phil you must know what happened to those who came before him.'

Jamie furrowed his brow. 'But...Uncle Rupert, he was the Daddy before Uncle Phil, wasn't he? And then it was Great-Uncle Alexander; your Ben never was the Daddy.'

Never-the-less he'd seen pictures of the man she mentioned, faded black and white stills with yellowed edges somewhere in the middle of a photo album mum kept under her bed, and one similar shot that took pride of place on Aunt Amanda's mantelpiece. He was fair and light-skinned, colouring almost identical to Jamie himself in fact, but his hair was worn long and swept in a kind of Elvis style, curling elegantly over his ears. As if reading his mind Aunt Amanda reached into her purse and took out just such a photograph, holding it up in front of them. 'That's him, right?' Jamie asked. 'I look a bit like him, don't I?'

'That's my twin brother,' she nodded. 'And like I said, he died in there, back when it was a nightclub. There was a shootout, and he was the one fatality; a lot of other people were hurt, but he was the only one who actually died.'

'I know he died,' Jamie said, disengaging himself from within the folds of her coat and thrusting his hands into the pockets of his hoodie, wandering up to the door of the newsagents and peering inside. 'I never knew he was shot. Mum never said…'

'…there's a lot your mother doesn't say, because there's a lot your mother doesn't know, bless her heart,' Aunt Amanda pulled him away, and turned them both towards the top of the Bethnal Green Road. 'Ben was twenty seven when he died, the age you'll be in a few years' time; twenty seven. That's no age at all, when you think about it.'

'I guess not.' he glanced up at her. She hadn't seemed this sad when Uncle Phil had been ill; there was another word he wanted to ascribe to her, but his burgeoning vocabulary still hadn't quite sorted out what meant what yet, but he was sure it sounded a lot like 'violin'. Perhaps it was true what he'd heard, that sudden deaths of loved ones were far more shocking than those you knew about in advance, when you had time to say your goodbyes. That hadn't made any difference with Uncle Phil though. Even when the doctors had warned the family that there was very little likelihood of him pulling through, Jamie had clung to the hope that he might, and spent the whole of Boxing Day and the day after sat on a bench outside the hospital mortuary, hoping that somehow a mistake had been made, and that the door would be flung open and Uncle Phil would be stood there in a halo of light, in his full West Ham strip. 'Who shot your brother?' he asked, to snap himself out of it.

Aunt Amanda cleared her throat. 'Your great-uncle…he fell in with rather a bad lot.'

Jamie's eyes sparkled. 'Not the Krays?' now this he had heard a bit about; every second or third person in the East End or Essex boasted some sort of connection with the Krays, but in the case of the Woodfields it was genuine; Aunt Amanda had lived a few doors down from them on Vallance Road since the Forties; there were pictures of her with Violet Kray in some of the old family albums, and even a shot with the twins themselves in it, seven or eight people outside the Grave Maurice pub on Whitechapel Road, Aunt Amanda on the far left in tumbling layers of red silk and big sunglasses.

'The very same,' she nodded. 'It was bound to happen I suppose, given the proximity. Although when this shooting happened Ronnie was inside and going sweetly out of his mind, and Reggie wasn't half as interested in Ben as his brother had been. The trouble was your great-uncle was always so easily led…'

'Yeah, but who shot him?' he asked again, as they crossed the road and passed the entrance to the Underground Station.

Aunt Amanda made a sound of dismissal. 'You know, that was hit by a bomb in the Blitz and they kept it quiet,' she said, nodding to the aforementioned entrance. 'So many people died in there. Of course we were in Oxford then; myself, my sister Andrea – your grandmother – and Ben, living with that lovely Atwell family in their hotel on the Abingdon Road. But the authorities covered it up about the bombing and we only found out years later, and nothing straight away when we got back. They thought it was bad for wartime morale, you see. Some of our friends died that day, and we never knew how, or why.'

Jamie squinted up at her. 'Aunt Amanda, who shot your brother?'

She seemed to collect herself and turned to him, smiling. 'I don't know, darling. There were so many people there that night, on both sides. But although this may sound strange, who shot your great-uncle doesn't really matter. He wouldn't have been shot at all, if not for…'

'…if not for what?'

They wandered a little way down the Bethnal Green Road before she answered, pushing open the door to Pellici's café and wandering inside, Aunt Amanda nodding her greetings to the staff, all of whom were clearly very pleased to see her. She took what the older man behind the counter called 'her table', by the window, and set her handbag down by the side of her chair. 'There was a girl there that night,' she said, making a steeple of her hands. 'Her name was Cindy Gatt. But that isn't important, and neither was Cindy, not really. Except that Cindy was seeing your great-uncle Ben at the time. They were sweethearts in a kind of old fashioned way that was dying out around 1960.'

Jamie gazed at her. 'Was the gunfight over her?'

'I'm not sure…I don't think so, no. Or maybe it was. But either way she was there, and the important thing is a girl like Cindy wouldn't have been there at all, if not for…'

These dramatic pauses were beginning to fray Jamie's nerves. 'If not for what?!'

'They say your great-uncle's body was riddled with bullets; seventeen was the count some of the papers put it at. Someone in the rival gang south of the river who liked Cindy Gatt tried to put a bullet in her; 'if I can't have her no one can', that sort of awful, garish gang mentality.'

'So…they were trying to shoot her and Ben got in the way? He threw himself in front of the bullets to shield her?'

Aunt Amanda sighed. She seemed to weary suddenly, and so old. 'No. It was the other way around, I'm afraid.'

'She threw herself in front of him? But you said they were shooting at her.'

'She wasn't sure what the bullets would do to her body, in the… 'condition' it was in at the time.'

'She was pregnant?' Jamie was fast losing the plot.

'Doubtful. No, she was scared of what the bullets might do the body with her essence or whatever still in it; she panicked, grabbed your great-uncle and pulled him into the line of fire. In effect she used his body to shield her own.'

They obviously weren't talking about Cindy Gatt in the literal sense anymore. 'Who did?'

Aunt Amanda's face tightened. 'Minty Hardcore.'

Chapter 15

Friday 31st March 2006

Jamie hadn't been able to look at the picture of his Great-Uncle Ben when they returned to the house on Vallance Road; as if somehow sensing his anxiety Aunt Amanda took several coloured candles from a cupboard under the sink and lit them in the living room. They gave off a scent that was different from normal candles, and the smelt kind of like the ones Marsha sold on her stall just down the way from his; when she demonstrated them for customers he'd often reap the benefits, standing there with his eyes closed and his little nose held up to the wind. 'Close your eyes, darling,' Aunt Amanda said, slipping her coat over the back of her favourite chair. 'We're going to do some relaxation techniques. I want you to unwind a little, and to visualise.'

'Visual what?' he sat down and tossed his Reeboks into a corner by the fire.

'Visualise,' she opened her hands. 'Like an exercise. I want you to concentrate on a happy memory, one that you can pinpoint and recall in times of stress, or of…psychic attack.'

'Psychic attack,' Jamie's eyes lit up. 'That's what happens to Derek Acorah when he visits haunted houses on 'Most Haunted'; he got beaten up by a poltergeist last week, Derek did! My mum loves that show!'

'Quite,' Aunt Amanda sighed. 'Now close your eyes and visualise; a happy, happy memory. One with your Uncle Phil should work as well as any other, and be rather apt, as it happens.'

Jamie nodded, closing his eyes and stretching his legs out. It took him a moment or two to sift through the recent trauma of Uncle Phil's funeral and go further back, back to happier times. A banner materialised in his mind's eye, the words 'HAPPY 16TH BIRTHDAY JACK AND JAMIE' slung across it in alternating rainbow colours, festooned from one end of the bar to the other. Uncle Phil hadn't taken up the option to close off the family area of the Barking Dog for a private party, because everyone knew the Woodfields and wanted to join in, to pat the boys on the back and shake their hands, offer their heartfelt congratulations. Jamie remembered jokes abounding about certain things now being legal, and Uncle Eddie had thought it a capital joke to buy them a ticket to the matinee show at the Raymond Revue Bar in Soho, for the following day. 'You're not taking my boys to see that filth!' mum had snapped, swinging for him with her handbag. 'You dirty old man!!'

Uncle Phil slapped his knees, laughing delightedly. 'I think it's fantastic, 'sis!'

'They're not going, Phil,' mum had stood her ground. 'You know I don't approve of things like that; some old slapper flashing her boobs in their faces, no thank you!! Not after last time.'

''ark at her!' Uncle Eddie was laughing too, his cigarette hanging out of the corner of his mouth. 'And with what she used to get up to back in the day as well!'

'Eddie!!' Aunt Delia had shot him one of her glances.

Then the memory diluted and it was just a little later on, and Jamie had downed a couple more pints, and was getting into the party mood. Aunt Sophie, sweet, shy Aunt Sophie had stepped forward and said, 'Here you go, my darlings, happy birthday', to him and to Jack, offering them a single present between them, a parcel of A4 size, topped off with a navy blue bow. Aunt Sophie and Uncle Heath never had much money, what they did earn going into buying her arts materials and paying for her evening classes. 'I hope you like it,' she said, and kissed the pair of them on the cheek.

Jack offered it to Jamie to unwrap but Jamie offered it back, for reasons he couldn't entirely recall. Jack tore the wrapping off and held up the result; one of Aunt Sophie's better watercolours, the two boys together, smiling, shoulder to shoulder but facing outwards, away from each other, arms folded. Jamie remembered the moment's silence as the crowd, growing larger all the time, gathered around and waited for their reaction. Jack had made a noise, something indiscernible, and had then held the picture to his chest. 'I love it,' he said. He'd handed it to Jamie and gone and picked Aunt Sophie up, literally picked her off her feet, and she a grown woman, and all. But Jack was well over six foot even then, and he held her aloft for almost a minute, showering her with kisses. Jack loved to do that, to pick people up, and spin them around.

'Yeah,' Jamie had nodded, screwing the wrapping paper up in his hands. 'It's great. Thanks, Aunt Sophie.'

'Let me see that,' Uncle Phil had taken it from him, studying it with the most serious expression; he'd looked for all the world like one of those toffs on 'The Antiques Roadshow' in that moment. 'Jack looks a little fat around the face, 'soph,' he said. 'You've been a little harsh, I think.'

'I'm not fat!!' Jack had gasped, gently lowering her down. 'I'm lean!!'

This reaction seemed to drive Uncle Phil into one of his usual riffs of laughter, slapping his knees whilst mum shook her head, moving off to the bar with Uncle Heath to order up another, larger round of drinks. Adam was serving, on tiptoe, trying to see the picture over the sea of heads. 'Is it any cop?' he'd asked mum as she dug into her purse. 'Hey,' he'd said, waving his hand at her, 'put your money away, Ms. Woodfield. The mangers set up a kitty for the boys. I put twenty quid into it myself.'

'Oh bless you my love,' mum had tweaked his cheek. 'I think it'll be the same for everyone then, and you get yourself a break and come and join us.'

'Will do,' he nodded, 'Jamie having a good time?'

'I'm so proud of Jack,' mum had turned and glanced over at them, now almost fighting over their cousin Laquisha's gift, a space-age style ghetto blaster with multi-deck CD system. 'For him to be on his way to college when he's only just turned sixteen, don't you think that's something? He's something, he really is. I think he'll be the first Woodfield to go to university, you know.'

'Jamie's a sound geezer too,' Adam added, making sure Jamie had heard him. 'My best mate, he is.'

Uncle Heath waited until mum had taken the first new tray of drinks back before leaning over the bar, and Jamie had heard all of this exchange too. 'Mate, you might as well be talking to thin air. Jamie could be bleeding from the eyeballs and she'd still have her tongue halfway down Jack's pants; metaphorically, 'course.'

The family itself was congregating into something of a circle, broken suddenly by shouts of 'Aunt Amanda's here!!', whereupon all heads turned to the entrance, through which Aunt Amanda veritably swished, followed up in short order by Aunt Hannah's eldest daughter, Sara Woodfield, who had been kind enough to drive over to Bethnal Green and pick her up. Aunt Amanda made a beeline for Jamie, clasping his face in both hands and kissing him fully on the lips. 'My darling!!' she declared, 'sixteen already! Where have the years gone, eh?! Where have they gone?! Why it seems like only yesterday I was hoisting you both out in that double buggy down Bethnal Green Road, the proudest aunt there ever was, I can assure you!!'

'Amanda,' Aunt Delia embraced her, the first in a queue of seven or eight and growing. 'It's been weeks!!'

'I refuse to let my advancing years slow me down,' Aunt Amanda handed the boys two large cards. 'I've been taking driving lessons; I think it's about time I learned. And once I pass I intend to buy a fast car, and Jamie and I will drive up and down the Roman Road, breaking the speed limit and making those funny yellow boxes take our picture.'

'They're called speed cameras, Aunt Amanda,' Jamie had said, pulling his card out. A cheque fell out, and he'd picked it up, eyes widening a couple of seconds later. 'Holy fuck!!' it had been for something like a hundred, maybe a hundred and fifty pounds or so; Jamie had never seen his name written down next to an amount of money like that in his entire life.

'Hey!!' he'd felt Jack leaning over his shoulder, the feel of his hand prising the cheque loose and waving it around indignantly. 'How come he's got more than me?! Forty quid more, he's got!'

'Because you got considerably more from your dear mother, am I right darling?' Aunt Amanda settled down and snapped her handbag shut. 'Am I right?'

'I haven't even given them their cards yet,' mum was aghast, 'how'd you know?!'

Aunt Amanda tapped the side of her nose. 'What can I say, darling? I'm a psychic.'

A ripple of laughter drifted through the crowd, and someone over near the bar hollered, 'You got that right, darlin'', and more laughter followed, all of it good natured. 'Thanks Aunt Amanda,' Jamie kissed her on the cheek. 'I'll invest it, I think. The new away strip's out next week, and I got to have that, so yeah, the rest I'll invest.'

'What are you investing for?!' Jack had shoved his own cheque back into the envelope.

Jamie shrugged. 'Dunno. Me and Adam…'

'Adam and I,' Jack had said.

'Aw bless them,' mum sighed, gazing dreamily from one to the other, and then at those around her. 'Brothers.'

'You go on holiday whenever you want, my darling,' Aunt Amanda ruffled Jamie's short spiky hair, a lot like she still did now, as matter of fact. 'Rome is always nice. I have friends in Rome. You can stay with them and make love to lots of nice Italian girls, and sit and hold hands on the Spanish Steps.'

As the evening wore on the crowd around the family grew larger still, until it became difficult to navigate the path to either the bar or the toilets. A round of applause went up when Uncle Richard Woodfield arrived from Brighton, although Uncle Eddie muttered something about '…the silly old faggot,' and received another slap around the head from Aunt Delia as a result; an even bigger burst of applause went to Aunt Queenie, the oldest living Woodfield, a rather comical little woman with rusty red hair and crinkled stockings, whose face rather resembled a chewed-up old toffee. Uncle Phil fed the jukebox with a fiver's worth of credits, all of them pub classics along the lines of ABBA, T-Rex, and various assorted songs that wouldn't have been out of place at any typical family wedding or general get-together. Where there was room to dance people danced; Aunt Amanda had embarrassed Jamie by pulling him up and jigging around rather nimbly to Bucks Fizz's 'Making your mind up', then falling back into her seat breathless, demanding that Uncle Heath bring her a gin and tonic at once.

Uncle Heath and Aunt Sophie's twins, Daniel and Debbie, had both fallen asleep on either side of Uncle Phil, nestling against him with their mouths open, effectively pinning him into the arrangement he'd been sharing with Uncle Heath, Uncle Brian, and cousins Springer and Clay. Jack was ensconced in a corner with his current girlfriend; Jamie opened his eyes during the 'visualisation' now and tried to recall her name from the endless list of girls Jack had been out with, had up against a wall, or brought off in the back row of the Warner Bros. cinema in Dagenham Leisure Park. He settled for 'Mandy' but might've been way off the mark, and closed his eyes again, searching for himself in this stage of the evening. He was chatting to Adam up at the bar now, knocking back far too many double Southern Comforts. When Whitney Houston's 'How will I know' kicked off, as last orders were called, Uncle Phil had gently slipped Daniel and Debbie to Uncle Brian and mounted the table with Uncle Heath, the pair of them hollering and shouting and making a general spectacle of themselves, several of their friends from the East Street market commandeering adjoining tables for a similar spectacle. Around 11.10pm the manager opted for a lock-in, news of which was greeted with cheers and clinking of glasses all round. By midnight Jamie was throwing up in the street outside; he remembered the awful nausea and that sense of the world tipping on its side every time he opened his eyes, sick mixing with the metallic taste of blood in his mouth; he'd been hit, and hit hard. He sitting against the wall and closed his eyes, moaning, 'I want to die!!'

Cousin Jessica was there, lighting up a cigarette. 'Serves you right, you spiteful little prick,' she was saying. 'What were you thinking of, in there?!?'

'Gimme a cig,' he groaned, 'might make me feel better.'

'Make you puke, they will,' she'd crouched down on her heels. 'And don't you tell my dad you saw me smoking either, or I'll say you brought them for me. Aunt Queenie gave me this, as it goes. She gets cigs for me whenever I ask her to.'

'Smoking at your age, Jessica?' Uncle Phil cast a shadow over her, materialising it seemed almost out of thin air, arms folded, sleeves rolled up. 'For shame.' He'd plucked it from her pretty, bee-stung lips and taken a generous puff. 'Go on, get back inside.'

'I'd shin you, Uncle Phil' she sighed, 'if you weren't so sexy.'

'For shame again,' he raised his eyebrows, a guaranteed crowd pleaser. 'There's a word for that, you know.'

'Yeah,' she stuck her big chest out as she made for the doors. 'It's called 'horny'.'

Uncle Phil had chuckled to himself, kneeling down beside Jamie. 'You ok, little fella?' he asked.

Jamie struggled to rise, then fell back, before jerking forward and throwing up all over his shoes. 'I'm sick, I think.'

'No kidding.'

'We drunk doubles; Adam's passed out in the toilets.'

'Silly silly,' Phil shook the spew from his shoes and crouched a little more comfortably. 'First time you've ever been really bladdered, far as I can recall.'

'And the last,' Jamie wailed. 'Everything keeps tipping sideways.'

'You're only just sixteen, little fella,' he'd felt Uncle Phil fondly gazing down at him, 'plenty of time for all this when you're older. Me and your Uncle Heath, well we snuck cider into our room when we were thirteen and drunk so much your Aunt Amanda thought we had alcohol poisoning. We sat in casualty on the Whitechapel Road for four hours, and when we sobered up, boy did she ever tan our hides. People thought we were ginger, we couldn't sit down for so long.'

'Don't tell mum,' Jamie held his stomach. 'Uncle Phil…I think I'm gonna hurl again.'

Uncle Phil held him as the inevitable inebriated convulsion came and went. Then he had shrugged his jacket off and used the sleeve of it to wipe Jamie's mouth. 'Better?'

'I think...' Either way Station Parade was relatively quiet, and private. 'Uncle Phil?' he'd said suddenly.

'Yes, little fella?'

'Why's everyone love Jack?'

Uncle Phil had pursed his lips, watched a Night Bus as it trundled past, picking up more people than it disgorged onto the opposite side of the road. 'That's the way it is, little fella.' He said.

'Why don't they love me like they do him?'

'It's just...the way things work out. Jack's going to be the Daddy one day, that's all.'

Jamie burped. 'I don't care anyway. I showed him tonight, good and proper.'

'I wasn't very proud of you then, Jamie. I think you've got a few people to apologise to, come the morning.'

Jamie had waved a hand dismissively. 'Uncle Phil?'

'Little fella?'

'I wish you were my dad.'

Uncle Phil had smiled softly, gazing down at him. 'I am; in all the ways that truly matter.'

Jamie had struggled to rise, falling against him, holding on by gripping Uncle Phil's shin in one hand and his arm in the other. 'I....'

'You what, little fella?'

Jamie had swallowed, sniffed. 'Don't matter. Boys don't say them things anyway.'

*

'That was weird,' Jamie said later, as he tucked into a dinner of sausages, mash and peas. 'I could remember some bits of it crystal clear, but there was tons missing as well. Nick must've been there, but I couldn't remember him being there at all. And I couldn't remember Marie or Laquisha being there either.'

'Was it your favourite memory of your Uncle Phil?' Aunt Amanda asked, pouring the gravy onto both their plates.

'It was my favourite memory full stop,' he grinned wickedly.

'Whenever you get stressed,' she said. 'Or worried or anxious, you must visualise that memory; recall it then as exactly as you tried to now. It'll be a good defence.'

'Defence against what?' he sniffed. 'Minty Hardcore's not really coming to get me, is she? You said you'd be there to get her, if she did.'

Aunt Amanda seemed to take his doubt all in her stride. 'We don't want you ending up like your Uncle Phil, is all.' She reached for the fridge door with her long fingers and pulled it open. 'She's a crafty little whore,' she reminded him. 'Just be glad I'm looking after you, and someone else is watching over Jack, although he's totally unaware of it.'

This little titbit almost made Jamie choke on his sausage. 'Who??'

'Never you mind,' she said, closing the fridge door and sprinkling her plate with some grated cheese. 'And you're not to mention that to a living soul, Jamie Woodfield.'

'Jack's tough,' he said through a mouthful of sausage. 'He doesn't need anyone to watch over him. He knocked out Craig Davies with one punch when Craig Davies said he had the teacher in his pocket; it wasn't Jack's fault Miss Parker fancied him. She used to give him 'A's' for everything, even if he'd copied it out of a book.'

Aunt Amanda narrowed her eyes, and the mouthful of potato she'd scooped up remained suspended, a couple of inches away from her mouth. 'Do you want to be like your brother, Jamie Woodfield? I mean, really?'

He knew it was serious when she said his full name like that, although his *full* full name was actually Jamie Benjamin – after Great-Uncle Ben, obviously – Nathan Alexander – after Great-Uncle Alexander – Woodfield; Jamie Benjamin Nathan Alexander Woodfield. He'd asked his mum tons of times if Nathan had been the name of his and Jack's father, but she'd always laughed and said, "It was probably just a passing salesman, sweetheart."

He liked Jack's name better; Jack Ewan Nathan Jeramiah Woodfield; Ewan was their grandfather's name on mum's side, although he'd died long before they'd been born, in an awful accident on the platform at Barking Underground Station; Jeramiah was Great-Great-Uncle Jeramiah, the one everyone spoke about with such reverence. Great-Great-Uncle Jeramiah had been friends with Aleister Crowley, some famous magician or occultist or other, although Aunt Amanda called him 'a stinking great fraud', and said that everything he'd done had actually been what Jeramiah had taught him, but that Jeramiah wasn't vain and was far more interested in making love to pretty girls than to having his name attached to various dubious cabals and black magic circles. There was a picture somewhere of Great-Great-Uncle Jeramiah, taken by Aleister Crowley, of Jeramiah making love to a girl in a punt in Cambridge, a girl who everyone said was Minty Hardcore, although Jamie had never actually seen the photo himself. Someone had said that Aunt Queenie used it as a coaster.

Jamie had shrugged, and tried to appear casual, fumbling for an answer to the question. '' course I want to be like Jack,' he said. 'Everyone loves Jack.' Then he caught the look on her face. 'What?!'

'You've said that before, darling. Now look, no one is here, so no one is going to think any the less of you; you're not 'Essex boy' here, you're just my little grandson, of sorts, and I'm your old gran. Now, do you want to be like your brother?'

He nodded. '"course I do. But I'm not, am I? I haven't got a six pack, or a square jaw, or…or…' he swallowed, and plucked up the courage. 'Aunt Amanda, if we're twins, why is Jack's dick bigger than mine?!'

'I want you to forge closer ties with your brother,' she said, dismissing his question out of hand. 'You going to university will help that, if we get you a place, that is. Go and see him. Ask him if he wants to come to a football match with you. Anything; the point is, build bridges. His advice on essays and exams will be invaluable to you.'

Jamie shrugged. 'If you want. But he thinks I'm dumb.'

'Doesn't matter what he thinks.' Aunt Amanda said. 'Just humour a mad old woman, will you? Humour me like you're humouring me over all this 'Minty Hardcore' madness.'

'Minty Hardcore isn't like, walking around, live and kicking, is she?' Jamie polished off his peas and pushed his plate to one side. 'She's not real as in, like, well…I mean, you said she was a whore. But like, a made-up whore, right?! Like one of them girls on the cards in a phone box, who never use their real name?!'

'She is a whore; first and foremost, and don't you ever forget it. A crafty little whore. As soon as you think of her as anything else, well you're halfway to becoming hers. Now, have you ever seen the Exorcist, darling?'

'Uh huh. Springer had it on pirate before it was legalised.'

'Well it's like that, only without the projectile peas.' Aunt Amanda collected their plates up and set about preparing dessert. She stopped at the sink however, and fixed him with a steely glare. 'I mean it, Jamie,' she said.

'She'll possess someone?!' visions abounded of Linda Blair impaling her nether regions with a crucifix, and of beds floating off the floor. 'Won't people like…well won't they notice?!'

'We're dealing with very, very crafty little whore here,' Aunt Amanda said. 'Now what is she?'

Jamie bowed his head. 'A crafty little whore.'

'Good. Now be vigilant. Possession is her favourite party piece. She isn't going to accept you as the Daddy without a fight, you know. Its Jack she wants, first and foremost. We must bring you up to Jack's level to stand a chance of swaying her, and then getting her off her guard…'

'Will they look funny, if they're possessed?' Jamie watched her dole out the ice-cream. 'How will I know?! Won't it be like Derek Acorah at all?!'

'I'll know, darling,' Aunt Amanda said, 'and the person watching over Jack? Well she'll know as well, and she'll be able to protect him, and he'll be none the wiser.'

'So it'll be someone who likes Jack?'

'Most likely.'

'Then that's like, well, millions of birds!'

'It'll be someone with that extra something,' Aunt Amanda said. 'Someone who can tempt him the way a million other 'birds' couldn't. The one that got away, something like that…'

'No girl ever escaped Jack,' Jamie said. 'No girl ever wanted to.'

'Oh, there's always one, darling. You're sure you have no idea who it might be?'

Jamie gazed down into his gravy, and saw his own reflection peering back up at him. 'No,' he said. 'No idea.'

Chapter 16

Sunday 2nd April 2006

'I had no idea London could be so charming,' Tiffany said, slipping her arm through Jack's and lightly stroking the hairs on his wrist. 'Why, Mr. Livingstone has given it back that picture-postcard quality, don't you think? But still...' she glanced up at him. 'It lacks the...organic ambience of Barking, don't you think?'

'Barking is a pit,' he sniffed. 'I love London. My life's here in London now. My friends are here; my career is here.'

'Well strictly speaking, Barking is in London,' she gazed up at the London Eye. 'Or are you one of those who insists that it's the on the cusp of Essex proper?'

He gazed down at her. 'It's Essex, of course; East London ends with Mile End, hence the name 'Mile End'.'

She gazed up at him, smirking. 'Is that an academic fact, or just a typical Jack Woodfield assumption?'

He beamed back down at her. 'Don't know. You tell me.'

'I do admit this makes a change,' she said, squeezing his arm a little harder, 'from always hanging around the Vicarage Fields shopping centre, and for the capital idea of a night out to be a 'two for the price of one' meal in the Barking Dog, and a DVD at your Uncle Phil's flat afterwards.'

Jack furrowed his brow. 'Are you and Jamie having problems?'

'Problems?' she allowed him to lead her up the steps onto Westminster Bridge, the wind whipping her hair about her face. 'No, he's just become a little...distant lately. Your Aunt Amanda has been filling his head with all sorts of nonsense and now when he isn't on the stall he's here, in the West End, learning to type and to read, which is all very commendable, but it's like he's forgotten I exist.'

Jack pondered on this for a moment, on the possibility of a cheesy, very much in-character response along the lines of, 'If you were mine I'd never neglect you' type answer, but settling in the end for, 'I think it's cool, that he's trying to better himself; a little late, but cool never-the-less.'

Tiffany laughed, taking in the spectacle of Big Ben with all the enthusiasm of someone who didn't get into the West End often enough. 'You try very hard to be indifferent when it comes to Jamie, but I can tell by the way your eyes sparkle that he could run a Stanley knife over every Beatles record you own, and you'd still forgive him.'

He shrugged. 'What makes you think that?'

Now it was her turn to shrug. 'Like I just said. I think it's a marvellous testament to your character that you even give him a passing thought, with everything he's done.'

'Speaking of sparkling eyes,' Jack said, quickly changing the subject. 'And lustrous hair, and a general all-pervading sense of vitality, have you been working out?'

'No...' she blushed, letting him grind the pair of them to a halt so that he could scrutinise her more closely.

'New foundation?' he raised an eyebrow.

'...you could say that, yes; a far more tried and tested one, if you like.'

'You look radiant,' Jack said. He couldn't resist bringing his hand up, and stroking the soft, taut flesh of her cheek. 'You've got...a blush.'

'Maybe it's the company I keep.'

They resumed their slow walk, reaching the far side of the bridge, and Jack stopped at a stall selling Union Jack flags and hats, policeman helmets, and the usual array of postcards with pictures of Princess Diana and the Queen on them, sun-faded and in the case of the former vaguely distasteful. 'I ought to get mum one of these,' he said, picking up a Union Jack tea-towel. 'Actually, I might get a set, 'coz when Aunt Rachel and Aunt Hannah see them they'll want one as well, and they're certainly kitsch enough for Aunt Delia...'

'I might get a tattoo,' she said offhandedly. 'What do you think?'

'What of?'

'Oh, I don't know,' she said. 'Why don't you give me a few ideas. I feel like putting this body of mine through a few...cosmetic changes, so that I feel more comfortable here. You've got a couple of tattoos, haven't you?'

'I got the West Ham logo on my shoulder,' he said, one ear with her and the other with the stall's owner as he explained the pricing system to him. 'My last, and almost aborted bonding attempt with Jamie, plus I got my cousin Jessica's name on my bicep. Me and 'jess, we're pretty close. She got mine, so I got hers.'

'She's a right old one, isn't she,' Tiffany laughed. 'Oh, the stories I've heard about Jessica Woodfield over the years; the modelling; the soft porn videos; and Barking's first ever Page Three Girl to boot!' she said this just loud enough that the stall owner might hear it, and wrinkle his old face up in delight at the tawdriness of it all.

Jack's eyes misted over, as he put the tea-towel back on the shelf. 'She's amazing.'

'Yes well,' Tiffany cleared her throat. 'I bet you don't see much of her these days.'

'Not as much as I'd like.'

'So anyway,' she said quickly, leading him away from the stall. 'Are you sure those two tattoos are the only ones you have?'

'How'd you mean?'

'Oh...' she slipped her free hand around to his back, untucked his Ben Sherman shirt and pulled it up, exposing a clear red lip print on the small of his back, just above his left buttock. 'What about that one?'

'Hey!!' he yanked the shirt down. 'What the hell are you doing?'

'Oh don't be mad,' she was rather amused. 'I think it's rather sweet. Jamie has one rather like it, only it's blurred, like the ink ran or something. Yours is perfect. Don't worry,' and here she glanced from left to right. 'I'm sure people just think it's a Henna tattoo or something.'

'Yeah well,' he exhaled heavily. 'It runs in our family, kind of like some congenital deficiency.'

'I wouldn't call it that,' she said, raising her hand to her eyes as the sun moved from behind a particularly large cloud bank. 'I've heard it's what being a Woodfield is all about.'

'It's what being one Woodfield in a generation is about,' he corrected her. 'But for me? No thanks.'

She stopped, ignoring the crowds, and faced him. 'Jack,' she said, taking his hand, and wrapping all her fingers around it, just about making them meet. 'I know what you are.'

He glanced over her shoulder. A student protest was forming in Parliament Square, placards proclaiming an end to tuition fees, and among them representatives from his own university, the London School of Economics. In fact, elected representatives from the LSE seemed to be heading the protest, or trying to at least, as they were slowly shoehorned into an ever tighter corner by the police, anxious of any kind of protest that took place a little too close to the seat of democracy, and all that.

'I know that fella,' Jack squinted. 'Robbie Ryan; he's head of the postgraduate union body.'

'He couldn't find his arse with both hands, by the looks of it,' Tiffany said, turning to follow his gaze. 'What an awful, ferrety little man. Look how he's letting the police box them in. What sort of a protest is that?!' she glanced up at him. 'I bet you could do a lot better.'

'Not my sort of thing really,' Jack shrugged. 'Aunt Amanda kind of gives me a blank cheque on that score. They can't pay, that's their problem. Use their initiative if they've got overheads, like I had to.'

'He has no authority,' she said. 'Look, he can't even get them to quiet down. He has no presence, and really it' no surprise, I mean, he can't be more than five foot six, at a push.'

He laughed. 'What's that got to do with the price of fish?!?'

'Oh Jack, you are naïve,' she let her hand fall on his chest, and from there trace the contours of his beautifully sculpted pecs. 'People would take far more notice if someone of your…stature were to climb up on that podium and plead for calm.'

He shoved his hands in his back pockets and shifted his weight from one foot to the other. 'You reckon?'

'Of course. What a lucky coincidence it was that we just happened to be passing.' she pressed her hands against his chest, taking great pains to reduce her stance to that of the demure female in the picture they now posed to passers-by. 'Go on Jack. Just for me, if not for them. Like you said, what excitement do I get with Jamie these days?!'

'Tiffany...' he stepped forward and embraced her, taking her weight against his own. 'I'm not sure...'

'Sssshhhhh,' she pressed a finger to his lips. 'Doubt is like a flaccid cock.'

He sniffed, and then rolled up his sleeves, exposing his thick, hairy forearms. He inhaled, then let it out slowly. 'I better not make a tit of myself,' he said. 'I've had a few drinks with Robbie, and he's okay.'

'You can do anything,' she patted him on the back, adding a little shove into the mix, and then almost thrust him forward bodily. 'Go and sort them out.'

Jack nodded, then turned, still unsure. He reached his arm out and pulled her close, locked his lips on hers, and slid his tongue inside. They kissed deeply, and he didn't want to leave when they'd finished, he was that excited. 'Now you're perfect,' she whispered in his ear. 'Engorged with testosterone; go and brush that silly little man aside, and tell those students that they need to fight for those fees to be abolished!'

He nodded, bounding off without another word, cleaving deftly through the crowd and mounting the podium a moment later, whispering something to Robbie Ryan, who considered momentarily and then made a bow and stepped aside with his dignity relatively intact. Tiffany tossed her head back, her strawberry blond hair whipped up into a veritable frenzy by the approach of the SKY News helicopter. 'Smile Jack,' she said to herself. 'You're on candid camera.'

Chapter 17

Sunday 2nd April 2006

Jamie's mum always cooked a mean Sunday roast, even if she left it until around four in the afternoon to actually get the thing going, preferring instead to spend the better part of the afternoon giving herself one of the facials she doled out to paying customers the other six days of the week. The soft steaming potatoes, thick beefy gravy, crisp cooled vegetables and lean side of pork were well worth the wait, especially when washed down with a can or Stella or two, or three. Uncle Phil had always taken Jamie over there for Sunday dinner, moreso since Aunt Rose had passed away. Uncle Phil himself had never been able to cook very well; a slice of toast or a tin of soup had been about his limit, and even then the toast was usually so burnt that Jamie would have to scrape the black bits off with a fork. Normally on a Sunday afternoon the dining table at mum's would be crammed with this or that cousin or uncle and aunt coming round for a free nosh-up and a gossip with Phil; today however, one of the first times since his death that she'd issued an open invite, it was relatively quiet, just herself and Jamie, her twin brother Heath, and Heath's sixteen year old son Daniel. Uncle Heath was every inch the classic Essex man, all scowl and jowls, who always had time for Jamie, although his lardy son was something less than a chip off the old block; Daniel made up for it as best he could with his Reebok t-shirt and bottoms, and the fake bling on almost every available finger, but the fact was that he was a bit of a spakker. All the Woodfield men were considered by their peers to be very fine specimens, but there were exceptions to every rule and, Aunt Delia's son Springer notwithstanding, Daniel was one of them. Aged just sixteen he spent his days hanging around the arcades, and the nights pouring over the latest issue of 'The Zoo' and that was about it. He was spotty, and he had bad breath, but he was harmless. He was someone Jamie could quite happily look down his nose at, although Uncle Phil had always told him that "…it's what's on the inside that counts, little fella," even though Uncle Phil's left eyebrow twitched when he said, which meant that he was lying, or at the very least struggling to convince himself that what he was saying was the truth.

The TV was on in the background, the omnibus edition of 'EastEnders', something mum didn't miss come hell or high water. While Daniel rattled on about his ambition to be a nightclub owner, and Jamie recited the list of books he now planned to read, she nodded and went, 'Uh huh' at intervals of forty seconds or so, her eyes never once deviating from the screen. Only when the end credits rolled did she give anyone her full attention, pouring the last of the by-then lukewarm gravy onto half empty plates and taking her own out to the kitchen and plopping it into the sink before pulling an ice cold can of Stella from the fridge.

'I could move into the West End like Jack,' Daniel was saying, scraping the remainder of his peas around the plate. 'Be like Peter Stringbean or whatever his name is. I'd never go out in the day, only at night. I could get a girlfriend like that Chantelle; she's well fit, man'

'If you didn't go out in the day then you'd be a vampire, my darling,' mum chuckled. 'And we don't want that, now do we?'

'We don't want you going to the West End either,' Uncle Heath said, wiping his mouth on the back of his hand. 'One's enough, right Bev?'

'Too right my darling,' she nodded. 'Us Woodfields…'

'…it's 'we Woodfields', mum,' Jamie pointed out. 'I'm learning proper grammar at the moment.'

'We Woodfields then,' she sighed, supping on her can, 'we weren't meant for the West End. We're Barking born and bred.'

'We're barking, that's for sure,' Daniel chuckled, followed shortly by Jamie, 'Barking mad!!'

'You lot go and sit yourselves down on the sofa,' mum said. 'I'll get the washing up going and then we can put our feet up, have some ice cream, and you can tell me when you're getting married again, Heath baby.'

'Dad isn't getting married again,' Daniel smirked, leaping up from the table. 'That's what he says when he's half cut and asleep in his chair, but he wants to give that Carol who sells DVDs on the stall near his a right good seeing to, I know it!'

'Hey!!' Uncle Heath fixed him with a steely gaze, 'less of that. You wouldn't speak that way if your sister was here.'

'No, I'd say worse.'

'Where is Debbie?' mum called out from the kitchen.

'With her stupid girlie mates,' Daniel said, swiftly performing the 'fingers down the throat' routine. Jamie laughed at that, because he knew full well that Daniel wouldn't have minded giving either Amber, Cheryl, or Sienna one; Amber was the cutest, if he'd been forced to pick. Daniel went on, 'But Debbie knows dad likes that Carol as well. She winds him up about it.'

'They're right you know, these kids of yours,' mum walked back into the living room, wiping her hands on a dishcloth, gazing at Uncle Heath as she did so. 'You're 39, not 59, my sweetheart; you need to find yourself someone. It's been six years since…'

'…how long has it been for you?' Uncle Heath raised an eyebrow.

'Actually…' she cleared her throat. 'I am seeing someone.'

'Since when?!' Jamie had slumped himself in one of the creamy white soft chairs but jerked upright at this news, as though someone had prodded a firework up his bum.

'Since…well, since!' she sat in the chair opposite. 'For a good while now anyway, and before you say anything I wasn't carrying on like some callous woman whilst your Uncle Phil was ill. I put this bloke off until I knew what was what, and Phil was very happy for me.'

'You're gonna have a stepdad, Jamie!' Daniel slapped his knees.

Mum made a face at him. 'I'll tell you more when we've found your dad here some nice girl. Carol's all right, you know. We've had a few drinks, and I've given her a facial or two. She's got good skin. Good tits, too. You could do a lot worse, Heath.'

'Who is this man you're seeing, mum?' Jamie asked. 'Does Jack know?'

'No he doesn't. His name, if you must know, is Chris. He's 40 and he's a writer. He works at some fancy college in the West End.'

'A writer?!' Uncle Heath laughed to himself, glancing at Jamie, and then supping on his Stella. 'Whatever floats your boat, 'darlin.'

Now it was mum's turn to make a face. 'He's very intellectual, as a matter of fact. He's opening me up to all sorts of things.'

'Are you gonna get with Carol, dad?' Daniel asked.

'Oh come on,' mum kicked out at him. 'You're 39, for heaven's sake! You're tall and handsome and you're not in bad shape, what woman wouldn't want to eat you up?!'

'Ew, mum!' Jamie gasped.

'What?!'

'Less of the eating!'

'It's a term of endearment, sweetheart. I don't know what they've been filling your head with in that fancy college of yours but…'

'No one would want to eat my dad,' Daniel chuckled.

'Thanks matey.'

'Well dad, it's…gross!'

'You say that when you've reached 39,' mum slumped back and stared into her Stella. 'God I feel much older than that though, I tell you. It's this family. It makes you feel ancient. There's always someone having a baby and reminding you of how old you really are.'

'Oh mum,' Jamie said, 'speaking of family, Aunt Amanda wants to come 'round one day next week and sort through the stuff in the loft. I think she wants to go to Aunt Rachel's and sort through her loft as well. She says she's looking for a pair of virgin's knickers.'

'Around these parts?!?' mum laughed. 'She'll be lucky.'

'Well she says she wants to come around, and as soon as possible.'

'Oh does she?! Can't she speak for herself anymore, or are you her intermediary or whatever they call it?!'

'She's as good as your own mum and you always moan when I mention her name,' Jamie kissed his lips. 'Have you had a falling out or something?'

'My darling,' mum sighed. 'As I've told you many times, your Uncle Heath, Uncle Phil and I were brought up almost single-handedly by that woman,' – to this Uncle Heath nodded his agreement and tipped his can of Stella in honour of the fact – '…but the fact is she can be a little…'

'...eccentric,' Uncle Heath nodded, finishing the can. 'And that is putting it mildly.'

'She's old, bless her,' mum said.

'You make her sound like some crazy old woman,' Jamie frowned.

'A crazy old witch,' Daniel grinned.

'Hey,' Uncle Heath tipped the empty can towards him, 'less of that too.'

'That's what Annie Woodfield says!' Daniel protested. 'Last week she saw me walking along on Shoreditch High Street and gave me a lift and she said not to worry 'coz she wouldn't drop me at the old witch's house!'

'I said hey!!' Uncle Heath sat up, scowling; he possessed one of those hard, overly masculine faces that looked a picture when riled, jowls clenching and unclenching like the workings of a machine. 'Like your aunt says, she was a mother to me, to her, and to Phil. And she adores the cotton socks off each and every one of you, although I fucking wonder why sometimes.'

'It's cool to be a witch!!' Daniel protested. 'I didn't mean it like I was 'dissing her!'

'And don't you go speaking to Annie Woodfield either,' Uncle Heath snapped, 'them 'Hackney Woodfields' are nothing but trouble.'

Daniel kissed his lips also, playing with the twin strings on his hoodie. 'It's not like everyone doesn't know about Aunt Amanda. Annie said she has a broomstick and at night you can see her riding it, 'round and 'round the gherkin building in the City, and then back again. And she said she killed her sister, your mum, with lethal poison!'

'You shut that hole in your face,' Uncle Heath stood up, tipping his can towards him as part of the gesture. 'Or we're going home, right now.'

'Dad!!'

'I mean it!!'

'Oh bless him, he means no harm,' mum laughed. 'It's Jamie here I'm more worried about, 'round there almost every other night. It isn't natural, a boy of your age, especially with a lovely girl like Tiffany waiting for you.'

'Aunt Amanda gets lonely,' Jamie said, fiddling with the buttons on the remote control and flicking from channel to channel, terrestrial to digital. 'You're all acting like Uncle Phil died years ago, not just at Christmas. Me and her are the only ones who care. We're the only ones who really loved Uncle Phil, proper like.'

As soon as he'd spoke he knew he'd said the wrong thing, but mum was by his side already, her normally soft, pouty features contorted with anger. 'How dare you!!' she snapped, 'how dare you say that to me, and to your Uncle Heath?!?'

'Bev...' Uncle Heath put out a large paw to restrain her.

'No Heath!' she went on, 'how dare you say that, Jamie Woodfield?! I loved that man, my brother, so much...I...you know how I cope, from day to day, well do you?!'

Jamie shook his head. 'No.'

'…I cope by not thinking about it, not thinking about the fact that he's gone for even a second, because if I do, if that thought gets into my head then for that day and maybe the next I'm finished, you understand?! I'm a mess! a bloody mess.' And she wiped the trickle of tears that slid down her big eyes and onto her carefully rouged cheek with the back of her hand.

'I'm sorry mum…' Jamie was crying too, soft soundless tears that he too quickly wiped away with the back of his hand. 'I miss him as much as you do, you know.'

'Oh I know you do my darling,' he knew nothing cut mum up more than the sight of either one of her boys crying. She sat on the arm of his chair and ruffled his crop, wiping away the odd tear he'd missed. 'I know you do. He was our rock, Phil was. Our rock.'

'Look at this!!' Daniel was distracted from the drama by a newsflash on SKY ONE. 'Something's happening at Big Ben; there's police choppers there and everything!! It might be fundamentalist Muslim ninja suicide bombers!!'

'Hey now, your cousin Laquisha is a Muslim now, didn't you know?!' mum turned to the TV. 'She brought a prayer mat for five pounds on the Romford Market, and a second-hand Koran from our Jamie's book stall here for a quid. That's a bargain, I say, a bargain! instant conversion for less than a tenner.'

'Mum,' Jamie rolled his eyes, 'she was a Christian last week, and a Pentecostal the week before that! Laquisha only does it to be controversial! She does it so's she's got something to write to Hayden in prison about. It makes him laugh, and he shows the letters around to all the other cons, and they hold communal readings of them in his cell! She told me!!'

'Look!' Daniel was whooping with delight. 'Look at them all!!'

'Protestors of one sort or another,' Uncle Heath sat back and laughed, gazing at the screen, 'probably animal rights or something, or 'Fathers for justice', maybe? I reckon I ought to hook up with them, get me some peace and quiet.'

Mum peered at the screen, as the camera came into focus on those heading up the protest, now almost shouting down the police as they continued to voice their demands. 'It's Jack!!' she almost fainted, her hand on her breast.

'And your Tiffany, Jamie!!' Daniel slapped the arms of his chair in delight, 'right behind him!'

Jamie glared at the screen, his frustration visible and mounting with every passing second. Finally he spoke, when the camera pulled away and the words 'student protest' filled the screen in bright white capitals. 'I wish I was an only child,' he said, softly at first, but then louder, loud enough for them to hear it; 'I wish I was an only child!!'

Chapter 18

Tuesday 4th April 2006

David was an only child, an only child from a rather cold and pointless marriage between two people who still lived together in their little house down in Bournemouth, but who essentially lived very separate lives. He had one aunt, a cousin he'd met once, maybe twice, and that was about it. The idea of a clan as large, as engulfing as Jack's, whilst to some perhaps a downright horrifying thought, was to him one of the most seductive, overpowering things he'd ever heard of in his entire life. He'd first read of the Woodfields – their names changed to the 'O'Brien' for the purposes of legality - in an old copy of Fortean Times left in a dentist's waiting room when his mother had taken him to have a filing, age twelve. That was thirteen years ago. In those thirteen years he'd gained a degree, a first, in media journalism from Bournemouth University, relocated to London aged twenty, and offered himself up to Fortean Times as a freelance journalist on a pittance commission as long as they gave him carte blanche access to everything they'd ever written on the Woodfield family. Someone high up was obviously very impressed by his sheer enthusiasm for his subject, either that or simply they'd been taken with his rather innocent south coast charm, his big blue eyes forever widening as he'd been escorted down into the dusty vaults to look over reams of paperwork, old photographs, property ledgers, movie reels, and books on the 'alternative' history of London, books that told a lot more than just the same old tales about Jack the Ripper, Sweeny Todd, and the stories about the Kray Twins that almost everyone knew.

This new employment dovetailed rather nicely with Jack approaching the magazine off his own back – it was just one in a number of calculated 'career moves' – whereupon he'd sell as much of his family's secrets, the gossip and the 'unknown histories', as much as was possible without getting into too much legal difficulty, in exchange for a cheque big enough to see his way through the first year of a degree in sociology at South Bank University. They hit it off during a lunch arranged by the head of David's department at the magazine, and within a fortnight they'd agreed to flatshare a property in Islington that Jack had come by through way of a distant cousin, one of 'the Hackney Woodfields', he'd said with a chuckle, something David didn't entirely understand. That autumn David got in at South Bank on 'the clearing' procedure, taking an MSc in sociology, with a leaning towards 'deviant' subcultures. David was essentially shy to the point of being withdrawn, and only enlivened by talk of the Woodfields or other supernatural ephemera as such, but Jack…well, Jack was everything he wasn't; Jack was confident and outgoing, lively and engaging, almost masterful in his approach to people, especially in awkward or difficult social situations. He didn't even have to try, most of the time. Jack was the kind of person who elicited the sounds of dropped dishes in a restaurant; David had written that in the back of one of his notebooks once, and never had he topped it for summing him up. Walking down the street on a hot summer's day with Jack, in one of his ill-fitting t-shirts and his jeans that hugged his rugby thighs was an experience all of its own.

But it was far beyond the sphere of the social, or the physical; Jack was instant and unashamed access to every aspect of the Woodfield life, to family photos and letters he'd never even dreamed off. In essence he was something of a Fortean Times fanboy's wet dream. After a few months hanging around with him it had even seemed as if some of the magic was rubbing off. It was through Jack that David found out for the first time that girls found him attractive, that he could wear nice clothes and look good in them, instead of still trying to squeeze into jumpers his mother, a rather brittle and put-upon woman, had stuffed into a carrier bag for him, in floods of tears, the day he'd left home. Of course this particular aspect of life didn't matter much to David, because he'd pretty much fallen in love with Jack that first lunchtime, nodding and listening intently over a shared 'Meat Feast stuffed crust' in the Pizza Hut at Cambridge Circus. David had known he was gay from a very young age, but that painfully shy manner had pretty much circumcised the opportunity to do anything about it, that and the prohibitions his parents had put upon him until he left home. He'd been with one, maybe two rather lacklustre guys when he met Jack, and for him it had been like meeting one of the men he'd fantasised over in the magazines he'd seen on the top shelves of newsagents back in Bournemouth. He'd kept quiet for as long as possible, until one day they'd been in the South Bank student union bar and the most gorgeous girl had walked in, turning everyone's head, and she'd walked past Jack and done a double-take at him. 'Mate, I'm gonna fuck her,' Jack had said. 'I am gonna fuck her badly.' And he'd looked at David and said, 'How about you?' and David had coloured and said, 'I'd rather watch.'

From South Bank they'd graduated and gone on to the London School of Economics, continuing their respective courses; Jack's graduation had been swamped by Woodfields, whereas all David could show for it were his two rather out of place parents, his photographs as a result rather Spartan in comparison to the ones Jack was hawking around a couple of days after the event.

He'd been secretly upset when Jack had begun to take an interest in a girl in his class within weeks of starting at the LSE, a girl called Dorothy, with whom he'd been paired to do a presentation on gender violence. Jack took an interest in girls all the time, almost always reciprocated, but Dorothy was different, because she didn't return it, and that made Jack all the more determined, and so talk of her became all the more frequent and intense, and so David became more and more upset as the prospect of something perhaps more and more intense, if and when it occurred, began to blossom. Dorothy was well-read, a great advocate of Judith Butler and radical gender theory, and didn't mince her words. She'd done her degree at an offshoot of UCL, somewhere called 'the Hopkins Institute', where gender theory and relational psychoanalysis were fused into a new form of therapy for a mainly female clientele. After allowing Jack to woo her for weeks she politely declined his advances; she had a little boy who took up all her time when she wasn't studying, and the parting with his father had been such a painful experience that she was off men for the foreseeable future. That didn't however put paid to a possible friendship, and she'd inserted herself into their twosome rather seamlessly.

Today was the first time Jack had actually taken David to Barking. Previous trips had been postponed and endless promises broken because this or that essay was due in, or rather more painfully, because this or that girl needed 'a good seeing to'. And so David had only seen Barking in books, and treated the whole experience as though it were some long-sought after holiday to an exotic locale in the South of France or something; to Jack it was nothing more than a dreary little town on the edge of London filled with chavs and market stalls selling piles of tat, that and a garish shopping centre – the Vicarage Fields - possibly outdone only by the pink monstrosity at the Elephant and Castle. Even the tower blocks were awful, huge sprawling edifices of a faded cream colour, blotting out the sun as they rose up on the right of the train line. 'My god, they're hideous,' David had said, his hand over his mouth.'

'That's the Murphy Estate,' Jack said. 'I grew up there.'

'You did?!' he gasped. The District Line train they'd picked up at Embankment pulled into Barking, the sun breaking out only occasionally behind large banks of smudged white cloud. David swallowed. 'I didn't mean…'

Jack just grinned, that near ear to ear dazzling display of perfect white teeth. 'I know, mate; it's a shithole. I totally agree with you.' He got up, and led them to the doors. 'Here we are,' he said, injecting about as much enthusiasm as he could muster into his voice. 'Just follow me, but don't go taking any pictures or people will think you're weird.'

'Well I'll need pictures at some point,' David slung his bag over his shoulder and quickly took a snap of the station platform on his camera phone anyway. 'Otherwise certain sections of the article, after it's been used as my dissertation, will look rather threadbare.'

'Plenty of time for photos later,' Jack hurried up the stone steps and turned left, swiping his way through the ticket gate, 'now, where do you want to see first?!'

'I don't know, I mean, there's so much…' David was gazing up and down the concourse, this way and that. 'What do you think?'

Jack sniffed, inhaled, and led him out to the taxi rank. 'Over there's the Vicarage Fields,' he said, nodding at the rusty red brick building on the adjacent side of the road; the garish shopping centre, in other words. 'My brother lives in our Uncle Phil's apartment just down there; my mum lives on the Murphy Estate, down the end of the road; there's the East Street market, and just behind that my Aunt Delia and Uncle Eddie live with...'

'Whoa!!' David laughed, patting him on the back. 'Information overload!'

'Just put your fanboy hard-on away, Davey boy' Jack chuckled, unaware how close to the truth he was skirting in more ways than one. 'To my mind this place is terminally dull and dreary, even in the height of summer. In fact summer only makes it looks worse, 'coz then it shines a light on exactly how tatty it really is.'

'Come on Jack...' David held up his camera phone to the Vicarage Fields and, after adjusting the contrast, took a couple of shots. 'You grew up here, you must have some affection for the place. It's your home. Bournemouth is still full of pensioners, despite what the tourist board would have you believe, but it's got a special place in my heart, always will have. I do feel like I'm home when I go there. Maybe you can come down with me one day, and see.'

'In summer?'

David nodded, his face flushing unexpectedly at the lack of rejection that usually came after suggesting something to Jack. 'In summer.'

They set off down Station Parade, Jack having to constantly stop so David could look at this or that shop, making little notes on a pocket sized pad he'd brought with him which, whilst slightly conspicuous, was nowhere near as embarrassing as the camera complete with zoom lens he'd threatened to bring. 'We're bound to see some cousin or uncle or other,' Jack was saying. 'My cousin Casey runs a photography shop back there in the station foyer; my Uncle Heath sells mobile phone covers down there on the East Street market, Jamie sells second-hand books there, and my Aunt Hannah sells doormats!' he smiled to himself. 'Oh, the glamour of it!' and the he nodded his head back and to the left. 'Cousin Bobby works in the KFC just there, and I think he's doing that to finance his way out of here because he's not that happy with his lot, but if we meet him don't say I said that 'coz he's ever so sensitive. In fact, I think he might be like you, you big poof.'

'I bet if he is then he hasn't come out,' David winced at the thought of it, 'gay, and in Barking?!'

'You want to meet his dad,' Jack rolled his eyes, 'my Uncle Brian; religious nut of the highest order, and an Essex man to boot. I'm surprised he hasn't had Bobby exorcised and done over at the same time. You want to hear the things he's done to my Jessica over the years.'

'Your Jessica?'

Jack coloured a little. 'I'm very close to her. I think you saw her at the graduation, but I can't wait for you to meet her properly.'

'What about Jamie? he isn't here, right? On weekdays, I mean.'

'Nope. He's sold the stall over to someone four days a week while he learns to read 'Jack & Jill', if you'll pardon the pun.'

'I don't think he liked me,' David said. 'He was so upset that Christmas Eve, although he wore it well. I felt a bit like an intruder, I have to say.'

'Don't go grey over it,' Jack waved a hand dismissively. 'He's gonna have to learn that life goes on; Jamie's problem is he's always existed in a little Uncle Phil-orientated bubble, and I'm afraid that bubble burst that day, rather abruptly.'

David made a sympathetic face. 'How about a look in the Vicarage Fields then?' he nodded past the post office. 'That's where Jake Woodfield uncovered the money his grandfather Jaden had hidden, the money he used to buy up the original family properties, right?'

'Is it?'

'Of course!!' he bounded over the road. 'You go in first; I feel like I might pass out.'

Jack followed on and pushed open the doors, one hand on each so that they swung open rather like the doors of a royal court swung open just before a monarch struts through them. Piped pop music played over the tannoy, and he walked at a brisk pace up the creamy coloured walkways, demonstrating to David how the ground floor rather strangely began tapering into the first floor, a phenomenon that culminated in the balcony overlooking Morelli's coffee counter and the ASDA store, one floor below them. Jack stopped at the balcony to glance down, but of Tiffany there was no sign. 'Is that of any significance?' David asked, following his gaze. 'Family hold court down there, or something?'

'No...' Jack's eyes had been drawn by a pair of rather busty young women supping coffee and sorting through their bags of shopping. 'Tiffany works here.'

'Ah.' David cleared his throat. 'Well anyway...you're lucky you got off with a caution, I mean, that student protest and all.' he shook his head, glancing up at the oversized glass baubles suspended from the ceiling. 'And that you kept your name out of the papers was a bloody miracle.'

'Sometimes it is handy to be a Woodfield,' Jack shot him a crafty glance. 'But LSE students have a long tradition of those sorts of protests, from what I've heard. They did gay liberation and all that guff, so I thought you'd have been sympathetic at least. Oh hell.'

'What?' David followed his gaze, down to where a rather mischievous looking black girl, cartoon pigtails cascading down over the back of her ASDA checkout uniform was chatting to several of her co-workers over an espresso and a rather enthusiastically sugared jam doughnut. 'You know her?' he asked 'Is she a Woodfield?'

'Uh huh,' Jack smiled fondly, 'that's my cousin Laquisha. She was at our graduation too; most of them were, as it goes.'

"I was too busy showing my parents around the War Museum," David sighed. He glanced back down at her. 'You're a racially divergent family, I must say, that's fascinating.'

"She's a real scream," Jack went on. "You want to meet her? From what mum tells me she's just converted to Islam, but only because she found a prayer mat she thought might look good in her bedroom, and she had to convince the stall owner she was Muslim before he'd let her buy it.'

'Does she know…well, you know, all about the family history?'

'Heck no. Or if she does she's never mentioned it to me. All 'quish really cares about is make-up and extensions, heels and handbags. Oh, and her boyfriend Gael, who is a top bloke and a good friend of the family. Want to meet her then?'

David felt his natural shyness coming into play, vying almost at once with the overwhelming desire to meet another Woodfield. 'Ok, but you do most of the talking.'

They went down the escalator, Laquisha spotting them before they disembarked, whispering to her friends, both of whom eyed Jack up like he was something good to eat. 'Girls,' he said, arms wide. 'This is my best mate David. We've come to…well, I've come to see mum, and he wanted to tag along. He thinks Barking's wonderful!' and at this he slapped David hard on the back, adding, "coz he's sick like that!'

Laquisha looked David up and down, twirling her pigtails like they were the rotors on a helicopter. 'Hello David,' she said.

'Hi,' he stuffed his hands in his pockets, and then remembered he really ought to be offering up a handshake. 'I've heard…well, you've been mentioned.'

'I have?' she giggled, and the other girls followed suit. 'Lovely. Are you as brainy as our Jack then?'

'Well I'm at LSE too…'

'That's good enough for me,' she splayed her painted fingernails all over his denim shirt. 'What's your phone number?' and at this the girls laughed again, louder.

'Hands off, 'quish',' Jack laughed. 'Davey boy's shy.'

'I can change that,' she said.

Jack exhaled, and then laughed. 'You heard from Hayden lately?' he asked.

Her mischievous attitude darkened a little. 'He's depressed,' she said. 'Nick's applied for a transfer to some open prison so he'll be all alone, even though Hayden hates him anyway, at least its company.'

'My cousin Hayden,' Jack said to David, over his shoulder. 'He's…away; cousin Nick too, as a matter of fact.'

'Nothing serious, I hope?' David said, in all seriousness, but Jack and Laquisha just laughed.

Jack said to her, 'When you write him again tell I was asking after him, and I'm thinking of him, and stuff; tell him I can't wait to see him too, and we'll hang and stuff.'

'You could write and tell him yourself,' Laquisha asked. 'I think it's beastly the way you flex your biceps at me, Jack, and expect me to do everything you ask!' then she glanced over his shoulder and her eyes widened. 'Shit. Mr Ferguson's on the prowl. We better get back to our tills, girls.' And with that she stood on tiptoe and kissed Jack gently on the lips, then turned on her tail, pausing only to twirl her pigtails a final time in David's direction, wiggling her rather shapely bum a little too much than was perhaps necessary as they headed back to ASDA, and to their respective tills.

'Well,' David fingered his collar. 'She's a little…'

'Oh believe me,' Jack grinned. 'She's a *lot*.'

'Jack!!' it was a girl's voice, lighter than Laquisha's, and without the artificiality of the Jafaican twang. Before David knew who was where, a white girl was waist-length brown hair streaked rather violently with flaxen, some of it dangling down over her big doe-eyes was standing in front of them, smiling a little shyly, her hands behind her back. She was looking David up and down rather uneasily, but broke out into a beaming smile at the sight of Jack, and proceeded to wrap her arms around him and bury her head against his chest. 'What are you doing here?!'

'Marie!!' Jack returned the embrace wholeheartedly. 'ASDA didn't get you too, did it?'

'Did it heck,' she twirled for him, showing off the clinician's tunic she wore. 'I work in the perfumery, just back there. I get more than her and she's jealous, but she just texted me that you were here so I thought I'd pop down and say hello.' She nodded at David. Who's this?'

Jack spread his arms wide. 'Marie, this is my best mate and flatmate, David; David, this is Marie, Laquisha's non-identical twin sister; second of three, and yeah, their mum wanted one of each!'

'A pleasure,' David shook her hand warmly. 'You must be Hannah's twins then?'

'Yeah, how'd you know?' she narrowed her eyes, but David caught Jack shaking his head over her shoulder just in time.

'Oh…I got Jack's Christmas card list mixed up with mine…' it sounded lame and they both knew it, but she seemed to buy it, and beamed. She had a lovely smile.

'Jack, you need to come and visit more often,' she said, leaning against him and squeezing his bicep. 'Your mum misses you so much it's untrue; and you know it isn't natural for a Woodfield to live in the West End; you're a fish out of water. And besides, I miss you. I miss having a mad crush on you.'

'Well I'm doing quite well thank you,' he made a theatrical bow. 'And you?'

'Still single,' she sighed, something David found hard to believe. 'I'm not like the other girls, Jack! I'm looking for love! why can't I just meet a nice librarian or something?!?'

Jack took her face in his hands. 'You're a beautiful girl, Marie,' he said, and David could see the old magic working, as it did for him, and for so many other; that deep, soothing voice, that near overwhelming physical presence...Jack was saying, 'You know I'd marry you myself, and you could make me raspberry ice cream until the cows come home, but...'

'Oh Jack I love you,' she sighed, flopping against his chest under the onslaught of tactically directed testosterone. 'I want to cook and clean for you, iron your shirts and straighten your underpants! I don't care what other women say! I want to be subservient!'

David smiled. He liked Marie. She was a girl after his own heart. Jack said, 'Now if you'll excuse us angel, we need to eat.'

'Text me,' she disengaged, making the sign of the mobile to her ear. 'Don't forget the plebs, 'cuz.'

'Will do,' he kissed her on both cheeks then watched her go, his head cocked to one side. 'Stay out of trouble.'

'Oh, I'm not Laquisha,' she giggled, and was gone.

'Well she was charming,' David said as they strolled up towards the Ripple Road exit.

'That she is,' Jack nodded. 'She's one, you know. Or so they say, anyway.'

'A witch?'

'Uh huh. Well, leastways I think so; this girl was giving her hassle at school one time, when we were in the juniors; St. Margaret's. Anyway, Marie lost her temper and when the girl laughed at her like, 'watch skinny go', she suddenly gets this awful rash, almost on the spot; turns out she'd developed scabies, like, instantly. She nearly died, I think; the scabs were so bad they got infected, or so I heard. Of course I think its utter horseshit that Marie had anything to do with it. Its transference, is what it is; the girl was a slut, obviously.'

'Wow.' David made a face of amazement. 'Sex magics? There was an article in Fortean Times a couple of years back; they said that sex magics were...'

'Transference,' Jack shook his head. 'Everyone was jealous of us in school because Uncle Phil was our uncle; we had as many enemies as friends.'

David glanced at him, loving these sudden and frank admissions. 'I bet you looked after all of them, when Uncle Phil wasn't around.'

Jack shrugged. 'Pretty much; me and Michael, and Hayden and Clay...'the Woodfield boys', they used to call us. We could take anyone. Ninety per cent of the time it never came to fisticuffs anyway, I mean, Hayden was like a fucking wild animal once he...' and then Jack checked himself, and they stopped at the doors and he was pushing them open in the same manner he'd done when they arrived. 'Come on,' he said, lolling an arm around David's shoulder. 'I'll take you to meet my mum now, and then Jessica, if she's not off on one of her fancy photo shoots.'

'I love your family,' David said, as the cold air hit his face. 'I don't care what you say, it must be wonderful to have so many different people who love you, unconditionally, and all.'

'Isn't it just,' Jack beamed, a little falsely.

The Daddy Dissertation Part 1

By David Samuels

The legend of Jake Woodfield

Wikipedia, the invaluable free online encyclopedia, defines Barking as being '...the *principal town in the London borough of Barking and Dagenham. It is a suburban development with a large retail and commercial centre situated to the west of the borough.*' (a full bibliography of sources can be found at the end of this dissertation).

It goes on to illuminate the casual reader to the fact that the town was built upon the site of Barking Abbey in the year 666; the dissolution of the monasteries in 1536 led to the destruction of the Abbey but St. Margaret's church stands now upon the old site, where some of the original foundations, including the ominous Curfew Tower, where local legends say that 'Minty Hardcore' flung herself to her death, remain. It's also worth noting that the current chaplain and residents of St. Margaret's are also among the subjects of this dissertation; the Reverend Brian Woodfield has been in the father of St. Margaret's since 1971, and lives there with his wife Betty, and his two youngest children, Bobby and Jessica.

Barking became an urban district from 1894, and a municipal borough in 1931; this was later abolished when it became the London Borough of Barking, and the '...and Dagenham' term came into use around 1980. It is on the District and Hammersmith & City line of the London Underground, and C2C services connect it out to Upminster and Dagenham Docks. The main shopping thoroughfares are immediately apparent on leaving the Underground station; here you have Station Parade, with the Vicarage Fields shopping centre, where many of the Woodfield family work, and further down the bandstand and a three-way divergence leading onto London Road on the far right – home of Barking's only nightclub, 'Legends,;' East Street in the middle, where more Woodfields run various stalls; and the Ripple Road on the left, where Rachel Woodfield and her son Michael continue to live in the oldest standing family property. In fact, you would be hard pressed to find one vein of life in Barking that the Woodfields were not involved in, in some capacity or other. There have been Woodfields in the area as far back as the mid-1700s.

However, this enormous clan started for the purposes of this dissertation with just one man; the oldest records I have been able to find and verify through multiple sources indicate that Jake Woodfield and his twin Julian were born in 1785 to unidentified parents and left in the care of the nuns of the former Barking Abbey. Such a move had been specified in the will of their grandfather, Jaden Woodfield, in the event that anything happened to his son and daughter-in-law. Almost nothing is known about

Jaden except that he was said to be something of a local 'Jack the lad', and that the rather strange clause in his will, one that didn't extend to his own son and was only made in provision for the grandchildren, was to be followed to the letter. The East End and Essex of this time were places of great poverty and it wasn't uncommon for children to be abandoned at birth or shortly after in this way, and for orphanages to be filled to the brim with such unwanted children, the sorts of places that would inspire Dickens only a couple of decades or so later in some of his most famous works of fiction. If I were to venture back further then parish records do indeed confirm that there were Woodfields in Barking as far back as 1666, when one John Woodfield was burnt at the stake in the area where the bandstand has since been erected, burnt before a public crowd shortly after Martha Driver or Chalke, both for charges of bewitching.

Whereas Jake was a boisterous and carefree child, Julian was said to be sickly and withdrawn, and kept to his bed much of the time. He clung to the skirts of the nuns and followed them around the orphanage night and day. Julian died from complications caused by croup when he was only eight years old, leaving his twin brother Jake essentially alone; there was scandalous rumours at the time that the nuns had abused or neglected Julian because he'd been so sickly, but these allegations were never proven. Jake left the care of the nuns when he was twelve years old, which in those days were perfectly normal practice. He eked out a living stealing and avoided the workhouse by sheer cunning, and by virtue of his angelic face, large dark eyes and wavy brown hair which all combined to give him the appearance of a rather shifty little cherub.

He soon turned from thievery to street entertainment, playing the lute and the fiddle, and sometimes dancing when he could find someone else to play for him; he toured all over Essex doing this and his sheer enthusiasm often won the most disheartened crowds over. He added card tricks and some simple sleight-of-hand to his act, and found he had a natural talent for illusion and won large amounts of money in street card games and the like, money which he wisely hid away to be invested at a later date; Jake was an early example of the traditional East End 'ducker and diver', if you will. By his late teens he had garnered something of a reputation and did nothing to ward off suggestions that he was descended from a great family of witches from the 1600s; it soon went about that he could give 'the evil eye' to those who poured scorn on his act, and float himself up into the air as if by magic, and all these stories only enhanced his reputation moreso, at a time when Essex was still highly superstitious and regarded as a haven for witches and their like despite the last burnings having taken place some hundred years previous.

By age twenty Jake Woodfield was said to be the most sought after man in all of Essex, with his deep set dark eyes set now almost hidden in a permanent broody frown, the upturned cheeky grin giving him a most disarming appearance. Those same deep set eyes, albeit ice blue, and the upturned cheeky grin can be found today in his ancestor Jack Woodfield, more of whom later. Jake's investments in sites destroyed by the Great Fire of London and left neglected for decades made him vast amounts of money for the time, but he continued to work the streets simply because he loved the thrill of the act, and the adulation of the crowd, although he became more choosy about where he worked, and was soon performing on the streets of London proper, entertaining vast crowds in Hyde Park and on the Strand. Agents even approached him for theatre work but he seemed reluctant, content in the main to live off the profits of charging rent to the destitute whose own homes had been burnt down in the aforementioned disaster. These properties were ramshackle and cheap, but Jake was a considerate landlord and was often willing to let months pass before calling to collect the money due him; more than one resident's daughter was romanced by Jake, some might say 'in lieu' of payment, and more than one of these girls was rumoured to have left London with more than she'd originally started there with, i.e. a child, probably twins. In fact, it seems Jake went out of his way to 'sow his seeds', and by the age of twenty five he was rumoured to have had at least thirteen illegitimate children, many of whom unfortunately died in childhood.

In 1805 he married a girl named Jodie Ferguson after a courtship lasting several years, the daughter of a local businessman investing in the-then burgeoning business of printing newssheets. The father was initially opposed to the union as Jake's reputation not just as a street performer but as penny ante magician and all-around lothario had spread from the East End to the West many years previous and cemented him as something of a 'bit of East End rough' (one wonder if the whole idea of 'a bit of rough' started off with Jake), but he respected his business savvy in regards to property and eventually allowed the marriage to go ahead. Within a year Jodie had given birth to twins, Joshua and Jackie. The trouble began almost within hours of their delivery, however. Jodie's mother noticed a faint mark on baby Joshua's buttock, like a lip print, a kiss and a bite combined. The same mark was present on the small of Jake's buttock as well, and he was loathe to explain it away, although Jodie was adamant it hadn't been there when they'd begun courting, and as a fairly respectable girl she certainly had had nothing to do with it.

Jodie gave birth to Christopher and Luke soon after, and they too bore the strange mark in various positions in the small of their backs, and in the case of the former directly on his left buttock, but Jake seemed determined to explain it away as a birthmark passed down in his family for generations, and Jodie, by now exhausted from two double pregnancies, wasn't in the mood to argue. The family moved from Jake's modest room on the Ripple Road in Barking to a larger house in Stratford.

Jake only ever told his son Christopher where the strange mark they all – all apart from Jackie, the lone daughter – bore, that it had come from his 'Minty Hardcore' during a night of '…the most unbridled passion'; that the bite or the kiss was her '...thanks for the thighs that thrilled me so thoroughly.'.

*

Jake is said to have seen Cecilia Pynder's face on the cover of one of the newssheets Jodie's father printed at a time when the couple were still in their early days of courtship, and to have brazenly asked his father-in-law, 'Who is that beautiful woman?'. Almost at the same time Cecilia Pynder is said to have seen Jake's face on a dog-eared poster advertising 'Great Magicians of the East End and Essex' whilst passing a theatre on the Strand in her carriage and, fanning herself lightly, gestured to her mother and asked, 'Who is that handsome man?!'

Cecilia was something of a legend on the debutante scene in London at the time, although it isn't known where she originally hailed from. Tall and fair, with hair, as one courtier put it, '...like a waterfall of gold all down her back', she saw off prospective husbands by the bucketload, but maintained her position by charming all those around her with her quick wit and easy ear, and when all else failed, simply by purring at them with her sugar-syrupy voice. The other girls were in awe of her and yet also fiercely disapproving; she made no secret of the fact that she despaired of finding a husband among the '...effete little specimens presented to me all through one long summer after another', and was convinced she would die an unmarried old hag. The kind of men she wanted, so she said, were not to be found in the courts of bourgeoisie but in the fields and the factories; large, burly men, she would coo, whose big rough, hairy hands thrilled her no end, whose breeding showed no respect for her finely laced up petticoats as they tore them off her in their lust. As debutantes went she is said to have been a remarkable figure, eschewing many of the fashions of the time for pastel combinations that offset her porcelain skin and accentuated her hourglass figure, 'shockingly', some of the other mothers said. Some people were wary of her, and attributed strange remarks to her bearing and attitude, saying, '...that girl has too much Minty Hardcore in her for her own good.'

Cecilia was in the audience when Jake wrestled a bear on the open grounds where the Vicarage Fields shopping centre stands today, during the Barking Fair of either 1803 or 1804, certainly before his marriage to Jodie Ferguson. He is said to have been so distracted by the sight of her in her bonnet and her pastels with her tresses done in curls down her shoulders that the bear almost tore half his face off. Following his triumph he was introduced to Cecilia, and at midnight that night, much to the alarm of her fellow debutantes, all of whom were huddled in a carriage and most fearful of being in '...such a place' after dark, she and Jake were declaring their undying love for each other under the glow of the full moon in the self-same spot where he'd fought the beast only hours earlier.

When Jodie Woodfield died of natural causes in 1814 her father blamed it almost entirely on Jake's lengthy 'dalliance' with the young debutante, and even attempted to take him to court for it. In actual fact it was far more than a dalliance, although sometimes months would go by before Jake and Cecilia were able to meet, always in the utmost secrecy, although she regaled her fellow debutantes afterwards with tales of '…his rough beard tickling my thigh', and of his '…masterful advances', which only served to highlight the nervous fumblings of the courtiers she was usually presented with for what they really were. Jodie had long suspected the affair and issued an ultimatum to Jake around 1810; he chose her over Cecilia, and this news is said to have devastated Cecilia. He told Cecilia that now was the time for both of them 'to grow up', and to face the responsibilities that their vastly differing worlds demanded.

Cecilia is said to have begged and pleaded with Jake, telling him that she was suffering unspeakable torments, that she was accosted by a strange woman wherever she went, that the woman even entered her bedroom at night and stood in the corner of the room glaring at her. The most appealing anecdote I have is that she came to Jake in Barking and pleaded with him to call off '…his evil familiar, his Minty Hardcore", but that her pleas fell on deaf ears, and that she either shot or hung herself in front of him, right there and then, on the very spot where they'd met, where the Vicarage Fields shopping centre now stands.

Following her death Jake is said to have been disturbed and withdrawn, and not much help to Jodie when her illness claimed her, some years after. As I have said, Jodie's father blamed Jake for her death; neighbours spoke of awful confrontations at the family house in Stratford, where Jake would come to the door flanked by Joshua and Jackie, and on either side of them the two younger twins, Christopher and Luke. Young Luke Woodfield was particularly handy with his fists and on one occasion laid Mr Ferguson out flat on his back, causing him to land badly in the open sewer that ran along the bottom of the street; this seemed to aggravate a heart condition Mr Ferguson had and he died several weeks later, but medical cause and effect being what it was in those days the link was never established.

Luke Woodfield nearly died in his teens from drinking water infected with cholera, sold to him as fresh water from the Thames in the hot summer of 1817, a common trick from street vendors of the times, which caused the deaths of thousands. Jake was upset – naturally – at his son's brush with death but nothing could have prepared him for the shock of losing his first-born son Joshua only two years later when he was beaten to death by the brothers of a Hackney family whose only daughter Joshua had been romantically linked to. Rather unwisely some of this family were living in Woodfield properties at the time and they were summarily evicted, the remaining Woodfield boys coming around in the early hours to unceremoniously turf them and their belongings out onto the streets. The daughter whom Joshua had romanced was pregnant by him and became caught in an awful tug of war between the two families. Luke Woodfield laid her father out with a single punch in Victoria Park, and he too died from complications caused by the blow; this time there were witnesses and Luke was sent to prison, where he died. One strange anecdote I have of Luke's time behind bars was that he was sent to the equivalent of solitary confinement for somehow sneaking a woman into his cell on several evenings, a comely young girl of about sixteen, whose description bears more than a passing resemblance to Cecilia Pynder, with her tumbling blond hair and her bonnet. Fellow prisoners were said to have heard this girl screeching in ecstasy from within Luke's cell, calling out such things as, 'Oh Luke, your big, rough arms!! Oh Luke!! Pin me down with them, Luke!!'

It was said that Jake sent his son Christopher to kidnap the baby Joshua had fathered the day it was born, and this he did, and that he then had the baby registered as being his own, and changed its name to Jonathon. The girl was bought off, and the scandal at the time even reached the local papers, such as they were.

Jake Woodfield died in 1834, some say by the stress brought on by the death of his beloved Joshua; he is said to have been in his final days almost a shell of his former self, his hair prematurely greying and his posture stooped, causing many people to remark that he was '...old before his time.' Christopher is said to have tried to carry on administering his father's many properties but to have '...completely messed things up', almost driving the family to the point of bankruptcy. Mad at the poverty and conditions his family were then forced to live in, Jake is said to have taken his grievances to Parliament, walking all the way there from Barking with just his cane to support him. Parliament burnt down soon after the fact, to which historical records can also attest; witnesses were said to have glimpsed '...a nymphet cavorting madly above the smoke and the chaos, whipping off her bonnet and waving it to the wind, and crying out, "I did it for you, Jake!! Oh how I loved you!!".'

Jake's funeral in St. Margaret's Cemetery, where the majority of the Woodfields are buried to this day, was a grand affair and attended by many local businessmen, his coffin borne by his remaining son Christopher and headed by the younger Jonathon, child of Joshua's disastrous dalliance with the Hackney family. Jake left everything to this child over Christopher, whom he is said to have called '...a hopeless lump.' Among the many items packaged up for the young Jonathon was a pillow, seemingly hand-stitched and full of the strangest feeling items, which Jake had instructed should be secreted under his grandson's own pillow at night when he slept.

Chapter 19

Tuesday 4th April 2006

Jack's mum's flat was a lot smaller than David had expected, and his admittedly optimistic visions of framed paintings of various family members all the way back to Jake and Jeramiah were way off the mark; he would have to settle for one of those painfully posed school shots of Jack and Jamie, smiling falsely for the camera, aged perhaps nine or ten, their hair pushed forwards French crop style, Jack as gorgeous as always, his jaw already squared and his brow somewhat prominent, but David been surprised by how beautiful Jamie had been, also. The only pictures he'd seen of him were the moody, scowling skinhead of recent years, and yet here was an angelic natural blond with large, almost sorrowful eyes, thin, seemingly pencil-drawn lips, and painfully exquisite cheekbones. The picture made Jack look like an older sibling rather than an actual twin, and seemed to validate the yawning social and sexual chasms between the two of them. David picked it up and waved it at Jack with a coo of delight. As he would be informed by Jack on the journey back, the majority of the paintings, photographs, tintypes and the like were in the loft of the house on the Ripple Road, now occupied by his Aunt Rachel; these would only be unearthed by someone with a lot of time on their hands, and the ability to sift through piles and piles of uninteresting local landscape shots taken by Casey Woodfield for a book provisionally entitled 'Barking through the ages', an idea he'd hatched as fledgling photographer and then forgotten about when he got married.

A further cursory glance around the room located Jack's graduation photo, several in fact; a solo shot and then one where he was flanked by his mother and his Uncle Phil. Jack was beaming broadly, almost cheekily in the solo shot. David recalled filing into the photography room behind him, Jack turning to him, peering out from under his mortar board and saying, 'This isn't just for me, you know, this degree; it's for Jamie too.'

The rest of the room was taken up with his mother's beauty therapy stuff; the massage table, the bottles and bottles of special massage oils and conditioners, piles and piles of carefully folded white towels, and boxes of disposable rubber gloves.

'Sit yourself down, David' Ms Woodfield – or Bev, as she would insist on at least two further occasions – said as she hurried into the kitchen, talking to them through the service hatch. 'I've only just eaten so there's still plenty more. Jamie's coming 'round later, Jack, and probably your Uncle Heath too, and Daniel, and Debbie…'

'Debbie!' Jack made a face, something just above the evolutionary ladder of the old fingers-down-the-throat routine.

She carried on regardless. '…I swear that brother of mine needs to find himself a new woman. I mean, I don't mind feeding his kids, because he slips me a tenner now and then but I haven't the heart to tell him that a tenner barely covers two people, let alone five or six…'

'Geez mum,' Jack seemed flustered. 'Maybe we'll just clear off, and…'

'Oh I'd love to meet Jamie again,' David beamed, 'and your Uncle Heath.'

'Fine,' he slumped in the nearest chair but stopped short of actually folding his arms in a show of complete annoyance. 'But I do have an essay to be doing, and postcolonialism isn't really my strong point.'

'One that isn't due in until the 27th, Jack,' David spread his arms out. 'This is your mum here!'

'Yeah, don't I know it.'

'So you're David,' Bev's head popped back out of the service hatch. 'I know we've spoken on the phone a few times, usually with you making excuses for this one when he doesn't want to speak to me…'

David blushed. 'He can be very persuasive.'

'I know he can,' she glanced at Jack and shook her head. 'One flash of those big blue eyes and he thinks he can charm the birds out of the trees. Well I tell you, that stopped working on me years ago…'

'Hasn't stopped working on me yet…' David said under his breath.

'I suppose a sub's out of the question then, mum?' Jack piped up.

She ignored him. 'Well, I hope you can cook, David, because I know for a fact that lazy article sitting there can't do much more than heat a can of beans up!'

'Mum, you make us sound like a bloody couple,' Jack sighed, unaware that David was becoming rather thrilled by her allusions to domestic bliss in Barnsbury. 'As it happens,' he went on, 'Davey boy here is a great cook; lasagne, spag-bol, fry-ups, you name it, he can do it, and with style. I'm getting fat, mum. My six pack is like, endangered. I reckon every straight lad should get a gay housemate!'

'You could do with putting on a bit of weight,' she dished out two hot plates and began to pile them with potatoes and sausages. 'And if I find out you've been trying to start a riot in Parliament Square again, or whatever it is you were up to the other day…'

'…student protest, mum!!' he slapped his brow in disbelief. 'They go on all the time! That's tame by LSE standards, I tell you.'

'…you could've been shot, like that poor Brazilian man on the Underground last year!' she shook her head. 'I thought that was awful, that was. I had half a mind to go down there and light a candle for him myself.'

'She's got a point,' David sat opposite him. 'I don't particularly want to see you with seven bullets in your head.'

Jack beamed. 'In the old days they used to burn us at the stake, right mum? Or dunk us?!'

'Oh don't listen to his nonsense,' she poured them both some fresh orange juice and set the condiments out. 'Now where is that brother of yours?!'

'I find if fascinating, Bev,' David beamed up at her. 'You're such an interesting family; real local colour, and all that.'

'I can tell you a few stories about this one here,' and she nodded at Jack, 'and make no mistake. I didn't get these crow's feet playing 'spot the ball' in the *News of the World* every Sunday, you know.'

'Mum…' Jack groaned.

'Oh bless him!' she nudged David's foot. 'He looks so handsome when he's ruffled! He hates to be foiled, he does! he absolutely hates it! He's so used to getting his own way, if it's not the eyes then he just jiggles his eyebrows and they all melt, but not me, no, I can see through him like a pane of glass!'

'This is splendid,' David dug into the meal with relish, blowing on the potatoes to cool them down. 'It's nice to be cooked for, for a change.'

'We can't stay too late, mum,' Jack said between mouthfuls. 'Like I said, I do have an essay due.'

'Always on the move…' she sat down and turned the telly on, flicking channels and settling eventually for 'the Simpsons'. 'I don't know.'

'You're welcome to write it for me, if you want,' he said. 'I wonder mum, what's your standpoint on the exploitation of the indigenous peoples of Thailand by white middle-aged sex tourists?!'

'I had a thing with a Gondolier from Venice once,' she said. 'Of course he was living in Stepney at the time, but he showed me all these pictures of him on his gondola in Venice. Does that make me a white middle-aged sex tourist then? It can't do, surely, because we split up before he actually took me there.'

'Have you lived here long?' David asked. He could see that Jack was trying to perform cerebral handstands over his poor mother just to prove the point that he didn't particularly want to be there, and as a result he felt for the woman. His own mother suffered a similar fate under his father more often than not, and she'd become a nervous wreck as a result. Still, he couldn't envisage this rather ballsy woman going down the same route, but one never knew.

'How long have we lived here?' Bev gazed into space. 'Oh, about as long as this one's been around,' she nodded at Jack. 'I can't say as I ever think I'll leave now.'

'And you live alone?'

'I'm afraid so, but you're never alone when you're a Woodfield, my darling,' she sighed wistfully. 'I don't get a moment's peace, really.'

'That's what Jack says,' he nodded, at which point Jack's face visibly tightened. 'I can't believe there are so many of you. I met four of his cousins alone while we were walking around; they all run up to him like he's the Second Coming or something!'

'Did you see Laquisha, Jack?' she asked. 'Her mum thinks she's taking the pill, you know. I said, well she's old enough now, it's not unheard of, but she wasn't having any of it. I don't think she wants her to end up like she did, saddled with a baby before she'd even reached twenty, and then two more by the time she was twenty five. Oh, and did I tell you she's become a Muslim too?! well we'll see how long that lasts, that's what I said to Hannah. She doesn't know whether to be more worried about the pill or the prayer mats!!'

'Laquisha's not that stupid,' Jack sighed, washing his food down with a big swig of orange juice. 'About the pill, I mean. But it's the way things are going, for kids her age. We did it the other week, you know, Britain has the largest numbers of single teenage mums anywhere in Europe. Combine that with how fashion conscious 'quish is and I'll bet she's got a sprog by Christmas.'

'Oh, speaking of Hannah's girls, your cousin Sara is engaged to that Ron fellow,' Bev went on. 'Party to be announced soon; you'll come too David?'

'Of course!'

'And you can bring that girlfriend of yours, Jack; Dorothy, is it?'

'Actually mum,' Jack went on. 'I think we're more likely ending up just friends.'

'You, friends with a girl?!' she shook her head in disbelief.

'I can be friends with a girl, mum!' he shook his head. 'It isn't all about sex, you know.'

'With you it usually is.'

Jack made a little noise. 'She's kind of old fashioned; not on the pill, if you know what I mean.'

'Well I'd love to meet her,' Bev said. 'You bring her next time. David, you make sure he brings her.'

'I will,' David said, at this point becoming slightly aware that the whole conversation was grating on Jack somewhat more than it had been for the last fifteen minutes or so. Jack had certain very distinct but not uncommon mannerisms that indicated when his rather generous patience was beginning to expire; usually he'd begin with two or three rapid outtakes of breath, followed by a brief running of his tongue around the circuit of his mouth, and finally his left leg would begin to jerk and the accompanying foot to tap rhythmically on the ground. At that point, David had found, it was best to bow to his wishes.

'Mum, how are Jamie and Tiffany getting on?' Jack asked.

'Well he wasn't best pleased to see her up on that riot with you,' she said. 'Although I said to him, she's your girlfriend, I said, but she's always been Jack's friend as well. She's quitting her Morelli's job, and trying to go into modelling full time; I think Jessica is giving her some pointers. She's been acting a bit funny lately as it goes, but maybe it's just the stress of all that posing and pouting. We don't want her ending up like that Kate Moss, do we?!'

'Does your Aunt Amanda come for tea at all?' David asked, rising and taking both his and Jack's plate into the kitchen. 'I've heard she's quite a character.'

'Oh she pops in now and again, but she's very self-sufficient for an old lady,' Bev sat back and loosened the elastic around her trackie bottoms. 'Jack can take you over to Bethnal Green one day to meet her. We used to live just down the road from the Krays, you know; their mum used to baby-sit for me and Heath when we were little.'

'If I must,' Jack sighed.

'Is this your Uncle Phil?' David was holding a framed photo as he came back from the kitchen, a framed photo showing a tall, slightly wiry man with large, dark eyes, wearing a green t-shirt and sunglasses, sandwiched in the middle of a beaming Bev and a smiling Heath; a sunny day, cars in the background, the faint edges of buildings and the overhang of a tree or two.

'Bless him, it is,' Bev studied the photo. 'He was handsome, wasn't he? And our baby brother there's not so bad either. Did you see Heath on the market, Jack?'

'Briefly,' Jack lied; he'd become so exhausted after the Laquisha and Marie that he'd edged David neatly around his Uncle Heath's stall, narrowly avoiding his Aunt Hannah's doormat emporium as well. 'Anything for pudding, mum?'

'He'll want his favourite,' David winked at her, 'raspberry ice cream with the chocolate sauce in the squirty bottle!'

'I always have some raspberry ice cream for my baby,' Bev was already on her way to the kitchen, just as the sound of another key twisting in the lock, jamming, and then being wrenched this way and that cut through the closing credits of 'the Simpsons'. She glanced over her shoulder. 'That'll be your Uncle Heath, or maybe your brother. God I hope it isn't Aunt Queenie.'

David followed her into the kitchen and watched as she dished out some raspberry ice cream for the both of them, taking extra care to put Jack's chocolate sauce on just as he liked it, in a funny kind of squiggly pattern that looked like the random scribbling of a child prodigy let loose with a coloured crayon. He folded his arms and peered through the service hatch, making sure Jack was totally absorbed in the latest news report on 'London Tonight' before leaning forward and saying, 'It's very nice of you to have me over at such short notice, Bev.'

'Oh think nothing of it, sweetheart,' she turned and smiled, and rubbed her knuckle lightly against his chest. 'I wouldn't see him,' and she nodded towards the service hatch, 'barely at all if you didn't remind him to ring, and such. Its bad blood that drove him away, you know. I wish they'd put it behind them, but that's boys for you.'

'Bad blood?'

At that point there was a yell from the living room; Bev ignored it, and put the two bowls of ice cream on a tray. A second yell and a brief volley of verbal abuse drifted through the service hatch, prompting David to go and see what was going on. A couple of seconds later he hurried back into the kitchen, his face creased with concern. 'Ms Woodfield…Bev, they're fighting!!' he gasped, his chest heaving, his finger pointing back over his shoulder, 'over Tiffany!!'

'They're what?!' she hurried into the living room, David right behind her, to find Jack and Jamie rolling around on the floor, trading rather hearty blows and yelling all sorts of obscenities at each other. One of the chairs was overturned, and as they watched the TV remote control went out the window, soaring over the landing, and ending up on the roof of a passing westbound District Line train.

Chapter 20

Tuesday 4th April 2006

It was almost dark as Jamie stormed out of the Murphy Estate, his lip swollen and a large rather nasty bruise forming just below his left eye. Mum had run after him in her slippers but he'd cranked up into a sprint and lost her just short of Aunt Queenie's flat on the Linton Road, taking a right and cutting around the back of the London Road car park, then passing the bandstand and diving into the door of Uncle Phil's flat so fast he almost broke the key in the lock. He bounded up the stairs and into the kitchen, stopping with his hands on his knees, almost bent double. When he had both breath and composure back he examined the damage to his face in the mirror over the sink; how much worse Jack had come off it was impossible to tell, he'd left that fast, been that flustered. The truth of the matter was he doubted he'd caused any real damage. Hitting Jack's stomach had felt a lot like pummelling a brick wall, and when he'd tried to catch him off guard by ducking to the left and then coming up with a right Jack had caught his fist in his open hand, closed his fingers around it, and then slowly bent Jamie's arm backwards until his eyes were watering, it hurt that much.

He spat into the sink, noting the pinkish colour of the spittle, and rinsed his mouth out with a swig of ASDA cola from the fridge. It was the first fight he'd had with Jack for…oh, at least nine years, and just like the last fight it had run the usual course of Jamie starting it and Jack finishing it, only this time there was no Uncle Phil around to wipe the blood away, and no Aunt Rose to smudge away the tears. It might have gone a whole lot worse for Jamie if it hadn't been for that friend of Jack's diving in between them and forcing Jack one way whilst mum had pulled him the other.

His mobile went off, caller ID showing it to be Aunt Amanda. 'Hello?' he said, suddenly remembering how hard it was to talk with a fat lip forming. 'Yeah,' he said, after letting her speak for a moment. 'I had a scrap with Jack. No. No I'm fine. I don't know. Yeah, he started it, as usual. I know. What? Where? Ok, if you reckon mum won't have chucked them out when she cleaned this place up. Ok. 'bye Aunt Amanda.'

He turned the mobile off and went up the stairs from the kitchen into Uncle Phil's bedroom, something he'd been avoiding doing for weeks. The pictures on the walls of the West Ham players and the 'Carry On' stars didn't wink when you looked at them anymore, as though they'd died when Uncle Phil had. Even the picture of Jamie in his junior kit with the youth academy team didn't have the grass blowing in the background as it had when Uncle Phil was alive. He ran his finger over the glass and when dust came off he spat on his hand and wiped the little pane clean. Somewhere downstairs the landline rang but he ignored it. As Aunt Amanda had directed he found a shoebox under the big metal framed double bed containing any number of old photographs, letters, official documents and the like. He emptied the contents of the shoebox onto the bed and sat there, sorting through it bit by bit.

He'd finished going through the shoebox by about eleven pm, and had stuffed everything he'd found into his rucksack for Aunt Amanda to inspect when next they met. It was all of the crazy stuff Uncle Phil used to always push under the bed whenever Jamie walked into the room, trinkets and little pouches, notebooks filled with things Jamie couldn't make head nor tail or even with his Sight & Sound book by his side ready to translate even the most indecipherable of scrawl. He left the room as quickly as possible, bolting the door behind him. It was his special space, and he didn't want anyone just wandering in there and upsetting it.

The buzzer went, and he peered cautiously out of the kitchen window, spotting Uncle Heath down on the street, his hands in his back jeans pockets, squinting at up the window. Jamie pressed the release button, and quickly checked his face. His wounds were coming up a treat, and he coloured a little when Uncle Heath caught sight of them his normally squinted eyes, squinting from too much time spent selling mobile phone fascias on the East Street market, widening suddenly. 'Shit Jamie, my little lad,' he said. 'What happened to you?'

Jamie knew he knew, of course; there wasn't much else reason for him to come around, not with Uncle Phil gone. Uncle Heath was a man of few words. It wouldn't have surprised him if mum hadn't assigned him to keep an eye on Jamie since he'd moved back. He glanced out of the corner of his eye at the table, normally pristine but now covered with the odd tea ring or two staining the wood, and the fruit in the bowl in the middle going slightly mouldy, to say the least. 'I got in a fight,' Jamie shrugged. He put the kettle on, stood on tiptoe to peer out through the window again, just in case the 'relief party' was in danger of growing any larger. 'You want a cup of tea, Uncle Heath?'

'Sure thing,' he leant against the sideboard, and folded his arms. 'This fight,' he went on, as he watched Jamie prepare the cups, 'wouldn't have been with your brother, would it?'

'What if it was?' he sniffed. 'He started it,' which basically meant Jamie had all but hurled himself at Jack the moment he'd come through the door and seen him sat there, and Jack had tried his utmost to restrain him before resorting to brute force, and finally losing his rag completely.

Uncle Heath made a little noise. He wasn't chewing gum like he normally did. 'I know all about fights with my brother, our old Phil. We used to fight like cat and dog when we was nippers, and your Aunt Amanda would have to literally come and stand between us, else we'd kill each other!'

Jamie couldn't imagine it, not really. All his life he'd only ever seen his two uncles as friends, not close, but always together at each and every West

Ham game, home and away. They'd crack open the occasional six pack and watch a video of the previous season's highlights, the sort of thing Jamie could never imagine doing with Jack. 'It was nothing,' he said, with a shrug.

'I was there,' Uncle Heath took the tea as it was handed to him. 'I saw the news thing, him 'an your Tiffany…'

'They're mates,' Jamie said. 'They was, when me 'an her were just…'

'Jamie,' Uncle Heath cleared his throat. 'When me and your Uncle Phil were your age, he got all the girls; now he was no beefcake or whatever you want to call it, like your Jack is, but he had the big brown eyes and the easy charm, and me? well I was the slow one, the awkward one; part of why I decided to bulk myself up a bit,' and here he gave a cursory flex of his bicep, under the faded denim shirt. 'But at the end of the day it don't mean nothing. Tiffany's with you; she's your bird, not his. I know that girl, her family live just around the corner from me, and they may not be Essex folk proper, but they're good, decent people, and she's a good, decent girl. She wouldn't do to you…what you're worrying she might be doing.'

Jamie leant against the sink, and sipped his own tea. These were more words than he'd heard Uncle Heath speak in years. 'Is that what everyone thinks of me?' he said. 'I'm the slow one? the awkward one?'

Uncle Heath ran a possible answer around his chapped lips, and then he leant forward and pulled up the back of his shirt, exposing the near clear lip print in the small of his back. 'You got one like that?' he said. 'I know you have. I was the first to hold you after Phil, when you were born. I saw it; we all saw it.'

'It's not like Jack's; Jack's is perfect, like a tattoo. Aunt Amanda said he should go to a derma…some place where they do skin stuff, and get it removed; get it lasered off and stuff.'

'So was your Uncle Phil's near perfect,' he said. ''and that's why he was the Daddy and not me. But I never minded much; I was happy doing my own thing, and when I found your Aunt Sophie, and she only had eyes for me…' he was in danger of drifting off now, as he did whenever she was mentioned; poor, tragic Aunt Sophie, whose talent as an artist was just beginning to be recognised when she took her own life.

'That's why Jack's the next Daddy,' Jamie said, 'isn't it? And not me.'

He nodded. 'You got to get on with your own life,' he said. 'Don't think about the how, or the why…'

'The why's 'coz Jack's taller'n me,' Jamie said. 'I know how it works. He's taller and he's better looking…'

'Jamie, you're a cracking looking kid…'

'Yeah, 'kid'; whenever they talk about Jack it's 'man', or 'bloke', but me, I'm always 'kid', or 'little Jamie'.' He could feel his hands gripping the edge of the sink. 'He's the Daddy 'coz he had to shave when he was thirteen, and 'coz he had big shoulders 'an a hairy chest by the time he was sixteen, ain't it?! And I'm just some silly kid.'

'Jamie…' Uncle Heath put his mug down. 'You can't think this way. I thought this way, for a while, and it was starting to chew me up, and your Aunt Amanda saw what was happening, and she sat me down and gave me a good talking to…'

'Aunt Amanda thinks I could be a good Daddy,' Jamie said, 'she says Jack's not interested…' and he found himself reeling off the same old spiel he'd given mum.

Uncle Heath had laughed. 'Jack ain't got no choice in the matter, same as your Uncle Phil didn't, even when he run away to Brighton…'

'Jack's at the LSE.'

'Jamie…once you've got that,' and he nodded down at his waist. 'You're the Daddy, and you don't got no say in the matter. There are things you don't know, things I hope you never know, or have to see…'

'Like what?'

Uncle Heath swallowed. He put his hand to his mouth as though he were actually readying himself to stem an unpleasant tide of truths. 'Like hearing a noise in the night and waking up and looking across at your brother's bed and seeing that he's got a woman there with him, who come from lord knows where, and she's waving her bonnet like a cowboy waves his hat as his horse completes the rodeo, 'an she's on Phil, you know, *on* him, and she looks across at me and laughs and giggles, pointing at me like I'm a silly joke.' He put his big paw on Jamie's shoulder. 'I don't never want you to see that. I reckon that's part of why your Uncle Phil took you when you got the scarlet fever that time, brought you here to live with him. You mum, she could never say no to Phil.'

'She only ever cared about Jack.'

'That isn't true, Jamie.'

'And you're just a sad old fart who sits around his house drinking himself silly, and crying over someone who died years ago,' Jamie said, his face reddening. 'I don't want to listen to what you got to say. You can go, like, right now.'

'You wouldn't speak to me like that, if your Uncle Phil was here…'

'Yeah well he ain't,' Jamie said, 'so you can just go!'

Uncle Heath towered over him. 'I'm gonna go easy on you on account of how we're all smarting over losing Phil, but…'

'Fuck off, you sad old cunt!' Jamie spat. 'I don't need you, or your stupid talks! Just go off back home and sit and drink Stella and cry over Aunt Sophie, like everyone knows you do every night! Put your stupid Status Quo records on, and drink and drink 'til Daniel or Debbie have to come down and throw cold water in your face!'

Uncle Heath raised his fist and pulled it back, and Jamie closed his eyes and braced himself for the blow, only it never came. He was fuming, shifting his posture from one way to the other, unsure of how to proceed. 'You're smarting,' he said, his finger raised and aimed at Jamie's nose, 'we all are, 'an we're all doing stupid things, saying stupid things, on account of how we can't believe Phil's gone...'

'I don't want hear people keep saying he's gone!!' Jamie suddenly shoved at him with the heels of his hands. 'I don't wanna hear it! He's still here when I'm here, and when you're not, coming around and telling me stuff I don't want to hear! I want you to go!' he screamed. 'Don't you understand?!? I want you to go!!'

The Daddy Dissertation Part 2

By David Samuels

The blowing up of Parliament

That the family eventually wanted Jonathon Woodfield would come as no surprise to anyone familiar with the sociological patterns surrounding the rough talking, hard drinking men of the East End and Essex. You see, Jonathon grew up to be the exact opposite of his grandfather Jake; indeed, he grew up to be quite unlike any Woodfield male the fledgling family had seen thus far. He was a fair-haired, fey, slight individual with little or no interest in girls, brawling or drinking, and even less in the family itself. He left the house in Stratford not long after Jake died and took up residence with another man in a room over a printing press in Shoreditch, in a social move quite blatant for the time, let alone the location. This caused great consternation to the family, and frequently the Woodfield boys – as they were now commonly called in the East End – went to see him, often dragging their sister, statuesque Jackie Woodfield, to mediate when they ran out of words, which didn't take long by all accounts. The split hadn't been resolved by 1837, at which time Christopher Woodfield lost his temper and throttled Jonathon in a row in the room over the printing press; Jonathon's male lover was said to have run screaming from the building and was half mad by the time he turned up in a pub in Dalston, claiming that '…a woman had appeared out of thin air while Christopher railed against Jonathon, and helped to hold Jonathon down'. There are also uncorroborated reports by some witnesses that a troupe of ghostly nuns was seen in the vicinity, further adding to the air of, in one person's words, '…black magic and mayhem.'

Christopher got away with murder quite literally; all the Woodfield boys told people that the two male lovers had in fact killed each other in a domestic, and no one was of a mind to question this account of things. However, further outrage was caused to the family name when it was revealed that Jonathon had sold a great many of their father's possessions, including a painting of Jake Woodfield and his 'evil familiar' Minty Hardcore, which later turned up in the British Museum. The family had tried to purchase it back over the years but have been continually refused since Jonathon by all accounts sold it to museum fair and square. The painting, a remarkable almost photographic likeness for the time, shows Jake, quite advanced in years considering the fact that he couldn't have been more than thirty or so, with heavy sideburns and smoking on a pipe, gazing mischievously out at the painter. On his right shoulder a comely young girl of about sixteen perches her chin and narrows her eyes, albeit with a slightly more malevolent gaze. She has large green eyes and the porcelain skin common amongst women of the time, an upturned nose with a slight dent in the end, but in no way detracting from the overall beauty of the whole. Blond hair in carefully constructed ringlets tumbles down over her shoulders, and onto his.

Christopher is said to have cursed Jonathon's soul and spat on his coffin, saying that '…this is what comes of going with *that* family', by which he meant the family Jonathon had been stolen from as a baby, the same family who had killed his brother Joshua over the pregnancy. This nameless family are not to be confused with 'the Hackney Woodfields', who emerged as a branch distinct and removed from the Barking Woodfields after the fall-out between Christopher and his nephew, Russell. Jonathon was not buried in St. Margaret's with the rest of the family, and there was even a rumour that circulated at the time that the Woodfield boys took his body from the coffin and dumped it in Victoria Park Lake, and sold the coffin second-hand to another bereaved family for a pittance, purely out of spite. Jonathon's male lover was found severely beaten in an alleyway near Hackney Wick a year or so after the funeral, and died a couple of days later from his injuries.

The Woodfields seems to have been at a loss due to the double blows of the death of Jake and the later betrayal by Jonathon, and several of Jake's illegitimate sons left London for good after the affair. Christopher became the unelected head of the family simply by virtue of being the oldest of Jake's surviving sons, and was married with a family of his own this time, including twins Jason and Jeffrey. After a period of relative financial and social uncertainty things seem to settle down around 1840 or so, and Christopher and his wife raised the twins along with their sister May in relative peace and quiet in the Stratford house; wills being what they were in those days, what Jonathon hadn't squandered on his male lover was claimed by Christopher, which he then eked out between himself and his sister Jackie, who had a large family of her own by this time. When Christopher signed a 'living will' in 1843, bequeathing the what was left of the Woodfield fortune – and it was a fortune in those days – to his only sons Jason and Jeffrey, they fought over it endlessly, finally ending up killing each other in bare-knuckle brawl witnessed by up to fifty people in Victoria Park. The prize possession of the fortune was apparently an old pillow stuffed with either horsehair or something slightly less salubrious, a pillow that disappeared soon after the tragic event, along with the rest of Christopher's living will.

Following the death of his sons, a distraught Christopher was approached by his nephew Russell Woodfield, the son of one of Jake's youngest illegitimate sons, to invest the squandered money further into property around the East End, Russell being an architect, and this Christopher did quite readily, now left alone with his daughter May and not a penny to his name; the Woodfield name can still be found in the records for properties in Bethnal Green, Mile End and Stepney to this day from the deal made between Christopher and Russell Woodfield.

Russell was a widower at an almost unfeasibly young age, and a crotchety old 'Scrooge'-style figure far older than he appeared, living alone in a dreary little two-up, two-down in Limehouse; Christopher is said to have poured his heart out to him, about the loss of his two sons and that no one '…knows the real reason they were always fighting', and to have inadvertently told him that his father Jake had been responsible for the burning of Parliament in 1834, for which the authorities were still seeking suspects.

Russell went to the authorities with the news on the basis of gaining a rather substantial reward, and lost favour with Christopher, but managed to con the rest of his money out of him and keep hold of what he'd signed over to him by a series of shrewd legal moves; some people said Russell was a witch who could read the future and bewitch people, and that he had bewitched his uncle Christopher. Christopher lost the rest of the family fortune; properties owned by various family members were reclaimed under various pre-existing agreements, or were sold to make ends meet when other, regular forms of income suddenly dried up. This began a family feud between the Barking Woodfields and Russell's family, who settled in Hackney, and that exists to this day. Great-Uncle Russell spent the money on developing his own businesses; no one knew what became of the rest of the money, or the deeds to the many properties owned by the family, only that that Russell suddenly became rich very quickly, whilst Christopher became very poor; Russell also boasted of '…tucking the pillow beneath my own,' whatever this statement is supposed to mean. For the first time the 'favourite son' Christopher was forced to go cap in hand to other family members for a job, for somewhere to live, indeed, for the very shirt on his back. He became an embittered drunk still devastated by the death of his two sons on top of everything else, and died soon after. His funeral at St. Margaret's was a pitiful affair, by all accounts. At his graveside his daughter May is said to have been the one who rallied the family at the behest of her aunt Jackie, and told them to '…hold our heads up high while we march back to Barking.' And, after deploying various nephews and nieces to pick up what few miserable possessions they still laid claim to, march back to Barking they did, and from there to all intents and purposes they have not strayed for the last one hundred and fifty years.

Chapter 21

Friday 7th April 2006

Aunt Amanda stirred her cappuccino until the froth built up to such a point that it spilt a little over the edge. She took a towelette and mopped up the excess, then dropped a couple of artificial sweeteners into the mix. Jamie pushed the notebook he'd been asked to bring across the metal table towards her, the rest of the stuff he'd packed into his rucksack being vetoed on account of it 'not being what we're looking for, darling'; apparently there was more than one shoebox stuffed under Uncle Phil's bed, full of weird and wonderful things. One or two of them seemed to have gone astray, perhaps when they'd moved him from the flat to mum's place on the Murphy Estate. 'Took me ages to find that, it did,' Jamie pointed out, nodding at the notebook. 'It wasn't where you thought it was going to be.'

'Never mind,' she purred, sucking the sugar off her silver spoon. 'Darling, your eye looks awful. I hope you did what I told you to, and put a cold steak on it.'

'I thought that was an old woman's tale.'

'And what am I?!'

'Well yeah...' he gazed up at the counter at Morelli's, a stark and uninteresting place without his Tiffany gliding to and fro, smiling sweetly at the customers and whistling a little tune as she mopped down the stainless steel surfaces. 'I put a cold flannel on it but you can tell I've been socked.'

Aunt Amanda made a little noise, and strummed her fingers against the side of her mug. The rings on her fingers made music of this simple gesture. 'I would've come around, but I was otherwise engaged, and besides, your mother said it wasn't so bad. I heard my adorable son looked in on you?'

'Uncle Heath?' he raised an eyebrow. 'He tried to give me a pep talk. I told him where to go.'

'Oh darling...'

'Well, I hate it when people talk about Uncle Phil in the past tense; I ain't ready for that yet!'

She shrugged. 'Fair enough. Neither am I, if you want the truth. Now,' she put her mug down. 'I can see how you came off in this fight, but tell me, how did your brother fare?'

'Mum says Jack's got a cut lip, but that's about it. I thought you wanted me to build bridges?!'

'It's sort of hereditary for Woodfield twins to fight,' Aunt Amanda sat back, and gazed around. 'In fact, it's a great tradition, if that's your idea of greatness. The only ones who got on all the time were my Grandfather Jacob and his brother, Jeramiah. I put that down to their mother, May, a woman whom I have always greatly admired. That's how I envision the two of you; like Jacob and Jeramiah. You'll have your scraps and your fallings out, but at the end of the day you'll be as thick as thieves.'

Jamie kissed his lips. 'We're meant to be going clubbing tonight, the whole lot of us.'

'Really? and Jack too?'

'Uh huh. He's bringing his fancy university friends, so they can look down their noses at us and talk about how common we are.'

'Darling I'm sure that isn't true,' she sighed. 'Anyway, you try and make sure you buy your brother a drink.'

'He should buy me one first!'

'Either way is building bridges,' Aunt Amanda smoothed out the notebook and opened it at the first page. 'Did you have a look at this?' she asked.

'I couldn't make head nor tail of what Uncle Phil wrote in there. I thought it was match scores and stuff, but I know most of them off by heart and the numbers don't match up. And what's all the religious stuff?'

'Ah, you found the crucifixes...' Aunt Amanda sat back, supping the cappuccino and gazing around at the midday shoppers. 'Was there a picture of Whoopi Goldberg from 'Sister Act' in there as well?'

'Don't think so. Uncle Phil wasn't religious, was he? He said religion was 'pants'!'

'Oh it meant nothing to us, darling...' she threw him a wicked grin, but he didn't flash one back. Aunt Amanda reached across the table and placed her hand on his. 'Jamie darling, what's wrong? You've had fights with Jack before and been right as rain in hours, but now...'

'It's nothing,' he sat back, rubbing at the cut on his lip until it looked red enough to bleed again.

'Jamie...'

'He beat me like a girl, Aunt Amanda!!'

'You said he had a cut lip.'

'Yeah well, there's cuts and there's cuts.' He bowed his head, and then peered up at her. 'He made me say, 'who's the Daddy'! He had me in a headlock, and he made me say it! And he didn't even mean it, it was just a joke to him.'

Her head titled slightly at an angle. 'Oh darling...'

'He's got bigger muscles than me, and everything. How am I gonna buff up like him, enough to make Minty Hardcore think she wants me?!?'

'This wouldn't be more to do with him going on that student protest with Tiffany as well?'

'Yeah...' Jamie sniffed. 'Kind of that too, but they've always been friends anyway.'

She nodded. '...and you miss your Uncle Phil still.'

Jamie sniffed, and then drank some of his own very sweetened tea. 'It seems to get worse, not better. At first it was like shock, you know? And now it's settled into this kind of awful, cold feeling. I don't feel like I'm really alive, but that I'm just going through the motions. No wonder Tiffany's hanging around with Jack instead, and that's without the fact that he's got bigger arms, 'an…'

'You were in shock when he died,' she said quickly. 'Even though you knew it was going to happen, we all knew. But it's now, as times goes on and birthdays and Easter come and go and he isn't here, it's now for the first time that it feels real, doesn't it?'

He nodded. 'I miss all the little rituals and stuff, you know? He used to buy all our match tickets, now I'm gonna have to do it. He used to fill in the subscriptions for the Hammers magazine, now I'm gonna have to do it, and fuck, it takes me ages. Stuff like that, you know? I think I'm gonna die when we hit June, and it's his birthday.'

'Do you want to come and stay with me for a while?'

Jamie thought about it, but couldn't figure out whether sleeping in Uncle Phil's old bed would be even more distressing than continuing to sleep just down the hall from his room, the room he'd come bounding out of every morning for the last twenty years or so. 'I don't know.' He made a face. Maybe. Can I get back to you on that one?'

'Of course you can darling,' she began leafing through the notebook, then frowned and reached into her handbag for a pair of spectacles which she perched on the end of her nose. 'Now let's see…'

'I've been looking out for possessed people too,' he told her, lowering his voice. 'But everyone's like, the same as they always were. Uncle Eddie's voice changes when he's drunk though, do you think that's important?'

She found the page she was looking for and spread it open; there was a sketch done in pencil of a leggy girl in pastels, a sun bonnet, and bare feet, bending over to smell a flower, her little skirt hitching up in her wake and offering a clear and concise view of her pert little rump. 'What do you think of her?' she said, turning it around and showing it to him.

Jamie stared at the picture. 'I don't remember her; but Uncle Phil had so many girlfriends…'

'This is Minty Hardcore; or your Uncle Rupert's rendition of her, at the very least. Look,' and here turned it over. 'It's dated; September 1st, 1970.' She tapped the picture. 'Know thine enemy.'

Jamie peered at it. 'I think I've had dreams about her, you know? When I was little, I mean. Or maybe Uncle Phil had a girlfriend who looked just like that. She used to stand in the doorway of my bedroom and look at me, and make this funny little sound, like she thought I was a joke or something. I didn't like her.'

Aunt Amanda scowled. 'Oh really? Well, let's just remind ourselves, Jamie Woodfield, what is she?'

Jamie gazed at the picture. 'A crafty little whore.'

Chapter 22

Friday 7th April 2006

'It's an awfully long way to go for a nightclub,' Dorothy said, reapplying her lipstick as the train pulled out of Mile End. 'And there are so many to choose from in the West End...'

'...that's the whole point of the exercise I think,' David said. 'Right Jack?'

Jack was staring out the window as the blackness of the tunnel roared by. 'Huh?'

'We're sampling Essex's 'exotic' nightlife, right?'

'Oh...yeah,' he nodded, a weak smile in place of the usual big, cheesy grin. 'Sure.'

'Well excuse me if I'm not blown away by your enthusiasm,' Dorothy said, clasping her Gucci handbag shut. 'And no one better try and nick this off me,' she held the rather expensive accoutrement to eye level. 'Or I'll bat them over the head with it!'

'What is this place like we're going to?' David asked. He was clearly gushing Woodfield fanboy enthusiasm all over again, and to his mind had taken yet another step into Jack's world with the invite of a night's clubbing, and even moreso, with the prospect of kipping on the couch in the Murphy Estate flat afterwards.

'Legends?' Jack raised an eyebrow. 'It's ok I guess; quite big, music's a bit retro and the girls are...'

'I thought Essex boys called them birds?' now it was Dorothy's turn to raise an eyebrow.

'I'm only an Essex boy by birth,' he seemed to lighten a little. 'You'll realise the full extent of the yawning social chasm between me and my family when you meet them.'

'I hope you're going to be nice to your brother,' David said. He almost reached out to touch the yellowy bruise on Jack's cheek but thought better of it. 'Jamie is coming, right?'

'It's Tiffany's idea,' Jack said. 'Partly to make things up between me and J, and partly 'coz she thinks I've been neglecting the family; and she's right, 'coz I have been. I was too busy having my own life, which is retrospect for a Woodfield is about as selfish as you can get.'

'Is that a tinge of guilt in your voice?' Dorothy studied his face carefully. 'Or sarcasm?'

'They're not such bad people,' he spread his arms wide, one over each of their shoulders. 'A little simple, maybe, a little insular...but hey, my cousin Jessica's coming tonight, D. You'll like her, she has aspirations, like me! She was in a pop group for about five minutes, kind of a poor man's Atomic Kitten, and now she's doing some glamour modelling...'

'…the word is porn, Jack,' Dorothy said dryly.

'Yeah, which kind of sucks considering her dad's a vicar; they call him 'the Pope', you know.'

'Try not to feel too guilty,' she crossed her legs. 'I still get pangs when I ask my parents to babysit, so I can do something like this; my dad looked at me like I was something he'd just trowelled off the bottom of his shoe.'

The light of a spring evening bathed the Murphy Estate as it came into view out of the windows. David shifted round in his seat, disturbing the suited gent next to him, in order to get a better view. Dorothy seemed lost in her own thoughts and decided to reapply her lipstick, while Jack was busy texting someone on his mobile. They disembarked last, allowing the remains of the rush hour crowds out ahead of them. 'It's chilly,' Dorothy said, pulling her coat tight. 'I don't think I'm going to like it here.'

'Oh hey give it a chance,' David said, watching Jack stride ahead of them. 'We're doing this for Jack.'

'…that's what worries me.'

'Huh?'

'Oh nothing,' she sighed. 'And you can haul your tongue off the pavement where it's fallen what with you staring at his behind and all.'

David stopped, caught short. 'What?'

'You know,' she stopped just short of the station café. 'Oh don't worry, I don't mind. It's awfully modern, as a matter of fact. Perhaps we could register under the new civil partnership scheme as some kind of bizarre threesome.'

David felt the colour rising to his cheeks. 'You won't tell him, will you? I mean, we flirt and that, but he thinks it's just a lark…'

'Of course I won't,' she tried not to snap. 'What do you take me for?'

'If he thought I really felt for him…'

'I don't think he does,' she said, pausing to light a cigarette and then getting annoyed when the breeze blew the flame of her lighter out. David obliged with a covering hand. 'Although by rights he ought to,' she went on, 'what with your gazing doe-eyed at him whenever his back's turned, hanging on his every word and all. Be careful, is all. He's still an Essex boy, whatever he says, and Essex boys aren't known for their gay friendly attitudes…'

'Noted,' he nodded. 'I just…he's so handsome, you know? And confident, and he knows what he wants. I've never really met anyone like that my age, you know? All the other boys my ages are really just stupid kids in men's bodies. Plus he has the blue eyes, and the big, hairy arms. I kind of have this thing for the big, hairy arms.'

Dorothy followed him up the stairs. 'If Jack wants to leave Barking behind then it's our duty as his sophisticated West End friends to help him in any way we can.'

'Don't you think he's gorgeous?!' David said. 'I know everyone else thinks he is.'

'Well I'm not everyone, am I?!' she raised an eyebrow, and puffed her smoke playfully at him.

Clay Woodfield, tall, handsome in a kind of vapid, thin-lipped way, was waiting for them in the station foyer, talking to their cousin-in-law Tamsin, cousin Casey's rather glamorous thirty-something wife. She was just shutting up their photography shop-come-studio for the day, Clay pulling the shutters while she attended to the padlocks. 'Get ready for the first of many introductions, guys,' Jack said over his shoulder, and then strode forward, arms wide. 'Guys, this is my cousin Clay, who's going to get us all in on the guest list 'coz he knows people who knows people, if you know what I mean. And this is our cousin by marriage, geez, does that sound too formal, Tamsin; Clay, Tam, these are my university mates, David and Dorothy!'

'Pleased to meet you,' Tamsin smiled, shaking first one hand and then the other. She was a warm, open person with a rather wide face, still, one of those people you couldn't help but like; 'wholesome' sprung to David's mind. 'I'd come with you tonight but...' she patted her stomach. 'Three months now.'

'Oh congratulations,' Dorothy smiled, dropping her cigarette and stamping it out beneath her heel, 'another Woodfield.'

'We breed like rabbits,' Jack threw Tamsin a sly wink that seemed to allude to something about cousin Casey's prowess that David at least didn't share, when he caught sight of her slightly podgy, dough-faced husband through the windows.

'Well I thought he was quite attractive,' Dorothy said afterwards. 'That Clay was too smarmy for my liking.'

Poor, 'smarmy' Clay led them around the corner to the Barking Dog, where most of the cousins had already commandeered the family section up the back, and were already on their second or third rounds respectively. Springer Woodfield, Clay's twin brother, skinnier and decidedly more unkempt, was entertaining the assembled throng by recounting one of his anecdotes about the attempts of various Woodfields who over the years had made the move from Barking to the great beyond, himself included, the punchline being that most of them ended up failing miserably and returning to the folds of the family within short order. Dorothy raised an eyebrow and turned to David, the both of them waiting for some kind of a personal twist on the punchline to give the thing a garnish, but Springer just sort of laughed like a punch-drunk hyena and reached for his pint, raising his eyebrows almost in apology. Hannah's twins Laquisha and Marie, whom David had already met, were giggling about something in a corner, sipping their drinks through straws; Laquisha's boyfriend, a rather stunning young black boy called Gael, was listening intently, laughing in that vaguely inane way straight boys did when they wanted to impress. Their elder sister Sara, a redheaded Goth sort with rather feline features, was whispering intently to her boyfriend Ron, a lanky, chiselled young man in geek chic and glasses.

Jack's favourite cousin Jessica rushed to greet them, flinging her arms around his neck and planting matching kisses on each cheek. Her twin brother Bobby, a rather withdrawn, almost apologetic individual with short wiry brown hair, bold blue eyes with tiny pupils, and rather cute big ears was being entertained by Jamie's best friend Adam, who was teaching him how to pour a pint on the spare pump at the far end of the bar. Jamie was nearby, whispering to Tiffany, but she broke away on catching sight of Jack and hurried over. 'Jack!!' she flung her arms around him, almost knocking Jessica and her on-going embrace sideways. 'They got you here, oh how fabulous! Oh we're going to have such a wonderful time tonight!'

'Yeah, guess we are!' he beamed, bashful of the bruise on his cheek. He nodded to Jamie, who nodded back, but neither of them made a move. A slap on the bum made him turn and he found himself confronted with Uncle Heath's little daughter Debbie, Daniel's twin, just sixteen although she looked more like twelve, all brown hair and freckles, and tarted up to the nines for her first ever 'official' nightclubbing experience. 'Oh no,' he gasped, in mock shock, 'who let the kids in?!'

'Bite me, cuz,' she popped her gum at him, the bubble nearly as big as her face. 'Daniel's coming too; Clay's going to swing it so we can get in; we've got fake ID and everything!'

'We'll look after them' Tiffany lopped an arm around her shoulder. 'I'll keep an eye on Debbie, and you can chaperone Daniel.'

Daniel came bounding over, high-fiving Jack and then doing the same to David before he'd even been introduced. At the sight of Dorothy he blushed and then, according to what Jack told them later, had whispered to him when she'd gone to the bar with David that she "…was fit as fuck, man!"

Jack and Jamie sat apart for most of the evening, but even if they weren't fresh from fisticuffs no one was under any illusions that they would ever be the best of friends. It was rather painful to watch the cousins gathering around Jack and hanging on his every word, hanging on his arms even, or at least Jessica was, gazing doe-eyed up at him, in her case sometimes leaning her head against his shoulder and snuggling there as though they were star-crossed lovers or something. Adam was the only one who didn't seem to have much time for Jack, keeping a discreet eye on Tiffany and calling her back under some pretence whenever he felt she was giving a little too much attention to the brother who wasn't actually her lover. Michael Woodfield, big and burly in a vaguely Neanderthal way, joined them off his bar manager duties around eleven, and an old friend of Jack's from St Margaret's called Craig arrived around eleven thirty, and the group was at that point to all intents and purposes complete. As they were walking down Station Parade Daniel tugged on the sleeve of Jack's Stone Island jacket and then held out his open hand, containing therein any number of pale blue pills. 'I got these, one for each of us! Although I didn't know your mate Craig was coming, but I'm dealing in Legends on Monday now anyway, so I can always get more! We could do doubles!!'

'You stupid little fuck!!' Jack gasped, pulling him into the station foyer and almost pinning him up against the window of cousin Casey's photography shop. 'And with your house just over the road, are you totally off your head?'

Daniel was taken aback. 'But I thought…I thought it'd be good!!'

'You're sixteen, do you want to go to prison?!'

'Well it's better than rotting in this place for the rest of my life!' his eyes reddened, as Tiffany came up behind them. 'Tell him,' he said. 'He's having a right go at me. He thinks he's the only one good enough to get out of this shit-hole.'

'Oh Jack don't be such a stuck in the mud,' she took the pills from Daniel's hand, held them up to the light and turned them over a couple of times, then slipped them in her purse. 'Are you telling me you've never popped an E in your entire life? not good enough for the London School of Economics, is that it?!'

''tiff, I thought you didn't care for drugs either way,' Jack stepped back. 'I don't know what's got into you lately.'

'I've loosened up a little,' she gave him a wink, the lifted Daniel's chin up with a ruby red nail. 'Come on handsome, let's get down to that club, pop these pills, and shake our booties!'

They arrived at Legends on the London Road at about twenty to midnight; Clay whispered something in the ear of the bouncer and the entire group was ushered in ahead of the rather modest queue, their names ticked off on a lengthy guest list. Mirrored steps led down to a coat check and one of two sets of rather shabby, smelly toilets, a booth selling records, and up to a balcony section that stretched off in both directions from where you could look through scratched plastic onto the dancefloor below, where huge plumes of choking dry ice were swamping an already heaving throng of clubbers. David saw Dorothy looking rather lost and lopped an arm around her neck. 'Thanks,' he said, kissing her cheek.

'What for?'

'For not saying anything to Jack; playful lusting is one thing, but full-blown unrequited love is quite another.'

'I can see it, you know,' she said, removing her coat. 'I'm starting to see why Jack wants to leave Barking. There's only a handful of his family here tonight and yet they're so…overwhelming. I know they're trying to be friendly, but they're like one huge entity. They giggle and chatter amongst themselves and don't realise they're totally leaving you out of it.'

'They're nice people, though,' he handed her coat in and turned back. 'Don't say anything, but I think that Bobby is gay, you know, the cute one with the big ears?'

'What makes you think that?'

David tapped the side of his head. 'Gaydar.'

'Well like I said, just be careful. They're still Essex boys, and they're also…'

'…also what?'

'…nothing. Come on,' she took his arm, made sure her cigarettes were handy. 'Let's go and get ourselves a drink.'

They made their way into the left-hand side bar, where most of the family seemed to have congregated. 'Guys!!' Jack was spread out on a long purple couch, Tiffany on one side and Jessica on the other, both hanging on his every word, each of them gripping the bicep of the arm draped around their respective shoulders, and stroking it up and down occasionally, glaring across the vast expanse of his chest at each other whenever his eyes wandered elsewhere. 'Pull up a pew!'

Dorothy sat near Jessica and the two girls sized each other up, both aware that alongside Tiffany they were undoubtedly three of the fittest specimens in the club. 'So,' Dorothy said, 'I hear you're looking to make the break too?'

Jessica frowned. 'Sorry?'

'She says you're gonna up and leave Barking too,' Jack had to shout to make himself heard over the music. He disengaged from Tiffany and slid his other arm around Jessica's shoulders and pulled her close, so that she was resting square on his chest, at which point Tiffany made a little noise and moved off. 'Jessica and I made a pact when were were…how old were we, 'jess?'

'Eleven!' she said, gazing up at him.

'…yeah, eleven! We made a pact that we were gonna make something of our lives and well, let's face it, you can't do that in Barking!!'

Jessica ran her fingers lightly over Jack's pecs, tracing the shape of them against his t-shirt. She turned back, and said, 'So…Dorothy, is it? You're in Jack's class, right? Psychology?'

'Sociology and psychoanalysis combined.' Dorothy sipped her tequila. 'MSc. I'm branching out.'

Jack beamed. 'Worth its weight in gold at our 'uni, although D here has a Masters in psychoanalysis already; I want to go into psychoanalysis proper, afterwards. I wouldn't mind opening my own practice.'

'And you…' Jessica turned her big liquid eyes on David, 'the same course?'

'Ah no…' David stared down into his drink, then uneasily at Jack. 'I'm doing…'

'Sociological theory,' Jack interjected. 'The way society is structured and all that; families and stuff.'

'Oh you should study our family!!' Jessica reached over and slapped his knee. 'You could write reams on us; we're the Woodfields, you know! 'The Woodfield witches'!'

Over the other side of the bar Jamie was downing one Southern Comfort after another, Adam keeping pace, watching the clock waiting for his girlfriend to arrive, and listening to Springer Woodfield reeling off another anecdote, this one about the time he'd found a woman in a wheelchair locked in the cargo hold of a train from Liverpool Street and had wheeled her all the way up the platform, and eventually, into his bedroom. As David walked past, in pursuit of the gents, he clearly heard Jamie say, 'Look at Jack, everyone crowding 'round like he's the fucking messiah or something. He doesn't give a shit about any of us. He's abandoned this family. Shit, listen to me. Do I sound bitter?'

'It's the drinking talking, J,' Adam took the glass from his hand. 'Slow down mate, it's only midnight.'

'Yeah,' Jamie had sniffed, 'the witching hour.'

*

'Is it real??' little Debbie Woodfield held the pale blue pull up to the light. 'It looks like a Smartie.'

'It's an E,' Daniel snatched it back, offended, 'and it costs a fiver.'

'I'm your sister!' she gasped.

'Two quid then.'

'You little shit,' she handed over the money and downed the pill with a swig of lemonade, swallowing hard. 'How long will it take to work?'

'Maybe an hour,' he shrugged, unlocking the cubicle door. 'You'll want to make love to every single person in the club! You won't even think giving a blowjob is gross when that kicks in!'

Debbie held her nose and swallowed again. 'It better work, or I'm telling dad you deal. He'll kick the shit out of you. And then he'll chuck you out.' And with that she turned on her heel, pushed the door open and marched out of the toilets. Daniel shrugged, popped one of the pills for himself, and followed suit.

*

Laquisha was having a full scale row with her boyfriend Gael in the right hand bar when David decided to stroll on through, spotting Bobby Woodfield on his own on the end of another of those long purple couches, peering through the plastic down at the dancefloor, where Marie was dancing around her fake Fendi pink handbag. 'You look about as out of place as I do,' he said, pulling up a chair. 'I'm David, Jack's flatmate/punching bag/crying pillow/secretary.'

'Bobby...' Bobby beamed. 'Jessica's brother, Brian and Betty's boy, Casey's little brother...'

'Yeah,' David nodded. 'I know.'

'You know?'

If he'd had a drink to hand then he would've taken a rather ample swig of it at just that moment. 'Uh...that is, Jack briefed me on you guys on the tube on the way here,' David supped his beer nervously. 'Do you come here often? And sorry if that sounds tacky but I'm guessing by your expression, you don't.'

'You're right, I don't,' he nodded. 'At this time of night I'd normally be tucked up with a cup of cocoa and a Doctor Who book. I like Doctor Who.'

'Oh. Right.'

Bobby's blue eyes widened, and the tiny pupils seemed to engorge suddenly. 'Did you see the new series? Well, since Jack said you were at university and all, I wonder what you made of it from a sociological perspective, given that the role of the female assistant has now been vastly expanded when you compare it to…'

*

The majority of the Woodfields, also with assorted boyfriends, girlfriends, and friends were down on the dancefloor now, and, coupled, with pub and club friends they'd simply bumped into since arriving, formed the largest clique in the place. Laquisha had made up with Gael and was snogging him passionately in one space, while Marie was trying to make eye contact with a boy she'd fancied for ages, a young Latino-type who sold rugs on the stall next to their mum on East Street, in another. Jack and Jessica were doing some kind of dance only they seemed to know the moves to, rocking and shimmying backwards and forwards and laughing their heads off at regular intervals. Great plumes of dry ice threatened to swallow David and Bobby up as they joined them, with Dorothy reluctantly following suit, although her heels made any real movement all but impossible and she ended up looking like she was jogging on the spot. Clay had his arms around the waist of some blond he'd been 'working on' for the past two hours, and judging by her expression she was more than up for the suggestions he was whispering in her ear in-between songs. Daniel was waving his arms giddily in the air, dancing in a little spot all of his own, and sister Debbie was nowhere to be seen.

Adam's girlfriend Mandy had arrived and was doing slow waltzes with her man, tossing her long blond hair backwards and forwards in direction competition with Jessica, who at one point almost jostled her bodily off the dancefloor. Tiffany joined in with Jack and Jessica, and the three of them quite happily did their own thing for the next fifteen minutes or so, 'happily' actually constituting of the two of them doing their level best to elbow each other out of the way and then wrap their arms around his waist, gazing doe-eyed up at him and gyrating their bootie suggestively.

Sara and her boyfriend Ron weren't much into the music, preferring something with a slightly harder edge, but they made an effort anyway, laughing at some of the DJ's choices but finally just chilling out and having fun anyway. David liked Sara, probably more than any of the others, sweet

Marie aside. Sara was clearly the eldest female cousin, and fulfilled a kind of pseudo-matriarchal role, that plus the fact that she seemed to think Jack every bit as 'cheesy', as Dorothy did, and to take his in David's eyes rather awe-inspiring masculinity all in her stride.

*

Dorothy finally gave up trying to dance around one am, and went to get herself a mineral water and freshen up in the toilets. On her way back she saw Jack and Tiffany talking down the corridor leading to the exit, Tiffany leant back against it with her arms folded and Jack was propping himself against it and leaning in on her rather suggestively, speaking hurriedly, Tiffany tracing the shape of his big chest through the strain of his t-shirt in much the same way Jessica had, only hours earlier. She could see from the two of them why Jamie got so jealous, but then from what she'd heard, Jack and Tiffany had been friends for almost as long as Jamie and Tiffany had been an item. Even so, it was to her complete astonishment that Jack suddenly leant in and kissed Tiffany full on, slowly at first but then in an embrace and with tongues, not caring a whit seemingly for who saw them. 'Uh oh,' said a voice beside her. 'Good thing Jamie's too busy down on the dancefloor having fun…'

It was little Debbie Woodfield, drinking rather over enthusiastically from a bottle of tap water and looking rather hot and flushed. 'Still it's no surprise; they've been fighting over that girl since the first day she started shelling out coffee and doughnuts on Morelli's.'

'Are you ok?' Dorothy asked her. 'You're sweating rather a lot.'

'I don't feel so good,' she wiped her forehead with the back of her hand. 'Hey Jack!!' she shouted. 'We can see you!!'

Jack and Tiffany parted rather suddenly, looking slightly flustered. They came over, trying to disguise their blushes, Jack wiping his mouth with his hand and still not managing to shift the lion's share of Tiffany's pink pastel lipstick. 'We were just…' he shrugged.

'What's it worth not to tell Jamie?!' Debbie folded her arms. 'I knew you two were up to something!'

'Debbie!' Tiffany sighed. 'It wasn't what you think anyway!! Jack and I, we were just…'

'Tongues at dawn, I know what I saw!' electro-pop began pouring out of the stairwells leading down to the dancefloor. 'I love Jack, but I love Jamie too, you know?! You can't fuck both brothers!' she turned to anyone who'd listen and said, 'She's like a kid in a candy store, this girl! just 'coz she's West London originally don't mean she can come here and fuck all the fit boys, treating them like they're just brainless bits of rough or something…' and in a fit of pique she turned and headed for the nearest stairwell, Tiffany in hot pursuit.

Dorothy folded her arms and turned and gazed at Jack, tongue firmly in her cheek.

'Don't look at me like that, D!!' he gasped, eyes wide, expression just like the aforementioned kid in a candy store, only this one was caught with his hand in the sweetie jar and no pennies in his pocket.

Jamie was dancing with Adam and Mandy, Springer lolling energetically around in the background when Tiffany came breaking through the crowds to grab him. 'Jamie!! Come quick, it's your Debbie!!'

'What?!' at this decibel even shouting was no guarantee of being heard. But it didn't matter; at that moment the crowd began to part even though the music carried on, and the people around ten feet away from them stopped dancing and made way for the in-house paramedics, running onto the dancefloor with their medical-kits in their hands. The crowd parted more fully to reveal Debbie sprawled out like a broken rag doll in the middle of the dancefloor, utterly limp, her bottled water hanging loosely from her fingers, the contents forming a puddle around her elbow.

'Debbie!!' Jack came pushing through the crowd, Dorothy hot on his heels. 'Fuck!! I told that stupid little shit!!'

'Told who?!' Jamie gasped.

'Her brother, our little twat of a cousin, selling his shit pills!!' he ground his teeth together, watching as the paramedics propped Debbie upright and began to administer mouth-to-mouth. Tiffany stood a little way behind him as the music died down altogether, her face a complete blank.

'Poor little Debbie,' she said, turning to Dorothy, her hands clasped before her like a nun. 'I do hope she'll be alright.'

Chapter 23

Sunday 9th April 2006

The slow, rhythmical ticking over of the heart monitor fell in tandem with Jamie's own heartbeat if he relaxed enough, closed his eyes and blocked out the subtle tick of the clock on the far wall. It was that quiet in here, that still. Uncle Heath was dozing in a chair in one corner, mum directly opposite, nodding off then jerking awake suddenly in that funny way some people do, rubbing Debbie's hand every now and again to make sure she was still with them, and then doubtless remembering that if she wasn't the machine would have made that awful wailing noise that it always did when some poor bugger at the end of 'Casualty' carked it, and the nurses would have all come running in with those electric shock thingies they put on the patient's chest.

Debbie had woken up for the first time around an hour ago, almost twenty four hours after passing out on the dancefloor, unable to remember almost anything of what had happened. Tests showed she had traces of an illegal substance in her system, some kind of amphetamine, something Jack had been able to concur was indeed the case; there had been some trouble with a rogue dealer in the club that night who had taken out his grievances by spiking the drinks of any number of clubbers involved, little Debbie unfortunately being one of them. His friend David had been affected as well, but being older had managed to fight of the worst of the effects, and was now quietly convalescing back at their flat in Islington. The first thing that had come to almost everyone's mind and to a fair few lips was that such a thing would never have happened if Aunt Delia's two youngest, Hayden and Nick, were still working on the door, only they weren't because they were 'away visiting' after doing their jobs just a little too well, this October just gone.

Jamie didn't know anything about a 'rogue dealer', but he and Adam had had a great time, out of their faces on E, the first time he'd done anything since Uncle Phil had died. The high had been somewhat neutered, but gorgeous never-the-less. He'd almost liked Jack, under the influence, but that had quickly dissolved when his big brother had taken to the dancefloor and had almost every fit bird in the place shimmying around him seconds later, severely pissing off Jessica, who almost got into a fight with a girl called Rachel from Romford.

Jamie hadn't much liked his university friends either, who to his mind were every bit as snobby as he'd imagined they were. The boy, David, well he was almost certainly a queer. He'd spent the better part of the evening talking to Bobby, and everyone knew Bobby wanted it up the arse. Jamie may not have gotten on much with 'absent' cousin Hayden, but he definitely concurred with his opinion of what ought to be done to Bobby, and had even helped him once, when all the boys were throwing Bobby's bag to each other over his head, and Hayden was the ringleader, and Jack wasn't around to wade in with his sanctimonious crap, and spoil all their fun. Jamie had thought up a chant and began the clapping as they emptied the contents of the bag all over the ground outside Cash Converters on East Street, and picked up his stuff and took the piss out of it. 'You gonna cry?!?' Hayden had said, pushing Bobby up against the shop window by his shoulders. 'You gonna cry like a queer, Bobby Woodfield?!?'

He hadn't cried though, not even when Hayden had whacked him in the gut and Bobby had lost all the day's food over the kerb, and fell down, clutching at Hayden's leg because he was so winded. Hayden had kicked him off and they'd walked away laughing, and said if he told Uncle Phil he was dead. Jamie had been able to provide some reassurance then, that Uncle Phil wouldn't believe it if he put a word in first, and if he did then he'd say that Bobby was making eyes at them or something.

'He fancies me anyway,' Hayden had said, his arm around the shoulders of the boys in his gang, 'he always has. I catch him checking me out all the time. It turns him on when I knock him around; I bet he's knocking one out over it now.' Now Jamie didn't know if that was true or not, but he doubted it was. Fact was, Bobby would have had the shit completely kicked out of him if he'd done anything like that, checking guys out and stuff. Jamie would've been there to put the boot in, right and proper, even though he was scared of Hayden himself, he would've helped, no questions asked. Hayden was beyond hard; Hayden had taken a knife to school before it became fashionable.

The girl, Dorothy, well she was a right snooty sort, in Jamie's opinion. She was weird looking too, like she was foreign or something, but only half, with her slitty eyes and her beauty spot. He didn't like the look of her one bit, no not at all, and he hadn't said anything beyond their initial introduction. Jack could keep the pair of them.

The nurse came into the room, and said, 'We should be able to discharge Debbie first thing tomorrow morning. The police will want to speak to her about what she was doing in the club in the first place, considering she's only sixteen.' She turned and looked at mum, and said, 'You ask me, you don't tell them nothing you don't have to, Mrs Woodfield.'

'It's 'Ms',' mum sighed, rubbing her hands together. 'And thanks, sweetheart.' She glanced over at Debbie. 'She's not going to suffer any permanent damage, is she? I mean, she won't be, well…like a moron?!'

'Not anymore than she already is,' Jamie said, despite himself.

'Oh I don't think so,' the nurse looked up as Aunt Amanda came into the room, a tray of steaming drinks in her hands. 'She's young, and resilient, bless her little heart. I was with her mother when she died here, you know? Sophie Woodfield, wasn't it? Awful that was. Just awful.'

'Will it put a lid on her big gob?' Jamie asked, but mum made a little face and he shut up again.

The nurse went on, 'What a lovely woman was, her mother. And so talented. She was an artist, wasn't she?'

Thank god Uncle Heath was asleep, that was Jamie's thought on hearing this, because any mention of his dead wife would send him into one of those long, boring reminiscences he always dove into when someone recalled her. Jamie didn't want to have to tell him what a sad old cunt he was a second time. Aunt Amanda set the tray down on the bedside table. 'Far too many deaths in this family,' she nodded, 'far too many.' And she turned and smiled at Uncle Heath, but he really was still out of it, mouth open, a fine line of spittle trickling slowly down his chin and onto the collar of his denim shirt.

'All right mum,' mum said. 'Let's try and keep things upbeat, shall we? Debbie's going to be all right, that's all that matters.'

'I'll check back in an hour,' the nurse turned and smiled as she left. 'You all should go home and get some rest. If there's any change you'll be told straight away.'

Mum stirred Uncle Heath in his chair and he mumbled something, swatted at something on the end of his nose. 'She's right, sweetheart,' she said. 'You look like death. Why don't you go on home now, the worst being over and all. I'll call you if anything happens.'

He sniffed, rubbed at his eyes. 'You make sure'n you do then,' and he reached for his battered brown leather jacket and slipped it on, bending over the bed to kiss Debbie on the forehead. 'See you soon kiddo,' he said, lingering only to take her hand and seemingly reassure himself by the warmth that emanated from it that she wasn't about to slip away in some dramatic fashion or other. He turned and gave Aunt Amanda a hug. 'See you, mum. You watch over her, okay?'

'Oh I will,' Aunt Amanda gazed sadly at the little figure on the bed. 'You go on and get some sleep, my darling.'

'I'll walk you out,' mum took her coat from behind the chair. 'Back in a minute, mum.'

Aunt Amanda waited until she heard their steps receding into the distance before turning to Jamie, fishing in her plain black handbag for something. 'It took me hours to put this together,' she said, with a sly little wink. She turned to the bed, and bent over Debbie. 'Here you go, my little darling,' she said, pulling a little silvery pouch strung with glittering ribbon from one of the inside pockets, kissing it and slipping it deftly under her pillow. 'This'll keep you safe if she tries any more of her...'

'Mum have you seen my purse?' mum blustered back into the room, eyes darting this way and that. 'I was going to give Heath money for a cab, but...what's that?'

Aunt Amanda pulled the little pouch out from under Debbie's pillow and passed it to Jamie, and he put it in his back pocket real quick, like that time Kevin Cossington had drawn a picture of Jessica's pussy on a piece of scrap paper and Jamie had had it in his hand when Jack peered over, and he'd had to hide it, 'coz Jack was sensitive about things like that, where Jessica was concerned, although everyone else knew she was a complete slut. 'This?' Aunt Amanda said. 'Just a little good luck charm; you know what a silly old woman I can be, I was just…'

'Oh none of that nonsense, mum please!!' mum snatched the pouch out of Jamie's back pocket and made ready to throw it into the bin, 'enough of that!! Do you want the nurses to think we're mad or something?!'

'The woman down the corridor is a practicing catholic and her bed is strewn with cheap, nasty rosaries!' Aunt Amanda snapped. 'What difference is there?'

'The difference is this,' she ripped the pouch open with her fingernails and emptied the contents – what appeared to be dust, the parings of nails, hair, and some dry earth – onto the floor and then kicked it under the bed with her shoe. 'That doesn't come from any religion I know of. It's your silly voodoo, mum.'

'The word is 'hoodoo' darling, if you must,' Aunt Amanda stooped down rather gracefully for a woman of her advanced years and retrieved the pouch. 'Although I must think of a name that more suits my humble East End origins.'

Mum grabbed her by the shoulders, a little too harshly, perhaps, in Jamie's opinion. 'You silly old woman! If there's anything wrong with this family then you're part of it, with your silly ideas and such.'

'Who said anything was wrong with this family?' Aunt Amanda raised an eyebrow.

Mum loosened her grip, exhaled. 'Mum, I want you to leave Jamie here alone. Stop filling his head with ideas that he can be the Daddy! Jack is the next Daddy. I may not like it, but that's the way it is.'

Aunt Amanda gestured to the prone form of little Debbie, utterly oblivious to the pair of them. 'Would the Daddy really let this happen?!'

'Yeah mum, Jack doesn't give a toss,' Jamie piped up. 'All he cared about last night was all the girls checking out his big arms, 'coz that's all Jack is, a pair of big arms screwed onto an 'Action Man' body, and about as boring as Superman to boot!'

'Hush now darling,' Aunt Amanda put a hand on his arm.

'You,' mum said, pointing a finger at Jamie, 'keep this,' and here she made a little move to her mouth, 'shut.'

'Uncle Phil would've sorted it, right and proper,' he went on, regardless. 'He would've talked to everyone in that nightclub 'til he found out who did it, but all Jack cared about was this bird he'd met with tits like…'

'Jamie, shut up!' mum snapped.

'He sucks,' Jamie folded his arms. 'Him and his queer friend even danced with Bobby! I didn't know where to look!' and it had been awful, that poof song by Hazell Dean on; 'They say it's gonna rain', and Jack doing pretend flirting with both of them, flashing his six-pack and stuff. He wouldn't have done that if Hayden had been around, 'coz him and Jack were tight. Jack was about the only person who wasn't scared of Hayden. They were best mates since they were kids, although that hadn't stopped Jack fucking off to his fancy university and his flat in Islington. And to think Hayden had blamed Jamie for that! Like anything Jamie had done would have driven a 'real man' like Jack away. Jack thought he was better than the rest of them, that was his trouble; that had always been his trouble. 'I hate Jack,' he found himself saying, suddenly and out of context given that mum and Aunt Amanda were arguing about something else entirely now. He looked at them, made sure they were looking at him. 'I hate him,' he said again. 'Aunt Amanda says I can be the Daddy, and I will! I'm gonna do it for Uncle Phil, and Jack can kiss my arse!'

The Daddy Dissertation Part 3

By David Samuels

From May to Agnes

May Woodfield seems to have been the magnate for the family from the get-go upon their return to Barking proper; her husband, a quiet, pliant man, an engineer by trade, seems to have been quite happy with the move, happy with her role as matriarch, and happier still when in 1858 he became the proud father to twin boys, Jacob and Jeramiah. The family settled in a rather grand house on the Ripple Road, grand for the times, albeit, where they'd moved before she became pregnant.

Before she died she had three more children, all girls, all of whose descendants remain in the Barking and Dagenham areas to this day. Jacob and Jeramiah were the first to be born in the house on the Ripple Road, and Jacob lived there with his wife Margaret after his parents' deaths; their children Avis, Agnes, and Gary were all born there too. Indeed, Woodfields are born and continue to live in the house up to and including the present day – the current occupant is May's Great-Great-Niece Rachel, and her son Michael.

The family deferred to May in all things, and backed her when she petitioned to have a statue of her grandfather Jake Woodfield erected near where the bandstand now occupies the junction between the Ripple Road, East Street, Linton Road, and Station Parade. The plans got as far as sketches being done by local architects but were blocked by those in council who had long memories of Jake's alleged involvement with the burning down of the Houses of Parliament; as a consolation a portrait of Jake was done that hung for a while in the hall of the house on the Ripple Road, until Agnes Woodfield became adamant that the eyes in the picture were following her wherever she went, and had it put in the loft. Sketches for the aborted statue are said to be among papers Phil Woodfield left to his brother Heath shortly before his death.

Jacob and Jeramiah broke the mould for twin boys in the family by being lifelong friends, soulmates even, virtually inseparable from the moment they were born. May seems to have taken the death of her brothers Jason and Jeffrey especially hard, and to have gone out of her way to make sure that her own boys became firm friends. Indeed, when Jeramiah was hospitalised with a mild case of bronchitis around the age of ten or so Jacob cried until he was physically sick, night after night, until they were reunited. Both boys were exceptionally handsome, but Jeramiah was said to have been 'exquisitely beautiful', with high cheekbones, piercing dark eyes and a perfectly shaped mouth, this on top of a powerful, sturdy frame made him the object of desire for almost every woman in Barking at the time. Again, there was never any jealousy or competition between the boys, and Jacob was said to have been quite amused by his brother's 'Romeo' reputation.

May left the house on the Ripple Road to Jacob and again no one seemed to question this, least of all Jeramiah and his sisters, all of whom were devoted to their brother come what may; 'Jacob will be just like my father,' May is reported to have said at one family gathering, when the boys were still babies; 'He'll be the Daddy, and he'll do us all right.' Certainly by the age of thirteen it was well-known in the area that Jacob was the Daddy, and this was confirmed when he turned sixteen and his Great-Uncle Russell was found hanged in his dreary little two-up, two-down in Limehouse, the suicide note saying only, 'I am spent; let someone else try, for I can no longer sate the harpy.'

Although the Woodfields were well liked and respected by their neighbours, and despite that fact that Jake Woodfield had become something of a local legend, having been immortalised in the aforementioned portraits, poems, and in print - rumour has it Dickens wrote a homoerotic short story about him that was either lost or destroyed - there were many people in outlying areas who feared the family, and especially May Woodfield. A washer-woman from Chingford who said that the return of the Woodfields was '...bound to bring nothing but trouble to Essex' was publicly humiliated by May Woodfield, who revealed to the entire town in market one Saturday morning that the child the woman was expecting was not her husband's. The woman confessed in shame, but said that there was no way May Woodfield could have known this and therefore that she must be a witch, and furthermore, that she was descended from witches and that her grandfather Jake Woodfield had been '...Satan himself.' The woman's child was stillborn.

In 1875, the year of the last Barking Fair, Jacob met seamstress Margaret Harrison and they were married four years later; a tintype exists of the two brothers on either side of the bride, a waif-like blond with porcelain skin, flanked by two of the most striking males I have ever seen in my entire life, especially Jeramiah. As May was still alive and well at the time, and managing the affairs of the family extremely adeptly, there seemed no need or necessity for Jacob and his new wife to produce any children, and so they were able to live a life of considerable leisure, visiting Woodfields all over the country, and helping May to assemble the most accurate family tree we have to this day, which has been published in a previous issue of Fortean Times.

May died in 1895 and was given an enormous send off in St. Margaret's, one to rival Jake Woodfield's, with the her inscription on the family gravestone reading, 'Our May; she brought us back home'.

Although Jacob and Margaret had a son by the time May died, this child was taken in 1898, and so Margaret hurriedly gave birth again in 1899, this time to twin girls, Avis and Agnes, in the front bedroom of the house on the Ripple Road. Both girls caught smallpox in the 1902 epidemic but Margaret nursed them night and day and they recovered, although as she became older Agnes appeared to be a little slower than Avis, and it was assumed that the illness had in some way damaged her. Margaret gave birth to another boy, Gary, in 1902, shortly after the girls recovered, and this was the first time that local gossips suggested that the Woodfields bred boys so that 'they could throw their weight around', or even more scandalously, '…because they have a whore in that family, a whore that can never be satisfied, no matter how handsome her suitor!'; further 'outrageous' gossip suggested that Jeramiah was in fact Gary's father, that Jacob had begged his brother to provide them with the son he seemed unable to.

Despite the gossip, Jacob was said to have still been an agreeable, amiable man, well-liked by everyone who met him, square-jawed and generally wholesome, but on the whole somewhat uninteresting. He made great headway in restoring the good name of the family as far as Jake Woodfield was concerned, having declared in public that no proof had ever been put forth as to Jake's direct involvement in the 1834 burning of Parliament apart from his having been very drunk and in possession of tinderboxes, in the vicinity at the time.

When Jeramiah died in 1910 Jacob was prostrate with grief for days on end, and both his daughters Avis and Agnes and Jeramiah's supposedly only child Felicity wept to see their father/uncle in such a state. 'Don't cry daddy,' Agnes was heard to say again and again, stroking her father's grey blond mane with her rather stubby, malformed fingers. 'Don't cry. She still thinks you're quite handsome.'

In 1912 Jacob awoke with a premonition of a sinking ocean liner and told Margaret on waking; knowing full well how many of her husband's dreams turned out to be portents she informed local authorities, but as much as she was a well-liked local figure, no one took much notice. Disheartened, she put a bet on it with a local bookie, and made sure all the details were written down in case she was proved right; when the bookie unfolded her paper and found the name 'Titanic' on it a little over two years later it the shock was said to have made his hair go white on the spot.

When the Great War broke out in 1914 their young son Gary signed up, against the wishes of both parents, and indeed the uncles and aunts and cousins, but he smuggled himself out of Essex with the aid of one of the Hackney Woodfields, further deepening the family feud. 'Who will satisfy her now, now that he is gone and Jeramiah is gone, and Jacob is too old?!?' the cousins cried. Gary died in trench warfare in 1917, and the night news of his death reached the family there was a massive explosion at nearby Barking Chemical Works. Jacob was seen sobbing openly in the street, comforted by a woman whom many witnesses were sure was 'not his wife, Margaret'. His nephew Alexander also saw trench warfare but returned home alive and relatively unscathed in 1918; he brought with him Gary's meagre possessions, his dented rifle and tin hat, and the sight of these are said to have driven Jacob almost wild with grief. He died a year later, and everyone put it down to the loss of his only son. Doubly traumatised, Margaret slowly lost her grip on reality and was admitted to an asylum the following year, leaving her two daughters, both as yet unmarried and unaware of the expectations placed upon them regarding the siring of sons, living alone together in the house on the Ripple Road.

Avis married a local bus driver in 1925, and their cousin Felicity married Father Billy Harkett in 1926, but Agnes had difficulty in finding a husband; people rather uncharitably put it down to her shuffling gait, the aforementioned claw-like hands, and the tick that had been with her since the smallpox, not to mention her rather alarming shade of red hair. The three girls are said to have been firm friends though, and were often seen cruising up and down the Ripple Road in the Cadillac Jeramiah brought Felicity for one of her birthdays. Felicity was an exceptionally striking young woman whose beauty far outshone that of her two cousins; her granddaughter Jessica is said to be 'her very double' by contemporary cousins.

Avis and her husband left Barking in 1927, against the wishes of the cousins, and moved to Barnsley where they had a boy, Richard, who later moved down south to Brighton and became something of a bohemian, and the first openly homosexual Woodfield who actually avoided getting his neck wrung by his more 'virile' cousins. Without a real friend in the world and shy of the somewhat cloying cousins, and in awe of beautiful Felicity, Agnes became a lonely and tragic figure and by age thirty she looked like an old woman, stooped and prematurely greying; local children teased her and called her 'that buckled old witch', and said that the house on the Ripple Road was '...where she cooked babies in her cauldron, and stuck pins into pictures of '...beautiful Minty Hardcore'.'. One night she was found lying by Barking Abbey ruins, in the shadow of the Curfew Tower, and there was evidence that she had been raped; the evidence was correct and she gave birth to twins, a boy and a girl, Amanda and Ben, strapped to the bed and with no sedative, as was custom in those days for women thought to be 'of unsound mind'. She was unable to name her assailant, if indeed there had been one at all; more unkind local gossip said that she was '...simple enough to be anyone's after a drink or two'. Two years later she fell pregnant again, and was again unable to name the father, giving birth to Andrea Woodfield in the front room of the house on the Ripple Road in December of 1935. Her children brought her some small level of comfort and despite the stigma of being an unmarried mother there were enough Woodfields to make sure that Agnes was never without some money in her purse, or someone to help her around the house; Felicity in particular seemed to have cleaved to her at this time despite the protests from her deeply religious husband, Father Billy, citing on more than one occasion that the woman was '...nothing but trouble.'. When the Second World War broke out Agnes confused it with the Great War and became increasingly hysterical, recalling the death of her brother Gary in the trenches. In fact she became so worked up that family members feared she might end up in an asylum like her mother Margaret, and the less kind cousins began to wonder if perhaps Margaret had brought some kind of congenital insanity with her into the family, and to begin to curse her name even though she had been loved by everyone. Although local lore says that Agnes died in the air raid that wrecked Beckton gas works, children at the time swore that '…that mad old witch flew her broomstick straight into the paths of them German bombers!'

Her three children were evacuated in 1942 along with Felicity's two toddlers, Brian and Delia, both of whom went to a family in Torquay. Ben, Amanda and Andrea were lucky enough to be kept together and housed with the well-to-do Atwell family, who ran the Lakeside boarding house on the Abingdon Road in Oxford. Rather than leave the house on the Ripple Road abandoned, Felicity herself moved into it despite enormous protests from Father Billy, who maintained that the place was '…a cesspit of witchcraft and adultery.'.

The children settled in well with the Atwells in Oxford, and Amanda attended the local schools; there is a charming photograph of Ben at the time, dressed up as a sailor. The girls doted on their little brother and took special care of him, as letters from the cousins back in London informed them that he '…was as special as Christmas pudding'; none of the letters mentioned what had happened to their mother in regards to the Beckton gas works incident, most of them centring around the adventures of Alexander's son Rupert, who received 'the call' in 1943 when he was just eighteen. Alexander's daughter Queenie – now the oldest living Woodfield, aged eighty six of this writing, in 2006 – was a member of the Women's Voluntary Service during the Blitz. There seems to have been an unspoken consensus since the death of Jacob that Alexander was the Daddy, and that same word of mouth persisted to Rupert when he hit puberty and sprouted into a rather striking young man of some 6'3 in height, with a fine, Roman nose and, in the words of Minty Hardcore, found scrawled on the sides of burnt-out buildings, '…a nice, thick neck!'

There were tears and tantrums aplenty when the War ended and Margaret's niece Barbara Corbett arrived in Oxford to take Amanda, Ben, and Andrea home. She was the only relative of the family willing to take all three children in after Father Billy had refused to do so, causing a rift between him and his wife Felicity that lasted until he died in 1961; Alexander died in 1948, full of regret that he had been unable to take the children in himself, but stating that his wife had never been the same since the birth of Rupert, when there are said to be have been scenes of 'wild jubilation' when a birthmark was located down near the child's right buttock, a large, clear lip print, only slightly smudged in one corner. 'My child is kissed by Satan!!' she is said to have cried, and the cousins are said to have laughed and said, 'No, by Minty Hardcore!!' Of Barbara Corbett, the cousins complained that it '...wasn't right, her not being a Woodfield and all.' But by all accounts the children came to adore their 'Aunt Barbara', and lived with her well into their twenties, along with her husband and two children in their house in Bethnal Green. This is the same house that Amanda Woodfield lives in to this day, the only surviving house on Vallance Road that escaped the mass demolitions of the Sixties, although how this was managed no one quite knows, when even the notorious Kray family, only a couple of doors down, were unable to prevent their own homes from falling before the bulldozer. Records of the time are either lost or incomplete, and Amanda Woodfield was always known to have had friends in high places; the official in charge of the demolitions in the area was found dead of a suspected heart attack in his home in Stepney in 1967, with '...severe chaffing to the genital area.' Other reports were that the relatively healthy young businessman had '...gone grey overnight', but these were never sufficiently corroborated to be included here as anything other than idle gossip.

Chapter 24

Sunday 9th April 2006

Daniel sat on his bed with his legs drawn up to his chest, rocking slowly backwards and forwards, listening to the sounds of the trains outside his window as they rumbled out of Barking and on towards Dagenham Dock and beyond, all the way to Upminster. A knock on the door ruptured his reverie and made him jump; visions of his dad, shirt sleeves rolled up to reveal finely veined muscled arms with fists clenched ready to give him a good battering on receipt of Debbie's confessions abounded in his mind. He tightened his stomach muscles as best he could and said quietly, 'Come in.'

But it wasn't dad after all. It was Jack, in faded jeans and a tight white t-shirt, one of those ones he always wore that showed off his taut biceps, his impressive deltoids; Daniel knew the name of every important muscle in the upper body because they were all encircled in marker pen on an anatomy poster on the opposite wall, as a kind of self-motivation technique that, as yet, hadn't really paid any dividends. He felt ashamed of it suddenly, almost as bashful as he was of his extensive DVD collection, most of them horror films, of which he was an ardent fan, particularly the gory remakes of Seventies classics.

Jack sat down on the edge of the bed, and flashed that big, cheesy smile he had, the one that always made the girls go all silly and gooey. 'Hey fella,' he said, 'how you doing?'

Daniel sniffed. He couldn't remember the last time Jack had been in his bedroom and more than being ashamed he was embarrassed suddenly, embarrassed by the big poster of Kelly Brook on the other side of the door, of the heaps of unfolded clothes in the corner, the bin full of wank tissues, things like that, things that may or may not have been entirely common in the bedroom of any sixteen year old boy. 'Not so bad,' he said. 'How's Debbie?'

'Up and eating,' Jack spread his arms wide. 'Don't worry, she hasn't said a word; no one has. And she won't grass you up, she's your sister.'

'Well sisters can be cunts sometimes,' Daniel stared down at his feet, at his left big toe pocking through his sock. 'I thought you'd have gone back to Islington by now.'

'Ah,' he shrugged. 'I had to stick around, don't I? what with the ruck and all. Just thought I'd pop in and see if you were sweet before I headed back.' He took out a piece of paper from his back pocket, on which he'd written his address, mobile, and email. 'You could probably get these off my mum but thought you'd like to have them for yourself. Anything happens, your dad gets on your case, whether he finds out or not, just give me a call and I'll be over here in a shot.'

Daniel seemed to brighten a little at this offering, and he tucked the paper in the back pocket of his trackie bottoms. 'Is it true then?'

'Is what true?'

'What someone heard Tiffany saying…that you're gonna come back and be the Daddy?'

'She said that?!'

Daniel faltered. 'Well no, but someone said she did…'

'Look mate,' Jack put a hand on his shoulder, hands as big as Daniel's dad's, if not bigger. 'I'm not being funny, but if you were me, would you be the Daddy?'

'I've never really thought about it…'

Jack relaxed, and then nudged him. 'Move over 'cuz, and I'll explain a few facts of Woodfield life to you.' And Daniel shifted over and allowed Jack space to rest on the headboard alongside him. 'You got anything?' Jack asked.

'Anything what?'

'Oh come on Danny boy; you know I know you deal. Got anything we can toke on, lighten the mood a little? It's not often I allow myself, so…'

Daniel grinned and reached under his bed, pulling a tobacco tin out. 'I hid it in here 'coz it's like, 'so obvious it's too obvious',' he said proudly, plucking a rather hefty joint from within and lighting it. 'I call this 'the Barking blowjob'.'

Jack took it and inhaled, letting the smoke rumble out of his nostrils. 'Ah, that's good. I needed that. So,' he lolled an arm around Daniel's shoulders, 'let me explain a few things to you. About being the Daddy, and stuff like that.'

'You're the Daddy,' Daniel said. 'Well, you know, you're supposed to be, now that Uncle Phil's gone…'

'Why do you think your dad isn't the Daddy?' Jack asked him.

'I don't know. I guess, 'coz Uncle Phil was. Uncle Phil was older, right?'

'Well yeah, there's that,' Jack pulled his t-shirt up at the back, exposing tanned skin and, just in the small of his back, above his left buttock, a clear red lip print. He leant away from Daniel so that he might get a better look at it. 'And there's also this.'

'Holy shit,' Daniel bent down and peered at the birthmark, before Jack pulled his t-shirt back over it. 'I always heard of that but never seen it before; my mum used to thank god I didn't have one of those. My dad has a little red mark there, he showed me once, but it's not clear and crisp like that!' he pulled his own t-shirt up. 'I got a pimple there, see?!'

'I've got an appointment at a Harley Street laser clinic pretty soon,' Jack said. 'To see about having it removed.'

'Harley Street?!'

'Uh huh…Dorothy, the fit bird I'm in class with? well she's subbing me some of the cash to get it lasered off. Reckon it'll hurt like hell, but it'll be worth it in the end.'

'But it means you're the Daddy, doesn't it,' Daniel was still staring at the spot through Jack's t-shirt. 'Uncle Phil had one of those; when he was playing footie with us that time and he pulled his shirt up over his head when his side won, like they do on TV, I saw it. It was just like yours too, really red and bright.'

'Yeah,' Jack handed him the joint. 'And look what happened to him.'

'Yeah,' Daniel puffed on the joint, coughed slightly, then puffed again. 'And my mum too.'

'Your mum wasn't a Woodfield,' Jack said. 'Not a proper one; she married into this family, the poor old cow.'

'I miss her.'

'Yeah...' Jack put his arm around the boy's shoulders again and jostled him. 'She was sweet, your mum; my aunt Sophie.'

Daniel's eyes reddened. He nodded, rubbed his nose, and then seemed to lose it. Better not to think about mum, the way dad always did, and end up in his cups every night. 'I really miss her,' he said, and began to cry, the tears coming thick and fast. The tears came for the piles of washing on the floor that six or seven years ago would have been picked up first thing by his mum and deposited in the washing machine; for the slices of toast his dad offered which replaced the full English fry-ups his mum had done for them each and every morning; for her soft face and her slightly slow way of speaking. Jack pulled him close and for the next minute or so the only sound, aside from the trains still rumbling past outside, was the sobbing of a confused, frightened, lost sixteen year old boy whose mum, his only real friend, had been dead six long years, and whose dad drank every night to try and dull the pain of that loss. Daniel wiped at his eyes with the back of his hand and looked up at Jack. 'You have to be the Daddy,' he said. 'You have to. Only you can do it, not Jamie; everyone says so, and they're all fed up of waiting.'

Chapter 25

Sunday 9th April 2006

Aunt Delia was fed up of waiting for Uncle Eddie to move them out of the pokey little flat on the Broadway, the one they'd lived in for the past thirty five years or so. But she couldn't move now if she'd wanted to, because as cramped and smelly as it was, directly over an Indian takeaway, it was home; it was where she'd raised her two sets of twins, Clay and Springer, and then Nick and Hayden. All four boys had gravitated towards Jack as everyone else did, Hayden forging an especially close bond with him, but Nick and Nick alone had favoured Jamie, and it was for this reason that Jamie been asked to undertake the task of sorting through his entire wardrobe for various items he'd asked to be mailed on to him in prison, where he and Hayden were currently serving nine months for a GBH that Hayden had had everything to do with, and Nick had been unfortunate enough to witness, and not to grass.

Jamie was sat cross-legged in front of his wardrobe, sorting through the stuff into two piles. From the open door he could hear Aunt Delia down in the kitchen, talking busily to Aunt Amanda, and the clatter of pots and pans as they prepared the Sunday roast. The phone went at around four in the afternoon, and it was the news everyone had been hoping for, that Debbie had woken up and, apart from a sore head and some nausea, would be fine to go home in a day or two.

Nick's room, the one he'd shared with Hayden since they were babies, overlooked the Broadway, and if you leant out the window and peered left you could see Aunt Betty in the window at St. Margaret's, also preparing the Sunday roast. Jamie liked his Aunt Delia best, although Jack preferred Aunt Betty; she was his godmother, and Aunt Delia was Jamie's. Aunt Delia was loud and brassy, her hair dyed a permanent shade of peach, her lipstick and eye-shadow to match, her wrists adorned with bangles and her earrings great big hoops that Nick had once claimed he had held onto as a toddler, and had her walk around the room with him dangling there, although even Jamie wasn't dim enough to fall for that one. If Aunt Amanda had a compatriot-in-arms then it was Delia; they were, as mum put it, '…as thick as thieves.'

Like mum, Aunt Delia opted until rather late in the day to begin the preparations for the Sunday roast, stuffing the chicken when other families were digging into it, the finished product not being served until well after six in the evening, with sticky toffee pudding coming served around eight, so much so that it was often dubbed 'supper' by guests. As the antique clock in the sitting room that had once belonged to her mother Felicity struck five forty five, the peas were being shelled and the gravy was slowly being stirred to a boil; Jamie could see Aunt Delia in his mind's eye, tottering around the kitchen in a kind of artful daze, whereas mum kind of ambled around; whereas Aunt Betty for instance glided gracefully, and Aunt Hannah kind of wandered begrudgingly from one cupboard to another. Aunt Rachel, well she always talked ten to the dozen when she was preparing food, so it was hard to imagine her performing any other, complimentary function.

Jamie closed Nick's cupboard up and piled the sought-after items into an ASDA carrier bag. Visits to Nick were painful, protracted affairs, although Aunt Delia always held her head up high as they sought out a seat on the special bus service that took them from East Ham to Buckinghamshire. She thought Nick quite capable of looking after himself, whereas Hayden, always her favourite, well him she constantly fretted and worried over, not quite realising what, in Jamie's own words, '...a vicious little shit' he actually was. Still, as Aunt Amanda had told him several months previous, you didn't contradict Aunt Delia where her beloved Hayden was concerned.

Jamie went downstairs with the carrier bag in his hand, and set in a pile near the window reserved for rations to be taken on the once-fortnightly visits. Uncle Eddie was snoring in his favourite chair nearby, the '*News of the World*' slipping slowly out of his grasp, slipping until it covered their dog Vinny like a little paper tent. Uncle Eddie was portly and loud and combed his hair over his balding head in a way that made everyone laugh, mostly behind his back. Aunt Delia, well she was blunt enough to tell him how ridiculous it looked to his face.

Aunt Amanda was sat in the chair by the window, overlooking the Broadway, reading one of the Sunday supplements, making little noises now and then, usually derision but occasionally something amused her enough to utter a little 'Ha!' instead. She sniffed, laughed at something to do with Chantelle, and then turned the page. Jamie sat down on the sofa and put his feet up on it, flicking from one channel to another with the remote, settling for something on Sky Sports, popping open a can of Stella left for him on the side table and necking almost the whole thing, letting out his delight in a slow sigh as the cold trickled down his gullet. The smell of the chicken was driving him crazy.

'Get your feet off that sofa young man,' Aunt Delia swiped his trainers with her oven-gloves as she breezed through. 'I vacuumed this morning. Now, do you want peas, or beans? I did both because I know you're easy, not like your brother, who only ever eats peas.'

'Beans!!' Jamie exclaimed. 'And lots of mash; pile it up, Aunt Delia.'

'I'll pile you up in a minute,' she winked, her big earrings jangling like wind chimes. 'Get yourself and Amanda a tray then; we don't eat at the table anymore, old face-ache there gets ants in his pants about something or other on the news,' she nodded down to Uncle Eddie, 'and he bangs the table with his fist and my Brussels sprouts going flying, so I just gave up. Besides, you don't need to make an effort at our age.' And she stood for a moment and puffed the air from her peach lips, and then turned back to Jamie. 'Did you find everything he wanted?'

He nodded. 'Uh huh. Everything except that grey sweater, the one with the black shoulders.'

'Oh Hayden liked that,' she smiled, folding her arms. 'I snuck it up to him last week. I didn't think Nick would miss it.'

'I'll pull the curtains,' Aunt Amanda rose with a sigh, bracing herself with both hands in a move that seemed to Jamie only to accentuate how old she was; then again, post-Uncle Phil he was experiencing an almost hyper-sensitivity to confessions of mortality. 'These old bones aren't getting any younger.'

'Tell me about it,' Aunt Delia drifted back into the kitchen. 'But we keep going.'

'That we do,' she sighed, half happy, half weary, it seemed to Jamie. 'That we do.'

She turned to him, and reached down for her handbag, took out her purse, and removed a folded ten-pound note from inside one of the pockets. 'Slip that in with Nick's things,' she said in a whisper.

'What about Hayden?'

She raised an eyebrow. 'What about him?'

Aunt Delia set out their plates on battered tin trays and then went to the fridge for something, returning moments later to make a grand re-entrance in her Day-Glo pink pinny, wielding a bottle of ASDA's finest champagne. 'I thought we'd have this in celebration of little Debbie coming through the worst! Eddie?' she tapped his leg with her heel. 'Be a dear and fetch the crystal out, will you?'

'Eh, what?!' Uncle Eddie awoke with a start. 'Who let the dogs out?!'

'You silly old fart,' she sighed. 'I'll get them myself.'

Jamie tucked into his roast chicken and sighed as the delicious gravy ran down the back of his throat, just like the Stella, only thicker. 'Great as always, Aunt Delia,' he sighed.

'You enjoy it my darling,' she sat down alongside him, delighted simply that he was here. 'You don't get enough square meals nowadays. Although having said that I know full well you and your Uncle Phil lived on nothing but take-away pizzas and bottles of lemonade…'

Uncle Eddie poured them all a glass of champagne and they toasted little Debbie; Aunt Amanda toasted Uncle Heath as well, for all he'd been through these last few years; 'I'll drink to that,' Aunt Delia nodded. 'That son of yours needs to find himself a good woman, 'mandy. It's a tragedy what happened to Sophie but its eight years past now and life goes on…'

'…that it does,' Uncle Eddie nodded, through a mouthful of potato.

'Don't be a bloody pig, Eddie,' Delia sighed, clattering her knife and fork on the plate. 'We have guests.'

'We had a good night at Legends, apart from what happened to Debbie,' Jamie said. 'I stayed over at Tiffany's afterwards, and everything.'

'She's a good girl, your Tiffany,' Aunt Delia nodded. 'I was talking to her mum down the market just the other day, and you know they say they like it here so much now they wouldn't move back to West London if they had the money?! She says it's much 'homier' here.'

'Jack's friends didn't think so,' he went on. 'They looked at everything and everyone like we were as common as muck.'

'Now did they really, Jamie Woodfield?' Aunt Amanda raised an eyebrow. 'Or is this just cheap point-scoring time?!'

He shrugged. 'I couldn't even tell what they were going on about, half the time. They kept talking big stuff to make the rest of us look stupid. The bloke, well I think he's queer, you know.'

'Well Jack should've introduced him to Bobby!' Aunt Delia laughed, and veritably rocked with amusement, as did Uncle Eddie, although Aunt Amanda just laughed lightly.

They finished up and left the plates on their trays, sat down and watched the news on ITV, Jamie nodding and making little noises of agreement as Uncle Eddie gave his running commentary and personal opinion on each and every news story, especially the bit on the BNP in Barking and Dagenham, until Aunt Delia slapped him 'round the back of the head and he shut up. Pudding was a promise but in traditional East End style the men put their feet up while the women went into the kitchen to do the washing-up. Jamie waved for silence and shifted in his chair, the better to hear what was being said. Aunt Amanda nodded to him as she passed, and mouthed something along the lines of, 'It'll be ok', and then, as she and Aunt Delia were putting the dishes in the sink, said to her, 'I don't think Jack will be coming back for a good while now. It gave him hives to be here just for this weekend, by all accounts.'

'Oh he'll be back,' Aunt Delia shook her head. 'We'll always come first, you know that 'mandy.'

'I'm not so sure...' Aunt Amanda took a sponge and began scrubbing at the largest pan, fighting with the grease stains. 'I know it's a cliché but things aren't what they used to be; traditions change and I think this family is going to have to change a few things as well, if we want to go on the way we have been, and to make things even better.'

'How do you mean, dear?' As Jamie peered around the door he saw Aunt Delia was eyeing her in a funny sort of way, peering over her shoulder, causing him to rather rapidly begin an impromptu drinking competition with Uncle Eddie, seeing who could down the rest of the champagne quicker.

'I think we need to offer Jack the chance to abdicate as the Daddy,' Aunt Amanda said firmly. 'And offer it to Jamie instead.'

'You can't do that!' Aunt Delia gasped, a little too loudly. 'Now even saying that I could see where you're coming from, it's tradition; it's always been tradition. Kings may abdicate, but the Woodfield men never do!'

'Would you want your boys, Clay or Springer, to be the Daddy?' she asked, 'how about Nick or Hayden?'

'Well no, but if they…if they, you know…'

'I just think Jack isn't the least bit interested in family,' Aunt Amanda went on to washing the next pan, catching Jamie's eye and winking. 'He's very modern that way, whereas our Jamie is very much more in the traditional, if slightly old-fashioned mode. And besides, he was Phil's favourite. Phil would have wanted it; Phil did want it, as a matter of fact.'

Aunt Delia began piling the cups on the draining board. 'But the Daddy…well the Daddy has always been predetermined, hasn't it?'

'If you can call a birthmark predestined,' Aunt Amanda said matter-of-factly. 'No one's ever put it to the test; I propose to.'

It was at that point that Aunt Delia closed the kitchen door; Aunt Amanda relayed the rest of what was said to Jamie when he drove her home later that night; 'Terrible things could happen, you know,' Aunt Delia had said, her brow wrinkled in consternation.

'Haven't terrible things happened already?' Aunt Amanda had replied. 'Phil; Sophie; my mother; my brother, and my sister; your Nick and Hayden locked up for a whole year. Jack can do what he likes, and be here to advise and counsel Jamie if he needs it, and Jamie…well he can be that Daddy without that crafty little whore, Minty Hardcore.'

If she'd been god-fearing like her brother, Aunt Delia might have crossed herself at the mere mention of that name. 'My mother said pretty much the same thing, 'mandy…'

Aunt Amanda had nodded. 'She was inspiration to us all, Felicity was. Now mark my words,' and here she'd moved closer, for greater emphasis. 'When Minty Hardcore kicks up a fuss about us making the switch, well that's when I'll get *her*; I'll pull that silly sun bonnet off her head and jump up and down it until it's flattened, and I don't care if I put my hip out doing it!! And that's just for starters!'

The Daddy Dissertation Part 4

By David Samuels

Aunt Amanda and the case of the Kray twins

While his sisters forged relatively benign careers for themselves, with Amanda working in various shops on the Bethnal Green Road, and Andrea training as a secretary, Ben Woodfield became friends with local toughs the Kray twins, who lived only a couple of doors down from them on Vallance Road; it was said that Ronnie Kray fell in love with the young lad's blond hair and twinkling blue eyes, and would embarrass him by buying him gifts and sometimes just sitting on the wall opposite their house and staring at him as he washed the outside step in his shorts and vest.

Andrea grew up to be a stunning leggy blond with porcelain skin and a very proper accent that she'd been determined to keep from her time as an evacuee with the well-to-do Atwells in Oxford. She became great friends with Rupert's wife Michele, having been '…the most gorgeous bridesmaid you'd ever seen' at their wedding in 1947. With Michele's help Andrea went to work as a secretary in the City and married an up and coming Fleet Street journalist with a flashy smile and a good line in snappy banter called Ewan Starks, in 1956. Her sister Amanda was a more sultry, smoky eyed brunette with just a strange tint of red in her hair that she inherited from their mother Agnes. She kept herself to her herself for the most part, and there are no instances of any romances, or even dalliances, on her part.

Although he never succumbed to Ronnie's advances, Ben never-the-less fell in with the Krays and was drinking and brawling with them well into the Fifties; he would often turn up on his Aunt Barbara's doorstep with his shirt ripped and his lip split, and she would usher him in whilst the boys would stand outside and laugh as the sound of her scolding echoed up and down the length of the road.

Amanda, who'd been telling people's fortunes with tea leaves 'just for a lark' for years, one day told Ronnie Kray that if he didn't ease off her brother that 'he'd end up in prison for at least thirty years'. When this didn't work she tried dating Reggie Kray and then telling him that Ben really wasn't suited to the kind of world the twins were rapidly immersing themselves in. Reggie was sympathetic but Ben was a grown man, although a little naïve for his twenty two odd years, but he would see what he could do, because Barbara Corbett was a good friend of the twins' mother Violet. When Ben was hurt in a rather vicious tussle in a club in Mile End, Woodfield cousins came down from Barking at the behest of Rupert and Felicity, and confronted the twins personally. There was another fight, with coshes, bayonets, and the like, and by morning all the beds at Royal London

Hospital on the Whitechapel Road were full of battered, bruised and cut up young men, Krays and Woodfields alike.

Ronnie Kray went to prison in 1959, and without his influence Reggie sobered up a little, and Amanda was able to prise Ben away from the gang relatively easily. There were rows in the street outside the Corbett house about 'family duty' and the like, and gossips back in Barking said that 'that boy simply isn't cut out to be what a Woodfield boy ought to be; he's far too easily led, when he should be the one doing the leading'. In 1960 there was some kind of a tussle between various second tier Kray gang members and the rival Richardson gang of South London, in a nightclub somewhere along the Roman Road. Apparently Ben was shot and killed during the gun fight when the one of the woman present used him as something of a human shield, apparently near hysterical that she was to be shot herself (eye witness accounts on what exactly occurred here are many and various, but I'll return to them later in some detail). Amanda blamed herself for letting her baby brother down, and Andrea seems to have concurred, whispering to her journalist husband at the graveside that '...no good ever comes to the poor boys in this family, and if Amanda had had any kind of conscience she'd have sent Ben back up to Oxford and the Atwells years ago.'.

Apparently Ewan Starks decided on the strength of her remarks – and possibly an awful lot of pillow talk, for which Andrea was apparently notorious - that there was some sort of story in his wife's family history, and he set about penning a piece about 'this tragic Essex family' in late 1962, at about the same time Andrea fell pregnant, after a rather nasty miscarriage the previous summer. At this point the core family was headed up in Barking by Felicity Woodfield and increasingly by her daughter Delia, as well as Rupert Woodfield (his wife Michele is said to have let her husband do whatever he wanted because '...the bloody family will always come first.'). Delia was a brassy, buxom matriarch in the mould of her mother, although she wasn't nearly as attractive as Felicity had been as a young woman, compensating for her lack of naturally blond locks by reaching for the bleach, with a hankering for peach; never-the-less she had a matter-of-fact approach that won people over, and it was on her insistence that Andrea, her husband, and their new baby Phil moved back to Barking from their Liverpool Street apartment in early 1964, taking over the house on the Ripple Road after Father Billy's death; Felicity moved in with Delia and her husband Eddie Dowden. Andrea wasn't overly keen on living in the house of the person she would only refer to as, 'my mad, dead mother'. Delia is said to have thought Andrea 'snooty', and not to have liked her husband at all, although to neighbours she would proudly proclaim him to be 'the family journalist'. In 1966 Andrea was pregnant again, giving birth to Heath and Beverly in the front bedroom. The entire family continued to dote on Phil Woodfield exclusively though, and rather unkindly referred to his little brother Heath as he grew up as 'that spare', or 'Daddy-lite'.

One morning in 1966 whilst heavily pregnant with the twins Andrea was said to have walked into her bedroom on the Ripple Road and found a strange woman who looked not unlike both her and her sister combined feeding the-then toddler Phil his mashed food, stroking his hair and cooing sweet nothings into his ear. Andrea's scream was heard outside and neighbours broke in through the front door and found her sobbing on the stairs, her little son standing over her, totally bemused, hitting her over the head with his wooden spoon; bemused, it turned out, because according to the few words he knew, 'that lady is always around mummy, 'specially when you're not, and she tells me I'm gonna be a heartbreaker when I grow up. She says I was baptised in the testosterone waterfall!'

Andrea turned to her sister for help. Amanda was now living alone in Aunt Barbara's house on Vallance Road, although there were always guests of one sort of another there, 'Amanda's strange friends', Andrea called them, and often in her presence. Now however the pretty young city secretary with the Oxford accent was sobbing into her sister's lap and begging her to remove 'the family curse' from her son. Some say the shock of finding Phil with the strange woman kicked her into premature labour, because Heath and Beverly certainly spent a month in hospital before they were allowed to go home, and Felicity's son Brian, training for the priesthood at the time, said prayers over their beds daily. Amanda agreed to help her sister only on the condition that she told her husband Ewan to 'stop writing that silly article of his', and to respect the family's privacy. But it was too late. The article was published in a local paper in Barking some time in early 1967, and pointed out the tragic run of early and unfortunate deaths of males in the Woodfield family, and even dredged up ancient gossip about Jake Woodfield being an incubus, and of there indeed being a 'testosterone spring' secreted in the grounds of St. Margaret's church.

Ewan Starks died in June 1967 when he fell in front of an Eastbound District line train at Barking Underground; Andrea was distraught, and accused her sister of being a witch, and of murdering her husband in revenge for having the article published. Aunt Delia slapped her in broad daylight on Station Parade the day of the funeral, and told her to pull herself together, that she was scaring little Phil with all of her 'silly talk'. Indeed Phil spent the entirety of his father's funeral on Delia's lap, with his Aunt Amanda on one side of him, feeding him slices of tangerine, and his Aunt Felicity on the other, administering occasional sips from a mug of sweet tea.

Andrea took an overdose in November 1967, around the time the Ripple Road library burned down, and was cold by the time Felicity found her, laid out on the bed in the front room of the house on the Ripple Road, with a picture of her wedding day clasped to her chest. The whole family decided it was for the best that Amanda take in all three of her sister's children, and Beverly and Heath never even knew who their mother was until they were teenagers, and apparently both of them only ever called their

Aunt Amanda 'mum'. The house on the Ripple Road stood vacant for a year or so, with Felicity letting it out to various families, who moved in but left almost as soon as they had arrived, and finally in 1969 Rupert moved in with his wife Michele and their teenage twins, Hannah and Rachel.

By this time and back in Bethnal Green Amanda was acting as Ronnie Kray's full time spiritual adviser, and there is a lovely photo of little Phil between the Kray twins, holding a toy Dalek from the television series 'Doctor Who' that they had brought for him, and which he later gave to his nephew Bobby. Amanda seemed to have buried her grudge with the twins; or not, as in 1969 they did indeed go down for thirty years for murder, as she had predicted. In the years that followed Amanda remained a friend of their mother Violet's, dining with her and her sisters regularly, doing the odd bit of shopping, and generally being a good neighbour.

In 1970 she legally adopted the Phil, Heath, and Bev; the only thing she refused to do was move back to Barking proper, stating that Bethnal Green was her home, and that the mentality of the locals was pretty much the same as Essex anyway. Between them she and Delia ran the family affairs all through the Seventies and early Eighties, even when Delia married and gave birth to two sets of twins in two years, Clay and Springer, and then Nick and Hayden. Rupert was regarded by all as being 'the Daddy', but deferred to the women in almost all things, a state of affairs that is said not to have gone down terribly well with the male cousins of the time. One of them is said to have confronted Amanda about it on one of her visits to see Felicity and Delia, and asked why she couldn't '…keep a woman's place, and let Rupert handle things?!'; Amanda is said to have regarded him in that dry, casual way she had, and to have said simply, 'I do it, darling, because it gets on *her* tits.'

Chapter 26

Tuesday 11th April 2006

Jamie's alarm clock went off at 7am, a recording he'd made some months previous on his mobile of West Ham fans chanting outside the grounds at Upton Park; the recording was staggered so it got louder the longer it took for him to switch it off. Sometimes he'd just lie there and let it reach something of a crescendo before he finally hit the 'off' button. Then he would allow himself perhaps five or ten minutes to wake up, the only thing he could deem a 'luxury' now that Uncle Phil was gone, because in those days the bedroom door would have been flung open the minute the alarm went and Uncle Phil would have come bounding in, in his entire home kit and started running on the spot at the end of the bed, and then maybe touching his toes, or doing star-jumps. Life was kind of a before and after affair now, the things he'd done when Uncle Phil was around, and the things he did now, which for the most part were a recreation of the things he'd done when Uncle Phil was around, simply because it was too painful to contemplate doing them any other way. Anything more than five or ten minutes lying in and he actually ended up getting so upset that he had to get up, or the possibility of curling up under the covers and simply doing nothing became too great a temptation.

Throwing his legs over the side of the bed he dropped down and did a couple of press-ups to wake himself up, a tried and trusted technique although recently Aunt Amanda had been encouraging him to do more and more reps; 'Minty Hardcore likes big shoulders, darling' she'd say, 'big shoulders and bigger biceps!! When you think you can't do any more reps, well you just think about that!! Think about being as big as your brother is!!' She'd been buying organic foods for him to eat as well, and ordering a set of second-hand weights on eBay, to push things further in this direction.

He got dressed after doing an extra set, opting for briefs under navy blue slacks, a white vest that showed off his rapidly improving physique under a West Ham hoodie, West Ham socks and Reebok trainers. His 'beauty' routine consisted of a splash of cold water and a shave if his bum fluff/stubble was turning into a little more of a proper beard than it ought to have been. Sometimes he used the face wash and 'revitalising cream' Tiffany had brought for him one Christmas but usually they ended up gathering dust in the back of the wash cabinet. He brushed his teeth, gargled with mouth wash, examined himself for maybe ten seconds until he heard Adam's voice in his mind saying something along the lines of, '…get away from that mirror, you big poof!' and then he hurried down the steps to the kitchen and switched the kettle on; Jamie, like most Woodfields, simply couldn't function without several cups of tea first thing in the morning, strong and sweet. Breakfast consisted of a couple of slices of poorly buttered toast, a fry-up if and when he could be bothered, and on week days there simply wasn't the time. Sometimes he'd still be eating the toast as he hurried up Station Parade towards the Underground, grabbing a Pepsi from WHSmith's, waving to cousin Casey in his photography studio before swiping his weekly ticket through the turnstiles and hurrying down the steps onto the Westbound District Line platform.

The journey from Barking to Mile End, then changing to the Central Line to get off at Tottenham Court Road was something of a drag, so he'd usually doze, sometimes reading one of the free papers left on the seat next to him, or trying to read it at the very least; he'd become self-conscious that people could see he was straining to decipher some of the more convoluted terms, and when he did that he mouthed the words, or so Louise had told him, something he found embarrassing. Sometimes he'd bump into cousin Jessica going into the West End for one of her photo shoots, all done up and radiating a kind of D-list star quality, but usually it was a fairly solitary experience. Jessica was only interested in one thing, and that was Jack, about the least exciting topic of conversation Jamie could possibly imagine, and it wasn't unknown for him to spot her on the platform and actually hide himself in the crowds so he didn't end up having to listen to how well Jack did on his last essay, or how amazingly defined his six-pack was.

He bounded up the steps at Tottenham Court Road and down Charing Cross Road, greeting Don the Doorman at Sight & Sound with a cheery wave before rushing up to the first floor, straight into one of the typing booths, fitting his headphones on and pulling his training manual out. Louise would blow him a kiss from her desk, and Omiros might nod in his direction, but usually the poor bugger needed all his wits about him to keep up with the monotone voice as it slowly got faster and faster, the keys on the big screen in front of them flashing quicker and quicker. Normally they'd end up typing pages of gobbledygook, but it was marked in a certain way and made sense to Karen and Eva, the two members of staff who supervised these sessions; the 'qwerty board method', they called it. For lunch they usually went to the McDonalds at the bottom end of Oxford Street, buying family meals in bulk and then simply sharing the lot out between them. Louise flirted with Jamie a lot but by now he'd told her he was going steady with a girl called Tiffany and she'd toned it down a little. Louise's best friend Maggie would laugh at all of Jamie's jokes but she was, without putting too fine a point on it, 'a bit of a minger'; still, with girls like that Jamie often felt more relaxed because there was no kind of sexual agenda, not on his part at least, and they could play silly games and laugh so hard that at one point their strawberry milkshakes came out through their noses. After lunch they'd slouch back to Sight & Sound and up to the second floor, a large room filled with people listening to various exercises on headphones, all connected to some rather retro whirring tape machines at the end of each desk. This part required less concentration than the morning's typing, so Jamie and Louise would often pass notes to each other back and forth on scrap paper, Louise becoming transfixed when Jamie told her he had a twin brother who'd '...bedded more birds than Casanova'. Maggie perked up at this news too, even moreso when he elaborated, stating that Jack was 'a bit of a player', and had in all sincerity probably bedded more than two hundred girls in his time. The other day one of the supervisors, a big, bubbly woman called Yhelena came over and rapped her knuckles firmly on the end of the table and they all shut up pretty quick; Louise said later that she dreaded her coming over one time and taking the notes she'd been scribbling to Jamie, so she'd begun a strict policy of shredding them after each and every lesson.

The Sight & Sound day ended around four o'clock; sometimes they went for a drink in the Wetherspoons over the other side of the road, sometimes Jamie would go into Blackwell's or Foyles and sit cross-legged reading various books Aunt Amanda had recommended to him; 'Teach yourself witchcraft'; 'Familiars of English witchcraft', that sort of thing. She'd given him an allowance with which to purchase such books, but he'd found that he usually spent most of that buying rounds and ended up trying to memorise as much as he could of the important bits there and then. One time Louise had shoplifted one of them for him, and he'd given her a lingering peck on the cheek by way of reward. Another time they'd spent hours in the medical section looking at horrific deformities in medical texts and laughing uneasily to each other; all a bit morbid and unnecessary, really, when he'd told Aunt Amanda about it, but Jamie still had a rather adolescent sense of humour in regards to certain matters.

By six he was on the train back to Barking, seated if he was lucky but more often than not standing until Mile End, one hand in his pocket and the other clamped around the safety railing, whistling 'I'm forever blowing bubbles' to keep himself amused. The change at Mile End to the District Line usually afforded a few more seats. Upon arrival back in Barking he would have tea with a different family member depending on which night of the week it was, something Aunt Amanda had also positively encouraged, along with trying to get Jack to come to a game with him; all his texts on that front had thus far gone unanswered. On Mondays it was usually pie and mash with his mum in the Murphy Estate, sometimes with one of her beauty therapy clients still present and undressed, their body covered head to toe in 'organic Dead Sea rejuvenating mud'; Tuesdays he stopped off with cousin Sara and her boyfriend Ron at East Ham and they ordered Pizza Hut and watched rock concerts on DVD; Wednesdays were with cousin Casey, his expectant wife Tamsin and their little girl Meggan, Casey favouring Italian dishes that his wife cooked up a treat, with a generous dessert as well. Thursdays, although not lately, given the rather harsh mouthful he'd administered when Uncle Heath had turned up at the flat after his fight with Jack, had seen him landing on Uncle Heath's doorstep in the house on Salisbury Avenue, and that was usually just fish and chips because Uncle Heath couldn't cook to save his life, and Daniel and Debbie loved fish and chips anyway; Friday was his favourite, a huge 'all day breakfast' with Aunt Delia, Uncle Eddie, and Clay, lashings of ketchup on greasy chips, rashers of bacon, mushrooms, all washed down with several chilled cans of Stella, then feet up in front of the TV for the rest of the evening. Sometimes they'd call Nick in Grendon and pass the phone around, but the conversation always tended to get a bit maudlin because everyone except the poor incarcerated Nick had lots to say, and, as Aunt Amanda had told him on more than one occasion, even Woodfields possessed some level of tact and social etiquette. When dining with mum he'd become bored of her incessant talk about Jack and be home by nine; with Sarah sometimes he'd get the last train out of East Ham around midnight; Casey and Tamsin would politely urge him to stay but he'd become bored of their domesticity and leave around ten; at Uncle Heath's he could play with Daniel on the Xbox for hours, and he often kipped the night there, as he did at Aunt Delia's, but in those cases only when he'd drunk so much he actually passed out, and she'd drape a large tea towel over him and let him sleep it off.

Tonight would have meant disembarking at East Ham and visiting Sara, but Jamie got a text just as the tube pulled into Whitechapel, out of the tunnels and into a light drizzle, a lengthy text from mum, saying that Aunt Amanda had had a nasty fall on the Bethnal Green Road, that she had slipped and twisted her ankle badly, landing in the road; her hip was fractured and at her age that could be bad news, and that she might be in hospital for weeks as a result. She had been taken to the Royal London Hospital in Whitechapel and Uncle Heath was with her, and could Jamie tell Sara he couldn't make it for tea tonight, and instead go straight to the hospital? Considering the convenience of his location he disembarked straight away, was in the hospital two minutes later, and by Aunt Amanda's bedside with Uncle Heath in a further four, and trying valiantly not meet his slightly disapproving eye. Aunt Amanda seemed in good spirits but she was in a bit of pain, for which the nurses were giving her a morphine injection just as Jamie arrived; the skin on the palms of her hands had been almost taken off by the fall, and she had a rather nasty yellowing bruise on her jaw that made her symmetrical features look distorted, like the reflection in a fun fair mirror. 'Women in this family,' she said with a weak smile, catching him catching sight of her. 'We can be so accident prone.'

'You can come and stay with me when you're well mum,' Uncle Heath was squeezing her hand. 'And no arguments, you hear me? plenty of room.'

Aunt Amanda seemed to consider this for a moment, looking fixedly at Jamie all the time. 'Maybe it won't be such a bad idea, just for a week or two until I'm on my feet again. My poor darling,' and she lifted Uncle Heath's jaw up with slender, slightly gnarled fingers, all her rings removed. 'Your daughter last week and your old mum today; I bet you're sick of the sight of hospitals, aren't you?'

'How did it happen?' Jamie asked, sitting on the opposite side of the bed. 'I mean, you're as fit as a...'

'...a fifty year old?' she raised an eyebrow. 'I know. I forget sometimes that I'm...' and here she cupped her hand to the side of her mouth in a mock whisper, '...seventy three!'

'That's no age these days, mum,' Uncle Heath said. 'But you're gonna come stay, right? Daniel and Debbie would love it.'

'Of course I will darling,' she nodded. 'And you and those little horrors of yours can have a decent meal in your bellies each night for a change. And as for you...' and she fixed Jamie with a steely glare. 'Have you been doing everything I told you do? When are you and Jack going to see 'the Mallets' play then?'

'It's the Hammers,' Jamie couldn't tell if she was still trying to cheer him up or not. 'I have been doing all the stuff though,' he nodded, aware that across from him Uncle Heath was utterly bemused by this exchange.

'Been reading the books I recommended?' she asked.

'Uh huh.'

'Changed your diet?'

He patted his marginally flat stomach. 'Yup.'

'Are you sure, Jamie Woodfield?'

'Well...mostly,' he blushed. 'I like pizza, Aunt Amanda. I can't help it. Especially 'meat feast'. It was mine and Uncle Phil's favourite; we used to eat it every week. I think Jack likes it too; it's about the only thing we have in common, I guess.'

'Well I'll be able to keep a proper eye on you for a while,' she said. 'Have the weights we ordered on eBay arrived yet?'

'The person emailed to say they're in the post. What happened exactly?' Jamie asked; it was the question he'd been dying to ask, in fact. His entire life he'd never known his Aunt Amanda to so much as even wobble on dry ice, let alone take a tumble headlong into the path of an oncoming number 8 bus, which was what had happened, she told them. She couldn't explain it, she went on, but one minute she was fine and then her legs gave out and she was in the road and her palms were bleeding, and thankfully people were rushing to help and they sat her down in McDonalds until the ambulance came.

'Go and get yourself and Jamie a cup of tea,' Aunt Amanda said to Uncle Heath, reaching for her purse, tucked in the dresser at the side. He refused her money but went anyway, that rather butch gait of his turning the heads of a few of the nurses. Aunt Amanda laughed to see them whispering to each other and said, as if to herself, 'Thank the lord she didn't get her hands on him as well; and lord only knows she tried.'

'Who tried?' Jamie asked.

'Who do you think?'

'Oh.'

'Exactly.'

Jamie thought about it for a bit. 'So…Uncle Heath might have been the Daddy then, and not Uncle Phil?'

'Oh heavens no,' Aunt Amanda chuckled. 'Your Uncle Phil had the kiss good and proper, but now if you ever happen to stay at your Uncle Heath's and he comes down in a state of undress…' and here she beckoned him closer, confidentially, 'you look for a little bump a lot like some sort of a mark in the same place. A lot like your one.'

'A little one…' Jamie said, a little embarrassed, 'more in the middle of my back than on my bum or anything. Nothing like what Jack's got.'

'They called it 'a witch's mark' in the old days,' she told him. 'And they'd strip you and scour your entire body until they found it, as proof of your possessing a familiar, whom they supposed would suckle on it. My brother Ben had one, although it was a little smeared; apparently Jacob and Jeramiah had matching ones, you know? Like where you draw one half of a butterfly in wet ink on a piece of paper and fold in on itself? I'm sure Jack would know what that was called.'

'Did you really slip?' Jamie asked her.

'Did I heck as like,' she narrowed her eyes. 'I felt two hands square on the middle of my back, giving me a hearty shove and you make no mistake; of course there was no one behind me at the time…'

'But you're usually so careful,' he said. 'In all these years…'

'Like I said my darling, I'm seventy three.' she held his hand between both of hers. 'I'm getting on a bit, to put it mildly. And I'm only really safe when I have all my…things around me. And I let my guard down sometimes, is all. It won't happen again.'

'Bad things always happen to the girls in this family,' Jamie sat back, his teeth grinding together. 'Maybe the person who pushed you was possessed! I'll find them and kick shit out of them! I'll get Uncle Phil's mates in the 'Dog to help me!'

'Don't you dare,' she narrowed her eyes. 'And then you get caught and go to prison, and where am I then?! All of us, even! No, you just keep doing exactly as I tell you, Jamie Woodfield. Sooner or later she'll make a mistake, and when she does, we'll pounce. Now, what is she?'

Jamie sniffed, inhaled, and thumped his fist against the metal frame of the bed. 'A crafty little whore!'

Last thing before bed, back in the Daddy flat, Jamie laid out on the sofa and watched TV, and he'd thought of Uncle Phil, of that memory Aunt Amanda had told him to 'visualise' and relive it, vicariously; she had said that was good therapy to do that, and not to think of the time when Uncle Phil had been ill, or the fact that he'd died on Christmas Day, or that Jack had been there to witness his grief on that awful afternoon. Before bed he texted Tiffany, although for the last couple of weeks he'd occasionally forgotten and she hadn't seemed bothered either way.

On this particular night he had a dream about meeting Uncle Phil on the pitch at Upton Park, and Uncle Phil had come together from all of his scattered ashes, and he was wearing his full home 2005 strip and looked the business in it, and he was grinning and his big eyes were wide, and his floppy brown hair blowing in a light breeze. He would cup his ear in his hand, and lean forward as though straining to catch something Jamie was about to say, although Jamie didn't know what on earth it was, and after a while Uncle Phil would shrug and raise his hands in a 'what's up?!' way and slowly dissolve, back into ashes. And Jamie woke up, and even though he tried not to, he ended up crying.

The Daddy Dissertation Part 5

By David Samuels

Behold, the Seventies!

Phil Woodfield was the apple of his Aunt Amanda's eye, and by all accounts had a similar effect on his countless uncles and aunts as he grew, all the way from a toddler to a teen, although Amanda didn't like too many visitors constantly cooing over him and '…those big brown eyes', visiting the house as they often did in their droves, piling into their cars at one end and then disembarking at the other with armfuls of presents, sweets and such; 'oh, those big brown eyes!!' they would cry out, 'I could just eat them up!!'. The somewhat faded pictures I have seen of Phil Woodfield in the early Seventies do indeed show these eyes to be almost femininely large, punctuated by a cute spray of freckles across his nose which only marginally faded as he grew older. He inherited his father Ewan's toothy grin and his journalist's gift of the gab, and his mother Andrea's long legs and slight but sturdy build, as well as her frank way of speaking.

One of his uncles, either Rupert but far more likely Delia's long suffering husband Eddie Dowden began taking Phil to see West Ham when he was still a toddler, planting in him a devotion to the team he kept up until the day he died; he was a permanent season ticket holder, and would attend matches come hell or high water. Heath sometimes went along and both boys could often be found on a Sunday afternoon round the back of their house on Vallance Road, kicking a football up and down the length of Weaver's Field, for hours at a time. With other local boys they formed sides and often held impromptu matches that would, on sunny days, bring the neighbours out with their wooden chairs and their bottles of flat lemonade.

Their Aunt Amanda was the woman whom many people in the area went to with their problems, and for them she represented the dying breed of East End matriarch that was fast becoming consigned to history, as the old houses of the area were demolished to make way for high rise tower blocks, and the traditional networks of the old East End families began to disintegrate. This idea is very much in keeping with the Woodfields today, with their large numbers and close-knit ways; they still resemble in their geography and social make-up a throwback to one of the large East End/Essex families of the Fifties or Sixties, when all else around them are nowadays busy sinking into a mire of 'alternative' or 'new' families. Having no children Amanda kept her looks and even to this day people are shocked to discover that she is in her early seventies; she is often mistaken for a woman in her mid-fifties, and a clean living one at that. In the early Seventies she was a familiar figure along Bethnal Green Road on a Saturday lunchtime, bags of shopping in each hand, little Beverly, all blond plaits and pink jumpsuit, holding onto her jacket tails; Heath and Phil would be tagging some way behind, still stuffing the sweets Mr Pellici had given them after the lunch in his café, shouting and hollering and kicking empty plastic cups around in the gutter, in the strips their Uncle Eddie had brought them.

Testimony from family members still living and the abundance of post-war records make descriptions about the Woodfields from the Forties until the present day remarkably vivid, and sometimes even bloated when compared to the few sketchy accounts of Jake Woodfield's life that I was able to glean from the on/off diary he kept. I feel obliged to include as much of this material as possible, in order to perhaps compensate for the aforementioned lack of it during the family's early years.

*

Back in Barking Delia continued in her role as secondary matriarch under the guidance of her increasingly senile mother Felicity, organising weddings and christenings, birthday parties, and even the odd funeral or two. Her two eldest sons, Clay and Springer were toddlers at this time, and the entire family lived in a two bedroom flat on the Broadway just behind the East Street market, swollen to capacity in the late seventies by the arrival of Nick and Hayden; Delia had a hysterectomy after this pregnancy due to complications from which she almost died. Her brother, Father Brian Woodfield lived almost adjacent to them in St. Margaret's with his wife Betty and their son Casey (Bobby and Jessica arrived some years later), where many members of the family were christened. He continues to be the father of this parish to this day, and held Phil Woodfield's funeral service there in the beginning of 2006. Rupert and Michele continued to live in the house on the Ripple Road with their two teenage daughters Hannah and Rachel; both girls were pregnant by twenty, with Hannah moving with her baby Sara to nearby Cranborne Road; she still lives there today with her two youngest daughters, Laquisha and Marie, Sara having moved to a flat in nearby East Ham. Hannah was the first Woodfield known to marry anyone outside of the family's own ethnic background, wedding Rhodesian born Edward James in 1980; Delia sided with her when other, less charitable members of the family spurned her for '…getting in the club by one of those bloody blacks'. Her sister Rachel is said to have been told by her husband to '…keep clear of the whole dirty affair' – the fact that she didn't, and took Delia's stance in standing up for her sister led in part to the breakdown of her marriage.

From here on the story of the family is essentially and also rather importantly – for reasons which will become clear - Phil Woodfield's story, and his siblings essentially fell by the wayside as his shadow loomed long and large over the entire clan. Whilst his sister Beverly certainly had her fair share of fun and excitement during the late Seventies and early Eighties (rumours abound she was pregnant at fourteen but had a secret abortion),

Heath was a quiet, rather brooding individual who never held any animosity towards his more popular, outgoing older brother, preferring to take long walks by himself and sharing the friends his brother had rather than actively seeking out any of his own.

The three children all did well at school, but for a time teachers thought Heath might be '...a little slow'. Phil excelled in most things but was said to be frequently bored by things that 'he already knows the answers to'. He began wear West Ham shirts around age seven and by age ten he wouldn't be seen in anything else, and Aunt Amanda had his bedroom done out in the team colours when he turned eleven, as a birthday present. If the children had any father figure as such then it was probably still Delia's husband Eddie, although relatives said Amanda couldn't bear to be in the room for him for more than ten minutes at a time. Eddie drank a lot, swore a lot, was sexist a lot, was racist fairly frequently, and was homophobic purely as a matter of course; he and Uncle Rupert often went on drinking bouts that lasted days rather than hours. In these respects he wasn't much different from the majority of East End men in the late Sixties and early Seventies, and shouldn't be singled out for special vilification. He was simply a product of his time. Things came to a head between him and Amanda when he made a pass at her during the Christmas festivities of 1971, and his wife Delia as a result chased him out of the house on Vallance Road and down the street, swinging at his rapidly receding backside with a particularly spiky branch of the Christmas tree.

Where Amanda Woodfield got much of her money from remains a mystery, but the children never went without anything. Although there was still money in the properties the Woodfields owned a lot of them had been sold to cover increasing debts, or lost through bad management and family rifts involving co-ownership with various 'Hackney Woodfields'. Rupert made a lot of money through gambling and it's rumoured some of this went to Amanda without his wife Michele ever knowing, even to the point where his own girls went without so that Phil might benefit, although the children were totally unaware of this. Some people say Amanda had a fortune stashed away in a secret place that Ronnie Kray had fed into on a yearly basis in return for telling his fortune; others simply said she was a witch who could conjure money up out of dried lettuce, simply by blowing on it; the bank-notes she used smelled of it, local shopkeepers told one another.

When Phil was ten and Heath and Beverly both seven Amanda took them to Brighton for a week during the summer holidays where they stayed with Amanda's journalist cousin, Avis's only child, Richard Woodfield. Richard was a gay man very much of the time and very much in the mould of a young Larry Grayson, but he doted on the children and indulged their every wish, penning stories of dragons and knights, witches and wizards, with themselves in the roles of heroes and heroine. Amanda apparently made a rather bizarre request of him during this visit, and asked him if there was any inkling that young Phil might be gay, or at the very least bisexual; in fact she was said to have been almost keen for his affirmation of her 'suspicion'. When he'd gotten over the sheer inappropriateness of the question, this being 1973 and all, he said that from what he could tell, no Phil probably wasn't gay, although exactly how much you could tell from a ten year old he wasn't at all sure. Amanda seemed almost disappointed to hear this, and quizzed Richard endlessly on his own development and then apparently reiterated the same questions in modified form to Phil during a walk along the beach the next day.

Upon their return to London things sailed along fairly smoothly, until Phil began to see a local girl when he was around the age of thirteen; his Aunt Amanda warned him off her without much in the way of explanation, and there ensued many rows and tantrums in the front room of the house on Vallance Road, with even the odd ornament being thrown. Half-baked excuses that the girl '...simply isn't good enough for my Phil' didn't cut much ice, and in defiance of her the pair of them even threatened to elope to Gretna Green to get married, despite being only thirteen and twelve apiece. When the girl in question suffered a serious fall off the open platform of a Routemaster bus going along the Roman Road, breaking her nose as a result, Phil accused his aunt of being 'a mean old witch', who'd done the deed on purpose in order to make the girl ugly so that he wouldn't fancy her anymore; 'Ah, well there you are,' Felicity is said to have told Amanda over tea and biscuits the following week, 'the shallow romances of the teenager.'

Chapter 27

Tuesday 11th April 2006

'It's a shallow romance,' Tiffany said, depositing her heaviest case in the hall. 'I'm leaving Jamie.'

'You're what?!' Jack stood aside so that she could properly follow up her dramatic statement with an equally dramatic entrance, breezing through into hallway of the Islington flat and tossing her heels neatly next to his loafers. "tiff…'

'Don't.' her handbag she slung down on the couch, crashing out alongside it. 'I haven't told him yet, of course. But I've made up my mind. I'm finished with him. He's like a kid; a teenager. He even looks like one!'

'Hello Tiffany!' David stuck his head around the door of the living room. 'You want a coffee or something?'

'Tea please,' she wiped at her eyes, which were faintly moist at the edges. Jack sat down on the edge of the couch. 'I mean…'

'He's a little boy,' Tiffany sighed, throwing her head back. 'And all the years I've been waiting for him to grow up and let's face it, if it hasn't happened by now it's never going to.' She glanced at him. He was in his dressing gown, barefoot. 'I expected it to be worse after Phil died,' she said. 'But its four months now, and he's no better. It sounds a little cruel but I thought the grief might…harden him, but it hasn't. Can I stay here tonight?'

He frowned. 'But you don't live with Jamie anyway.'

'I know, but I'm not ready to see him until I'm ready to tell him, which may not be for a little while yet; but I just had to tell someone. My flatmate Elisha, well she's…away, so I couldn't tell her.'

'Well sure you can stay here, for tonight anyway,' Jack spread his hands wide. 'You can have David's bed,' and he turned and reiterated the suggestion around the kitchen door.

David hurried in with a tray filled with cups and biscuits. 'I guess…I mean, if it's just for tonight.'

'I won't get in your way, I promise,' she picked up her designated cup and blew the steam off the surface. 'I just had to get out of Essex for a while.'

'Tell me about it,' Jack grinned.

'You know about your Aunt Amanda, right?' she asked.

'Yeah, mum texted me.'

'Your family's really going through it,' Tiffany said. 'What with little Debbie, and all; you know she had a blazing row with your Uncle Heath the day she came out of hospital? She told him doing an E was the most excitement she'd had since her mum died, and he hit her; nothing too hard, just a slap on the thigh, but even so. You should go and sort things…don't you have an Easter break coming up?'

'We're kind of on it now,' David explained, sitting himself on the couch opposite, traditionally Jack's couch, but since she was on his he didn't have much choice. 'But we have coursework, and Jack and I...well, we're kind of working on a joint special project; my dissertation, as it happens. It's heading for publication.'

Jack blushed, spread his arms wide. 'Uh yeah, so I'd love to help but...'

'S'ok...' she eyed the pair of them suspiciously, then supped a little more of her tea. 'Like I said, it'll just be for tonight. But please don't tell Jamie yet; these sorts of things, you have to pick the right moment, especially where you Woodfields are concerned.'

*

Tiffany had a shower around eleven, and walked around the flat in a towel for about twenty minutes, something Jack didn't mind at all, but David found it rather distracting and in the end he switched 'Newsnight' off and set about making a temporary bed for himself on Jack's couch, which was the longer of the two by about a good foot or so. He'd never been entirely comfortable around girls, and even dear Dorothy had taken a certain amount of getting used to, but Tiffany was something else entirely. She had very large breasts that seemed almost to cry out to be looked at, that and her large saucer-like eyes, her blond hair wet down her back, it was all very comely, and in such an overtly fascinating manner that he found himself taking far longer than he ought to have in finding the sheets necessary to make up the aforementioned bed. He wondered if perhaps somewhere deep down he perhaps wasn't that tiny bit bi-curious.

Around eleven thirty he heard noises coming from the bedroom and went to listen, removing his shoes so he could pad across the carpet in complete silence. Pressing his ear to the door he could hear the sound of one of the beds creaking, slowly at first but building up momentum the more he listened. Clearly they were having sex. He sniffed and stepped back, tried not to cry, and went and sat back down on the couch. After a few moments he curled up in a foetal position and turned the TV back on, with the volume up to drown out any more unwanted noise. At around midnight Tiffany peered around the door. David was watching some documentary on Channel Five about female to male transsexual priests, and he looked up with a start. 'Sorry about that,' she whispered, her face pressed hard against the partition. 'Jack and I...well it's been coming for a long time, you might say.'

'I gathered that...' he found himself welling up again, and before he could say or do anything else she was sitting next to him. 'I'm sorry,' David wiped his eyes with the back of his hand. 'You might say this has been coming for a long time too...'

'Here,' she offered him the edge of her nightie. 'It can't be all that bad, surely.'

'Can't it?' he blew onto the fine pink material. 'I love him.'

'You what?!' her eyes widened; in fact she looked about as shocked as a deer in the headlights.

'I love Jack.' He lowered his voice to a whisper, secure that the bedroom door was shut. 'I have done for…well, for ages, probably the first time I saw him, if you want the truth. Of course he doesn't know. What he'd do if he did find out, I don't know, but I'd rather he didn't, so…'

'…I won't.' she seemed totally thrown by this revelation. 'I mean…look, Jack's very modern and all for an Essex man but exactly how progressive he is, is open to debate.'

'You don't have to spell it out,' David laughed uneasily. 'But I love him as a friend too and I don't want to lose that, so please, don't say anything.'

'I won't.' she placed her hand on top of his. 'Don't worry. I'm sure it will all work out in the end. In fact, you can count on it.'

Jack wandered into the living room at about two thirty in the morning; David was a light sleeper, and had had an eye alert ever since he'd heard the bedroom door being slowly opened. He pretended to be awoken properly by the squeak of his own couch as Jack sat down on it. 'Sorry,' Jack said, 'thought you were out for the count.'

David propped himself up onto his elbow. 'What's up?'

Jack edged forward, then pivoted a little; fresh scratches on his back, so many in fact, that his back looked like it might have belonged to a gamekeeper who'd accidentally freed one of his more ferocious beasts and come off worse in the resulting recapture. 'You got any more of that cream?' he asked.

'Oh god Jack…' David leant forward, as his eyes began adjusting to the dark. 'What is this?!'

'It's called passion, mate.' he sniffed. 'But it sure does smart.'

'I guess I've led a pretty sheltered life,' David got up, navigated his way past the table and into the kitchen, returning a few moments later with the appropriate ointment. 'We're going to have to get some more of this soon, if you and her don't cool it a little,' he said. 'You want me to put it on?'

'Nah mate,' Jack shook his head. 'Better not, you know?'

'Okay.'

They sat in silence for a while, the only sound that of Jack squeezing pea-sized amounts of the stuff onto his fingers and then applying it as best he could. Eventually, after a prolonged struggle, he handed the tube to David. 'Do my back, will you?'

David shifted himself onto the couch and began rubbing the ointment to the scratches further down, these ones, near Jack's buttocks, were again so deep that the blood rose easily to the surface when the cream was applied, and Jack had to put his hand over his mouth to prevent little gasps of pain from issuing through his tightly clenched lips.

'I wonder if Jamie ever suffered like this with her?' he whispered. Outside a car pulled away, and they heard Wolvie scratching on the front door. David went to let him in and then returned a few moments later, the cat now coming to investigate what was going on and jumping up onto Jack's lap, where he curled gracefully under a prolonged chin scratch assault. 'I'd ring him and ask,' he went on, 'but I don't think he'd appreciate the context of the query, you know?'

'Someone's going to get hurt in all this,' David said. He twisted the cap back on the tube and put it to one side. 'I don't want it to be you.'

Jack made a little noise, something between agreement and maybe even a little derision. 'Maybe she's right; maybe Jamie does need to grow up a bit.'

'And you're the one to teach him?'

'It isn't like that,' Jack said. 'Me and 'tiff go back a fair bit ourselves.'

'Jack, she's Jamie's girl. We had this very same conversation only…'

'I know, I know,' he nearly waved him away. From behind David gazed at his beautifully muscled neck, the way the sinew tapered down into those mighty shoulder-blades, then inwards in the classic triangular form of a well-honed physique.

He said, 'Jack, you know I'm here for you, whatever happens?'

Jack nodded. His hand reached back and took David's hand, squeezed it, even the fingers coming into play, tickling his palm. That was the wonderful thing about Jack; not just that he was so touchy-feely with everyone, but that he was totally unselfconscious, even when it came to a gay guy. It was a mixture of innocence, doubtless brought about by the minimum of exposure to homosexuals in Essex, and the sheer belief in his own masculinity, that boiled together to produce such a wonderful temperament. After a minute he sort of sniffed, and said, 'How's the paper coming? The article, I mean.'

'I'm midway through Uncle Phil,' David said. 'There's more detail here because you knew him, so the text is deeper, more intimate.'

Jack made another one of his little noises. He gave David's hand a last reassuring squeeze and then pulled it away; the unselfconscious firmness slid slowly out of David's grasp, but he would never forget what it was like, to have Jack Woodfield hold your hand like that. He watched him go to the door, and then he turned. 'Night, Davey boy,' he said, smiling at him.

The Daddy Dissertation Part 6

By David Samuels

The life and times of Phil Woodfield

By the age of fifteen Phil Woodfield was already 6'1 and cut a dashing and overly manly figure, with his heavy arched eyebrows and his greyish five o'clock shadow, opting for the mod revival look, with his brownish hair spiked up wildly, a long trenchcoat slung over a scruffy suit and tie, topped off with Doc Martens, and on hot days t-shirts instead of the shirt, sporting various slogans of the era. He was still sharing the upstairs bedroom overlooking the street on Vallance Road with his brother Heath, with Beverly in the back bedroom and Aunt Amanda downstairs. Sometime in 1977 Barbara Corbett's eldest daughter Eva, recently widowed, came to stay for a couple of weeks, and ended up living there for seven years. She was a couple of years younger than Amanda and still extremely attractive, with large dark eyes and wavy brown hair. She'd had no children, her husband had killed himself due to debt, and her house had been repossessed. It was Amanda's idea that she come and stay with them, moving from Stoke Newington to Bethnal Green. Although she was thirty six she made almost no bones from the get-go that she found Phil, who was, as said, very physically mature for his age, extremely attractive.

Having Eva around the house meant that Amanda could now work-part time and took up a position in the Woolworths on the Bethnal Green Road merely on a whim, beginning on the tills and then graduating to assistant manager a couple of years later. Phil was just leaving school when Eva came to stay and didn't fall headlong into work, instead preferring to immerse himself in the aftermath of the teen angst rebellion mood the Sex Pistols had stirred up, reinvigorated to some extent by the mod revival that was beginning to sweep the country at the time. Eva was 'recuperating' and spent most her day around the house, doing all the menial chores, on hot days in little more than one of Phil's West Ham strip shirts stretched tight over her rather well-endowed frame. During August neighbours recall incidences of her washing Phil's scooter in little more than the aforementioned shirt, pulled low over her knickers, splashing herself with water from the blue plastic bucket while Phil did work on the tailpipe. Within a matter of weeks they were sleeping together rather indiscreetly; Beverly once found them in her room on arriving home from school and proceeded to blackmail her brother twenty pence a week in order to 'keep schtum'. Eva paid. Phil made no bones about the fact that he had lost his virginity with Eva, and that he was in fact privileged to have such an experienced teacher; she was schooling him in things his other friends could only talk rather uneasily about, thumbing through their pictures of Debbie

Harry and Suzi Quatro. He referred to the arrangement almost as something of a transaction, boasting that she was enjoying the vigour of a healthy young man in the full flush of puberty whilst he was gaining the many years of married experience she had to offer garnered during the sexual liberation of the Sixties.

All hell broke loose when Aunt Amanda came home early with a headache one afternoon and found the two of them 'cavorting' in her bed. Apparently the shouting could be heard from one end of Vallance Road to the other, and moments later she stormed out of the front door and pushed Phil's scooter over into the road, denting the paintwork; according to eyewitnesses she had to be pulled bodily off '...that wretched machine' when she began laying into the spokes with her heels. Phil had a full-scale slanging match with his aunt/adopted mother in the middle of the street, demanding to know why she seemed so determined that he should never have a girlfriend. Amanda tried the route of '...she's old enough to be your mother', but it didn't really wash, Eva all the time slouched in the doorway in a Jam t-shirt, her finger in her mouth, mildly amused by the whole exchange. Amanda responded by stating that she didn't really want to discuss 'family matters' in the middle of the street; matters were made worse when a neighbour shouted out, '...buggering it up the way you did with your kid brother aren't you?!'. Apparently Amanda had to be physically restrained a second time, threatening as she was to scratch the woman's eyes out.

At around 11pm that night more shouting was heard from inside the house. Phil stormed out around midnight, a knapsack in one hand and his trenchcoat in the other. He quickly tied both to the back of his battered scooter, which he then mounted, fired up and sped away on, down Vallance Road and towards Whitechapel. He turned up on his Uncle Richard's doorstep in Brighton during a torrential downpour at around four in the morning, ringing the buzzer repeatedly and not the slightest bit flustered to have the door answered by his uncle in a state of undress, and to find a labourer currently employed fitting arcade machines on the seafront in the master bedroom, smoking a joint. Phil was extremely tired and he apparently broke down when asked by his uncle what had happened. He then sat on the bed with his Uncle Richard and the labourer and whilst helping them finish the joint told them in one long breath that his Aunt Amanda had '...told him he'd never be able to have a normal girlfriend, that was he was going to have to grow up fast, as being a Woodfield male held special connotations, and that, worst of all, any girlfriend he did have was more than likely to become the victim of foul play.'. His Uncle Richard is said to have mused on this as he toked up and then grinned cheekily and said, 'Well I think you've come to the right place, my dear. We offer refuge here to those baptised in the testosterone fount.'

Richard didn't receive a phone call from Amanda until late the next day, as there were simply too many Woodfields, friends and even acquaintances to go through before she figured that Phil might actually take refuge with the person whom he'd only ever in the past referred to as 'my funny uncle'. Since Phil was soon to turn sixteen she didn't threaten Richard with any kind of legalities, but simply told him that, '…by all means have him as your unpaying house guest, but I guarantee you'll be calling me in a week begging me to come and collect him.'

Seven days later and Richard was rather enjoying having his young nephew (or second nephew) around the house, his Purple Hearts records blaring out the front window on the modest little house off St James Street. Richard was at the time involved with the burgeoning gay press in the area, and Brighton itself was fast becoming the 'gay capital' of the south. Phil found his Uncle's rebellious nature rather in line with his own mod revival attitudes, and it wasn't long before Richard had found him a job as an office boy at the local gay information centre, something which would have lasted a lot longer than it did if one of the volunteers hadn't taken such a shine to '…that lovely tall lad with the big brown eyes', and gotten a sock in the jaw from Phil for his troubles. Phil then got a job on Brighton Pier on one of the fairground rides, and didn't go back to Bethnal Green or Barking even until 1979, when he popped by on his way back from a mod weekend in Southend. Aunt Amanda refused to speak to him, but Beverly was overjoyed to see her big brother again and spent hours telling him how awful mods were and that he really ought to give ABBA a try; he conceded and took her 'Arrival' album back with him but returned it by post from somewhere in Hove a week or so later. Before he left London Uncle Rupert slipped him £100 in a folded brown envelope.

When 'Quadrophenia' filmed in Brighton the same year Phil was among many local mods to secure a background part, recreating one of the famous beach scenes of the Sixties. With him and clearly caught on film was a buxom strawberry blond in pretty pink pastels and a large sun bonnet, a girl whom both he and others referred to on more than one occasion as 'Minty Hardcore'. The star of the film, Phil Daniels, was said to have made a pass at this extra during filming but she only had eyes for Phil, in-between takes throwing her arms around his neck and kissing him wildly, one leg raised and arched almost back upon itself. Closer scrutiny of the beach scenes in the film shows Phil and his companion quite clearly, and for prolonged periods. Fortean Times asked an African spirit guide called Chuchie Miyamba Kasongo to examine the film, and she concluded that '…the boy is a powerful witch, and the creature with him is an abomination.' She searched her books on witch familiars – English and otherwise - but could find no reference however, to any such entity by the name of 'Minty Hardcore'.

Phil had any number of girlfriends between 1979 and 1981, but most notable among them was Nancy Smith, who spent her days tossing burgers at a little café near Brighton Pavilion, and her nights all dressed up as a proper mod revival girl in a long black trenchcoat, peroxide hair all fluffed up from being stuffed under the hat she'd worn for the last eight and a half hours. They became known as 'Phil'n'Nancy' pretty soon and were inseparable by the beginning of 1980, when Phil is said to have proposed to her down on one knee on the shingle under the pier after he'd finished his shift on the dodgems. Richard Woodfield found the couple adorable and was quite happy for Nancy to move in, and said he didn't mind in the slightest being kept awake half the night by the bash of Phil's headboard as it pounded repeatedly against the wall next to his own. However, in February of 1980 Nancy was killed when the carriage of the waltzer she was riding on with her several of her girlfriends came loose and flew off the side of the pier and into the sea. The incident made the local papers and was even a footnote in several national tabloids, with Nancy the only fatality, and for a week or so the entire funfair at the end of the pier was closed off whilst extensive safety checks were carried out. Phil was said to be distraught by Nancy's death and would not eat or speak for five whole days, sitting in his room with his legs drawn up close to his chest, rocking backwards and forwards. Aunt Amanda came to visit him and he broke down in her company; she reportedly held him for almost an hour while he sobbed against her shoulder, moving Richard to tears as well when he came into the room with a tray of tea and biscuits. She then spent several days down in Brighton, and the three of them took long walks on the beach together; Amanda brought a scooter helmet from a charity shop on St James Street and Phil drove her up to Beachy Head, where they spread out a West Ham towel and ate ham and cheese sandwiches and drank cider from a flask normally reserved for her lunchtime tea breaks in Woolworths.

Amanda couldn't persuade Phil to return to London with her but she had at least built some bridges between them, and after Nancy's death letters and phone calls were exchanged on a weekly basis, the calls sometimes lasting as much as an hour, and the letters running to fourteen or fifteen handwritten pages, both sides of the sheet filled. However, if his aunt couldn't persuade Phil to return to London then his baby sister Beverly most certainly could, when, in January 1981, aged just fifteen, she announced she was pregnant, that she wasn't going to name the father, and that she fully intended on having the baby. Amanda was by all accounts furious, not so much with Beverly, as she had often been easily led, but with her brother Heath for not keeping an eye on her, and she apparently made his life hell for a number of weeks after the pregnancy was announced. Heath was a rather easy-going individual who, like Phil, was very physically mature for his age, but he seemed in genuine fear of his aunt's wrath, and was reduced to tears on more than one occasion by her furious outbursts.

Phil moved back into the house on Vallance Road but Richard kept his room open for him down in Brighton, and was said to have been extremely upset at Phil's sudden departure, taking the train from Brighton to Victoria Station a week or so later, and then the underground to Bethnal Green, to see if he could offer any assistance. Beverly began to get very large very quickly, relatives spotting before the doctors that she was expecting twins, common enough in the Woodfield family by that time as to be something of a localised medical phenomenon. Boy twins however, were still relatively rare, with most Woodfields ending up with one of each. Amanda and Aunt Delia argued about where the babies should be delivered, Amanda citing the Royal London Hospital, but Delia insisting that Beverly be brought to Barking to give birth, preferably in the front bedroom in the house on the Ripple Road, being due sometime in early July. As it was Jack and Jamie Woodfield were delivered in East Ham Memorial Hospital in the early hours of Saturday 11th July, 1981. The birth presented no problems and Phil was by his baby sister's side during the delivery, holding her hand; in fact the delivery room was full of Woodfields, all of whom cheered and shouted when first one boy was held aloft by the nurse, an enthusiastic Jamaican woman by the name of Joy, and then the other. Eddie Dowden ran out into the street and waved his West Ham rattle until a policeman told him to calm down; upon hearing the reason for the outburst, the policeman then excused him and allowed him to whirl the thing for a further few minutes. Phil was the first to hold both babies, before they'd even been washed down and mere minutes after the cord had been cut; he apparently bemused Joy by searching for 'a particular birthmark' on both boys, locating it pretty quickly in the small of the back of the elder boy, whom Delia's mother Felicity was urging should be called 'Jack'. Phil quickly handed the baby to Beverly and made a beeline for the younger twin, whom he took to the far corner of the room and cooed and fussed over for what seemed like ages, returning him to the nurses to be examined only reluctantly, informing them and indeed his exhausted sister that this was 'Jamie'.

Phil was often caught singing Aneka's 'Japanese Boy' to the wide-eyed gurgling little baby as he lay in his cot in the maternity ward; and for several months after as well (it was a big hit at the time!).

Try as they might the family were never able to prise from Beverly the identity of the father. All she would tell them was that it was someone at school and it had all been 'a silly mistake'. She took to motherhood remarkably well and cheered up considerably when various family members, headed by Phil, clubbed together to buy her a modest flat in the Murphy Estate in Barking, where she lives to this day, usually with one boyfriend or other but more recently alone. Uncle Rupert had initially offered her the house on the Ripple Road but Beverly refused, stating simply that it '…gave her the willies.'

Using money lent to him by Uncle Richard, Phil brought a two-floor flat on the bottom end of nearby Station Parade, where Jamie Woodfield continues to live after his death in 2005.

Phil was eighteen at the time of the twins' birth, and helped his sister out when and where he could, babysitting them so she could still enjoy nights out with her girlfriends, and between the two of them they even persuaded Aunt Delia to have them two days a week despite the fact she had four boys of her own, so Beverly could go on a beauty therapy City & Guilds, which she completed successfully in 1983. No one made such allowances for Hannah or Rachel with their sets of twins.

Felicity died in 1983 at the age of eighty three; she had Alzheimer's in her last few years and had been found more than once in her nightgown by the bandstand or halfway down the Ripple Road in the early hours of the morning talking '...to the empty air', shouting and yelling that '...she should leave our beautiful boys alone'. Delia and Father Brian, along with his wife Betty, took turns caring for her; never was there any mention of putting her in a home, and the entire Woodfield clan turned out for her funeral, where she was interred alongside her father Jeramiah and her mother Karen. At this time Heath was still living in Bethnal Green with Amanda, and was heavily involved with a local girl studying art in Barking college, Sophie Catherall. They were engaged in 1987, married in 1988, and in late 1989 she gave birth to twins, Daniel and Debbie. They moved from Bethnal Green to Barking shortly after the birth, living just off Station Parade on Salisbury Avenue.

Rupert died in 1990 (his wife Michele is said by her friends to have '...escaped from this monster of a family' back in 1978, when she died from breast cancer), but his daughter Rachel decided to stay in the house on the Ripple Road with her twins Michael and Tracey, where she lives to this day.

Phil doted on his nephew Jamie constantly; when he was just seven months old he brought him his first West Ham strip, a special line in toddler clothes the club had only just started up at the time. Many locals who didn't know they were brother and sister assumed Phil to be the father when he was seen out walking with Beverly, the twins in their stroller and their matching hats, one blue and one purple. Although she had a long line of boyfriends after the twins were born Beverly refused to settle down and this caused something a ruck between her and Phil, and in 1984 when Jamie was still a toddler and recovering from a rather nasty and sudden bout of scarlet fever, she made the drastic decision of allowing Phil to take him to live with him just a couple of hundred yards away in the Station Parade flat, now referred to by one and all as 'the Daddy flat'. With less of a workload Beverly brightened considerably, and went to work part-time at a hairdresser's on East Ham's own Station Parade.

Rather disconcertingly was the fact that the twins didn't seem to miss each other at all; some twins were like that, Father Brian said when he christened them. Some were inseparable, he told the congregation, whereas others couldn't stand the sight of each other. The whole family seemed to support Phil's taking Jamie in, although his argument that Beverly's reams of 'men friends' were upsetting to the twins seemed a little flaccid given his own subsequent dalliances with almost every girl working the East Street market, and a little more besides. Phil refused to send Jamie to nursery, declaring that he could amuse the child far better than some paid-up 'do-gooder'. There is a charming photograph taken in 1984 of Phil and the then three year old Jamie, shot by Father Brian's eldest son Casey, the toddler sat on Phil's lap in the stands at Upton Park, a little purple and blue bobble hat on his head and a delighted expression on his face. Phil is staring down at the boy with his big brown eyes, looking to all the world like the proudest father there ever was. But where Phil doted endlessly on Jamie, the rest of the family seemed to gravitate almost naturally towards Jack. Beverly was always saying how her eldest son – as if she only had the one - was headed for 'great things', and she began to lay out a meticulous plan of action for his schooling and subsequent further education soon after Jamie left, most of which, to her credit, has come true. Rachel was even persuaded to sign the house on the Ripple Road over to Jack in her will, over her own son Michael.

Phil enrolled Jamie in the West Ham youth academy when he was just five, and on Saturday afternoons, home matches or away, the entire male Woodfield local clan, numbering some thirty-odd individuals, and often including girlfriends and other assorted mates, would descend on Upton Park and then end up in the Barking Dog, drinking 'til last orders and then on with the occasional lock-in. Phil went through a number of odd jobs in the early Eighties, working for a while as a handyman, until he got in trouble for bedding the wife of a local Barking councillor, whose drains he'd been paid to clear on the cheap. Following this he tried his hand at office work based on a reference from Uncle Richard, but was said to been '...bored shitless' by the whole affair. Like his Aunt Amanda he was able to live quite comfortably off these odd jobs simply because the Woodfields, through means that others found frankly bemusing, could... 'make fivers multiply in their pockets!' or so one of Phil's drinking partners in the Barking Dog said of him; 'get two tenners in his wallet and they're like a couple of rabbits, 'coz when he opens it up later, there'll be four, and make no mistake!'

Phil finally seemed to settle down when he began working in a second-hand record shop on East Street, one that was eventually taken over and became one of the chain of Superdrug stores. This record shop was a bit of nostalgia-fest for mods of the Sixties and Seventies and he was soon managing the place part-time. Often he'd bring Jamie with him and the boy would sit on the counter and play with his Star Wars figures whilst Phil exchanged reminiscences of filming 'Quadrophenia' on Brighton beach with various customers. Nancy's sister came to visit in the summer of 1985 and Phil had a brief fling with her as well.

Jamie's early education seems to have been somewhat haphazard, with, according to staff reports, Phil only bringing Jamie in '…when there was nothing more exciting that they could be doing.'

Phil began seeing a girl called Rose Hamilton sometime in the late 80s, an on/off thing for a while but it soon became serious enough for her to move in with him and Jamie around 1989. The family got on extremely well with Rose, once she'd passed the initial test for one of Phil's girlfriends of not being given her marching orders after a two-month trial period, the usual time slot during which Phil got bored of his girls and was off looking for 'the latest model'. Rose was a stunning and leggy blond with pouty, bee-stung lips years before bee-stung became fashionable. Jamie got on well with her, but never enough to call her 'mum'; maybe he'd been too burnt by getting attached to the previous girlfriends.

'The Daddy flat', in which the three of them lived, was large and airy, an initial staircase leading to double doors with opened to the left onto a modernised kitchen, and to the right onto the living room. A staircase in the kitchen led up to the two bedrooms and the bathroom. Beverly's flat on the Murphy Estate had a larger living room, a slightly smaller kitchen with a handy service hatch, two bedrooms and a bathroom. Jack seemed entirely happy there but the twins still played together most days of the week, although more often than not they ended up fighting; on one occasion Jack kicked Jamie in the shin and took all the skin off, and on another Jamie pushed Jack off his bike the day Beverly took the stabilisers off, causing him to chip three of his front teeth. The boys both went to St. Margaret's primary school, along with Delia's sons Clay, Springer, Nick, and Hayden (Delia's four sons being the modern version Jake Woodfield's 'the Woodfield boys'); also in attendance were Rachel's twins Michael and Tracy; Hannah's eldest, Sara, and Father Brian's two youngest, Jessica and Bobby. Father Brian's eldest, Casey, left in the term before the twins began, and straight away applied for a grant to open a photography studio on Station Parade, which he still runs to this day.

Jack excelled at almost every subject put his way but Jamie proved exceedingly slow, although no one seemed to have noticed by the age of ten or eleven that he could barely even write his own name, and seemed far more interested in playing football after school – or during school sometimes – than with excelling academically. Jack embraced school wholeheartedly, although he was savvy enough not to end up being labelled 'teacher's pet', and still played football with the cousins after class, although some said that his heart obviously wasn't in it. He got on very well with his second or third cousin Jessica, and she seemed to share his ideas that they would get out of Essex one day and move on to something a whole lot better.

On Saturdays when West Ham weren't playing, and usually out of season, Phil would often take the entire junior Woodfield clan, usually comprising a core of Jamie, Jack, Springer, Clay, Hayden, Nick, Michael, Tracy, Jessica, Bobby, and Sara into the West End for cinema trips, museum trips (very occasionally), and on one or two occasions further afield, to Chessington or Thorpe Park. Around forty five Woodfields descended on Chessington World of Adventures in the hot summer of 1990; Jack and Jamie had a fight in the queue for the Vampire ride, and a badly misjudged punch from the former landed nearby Nick Woodfield with a nice gap in his front teeth when he tried to intervene; Aunt Delia was sick after going on the Runaway Train ride; and a panic was caused when a woman in the changing rooms picked up Heath and Sophie's daughter Debbie thinking it was her own, whilst the family therefore walked around with this other woman's baby for over an hour before they realised that she was actually a he, when another change was rather prematurely called for, and the alarm was raised.

At almost no point during this time did the paths of the core family in Barking cross with those of 'the Hackney Woodfields', descendants of 'Great-Uncle' Russell. Although Hackney has had a 'colourful' social history to say the least, the Hackney Woodfields never-the-less looked down their noses on the Barking Woodfields, what little contact there was usually coming by with Aunt Amanda acting as a go-between. The Hackney Woodfields aspired to great things and many of them moved into education, becoming teachers, lecturers, welfare workers, and the like. They seem to have viewed the Barking Woodfields as 'eccentric', and 'not all there' in certain matters. The Hackney Woodfields were also very savvy in all things monetary, and to this day they own several shops and small businesses in the Hackney and Dalston areas, one hotel, and have two family members in their local council, and one training to be a lawyer, whereas the Barking Woodfields, for all their popularity in Essex, seem, Jack aside, to aspire to little more than running stalls on the East Street market.

By the mid Nineties the number of Woodfields marrying and/or having children had calmed down a little from what it had been in the Seventies and early Eighties, the exceptions being Heath and his wife Sophie with their twins Daniel and Debbie, and Casey, who married Tamsin Parish from Bow in 1998; their daughter Meggan was born in 2001 and as of this writing she is said to be expecting a second girl. Although relatives urged Phil and Rose to at the very least get engaged they seemed quite happy to live together 'in sin', as Aunt Delia referred to it behind brother Brian's back, with nudge and a wink.

Chapter 28

Wednesday 3rd May 2006

An enormous spiral staircase wound its way down the centre of the library at the London School of Economics, huge flared steps covered in plush rug that students would often tackle instead of taking the lift in order to burn the calories off from the previous night's excesses. Jack was staring at a girl considering taking the lift as she all but staggered up to the second floor landing, the huge steps hitching her skirt up each time she attempted to move forward, affording him a near perfect view of the navy blue lace of her knickers, although the gentle bounce of her breasts as she navigated her way onwards was far more enticing. A shadow fell across his contemplations and the pencil he'd been twanging against his teeth abruptly fell onto the keyboard of his laptop, stirring the silent musings of several other students nearby. His Aunt Hannah was standing over him, a rather statuesque bottle blond with a stern face in her late forties, well made-up, a fake Louis Vuitton handbag slung over her shoulder. Her arms were folded and the bangles on her wrist broke the silence almost excruciatingly as she rhythmically strummed the fingers of her left arm onto the forearm of her right.

'Hello Jack,' she said, her voice just about the loudest thing in the immediate vicinity.

'Uh...Aunt Hannah,' he rose, wincing as the fabric of his shirt brushed over the scratches on his back. He made a move to guide her to somewhere more discreet, a move she resisted. 'What brings you here?'

'Our Laquisha,' she said, still strumming.

'Is she ok?' a note of concern rose in his voice, genuine.

'Oh she's fine, no thanks to you,' Aunt Hannah pulled up a chair, ignoring the disgruntled look of the girl adjacent, who was clearly not used to having her study time interrupted by family disputes. 'She's at home today when she should be at work, though.'

'She is?' he closed the examination studies file he's been perusing and then closed the lid of his laptop as well.

'She is,' she nodded, reaching for her cigarettes.

'Uh, you can't smoke in her, Aunt Hannah,' Jack cringed.

'Fine,' she reached for the Nicorette gum. 'Want one?'

'I'll pass; so, Laquisha...?'

Aunt Hannah crossed her legs. 'She's at home. While she was at work yesterday, on the tills in ASDA, a customer said she'd charged her twice for something, a bloody packet of Corn Flakes or something. Now my Laquisha hadn't, but even if she accidentally had that's not the point. This woman called her 'a fucking nigger', and then she threw the packet of flour she'd brought all over her, and told her that 'that look' suited her much better.'

The girl adjacent put her hand over her mouth. 'You're joking,' Jack said.

'No I'm not. The woman legged it, and they gave Laquisha the rest of the day – this was yesterday – and today off. And you know what the first thing she said was when she called me?'

'No...' but it was sure to involve either him in a rather disparaging sense, or a testimony to Uncle Phil, if not both.

'...that it wouldn't have happened if Phil had been around, but since it isn't...well, it wouldn't have happened if you'd been around.'

The girl adjacent was clearly lost on this point but she fixed Jack with an accusatory stare anyway. 'Aunt Hannah...I'm here,' he shrugged. 'It's awful what happened but...well, what do you expect me to do about it?!'

'...what do I?!' she was aghast. 'You know damn well what I think about it, young man.'

'Actually I don't,' he scratched his hair, the buzz cut grown out slightly and swept over in a Fifties retro style that gave him a rather more dashing, cinematic appearance.

She leant forward and he caught a whiff of the fake scent she'd probably picked up on the East Street market, several stalls down from her own, no doubt. 'The Daddy, Jack Woodfield,' she said. The girl made an audible gasp; obviously she hadn't figured that someone as popular as Jack would abandon his own mixed race daughter to suffer a racist attack; despite having the wrong end of the stick entirely she shut down the file she was working on and gave the two of them her undivided attention.

'Well I'm not her 'Daddy',' Jack sighed, cooling down a little. 'I'm not anyone's daddy. I'm just me, trying to get on with my life. MY life, you get?'

Aunt Hannah folded her arms, cleared her throat. 'You are a selfish little git, Jack Woodfield.'

'No,' he said, 'I'm just a normal fella trying to get on with his life and not bowing down to some crazy notion a sad old Essex family has about enforced patriarchy,' and he sat back, confident he'd dazzled her with his deft take on things.

'Don't you come the clever dick with me,' she said, hoisting her handbag up onto her shoulder. 'You know how it is; how it's always been.'

'Yeah?' he raised an eyebrow, unaware his voice was raising too. 'Well things change. It's called progress. You might try and spread the word a little when you get off at Barking Underground and trot on down Station Parade to that dreary little market.'

'As dreary as all that?' she raised an eyebrow. 'Funny. We've been seeing you around a lot more lately, at least, when Tiffany's around...'

'Yeah?' he deflected this easily, but his mind raced as to why Tiffany had been talking when they'd mutually sworn their 'dalliances' to the utmost secrecy. 'Well I guess you all have nothing else to do except gossip, but leave me out of all the silly little fantasies, will you?'

'Tradition, Jack,' she fixed a finger and the long painted nail at the end of it firmly against his chest. 'It's all about tradition, and even you can't escape that, with all your brains and your books.' And that said she turned on her heel and made to leave.

'Aunt Hannah?' Jack rose from his seat, glaring across at the girl, who abruptly made to turn her laptop back on.

'Mmmmmm?' Aunt Hannah turned back, her tongue in her cheek.

'Tell Laquisha I'll pop over, by the weekend at the latest.'

Jack took to his couch upon arriving back at the flat in Islington, and refused to move there for the rest of the evening. Tiffany sat on the floor by his head, her left hand lolled up and the fingers absent-mindedly playing with his newly grown hair. 'I think you should shave it again,' she said, her eyes fixed on the TV, on some programme about female body dysmorphia. 'It's ever so butch, the crop.'

He sniffed, and rubbed his nose with the back of his hand. 'Go get the clippers then,' he said. 'They're under the sink. David usually does it for me, but he's researching 'til late at the British Library tonight. He got his membership last week, and he can't keep away.'

She turned, her eyebrow raised. 'So we're alone?'

He nodded. 'Yup.'

'That awful Dorothy isn't coming over, is she?'

'Hey, she's alright, is D!' Jack propped himself up onto his elbow. 'She's a good...'

'...a good what?'

'...a good egg,' he caught that look. 'I haven't screwed her, if that's what you're asking.'

'Well that's a first,' Tiffany got up, smiling. 'A female Jack hasn't fucked.'

'Go get the clippers,' he said, grinning. Whilst she rooted among the pots and pans he followed her out, pulled up a chair from the kitchen table and found a spare towel in the ironing and draped it over his shoulders, then sat down.

She found the clippers, put the no.1 guard on, plugged them in, and stood over him.

'Take your shirt off,' she said.

'Why?'

'You'll get hair all over it.'

He sighed, and pulled the light striped Fred Perry number over his head and slung it on the table. 'Better?'

'Very,' her fingers slid down his shoulder and into the thick dark blond chest hair, curling it, scratching at the taut muscle underneath. 'What a gorgeous hairy chest you've got, Jack. It drives me wild.'

'Shut up and shave,' he said, with a wink. Then he turned up and looked at her, and said, 'I know you love it when I boss you around.'

'Love it?' she said. 'It's trickling down my leg, is what it is!'

'Oh 'tiff!!'

She began cutting. 'You're in a mood,' she said. 'You have been since you got back. What's up?'

'My Aunt Hannah...'

'The stern one?'

'That's the one.'

'Jamie doesn't like her much; he keeps out of her way.'

'Can't say as I blame him. Well she had a go at me, 'coz someone had a go at Laquisha, called her a 'nigger'. I tell you, if Hayden weren't in the nick there'd have been a murder in that ASDA when it happened; did I ever tell you what he did to this boy who called her that in school?'

'Knowing your cousin Hayden I imagine it was something awful,' she said, and shaved a little harder.

'He set this boy on fire.'

'Really?'

'Yup. Awful, it was. Of course no one grassed him up.'

'Well you don't, do you? boys, I mean.'

'Well exactly,' he said, 'he always brought 'the Barking boy' mentality out in me. Still,' he sniffed, 'despite his many faults, he's my closest 'cuz; my 'bruddah', that's what we call each other.'

'You miss him?'

Jack nodded. 'Yeah.'

'Never mind, my pet,' she finished shearing and blew the hair off the top of his head.

He laughed. 'What's this 'my pet' lark?!'

Tiffany's left leg cocked. 'I don't know...' and she held the little round blue mirror up. 'There. What do you think?'

'Cheers,' he nodded. 'It does suit me, yeah.' And he got up, and turned to face her.

'Hold me,' she said, and she seemed almost to wilt as he towered over her. 'Put your big, hairy arms around me, and squeeze me like a zit!'

He laughed. 'You're so weird lately.'

'You've been away from Barking so long,' she curled her fingers into his chest hair again, 'you just forgot.'

'No,' he said. 'Something's...different.'

She raised an eyebrow, and then suddenly picked up the clippers and turned them on, moving them toward his chest. 'What are you doing?!' he said.

'Let me shave your chest,' she said.

'I thought you liked it!'

'I do! it'll grow back even hairier if I shave it with these!!'

He shook his head, laughing. 'You are crazy, Tiffany Grieve. I don't know what's the matter with you, but I think you're crazy.'

She moved her hands up, around his thick neck, and locked them behind it. 'I am,' she said. 'But do you love me?'

He paused. 'I...'

'Well I love you,' she said. 'That's what the matter is. I love you, and I always have...' and she closed her eyes and brushed her lips slowly over his. 'And if I don't have you,' she said with a giggle, playing he felt sure on his teasing accusations of mock insanity, 'if I don't have you, simply awful things will happen.'

He resisted a moment, the mention of Jamie seconds ago circumcising his desire, but when her breasts pressed against his own he lifted her up, onto the table, and his hands went up her skirt, and her panties then came down over her knees.

Chapter 29

Thursday 4th May 2006

Uncle Heath had a date on Thursday night, so Jamie swapped his evenings over and spent the evening with cousin Casey, his wife Tamsin, along with their little girl Meggan, at their house on Somerby Road, just around the corner from Uncle Heath's. Tamsin was showing her pregnancy a little more than when he'd last seen her, and the bump even stuck out from underneath her plastic pinny as she prepared the dinner of cold chicken and salad; temperatures in London had topped twenty five degrees today and no one was much in the mood for anything overly hot. Jamie and little Meggan, all blond curls and ribbons, were on the 'PlayStation' in the front room, both cross-legged, brows furrowed deep in concentration as they gave their thumbs a good working out. Casey was in his studio in the basement developing some a portfolio for a well-paying customer.

The phone rang and Tamsin took it on the extension in the kitchen. She talked for about five minutes or so and then when the call was finished came and sat on the edge of the sofa. 'Oh dear me,' she sighed, brushing her hair back over her ear.

's'up?' Jamie asked, his eyes not veering from the screen.

'Casey's little brother...'

'...Bobby?'

'Uh huh. Seems he's decided to tell his dad he's gay and was just letting us know before he went ahead and did it; now I'm as sophisticated as your next West End girl gone east, but Brian...well, he's a man of the cloth and all, *and* an Essex man. Bit of a no-no really, I would have thought.'

'Bobby is gay?!'

'Oh Jamie!' she sighed, 'as if you didn't know. He's never had a girlfriend, he likes Doctor Who...do I really need to go on?'

'Well no...' Jamie froze the screen despite a squeal of protest from little Meggan. He was faking it despite the fact that it was about the worse kept secret in the family, faking it for reasons that escaped him at present, but probably had to something to do with the fact that Tamsin got on well with Bobby, even if he was a dirty rotten queer. 'Does Casey know?' he asked.

'Of course!' she laughed. 'We all know! Betty knows, Jessica knows; it's just his father who doesn't.'

'Well I didn't know either.' He pursed his lips, and tried not to think of the time Hayden had taken Laquisha's lipstick on her say-so, and painted it on the dozing Bobby's lips when he'd fallen asleep on a family picnic in St. Margaret's park, and let him walk around with it on for about ten minutes before someone saw and wiped it off. 'I didn't think there were any gay Woodfields,' he went on.

'What's a gay, mummy?' little Meggan asked.

'Well, it's...' she broke off as Casey came through the door, still in his shirt and tie, albeit loosened at the collar; cousin Casey, as big and burly as Uncle Heath, but his features somewhat softer, and his dark brown hair more styled; cleaner cut, really. 'Ah,' she said, 'your father can explain to you,' and she hopped off the arm of the chair. 'I need to see how the chicken is doing.'

'Oh what's this I can explain?' Casey picked his daughter up and planted a kiss on her cheek. 'What are you and mummy hiding from daddy?!'

'Bobby,' Jamie piped up, sipping his fresh orange juice. 'I mean, well they say every family has one...'

'Oh right,' Casey half grinned. 'Yeah, he's 'one'.'

'He says he's going to tell your father,' Tamsin called out from the kitchen. 'Now I think you should be there if he does, in case he flies off the handle, because you know Betty won't be able to handle him and he'll only go on at her because she knew anyway.'

'Couldn't 'jess do it?' he sighed. 'She has lots of gay friends up West, doesn't she?'

'Well really Jack should be there,' Jamie sighed. 'I mean, duty and all. That's what Aunt Hannah says, and she's spitting chips 'coz Laquisha got accosted in ASDA and a woman called her a nigger, and so Aunt Hannah went to see him at his fancy university, and did he come back with her to help?! did he heck as like.'

'Oh Jamie!!' Tamsin was serving up. 'It's so cute the way you two pretend to have no time for each other but really, well I bet you're a platonic little love story all your own, aren't you?!'

'Oh gross!' he gasped, and Meggan squealed with delight as he pulled an overly exaggerated denial expression in her direction.

'I'll call mum after dinner,' Casey decided, pulling up the chairs. 'I mean, I have nothing against gays and all, but...'

'...he's your little brother,' Tamsin served up his dinner first, threatening to drop the salad right into his lip with just a gentle tilt of the spoon. 'You do right by him, or mummy won't be so nice to you, will she?'

'No she won't,' Meggan nodded, strumming her knife and fork up and down on the table.

'Anything else I've missed out on?' Casey said with a little grin.

'Well...let's see now,' she ladled out Jamie's next. 'Oh, your cousin Marie has a lovely new boyfriend; his name's Scott, and he works in the library in the Vicarage Fields...'

'A librarian?!' Jamie made a face.

'He's very cute,' Tamsin went on. 'Looks Italian, so I've heard; dark eyes, dark hair, chiselled...' she put her chin on her fist and stared into the distance with mock longing, then caught Casey's eye and winked. 'Anyway, she's made up about it.'

'I love Marie,' Jamie said through a mouthful of potato and chicken.

'I love Marie,' little Meggan nodded.

'Well I love Marie too,' Casey concluded. 'And I guess that means we all love Marie then. Good for her.'

Jamie glanced at the TV; he still found it odd that they ate dinner without it on in the background, but it was probably a habit Casey had taken from his dad; at St. Margaret's they all ate dinner in almost abject silence, one of the reasons he never took up their invitations to visit. 'Aunt Amanda's back home today,' he said. 'After her fall, I mean. She rung me, said she's got me a kitten, says I need company in the flat now that Uncle Phil's not there.'

'Aunt Amanda's a witch!' little Meggan said suddenly, glancing around for a reaction.

'Oh Meggan!' Tamsin laughed, glancing at Casey, but he wasn't smiling

'Eat your salad,' he said, reaching over with his own knife and fork to mix it up with her chicken. 'There's a good girl.'

'Does she wear a pointy hat?' Meggan went on, fixing her eyes on Jamie. 'Does she have a broomstick?'

'Meggan, that's enough...' Casey's brow furrowed.

'She's making Jamie into a witch too!' she giggled. 'Like Harry Potter!'

'Right,' Casey stood up, 'to your room, now.'

'Casey...' Tamsin sighed, exhaling heavily.

Jamie kind of concentrated on his chicken as Meggan burst into tears and was escorted up the stairs by her father, wailing and protesting along the lines of '...but she is a witch!! Everyone says so!' all the way. He waited until they were out of earshot before turning to Tamsin. 'Sorry,' he said sheepishly.

'No worries,' she threw him a wink. 'You know I think this whole family's barmy sometimes, but hey, I'm a sucker for tall, dark men, and at 6'4 your cousin kind of swept me off my feet so I kind of have to deal with it...'

Jamie giggled, and then noticed she was holding herself. 'You ok?'

'Just a little...cramp,' she seemed uncertain. 'Eating too fast, I think.'

'I bet being pregnant is weird,' he said. 'I can't imagine it. And as for giving birth....'

'Tell me about it,' she rose from her chair a little unsteadily, then looked down at the seat, her face curdling in horror. The space below was wet with a little red circle of blood, and the slow but steady trickle of it from Tamsin herself was just audible over the distant wailing of Meggan's tantrum. 'Oh god,' she put her hand against the wall. 'Jamie...Jamie, get Casey.'

Jamie sprang out of his seat, opened the door to upstairs and took them three at a time. Tamsin steadied herself against the wall, but when a sudden, larger gush of blood began to issue she sank back down into her chair and began to sob.

Chapter 30

Friday 5th May 2006

David was awoken at around 6:45am – only a quarter of an hour before the alarm was due to go off anyway – to the sound of Jack groaning and then suddenly yelping, hands out as if to ward off an imaginary assailant. He propped himself up onto his elbow and peered over the partition between their two beds. Jack was having a nightmare, and not a wank, as he'd first hoped might be the case; Jack had once boasted that he never wanked as a point of principal, that he simply had far too many willing partners to ever consider entertaining such a 'juvenile idea'. He was talking too, and through the stream of mainly indecipherable words David heard a few things along the line of, '…mum no, no please, Aunt Hannah…mmmmm' staying here…keep away you all, keep away; not you Tiffany, not you…part time Daddy? No help! No help me!!' and at that point he woke, tossing the covers off with a decidedly unmanly little shriek, and then slumped back in a cold sweat, chest heaving, left leg twitching.

'Wow.' David cleared his throat, then reached forward and turned the alarm off. 'You ok?'

'Um…yeah,' Jack struggled to rise, 'God, that was a doozy. What was I saying?'

'I think you have Daddy issues,' David grinned, 'something about your Aunt Hannah as well?'

'Yeah,' he wiped at his forehead and seemed shocked by the clingy film of sweat that came off on the back of his hand. 'I told you the old battle-axe had a go at me right in the middle of the fucking library the other day.' he reached into his side drawer and pulled out a pair of Gucci briefs. 'And then, in this nightmare, they were coming at me, all my family, arms outstretched like zombies, all begging for help, begging for me to look after them and I'm like, '…get to fuck!!', but they wouldn't listen! They tried to consume me.'

'What's the Freudian take on a dream like that?'

Jack stood up, stretched. He went to the window and opened it, whistling for Wolvie. 'Fuck knows,' he said. 'It can't be internalised, 'coz I externalised all that shit on a daily basis.'

'Check your mobile,' David said, reclining momentarily and enjoying the view. 'There might be news about your cousin Tamsin and her baby.'

'Mum would've rung on the landline if there was any news,' Jack replied, switching his Nokia on anyway. A moment later he flashed in front of David's face a text from his mum, the two words 'no news' emblazoned over the 'buxom babe' screensaver. 'Told ya,' he said, and slung it on the sheets. 'Get the fry up on,' he said, jostling David's shoulder. 'There's a good chap!'

'Sausages?'

Jack trotted off into the bathroom, doubtless to splash his face with cold water. 'Yup!' he called out.

'Peas?'

'Sure,' he sure to be applying a liberal amount of the Clinique toning balm Jessica had sent him from her first week on the company's counter in Selfridges, and rubbing it into his pores.

David rose and pulled open his side drawer, selecting his t-shirt and underwear for the day. 'Eggs like titties?' he asked.

'Always with the eggs like titties,' Jack would be giving it the big, cheesy grin as he said that. And now he was rinsing with mouthwash, David could hear the cap being unscrewed and then filled, and then he would give his teeth a cursory brush, and then probably examine his reflection in the little round mirror that stuck out of the wall like a kind of reclining lever. Jack's beard grew quite dark for a natural blond, and as David tried to walk casually past the bathroom door he saw him running a disposable razor over it a couple of times, then sponging it down with cold water. Wolvie was waiting in the kitchen for his breakfast, something David always did first, before boiling the kettle and sugaring a couple of mugs. He failed to register until it was too late Jack, still in his briefs, creeping up behind him, throwing both arms around his waist at the moment of discovery, grinding his crotch up against him and asking, 'Do I get a newspaper with the fry-up, darling?!'

'Don't!!' David swiped out and nearly scalded himself in the process. 'Just don't Jack, ok?!'

'What?!' Jack folded his arms, and then seemed to think of a better idea, leaning against the counter and slowly flexing his ample right bicep. ''coz you don't like it...or 'coz you do?'

'Just don't,' David tried to hide his hard-on but in a pair of tight fitting GAP briefs it was kind of futile. 'Shit,' he said, and turned away.

'Hey mate, its ok,' Jack patted him on the back. 'I'm cool; I'm metrosexual now, you dig? Plus I'm the Daddy, in theory at least. I can take it. I know I'm a hunk, so be cool. I was baptised in a testosterone spring, so they tell me.'

'The fact that you didn't wink after that last statement is a little alarming,' David said.

'Which one? the Daddy, or the testosterone spring?!'

'Either!' he laughed uneasily. 'Now can we change the subject?' he made a beeline for a pair of his unironed trousers slung over the table, hurriedly putting them on, and tucking his embarrassment as far out of sight as possible. 'You want mushrooms?'

'Sure,' Jack began posing, then dropped onto the linoleum and commenced doing a quick series of press-ups, one-handed, switching from left to right every five repetitions or so.

David bit his lip, becoming quite transfixed by the sight of the muscles of Jack's thick, hairy forearms rippling and tensing. 'Bacon?'

'Please.' he stopped doing the press-ups and sat back, folding his arms behind his head and beginning a series of crunches. 'Just to verify,' he said between repetitions, 'because us straight blokes are curious that way, and you might've mentioned it before and all, but are you Arthur or Martha?'

'Um...' David slid the bacon into the pan, and followed it on with a little lump of lard to get it going. 'Martha, I guess...didn't I tell you that the time I was rubbing cream into your back, and you thought I was going to try and slip it to you?!'

'Ah yes, he takes it up the shitter!!' Jack sprang to his feet, a grin from ear to ear, and then obviously caught the pained glance David threw him. 'Sorry mate.' He came up behind him again and rested a hand gently on his shoulder. 'I'd slip you a Woodfield sausage myself, but you know I prefer the pussy; and the titties. Let's never forget the titties.'

'Turn the radio on,' David nodded to the battered portable next to the cat litter tray. 'Don't you want to hear about how the BNP did in Barking? None of your family would have voted for them, surely?'

'No way,' Jack sat down at the table, 'especially not with what happened to Laquisha the other day. And if any of them did, well I'd box their heads in; heck, Aunt Hannah would box their heads in for me.'

David turned, beaming. 'That sounds like Daddy talk!'

'It does?!' he made a face. 'Shit.'

'With this run of bad luck you might want to nip back more often than you do,' David went on. 'They need you at the moment, it's obvious. Isn't the Daddy supposed to be around in times of crisis?'

Jack was examining the flex of his left bicep and comparing it to his right, disgruntled by the minute difference in the bulge. 'Eh?'

There was a knock at the door. 'Postman probably,' David cracked the eggs into the pan, pouring a little pepper on them. 'Can you get it?'

'Or it might be Tiffany,' Jack sprung up, 'she can't get enough of it, you know!'

On receipt of these words David set the eggs to cook and followed him through, praying his prediction was right and that Jack's wasn't. Tiffany had gone home late last night, back to Barking, but not before spending the majority of the evening curled up in Jack's lap in much the same way Wolvie often did, and running her hand over his hair and commenting constantly on what a good job she'd done with his crop.

Jack strutted through the living room, to the front door, pulling it open, revealing his young cousin Daniel, dumpy, dishevelled and red-eyed, and clutching against his chest a little Nike rucksack, gazing forlornly up at them. 'Jack,' he said, voice full of woe. 'I've run away. Debbie told dad it was me who gave her that duff E, and he whacked me. So I ran away last night, got the Night Bus all the way here, but I fell asleep and ended up in Trafalgar Square!'

'Danny boy…' Jack scratched the back of his head, peering past him and up the stone steps. 'Geez, little fella…'

'Can I come in? Tiffany said you'd understand,' Daniel pushed past him. 'She was here the other night, right? And you said I could come 'round whenever I wanted. You gave me your address and email and everything.'

'Seven am wasn't what I had in mind…' Jack followed him into the living room, whilst David framed himself strategically in the kitchen doorway, like one half of a concerned couple.

Daniel dumped his rucksack in the middle of the floor and shrugged. 'But you're the Daddy, Jack. Despite what you say; you're the Daddy. You haven't got a girl here, have you?'

'Mate…' Jack took him by the shoulders. 'I'm not the Daddy. Really, I'm not. And no, I haven't got a bird here.'

'You are the Daddy.' Daniel was gazing around, taking in everything. 'Everyone knows it.'

'Well ok, so I'm meant to be, but…'

Daniel turned and looked up at him. His face began to twitch, his eye first, and then his lower lip, and he began to cry. In a vain attempt to disguise the fact he moved forward suddenly and buried his head against Jack's shoulder, and seemed to be pretending that it was some sort of impromptu hug, although he could barely get his chunky little arms to link up, even around Jack's waist. 'It's all gone to fuck,' he sobbed, turning his head to the side so his words weren't drowned in Jack's chest hair. 'Dad hates me,' he sniffed, glancing up at him, 'and they say Tamsin's gonna lose her baby; Bobby's a queer; Laquisha's scared that the BNP are gonna beat her up…it's all gone to fuck, Jack.' And the sobs became more real now, more violent, and his whole body shook, and Jack wrapped his own arms around the boy and comforted him, whispering and shushing in his ear.

*

The sun wasn't as hot as it had been yesterday, the air not quite so heavy, but it was still nice enough to take a walk from Jack's flat instead of catching the bus, setting off down Offord Road at a leisurely pace, turning right then left, and hitting Upper Street just as the afternoon sun did. Daniel ran on a little ahead of Tiffany, then slowed his step while she set her sunglasses in place, then kept a more discreet pace. 'The shops here are so cool,' he said. 'I could live here. Do you live here now, 'tiff? With Jack, I mean? And if you do, does Jamie know?'

'No I don't, and no he doesn't,' she said. 'I just visit. A lot.'

'Uh huh…' he undid his hoodie and slung it over his shoulder. 'So are you and Jack…'

She smiled. '…yes we are. And that's between him and me, and you and David, and no one else besides.'

'I think that David is a queer,' Daniel shielded his eyes from the sun as it bounced off the side of a passing no.38 bus, 'the way he looks at Jack...gives me the creeps.'

'Doesn't it just.'

'You think so too?'

'Hhhmmm?' Tiffany lowered her sunglasses, hoisted the straps of her flimsy dress up. 'I was thinking,' she said, resting her hand on his shoulder, 'that you need to lose some weight, young man. You're a little...'

'...chunky?'

'Lardy was the word I was looking for.'

His face fell, but then sprang up as though buoyed by the very flab she'd just condemned. 'Bobby's a queer too, you know,' he went on. 'Everyone knows, except his dad. I reckon he's gonna run away as well. He might end up at Jack's too, and he can get it together with that David!'

'You talk too much,' she sighed. 'Take it easy. I didn't agree to baby-sit just so's I could have my eardrums assaulted by your erudite little opinions.'

'Sorry,' he shrugged. 'Everyone says I talk too much, but in our family there's always so much to talk about. What does 'erudite' mean?'

'Isn't that true. And I was being ironic.'

'Where are we going?' he asked, suddenly cottoning on to the fact that here he was walking down Upper Street with one of the fittest birds in Barking, even if she was older, taller, and strictly off limits. He puffed his chest out and lifted up his chin. 'Are we gonna go for something to eat? Pizza Hut?'

'Daniel,' Tiffany placed a hand lightly on his shoulder. 'Give me a moment to think. I was hoping to talk to you anyway, about things; about Jack, as a matter of fact.'

'I love Jack,' Daniel said. 'I wish he was my brother. I don't have a brother. Just a stupid sister who blabs about me selling E and gets me chucked out even though she took one herself, not like it's my fault she nearly died...I bet they'd blame me for Tamsin and her baby too, if they could.'

'I know about Debbie; I was there, remember?'

'Oh yeah!'

'I think Jack is going to come back to Barking,' she tossed her hair back, drank in the admiring glances of passers-by. 'It's his summer break soon so it's not like he'll miss anything, and he's going to need our support.'

'He is?' Daniel was peering into the window of a Subway restaurant but she pulled him on, oblivious to his squeal of protest.

'That's right,' she nodded. 'I think Jack's going to be the Daddy.'

'He is?!' Daniel stopped, did some movement with his fist that clearly left her utterly bemused. 'Wicked!!'

'My thoughts exactly. But like I said, he's going to need support. There are those in the family who...resent his decision to leave and study at the LSE, like it was a crime to better himself. Are you going to stand by him?'

'Me?' Daniel stopped short. 'Like I said, I love Jack. He's the man. He's hard!!'

'He's the Daddy.'

'Yeah, the Daddy!' he raised his fist. 'Who's the Daddy?!?'

Tiffany ran her tongue the circuit of her lips, then glanced down at her fingernails. When she looked back at him there were frown lines aplenty. 'There's some silly idea that Jamie could be the Daddy,' she said, 'because Jack didn't seem interested, but the idea has no wings. It mustn't come to pass. Jamie is...a child.'

'Jamie's a waster,' Daniel said. 'And coming from me that's really saying something.'

Tiffany said, 'We must make sure Jack has our full support. The family needs him right now, and I hate to say it but Jamie couldn't find his arse with both hands.'

Daniel squinted, followed her across the road. 'Don't you love Jamie no more?'

'As a friend yes, but our romance...well let's just say it disintegrated rather abruptly.'

'That sucks.'

'Doesn't it just.' She took his hand and smiled down at him. 'Jack will be so glad to know he can count on you, Daniel. And we must win the others over too.'

'Everyone loves Jack anyway,' he said, 'they won't need winning over, and like you said he is rightfully the Daddy anyway.'

'I did, but I also mentioned a bit of bad blood his leaving to do this MSc caused, but that's mainly the older ones anyway, and they're just jealous. We must disregard them. We must try and envision a future where Jack is the Daddy and where they...well, where they've simply been wiped off the map.'

'Uh huh.'

'Bobby adores Jack so there's no problem there; the same goes for Sara, Laquisha, and Marie, and Clay and Springer...still, you can never have too many fans. Tell me, has there been any word from your Aunt Delia's youngest twins?'

'Not that I know of...' Daniel shifted uncomfortably. 'We kind of don't mention them 'coz...well, it upsets Aunt Delia, 'coz they're...'

'...doing time?'

'Uh, yeah.'

'Well we must keep our ear to the ground for when they come out; and there's also the 'Hackney Woodfields' to consider.'

'Uggh, they suck!' Daniel spat rather dramatically into the kerb. 'We hate them!'

'Well that was all a long time ago,' she nodded to the bus-stop. 'Long before you were born. There are lots of twins on that side of the family too, you know.'

'Twins, like Jack and Jamie?'

'Like Jack and Jamie, like you and Debbie…your gene pool loves the twin thing. Anyway back to your Aunt Delia's youngest; Hayden and Nick are a pair of fine, sterling young men, and they both have certain…attributes Jack may find useful in cementing his foothold once he returns, especially Hayden.' She smiled to herself. 'I'm very fond of Hayden, as a matter of fact.'

'Hayden set a boy at school on fire once,' Daniel said. 'I was too young, still at St. Margaret's, and this was at Eastbury; he did it 'coz this kid called Laquisha 'a nigger', and Hayden and Laquisha are like, well close. She never knew he did it though.'

'He always was very…enthusiastic,' Tiffany narrowed her eyes.

'You speak real funny, Tiffany,' Daniel squinted up at her as they sat at the bus-stop.

'I got an education,' she winked. 'Will you do that for me, Daniel? enquire about Hayden and Nick's release date? And as for the 'Hackney Woodfields', I know where most of them live, and really you must forget this silly feud; Christopher and Russell have been dead for positively ages…'

'If you say so…' he said. 'But if they kick my head, well you owe me dinner!'

'Silly goose,' she ruffled his Hoxton fin lovingly. 'I'm taking you to dinner anyway.'

'You are? up West?'

'Up West,' she nodded, glancing to see when the next bus was due.

'Wicked.'

'Oh I am,' Tiffany sat back, satisfied. 'But it's the least I can do for one of my lovely little Woodfield boys.'

Chapter 31

Friday 5th May 2006

'Such a lovely evening,' Aunt Amanda said, sticking her head out the front room window. 'It seems a shame to have to stay in, but...well we can't very well do what we're going to do in the middle of Victoria Park, can we?!'

Jamie was sat in his big armchair opposite, Uncle Heath's old chair, clad in a green GAP t-shirt and jeans, Converse trainers, admiring the new watch with the chunky leather strap she'd brought him, from what she'd called '...a shifty sort selling such things out of a briefcase on the Whitechapel Road'. Around his feet a fluffy little tortoiseshell kitten purred and rubbed itself against his ankle; Tiggy. 'What are we going to do?' he asked.

'A séance, darling,' she drew the window frame down, then turned and folded her arms. 'It's time to practice what we preach; I'm going to sift through the ether and look for possessions, thing of that ilk. I'm not going arse over tit onto the Bethnal Green Road again for anyone, I can assure you.' And as if to punctuate the point she gave her bandaged hip a cursory rub, and thanked some obscure deity for the healing properties of certain odd sounding oils.

'Do we have to?' Jamie sighed. 'I'm tired. I've been typing all day and...'

'What's your typing speed?'

'Thirty five words per minute.'

'Oh darling,' she cupped his chin in her hands, the cold of her many rings almost making him jump. 'That's wonderful. I got a prospectus from South Bank today, where Jack did his degree; I don't see any reason why you couldn't go there as well, so I took the liberty of arranging an interview for you...'

Jamie picked Tiggy up and kissed him on the nose. 'I'll need a suit...'

'Well probably not, but you're angling so I'll buy you one anyway,' she went out to the kitchen and poured the tea, set some biscuits out on a tray and came back, then went upstairs, taking it slow due to her hip. Jamie bounced Tiggy up and down from one knee to the other, giggling as the kitten mewed playfully. Aunt Amanda returned moments later with a selection of coloured candles, some sachets of coloured powder, a blue urn decorated with star symbols, and some incense sticks. 'Dim the lights,' she said. 'And keep Tiggy back; he's ever so curious and I don't want him burning his nose.'

'I can keep him, right?' Jamie closed the door on the curious kitten.

'Of course, darling. Now sit opposite me cross-legged and think sweet thoughts; we must purify ourselves.'

'I'll try,' he slung his trainers into the corner. 'I read that book 'the witch's familiar', so I kind of…well…I mean, I never saw Uncle Phil do this.'

'He was a professional, and besides, he didn't want you involved in such things when you were younger,' she said, sitting cross-legged with some difficulty. 'Now, light the candles and the incense, and I'll put the powders on a slow burn.'

Jamie sighed, more through tiredness than boredom. 'Ok.'

'Oh darling,' she jostled him. 'I know you should be anywhere but here with an old woman on a Friday evening, but this has to be done; we agreed, didn't we? For Phil?'

He nodded. 'For Uncle Phil.'

'And for my Ben too,' she set the candle in the centre between them, and then put a match to the purple powder. 'Not to mention the countless others…'

Jamie's phone went off, a text to the tune of the 'Crazy Frog'; he read it, his face falling. 'It's mum,' he said, tucking it back into his pocket. 'She says Tamsin lost the baby.'

Aunt Amanda's face fell too, and at her age it took a lot longer for the musculature to reassert itself. For a moment he thought she was going to sweep the candles aside, but something passed over her face and she regained her composure. 'No,' she said, 'no, we have to do this.'

'Mum wants me to go over,' he said, 'she said 'come over'; I think Casey needs a few shoulders to cry on.'

'He'll have plenty of those,' she blew on the incense. 'He's probably got a houseful already. Now, close your eyes.'

Jamie did as he was told, but his mind was elsewhere; in times of strife the Woodfields always congregated in the Barking Dog, and he could see mum at the bar now, in her finest, a ribbon in her hair, being served by Adam; Uncle Eddie would down his first pint and then raise the second in toast to Tamsin, and before long the entire pub would join them in commiserating. 'What happens now?' he asked.

'Remember what you read; forget where you are.'

Jamie sat back; he could hear Tiggy clawing on the other side of the door. Somewhere outside a woman was shouting, and not far down the road a train from Liverpool Street rumbled over the viaduct; a taxi beeped its horn for someone in the flats opposite. He thought of Aunt Delia ruffling Casey's hair, kissing him on the cheek, telling him everything was going to be ok. He didn't know what he expected to happen; chancing a look he opened one eye and saw Aunt Amanda, legs crossed, fingers poised, rocking backwards and forward, her lips moving ever so slightly, the candle flickering in the breeze from the window. Maybe five more minutes passed, another train rumbled along. Aunt Amanda opened her eyes. 'Nothing,' she sighed. 'Absolutely nothing.'

'Guess my mind's not really on it,' he sighed. 'I really ought to go. If...well if I'm gonna be the Daddy maybe I should at least show up. Uncle Phil would be there, wouldn't he? I mean...'

Aunt Amanda smiled, reaching forward and squeezing his hand. 'Good boy. That's exactly what the Daddy would do. Will Tiffany be there, do you think?'

'Dunno...' he said. 'I haven't seen her for almost a fortnight. I'd say we were going through a rough patch but we're not even speaking. She has some modelling gigs, I think, I mean, no one wants to work on Morelli's forever...'

'People change,' Aunt Amanda blew the candle out, wet her finger and put it on the powder. 'Life goes on; I wonder, though...'

'I don't want her to change,' Jamie said. 'She's been with me all through so much; Uncle Phil; learning to read; and well, she's so damn fit...'

'You're not so bad yourself, Jamie darling.'

'Yeah but I'm...well I'm not Jack, am I? I'm not a hunk.'

'Oh please,' she rolled her eyes. 'My little sister, your Great-Aunt Andrea, well everyone said the same about her, that she was so dazzling, and I was always the plain one, or the 'slightly odd' one, but I did ok. Despite what all those glossy magazines your mum reads tell you, beauty isn't everything. You care about the family, and that's worth its weight in gold.'

'Yeah but I got to be a hunk for Minty Hardcore, that's what you said.' He swallowed. 'We have to make it look like I was baptised in the testosterone spring, don't we?!'

She gave his bicep a little squeeze. 'Feels quite hunky to me, darling. Not quite Jack yet, I admit, but not the Jamie of old either.' She gathered the things up, kissing him on the forehead as she went past. 'It's going to rain for the next few days, so come 'round one dreary evening when it does. And as for him,' and here she nodded to Tiggy, gazing up at them with large, quizzical eyes, 'you give him a good home; every witch should have a cat!'

Jamie beamed, pulled his hoodie on. 'Oh, the weights we won on eBay came,' he said. 'They're in pretty good nick. I've started using them,' he pulled his sleeve down and flexed, revealing a rather impressive bicep with a particularly pronounced blue vein running right down the middle. 'What d'you reckon? Feel it again!'

'Tiffany doesn't know what she's missing,' Aunt Amanda took the stuff out to the kitchen. 'You're a catch, Jamie Woodfield.'

'I still don't work out as much as Jack does though,' he examined the vein curiously. 'He's got abs you could grate cheese on, that's what Jessica says; she's always going on about how fit he is. Mine are just...well, just flat but undefined, you know.'

'Give it time,' she called out. 'Rome wasn't built in a day.'

'Tell me about it,' he gathered Tiggy up and tucked him inside his hoodie, checked his phone was on and made for the door, pausing to kiss her on the cheek as he went. '"bye, Aunt Amanda.' And then on the doorstep he paused. 'Aunt Amanda?'

She raised an eyebrow. 'Darling?'

'I keep having this dream...' he shifted uncomfortably, 'about Uncle Phil, where we scattered his ashes.'

'Tell me the dream,' she said.

'He reforms,' he looked up at her, 'and he's waiting for me to say something, and I don't know what it is, and in the end he gets fed up and goes, and when he goes I know he's gone forever, and sometimes then when I wake up, I cry.'

'It's normal,' she said. 'You have things you still want to say to him, I'm sure. There was so much I wanted to say to my brother before he died...'

'I guess...' he wasn't entirely satisfied with the answer, and felt that he might have it, that it might be on the tip of his tongue, only he couldn't quite clarify it. 'I better go,' he said.

'Goodbye my darling...' she folded her arms, leant against the frame of the door and watched him hurry up Vallance Road in the late evening light, and turn right at the top into Bethnal Green Road. 'God bless you, Jamie Woodfield,' she said. 'And may God forgive me.'

Chapter 32

Sunday 7th May 2006

Jamie had the dream about Uncle Phil again on Saturday night, and woke up around midday on the Sunday with a crushing hangover, the result of a rather riotous night 'up West' with some of his cousins and their collective mates. Even Jack and his friend David had popped in, with a bashful looking Daniel, who declared to one and all that he was 'a fugitive', around midnight. They'd been in the queue for Elysium for several hours, Clay trying his best to blag their way in but realising to his chagrin that the Woodfield name didn't hold as much weight in the West End as it did in Essex; that said, one of the doormen had done time with his brothers Nick and Hayden in the 'Scrubs, and promised to get them in next week at a discount price. They'd ended up in Sugar Reef on Great Windmill Street on David's advice, after his initial idea of Heaven had been vetoed on account of it being, '...for poofters', or so Jamie's best mate Adam told them, chewing gum and spitting in the kerb every time David so much as opened his mouth; this got the idea into a lot of their heads that Jack's mate David might be, '...one of them', but no one was prepared to say it to Jack's face. Jack himself spent most of the night snogging the face off one of the Sugar Reef barmaids; no one was questioning Jack's sexuality, but they were questioning his judgement in the company he chose to keep; '...the sooner he's away from that poof and back in Barking the better,' Daniel had told everyone, sipping tequila through a curly straw, although he did it when David wasn't around because in the weekend he'd spent at the flat in Islington he admitted a little later to actually finding David to be '...a sound geezer.', someone who laughed at his jokes when no one else did, and who'd told him he actually wasn't bad looking, when certainly no one else ever did.

Jamie had spent most of the evening downing everything on the cocktail menu with Adam and Michael, the latter pulling a rather fit piece around ten after midnight, and off they went in a taxi. Adam pulled just before closing. Jamie wore a tight black t-shirt to show off his improving biceps, firm enough now so that the veins stood out all the time and in regards to his wrists, well he'd had to adjust the strap on the watch Aunt Amanda had given him already. He'd had his hair newly cropped to a no.2 and used the last of the face cream Tiffany had given him for Christmas, keeping the tube in some kind of weird moment of sentimentality usually only reserved for gifts from Uncle Phil. Tiffany hadn't answered his texts in four days now; knocking at the flat was fruitless, her flatmate Elisha seeming to have vanished off the face of the earth, and the lights were never on even when he took a stroll past on his way back from Aunt Delia's. He thought about texting Louise from Sight & Sound and asking her out instead, but left the invitation in his draft texts, for another time. He hadn't had sex for well over a month now, and the last time with Tiffany had felt like going through the motions, on her part at least. He'd mentioned twice that he'd been working out, and with his physique having been pretty good before he thought she might've made the connection that he was now 'buff' without much prompting, but obviously it wasn't to be the case. No matter how 'buff' he was, it was still Jack who got all the looks in Sugar Reef, who elicited all the comments, and even had a couple of girls passing their numbers to him in full view of their boyfriends, pretending they were shaking his hand in greeting and then deftly slipping the folded up piece of paper between their professionally polished nails.

A girl called Natasha made a beeline for Jamie around eleven, after whispering with her girlfriends for about half an hour, glancing over at him and Adam in-between riffs of girly giggles; she'd been heavy on the eye contact and even asked if she could squeeze his bicep; he'd let her, to which she'd made an '…mmmmm' noise as her painted fingernails almost dug into the hard flesh. She'd been even more excited by the idea that he was an Essex boy, and for a moment he'd let himself envision her out of the one-piece white dress she was wearing, running his hands up and down her firm little tits and then licking at the nipples, tickling them with his boyish stubble. And then he'd thought of Tiffany, which had given him pause; then a wave of grief over Uncle Phil followed, as it often did at totally random moments, and he drew back, made his excuses, and found himself on Shaftesbury Avenue, looking for a minicab, hands in his pockets and his gaze downcast. A Romanian had taken him as far as the Bow Road, and from there he'd considered stopping off at Aunt Amanda's, but that was a walk all its own. Another minicab had taken him to the Station Parade on East Ham where he'd tried to knock up Sara Woodfield, but there was no answer; he had visions of her being screwed by her lank boyfriend Ron, and had gotten a hard-on over that and the fast fading image of Natasha, with a little bit of Tiffany thrown in just for good measure. Then he'd walked back to Barking and fallen asleep with Tiggy on his lap on the sofa in the living room, fully clothed.

After waking he undressed and took a shower, had some toast and then pulled on a pair of briefs and did his exercises, using the weight he'd won on eBay for around half an hour just on his arms before doing sit-ups, press-ups, and crunches. He was particularly proud of his up-and-coming deltoids. Then he tried texting Tiffany again, but got no response. He had to do something to take his mind off her, off the distinct lack of her; the lack of Uncle Phil was bad enough, but this new double-lack was all but set to finish him off, on the sly.

He'd put a corkboard up in the kitchen but as yet it was bare; he'd been putting off opening the envelope with the pictures he'd selected for it, but felt 'sound' enough now to give it a go. The brown envelope gave up around twenty photographs, and Tiggy danced in them when they missed the counter and fell all over the floor. The first was a picture of him and Tiffany at Casey and Tamsin's wedding, only a few weeks after they'd begun dating; Tiffany was beaming, and Jamie looked as if he couldn't believe his luck, which to tell the truth had been his state of mind for almost the first year of their relationship. The gradual disillusion of affections of the past few weeks had almost been expected, in a sad sort of way, as though she'd 'wised up' to him, and the initial physical attraction had worn off and she'd found that there was nothing beneath the baby-faced grin and the pale blue eyes. Jamie put the picture back in the envelope and selected another, he and Tiffany on the tube going from Barking to Upton Park, summer 2004; him in a white vest, she in a skimpy red outfit, laughing, half kissing, half posing for the picture he was pretty sure Uncle Phil must have taken.

He pinned the picture dead centre of the corkboard and placed a second tack in-between his teeth while he selected the second picture, one of mum at a barbecue Uncle Brian and Aunt Betty had held as part of Casey's wedding celebrations; mum had a glass in her hand and the little pink umbrella tucked behind her ear, and just behind her Daniel was doing a double-fingered salute over her head.

A picture of Uncle Phil in his West Ham away strip from '97 or '98 had proven too much; he'd spat the tack into the sink and slipped the picture back into the envelope and closed it, tucking it back in the draw. Then he sat down at the kitchen table and took a couple of Nurofen.

The buzzer downstairs sounded. He wasn't really in the mood to see anyone, so he vetted it, answering via the intercom. 'Hello?'

'It's Debbie!' was the reply. 'Let me in!'

Jamie sighed, exhaled. 'Why?'

'Just 'coz!!'

'Shit's sake.' he pressed the buzzer, heard the door downstairs open and moments later Debbie burst though. She'd dropped the bob in favour of some shoulder-length extensions, and shelved the awful shell-suits Uncle Heath brought her on the East Street market for a rather fetching little gold dress; unfortunately, on Debbie this still had the effect of making her looking like a very little girl trying to be a very grown-up woman.

'Hey!!' she beamed, cracking her gum, giving him a little twirl. 'Wow Jamie, you look like shit.'

'Thanks.' He suddenly realised he had on nothing but his briefs. 'Let me go get dressed,' he said.

'Don't hurry on my account,' she beamed, balancing on the very tips of her kitten heels. 'Lucky Tiffany.' And then she giggled to herself, as though laughing at a joke everyone was in on except her, although all Debbie's laughs sounded a little like that.

He returned around five minutes later to find her helping herself to a can of ASDA cola from the fridge, removing her gum and sticking it on her elbow while she took hearty swigs, then wiping her mouth with the back of her hand.

'How've you been then?' he asked. 'Not taking any more duff Es?'

'Bite me,' she sighed. 'Just had to get out of the house; dad's been seeing that Carol who sells DVDs on the stall down from his, and I could hear them fucking this morning; she makes so much noise I almost knocked on the wall. I had to get out of there. Is Daniel still at Jack's?'

'Far as I know,' he got himself one of the remaining cans. 'Last I saw him he was trying to chat up some bird way too fit for him and getting the mother of all knockbacks.'

'He's a prick, my brother,' she sighed, elbows on the table, 'an ugly, fat prick.'

'He's harmless.' He'd been dying to agree, but in line with his new fledgling Daddy policy it was better to tow the tact line.

'Dad says when he comes back he's got to shape up or he'll smack him one again; and he says that he's told Clay to make sure he's barred from Legends. Dad says he's got to get a proper job, on the market or something.'

'Your dad's right,' Jamie had a sudden visceral flash of himself as the Daddy, the wise sage in the guise of a bit of rough to whom the family came to with all their problems. He clasped his hands before him as though in prayer and said, 'He could apply to go to Sight & Sound, where I am; learn to type, office skills, stuff like that.'

'Tell him, not me,' she removed her gum from her elbow and began chewing. 'Ohhh, you've got a kitten!' she scooped Tiggy up off the floor and kissed him, 'wet nose kitten!'

'Aunt Amanda gave him me.'

'Ew!' Debbie placed him back on the floor. 'He's a proper witches' cat then!'

'He's my baby,' Jamie waggled his bare toes and felt Tiggy snuffle them a moment or so later. 'So anyway, what's up 'cuz?'

'Like I said,' she shrugged. 'I just needed to give my ears a rest from the sound of my own dad making out. You have no idea of how gross that is.'

'You haven't spent a night in the room next to Uncle Phil then...'

'I did once,' she piped up, and then saw the look on his face at the mention of Uncle Phil, talk of Uncle Phil as if he'd just popped off down to the cashpoint or something. 'Well anyway. How's Tiffany these days?'

'She's good.'

'Yeah?' she looked at him as though he were slightly off-centre. 'Where is she then?'

Jamie frowned. 'What d'you mean?'

'Well, she ain't here checking out your new biceps, is she?'

'She's busy.'

'Where?'

'Up west; her and Jessica are doing a modelling shoot.'

'That's bull,' Debbie sniffed, 'Jessica's getting fucked by the photographer but Tiffany isn't even there. And it's porn, for the record;

Jessica does soft porn, and if her dad ever finds out he's gonna go ape, and Jack just thinks it's funny.'

'Yeah?' Jamie tried to remain cool, but he was getting wound up at a rather alarming velocity. 'Where is Tiffany then?'

Debbie shrugged. 'Dunno. You're her boyfriend, how come you don't know? Or isn't your brain as big as your biceps?'

Jamie breathed in, deeply. 'What are you trying to say?'

'Nothing dummy,' she cracked her gum, twirling her kitten heels on the linoleum. 'Nothing you'd want to know, leastways.' She sniffed. 'So anyway, when are we all going to Legends for another boogie? You reckon we could get Jack down here again, and his funny friend David, and that frosty Dorothy?!'

Chapter 33

Sunday 7th May 2006

Dorothy unscrewed the cap of the bottle of Evian and took a hearty swig. The bottle didn't stand well on the grass after the fact and in the end she had to balance it delicately on top of the packets of assorted finger foods. Directly opposite her and unpacking the rest of the picnic was a woman in her late forties, not unattractive, but rather primly dressed for a relaxed Sunday evening by the Serpentine, her dry blond hair styled in little waves that just touched the collar of her tailored blue suit. Her name was Ruth Fremantle and she was, among other things, a highly respected psychoanalyst, one who worked out of the Hopkins Institute near Russell Square. They'd only just arrived, and it had taken almost fifteen minutes to find a clear spot safely out of earshot from the couples, families and assorted odds and ends enjoying the sunset over the waters as the last of the boaters were called in. Dorothy had picked the spot personally; she felt an affinity with the place she couldn't quite explain, and this sense of uneasy well-being was still troubling her when Ruth made a general enquiry as to her wellbeing. Dorothy shielded her eyes from the glare of the setting sun.

'Not so good; or, great, it depends from which angle you're enquiring.'

Ruth smiled easily. 'A Personal angle, to begin with. Your dad says you're under some stress, juggling this new MSc with your duties as...well, as a single mother.'

'Well I'm not stressed about the exam, but I haven't really begun to revise yet either,' Dorothy screwed the cap back down on the Evian. 'My weight is down so that's great, which means I can finally buy those cut-off slacks I want for when it gets really hot. What else did dad say?'

'...aren't we in the professional territory now?'

'Are we?' Dorothy squinted at her. 'You tell me.'

'How's Jack?'

'I wouldn't know,' Dorothy licked her lips, studied the array of finger foods on offer. 'I hardly see him these days.'

'And why's that?'

'He's kind of getting fresh with his brother's girlfriend; apparently she turned up at the flat in Islington out of the blue one night and told him it was over between her and Jamie, and there you have it, ever since she and Jack have been getting fresh.'

'Getting fresh?'

'They're fucking, in layman's terms.'

'Oh.' Ruth seemed to consider this for a moment. 'And how does that make you feel?'

'Well Jack and I never really got past first base; we were very old-fashioned that way, so I can't say that I'm exactly heartbroken.' And here she laughed to herself. 'He's ever so handsome and all, ever so charming in a very basic kind of a way, but ever so cheesy as well. He knows it too, but he just can't help himself.' And then her face darkened. 'Professionally speaking…well something's not quite right.'

'Explain?'

Dorothy mused, opting for a slice of what looked like cheese wrapped in a very wet slice of ham. 'There's just something…odd about this girl, Tiffany.'

Ruth made a steeple of her hands. 'Well it wouldn't be the first time a pair of Woodfield twins have been seeing the same woman.'

'It's not that…' Dorothy couldn't find the words. 'She's just…odd; very beautiful, but very odd. Hardly your average Essex girl, let's put it that way. I mean, without being too offensive, but she has class. She's like a Sloanie who got lost and ended up in Barking by mistake.'

'Tiffany…Tiffany what?'

'Tiffany Grieve. I know she's not Essex originally, but as to where she does hail from, well I'm clueless.'

'I'll see what I can dig up, but I think you're worrying unnecessarily; it's Jack we're concerned with.'

'Who said I was worried?'

Ruth raised an eyebrow. 'Jealous then?'

Dorothy considered. 'I'm very fond of Jack, but like I said, far too cheesy. I prefer my men a little more…roguish. Anyway, does it matter? We don't have to be lovers for me to be close, to have influence. Next to David and Frank from South Bank I'm his best friend.'

'That's good to hear,' she nodded. 'And how is Jack otherwise?'

'Same as me, a little stressed about the exam. They all went to Sugar Reef last night, so I heard. Jack wants to go abroad over summer, and David's up for it, so I guess I'll have to tag along, I'm sure Justin will love it; what's the data on Woodfields abroad?'

Ruth considered for a moment, half smiling, half serious. 'I'll have to get back to you on that one, but I know for a fact about forty of them went to Los Angeles in 2001; can you imagine that? Forty people, all of the same ilk, descending on some resort like a swarm!'

'I quite envy him,' Dorothy said. 'I've told him as much on more than one occasion; I come from such a tiny family…'

'…oh Dorothy,' Ruth reached out and lifted her chin up. 'You know that isn't true.'

'Well it sort of is; anyway, David very definitely does, and it fascinates him.'

'Well it's true when all around us the modern idea of the family is all but disintegrating. The Woodfields are quite an exemplary example of the classic British/East End clan, wonderfully preserved and with their corporate identity still relatively…'

'…except that they're patriarchal as opposed to the traditional East End matriarchy.'

Ruth raised an eyebrow. 'You'd say that to Delia Woodfield, would you? Or Amanda?'

'You know what I mean.'

Ruth opened a flask of tea and poured them both a mug. 'That I do. Anyway, so Jack is well?'

'He is. David adores him and waits on him hand and foot; David types his notes up for him, does his washing and his ironing; brings him breakfast in bed on a Sunday…'

'…and David is still doing his own occult studies MA, with a dissertation on the Woodfields?'

'With Jack's help, no less.'

'And no one in the Woodfield family knows?'

'No way.'

Ruth jutted her chin out. 'I wonder what the reaction would be. I mean, Jack's to be applauded for such an original method of financing his way through university, but the Woodfields have their secrets, much more than your average family, as you and I well know.'

'Well David doesn't even have to hand the rough draft in until the end of June.'

'Keep me posted. I'd very much like to see it.'

Dorothy nodded, sipped her tea. 'What's my next move?'

'You haven't mentioned the Hopkins Institute to either of them, have you?'

'Again, no way.'

Ruth nodded. 'Good. As to your next move…wait for me to furnish you with what I know about this Tiffany girl, but I think you're worrying unnecessarily. Just try and insinuate yourself into things a little more even if you and Jack aren't going anywhere romantically. See how he feels about these pressures…'

'What pressures?'

'You said in your last email he'd been going back to Barking a lot more, lately.'

'Definitely,' Dorothy said. 'One of the cousins, Daniel, has run away and he's staying in their flat at the moment, and several of them popped in yesterday to see him. Jack was in Barking yesterday too, I think because one of the other cousins had a miscarriage or something. They decided to go to Sugar Reef on a whim, I think, to chill out.'

Ruth mused. 'His family have been having quite the run of bad luck lately.'

'Well I was there when his little cousin Debbie almost died from a duff Ecstasy pill.'

'And so they're clamouring for him to come back and take charge?'

Dorothy laughed softly. 'I wouldn't say clamouring, but Phil Woodfield has been dead nearly six months now. There's a Daddy-shaped gap where he used to be.'

Ruth drank her tea, stared out over the Serpentine. 'This could be very bad, Dorothy. This could be the opposite of what we've intended. Keep me posted on the slightest change; I want to know how often Jack goes to Barking, and for how long. If anything happens to anyone in that family I need to know about it. Do you understand?'

She nodded. 'I'll tell you straight away.' She finished her tea. 'What about Jamie Woodfield?'

Ruth sniffed, considered, and finished her tea too. 'What about him?'

Chapter 34

Sunday 7th May 2006

Bobby Woodfield sat on his bed in his little square room in St. Margaret's and thought to himself, What could he take? What could he fit that he valued the most into the Nike rucksack that Daniel sold him several months ago, when he'd first hatched this crazy idea of running away and joining up with Jack and his friend David? David, who had clearly been 'one of them' the same way Bobby had known pretty much since the age of thirteen that he was 'one of them' too. If David was Jack's friend then Jack would be sympathetic; Jack was the Daddy, although no one had said that yet because everyone was still smarting from Uncle Phil's death.

As it turned out there wasn't a great deal he could squeeze into the Nike rucksack besides his clothes and his toiletries; his Doctor Who stuff was going to have to stay behind, and for a moment he was swamped with apocalyptic visions of his dad, Father Brian Woodfield, burning the lot of it on a pyre whilst quoting randomly from the Good Book.

Of course the whole family knew that Daniel had run away to Jack's already, ever since Debbie had blabbed about him selling Es – and selling her a duff one at that – at Legends the other week, but Bobby was sure there would be room for him at the flat in Islington as well. If the Daddy wouldn't come to them then he'd just have to go to the Daddy. Not that he'd ever say that to Jack's face because everyone knew Jack had better things to do than be the Daddy, really. Jack was going to be a famous psychoanalyst, and create a whole new term for his unique metrosexual way of thinking; the way there was Freudian thought and Lacanian thought, well pretty soon there'd be 'Woodfield thought' as well.

Bobby settled for his favourite Doctor Who story on DVD and his blue and silver remote control Dalek, zipping the Nike rucksack shut and then opening his door and listening out for signs of discovery. In the living room he could hear his father and his mum watching 'Antiques Roadshow' like they always did on a Sunday evening, drinking cocoa and leafing through the Sunday papers, just like a pair of old people, which was, when you thought about it, exactly what they were. His mum was in her early sixties, but dad was seventy if he was a day, although he still took mass every Sunday and confession most nights of the week too. Bobby was finding it suffocating, living here with them, especially since he'd had the idea that he might work his way to university, the way Jack had done years ago, in a bid to escape Barking. Bobby himself didn't want to escape Barking as much as all that though, but he did want to move out, maybe share a flat with one of the cousins, someone who would be sympathetic to his 'plight'. The thing was, whenever someone mentioned 'queers' it was always disparagingly; this was Essex, after all. Bobby's education may not have extended much past college but he knew exactly the sort of social climate he'd been brought up in. Now everyone in the family except his dad knew he was a 'Nancy', thanks to Debbie and her distorted view of cousinly discretion. Bobby couldn't actually believe he'd been stupid enough to think she'd keep it a secret after she'd told everyone where Daniel had run off to, holding her sides and laughing like some crazy cartoon.

Long before that he'd had an idea that Uncle Phil knew he was gay. One summer the family had gone and played Rounders in Barking Park and all the boys – Jack, Jamie, Michael, Clay, Nick, Hayden, even Uncle Heath – had all taken their shirts off as the midday sun beat down on them. He'd blushed when Uncle Phil had asked him if he was going to strip off too, and when he'd declined Uncle Phil had ruffled his hair and said with that twinkle in his eye, 'You're all right, matey.'

He missed Uncle Phil too. Uncle Phil would have understood about his having to run away now; he'd run away to Brighton himself when he was a teenager and gone to live with Uncle Richard, whom Uncle Eddie always called, '…that bleeding poofter!' Uncle Phil would have made things all right.

Bobby hauled the Nike rucksack over his shoulder and tip-toed down the stairs to the front door, letting himself out as quietly as possible. Once up the path and out of the graveyard his Aunt Delia's flat was almost directly opposite, and their window was wide open; he could hear her shouting at Uncle Eddie about something or other, which was the norm for them most days. He headed right, turning into East Street and then slowing his walk up towards Station Parade and the Underground station. No one would miss him anyway; everyone was busy fretting over his big brother Casey's wife, who was trying to pretend everything was fine even though she'd just miscarried, checking herself out of the hospital when they'd wanted to keep her in for observation because they said there was something 'unusual' about what had happened to her. Dad had said it was a matter for the Lord, but mum had simply sighed and gotten on with her knitting. Dad didn't mean to be…well, mean, but he thought everything that happened had God's hand in it in one way or the other, and so he never really felt sorry about anything. Except when it was something strange, something like Jamie telling everyone that Uncle Phil had taken him to the World Cup final in 1966, or that Uncle Phil had a secret girlfriend called 'Minty Hardcore', whom he met for illicit trysts in the Vicarage Fields when it was closed and Jamie was fast asleep in bed. Dad always made the sign of the cross whenever someone said 'Minty Hardcore', which wasn't all that often, as it happened, maybe even only once a year. No one had ever told Bobby who 'Minty Hardcore' was. Dad was always sorry that anyone would want to mention such a subject.

Bobby reached the band stand at the bottom of Station Parade, just as the door to Uncle Phil's flat opened and Jamie came out, wearing jeans and white trainers, a tight-fitting black t-shirt barely concealing his new and marginally improved physique. In the moment it took Bobby to blush at the sight of his rather buffed cousin Jamie had clocked him, jogging on over all butch like and slapping him on the back. 'Hey!!' he said. 'Where are you off to with a bulging rucksack?!'

Bobby tried to regain his composure. 'I'm running away,' he said matter-of-factly.

'Oh for fuck's sake!' Jamie slapped his brow in disbelief, 'not you as well!'

'I'm going to Jack's,' he went on. 'His friend David is...well, you know...'

'Queer?'

'Yeah.'

'Well my friend at Sight & Sound - Louise - her brother's friend is queer so I'm kind of learning...' Jamie shrugged, leant up against the bandstand and folded his arms, which to Bobby only made his biceps look even bigger. 'But you know...running away isn't the answer. Everyone knows about you anyway.'

'Everyone except my dad.'

'Yeah well...word of God and all that.'

'He'll try to have me exorcised or something, Jamie.'

Jamie laughed. 'No he won't! Aunt Delia will shout him down...'

'...unless she hates gays too.'

'Look,' Jamie lopped an arm around his shoulders, copying a move he'd clearly seen Jack do a dozen times, 'listen to me. I'll come down there with you now and we'll tell your dad together, ok? And if he has a go at you, well you can come and stay at mine, ok? For as long as you want, there's tons of room now that Uncle Phil's...well, you know.'

Bobby thought about it for a moment; he liked the squeeze of Jamie's arm around his rather slender shoulders, but he'd never looked up to Jamie the way he had to Jack; Jack was clever, Jack knew stuff, Jack always knew what to say, whereas Jamie was just kind of like the dumb, not quite so sexy carbon copy, even if he was buffing up now to match his brother, almost like it was a competition between them or something. But no, he'd made up his mind. 'I'll go to Jack's, thanks Jamie,' he said, disengaging himself and making a beeline for Station Parade proper. 'I mean, no offence and all, but it's not like you're the Daddy or anything, is it?'

Chapter 35

Monday 8th May 2006

Jamie gazed at his reflection in the window of the Underground train he was on, scrutinising in a way he hadn't since that awful Christmas Eve when he'd been sent to find Jack, up West. Bobby's word, '…it's not like you're the Daddy or anything, is it?!?' bounced around his brain, and in the empty carriage he found himself whispering under his breath, 'well it'd never be you either would it, you stupid little queer.'

On arriving it took him around ten minutes just to find his way out of the station at Elephant and Castle, as he navigated the cream-coloured stone passages, turned corners and found himself back on the Bakerloo line platform, or to lifts that only took you up to the mainline station; eventually he found a lift that took him up to London Road and after asking for directions from a nearby newsstand, he made a right and entered the building adjacent to South Bank University's new Keyworth building, flashing his interview letter to the woman on the reception desk, who buzzed him through.

Once inside he found himself lost in yet another labyrinth of corridors, leading off to classrooms and the like; he peered into a vacant lecture hall and found himself marvelling at the thought that in four or five months' time he could be seated in one of those with his notebook – or even his laptop, if Aunt Amanda could swing it – jotting down theories on literary criticism, or something along those lines, depending on when he finally made his mind up about what course he was actually going to do.

He found a toilet and slipped inside to adjust his tie; the suit he was wearing wasn't even new; it was one of Uncle Phil's old Brighton suits, kind of brown with blue pinstripes, the sort that would have been wildly out of fashion in the Nineties but thanks to the likes of Pete Doherty had recently come back into vogue. He'd kept his stubble but trimmed it into shape, and last night mum had run her clippers over his buzz cut, although while she'd done so she'd gone on once again that his idea of going to university was '…a waste of time when your stall is there waiting for you, and if you don't reclaim it soon someone else will take up the patch and then where will you be?!'. Uncle Phil would have understood, though.

He found himself in a hall adjacent to the large canteen, surprisingly busy given that according to the interview letter term time was now over until September and it was basically just examinations. He asked a young Brazilian girl where the main office was and showed her his letter, and she sent him off down a glass walkway overlooking Borough Road, and up a stone staircase. It was hard to imagine Jack here at one time, several years ago, Jack hurrying up and down these selfsame corridors, handing his essays in and stuff like that; Jack here with all his friends of whom Jamie knew little, or nothing; Jack cracking sociological theory while Jamie sold second-hand paperbacks that he couldn't even read on a stall on the East Street market, just opposite to Uncle Heath and a couple down from Aunt Hannah's doormat emporium. He'd come a long way all right, even if he had had to finish 'the Wizard of Oz' all by himself. He was reading 'Interview with the Vampire' now and enjoying it very much, using the picture of himself and Tiffany on the tube as a bookmark.

He handed his letter in to the office and the burly black guy behind the counter directed him off to his left, then suddenly called out almost as an afterthought, 'Hey! Did you say Woodfield?'

Jamie nodded. 'Uh huh.'

He turned over Jamie's letter in his hands, scanning the name and address. 'Are you Jack Woodfield's brother, by any chance?'

Jamie half grinned, half kind of thought, 'oh god!', but said anyway, 'Yeah, yeah I am.'

The man extended his hand. 'Pleased to meet you; Jack left quite a void when he graduated here a couple of years back. He was quite a character; 'big man on campus' I think they'd call it, if we were Stateside.'

'Yeah, that'd be Jack…' he caught a whiff in the man's memory of Jack's swaggering brand of confidence, where he simply let his height and his shoulders do the talking, and everyone just fell at his feet.

'He said he had a twin brother once, I think,' the man was nodding.

'Yeah I can see it, I really can.' He made a camera lens of his hands and framed Jamie's face in it. 'He doing ok?'

'He's at the London School of Economics now,' Jamie said, trying to sound enthusiastic. 'He's doing his Masters, same subject.'

'Good old Jack,' the man nodded again. 'Bet he's 'BMOC' there too.'

''BMOC'?'

'…like I said, 'big man on campus'.'

'Oh,' Jamie nodded. 'Right.'

'Well,' the man extended his hand. 'Nice to meet you, Jamie. Good luck with the interview, and hope we'll be seeing a lot more of you around here. I'm Alan, by the way.'

Jamie followed the directions given him, found the door marked 'Patricia Van Dyke', and knocked several times. An American accent bade him enter and he did so, finding therein a woman in her fifties or so, long greying hair framing an enthusiastic face, sitting at a desk finishing up something on the laptop on front of her. 'You must be Jamie,' she extended her hand. 'I'm Patricia, head of new inductions, part time sociology lecturer; I hear you're thinking of taking up a degree position with us?'

Jamie sat opposite, wondered whether or not to cross his legs but then thought better of it and clasped his hands reverently before him as Aunt Amanda had showed him. 'Uh huh,' he nodded. 'For the September academic year, I think it is.'

'That it is,' she nodded. 'Now...Woodfield? That name is awfully familiar. Come to think of it, you look awfully familiar.'

'You must be thinking of my brother Jack,' Jamie beamed his most insincere smile. 'He did Sociology here a couple of years back.'

'Of course!' Patricia almost slammed both her hands on the desk. 'Jack Woodfield!! He was on a couple of my courses; charming, absolutely charming, and such a brilliant mind! Never afraid to argue the point and put his own opinion forward, that was Jack.'

'Yeah, that'll be Jack.'

'And you're thinking of doing the same?'

'Well...yeah, I guess I am. I was thinking,' Jamie opened his hands. 'Well I actually quite like reading too. My Aunt Amanda thinks I should take sociology 'coz I'd have all of Jack's notes, but...well, is there a writing course or something?'

'Well,' Patricia said, 'you've got a glowing reference from...Monique, is it, at Sight & Sound. And if I'm to be honest, being Jack Woodfield's brother is good enough for me. Where is he now, by the way?'

'The London School of Economics.'

'Of course; well it was either that or Oxford for Jack. Sociology still?'

'Yeah,' Jamie felt a sudden urge to remind her that this was his interview and not a retrospective on Jack's academic career, but the thought of Aunt Amanda scowling when he told her he'd fluffed it silenced him somewhat.

'Marvellous,' Patricia nodded. 'Well you don't have all the usual qualifications we look for, but I'm willing to go with my gut instinct and say that I'll put your name forward for a place on sociology BSc beginning September, and I'll also put your name to the English Literature department in case you change your mind on that score too.'

'Wow!' Jamie lightened up a little. 'Well that was easy!! I was cacking it...sorry, I mean...'

'It's ok,' she smiled at him. 'I know what you mean, but when you've gone I want you to do something for me.'

Jamie was feeling awfully proud of himself. 'Name it,' he said.

'Thank Jack for sending you here. It was Jack, am I right? Well thank him because if you're a chip off the old block then I want as much Woodfield as I can get in my department. Jack graduated with an upper class 2:1, as I'm sure you know, and those kind of results look great on our overall achievement boards...'

'I'll be sure to tell him,' Jamie licked his lips, promising to himself to do nothing of the sort. 'Will...will I get a letter of confirmation about the offer? My aunt...I mean, well it'd be nice just to see it in writing, you know. I don't get many official looking letters with my name on them.'

'Tell you what,' she began typing an email and sent it through the printer on her laptop. 'There. I've recommended you straight away to Stina Lyon, overall head of sociology; there's no reason why she won't okay my recommendation and you should hear by the end of the week. I've copied the email and also sent it to Russell Bell, head of English Lit, so likewise, maybe depending on who end up you hearing from first?'

Jamie left the office and made a 'Yes!' gesture with his fist, pulling the proverbial jackpot lever. He took his Nike wallet from his back pocket and opened it, kissing the picture of Tiffany behind the plastic plate; then for good measure he kissed the adjacent picture of Uncle Phil as well, and then hurried up the steps, looking for someone to direct him to the student union bar and a nice cold pint.

Chapter 36

Monday 8th May 2006

'How do I look?' Bev asked, adjusting her cardigan so that less cleavage showed, and less belly too.

'You look fine,' Heath sighed, striding on ahead of her, his hands bunched up into fists. 'This isn't a party we're going to.' He stopped at Aunt Amanda's house and rapped firmly on the door with his rather large, meaty knuckles. 'Wish she'd get a doorbell,' he muttered under his breath. 'And,' he turned to Bev, 'this better not take too long; Carol's cooking a surprise for me, and...'

'...oohhh I bet she is,' she winked, folding her arms, scraping her heel along on the pavement. 'Finally you've gone and got yourself a new woman.' She nudged him playfully in the ribs. 'Good on you, big brother.'

He was about to rap on the door again when it opened and there was Aunt Amanda in a kind of fiery red dress with matching shawl, matching bracelets on her wrists, both of these things matching her fiery dark red hair. 'Well, this is an unexpected pleasure,' she said, folding her arms and making the bracelets rattle. 'I can't remember the last time my own two children popped in to see me.'

'Hello mum,' Heath kissed her on both cheeks, moving past her into the front room, Bev administering the same greeting and coming in close behind. 'I know, we should've visited ages ago, but things have been...well, hectic.'

Aunt Amanda carried on down the hall to the kitchen. 'I was just making some tea...'

'I'd love a cup,' Heath made himself comfortable in the big chair in the front room, the one that faced the window and in which he'd often lolled as a child on long hot summer evenings, sometimes hanging over the sill and chatting to his friends out on the street. Bev nudged him and mouthed 'the hip!!' He nodded, and called out, 'How are you feeling, mum? How's the hip?'

'Much better,' she called out. 'I hear you're seeing someone; Carol, is it?'

He blushed. 'Well yeah, we've...made a connection.'

'She stayed over at his at the weekend, mum!' Bev called out, making herself comfortable in her own old chair. 'They've been at it like rabbits!'

"sis!!' he almost choked.

'Glad to hear it,' Aunt Amanda returned with a silver pot on a tray, and a side order of digestive biscuits, which she set down on the table. 'Be careful,' she said. 'I just had this re-done this weekend; Mr Weeks up the top, his son is into restoring old furniture and well, this used to belong to dear old Felicity...'

'Mum…' Bev dunked a biscuit in her tea. 'Heath and I…well, we're worried about you. And not about the hip, 'coz you're clearly over that, but just…'

Aunt Amanda raised an eyebrow, settling back into her own chair. 'Just what, darling?'

'Things are a bit of a mess now,' Heath said, leaning back, loving the feel of his childhood chair and thinking whether he might ask if he could have it, one day anyway. 'My Daniel's off with Jack, so is Bobby now…'

Aunt Amanda sighed. '…if Bobby wants me to talk to his father about his being gay then all he has to do is ask.'

'That's just it mum,' Bev said. 'That isn't your job.'

'No?' she raised an eyebrow, 'and whose is it, pray tell?'

'Well,' Bev said, catching sight of the picture of her other brother on the mantelpiece. 'It would have been Phil's…'

'…and now it's Jack's, is that what you're going to say?'

She nodded. 'Mum, you're pulling in one direction and the rest of the family is pulling in another and…and well it has to stop!' she gripped the arms of the chair. 'Stop filling Jamie's head with silly ideas about being the Daddy, that's Jack's job; Phil…well Phil's been gone nearly six months now, and the family needs a Daddy. Jack is off for summer soon and he's going to come back.'

'…because Jack has always put this family before his own interests, am I right?' Aunt Amanda sipped a little of her tea and nodded. 'Of course he has.'

'Well not always,' Bev conceded. 'He had to find himself…'

'Find himself,' Aunt Amanda scoffed. 'Darling, that boy took the money I offered him to go to university without even batting an eyelid. You know what Jack wants? Jack wants a nice well paid office job somewhere fancy, like Cheapside or Canon Street, like where your mother used to work, God rest her soul; he wants a suit from Saville Row and a flat in Islington – a better flat than the one he was at present – perhaps a wife and kids; what Jack doesn't want is to come back here and be wiping all your noses every five minutes. We're too common for him, simply too common.'

Bev reddened. 'Mum, why are you filling Jamie's head with the idea that he can be the Daddy, when you know it can't be so?'

'Because Jamie cares about the family; Jamie cared about Phil; Jamie hasn't got a mean or selfish bone in his body.'

'We all cared about Phil,' Bev said. 'We adored Phil.'

'Jack didn't. Jack couldn't stand to be near him most of the time; a fraud, is what Jack used to call him.'

'Mum that isn't true!!'

'Hey hey!!' Uncle Heath waved his large paws in a calming gesture. 'Let's just snuff out the touch paper, step back and take stock, shall we?'

'What a splendid idea,' Aunt Amanda sipped her tea. 'I should've realised you hadn't come 'round just to see me. You've no idea how lonely it gets here. The Corbetts call on me more than either of you two do.'

'...and that's another thing,' Bev went on. 'If you're so concerned about the family why do you maintain your little outpost here when the rest of us are in Barking, helping Tamsin get over her miscarriage, telling little Laquisha that the fact half our bloody council is now BNP won't put her in any danger...'

'Just give Jamie a little more time,' Aunt Amanda said. 'You have no idea of the progress he's made...'

'No I don't, because he doesn't talk to me,' Bev said. 'And I'm only his bloody mother! What you and him get up to here lord only knows, filling his heads with ideas and nonsense...'

'Now it's my turn to get 'a cob on', as the youngsters say,' Aunt Amanda straightened herself out, smoothed the hem of her skirt with her long, bony fingers. 'Your whole life, Beverly Woodfield, you've thought you knew what went on with this family, what really went on, but you haven't got a clue; no, you always left it to me and to Phil, to your Aunt Delia and Felicity, to poor old Uncle Rupert...well now how about you just carry on leaving things to Delia and I?!'

'Mum,' Heath cleared his throat. 'Jamie isn't the Daddy. We all love him to bits but he isn't the Daddy.'

'And what do you know about who is and who isn't the Daddy?!' Aunt Amanda turned her flaring anger on him. 'You were bloody lucky it wasn't you!'

'That's what I told Jamie,' Bev tried to reason with her. 'It's something of a thankless job, I told him, and...'

'...far too thankless for someone as selfish as Jack,' she laughed. 'He's modern, to him the concept of family is quaint, a bit silly; 'naff', is that the right word? Well thankfully Jamie loved his Uncle Phil enough to know what it really means. It means sticking together, helping each other...'

'I knew she'd be like this,' Bev sighed, finishing her tea, turning to her brother. 'Waste of time, this was. I'm missing 'EastEnders' for this, you know.'

'You're living it, my darling,' Aunt Amanda snapped.

'What she's trying to say is, give Jack a chance,' Heath implored. 'Jack gave my Daniel a good talking to about peddling drugs just the way the Daddy ought to give a pep talk; I guess that's why he legged it down there to him when I gave him a good hiding...'

'Jamie's going to South Bank University in September,' Aunt Amanda told them. 'He went for his interview today and by all accounts it went very well, and the woman recommended him to two departments. I think he'll have a place by the end of the week, either sociology or English literature, depending on what he wants to do. What do you think of that then?'

'Mum,' Bev rolled her eyes. 'Jack was there years ago; Jack's thinking about his PHD now…'

'…Jack's thinking about himself. Let me tell you something, something only Delia, Felicity, Rupert and I really ever knew,' and she leant forward for emphasis. 'You know, the Daddy…how can I put it…it isn't always the one with the clearest kiss on their arse, you know.'

'What do you mean?!'

Aunt Amanda made ample opportunity of this advantage, although in truth it had only ever been hearsay, an idea even. 'Oh, they can be the Daddy in name, but someone else is doing the real stuff, the hard graft, sorting out the rows, the finances…do you think my brother Ben was ever really the Daddy? Your Uncle Ben, who died before either of you were born?' she nodded to one of the many pictures on the mantelpiece, the sandy-blond boy with the beaming smile, the swept over Fifties hair-style. 'He was meant to be the Daddy,' she said. 'But he wasn't capable; he was a little boy most of his life. Your Uncle Rupert was the Daddy to all intents and purposes, even though the only thing he had on his bum was a bit of a port wine stain!'

'Jack can be a proper Daddy,' Bev stood her ground, 'every bit as good as Phil was. Jack has that…that 'kiss', whatever it means!'

'Oh please,' Aunt Amanda swigged down the last of her tea. 'Jack isn't worthy to kiss Phil's soccer shoes, God rest his soul.'

'Mum,' Bev said. 'Jack is going to be the Daddy, and that's that. I've said many times, I may not like it, I may not understand it, but that's the way it has to be.'

'Over my dead body.'

Heath sighed; his mobile went and he replied to the text while Aunt Amanda strummed her long red nails on the table. 'Careful mum,' Bev said, trying to lighten the mood. 'You just paid through the arse for that varnish.'

'That was Carol,' Heath said, stuffing the phone back in his shirt pocket. 'My dinner's up.'

'Are you going to give Jamie a chance?' Aunt Amanda asked. 'He's good for more than selling tatty old paperbacks on that grotty old market, you know. No offence, my darling.'

'None taken, mum,' Heath said.

'Jamie's my baby just the way Jack is,' Bev said. 'But Jack…well you know mum…it's like you say, Jack has the kiss. Jack has the big arms, and the big chest….'

'Silly girl,' Aunt Amanda sighed. 'And like you said, you don't even know what that kiss means.'

'No I don't,' she said. 'You old farts never deemed to tell us.'

'And like I said,' and here she nodded to Heath, 'be glad that yours was blurred, indistinct. That's the reason you're alive now and Phil isn't.'

'Mum' Bev said, 'I'm not saying Jamie can't do better for himself, but…'

'…do you never wonder why Phil adored Jamie and not Jack?'

'...well, no but...maybe he just felt sorry for him. Everyone knew Jack was the Daddy. Maybe he thought Jamie needed a little loving too.'

'No my darling,' Aunt Amanda fixed her with a steely gaze. 'He knew Jamie had it in him to break the mould, to get rid of...'

'...rid of what?'

'Nothing.' Aunt Amanda said back and folded her arms, puffing air out of her mouth in short, regular bursts, 'nothing at all.'

Bev shook her head. 'You spend too much time alone here mum. Please. Sell this house. Come and live with me, or...or buy a little flat on the Ripple Road, or why not move in to Rachel's? She has plenty of room now that her Tracy's gone up north. I'm sure she'd love to have you.'

'I'm happy here.'

'You have too much time on your hands, mum' Heath glanced out of the window, as life on Vallance Road passed them by; kids laughing, the occasional car going past, maybe even someone come to see where the Krays used to live. 'Who's to say if you have another fall...what if its worse next time?'

'I tell you what,' Aunt Amanda snapped, 'why don't I just hurry up and die and get out of all your hair?! Look, I've had enough of this. You haven't paid me a genuine social call since before Phil died, and all of a sudden I'm glad. Let's have another six months out of each other's way, shall we? Now, don't let me keep you.'

'Mum!!' Heath rose only reluctantly. 'Please...be reasonable.'

'You all keep on looking out for Jack when he doesn't give a damn about any of you,' she ushered them towards the front door. 'I'll watch over Jamie, take the time and effort to see he learns to read, learns to read in his mid-twenties I say, that he betters himself...'

'Oh shut up mum' Bev sighed as she stepped onto the pavement, 'if you could only hear yourself. I swear you've got whatever it was Felicity had, what is they call it?! Alzheimer's?'

'My faculties are just fine, thank you,' Aunt Amanda folded her arms, stood her ground. 'Don't let me hold you up.'

'It's Delia's birthday in a couple of weeks, mum,' Heath said. 'We're planning...'

'She's my best friend,' Aunt Amanda sighed. 'I know all about the surprise party; it was my idea.'

'Oh mum stop being so bloody confrontational!' Bev snapped, hoisting her handbag up. 'You just call me when you've cooled off.'

'Don't hold your breath, my darling.' she watched them turn and head up towards the Bethnal Green Road. And then she laughed. 'For a moment,' she said, 'a moment that just seemed to jump at me suddenly, I saw you as children again, Phil suddenly in the middle, with an arm around either of your shoulders, both you boys in your West Ham strips, you Bev with your pigtails and one of your pretty dresses...' she wiped her knuckle across her cheek in anticipation of a tear, but none came. Then she turned on her heel and went inside, slamming the door behind her and double-bolting it. Bev and Heath exchanged glances, a simple shrug, and then carried on up the road.

Chapter 37

Tuesday 9th May 2006

The drive down from Islington to Brighton took about two hours, taking into account the stop-off at a services near the Sutton turn-off so that Bobby could run out and have a pee, and Jack could buy a lighter with which to ignite the joint he'd spent the last ten minutes painstakingly rolling, letting out an enormous 'Aaaahhhh!' as he exhaled, slumping back against the car and gazing up at the cloudless blue sky. Bobby hurried back to the car and climbed in the back, where Daniel was leafing through a copy of Sunday's *'News of the World'*. David was strumming his fingers on the steering wheel, wondering whether or not he was going to be warm in just a tight black t-shirt and slacks, something he'd opted for only to be in tandem with Jack's own cream coloured Reebok top and knee-length beach briefs, so that they presented – in his mind at least – a kind of beautifully buff London couple on a wistful mid-week excursion to the coast.

Jack clambered into the passenger seat and slammed the door shut, fiddling with his seatbelt and growingly increasingly frustrated, until he discovered he'd half shut it in the door. 'Okay mummy,' he beamed at David, after freeing himself. 'The children are getting fidgety,' and here he nodded to Daniel and Bobby. 'Crank the radio up and hit the accelerator. The alternative Woodfield family is off on a day out!'

'Bite me!' Daniel swiped at him with the edge of the paper.

'Okay daddy,' David nodded obediently. 'Brighton here we come!!'

By the time they were pulling into the city centre David had managed to rouse them all into wailing the lyrics to Katrina & the Waves 'love shine a light' with the windows down, and even Bobby was lightening up a little; the last time he'd asked if Jack thought anyone had told his dad the real reason he'd run away was somewhere back near Gatwick. His mum – Aunt Betty to the others, sans David – called as they were coasting past the Pavilion looking for somewhere to park, and again sans David the phone was passed around so that she could chat and giggle with them, reassure Bobby that the manager of KFC thought he was just a little '…under the weather', and in regards to this father that he thought the trip to Jack's entirely legitimate and prearranged. Jack even held the phone to David's ear, to give him a taste of exactly what his 'dotty old aunt' sounded like; Aunt Betty was prone to sudden fits of giggling and going off on complete tangents and she was discussing her shopping list with David as he tried to edge the car into a space between a white van and a Volvo near a billboard for 'The Ladyboys of Bangkok'.

'I want the Lanes,' Jack declared, pulling his Ray-Bans down over his eyes and glancing from left to right. 'I want second-hand record shops, and I want them now.'

'Let's find fit birds!' Daniel suggested, to which Bobby rolled his eyes. 'You said we'd find fit birds when we got here. Like that Dorothy friend of yours, the one you say you haven't shagged.'

'I haven't,' he said matter-of-factly.

'She's so fit, that Dorothy,' Daniel hurried to keep up with them. 'Reckon she'll be up for a chance with me now, then?'

'Oh please,' Bobby all but slapped his brow in disbelief. 'You're short and well...semi-fat; look at Jack! You're not even in the running.'

'Yeah?' he spat in the kerb. 'Well at least I'm not some skanky old queer.'

'Hey now,' David frowned, fumbling for his own sunglasses. 'Can we lose the Essex lingo for an hour or so at least? Call Bobby and I 'homosexuals', if you have to.'

'I still can't get used to people knowing about me,' Bobby shielded his eyes from the sun, suddenly realising with a little thrill how tall and dark David actually was. 'Maybe you could come with me when I come back to Barking, and...well, talk to my dad. He's a Father, you know; as in a priest, vicar-type thing.'

'Father Brian Woodfield,' David nodded, lolling an arm around his slight shoulders. 'I've heard...well...'

'He's a stubborn old cunt,' Jack said, making a beeline for a HSBC cashpoint. 'He always puts Aunt Betty down. Don't get me wrong, I don't think he means to, it's just habit. No wonder Jessica's pulling all the stops out to get away. The day we made our vow that we were gonna get out of Barking, well that was 'coz he'd bawled her out for hitching her school skirt up once she'd left the house and got 'round the corner. He even threw all her make-up in the bin, she found out when she'd got home.'

'He sounds like a perfect monster,' David said.

'You should try having him for a dad,' Bobby said, liking the feel of his rather brawny arm guiding him down past shops filled with ornately designed hash pipes and necklaces made of shark teeth and bits of coloured glass. 'He'll go ballistic when he finds out I'm gay. He goes all red and all the veins on his neck stand up, and he looks like he's gonna explode. I'll have to leave home. Hey!' and at this his blue eyes widened. 'I could move in with you and Jack like, full time!'

'I was there first, 'lady boy'' Daniel sneered.

'Daniel's very much in the traditional Essex boy breed, ain'tcha Danny boy?' Jack tugged his little cousin to the fore. 'But don't you think David's cool? Go on, even though you know he enjoys it up the shitter, ain't he just a hoot?!'

'I'm thinking of going versatile,' David said, winking at Jack. 'Maybe Daniel will bend over for me and give a novice his first try at the top spot?!'

'Get your queer hands away from me!!' Daniel darted ahead of them. 'Jesus H!!'

They wandered down the Lanes for about twenty minutes before Jack found a second-hand record shop selling genuine Beatles LPs. He was looking for a replacement copy of 'Revolver', his original having been ruined when Aunt Queenie had inadvertently used it as a coaster for her mug in his mum's flat, News Year's Eve '98. He'd bawled her out in front of everyone and called her 'a silly old bag', something he wouldn't have done prior to his and Jamie's sixteenth, the less said about which the better. 'They have one, Jack,' David located the dusty LP with its pencil art cover on a wall. 'Eight quid?'

'Five on eBay,' Jack lowered his sunglasses and chewed thoughtfully on the tips of them. 'But then again, well, remember that picture disc of John and Yoko I won last month, that was cracked when it arrived in the post? I left the cunt bad feedback and he had the cheek to do the same! I'm through with eBay, I tell you. I'm getting it here.'

'Oh. My. Fuck.' David had found something in the books section; he held it up for Jack to admire, a first edition copy of 'Magick without tears' by Aleister Crowley. 'I have to have this,' he said. 'It's rare as rocking horse shit, and look at the condition; it's 'as new'!'

'My Great-Great-Uncle Jeramiah knew him,' Jack said offhandedly. 'In fact, he taught him most of what he knew. Uncle Jeramiah went to stay with him in Cambridge when he was at Trinity College, and they used to conjure up familiars in their lunch break! Apparently Aleister made an early film of Uncle Jeramiah having sex with Minty Hardcore in the back of a punt. That is, if you believe in that sort of shite.'

David almost dropped the book. 'You never told me that!'

'Well I didn't remember it 'til just now,' he unhooked the 'Revolver' album off the wall and gently slipped it out, weighing the vinyl up and holding it to the light. 'Does it matter?'

'Oh yeah, just a little,' David slapped his brow in disbelief. 'We're meant to be compiling a comprehensive history of your family for my dissertation, the selfsame dissertation that might make it into book form if Fortean Times gives it the green light, and you just happen to leave out that your Great-Great-Uncle was pals with one of the most famous magicians in modern western society. Jesus! Aleister Crowley!! And you say Jeramiah taught him?!? Do you know how many books that information could rubbish, how many theories…'

'Take it easy!!' Jack seemed satisfied with the condition of the LP and took it to the counter. 'And keep your voice down; we don't want 'the children' twigging our little secret, do we?'

They wandered out into the busy little street, clocking Bobby and Daniel some way ahead, checking out hash pipes being sold on a rug on the side of the pavement. 'I'm sorry,' Jack said. 'I'm doing my own Masters, you know. These things slip my mind occasionally, and I've only got memory to recall these things from. I think it was Aunt Felicity who told me that. Jeramiah was her dad, you know.'

'I know, Jack,' David sighed; he found it so hard to be angry with him. 'I probably know more about your family's lineage than you do.'

Jack lolled an arm around his shoulder and squeezed, almost purring in his ear. 'I know you do, and I think it's marvellous. Just try and remember I have my own shit to deal with, and...'

'I kind of thought my dissertation was 'our shit," David said.

'Dave...I'm fucking my twin brother's girlfriend! Forgive me if I occasionally forget some fragment of a conversation from twenty years ago or something.' He set off down the path, shaking his head, 'Jesus, man.'

David watched him go, then bowed his head and removed himself from the crowd, from the relentless glare of the early summer sun. Jack's moods were like mercury lately, and for that he blamed Tiffany entirely. Why she couldn't settle for just one twin he didn't know, although just watching those big, broad shoulders receding into the sunlight was answer enough. David had visions of running off down the path after Jack, pivoting him around by the shoulders and saying to his face, 'Look, I love you. Do you know that? I love you. I always have, only you're too stupid to see it, you big dumb hunk of Essex man. You're the most exciting thing that's ever happened in my boring dumb-ass life...', only he didn't. He sniffed, went back in the shop and brought the Aleister Crowley book, then hurried down the path to find the three of them checking out graphic novels and trading cards in the window of the local comic shop. Apparently Daniel collected trading cards – mainly horror movie ones – and they had a cheap selection inside, and, after bumming a fiver from Jack he set to work examining each and every one, crouched next to a row of dusty cardboard boxes containing old copies of 'Booster Gold'. Jack turned to David and threw him that disarming smile, then slapped him on the back. 'Sorry mate. You know I love you, don't you? You're my best buddy.'

'I love you too,' David said.

They quit the Lanes in the mid afternoon and went to find somewhere to eat; 'the children' wanted pizza so they settled for the Pizza Hut near Churchill Square. Daniel's phone went off. 'It's Debbie,' he grinned. 'Hang on a sec...' what followed was maybe thirty or forty seconds of, 'Well we're in Brighton; at least it's not raining here,' and the like before he winced as she obviously hung up on him. 'She hung up on me!' he slapped the table with both hands, 'called me a fucking cunt for not inviting her! I hate my sister.'

'Be lucky you've got a sister,' David glanced at him over the top of the menu. 'I'm an only child, and believe me, it sucks, big time.'

'I'd love to be an only child...' Bobby gazed off into the distance, at the shoppers in the sunlight. 'Can you imagine that, Jack? Not to have all our cousins and aunts and uncles in our hair all the time?! To be able to walk down the street without someone calling your name, running over and asking what you're doing, where you're going...not having to remember a birthday or wedding anniversary almost every week...'

'...I should think that would be wonderful, to have that,' David sighed.

'It is!' Daniel declared. 'You get tons of birthday presents, and Christmas is like...well, fuck me, man! Especially when your mum's dead like mine is, and everyone feels sorry for you. I rake it in!'

'Yeah but you'd trade it for Aunt Sophie back, right?' Jack gazed at him. 'She was one'a my favourites, your old mum. She 'got' me, you know?'

'Yeah...' his face fell. 'Now it looks like I'm getting a new mum, too. And she's black!! or half-caste, or whatever.'

'The correct term is 'mixed race', dear child,' David folded the menu shut. 'Is that Carol, off the market?'

'Uh huh. Shit,' Daniel eyed him suspiciously. 'You know like, more about what's going on with us than we do!' he turned to Jack. 'Pillow talk?!'

'Well that was almost witty! Now go fuck yourself,' Jack slapped him with the menu, and therein ensued around a minute or so of the two of them jousting with the dessert menus, until the waiter came over and David coughed rather loudly, and they ordered their pizzas, not to mention their starters; garlic breads and 'cheesy wraps', their cokes and their fresh orange juices.

'I might give Uncle Richard a ring, see if wants to meet up,' Jack said suddenly. 'I bet the poor old queen gets all lonely down here.' He flipped open his mobile and made a quick call, then shut it and turned to David. 'The Bulldog?'

'Oh god it's terrible,' he said. 'I went there a couple times on weekends away from my parents. We want somewhere quiet, really. Tell him the Queens Arms.'

'Uncle Richard is a right old queer,' Daniel said, waggling his thumbs together. He glanced at Bobby. 'Maybe he can fix you up with someone, or you could move down here with him and leave me and Jack in peace!'

'Oh grow up,' Bobby sighed. 'You're such a wanky little child.'

'And you suck cock! Or you want to 'coz you're also a virgin!'

'The Queens Arms it is,' Jack said, turning his phone off. 'Five.'

'When did you last see your Uncle Richard?' David asked him.

'God...Uncle Phil's funeral, I think. Of course you know Uncle Phil lived down here with him in the Seventies...'

'Uncle Phil wasn't a homo as well, was he?' Daniel asked, sipping at his coke with a straw.

'Heck no,' Jack almost laughed. 'He ran away from Aunt Amanda's 'coz...'

'...'coz she was a creepy old witch!'

'...'coz he was fucking some girl in her bed when she was out working at Woolworths or something!'

'Good old Uncle Phil!' Daniel and Bobby almost said it in unison, and even high-fived each other.

'Uncle Richard's what you might call an 'old dandy',' Jack leant back as the starters arrived. 'One of those Joe Orton style caps, leather jacket, keychain on the belt and all that. It's quite sad really; I think he was born in the same year as Aunt Delia, so that'd make him…'

'…sixty eight,' David said through a mouthful of garlic bread.

'Uh huh.' Jack winked at Bobby. 'He might be able to give you a few pointers!'

'David's going to take me to the bars in Soho,' Bobby said proudly. 'He promised.'

'Yeah, I did at that…' he nodded, making a gesture of appeasement. 'We need to get you a better outfit too, maybe get you to a gym or something; how about a crop?'

'I want big arms, like Jack has,' Bobby said. 'You get tons of looks, Jack, but you don't even seem bothered; that girl nearly flashed her tits at you while we were in Next!'

'Oh I noticed,' Jack winked. 'But as tits go, well you can't beat Tiffany. You just can't; what do I call them, Davey?'

'Marvellous mammaries.'

'That's it; 'marvellous mammaries'. Jesus, change the conversation or I'll be packing it in a minute.'

'Someone ought to change the piped music in here,' David said quickly. 'Is this Whitney Houston?!'

'It is,' Bobby said wistfully.

'First record I ever brought was a Whitney single,' David went on. 'I think it was this one as well; 'Didn't we almost have it all'. Ah Whitney, you saw me through many lonely nights in my Bournemouth bedroom…'

'Whitney's on crack,' Daniel said matter-of-factly, and killed the conversation, such as it was, stone dead. They gorged themselves on slices of pizza for the next hour or so. Jack received several calls, one from his mum, one from Dorothy, and several texts from Tiffany; by the time the first call from cousin Jessica came in he was ready to switch the thing off but talked to her for five minutes 'coz she was his favourite, but by the time Aunt Betty was ringing to see how Bobby was now he'd put it on 'silent' and stuffed it in his pocket. She rang Bobby direct after that and he spent ten minutes reassuring her that all was well, that Jack and David had picked up a syllabus from South Bank University for him on the way down and he was going to look at it tonight, that he was through shovelling chicken at KFC, and had anyone told dad he was gay yet, the answer to which still proved to be a resounding negative.

'Apparently Jamie's got a place at South Bank,' he said as he came off the line. 'He's doing sociology, same as you did, Jack!'

'Oh please,' Jack almost choked on a slice of pepperoni. 'That is so dumb. J won't last five minutes doing a degree; he can barely read!! He must've got through on the clearing.'

'I told you Jamie came on like he was the Daddy or something when he saw me legging it to you,' Bobby said. 'I said, 'J you're not the Daddy; Jack is the Daddy'.'

'In theory,' Jack said. 'Everyone decided it but me, and I'm like, 'get to fuck!!"

'But you are the Daddy,' Bobby said.

'Well yeah,' he spread his arms, 'but I kind of want my own life...'

'You said you'd maybe be the Daddy for summer,' Daniel leant forward. 'You said you told Tiffany you would, 'coz Tiffany thinks we all really need a Daddy right now what with Uncle Phil gone almost six months and it's true we do, and you love Tiffany even though she's Jamie's girl so you'll come back after your exams and be the Daddy for summer, right? And then we can go to Chessington and Alton Towers and stuff, like we did with Uncle Phil; we can play Rounders and go to the cinema and you'll organise everything, and look after us all and...'

'Whoa, time out!!' Jack raised his hands. 'I said I was thinking about it! And only 'coz you two are giving me such a headache.'

'I bet you think we're mad, all this 'Daddy' talk,' Bobby said to David.

'Actually no,' he shrugged. 'Jack's told me all about it, and I think it's fascinating. The way that patriarchy dominates in your family is, from an East End perspective, both right and yet so very wrong at the same time, but having said that...'

'Chill!' Jack almost thumped his fist on the table. 'This was supposed to be a nice day out before I get my head down to revise, guys! less of the suffocating Woodfield talk!'

'You could be a part-time Daddy,' David had to say it. 'Aren't the majority of daddies estranged these days anyway; single parent families and all...'

'Bite me.'

They finished the rest of their pizzas in relative silence, with only Daniel complaining that the people on the top decks of the buses passing outside were staring in through the windows, but Jack told him to 'shut it' as he wasn't paying for the meal anyway. They left and wandered around the Churchill Square shopping centre for around half an hour. Jack brought some t-shirts in River Island, and David stood there admiring him as he tried them on, nodding and mouthing the word 'marvellous' over and over again. One of the shop floor girls made a blatant pass at Jack, and as they were leaving the shop one of her friends ran out and gave him the girl's number written on the back of a smudged till receipt. 'Vicki,' Jack said, turning it over in his hands as they mounted an escalator, then slipping it in his back pocket for future reference. 'She was ok. I'm not so keen on pure brunettes though, you know? I like strawberry blond, like Tiffany, or just plain blond, like my 'jess. That bird was kind of...well...'

'She looked like Katie Holmes,' David added helpfully.

'Yeah. I mean, I'd fuck her, but not in any great hurry.'

'I'd fuck her like, right now!!' Daniel craned his head around for another glimpse.

'Yeah but she wouldn't fuck you,' Bobby sighed. 'She's pretty.'

'At least she'd get fucked with me, with you she'd get fuck all!'

'Jesus, "children"!!' David stepped between them. 'You're making me glad I probably won't ever be a parent. Can't you play nicely, just for five minutes?!'

'He started it,' Daniel pouted. 'He keeps hinting I'm fat and ugly.'

'You are fat and ugly,' Bobby scowled. 'And you're homophobic. You have no redeeming features.'

'Am I ugly?' Daniel turned to David, mussing his hair in the reflection afforded by the escalator's glass divide. 'Would you...?'

'You're sixteen, right?' David mused, his chin in his hand in a slightly theatrical pose of thought. 'Far too young, and you could lose the trackie bottoms, but with a little work, and a little less of the Essex boy attitude, I think you could be quite passable.'

'Did you hear that?!' Daniel tugged at Jack's arm. 'Your mate wants to stick his cock up my arse!'

Jack tried on a blue pinstripe suit in 'Suits You', something he had in mind for that job he'd start on Cheapside or Cannon Street in the autumn; the price tag made him flinch but David offered to put it on his credit card, but they left the shop undecided, and began to make their way back towards the Pavilion, and St James Street. After a quick look in a couple of the gay sex stores, wherein David and Daniel engaged in a spirited duel with some rather oversized dildos, the initial handling of which caused Daniel to squeal in disgust, they ended up in the Queens Arms. The pub was a rather homey, almost traditional low-ceilinged affair, stuck up one of the side streets. They settled down to wait for Uncle Richard in a big seat right in front of the main window, with a round comprising alcopops for Bobby and Daniel, and pints for Jack and David. 'My feet ache,' Daniel said. 'I haven't walked so much in like, ages.'

David sat back, scrutinising him. 'What do you want to do, Daniel? I mean, you left school recently, right? What does your sister do?'

'She opens her big gob a lot.'

'No, really.'

'I wanna...I don't know. I can't sell no more stuff 'coz dad'll beat me so bad next time he'll leave marks!'

'Come to uni with me, and with Jamie,' Bobby suggested.

Daniel considered. 'What should I do, Jack?'

Jack sat back, running his fingers over his newly cropped hair. 'What would the Daddy say...'

It was just at this juncture that Uncle Richard walked, or rather, hobbled, into the pub. He looked a lot older than when they'd last seen him, and that had only been January; so old in fact that Bobby almost gasped audibly, and put his hand up to his mouth 'girlie style', as Daniel would comment on the way home. His face had little pits in it and his eyes were sunken; only with the aid of a cane did he navigate the few steps from the door to their seat, Jack jumping up quickly to make room for him and to provide a shoulder to lean on as he settled down, coughing suddenly and uncontrollably for almost a minute before patting his chest and smiling up at them over wire-rimmed glasses.

'Well you make me feel even older than I am,' he smiled, dabbing at the corners of his mouth with a spotted handkerchief. He looked up as David returned from the bar with a tray of drinks. 'And who's this strapping young man?!'

'Ah, Uncle Richard, this is David; David Samuels,' Jack stood up as if to emphasise his own 'strapping-ness'; 'he's my flatmate, best buddy, uni buddy, etc etc.'

'Ah!' Uncle Richard nodded. 'So are you two…?'

'Ah no,' David almost blushed, but he too hadn't been expecting such a wreck of an old man, and the flush didn't really fight its way to his cheeks. 'I am, and Jack still isn't, but I'm working on him,' and he winked and they all laughed. 'But Bobby here is,' he added helpfully. 'He's only just 'come out'.'

Uncle Richard looked at Bobby over the top of his glasses. 'So your Aunt Amanda was telling me. And have you told 'the Pope' yet?' 'the Pope' being his personal nickname for Bobby's father.

'Have I heck as like!' Bobby gasped, making way for David to return to the bar for Richard's tipple. 'I was thinking Jack was going to do the Daddy with me and, well, tell him for me or something…'

'You're looking very strapping yourself Jack,' Uncle Richard nodded. 'What lovely big arms you have, could set an old queen's heart aflutter.'

Jack nodded, satisfied. 'You're looking…'

'…like a dried-up piece of toast, I know, you don't have to say it.'

'Are you well?'

'Actually, no.' he settled, shifted a little, and looked up at them. 'I have full-blown AIDS.'

The silence was palpable, punctuated only by Daniel as he shifted uncomfortably in his seat. David broke it, handing him his wine and saying, 'I'm very sorry to hear that, Mr Woodfield.'

'Richard, please. There are so many Mr Woodfields.'

'I take it the family didn't…'

'No we didn't,' Jack was still digesting the information, running his eyes unashamedly over the skeletal form beside him. 'Does Aunt Amanda know?'

'Oh I think so,' he waved a hand dismissively. 'Yes I think I told her when I was diagnosed HIV positive, a long, long time ago; I may even have been one of the first. What an accolade. But I made her swear not to tell, although I can't even remember why. I could use a good bout of sympathy right now, especially off you hunky young boys,' and here he squeezed Jack's bulging bicep playfully, looking at David much as if he wanted to do the same to him. 'How is the old witch, by the way? She wasn't in much of a mood to talk the other night.'

'Well I haven't seen her since…well since the funeral, when I last saw you,' Jack felt a little uncomfortable, David could tell. He wanted to ask questions, everything he'd ever heard about AIDS. He doubtless wanted to ask how long his uncle had left; he was no spring chicken, after all. 'I'm kind of a West End boy now, Uncle Richard.'

'So I hear, so I hear,' he supped his white wine delicately, then went to coughing again. The boy exchanged nervous glances, as though he were about to cease on this very table. 'And the LSE too. I take it you're a student there too, David?'

'That's right; sociology, with a little bit of an occult twist.'

'Oh well you'll love our family then,' he laughed, "the wacky Woodfields!"

'David wants to study us,' Jack winked at him playfully. 'He thinks we're a fascinating throwback to a way of life that's fast being engulfed by modern, 'alternative' families; the fall of 'Essex man' and all that.'

'Belonging to this family is both a blessing and a curse,' Uncle Richard sat back, dropped his cane and waiting for Bobby to pick it up for him. 'When you want someone to talk to there's always someone there, but then again them always being there can really get on your tits.' They all laughed. 'But it's peaceful down here; I'm the only Woodfield on the south coast, so far as I know. I have my books, my little circle of friends, my dog, my partner Owen…I'm content. You don't want for so much when you reach my age; a kind of grim acceptance sets in.' he looked up to find the four of them gazing at him almost in horror. 'Sorry. I suppose this isn't exactly riveting conversation for a bunch of young lads, is it.' He patted Daniel's little belly. 'And you, you little horror. If you don't stop eating the fish and chips you're going to end up as big as…well, we Woodfields don't really do the fat, do we? We're all quite fit, one way or another.'

'Am I really that fat?!' Daniel looked crestfallen.

'No, dear child, just a little…rotund.' He chuckled. 'And I suppose you want to know a little more about how I came to be this unfortunate shell of my former glorious self, aren't you?'

'Actually yeah,' Jack was becoming visibly concerned for someone who had always been more of a favourite of Jamie's than of his. 'Does my mum know? Is anyone looking after you?'

'You'd have to ask Amanda. As for care, well there are health services of course, down here…well it's the gay capital, isn't it, so there's no shortage of shoulders to cry on, and those with similar stories, well they're an abundance. I take around twenty five pills a day,' he glanced at his watch, which seemed only to emphasise his skinny wrist with its great big leather straps. 'And I need to take one in a minute or two…' he fished in his tweed jacket for a bottle containing some large blue pills, one of which he washed down with a swig of the wine. 'Ah, better. How is Jamie, by the way? I do worry about Jamie now that Phil is gone; he idolised him, you know. We all did. He was…well, he just was, you know. He was the son I never had, Phil was. Listen to me. What a corny old queen I sound!' 'Anyone who had a heart' by Dusty Springfield was playing on the jukebox and he began to sway to it, knocking into their shoulders until they all repeated his movements, and when the song ended he burst out laughing and clapped appreciatively.

'Jamie's ok…' Jack said. 'He's…'

'…they had a fight last month,' Daniel grinned, 'over Tiffany!!'

'Oh boys!!' Uncle Richard's face might have been mock concern. 'There's plenty of pussy, isn't that what they say. Well how vulgar. But you and Jamie never did really get on, did you ?'

'It's not that…' Jack shifted awkwardly. 'We just have nothing in common. Nothing except the family, that is, and the family…'

'…scares you?'

'Suffocates.'

'Quite. But I'm still your old 'Uncle Monty', am I right?!' and he here went to squeezing Jack's thigh. 'What powerful thighs you have, on top of your big arms and your broad chest. Very much the Woodfield male, you are, baptised in the testosterone spring and all that. Now you know of course that you're the exact double of Jeramiah Woodfield, who was ever so beautiful; people used to weep in the street to see him pass, in his coat and tails; what cheekbones, and all that. You know of course I have some old photographs if you'd like to…'

'Oh we'd love to,' David beamed.

'No we wouldn't.' Jack said firmly.

They spent the next hour so talking about various family members; about Bobby's 'coming out' dilemma; about Uncle Heath's new girlfriend Carol; about Tamsin's miscarriage; about the upcoming surprise party for Aunt Delia's birthday; and about how everyone was doing without Uncle Phil around, basically. They didn't talk much more about how long Uncle Richard had been full-blown, about what kind of pain – if any – he was in; he seemed to pick up the longer he was there, the more wine he drank, almost as though he were leeching the youth and vigour out of the rest of them. When Jack went to the toilet and David to the bar he followed the latter and stood next to him, sliding a twenty pound note in his hand. 'This round is mine,' he said, squeezing the money into his hand. 'Well you are a lovely young man, of course Jack's never mentioned you before but Jack has taken it upon himself to personally abdicate all family responsibility, and the like. And in some ways I don't blame him. I don't envy him one bit. You know Phil used to live with me when he was a teenager, and all this 'Daddy' nonsense used to grind him down…do you know about this?'

David nodded, cleared his throat. 'I know…well, bits and bobs. As Jack said, I find it quite fascinating actually.'

'It's all a load of old crock if you ask me,' Uncle Richard laughed to himself. 'Although the idea of having a big strong man to look over the whole family and make sure everyone is alright does have a certain homoerotic appeal...' they laughed freely, easily. 'You're fond of Jack?'

'Well he's my best friend,' David paid for the round but remained at the bar. 'I care for him.'

'I can tell. You care a lot.'

David felt the colour rising to his cheek, and he turned to make sure Jack was still in the toilets. 'Does it show?'

'We stately old homos have a way of knowing these things. Just...be careful.'

'Careful?'

Uncle Richard nodded, and sipped his wine, made a face. 'That's a little off.'

'Do you want another?'

'No it's fine. No...it's just this enormous family of ours; some people in it tend to believe some very strange things.'

'Oh I'm no stranger to the odd bit of snickering and name-calling.'

'I'm not talking about that, dear boy,' Uncle Richard sipped a little more wine. 'Oh they're Essex in their attitude as much as the next man, no...just...be careful, please? Like I said, some of the people in this family of mine believe some very strange things, and sometimes it's all very cute and sexy, and other times...well at other times it isn't.' he squeezed David's shoulder and made his way back to the seats, waiting for him to join them before he resumed the conversation.

The evening drifted on at a pleasant speed, as the light outside gradually turned from a clear blue to a more mellow shade, and the shadows of those passing by outside grew long and leaner, and cast the most extraordinary patterns on the walls inside as they went on their way. Bobby didn't really drink but Uncle Richard told him in no uncertain terms that he deserved a stiff drink – and perhaps a stiff cock – or two for putting up with 'the Pope' for all these years, and so by around eight thirty his little cheeks were glowing and his he was grinning inanely and pouring forth that yes, he did in fact have a bit of a crush on David, and that in fact he wanted nothing more than to climb over the table and sit on his lap. Daniel was downing them at a rate of knots and getting louder and more leery every time he spoke. He admitted missing his dad but not his sister, and suddenly his mood swung and he became all teary eyed and began talking about his mother, before falling asleep against Uncle Richard's shoulder, his mouth wide open. Jack began to grill Richard a little more on his condition, while David listened intently and tried to ignore the fact that Bobby was all but making goo-goo eyes at him. The kid was cute, but a little too young, a little too skinny, and a little too inexperienced.

'...I shall want to die at home, of course,' Uncle Richard was saying, 'surrounded by Woodfields, but only those whom I ever got on with, of course. I should like to have ice cold water pressed gently to my lips on a flannel, by you Jack, I think, wearing only a leather thong, and with your brother Jamie close by, in white briefs. He's ever so pretty, is Jamie; you are ever so handsome, and Jamie is ever so pretty. Yes, I think that'll do nicely...'

'Nonsense,' David said. 'With the drugs they have today there's no reason why you won't see out your natural life span...'

'...oh there's nothing natural about a Woodfield's life span, my handsome young duck.'

'You'll want a lift back to your place?' Jack asked.

'Of course. Owen, my dear, dear Owen, well he's entertaining elsewhere tonight, so I have the place to myself, if you boys want to stop over; poor David here can't drink because he has to drive you all back to London...'

'We'll see how we go,' David smiled politely. He desperately wanted to take him up on the offer, to see the old photographs of Jeramiah, and to rifle through the other memorabilia sure to be found there, doubtless a few keepsakes left from Phil's time as lodger. 'It's up to Jack, really.'

'I'll get a round in,' Jack replied, his mind somewhere else. Uncle Richard followed him to the bar, a little unsteadily due to the drink, and when he reached it he had to brace himself on Jack's shoulder. David leant over to listen and squeezed Bobby's outstretched hand absent-mindedly.

'I want a firm word with you, my boy,' Richard was saying, his voice slightly slurred. 'You will indulge a silly old queen, won't you?'

Jack frowned, then threw him a cheery wink. From the look on his face, David knew him so well, that he was feeling that awfully amoral something, about being young and tall and blond and muscular when the person standing next to you was on death's door, literally. 'Go for it, 'unc,' he said.

'Those boys,' he said, nodding back to the table, to Daniel and Bobby in particular. 'It's written all over their faces.'

'It is?'

'It is, only you're so wrapped up in yourself you can't see it.'

'I don't...'

'Oh you do my boy, you do. I'm not the silly old fool you think I am. I know how marvellous it is to be young and handsome and to have heads turn as you walk down the street; to never have doubted myself for one instant, I've known how that felt as well. To be the one everyone looks up to and admires, when all you are is a conceited little shit who can't see anything because he's too busy staring at his own bloody biceps!!'

Jack ran his tongue the circuit of his mouth. 'No offence 'unc, but you were never in my league.'

'Oh I know I was never as tall as you, I was never blond...and I don't have a clear lip print on my bum, which is as smooth as a baby's, am I right? I can tell by your expression you know what's coming. But see, I do have a mark there, a little fleshy pimple. Enough, just enough to mark me out as a little bit different, a little bit interesting, you know…to those who notice such things.'

Jack shrugged, and he glanced at David, who met his eye worriedly. 'It's just a birthmark.'

'Maybe you're right. If you want my opinion then yes it is, that's all it is, and all of the bull that goes with it is just that; bull. But our family…we do things a certain way, you know?'

'Tell me about it.'

'Right. And like it or not it's you those two little bleeders over there are looking to to solve their problems; Daniel needs a direction 'coz for whatever reason or other Heath just doesn't seem to be able to give it to him, and Bobby…well Bobby needs you there when he confronts 'the Pope', and to show that he can be a Woodfield and gay and that it doesn't really matter. Do you understand me, Jack?'

Jack pursed his lips. 'Yeah…I think I do.'

'Good. And are you man enough to do it? to think about someone other than yourself for a change? Do you even think about that handsome young David, who clearly thinks the sun shines out of your proverbial, ever? Or is he just someone to ferry you around, to tell you how good you look, and to buy you drinks, hmmm?' and he glanced back at David, who managed to turn his head away and pretend to be listening to Bobby just in time.

'Alright, I get the picture,' Jack had raised a hand as if to ward off a blow. 'Look, I have some shit I have to deal with, but when that's done…'

'…when that's done you get on that District Line, or in his car; in fact, I don't care how you get there, you just get to Barking and you present yourself and you say, 'here I am, I'm the Daddy, now what do you want me to do?!'.'

Chapter 38

Thursday 11th May 2006

'I'm the Daddy,' Jamie said to himself, over and over, in-between glancing at his watch and wiping the sweat from his brow with the back of his arm. 'I'm the Daddy; now what do you want me to do?!?'

A mini heat wave had erupted in the last day or so, and as the relentless sun all but melted tube tracks together he was totally unaware that Aunt Amanda was being forced to spend forty-odd minutes somewhere between St Paul's and Holborn fanning herself with a copy of the free *'Metro'* newspaper, until the problem was rectified, by which time one woman had almost passed out, and a young Asian man had had a panic attack. He was still waiting for her at the Charing Cross Road exit just under Centre Point when she finally emerged, lowering her sunglasses to catch sight of him in his tight white t-shirt and cut-off shorts, arms folded, chewing gum. 'Darling!' she all but collapsed against him. 'I thought I was finished, for sure. Times like this it almost galls me that I look twenty years younger than I actually am, because no one made any allowances for me when the air conditioning ran out. I thought I was going to come out crispy-fried!'

''I'm the Daddy,' he declared, well out of earshot of passers-by. 'Now what do you want me to do?!?' and then he folded his arms and scowled. 'What do you think?!'

She made a 'hhhmmmm' noise, then stepped back, rubbing her chin. 'It needs some work...' and then she caught the look of woe that passed over his face and moved in, grabbing his shoulders and shaking him. 'Oh darling, don't be such a drama queen! It's still early days yet; early days.'

'We can go and sit in Soho Square,' he suggested, threading his arm through hers. 'I got mineral water and sandwiches from Boots, all low-cal, so's it doesn't fuck with my new diet. I'm watching my body fat intake and everything.'

'I did have chocolate,' she peered into her carrier bag. 'But I suspect it may have liquefied. Let's pop in somewhere and get some more, and perhaps a little bottle of bubbly; we need to toast your acceptance to South Bank!'

'It's only a conditional offer,' he led her across the road, 'subject to my getting the pass certificate from Sight & Sound.'

'A mere formality,' they cut past the Astoria and set about finding a vacant patch of grass. 'You look wonderful darling, you do know that? You weren't in bad shape before but with the diet and the weights...well, look at all the heads you're turning! You're up for giving that brother of yours some serious competition.'

'Most of them 'round here are queers,' Jamie whispered, spreading the cloth he offered her a safe distance from the nearest sprinkler. 'All this muscle posing and stuff, like you said, it's more Jack's thing than mine. He's even got his very own gay slave, that David person! He does everything for Jack, so mum reckons! He does his washing and ironing and all Jack has to do is walk around the flat topless now and again!' he made a little noise. 'I don't see why I have to be ripped just to be the Daddy.'

'Ripped?' she lowered her sunglasses.

'Muscled; toned, you know. Do I actually have to get as big as Jack is?'

'Well the Daddy has to be someone you can look up to, physically as well as spiritually, emotionally, and all that,' Aunt Amanda produced two wine glasses from the bag and began to pour the champagne into them. 'I don't recall a skinny Daddy, not ever, I don't think. It just isn't done, darling. It's all about hyper-masculinity.'

'Yeah but Uncle Phil…well he wasn't exactly the Rock, was he?!'

'No,' she handed him his glass. 'But he was still physically fit, and he was tall too; that went in his favour. Minty Hardcore simply can't abide anything under six foot. Here darling,' she raised her own glass, and then raised her voice loud enough for those in the immediate vicinity to hear exactly what she was saying. 'Congratulations on your university offer, my darling Jamie; here's to many years of academic achievement ahead!'

'Cheers,' he nodded, grinning despite himself as several of the young lads whom he'd cheerfully referred to as 'queers' hollered out, '…cheers Jamie; well done sweetheart!'.

'It's sweet,' he licked his lips. 'I like sweet.'

'You're so 'twin-ish',' she laughed, tossing back her hair and resting on the flats of her hands. 'Jack prefers sour.'

'They went to Brighton the other day,' Jamie said. 'Him, Daniel, Bobby, and that David, and I bet he had to drive. I wasn't invited, as usual. Jack doesn't reply to any of my texts.'

'How many have you sent?'

'Two.' And that in itself was something of an exaggeration.

'Darling,' she sighed, 'since you were plucked from your mother's body you and Jack have gone your own separate ways, so why should now be any different. You can't say as he didn't make the effort, in the past, but you were…well, let's just say you weren't always as agreeable as you are now.'

'I guess, it's just…' he cracked open the sandwiches – a rather squashed selection of cucumber and ham – and offered her one. 'I think Tiffany is spending a lot of time there too, you know? It was something Debbie said…'

'…Debbie is always saying something, darling; her tongue is practically athletic. If anyone's possessed it's her, the only problem is no one would notice.'

Jamie looked at her. 'I think Tiffany is through with me.'

Aunt Amanda peered into his face, but it was so hard to read. 'You don't seem heartbroken, darling. Don't think I haven't seen you with that girl…Louise, is it? Laughing and joking; holding hands once or twice, so I recall!'

He shrugged. 'After losing Uncle Phil I'm kind of numb. Louise is just a mate.'

'You're going your own way,' she said. 'And Tiffany, with her modelling, is going hers. This is life at its most tragic and it's most beautiful. Enjoy the time you had together, that you had each other for as long as you did, and then move on.'

Jamie peeled the bread off his sandwich and set about removing the cucumber slices. 'I mean I might be wrong, and she is just really busy, but still…' he stared off into space. 'Anyway, you're right, things are going great for me right now; I look great, so I'm told, I feel great, I'm doing great, you know I'm reading a book by myself now?! It's Jordan's autobiography! I finished my horror book that Daniel lent me already! It's got some well big words in it. I sit there sometimes with a dictionary or look them up online, but I'm getting it. I'm joining the library down Charing Cross Road too, 'coz they've got a bigger selection.'

'Wonderful,' she nodded. 'Try some Dickens next; Dickens is marvellous. I envy you almost, for all the books I've read that you've yet to.'

He swigged a little more of the champagne. 'It still feels a bit…poncey, you know?'

Aunt Amanda smiled. 'That's your inner Essex man fighting it, bit you must resist. Your Uncle Phil was quite cultured as well you know; I bet you didn't know he tried to write a book on the Mod revival, but the manuscript got lost. The trick,' and here she leant forward as if to emphasise her point, 'is to strike a healthy balance between the Neanderthal and the metrosexual, which I think we're achieving to marvellous effect, if I do say so myself.'

'It's Aunt Delia's big birthday bash in a few weeks,' he said. 'You will come won't you? I mean I heard you and mum had a few words the other night…'

'Your dear mother's heart is in the right place,' Aunt Amanda said. 'But she knows nothing about some things, and plenty about nothing, if you catch my drift. But I'll be there; Delia is my closest living relative. You know she knows what I'm doing too, grooming you as the Daddy.'

'What did she say?'

'Well she's right in that it's never been done before, but then we've never had a Daddy like Jack before, darling, simply too far up his own anus to even realise his family exists.'

He shifted a little. 'Has this really never happened before? I mean, where the Daddy just didn't want to do it, so they had to get someone else?'

Aunt Amanda paused. 'My baby brother Ben, as I've told you, was never fit to be the Daddy and I wouldn't have let him anyway. I didn't know enough then, and I wasn't ready to take *her* on, so he kind of got cajoled into it anyway, and you know how that turned out. Now I am ready, however.'

'When I'm the Daddy, and she likes my arms and stuff enough...well you'll jump her or whatever, won't you?!'

'Darling, I shall be on her quicker than...well, pretty damn quick, anyway.'

'Quicker than flies on shit?'

'I'd rather not think of myself as a fly darling, but yes.'

'I feel a bit like bait,' Jamie laid back, his hand on his stomach.

'Try not to see it like that,' she said. 'When the dust settles you'll still be the Daddy, and you'll be a Daddy that doesn't need her; now, what is she?'

'...a crafty little whore.'

'Exactly. And I think Jack will thank you for what you're doing, because then he'll be free to do whatever he wants without anyone ever getting on his case. Perhaps when all is said and done, you and Jack might be the best of friends.'

'It's not really his fault, is it?' Jamie gazed up at her. 'I mean, when Jack's an arse...well I think I would be too, if I had all that weight and expectation on me; he's had it his whole life, I've only had it off you for a few months.'

'Don't feel too sorry for him,' she said. 'Phil only died Christmas gone, so he'd had years to get used to the idea.'

'Like Prince William, and I'm Harry the spare; the heir and the spare.'

'Well look at it this way darling,' she took his hand and squeezed it gently. 'At least you don't look like a horse.'

He laughed, glanced at his watch. 'I have to get back soon.'

'I think I'll stay here,' she took some sun-block from her bag and began to apply it on her arms and shoulders. 'It's gorgeous, and there are all these beautiful people to ogle. When you get to my age you can ogle indiscriminately, darling, and if you're caught then people just feel sorry for you.'

'What happens next?' he asked. 'I mean, when are we going to 'go public'?'

'I'm thinking of making the grand announcement on your Aunt Delia's birthday,' Aunt Amanda said. 'There'll be a fair few nice surprises that day; her Hayden is being released from the 'Scrubs two days before and I'm going to hide him so he can show up and surprise her. Now having Hayden Woodfield as your surprise guest would be most people's idea of a nightmare, but your Aunt Delia and her blind spot...'

'What about Nick?'

'Oh he didn't do so well, which is quite surprising when you consider Nick's the angel, and Hayden's the rabid little animal and all. They sent Nick to a place called Grendon, which is some sort of special prison up past Oxford. I dread to think what he told the prison shrink to end up being carted off there, but I wouldn't have been at all surprised if he didn't do it just to get away from his brother.'

Jamie grinned. 'I bet he said he came from a family of male witches from Essex or something...'

She raised her champagne, and smiled. '...we're Harry Potter for chavs, darling.'

Chapter 39

Friday 12th May 2006

The floor length windows up at the back of the Barking Dog were thrown wide open on the Friday evening before the FA Cup Final, and the place was full of Hammers fans ready to board the coach or train to Cardiff in the morning; Jamie was among the lucky ticket holders, along with Uncle Eddie, Uncle Heath, and cousins Casey, Michael, Clay, Sara and her boyfriend Ron, as well as Jamie's best mate Adam. Tonight's drinking was a celebration both of this and a little impromptu congratulation on his getting a conditional offer from South Bank University, news which Aunt Amanda had spread by way of one strategically placed phone call, that therein led to another, and another, and so on and so forth, via the family grapevine. Most of the cousins and uncles and aunts had pitched up, all but engulfing the family area of the bar, the numbers swollen by their friends and well-wishers, and other locals; at one point it seemed as if there wasn't a person in the place who hadn't slapped Jamie on the back and bellowed, 'Congratulations lad!!' in his ear. The only notable absences were Jack – who had been unlikely to show up anyway – and Bobby and Daniel, the latter's ticket for tomorrow waiting for him on his dad Heath's sideboard. Aunt Amanda had made a rare trip from Bethnal Green after being picked up by Springer Woodfield, and was holding court up at the back along with Aunt Delia and some of their friends from 'the good old days'. Mum was in a somewhat restrained mood, and when Jamie asked her when they were finally going to meet her new boyfriend she waved a hand dismissively and said, 'Soon my darling, soon.'

Half an hour earlier Aunt Amanda had clutched him by the shoulders and whispered in his ear, 'This is your night darling, so enjoy it; it'll be Aunt Delia's birthday all too soon and then someone else's after that; you know how it is in this family, so lap it up.' he'd been about to mention that it was his and Jack's birthday in early July but it seemed a little off, so he nodded and smiled and took a hearty swig of his pint. He'd texted an invite to Tiffany but she hadn't responded, and he was looking out for Debbie to see if she was of a mind to offer up any more of her cryptic comments, flitting from person to person and talking through a mouthful of gum, blowing bubbles that got larger in relation to how bored she was. No sign of her tonight though, and maybe that was for the best.

He wondered how Daniel was going to get to the coach tomorrow, coming from Jack's, and whether or not Uncle Heath would give him another slap 'round the back of the head when he laid eyes on him, although he'd promised not to. Uncle Heath's new girlfriend Carol, the one who ran the second-hand DVD stall on the East Street market was with him; she was quite a stunner, mixed race and straight out of the Halle Berry mould, and the whole family seemed to take to her. There was of course always the danger that she might be overwhelmed, as so many other had been, by the sheer number of Woodfields pressing their hands to hers and introducing themselves, but as yet she seemed to be taking it in her stride, deferring to Uncle Heath only occasionally to ask him who this or that one was in relation to his good self.

Someone toasted Uncle Phil over near the bar and almost forty or fifty glasses went upwards to a chorus of 'Uncle Phil', or just plain 'Phil', depending on who it was. Jamie was at a point now where he could hear his name and smile a little instead of feeling like he was going to burst into tears. Aunt Amanda raised a glass and toasted her brother Ben and others followed suit, and pretty soon they were toasting anyone and everyone who had passed away in the last forty years, from Felicity to Rupert, Sophie to Andrea.

He felt a hand on his shoulder and looked up to see cousin Clay angling in on him from on high. 'Congrats, 'cuz,' he beamed. 'You're finally doing the sensible thing and getting out of here. Now, did you hear about Hayden's release?'

'Aunt Amanda mentioned something; a surprise for Aunt Delia's birthday?'

'That's right, she's hiding him out so's we can present him at the party, so not a word of it, 'k?'

'You got it, mate.' It wasn't the right time or place to make some comment about how unexcited he was by the whole idea of Hayden back in the family midst, although if Clay had said something, which wasn't unknown but usually in a semi-affectionate way, well then he would've jumped on it at once.

Clay ambled off and was replaced seconds later by Adam, utilising his bar break to join in the revelry. 'Alright?' he lolled an arm around Jamie's shoulders. 'Turn out did you proud, didn't it? Let's just hope the team does the same for us tomorrow.'

'You bet.'

'You heard anything from Tiffany?'

Jamie shook his head, took a particularly large swig of his pint. 'Nothing. Makes me seem a right sad old fucker, doesn't it?!'

Adam jostled him in a kind of semi-affectionate manner. 'It'll sort itself out, mate.'

'Yeah,' he nodded, nearly gnashing his teeth on the rim of the glass. 'That's what I keep telling myself.'

Jamie went off to the toilets a couple of minutes later and ended up chatting about the possibilities of a Hammers win with one of the guys in the urinal, then pretty much the same with cousin Michael as he did the hourly toilet check, high-fiving him before returning to the bar to be handed a fresh pint by Adam as he went back on duty.

'You ready for tomorrow then, matey?' Uncle Heath asked, again with the lolling arm thing. 'That little bleeder of mine better get his arse up here for eight or…well, it'd be too late to sell his ticket on eBay, wouldn't it?' and he laughed and jostled Jamie a little. 'You know all about eBay, don't you?!'

'Reckon so,' Jamie nodded, indeed now something of an eBay whiz, with several bids on West Ham memorabilia in the pipeline. 'We could always flog it here though, first thing, if he doesn't show up; reckon he'd be gutted though.'

'Wish Phil could be here to see it.'

'Uh huh.'

Uncle Heath squeezed a little tighter. 'They'll win it for him.'

'They better. It's Gerrard I'm worried about; the man is lethal.'

'What do you think of Carol?' he inclined his head over to where the woman in question was being formally introduced to Aunt Amanda as if she were royalty or something. 'She's beautiful, ain't she?'

'Uh huh.'

'You heard from that bird of yours, Jamie?'

'No. She's doing lots of modelling, I think.' He shifted a little and tried not to think that Uncle Heath might be trying to score a cheap point or two on account of being called 'a sad old bastard' the other week, but he didn't imagine that was the case; Uncle Heath was above all that sort of thing. 'She's fed up of working on Morelli's,' he went on. 'And she's good looking enough to model, so…"

Uncle Heath sniffed. 'Well she is a looker, I'll give her that.'

'Yeah she is. Is Debbie around?'

'Nope; went out with her girly mates, went to the flicks or something.'

''k.'

As Uncle Heath departed he was replaced by cousin Laquisha, her boyfriend Gael notable by his absence. 'How's it hanging, cuz?' she planted a smacker on his cheek. 'Taking a leaf out of Jack's book at last, eh? Bet you won't be back here in a hurry, leave me and the others with this crazy arse family of ours.'

'It's only a conditional offer,' and it was only about the thirteenth time he'd said it. 'And it won't be 'til September anyway; either sociology or English literature.'

'I want to get out of this shit-hole now too,' she whispered. 'Bloody BNP and all; you heard what happened to me at work the other week?!'

'Yeah it sucks,' now it was his turn to do the lolling arm thing, although he caught her looking at his hand as it rested on her shoulder as though it were some kind of foreign object, and quickly pulled back a little. 'But most people don't think like that, 'quish,' he said.

'Enough do to make me think about it,' she said. 'Reckon I might see if there's any more room at Jack's!'

'I hear it's becoming a regular hotel.'

'I miss him,' she sighed. 'You think with Uncle Phil gone he might come back a bit more; it was really great when we all went clubbing the other week, just like old times, apart from Debbie doing the convulsion dance, of course.'

'Yeah,' he half smiled. 'But I don't think he'll be back. He likes it in the West End too much.'

She studied him. 'Do you speak at all?'

'Nah,' he sniffed. 'Aunt Amanda says Woodfield twins either love or loathe each other; I guess we're more on the 'loathe' end of the scale.'

'How can you not love Jack?!' she leant back, the better to flash her big chocolate eyes at him. 'He's like, the Daddy in waiting!!'

'Well…'

'Ah there's my man,' she nodded up the front near the doors, where Gael was pushing through the throng. 'I got a lap to straddle; see ya gorgeous,' she planted a kiss on his cheek. 'Nice baby biceps, by the way.'

Jamie smiled, and sipped a little more of his pint, the wondered exactly what she'd meant by 'baby'. He saw mum near one of the windows, lighting up and gazing out at the Job Centre on the opposite side of Wakering Road. He walked over and put an arm around her. 'You ok mum?' he asked. 'You seem sort of out of it.'

'Hello my sweetheart.' She rubbed his hand. 'I was miles away.'

'Not enjoying yourself?'

'Of course I am,' although she looked like it about as much as someone looks like they enjoy being held up at gunpoint. 'It's your night and I'm happy for you. I just have a lot on my mind, is all. Your Uncle Heath seems made up with that Carol, doesn't he?'

'He does,' Jamie nodded, breathing in the thick night air. He turned and gazed at her face, soft and sweet and framed by that lovely familiar lemon-blond hair. 'I love you, mum,' he said suddenly.

'Oh sweetheart I love you too,' she returned the kiss and threw in a hug for good measure, rubbing her hands up and down his back. 'Don't take any notice of me; time of the month and all that.'

'Right!'

Aunt Amanda was beside them suddenly, a wine glass in each hand. 'Darlings,' she purred, clearly half cut. 'I'm having a wonderful time; Springer has gone off with some girl so I'll stay at yours tonight, is that ok Jamie darling?'

'S'always ok,' he said. 'I have to be off early for the cup final tomorrow; you can look after Tiggy for me.'

'Tiggy,' mum shook her head. 'What sort of a name is that for a cat, I ask you!'

Jamie grinned. 'It's wicked mum, trust me.'

'I'm sure it is,' she slipped out from in-between them, making a beeline for the toilet. 'Excuse me, you two.'

Aunt Amanda watched her go, then turned back, and handed Jamie one of the wine glasses. 'I think she still thinks we're crazy,' she said, winking at him. 'But if we want to be crazy that's our look out, right?'

Jamie clinked his glass to hers. 'Right.'

'Your life is about to change, my darling,' she went on. 'Forever.'

Chapter 40

Saturday 13th May 2006

Dorothy rapped hard on the black panelled front door of Jack's flat and waited. When after a minute or more no answer came she crouched down and opened the letterbox, peering through it and calling out, 'Jack?' followed a few seconds later by 'David?', and, as an afterthought, 'Bobby? Daniel?' until it dawned on her that West Ham were in the FA Cup Final today and they were most likely at the nearest bar on Upper Street watching it, tanked up to the gills and hollering their heads off, although Bobby hadn't really struck her as the football type; nor had Jack, for that matter, but perhaps he was having one of his 'Barking boy' moments.

She opened her Gucci handbag and reached inside for a flat key with several indentations at both ends and, as she'd been taught, slid it into the lock and made a couple of abrupt turns. The door swung open almost at once and she went inside, closing it firmly behind her.

'Wolvie' the cat was asleep on the floor by the bathroom door, and didn't stir as she passed, peering first into the bedroom and then the living room before tip-toeing into the kitchen. The flat was deserted, and in a right state. There were assorted empty Pizza Hut boxes on the coffee table and as she soon discovered, on the sideboard in the kitchen as well, some with stale left-overs still inside them. Jack's psychoanalysis exam notes, the ones David apparently read out to him every night, were in a dishevelled pile on the arm of the leather sofa adjacent to the window, 'Jack's sofa'. Bobby's sleeping bag was rolled up by the TV, and the pile of blankets Daniel threw over himself when he slept on the other sofa – 'David's sofa' - were rolled up in a pile underneath the window.

The phone rang and scared the shit out of her, but after she'd regained her composure she glared it out until whoever was at the other end gave up and rang off. She thought about picking it up and doing a '1471' but then wondered what might happen if the person tried to ring again and found it to be engaged. There were any number of places to find what she was looking for, but she began with the most obvious choice, the computer in the kitchen. She switched it on and boiled the kettle while the thing sprang to life, making herself a nice cup of coffee; the screensaver on the monitor made her smile; it was Jack and David, Bobby and Daniel down in Brighton from just a few days ago, taken on one of their phones, the four of them crammed into the corner of a pub whose ceilings were adorned with tinsel, raising their glasses and hollering wildly. She scanned the desktop files and quickly found what she was looking for; 'Who's the Daddy, Minty Hardcore - A dissertation – by David Samuels', parts one through to eleven. She took a CD from her handbag, inserted it into the tray and quickly made copies for herself, then turned the computer off.

The other things she was looking for – rough notes and the like – would be a lot harder to locate, but they might contained material that whilst being pruned would be of inestimable value both to her and the people she was gathering it for. She made a rudimentary search of the kitchen but ended up in the bedroom. Both Jack and David's beds were unmade, and various items of clothing including briefs, socks, the odd loafer or two were thrown around the floor. She searched the cupboards and then made a beeline for the drawer beside David's bed first. Inside she found a pile of photographs of him and Jack and various other friends, herself included. There was a train timetable with routes from Waterloo to Bournemouth underlined; a packet of condoms; an inhaler, a copy of a free weekly gay periodical, and little else besides. A quick rifle through Jack's draw gave up the same odd assortment of photographs, peppered with shots of various Woodfields, most notably his slightly slutty cousin Jessica. There were also a bundle of photographs of Jamie, carefully wrapped up in an elastic band and shoved to the back. There was an exam timetable, a bottle of Hugo Boss scent, and some old bank statements. Not what she was looking for. She bent down and looked under his bed and spied a shoebox; a Doctor Marten shoebox with the words 'property of Phil Woodfield' stencilled on it in Day-Glo early Eighties neon green. Now that was more like it. She prised it open gently and peered inside; there was a whole pile of photographs, again bound up in elastic bands which she removed and then thumbed through; countless shots of a young Phil Woodfield, many of them posed on his motorbike outside what she presumed was his Aunt Amanda's house in Bethnal Green; some shots in Brighton, several with different women and one or two with a middle-aged dandy who was probably his uncle, Richard Woodfield. She couldn't help but warm to the sight of Phil's cheery grin, hands thrust deep in the pockets of his Mod trenchcoat, big brown eyes reduced to a squint from the sun coming down from behind whoever was taking the picture, his fringe flopping casually over his forehead. She sat with her back to the wall and leafed through the selection of shots several times over, finding what she was looking for almost by accident; shots of 'Quadrophenia' being filmed on Brighton Beach, shots with Phil in them, Phil with a tall leggy Barbie-style blond in multi-coloured pastels and a huge sun bonnet, draped all over him, her long blond hair tumbling down around them as she rested her chin on his shoulder. The shots with this woman in them looked a little over-exposed, and there were bursts of light on some of them that obscured either her face or Phil's altogether. Dorothy took one and slipped it in her handbag, confident it wouldn't be missed. Then she took another, solo shot of Phil and slipped that in a different compartment. She texted Ruth Fremantle and said she'd come across something '…very interesting', and was replacing the lid of the shoebox when something else caught her eye, underneath a couple of old West Ham match programmes. It was a ring-bound red exercise book with the words 'Phil's Book of Shadows, 1977 – 1981' on the cover in scratchy black biro. She held it up to the light streaming in from the garden and pondered on what she should do. Then, moistening her lips with her tongue, she took a deep breath and slipped it in her handbag, then shoved the shoebox back under the bed and hurried out of the flat, pausing only to pat Wolvie as she passed him.

Chapter 41

Saturday 13th May 2006

The cool, scratched glass of the coach window kept Jamie awake if he leant his head against it, letting it squash his cheek into some funny, wind-tunnel sort of a shape, and it stopped him from feeling quite so sick as well. After the Hammers had lost the game on penalties they'd gone for a marathon drinking session around Cardiff city centre, cursing Steven Gerrard so vociferously that they'd inevitably drawn the attentions of some adjacent Liverpool fans, and a massive punch-up had ensued. Jamie had been holding his own with a fan roughly his age but slightly burlier before someone had smacked a chair over the back of his head and it all went a bit hazy after that, half-cut as he already was. He came to 'round a back alley where Adam had dragged him in order to avoid the police; Uncle Heath, who had been the last to throw a punch, had been the first arrested and hauled off along with cousin Michael and several of the Liverpool fans. They'd gone to the station to find them but were told there was no point in hanging around, as the two of them were going to be kept in overnight. And so he'd slouched off to the coach station with Adam in tow, as well as Uncle Eddie, cousins Clay, Casey and Sara, her boyfriend Ron, and Daniel, who had asked the coach driver if he could be dropped off in Islington once they hit London, but his request had been rather impolitely refused.

Jamie had no idea where they were now, the motorway outside was poorly lit and the moon was obscured by wreaths of tawdry looking grey could. He had no idea how long he'd been asleep, might have been minutes, or hours; they could be seconds away from pulling into the coach station in Barking right now for all he knew. Adam was in the seat in front swigging on a bottle of Evian; Jamie considered asking for a bit but then the thought of any fluid touching his lips made him feel sick.

'You look like I feel, young Jamie me lad,' Uncle Eddie sighed, leaning in through the gap in the seat behind. 'Actually, I probably look how you feel too. You ok?'

Jamie sniffed, nodded. 'Shit, wasn't it? We were so close, the tossers scored an own goal, but we still managed to fuck it up. Uncle Phil would have turned in his grave.'

'That he would,' Uncle Eddie nodded, sniffed and took a swig from a bottle of something alcoholic, wrapped up in a brown paper bag. 'Knew it was gonna be tough on you, kiddo; saw the tears welling up in your eyes when Gerrard scored for them right at the end.'

'I'll be crying even more when we get back,' he forced a smile. 'And we have to face mum and Aunt Rachel; shit, I mean Michael has to work tomorrow; he has to open the bloody pub!'

'We'll go elsewhere to drown our sorrows,' Uncle Eddie laughed to himself. 'Lord knows I need to.'

'How so?'

Uncle Eddie looked so old all of a sudden; Jamie had always thought of him as being in his early fifties or something, with his hair still naturally brown and swept over in that style balding men of the bygone years seemed to favour, but now he could see the flesh crinkled up around his eyes, the liver spots on his hands, and the length in his yellowing gums. He seemed to have aged enormously. The man seemed to sense the scrutiny he was under and smiled half-heartedly. 'I know, young fella me lad. I look like shit; bloody fucking shit, don't I?!'

'How long have you been married to Aunt Delia?'

'Too bloody long, kiddo.' He laughed, and shook his head, gazing out of the window. 'Too bloody long.'

'I hope you got her something for the big birthday bash next month.'

'I'm working on it,' he nodded. 'You know about Hayden, right? Pity we couldn't get Nick out as well and do a double. Two bloody kids in prison, eh? What the fucking sort of luck is that. You still write to Nick, right? You know they sent him to Grendon, don't you? I hear Grendon's a nuthouse. It should have been Hayden that was sent there, and not our Nick, but don't you tell your Aunt Delia I said that, because you know how she thinks where our Hayden's concerned, that the sun shines out of his proverbial, whereas to the rest of us it's just another bloody chocolate starfish.'

Jamie nodded, and then shrugged; he'd never heard the normally robust and upbeat Uncle Eddie spill his guts like this, not even when Aunt Delia had bawled him out when he was drunk or something, when she'd lock him out of the flat, or chase him down the London Road trying to splash him with a bucket of cold water. 'Do you miss Uncle Phil as much as I do?' he asked, after a moment.

''course I bloody do,' he nodded. 'He was like a son to me years before Delia and I ever had any of our own; Rupert and I took him to games almost every week, him and your Uncle Heath. You know if he were here now he'd be up the front with a bottle of wine in one hand and a rolled up newspaper to use as a megaphone in the other, and despite the fact we'd lost he'd have us singing in the aisles!! As it is, look at us; we've had the shit kicked out of us mentally and physically.' He laughed, shook his head. When he spoke next though, he wasn't laughing. 'Sometimes I think the Woodfields are finished. We used to breed like we were rabbits, all pretty bunny rabbits; now we're just flies on shit.' And he folded his arms, and said it again; 'Flies on shit.'

'Things'll get better,' Jamie was sobering up a little now, and when Adam tapped him on the shoulder and offered him the mineral water he took it gladly. 'You know, everyone thought Jack fucking off to the West End to do his fancy degree was the end of everything, once they knew

Uncle Phil was gonna die and there might not be a Daddy, but it might be for the best; you see, Aunt Amanda and me, we've got this idea…'

'I've got cancer, Jamie me lad,' Uncle Eddie said suddenly, softly enough for no one else to hear, but emphatically enough to knock the lad in front of him for six, causing him to splutter as he took another swig on the water. 'I've got prostate cancer.'

Jamie frowned, not sure if he'd heard right over the dull but continuous churn of the engine. He wiped his mouth with the back of his hand. 'Say what?'

Uncle Eddie nodded. 'The 'big C'; prostate cancer, and how advanced it is lord only knows.' And he took a hearty swig on whatever his secret tipple was. 'Your Aunt Delia doesn't know; she isn't to know until I decide to tell her, ok? Nobody knows, come to think of it. I'm only telling you because…well, because like you said, you're Phil's boy, as good as, and Phil was the Daddy.'

Jamie nodded, and sank back in his seat. He turned and looked at Uncle Eddie again but he'd closed his eyes and was shifting uncomfortably in his chair, pulling the old tweed jacket he seemed to have worn his entire life over him like some sort of shawl.

Chapter 42

Sunday 14th May 2006

'What is psychoanalysis?' David asked, peering at Jack over a sheaf of papers held together by a bright blue paperclip.

'Psychoanalysis is…' Jack scratched the soft ark blond hair under his belly button thoughtfully. 'Um…psychoanalysis is…'a technocratic discipline that can help society'?'

'Right,' David nodded. 'Who originated it?'

'Freud.' He gave a little laugh, 'Christ, Davey, this is easy.'

'Shush. What was the most important period in terms of the construction of the ideas in psychoanalysis?'

'1890 to 1939.'

'Great stuff. What was the main theory that Freud put forward as the motivation for everything we do?'

'Sexuality?'

'Be more specific.'

'…the libido?'

'Right,' he turned to the second page, at about the same time Daniel, cross-legged in front of the TV and busy on the PlayStation, kissed his lips loudly. David peered over the top of the paper at him. 'Something up, child?'

'I buggered up level four, got to start from scratch now,' he sniffed. 'And I feel like shit. My head still hurts from yesterday; you know my dad's still in Cardiff probably, in a police cell?! It wouldn't have happened if Uncle Phil had been there.' He glanced at Jack. 'It wouldn't have happened if you'd been there either, Jack.'

'I thought Jamie was there,' Jack winked at him. 'He could have sorted it.'

'He got clonked on the head,' Daniel said. 'But he laid a bloke out good before he did; he's a fair bit ripped now, almost on the way to being like you.'

Jack flexed one of his biceps lovingly, marvelling how the vein rose to the surface so readily. 'Almost.'

'Quite,' David cleared his throat. 'Ok. What is the biggest threat to psychoanalysis today, Jack?'

He let his arm relax. 'Self-help techniques?'

'Correct. What would you say the difference was between psychoanalysis here and psychoanalysis in the States?'

'In the States it's…' he was interrupted by a firm rapping on the door. 'Go see who that is will you, Danny boy?' he nodded down at Daniel. 'There's a good chav.'

Daniel kissed his lips again and ambled out of the room. David cleared his throat and went on. 'Typify the main aim of psychoanalysis for me.'

Jack sniffed. ''...to make the unconscious conscious'.'

'Hello Jack.' Father Brian was standing dead centre of the doorway to the hall, dog collar and all, his hands folded, looking as gaunt and ghoulish as ever. 'Is Bobby here?'

'Uh...he's in the bath,' Jack rose off David's couch, suddenly realising he was only wearing a towel himself. 'Hi Uncle Brian, it's been a while.'

'Since Phil's funeral actually,' the man made a slight bow. 'You're looking well.'

'Ta.' He smiled, and threw an arm over David's shoulder purely because he knew man-on-man contact was sure to wind the old fart up. 'Oh, this is my best mate David; Dave, this is Father Brian, Jessica's dad; and Bobby's; and Casey's...'

'Pleased to meet you sir,' David offered his hand but Father Brian seemed a little backward about coming forward in returning it, and David winced at the cold of the rings on his fingers when he did.

'Hi Uncle Brian,' Daniel looked up a little sheepishly from his cross-legged position in front of the telly.

'Daniel,' he nodded, peering down at him. 'I hear your dad's landed himself in a spot of bother with the Cardiff constabulary.'

'I'll go and get Bobby,' David said awkwardly, and slipped out of the room; he pulled a face at Jack behind Father Brian's back, something along the lines of 'Christ, what a solemn old cunt!' and Jack suppressed a sly grin.

Uncle Brian produced an envelope from inside his jacket and handed it to Jack. 'This should about cover Bobby's board for the past week. I've come to take him home.'

'Thank Christ...' Jack exhaled sharply. 'You want to take this one while you're at it?' and he nodded down at Daniel, who made a little noise of protest. David returned with Bobby, hastily dressed in his slacks and a white Umbro t-shirt. Jack turned, and stepped back. 'Bobster, your old man's come to take you home.'

'Bobby's a bit old for that,' Uncle Brian shrugged apologetically. 'Let's just say I've come to take him off your hands.'

'I don't wanna go, dad,' Bobby sighed, steeling himself. 'I like it here.'

'Bobby now come on,' Uncle Brian made to take him by the arm. 'I'm not having you saddling Jack and his friend with your problems and your perversions. Get your things and meet me outside in the car.'

'Excuse me?!' David's eyes flashed, 'his what?'

'Bobby's cousin Debbie let it slip the other day,' Uncle Brian straightened, and let go of Bobby's arm. 'Apparently I'm the last to know, as usual; I guess I'm always a bit of a laughing stock in this family, but I adhere to certain code of living and I expect my children to do the same.'

'My big-mouthed sis strikes again,' Daniel made a face.

'Excuse me Mr Woodfield, but I take offence at some of your language,' David stepped forward and folded his arms. 'I'm gay myself, as it happens.'

'Are you?' Uncle Brian raised an eyebrow dubiously. 'Well that's your lookout. You're not my son. And I would have thought better of you Jack,' and here he turned his gaze on the both of them. 'Are these the sort of people you share a flat with these days? Your Uncle Phil would be ashamed of you.'

'Uncle Phil thought queers were ok...' Daniel murmured, gazing ruefully at his uncle's pressed trouser leg. 'He lived with Uncle Richard in Brighton, ya know, and Jack said Uncle Richard was like Joe Orton, whoever that is!'

'Now wait a sec,' Jack stepped forward and issued himself before Father Brian in all his ripped glory. 'You can come and get Bobby if you like but don't go cussing my friends, ok? Go be the 'Pope' back in Barking where there's still some sad losers crazy enough to listen to you.' And he looked him up and down and then shook his head. 'God I feel sorry for Aunt Betty.'

'Jack, I don't wanna go...' Bobby protested, but even as he said it he was making a beeline for his things. 'I like it here.'

'Mate...' Jack laid a hand on his shoulder. 'I'm trying to study for an exam here. I don't need this kind of hassle. Sorry Bobster, but that's just the way it has to be. David helped you get your shit together, you have the university prospectuses, make the calls when you get home, and go for that job in HMV to tide you over.'

'He walked out on his job at KFC, did he tell you that?' Father Brian glared at both of them. 'I had to apologise on his behalf, but if he thinks he's going to university he's got another thing coming. Who is going to pay for it, for starters?'

'That's Bobby's lookout,' David said. 'He is an adult, after all.'

'While he's living under my roof he'll live by my law,' Uncle Brian nodded. 'I'm sure you're a very nice person David but I think it's about time Bobby left here, before you really begin to fill his heads with all sorts of modern nonsense about 'gay liberation'.'

'With all due respect Mr Woodfield, this is 2005,' David spread his arms out in a show of muted understanding. 'Bobby could find that anywhere. There's nothing wrong with being gay, you know.'

'Ya said the wrong thing there...' Daniel muttered under his breath, turning the PlayStation back on.

'Nothing wrong with being a sodomite?!' Father Brian's face creased up, so that it looked a little like a chewed-up toffee. 'I'm afraid the Good Book says otherwise, young man. I realise you're obviously one of these university types who are always trying to upset the status quo...'

'I'm majoring at the LSE if that's what you mean, sir.' David folded his arms, obviously counting on Jack to back him up. 'The home of gay liberation, if you like, thanks to Professor Jeffrey Weeks and Professor Patrick Pollard, to name but a few.'

'Buggers, the lot of them!' Father Brian pulled Bobby to the door. 'He'll see sense when he gets home.'

'No wonder my Jessica can't wait to move out, you miserable old fart,' Jack snapped.

'What did you say?!' Uncle Brian cranked up the righteous wrath a notch. 'So you can fill her head with all sorts of nonsense, like you did when you were little?! That you were going to run away and abandon the family?' and he took a step forward. 'The way she idolises you,' he sneered, 'with some silly crush, and your picture by her bed…' and he peered over Jack's shoulder, at the one of Jessica on the bookcase. 'And you for her, I see,' as Jack followed his gaze. 'Did you know my daughter?' he asked.

'You what?!' Jack's face screwed up pretty toffee-like too.

'I said, did you know my daughter…either when you kidnapped her and took her to Paris, or before?!'

Jack stood right in front of him, gazing down. 'None of your fucking business, you sick old coot.' And then he felt David's hand on his shoulder and cooled a little. 'Look,' he said, 'just take Bobby and go, okay.'

'You're not actually going to let him take him?!' David was staggered. 'Jack, he's a fucking religious homophobe of the worst kind! He'll fuck Bobby's head up right and proper!! We can't allow this.'

Jack's jowls were clenching and unclenching, but he made no move to stop Father Brian as he began leading Bobby to the door. 'It's not my problem. Bobby's not a kid.'

David waited until the door had slammed before turning on him. 'Maybe he isn't a kid,' he said. 'But he's a fucking little scrap of a young man who can't stand up to someone like that. I know because my dad was pretty much the same, only without the religious BS, but what does that matter? He'll make sure Bobby's back at the KFC tomorrow morning and sat at home with him and your Aunt Betty by five for tea, then in his room for eight. You're right, screw him.' He picked up the exam revision notes and slammed them against Jack's bare chest. 'And screw you too.'

'Everyone get off my fucking case!!' Jack snapped, watching the individual sheets flutter to the floor. 'It isn't my fucking problem, ok?? I have my own life to worry about, this fucking exam stress is doing my head in and everyone wants me to wipe their nose for them! I'm not the fucking Daddy, for fuck's sake!!' as he said this, his towel disengaged and slipped around his ankles. As he bent to pick it up the clear red lip print on the small of his back was clearly exposed.

'Uh…that kind of says you are,' Daniel sniffed, leaning over for another look. 'Guess the laser treatment didn't go so well, huh?'

'Piss off,' Jack snapped. 'You can go home too, while you're at it. I'm fed up of everyone thinking this is some kind of refuge from boring old Barking.'

There came the sound of shouting from outside; Uncle Brian's voice audible as a car door was opened; '...you'll get in there and you'll do as you're told, you bloody little bugger!'

Daniel looked up at Jack. 'It isn't right, Jack,' he said. 'Uncle Phil would have stopped him.'

'Yeah well I'm not Uncle Phil,' Jack said. 'Let Jamie try and be Uncle Phil if he wants.'

'But you've got the kiss,' Daniel pressed. 'You're the Daddy. I don't know what that means, but it means you're the Daddy; everyone knows it.'

'He just hit him,' David was peering through the net curtains, 'cracked him around the face good and proper. I'm going out there.'

'I'll do it,' Jack rolled his eyes and then pushed past them, still clad in his towel. He opened the door and hurried up the leafy stone steps, barefoot. Bobby was on one side of Uncle Brian's battered old Ford Fiesta, his father on the other, his face even redder than it had been before. 'Hey!' he shouted. 'You don't have to hit him, ok?'

'Keep out of this Jack,' Uncle Brian said. 'You've made your position in the family perfectly clear.'

'Go back in the flat, Bobby,' Jack said.

'Get in the car Bobby,' Uncle Brain said.

Jack stepped in front of Bobby. 'Bobby, go back inside.'

Bobby peered over Jack's shoulder. 'I wanna stay here, dad. I wanna stay with Jack.'

'You're coming home right this minute, you blasted bugger.'

'Piss off,' Jack said.

'What?!'

'You heard me,' he drew himself up to his full height, considerably taller than that of his uncle, and peered down at him. 'You stupid little man. Piss off back to Barking, back to your congregation, but tell Aunt Betty hello from me, 'k? 'coz to fuck, she needs a medal putting up with you all these years.'

'How dare you speak to me like that?!' Father Brian waved his fist under Jack's nose. 'You spoilt little shit! Who's paying for you to go all the way through university, Jack? We are! All of us, the family you seem to have such a dislike for. All because we're labouring under some silly misapprehension about you doing your duty, something that I'll have nothing to do with anyway, as God is my witness.' And he spat in the kerb suddenly. 'Black magic, that's what it is, and what it's always been; black magic! You're as bad as your Uncle Phil! He was a sorcerer, and your Aunt Amanda too, may God strike me down for saying it! And your Uncle Rupert and my mother Felicity too, God rest their souls! They were all witches!!'

'Go back in the flat Bobby,' Jack said firmly, and this time Bobby did as he was told.

'You come back here, you blasted little bugger!' Father Brian called after him. 'Oh God bless him, left in a flat with the likes of you, Jack Woodfield! God bless him.'

'Bless this,' Jack said, and laid him out with one punch.

Daniel, peering at proceedings from behind the net curtains, now bounded out the front door and up the steps in his bare feet, punching at the air with his hand. 'Who's the Daddy!!' he yelled, jumping up and down. 'Who's the Daddy!?!'

Chapter 43

Sunday 14th May 2006

'I thought I was never gonna see you again,' Jamie said, watching her dart around the kitchen, preparing mugs and putting the kettle on the boil. 'You haven't answered a text in weeks; not properly anyway.'

Tiffany pulled the milk from the fridge and poured it into said mugs, then drank a little for herself, straight from the bottle; the overspill trickled down either side of her mouth. 'I've been awfully busy, Jamie,' she said, wiping her chin with the back of her hand. 'I thought you knew. I'm the verge on winning a contract to model George at ASDA's autumn line.'

He shrugged. 'You kind of kept me in the dark,' he said.

'It's really taken off,' she said. 'It's like they're all just seeing me again, like I'm a new person on the market. On top of that I've decided to go back to college in October, take up where I left off. Mum's got a bit of cash, so even if the modelling doesn't pan out I should be okay. I'm going to do radical gender theory!'

'Congrats…' he sniffed. 'You're still my 'tiff to me, though.'

'Your eye looks awful,' she reached over and stroked the bruise with her thumb.

'We got in a barney in Cardiff city centre yesterday,' he brightened a little. 'I got my licks in though, don't you worry. Uncle Heath and Michael spent the night in the cells; they're only just on their way back home now!'

She handed him his tea. 'Jamie…I'm awfully busy. Is there a point to this visit?'

'A point?' he gazed at her. 'I'm your boyfriend, in't I?!'

'We haven't seen in each other in weeks.'

'Yeah, and we've been steady for nearly four years.'

She drank a little of her own tea. 'We've been drifting apart for a good while now. You've had your thing going at Sight & Sound and my modelling's doing so well; you must have seen I quit Morelli's.'

He glanced around. Her flat, here on the London Road, seemed emptier than before. 'Where's Elisha?' he asked.

'Elisha?' she followed his own gaze, watching what he was watching. 'Oh…she left in rather a hurry.'

'She left?'

Tiffany nodded. 'She got an offer she couldn't refuse.'

''tiff…are you ok? You seem kind of…different.'

'Actually I feel fantastic,' she threw back her head, letting those strawberry blond tresses jump into life and fall all over her shoulders. 'Don't you?'

'Well…yeah, I guess. I can read now, you know; by myself. I can read whatever I like. I've joined the library over in the Vicarage Fields.'

'Fantastic.'

'Yeah…so many books too, you know. And that's on top of all the ones Aunt Amanda wants me to read.'

'I wondered what you and her have been up to,' she narrowed her eyes. 'What sort of books is she asking you to read then?'

'Don't tell anyone this,' Jamie beckoned her closer. 'But me and her…well, she reckons I might be good enough to be the Daddy, since Jack isn't interested. She actually thinks that.'

'Oh does she?!'

Jamie beamed. 'Yeah!! Only it's a secret, although I think she's told Aunt Delia. I'm gonna be as good as Uncle Phil ever was, better even! She says there's a curse on this family and it has to be broken.'

Tiffany let her head flop to one side, eyeing him from a different angle. 'Jamie…have you been working out?'

He shifted himself off the stool and moved back a little from the kitchen unit. He pulled up the sleeve of his t-shirt and flexed his already rather impressive bicep until it veritably bulged. 'Not bad, eh?' he said. 'Wanna see my abs as well? They're almost as flat as Jack's!' and then he paused. 'But the pecs…well the pecs are harder to get, and so are the shoulders; I have a boyish build, that's what she told me, and Laquisha, she said I had 'baby biceps' when I showed in the 'Dog, the other day!'

She seemed deep in thought. 'It's true, you do look bigger; brawnier, even. I like it.'

Jamie moved closer. 'Yeah?'

She nodded, and ran her fingers lightly over his chest. 'Once more, for old times' sake?'

He nodded. ''k.'

Jamie and Tiffany had been together almost four years, and for most of those been reasonably sexually active. In the bedroom she'd always been a little restrained and unsure of herself, and a little of that had rubbed off on Jamie, who'd only been with one or two other girls before her anyway. This time was different though; he got all the enthusiasm he'd hoped for regarding his new and improved physique, and then some. She wrapped her legs around his back, and scratched there so hard with her nails that he pulled a face more than once; she was very vocal with her appreciation too, usually along the lines of, '…my beautiful butch Woodfield boy; oh, your big arms!!', punctuated with an awful lot of head gyrations and yelping. In retrospect it was a lot like doing it with someone who'd just read a good sex guide from cover to cover, and memorised all the best bits.

'I guess you enjoyed that,' Jamie said afterwards, pulling his jeans on. 'I sure did.'

She sat with the covers bundled around her, new sheets of a kind of pastel pink. 'You've come a long way,' she nodded. 'No hard feelings?'

He sat on the side of the bed. 'I still love you, only...it's different now, you know?'

Tiffany nodded again. 'Friends always?'

It was kind of what he'd been expecting, and as much as it hurt, to hear it finally confirmed was something of a relief. 'The best,' he said.

'Off you go then,' she patted his rear. 'I have so much to do, and well...so much time to do it in.'

Jamie stopped at the top of the staircase that led down to the street. ''tiff...'

She looked up. 'Mmmmm?'

'There was never anyone else, was there?'

'Anyone else?'

'Yeah,' he shifted uncomfortably. 'You know...it was always just me, wasn't it? The reason we're sort of over...well there was no one else, was there?'

She smiled. 'Of course not.'

Jamie nodded. ''coz I can just about take us finishing, but if it was 'coz you've met some other guy; well that would just about finish me off, you know? that on top of Uncle Phil and all.'

Tiffany pulled her knees up to her chest. 'Jamie, I swear. There was never anyone else.'

*

Tiffany threw her head sideways onto the pillow, arching her back into an almost perfect crescent. 'Fuck me, Jack!!' she moaned. 'Fuck me!!'

'Shit I'm close,' he wiped the sweat on his brow with the back of his hand, the other supporting himself just above her. 'Are you close?!'

'Baby, I've already come twice,' she heaved her legs up and around his back. 'Do me a hat-trick.'

Jack was a little restrained despite her pleas, fully aware that David, Bobby and Daniel could return from 'Vulture's Videos' on Upper Street with their choice of DVD for the evening at any moment. 'I'm gonna come soon,' he gasped. 'Let me make you come again then.'

'Tell me how you were today,' she gazed up at him, loving the sight and feel of his taut body over her own. 'Tell me what it felt like.'

'How what felt like?!'

'When you laid your Uncle Brian out,' she crooned. 'Tell me how big and strong it made you feel.'

Jack frowned, but kept his increasingly frenetic rhythm. 'It was just a punch...he was being an arse, so I...'

'...you were the Daddy,' she dug her fingernails into his back so hard he almost made a face. 'You were in charge. I want you to be in charge of me!'

'Did Daniel flog you one of his Es?!' Jack shook his head. 'You're crazy this afternoon.'

'You're bigger than Jamie,' she rubbed his chest. 'You'll always be bigger. No matter how much he exercises, you can't stretch bone, or grow hair where there isn't any!'

Jack stopped pumping. 'Have you told him? About us?!'

'No silly,' she sighed. 'But we mutually called it a day anyway. Of course if he knew it was because I was madly in love with you it'd devastate him, but that isn't going to happen. It's just when I'm with you now....well like I said, I realise he can work-out all he likes, but it'll never make him the man you are.'

'You're turning me on,' he grinned, 'wildly.'

'That's good,' she nodded. 'That's how it should be. Now tell me how big and strong you felt when you laid that awful old man out…'

The five of them spent the evening eating popcorn and nachos and watching the several DVDs that had been picked from 'Vulture's Videos'; 'Walk the line' and 'Jarhead', the latter a personal favourite of Jack's. Dorothy arrived around seven with several bottles of wine and these were knocked back in short order. Daniel was going on and on about Jack's knockout blow to Uncle Brian; Jessica had called earlier to say that their father was sporting the mother of all black eyes, and lord only knows what he was going to say to his parishioners. Jack had taken the phone into the kitchen to speak to her, and closed the door behind him.

'They're very close, aren't they?' Dorothy had asked, looking over the rim of her glass, 'Jack and his cousin Jessica?'

'He's more her brother than I am,' Bobby was on David's sofa, clutching a pillow to his chest. 'But it's cool, there's so many cousins and stuff in our family it's like that. I'm more close to my cousin Debbie, Daniel's sister.'

'I'm close to Jack,' Daniel proclaimed. 'I'm in his posse!'

'Are you fuck.' Bobby rolled his eyes.

Tiffany was curled up on the other couch, swirling the last of her wine around in the bottom of her glass, seemingly a million miles away. 'He's a natural.'

Dorothy glanced up at her. 'Who is?'

'Jack. He's a natural leader. It's inevitable, really.'

'Jack's gonna be the Daddy,' Daniel nodded. 'We're gonna march on Barking!!'

Jack strutted back into the living room and replaced the portable landline on its rest. 'Jessica reckons it's gonna be hell on earth at home now, so I said she could come and kip here as well if she likes.'

'There won't be room to swing a cat!' Dorothy laughed.

'They're flocking to him…' Tiffany was gazing at Jack like he was something good to eat. 'As their world crumbles he, like Atlas, hefts it onto his brawny shoulders and makes all right…'

'Does Jessica have to come here?' Bobby groaned. 'She could go to Casey's.'

'Tamsin's just had a miscarriage,' Jack sat down next to Tiffany and threw his arm around her. 'I think they've got their hands full right now.'

'There's a spare bed at mine,' Daniel pointed out.

'She's coming here, if she wants,' he said firmly, playing with a loose strand of Tiffany's hair. 'She can have my bed and David and I can take turns in his; you two can keep your sofas and whoever doesn't get the bed on alternate nights gets the floor.'

'My sis is a prig to live with!!' Bobby moaned. 'She takes hours in the bathroom!!'

'Not half as long as David does,' Jack threw his best mate a cheery wink. 'They can scratch each other's eyes out for the privilege.'

'You know I have plenty of room in my place at Queens Park,' Dorothy suggested. 'She...any one of you could always come there, if you want. My little lad would love someone to lark around on the PlayStation with.'

'That's so thoughtful,' Tiffany was gazing at her. 'Isn't that thoughtful, Jack?'

'I'll keep you posted,' Jack nodded, reaching out to pick up the wine and refill Dorothy's glass. 'I'm gonna have a review of things once our exams are over.'

'I thought we were thinking about a trip to Europe when the exams were over?' she said.

'Europe?!' Tiffany peered at Jack through narrowed eyes. 'You never mentioned...'

'It was just an idea we were toying with,' David came in with some fresh sauce for the nachos, 'Rome, right Jack?'

He nodded. 'I want to see the Sistine Chapel.'

'You can meet the real Pope!' Daniel giggled. 'Maybe you can deck him too!'

Dorothy licked her lips and looked up at Jack and Tiffany as though she were studying them. 'So are you two an official item then?'

They exchanged nervy glances, and then Tiffany whispered something in his ear. 'Uh huh,' Jack nodded. 'We'll make a formal announcement...'

'...when I figure out how to tell Jamie,' Tiffany nodded. 'Even though we're not an item anymore, let's just say; if it was anyone but his big brother...'

'...he'll be gutted regardless,' Jack chewed his lip. 'Maybe we should just keep it between us lot. I don't want to hurt J, not really.'

'You're not scared, are you?!' Tiffany was most amused, 'of Jamie?!'

'No, but...' he looked pained, pained and a little embarrassed. 'I just don't see that he has to be hurt.'

'You should have thought of that before you pinned me to the bed and gave it to me like I was some sort of 'ho!' she said, then caught the look of shock on the faces of the others. 'What?!'

'I want a girlfriend like you,' Daniel said, leaning back and gazing up at her with love in his eyes. 'Do you have any little sisters?!'

*

Dorothy was having a cigarette out in what passed for the flat's back garden, one Jack and David shared with the people on the ground floor, whilst trying to find a decent signal for her mobile. Bypassing the screensaver of her little boy, she singled out Ruth Fremantle's name and number and began to type a message when she was joined by Tiffany, one of Jack's Fred Perry jumpers pulled over her ample chest, her arms folded. 'It's chilly out here,' she said. 'I hope that wasn't summer last week, all used up already.'

'Tell me about it,' Dorothy nodded, still fiddling with her phone. 'Summers here are brief enough as it is. I hope we do get to Rome.'

'Are you English?' Tiffany asked her, pausing at the brick wall at the back and running her fingertips lightly against the crumbling red brick. 'I mean, you have such fantastic colouring…'

'I think there's some Brazilian somewhere down the line,' Dorothy cocked a smile. 'That's where I get that 'exotic' look.'

'Right,' she smiled. 'Bad signal in the flat?'

'Terrible.'

'Listen,' Tiffany walked back from the wall, and folded her arms. 'Are you ok? I mean, with me and Jack? I know you two were sort of seeing each other…'

'…'sort of' being the operative word, or phrase,' Dorothy nodded. 'It's cool. We're better as friends. I'm too busy with this Masters for anything heavy right now anyway. That, and raising a kid.'

'Well I'm glad Jack's got you to help him,' Tiffany nodded. 'I know how his mind can wander; he thinks he's in his Saville Row suit and in his job on Cheapside already.'

'Tell me about it.'

'What does David do again? He's at LSE as well, right?'

'Oh…occult studies,' Dorothy snapped her mobile shut. 'It's kind of an offshoot of sociology as it is, with a little history thrown in. Detractors call it a pseudoscience in the same way they do with something like psychoanalysis, which is the first exam Jack and I have, but it's actually rather more in-depth; 'occult' is just their way of being theatrical. It's more like the history of witchcraft in England.'

'I'm not sure if I believe in all that sort of thing,' Tiffany said, folding her arms, the longer sleeves flopping over her own hands, 'ghosts and all that. I saw this programme once where they tried to test it scientifically, and they thought ghosts were made up of electricity, you know, the brain-waves we have in our head, only floating around disembodied.'

Dorothy raised an eyebrow. 'Really?'

'Uh huh.' She nodded. 'Isn't that amazing? To think that there could be ghosts floating around this garden right now. And they're electric.'

'I'm sure David knows more about it than I do.'

'...all mixed up with all the other electricity we produce as humans,' Tiffany went on, twirling a length of cobweb that hung from the brick behind her around her finger. 'Like that text you sent, for instance; if there was a ghost nearby they'd know exactly what you'd said in it.'

Dorothy smiled slightly, and looked back down the steps to where she could see David in the kitchen, struggling with the cork of another bottle. 'God, can you imagine that.'

Tiffany nodded. 'Just imagine.'

The Daddy Dissertation Part 7

By David Samuels

Jack and Jamie; the Woodfields in the Nineties

The story of the Woodfields in the Nineties begins with a death, and it ends for the purposes of this narrative in 2005 with another death, the latter having considerably more impact than the former. In 1990 it was Uncle Rupert who died, after years of increasingly poor health; in the end a fall in the bath at the house on the Ripple Road caused massive head trauma, and his daughter Rachel for years after blamed herself for what she perceived to be poor supervision on her part, when in fact nothing could have been further from the truth; she was a devoted daughter who had turned her back only for a second when it happened.

Rupert was senile in his last days and is said not to have recognised either Jack or Jamie when they were brought to visit him; his condition distressed Jamie in particular, but Jack seemed fascinated and would often ask Rupert what day of the week it was, or who the Prime Minister was – it was Thatcher, just – and double up in a fit of laughter when his Uncle Rupert insisted it was Harold Wilson, or worse, Winston Churchill. Rupert's funeral was the first one Jack could remember attending and it was his turn then to be alarmed by the sheer number of Woodfields who turned out for the event, including even the 'Hackney Woodfields'. It hadn't yet been explained to him why almost every uncle, aunt or cousin wanted to be introduced to him and why they largely ignored Jamie, only taking notice of him when Phil would lift him up and introduce him into the conversation almost bodily.

Of the next generation of Woodfields Father Brian's son Casey was the first to leave school, and he took a job on a local paper as photographer, freelance at first but it soon turned into a permanent position on the strength of his work. Almost all of the photographs taken at weddings, christenings, and the like from 1990 onwards are Casey's work. He married Tamsin Parish from Bow in 1998 after a whirlwind courtship; she was a PA who worked near Tower Bridge, he was the dashing young photographer and their wedding was the first in the family for many years. As stated in the previous chapter, their daughter Meggan was born in 2001.

Returning to the early Nineties, the next generation of Woodfields continued to do well academically; most of them had left St. Margaret's primary school by now, with the exception of Heath's children Daniel and Debbie, who were only just starting there. Jack and Jamie went to Eastbury secondary school, along with the rest of their cousins. As per usual Jack excelled at almost everything, and began to take an interest in sociology, citing a particular fascination for the changes wrought by the Sixties and

Seventies as a personal favourite, and of how subcultures eroded social norms.

Jamie in the meantime excelled at being a devout supporter of West Ham; if anything his entire life revolved around the club, that and his love for his Uncle Phil, the two dovetailing beautifully with Phil's own obsession for the Hammers. They went to every home game, every away game, brought home and away strips regularly – and wore them out almost all the time in one form or another – and mounted autographs and pictures all over the walls of the flat on Station Parade. Pride of place went to a picture of the two of them with manager Harry Redknapp, Phil on one side and the-then thirteen year old Jamie on the other, their interlinking arms all managing to somehow find their respective hands and delivering a hearty congratulation on the new manager's promotion. Uncle Heath went to most of the games with them, sometimes with Daniel, then just four or five years old, along with Delia's four boys and Rachel's son Michael. Heath's wife Sophie was an aspiring artist who worked part-time at Cousin Casey's photography studio and painted in her spare time; some of her work was exhibited in exhibitions in galleries in Whitechapel in Stepney, and several were brought by members of the Woodfield family. Bev has a watercolour of Jack and Jamie hanging in the front hall of the Murphy Estate flat that was given to them by Sophie on their sixteenth birthday, although apparently this is not the original copy; the original, so the story goes, was torn in two by the twins in a drunken brawl between the two of them on the night of their surprise party, and Sophie had to hastily remount an earlier draft as the real thing as a result.

Sometime during Christmas 1994 Jack had the news broken to him that '…all this will one day be yours', and to have had Uncle Phil's arm make a dramatic sweep on the landscape visible from Station Parade, a view that encompassed all of Barking and back towards the heart of the East End. Jack's reaction of, 'I don't want it. Why can't it be Jamie's?!' is said to have provoked a similar response from Phil, followed by a shrug and something along the lines of 'The rules are the rules.' Aunt Amanda sat Jack down after the Christmas dinner and unveiled to him the full list of duties to which he'd be forced to partake of when was 'the Daddy', which they hoped wouldn't be for a long time as Phil was a vigorous young man with plenty of years ahead of him. Jack balked at the idea of members of the family coming to him with their problems, of approving marriages and partnerships and business ventures, of sorting out disputes and disagreements both within the family and without, and generally making his presence felt where it might not actually be wanted. 'I don't want to make my presence felt,' he told her. 'I want to be a sociologist, or a psychotherapist; I want to write books, and I certainly can't do that in this shit-hole, and with you lot breathing down my neck all the time.' Aunt Amanda is said to have replied with something along the lines of, 'Off the record there's nothing I'd like more than to see you do all of that, darling, but as your Uncle Phil told you, the rules are the rules. And if you ever need reminding of that then go to a full-length mirror and pull your pants down and take a good look at that kiss you have on your backside.'

One cold, snowy morning during January 1995 Phil, Rose, and Jamie were awoken by a furious banging on the door of their flat on Station Parade. It was Betty, wife of Father Brian and mother of Casey, Jessica, and Bobby. Normally a frivolous, slightly dizzy individual, Betty was this morning wracked with tears, telling Phil that Jessica had run away from home, that all of her things were gone, that somehow she had snuck away in the middle of the night, taking both her parents' credit cards and any and all cash they had in the house at the time. Ten minutes later Beverly was at the flat reporting much the same in regards to Jack, and it was quickly established that the two of them had fled together, although no one had a clue as to where.

Jack and Jessica had been close since childhood; the favourite anecdote about the two of them revolves around a photograph taken during the family trip to Chessington World of Adventures in 1990, depicting Jessica in pink and with pigtails, gazing adoringly up at the-then slightly skinny Jack, a big cheesy grin on his face and his arm protectively around her shoulders. She is said to have been closer to Jack than to her own brothers; Casey was 'too old', she is quoted as saying, and 'Bobby loves Doctor Who more than he loves me'. She was Bobby's older twin by twenty minutes or so, and beautiful in a pouting, slightly pornographic way, with large breasts and pouty, bee-stung lips all topped off with golden blond tresses. Many family members said she resembled her grandmother Felicity in her youth, although Felicity was a brunette; certainly though she has Felicity's liquid eyes and boyish little hips. For most of her young life her father had attempted to tone down what he saw as her 'excessive' behaviour; excess to Father Brian Woodfield in reality meant catching her trying her mother's lipstick on when she was seven, and throwing a fit when he discovered she'd raised her school skirts an inch or two. Jack was said to have been in awe of her spirit in the face of '…that miserable old bastard,' and to have likened it to his own struggle against the impending role of the Daddy.

When she was twelve and Jack was eleven they declared their intention to marry as soon as possible, and even held an impromptu wedding in the bandstand at the bottom of Station Parade, with cousins Marie and Laquisha acting as bridesmaids, whilst the role of best man went to Hayden Woodfield, the youngest of Aunt Delia's second set of twins, and probably Jack's closest male cousin.

Jessica's journal, found on the evening she absconded to Paris with Jack - revealed that they had made a pact not only to get married – just to spite their parents, it seemed – but to get out of Barking and stay out at the first opportunity. Jack wanted to travel the world conducting vast sociological surveys of different youth movements, and Jessica would be his exotic companion.

The credit cards were cancelled as quickly as possible, but both Beverly and Betty's accounts had been cleared. 'Jack's cunning,' Phil told them as he called a family crisis conference. 'If they're buying tickets he'll do it with cash, so as not to leave a trail.'

And he was right. Jack and Jessica were on the Eurostar bound for Paris even as he was putting out the 'all points alert' to Woodfields far and wide, although it was Aunt Amanda who rather sensibly pointed out, given Jessica's journal, that the last place they were likely to go was to other members of the family. Further perusal of the journal revealed plans for Hayden to join them several days later, but Aunt Delia soon put the kibosh on that by grounding him for the next two months. Hayden retaliated by beating his twin brother Nick almost black and blue in a fit of pique, and blaming it on a gang from the Murphy Estate who were at the time causing considerable trouble in the area. Nick never grassed.

Jack and Jessica arrived in Paris on a wet Thursday afternoon with all their worldly possessions packed into two suitcases. He eked out their money frugally, and lived on croissants and cola for more than a week, only occasionally treating themselves to a proper meal when they ran 'under their projected budget'. They stayed in a cheap hotel near the station, sharing a bed in order to cut corners. They told the manager they were newlyweds on '…the adventure of a lifetime'. Aged fourteen Jack was already pushing six foot, and had been working out for a year or so already; he had a naturally athletic body that easily developed when pushed. Jessica too was already rather buxom and with a well-crafted act they easily passed themselves off as a young couple in their early twenties. She did her hair up too, and said things like, 'Oh well I think we should go there today darling,' loudly whenever someone new came into their vicinity; 'darling' seems to have been the byword for the holiday, something they enjoyed aping from Aunt Amanda, who called anyone and everyone darling; they felt it lent them an air of Parisian sophistication.

Jessica was spotted on the Champs-Elysees by a young artist called Andrei and he painted her more than once at his pokey apartment on Des Mauvais Garcons. She resisted his advances for weeks and is said to have cried on his chest over her love of her cousin Jack, whom she referred to as 'the most handsome boy in the whole wide world!' Andrei was their key to sustaining their Paris adventure for as long as it went on; he got Jessica work as a life model in several establishments, and even taught Jack how to 'clip' in gay bars, that is, to lure men on the promise of paid sex and then take the money and run without giving up the goods. Jack was a sure-fire winner on that score, although once one of the men he'd 'clipped' caught up with him near Notre Dame one night and beat him soundly around the face and head with a copy of a Parisian art guide. Needless to say Jack didn't do any clipping for several weeks after that.

They toyed with the idea of moving on but both seemed to genuinely love Paris, and for Paris to have loved them; they were a permanent fixture at the Boho parties at the lower end of the market, and even the odd orgy or two; Jack fell in with the artist crowd in Montmartre and he asked Andrei to help secure them a flat nearer there so that he could 'fully explore himself'. Jessica is said to have been thrilled by the idea and began playing with the idea of becoming a showgirl at the Moulin Rouge. At a party in March 1995 Jack is said to have caused a minor sensation when he made a bet with a poet called Lucas that he couldn't perform a 'supernatural parlour trick', and to have netted almost two hundred pounds worth in Francs when he convinced the absinthe-sodden crowd that he had successfully levitated Jessica's pigtails and unravelled them, all with the power of his mind.

With Lucas's help and Andrei's good wishes Jack and Jessica soon ended up sharing a room in a stuffy loft that never-the-less afforded them a splendid view just adjacent to the Sacre-Coeur. Jessica didn't make it to the Moulin Rouge – although she and Jack did take in a show there – but she managed to secure work in a peep show on the Rue Gabrielle, and spent six days out of seven having to gyrate around a simple wooden pole for the delights of the gentlemen who frequented such establishments. Jack found he had a natural talent for sleight-of-hand, for elaborate tomfoolery and holding the attentions of a crowd and soon established himself as a credible street performer in his own right, a kind of latter-day Jake Woodfield, only without the bear-wrestling and the bare-knuckle fighting, although he did once walk over hot coals but apparently didn't share Jake's talent in this and burnt his feet rather badly. He refused to go to hospital in case they were traced, and is said to have '...bitten back tears' as Jessica gently and lovingly bathed the charred soles of his feet with a cold, wet sponge, the privacy of their little room.

One day a man in dark glasses and a trenchcoat challenged Jack to a fairly elaborate card trick, Jack rapidly rising to the challenge in his slacks and his hooded raincoat. However, the stranger was more than a match for him and was three steps ahead all the way; a dumbfounded Jack was forced to hand over his day's takings and then, when the crowd had dispersed, suffered the second indignation of having the man reveal himself to be a rather pissed-off Uncle Phil. 'Holiday's over, Jack,' were his words as he tossed his fedora onto the steps of the Sacre-Coeur and then rolled the sleeves of his trenchcoat up. 'You're coming back to Barking; your mother's bloody hysterical over you. She's been hospitalised twice.'

Jack is said to have bitten back more tears when he'd heard how much trouble their disappearance had caused; not only had his mother been so worried she'd been taken to hospital under sedation but the family had spent hundreds on poster appeals, even securing them a spot on the ITV local news spot 'London Tonight' on their 'missing file' section. Phil had had to build bridges with the 'Hackney Woodfields', travelled up to Barnsley to visit Great-Aunt Avis Woodfield, Uncle Richard's mother, then almost ninety six years old, to see if they were hiding out there; he'd been to relatives of Barbara Corbett, Margaret's niece, and to the Atwell family in Oxford that Aunt Amanda, Andrea and Ben had been evacuated to, again to see if there were any leads. He and Aunt Amanda had consulted private detectives and Father Brian had put out tearful appeals for his daughter to come home at the end of every Sunday service. 'For a family of so-called witches,' Jack said after he'd wiped away his tears, 'you're not much cop at fortune-telling, are you?!'

'Let me give you a few words of advice,' Phil replied, sitting them both down on the steps and shelling the money he'd won back out to Jack, occasionally performing some little sleight-of-hand routine with it himself. 'Don't fight this. Let...let your Aunt Amanda and me worry about it.'

'I don't want to be the fucking 'Daddy',' he said. 'It sucks. It's stupid. Why do I need to be the Daddy anyway? You're the Daddy.'

'Well I won't be around forever,' Uncle Phil said. 'In fact, I might pop off at any moment, if...well, just if.'

'So let Jamie do it.'

'Believe me, we would if we could. But as you know...'

'...yeah yeah, I have 'the kiss'.'

Phil had lolled an arm around his shoulders. 'You and I haven't always seen eye to eye Jack, but let me tell you, if I could find a way for you not to be the Daddy then I would. Can't you just...play along with the idea, at least for a while?'

'Until Jamie can be the Daddy?'

'We'd rather not have that either,' he said. 'It isn't the Daddy that's the problem. The position is fine, if a little...'

'...antiquated and overly patriarchal?'

'Well yeah, but like I said, it's not so bad; it's what goes with being the Daddy that's the problem; upholding the 'good name' of Minty Hardcore, and all that.'

'But that's all bollocks,' Jack said. 'I don't believe in all that.'

Phil then shrugged, kind of ran his tongue the circuit of his mouth. He looked tired. His big brown eyes had big grey bags underneath them, and his hair was untrimmed, floppy and foppish. He fixed Jack with his most serious expression, arched eyebrows knitting in the centre of his forehead. 'You will do,' he said simply.

Jack and Jessica returned to Barking along with their Uncle Phil in mid-April of 1995, around five days after he'd called to say he'd found them; apparently Phil had always wanted to see Paris, and also he wanted everyone at home to have time to 'cool down', so he extended his visit and took in the sights. When they stepped off the Airbus at Victoria Station

Father Brian was waiting, along with Beverly and Aunt Amanda. Father Brian is said to have been ready to lay into Jack verbally – physically wasn't his style – but Phil responded by asserting himself as the Daddy and saying that Jack and Jessica were upset and needed time to chill out and think about what they'd done. On arrival in Barking Jessica went to stay with Phil, Jamie, and Rose for a month until her father had sufficiently calmed down; she swore her Uncle Phil never to tell that she'd worked as a pole-dancer, something he was said to have found 'hilarious'.

As for Jamie, since leaving school he'd worked on various stalls on the East Street market; he held a Saturday job in the West Ham club shop in Upton Park, and finally in 1998 he got his own stall adjacent to the bandstand and just behind the big Boots store, selling second-hand paperbacks. A month or so after Jack and Jessica returned from Paris Phil took him and Rose to Blackpool for a week, along with Jamie's best friend Adam. Phil, Jamie, and Adam rode every ride in the Pleasure Beach at least several times over, while Rose held their candy floss and took pictures and laughed; only once did they get her on a ride herself, and that was the Steeplechase, riding behind Phil and screaming the whole way around the course. She and Phil were toying with the idea of getting engaged around this time, and were about to announce it officially in 1999 when tragedy struck the family, suddenly and viciously.

Heath's wife Sophie – Daniel and Debbie's mother – is said to have told her husband that she thought someone was in the house, and watching her; they lived in a two-up two-down on Salisbury Avenue, a stone's throw from the Barking Dog and Casey's house on Somerby Road. She said she'd heard someone '…whispering and laughing to themselves' whenever her back was turned, that she'd caught glimpses of someone in a mirror or the glass in the window, and that things were going missing, or being moved, and strange messages were being written in lipstick on various pictures and mirrors. Neither Heath nor the children noticed anything wrong, and on this basis Sophie is said to have begun to fear for her sanity.

Heath is said to have been reluctant to go to his brother over the matter and instead consulted Aunt Amanda, his adopted mother, who went straight to Phil with the matter anyway. There was never any animosity between Phil and Heath, indeed they were quite close, but Heath is said never to have understood what it meant that his brother was 'the Daddy', and that in times of even the most personal crisis to have been unable to accept that even his own children might turn to Phil for help over himself.

Phil found nothing unusual in the house but asked to be left alone there '…for a time', and when the family returned they found he'd sprinkled salt in all the doorways, and to have placed gris-gris bags under all the pillows in the house, these being little cloth pouches native to New Orleans hoodoo, filled with whatever substances the spells they were to countermand called for.

On the morning of November 10th 1999 Heath left the house at nine in the morning as usual, to make the short walk down to the East Street market and his stall selling toiletries and the like (he now sells mobile phone covers and Bluetooth headsets). Daniel and Debbie were at St Margaret's and had left half an hour earlier, and Sophie was alone in the house. Around eleven am neighbours heard the sounds of crashing, like every object in the house was being thrown around. They knocked on the doors to investigate, but were unable to raise an answer. When Daniel returned home during his lunch hour for his horror movie 'swapsies' cards he found several police cars and an ambulance outside the house, as well as a fairly large crowd. Miss Law, their neighbour, is said to have pulled the boy away, and only to have said that, '...something dreadful has happened to your poor mother'. It transpired that Sophie had run out of the house barefoot and hysterical, past her neighbours, and scrambled up the wall overlooking the train lines leading out of Barking Underground station. Miss Law told Daniel she'd lost her footing and fallen into the path of an oncoming c2c train from Dagenham Dock, that she'd almost certainly been killed by the fall alone, and so hadn't felt anything when the train, travelling at a good speed, had passed over her.

Some family members say that Heath never really recovered from his wife's death; the verdict reached by the coroner was that Sophie had killed herself whilst the '...normal balance of the mind was disturbed', although she had no history of mental problems either personally, or in her own family. Her entire family travelled from Laindon to Barking for the funeral, where ugly scenes ensued at the graveside at St. Margaret's. Her parents wanted her buried in their own family plot but they had been overruled by Aunt Amanda, who told them that Sophie had died a Woodfield, and all the Woodfields were buried together in the cemetery at St. Margaret's, and always would be, as far back as Jaden Woodfield.

Sophie's eldest brother faced off in a violent confrontation with a deeply grieving Heath, who laid him out for '...getting in my face like that', and Phil is said to have had to come between his brother and Sophie's father before the same thing happened there. Sophie's mother is said to have screamed at the assembled Woodfields that '...living with you lot would drive anyone out of their minds!!'

Of Sophie's two children, Debbie seemed to recover relatively quickly, having always been 'her daddy's girl'. Daniel on the other hand, was devastated by his mother's death, and began to pile an enormous amount of weight on in the weeks and months that followed, to miss a lot of school, and to generally cause a great deal of trouble for his father when he found him smoking joints in his bedroom, joints reportedly brought for by his cousin Hayden. Daniel didn't grass, though; no one ever grassed on Hayden.

Chapter 44

Thursday 18th May 2006

'It should be around here somewhere...' said Jack.

Tiffany clung to his arm, and peered into the failing light. 'There's the Serpentine, just over there.'

He held up the scrap of paper that had fallen out of the brown envelope, the brown envelope brought to him by Jamie all the way back on that awful Christmas Eve, along with the two keys inside it. 'Read me the exact instructions,' he said.

Tiffany narrowed her eyes. 'It says, "...walk to the bank and stand dead centre in the middle, so that your toes touch the water; then face the slope leading upwards and walk twenty two paces, and then dig".'

Jack strode on ahead of her and she hurried to keep up. It was a fairly warm, if slightly windy evening, and there weren't as many people around as there might have been. 'I totally forgot I had that envelope,' he said, reaching the bank and trying to figure out where the middle point was. 'Jamie gave it to me at Christmas; it was from Uncle Phil. I tucked it into my jacket pocket and totally forgot it was there. I think it fell inside the stitching or something.'

'Good thing I found it then,' Tiffany said, draping her arms over his broad shoulders. 'I think you'd be lost without me, Jack.'

'I think you're right.' He turned, and kissed her; tongues quickly entwined, and the odd little groan or two followed on. 'I do love you,' he whispered.

'I love you too,' she said. 'I always have.'

'Yeah?' he raised an eyebrow quizzically. 'How come you spent so much time with Jamie instead...'

'SShhhhhh.' she pressed a finger to his lips. 'Let's walk twenty two paces and then dig.'

Jack shrugged, then strode up the hill, counting his steps meticulously. He came to a halt on a flat sloping area of grass that looked just like any other. A woman nearby walking her dog glanced at him for a moment, and then moved away. 'I think she thinks we're looking for a prime spot to fuck in,' he said.

'She might be right,' Tiffany giggled. 'Come on, dig. I'm really curious. Knowing your Uncle Phil it could be buried treasure or something.'

'Or it could be a box full of potato peelings; Uncle Phil had a wicked sense of humour, you know.' He bent down and tested the earth, then slipped the trowel out of his pocket. 'Keep watch.'

Tiffany thrust her hands in her jeans pockets and swivelled on the point of her heel, glancing left and right. The last few people enjoying the sunset had moved on and apart from the woman walking the dog they were alone.

She glanced down and found herself admiring Jack from above, the nape of his neck finely muscled and a sole bead of sweat glinting in the light of the moon. Some men had awfully shaped heads that a crop only accentuated, but Jack's head was beautiful, the neck long and thick, the jawline so firm. She reached down and stroked the nape with her fingertip. 'Found anything?'

'Yeah,' he said. 'It's metal. I think it's a strongbox or something. Give me a hand, will you.'

'I'll get my knees dirty.'

He grinned up at her. 'You'll have grass stains in other places when I'm finished with you.'

'Promises promises,' she bent down and hooked her fingers under the length of greyish steel. 'You're right,' she said, 'it is a strongbox.'

'I know.' He strained but couldn't get ample leverage. 'I wonder how long it's been here?'

'Let's open it and find out.'

'Okay. Take the strain...' Jack pulled as hard as he could and in a little explosion of earth the strongbox came free; it was entwined by a single chain with a rusted metal lock, the keyhole of which they had to clean out with the tweezers Tiffany carried in her handbag. 'Two keys,' Jack nodded, 'one for the chain and one for the lock itself.'

'Open it,' she jostled him. 'I'm excited!!'

The chain came off easily, but the mud in the actual lock of the box had hardened considerably and it took them about ten minutes to scrape it out. A jogger came past and had almost done a return circuit by the time the lid swung open, revealing something large and soft all wrapped up in a Tesco carrier bag. 'Here it comes...' Jack unfolded the edges of the bag and held it up. What appeared to be a pillow fell out, not your standard sized pillow but something slightly trimmed down, and clearly sewn together by hand. It was yellowed with age and there was a clear, almost eerie head-shaped imprinted near a patch of discolouration on one side. He shook the carrier bag and peered inside it but nothing else fell out, and the same went for the strongbox too, when he turned it upside down. 'That's it?!' he almost threw it aside in disgust, 'a fucking pillow?!'

'Jack, don't!!' Tiffany scrambled to retrieve it, and slipped it back in the carrier bag. 'Your Uncle Phil obviously buried it for a reason. Maybe it belonged to someone...special.'

'Maybe there's something inside it,' he narrowed his eyes. 'Gimme those tweezers, I'll splice it open. It feels like there was something inside it.'

'No don't!!' she pressed the pillow to her chest.

'Huh? Why not?!'

'It might be valuable!!' she said. 'Look at it!' and she held the top of the carrier bag open. 'It's ancient, I know it is.'

'It's a pillow, 'tiff!!' he gasped. 'For fuck's sake!' and he all but slapped his brow in disbelief.

'Let's let David have a look at it,' she slipped it back in the strongbox and snapped the lid shut. 'Maybe it's magic or something; he might be able to identify it.'

'A magic pillow?!' he raised an eyebrow dubiously.

'Well...wasn't Uncle Phil...you know...a witch?'

'He was a crazy mutha, is what he was,' Jack shook his head, rose, and dusted the dirt off his knees. 'Burying a mouldy old pillow on the banks of the Serpentine, how autistic is that?!'

'Well I think it's exciting,' she remained on her knees. 'Are we going to get David to look at it? It might be in an old issue of Fortean Times for all we know.'

'Okay,' he sighed. 'You know I can't refuse you. So,' he thrust his hands in his pockets, 'are you gonna get up or what?'

'Oh I don't know...' her lips sealed in a wry grin. 'I'm kind of enjoying the view down here...'

'Oh you naughty little girl,' Jack fiddled with his fly. 'You just stay right there then.'

David was watching 'Question Time' when Jack got in; Daniel was in the kitchen on the computer, chatting to a girl in Japan and pretending he was tall and ripped, and Bobby was on Jack's couch, reading 'Tales of the City' by Armistead Maupin. Jack went straight into the bedroom and tucked the pillow, still in its carrier bag – Tiffany had taken the strongbox – under the bed. He took Will Young's latest album from David's bedside CD collection and put it on the player, selecting 'Who am I' to play on auto-repeat while he undressed for his nightly bath, forgetting that the volume was up quite high, and not really caring when he finally took note. David peeped his head around the door a few seconds later. 'You ok fella?' he asked.

'Gonna have my bath,' Jack stripped down to his briefs and rolled the soiled trousers up into a ball. 'Chuck them in the washing for me, will you? They might need something a little stronger than Sainsbury's own brand to clean them up.'

'Always,' David nodded, and then furrowed his brow. 'Jack...are you ok? You only play Will Young when you're like...well, fucked in the head.'

'I love this song,' he said, moving past him into the bathroom and turning the taps on. 'Kind of makes me want to cry, you know?'

David glanced into the living room, but the 'children' were still preoccupied. He thrust his hands deep in his jeans pockets and leant against the frame of the bathroom door. 'What's up?'

Jack tested the water with his fingers, then turned the cold tap on a little more. 'Everything,' he said, climbing in and letting out a slow, troubled sigh. 'Everything.'

Chapter 45

Friday 19th May 2006

'Don't I need a broomstick or something?!' Jamie asked.

'A broomstick, darling?!' Aunt Amanda braced him with both hands.

'Yeah...you know, to fly. They always have them in books, and in the movies.'

'And there you have your own answer,' she adjusted his posture and stepped back, seemingly satisfied. 'This is real life. That you can do it at all will be enough, believe me.'

It seemed such a long way down, and below them the commuters went in and out of Liverpool Street station none-the-wiser. 'I need it to brace myself though, don't I?!' he asked.

She sighed. 'Darling, witches only used the broomsticks because they enjoyed the feel of something long and hard between their legs; I wasn't aware you were 'on the turn', but if you are...'

'Bite me.' He stepped out onto the edge, and put one foot out, finding much to his astonishment the feeling of being about to tread empty air was much the same as that of pushing his foot into the muddy ground of a football pitch; it was going to be slow going but entirely possible. 'Hey look!' he peered over his shoulder at her. 'I think I can do it!'

'Very good,' she took her place on the parapet beside him. 'Now, don't let your concentration slip for instant, or we'll be on the pavement and on 'London Tonight' in a two-minute segment at about six seventeen this evening, understand?!'

'Uh huh. Aunt Amanda?' he turned, still with just the one foot out.

'Yes darling?'

'Did you know Uncle Eddie has prostate cancer?'

'What?!' she let herself slip, just for a moment, and she fell forwards. Jamie's arm shot out to grab her and caught her by the wrist. He dove onto his stomach and his other arm went out to the side of the parapet and with considerable difficulty – although not as much if he hadn't been buffed – he hauled them to safety. Aunt Amanda rolled onto her back and exhaled heavily. 'What did I just tell you?!?'

'But I was concentrating!!'

'Well I wasn't!' she slapped her brow in disbelief. 'Who told you this?'

'Uncle Eddie did, on the way back from Cardiff.' Jamie drew his knees up to his chest. 'Even Aunt Delia doesn't know; he doesn't want to spoil her big birthday. Don't you think it's good that he told me though? That maybe people are starting to see me as the Daddy?! I mean, he didn't go and tell Jack, did he?'

'How bad is it?' she rolled the news over in her mind. 'What else did he say? Damn that Eddie Dowden!!'

'It's only early stages,' Jamie went on. 'And it takes years apparently; he's seeing a specialist next week, in secret, like. They're going to stick something up his bum, a camera or something, and he's not happy about it! He says it's not a Kodak moment!'

'This isn't good, Jamie darling, and least of all for your Uncle Eddie.' Aunt Amanda glanced at her watch. 'The family seems to be shambling from one crisis to another; if I were of paranoid mind I'd almost say someone wanted it that way...'

'Uh, Aunt Amanda?' Jamie was peering over her shoulder. 'I think we've been rumbled...' and he gave a cursory nod to the two security guards marching towards them, their faces set in grim determination.

Aunt Amanda gathered her skirts up and wet her lips. 'Let me handle this, darling.'

*

'Tell me darling, has your brother mentioned anything about a pillow?' Aunt Amanda sloshed the wine in her mouth and then nodded to the waiter, who smiled cordially, and refilled her glass. Jamie watched her, quite fascinated, until she raised an eyebrow quizzically 'A pillow, darling?'

'A pillow?' he ran his eyes over the City Limits' restaurant's menu, sniffing and then rubbing his runny nose with the back of his hand. 'I got hay fever, shit.' He dabbed with the napkin and then coughed hard. 'You know I speak to Jack like, once every six months, and that's being generous. Don't see as how a pillow would be top of the list of things to catch up on when we do finally get around to it.'

'Funny, she never mentioned one either...' Aunt Amanda poured him a little of the wine. 'Try that.'

'"she"?' Jamie frowned.

'Oh, nothing doing, darling. Just try the wine.'

'Do you mean 'she' as in Minty Hardcore?' he tasted, then grimaced. 'You usually do when you say 'she', like you can't bear to actually say her name or something.'

'I'm not referring to that crafty little whore in this instance,' Aunt Amanda said. 'As I told you a while ago, darling, I have one or two other people helping us in our cause, and it's to one of them that the 'she' in this instance refers to; call her Jack's guardian angel, if you like.'

'Cool!' Jamie brightened considerably. 'When do we meet them??'

'We don't...yet, anyway. Their cover is of considerable importance.'

'It's all so cloak and knife,' he rubbed his nose again. 'It's better than TV, hanging around with you!'

'Cloak and dagger, darling,' she waved the menu in his face. 'You do have hay-fever bad, don't you? I have a few remedies for that back at home. We'll fix you up later.'

'Are we still gonna unveil me on Aunt Delia's birthday?' he asked.

'Of course.'

'Do you think my arms are big enough?!' he gave a brief flex. 'They still don't look nowhere near as big as Jack's; Jack's arms are so big you can't even make your fingers meet if you wrap both hands around his biceps, I know 'coz I saw Hayden try it once, and Clay too, and Clay's got like, massive hands, but even he couldn't manage it!'

She smiled. 'They were strong enough to haul me up the side of that building, weren't they?' she was grinning, and he suddenly realised he'd been had.

'You fell on purpose!' he said. 'Just to see if my arms were strong enough to catch you!'

Aunt Amanda made a steeple of her hands. 'What a suspicious mind you have, Jamie Woodfield!'

'I bet we weren't going to tread air at all,' he did a 'Jafaican' wrist-flick thing. 'I might have fallen! You should have told me, I could have just lifted you normally or something…'

She leant forward, hands still clasped. 'Minty Hardcore will want to see those biceps really bulge, darling!' she said. 'And so I had to make sure they did!'

'Crafty,' he shook his head, laughing, and folded his arms.

She let him have his little laugh, and then after a few moments said again, 'Darling, are you sure when you last spoke to Jack he never mentioned a pillow?'

'No,' Jamie frowned. 'What is this crazy pillow talk all of a sudden?!'

'You know, I do believe you cracked one there,' she smiled. 'But don't worry about it. It's all to do with that envelope you passed to him at Christmas, do you remember? the one with the keys in it?'

'Vaguely…'

She pursed her lips. 'Maybe he lost it. Let's hope he did.'

'You talk in riddles sometimes, Aunt Amanda,' he sighed.

'Let me worry about the details, darling,' she called the waiter over with a quick motion of her hand. 'You worry about getting big and strong and wise and being the Daddy. Minty Hardcore will want you big and strong, you know. And yes, I do think your arms are big enough now, so no more tricks on the ledges of tall buildings.'

'Jack's got really hairy arms too,' he said. 'A man's arms, that's what Jessica calls them. I've got a kid's arms.'

'Pardon me Madame,' the waiter cut in, nodding at Jamie, 'but him, the Daddy? no no, I'm sorry, but no. Perhaps however we can put him on a leash at Jack's side, like a pet; Jeramiah used to do the same with his brother Jacob when he was bad, if I recall.'

Aunt Amanda's eyes widened, gazing up at him. 'What did you say?!?'

The waiter smiled down at Jamie, who seemed blissfully unaware of the whole exchange. 'I don't do second best anymore. Although, I did enjoy him last Sunday, I have to confess. He lacks Jack's masterful technique, of course, but he more than made up for it with his sheer gusto...'

'You keep your filthy old hands off of him!!' Aunt Amanda rose, and gripped the edges of the table. 'You hear me?!'

'Aunt Amanda?!' Jamie's eyes widened. 'He's asking if you want to try the white!'

She started. 'The white?!'

'The white wine, madam,' the waiter made an apologetic bow. 'You seemed quite lost to us there for a moment.'

'Yes yes,' Aunt Amanda waved him away dismissively, grabbing the edge of the table with both hands and bracing herself a moment. 'We'll order in a minute, thank you.'

Jamie watched her settle back into her seat. 'You really lost it there for a moment, you know!' he gasped, 'you totally spaced-out on me!! People were looking!!'

'I'm sorry darling.' She dabbed at the corners of her mouth with the napkin. 'I don't know quite what came over me, I must confess.' She spent a moment or two more regaining her composure, and then looked up at him with a weak smile. 'Shall we order?'

Jamie needed some help pronouncing the name of the dish he wanted, but he seemed satisfied with the choice, especially when a different waiter, a rather leggy French girl, took the time to teach him to pronounce it properly, scruffling his hair by way of congratulations. After a lull in the conversation he said, 'Tiffany and me called it a day, you know. But I'm cool, see? I was worried she was seeing someone else behind my back, but she definitely isn't. We're still friends now, anyhow; close friends. I told her I was happy she was going back to college.'

'That's the best way,' Aunt Amanda nodded. 'Are you sad?'

'Kind of...still numb, you know? Uncle Phil going was so bad nothing can touch that.'

'I know what you mean,' she raised a glass. 'Still, let's think of him fondly. You have to remember the good times, Jamie darling.' And she touched her glass to his. 'Cheers, to my wayward 'son', your Uncle Phil.'

Jamie beamed broadly. 'To Uncle Phil!'

Chapter 46

Friday 19th May 2006

'He spends far too much time talking about your Uncle Phil,' mum said, 'far too much time. What's that word, sweetheart, when people mope too much? It begins with 'm' as well, but it's much more fancy than that...'

'Maudlin?' Jack ventured.

'That's it. Maudlin. I think you ought to have a word.'

'With Jamie?'

'Who else?! You know you can't tell your Aunt Amanda anything, and lord only knows your Uncle Heath and I have tried.' She turned and gazed at Jack, leant against the sink with his arms folded, his face set in something a little like a scowl. 'What's up, sweetheart?' she wandered over, placing her hands on his forearms.

'I can't see Jamie, mum,' he said. 'Not right now.'

'Why not?'

'Well, aside from the fact we haven't had a conversation in about six years, 'coz...'coz I'm seeing Tiffany.'

Mum shrugged, tossing her dishcloth over her shoulder. 'Well of course, she's your friend as well as being his girlfriend, wasn't I telling your funny friend David that just the other week?!'

'I'm not seeing her as friends, mum.'

'I mean, seeing as how you're friends and all...'

'Mum, I'm fucking her,' Jack leant forward. 'Alright? I'm fucking her; almost every day, if you must know.'

'Well there's no need to be so graphic!' she gasped, her hand to her breast.

He slapped his brow in disbelief. 'I give up.'

She gazed up at him. 'You're not joking, are you?' and when she shook his head, she shook hers. 'Oh Jack...'

'I know, mum.'

'Oh Jack...'

'I know, mum!!'

'This isn't the first time either,' she leant past him and switched the kettle on. 'I remember the time Clay met that nice girl from Chelmsford and they were dating and it was all serious, and she catches sight of you at a party one time and she's all over you, and did you resist?! Did you heck as like!'

'Alright mum!!' he threw his hands up. 'If this is a lecture then I'm out of here. I only popped in 'coz you said you had something important to tell me.'

'It hardly seems to matter now,' she began sugaring some cups. 'Oh Jack, how could you?! It's not some fling, him and Tiffany; it's serious! He needs her now more than ever.'

'Mum, she came on to me!'

'She did?!' her eyes widened. 'Well then she's a slut, and he's well rid of her. I never really liked her anyway, too sweet by half. Never trust anyone that sweet, your Aunt Amanda told me that when I was a little girl and God help me I haven't been able to shake it.'

'Mum, she's not a slut,' Jack sighed, handing her the milk. 'Me and her, well it's serious...'

'Like it was serious between you and that Toni Harrison? Or Chloe Astin?! Or...'

'Alright already!'

'Well I'm just saying.' She poured the cup. 'I hope you know what you're doing.'

'I do.'

'Well you don't sound like it. In fact you look bloody miserable.'

'Well yeah, 'coz I'm well aware at some point Jamie's got to be told,' he said. 'I'm not the total cunt he thinks I am. I happen to care...ah, it doesn't matter.'

'Jamie loves you, really,' mum handed him his tea. 'Only he'd never say it. He's waiting for you to be the Daddy, same as we all are. You really ought to put all that bad blood between the two of you in the past, where it belongs.'

'Don't start that again, mum.' He took a sip. 'Now, why have I been summoned?'

She cleared her throat. 'I have...I have...'

'...breast augmentation next Tuesday?!'

'Oh stop it,' she swiped his arm. 'No, I have...well, I have a boyfriend, sweetheart. And he's asked me to marry him.'

'Really?!' Jack raised an eyebrow. 'What's he like?'

'His name's Chris,' she said, 'and he's tall, just the way I like them, tall and handsome, a writer who made ends meet by lecturing students in creative writing at somewhere called Birkbeck, I think. We met by chance when he'd been visiting his sister in Upney, who had a couple of facials off me once.'

'He know you have two grown-up sons?'

'Oh of course!' she swiped his arm playfully, then clung to it. 'You're at the London School of Economics, I told him that.'

'Did you tell him Jamie's going to South Bank?'

Mum made a face. 'I think Jamie should stick to working in the market, he isn't cut out for an academic life; know your limitations, that's what I always say.'

'I think it might be the making of him,' Jack took two cups off the wall, one of them his favourite old mug that he'd left there for sentimentality's sake, ice blue, and chipped. 'Of course, he'd quit in a second if he heard me say so...'

'I told him all about Jamie, as a matter of fact,' she folded her arms, watched him sugar the cups ready for their next brew. 'So there, I wasn't singing your praises all the time. I told him Jamie was a little sensitive, not very world wise, that he's lived his whole life in Barking; well, we all have but somehow Jamie seems never to have moved beyond it, if you know what I mean. He's just been lost ever since Phil died, I told him that too.' and she sighed. 'Sometimes I wonder if all this learning to read and going to university isn't him just Jamie struggling for some sort of direction.'

'What did you say about me then?' he turned back, his big cheesy grin in full swing.

She smiled. 'Jack is more intense, more focused, that's what I said. He knew when he was little that he wanted to go to university, and leave Barking someday; he always wanted a job in some big office on Cheapside or Cannon Street. A psychotherapist, that's what he always wanted to be. Only trouble was...'

'...was what?'

'...nothing,' she shook her head, 'You know what I mean, sweetheart. No, I just said you were more intense, focused, academic. I said you were quick, verbally I mean, and very sure of yourself whereas Jamie isn't. He knows just what to say and do, I said, walks into a situation and takes control. He could have all the friends he wanted but he sort of kept himself to himself, kind of knowing he'd never want for company, and that's all.'

'Didn't you tell him what a stud I was?!'

'Oh get you,' she laughed. 'I told him about all the others, all the twins we have in our family, He was dead impressed that we were going to be on that programme on BBC2 that time, but remember the makers found a family in Leeds who had more twins than we did and they dropped us like a hot potato?!' she gave a little laugh. 'I think they thought we were a bit common.'

'And he's asked you to marry him,' Jack was pouring the teas, 'this Chris, I mean.'

She reached into her jeans pocket and produced a little gold band with an indent where a pure diamond had been fitted and sat rather jaggedly at one angle. 'We're going to the Barking Dog tonight,' she said proudly, 'I'm going to unveil it, and him, and I was hoping you at least would be there; Jamie's off doing God knows whatever it is he does with his Aunt Amanda, I dread to think...'

'I can't mum,' he said. 'Me and 'tiff, tonight; I'm taking her to this new place on Upper Street, it's Lebanese...'

'What do you want to take her to a lesbian place for?!' mum's eyes widened, and she almost dropped the ring. 'Oh God, you're not into that as well, are you?! 'coz I've seen the covers of those 'lad mags', I know what boys like you like...'

'Oh please. I don't need to look at the pictures.'

'Well anyway,' she said. 'I've got a man, and perhaps a fiancée. Are you happy for me?' and she grinned. 'I asked you to marry me years ago and you refused, if you remember!' she threw him a wink, then tweaked his cheek. 'Oh look at your face, my handsome pride and joy!!'

'Mum!!' he laughed. 'They call that the Oedipus Complex, only you're doing it in reverse; I'm meant to be the one wanting to marry you, and kill him!'

'You did want to marry me when you were little,' she smiled at the memory. 'You and Jamie used to fight over that as well.'

Jack exhaled. He gazed past her, out of the kitchen window; a District Line train rumbled past, out of Barking and on towards East Ham. 'Does he treat you ok, this Chris?'

'He treats me wonderfully,' she said. 'He's teaching me all sorts of things. I might even take up a night class at Birkbeck myself.'

'Oh, so he's canvassing?'

'Oh sweetheart,' she sighed. 'Please, try and be happy for me. I've been on my own for so long now, I'd almost given up hope.'

'Mum, you've had tons of guys on the go,' he said. 'What's so special about this one?'

'You're sorted, that's what's special,' she said. 'You're at the LSE now, you've got your interview for that summer job coming up...I feel, well I feel like I can relax, take a look at my own life.'

'You could always do that.' He put his cup down and put his hands on her shoulder. 'I'm big and strong enough to look after myself, mum. I always have been.'

She rubbed his hand. 'I know sweetheart, but I had to see you get there myself. It's so easy with Jamie because he never had any ambition, but you...well you've always wanted to go so far, do so much, see so much; I don't think there's ever been a Woodfield quite like you.'

'So,' he said, 'you're gonna tell everyone tonight?'

'Oh no,' she shook her head. 'Only the introduction tonight; we're saving the engagement announcement for your Aunt Delia's birthday party; any excuse to keep things going until four am at least!'

'Well he better treat you right,' Jack said. 'That's all I can say; because if he doesn't, well then I'll be back around here to kick his head in, and make no mistake.'

'It won't be necessary, sweetheart,' she said. 'This one's for real.'

'Yeah well...' he gave her shoulders a gentle squeeze and then kissed her gently on the forehead, his eyes closed. 'You'll always be my number one girl.'

'And Jessica's your number two...' she ran a little theory through her head. 'So Tiffany runs a very poor third?'

Jack cleared his throat. 'Family first, mum. It's always been that way with us, and even I can abide by it when I have to.'

'Let's just hope she sees it that way.'

'Mum, don't sweat it. I'll be cool; it'll be cool. I love you.'

She sighed, gazing up at him. 'I love you too, sweetheart.'

*

'We're not telling them about the engagement tonight,' Bev said, urging Chris toward the doors of the Barking Dog. 'This is just to introduce you to whoever's here, which I suspect may be quite a lot, but that's my family for you, nothing better to do on a Friday night than drink themselves under the table...'

'Are Jack and Jamie here?' he straightened his collar. 'Do you think I look ok; smart casual?'

'You'll knock them dead, sweetheart' she stopped short of the doors. 'But don't ask me where those boys of mine are. If I know Jamie of late he's with his Aunt Amanda, talking far too much about our Phil than is healthy. As for Jack, well he could be anywhere; probably romancing some beautiful girl or other, a rose between his teeth and a packet of Durex in his back pocket!' She didn't want to mention anything she'd learnt this afternoon; that would deal with itself in its own time, she figured. She pushed the double doors open and beamed as a multitude of familiar faces turned to take them in. 'Here he is,' she declared, giving Chris a hearty shove forward. 'Meet my boyfriend!!'

'Oh here he is!!' Aunt Delia declared, snaking forward in a cloud of perfume and gaudy colours. 'Ohhhhh isn't he handsome?!' she fingered the lapels of Chris's jacket. 'It's not fake either, girls!! quality all the way here!'

'Leave him alone, you,' Bev gave her a cheery wink. 'He'll have a rum and coke and I'll have the same, I think.'

'Eddie!!' Aunt Delia nodded to her long-suffering husband, 'three rum and cokes!'

'Sit yourself down over there, sweetheart,' Bev directed him to the nearest table, already commandeered by a good many Woodfields and their friends. 'The introductions are going to take the best part of an evening as it is.'

Chris found a spot between Tamsin and Casey Woodfield, craftily planted there earlier by Bev to give her husband-to-be the most sober introduction possible to her rather overwhelming family. The idea was that he might have quite a lot in common with Casey; they were of similar ages and both of them shared something of an artistic flourish. Meanwhile, Tamsin's skills as a PA would be sure to smooth over any of the rough edges that the other cousins would doubtless provide. Chris glanced around a little nervously; she could tell from the look on his face that he'd thought she was exaggerating about how many cousins and aunts and uncles and nephews and nieces she actually had, but now he could see she wasn't; that on top of all of their friends and the like, it seemed there wasn't a person in the bar who didn't want in on meeting him in some shape or form.

'You get that down you,' Aunt Delia all but shoved the rum and coke into his hand. 'There's plenty more where that came from.'

'Don't get him too merry, girls,' Bev draped herself over his shoulder. 'I might need him later, you know?!'

'Get her!!' Aunt Delia jostled Aunt Rachel playfully, and the two of them erupted into near-helpless laughter. 'I could do with one of these myself; feel his muscles, Rache'!!'

'Only if you let me feel yours,' Chris threw her a come-hither look; best to play these women at their own game, Bev had warned him, 'how about it, Delia?!'

'Ah, she's built like a trucker, is our Delia,' Casey winked her way playfully. 'Isn't that right?!'

'Cheeky sod!' she swiped him with the back of her hand. 'I've had you over my knee when you were a boy, and I still could, Casey Woodfield!'

'So what do you do then, Chris?' Tamsin asked him. 'We've heard next-to-nothing about you. It's all been very covert, in fact.'

'I lecture in creative writing,' he nodded, 'at Birkbeck College. And in my spare time I write my own novels and hope one day to have one of them published.'

'A writer!!' Aunt Delia's eyes widened. 'What's he doing with our Bev then, I wonder?!'

'Less of that, you cheeky old cow,' now it was Bev's turn to swipe her arm out. 'I've had poems written about me by this man, let me tell you; he could charm the birds out of the trees with his lengthy prose!'

'What do you do, Delia?' Chris asked.

Aunt Delia made a face, ran her tongue inside the circuit of her mouth. 'Well officially I'm retired, but I can't be sitting around on my arse all day,' she lit up a cigarette and blew the smoke out in a theatrical plume. 'So I make ends meet by doing two or three days a week on the till in the Superdrug on East Street. Not very grand I get you right, but there you go.'

'Britain will always need women on tills,' he winked again, 'good, stout British stock like you.'

'He's turning my head now, he bloody well is!!' she laughed, a great cloud of smoke flaring from her nostrils. 'Gordon Bennett, so he is!!'

'Here comes your brother, Aunt Bev,' Casey nodded to the door.

'He's a pussycat,' she whispered to Chris as she sidled out of the seat; he'd been nervous of meeting her twin brother. 'Trust me.'

'He looks very...' Chris looked from Uncle Heath to Tamsin, who was smiling, and then back again.

'Essex man?' Tamsin raised an eyebrow dubiously.

'My thoughts exactly.'

'Oh, and what am I then?!' Casey puffed his chest up and clenched his jaw, 'not Essex enough for you, Mrs Woodfield?!'

'Plenty enough', Tamsin blew him a kiss. 'But I know how Chris feels; coming into this family...it's an experience all its own. He can reap the benefit of my years of experience.'

Heath strode up to the table in that almost comically masculine gait of his, paw outstretched. 'Hey,' he nodded, 'Pleased to meet you, Chris.'

'Heath', Chris rose to return the shake. 'The big brother revealed at last; now all I need to meet are Jack and Jamie and maybe my palpitations will die down a bit.'

'Oh you'll be lucky to see Jack, like ever,' cousin Marie interjected, leaning over from the adjacent table, where she'd been canoodling with her librarian boyfriend Scott. 'He's long since left for pastures new.'

'So I've heard...he doesn't pop in at all?'

'He will if I bloody well text him' Bev pulled her mobile out. 'I could have at least one of my blessed sons here with me; I don't care if he's on the job, either.'

'Jack's an academic as well,' Marie went on. 'He thinks we're all common. He thinks we all need therapy, and stuff. He's going to be a psychotherapist, you know. He's going to analyse us all and publish his findings in *The Sunday Sport*!'

'Marie!!' Aunt Rachel gasped.

'Oh you'll be strung up for that,' Tamsin threw her a cheery wink. 'We mustn't talk out of turn about Jack, must we?!'

'He's turned his phone off,' Bev sighed, slumping back down in her seat. 'I guess he was on the job after all. Oh well, there's plenty for you here to be going on with.'

'No Jamie?' Chris asked.

'Well...'

'Text him, Aunt Bev,' Marie said. 'Poor Jamie just sits in that flat every night wishing Uncle Phil was back, you know he does. He'll be grateful for the invite.'

'Bless his heart,' Aunt Delia sighed, stubbing her cigarette out in the nearest ash-tray, twisting and turning the butt until the last spark was extinguished. 'I sometimes think we forget all about Jamie.'

Chapter 47

Sunday 21ˢᵗ May 2006

They'd all forgotten about Aunt Queenie, and it wasn't hard to see why; her flat above the 'At Barking' bar on Linton Road smelt of cats piss and old people. The carpet on the stairs was peeling and curled at the corners, and Jamie had to navigate large piles of old newspaper in order to reach the room at the top, wherein the aforementioned smell became almost overpowering. 'Aunt Queenie?' he glanced about, but the room was so dank that all he could make out were vague shadows, the hum of a radio coming from the kitchen. 'Are you here?'

His foot hit a chair and he reached out and felt something soft, soft flesh under a loose lace garment; Aunt Queenie, in her nightie, fast asleep. He prodded her gently. 'Aunt Queenie?'

'Piss 'awfl!' she gasped, her eyes widening, meaty little hands flailing. 'My 'usband will be back soon, so just you piss 'awfl!'

'It's Jamie, Aunt Queenie,' he crouched, fumbling for the switch on the nearby lamp. 'I've come to see how you are.'

'Is that Jack?' she leant forward and grabbed his chin in her hand, turning his face this way and that. 'About bleedin' time you came back, me old lad. Go put the kettle on and we'll have a cuppa. What time is it?!'

'It's Jamie, Aunt Queenie,' Jamie sighed, exhaled slowly.

'Jamie who?'

'Jamie Woodfield. You know, Bev's son…Jack's brother.'

She leant forward, her beady little eyes focusing on him. 'You look familiar…are you Jack's brother?'

'Uh huh.'

'Well why didn't you say so?!' with great effort the rotund, almost comical little woman hoisted herself out of her chair. 'I'll go and make some tea then!'

Jamie followed her out into the kitchen. The floor was wet, milk and water combining from the upturned cat bowls tucked in the gap between the washing machine and the sink. The sink itself was piled high with washing, old tea bags and even little cartons of milk and juice. The surfaces were dusty and the corners of the units were threaded with cobwebs. 'Doesn't Aunt Rachel pop in here and sort you out, Aunt Queenie?' Jamie asked.

'Oh she gets on my bleedin' tits, she does,' she filled the kettle with water and set it to boil. 'Always cleans up and moves everything and I can't bloody well find nothing; I told her not to come about a month ago. I can look after meself, so I told her. And then I think she forgot I was 'ere to begin with!'

Jamie felt like saying something about how Aunt Rachel had spent years looking after her father, Aunt Queenie's brother Rupert, in much the same fashion, and that she was to be congratulated for offering to do the same here, but he thought better of it. Aunt Rachel had even offered Aunt Queenie a room in the house on the Ripple Road but she'd refused it; Aunt Queenie was waiting here for her husband, so the family lore said, who'd gone out for a pint of milk in 1966 and never come back. It gave him a swell of pride though, reinforcing his notion of her as a forgotten casualty of the vast Woodfield clan, whom he would rediscover, and reintroduce into the fold 'Do you need any shopping doing?' he asked. 'Anything you want, just let me know and I'll do it.'

'Ah you're a good boy Jack, that you are' she squeezed his chin hard, leaving nail marks in it.

'Jamie.'

'That's right,' she nodded, preparing the mugs. 'How is Jamie?'

'Aunt Queenie...I am Jamie.'

'Are you?' she leant forward, squinted. 'Well never mind.'

'Jack lives in Islington, Aunt Queenie,' Jamie pointed out. 'He doesn't stop by here much these days. He's at the London School of Economics now; he's going to be a famous psychoanalyst.'

'Good for you.' She handed him his tea and ambled off into the living room. 'Where are me fags?!'

'Are you keeping well?' Jamie cleared the magazines off a chair opposite and sat down, wincing as a spring all but inserted itself up his bum. 'You look well.'

'My bleedin' knee is killing me' she said, finally finding a packet of Bensons and lighting up. 'You want one?'

'I don't smoke, Aunt Queenie.'

'Good for you,' she inhaled, and sighed, her eyes seeming to clear. She looked at him and it was as though a light had gone on in her head. 'Jamie!!' she gasped. 'I've not seen you since...well, probably since Phil's funeral. How are you coping, bless you? 'coz he was like a father to you, wasn't he?!'

'I'm ok...' he noticed the picture of Phil on the mantelpiece, one among many; Uncle Phil on his scooter down in Brighton, Uncle Richard in the background, arms folded and gazing fondly at down at the young man, his face almost obscured by his big 70s moustache. 'I've not seen that picture before, Aunt Queenie.'

'Ah he was a handsome bloke, your Uncle Phil,' she reached over and picked it up, wiping the dust off it with her thumb and then taking another drag on her cigarette. 'Bleedin' beautiful big brown eyes he had. How's Richard?'

'Fine,' Jamie nodded. 'Jack, Bobby, and Daniel saw him about a month ago, said he was...well, he's fine, I guess.'

'He took it up the bleedin' shitter, he did,' Aunt Queenie replaced the picture, 'tulips from Amsterdam and all that.'

'Who's that?' Jamie nodded to the picture next to Uncle Phil's; black and white, a handsome man with a proud, roman nose and a large forehead, slightly wonky teeth. 'That's me dad,' Aunt Queenie nodded proudly. 'He'd have been your Great-Uncle Alexander, I think; or would he have been your great-great-uncle?!'

'Yours and Uncle Rupert's dad?'

'That's right.'

Jamie leant forward and studied the picture. 'When was this taken?'

'Must be in the 1920s,' she ran her tongue over her stained false teeth. 'Back when he was the Daddy.'

'He was the Daddy?!'

'"course he bleedin' well was,' she laughed to herself. 'Bloody Jacob went crackers in the end, same as Margaret, he had no choice, did he? There has to be a Daddy.'

'I thought Ben was to be the Daddy then,' Jamie struggled to reconcile dates. 'You know, Aunt Amanda's brother.'

'Hah!' Aunt Queenie threw back her head and laughed so hard Jamie could see all the way down her throat. 'He weren't even born then! And that mad old mother of his; Agnes, batty as a fruitcake and living all along in that house, no kids, no bleedin' job; well someone had to be the Daddy, didn't they?!' and here she fixed him with a steely glare. 'You ought to be telling that to that brother of yours the next time you see him. I was there when you was born, you and Jack, and they said about Jack before they'd even cut the cord that he was gonna be the Daddy once Phil was spent.'

'Well that's what I was going to mention…' Jamie made a steeple of his fingers. 'You see, Aunt Amanda, she thinks…'

'She's a bleedin' old witch, she is,' Aunt Queenie finished her fag and promptly lit another. 'And you know there's no way on god's earth she would have let her brother Ben be the Daddy anyway, so my dear old dad was the Daddy 'til he died. Breaking tradition is all she's ever been interested in. She never could bear to see anyone having a good time, and getting their end away.'

'That's not true,' Jamie said. 'There are things you don't understand…'

'…. there are things *you* don't understand,' Aunt Queenie shifted in her seat, propped herself up and leant forward. 'I could tell you things about your Aunt Amanda that'd make your hair curl, if it weren't so short already!'

'Aunt Amanda wants me to be the Daddy,' Jamie said, bowing his head and then fixing her gaze against his own. 'She said there are some things that have to change, and some things that have to stay the same, and that I'm the one to do it. Jack doesn't want to do it, so I'm gonna do it; I'm gonna do it for Uncle Phil. She says Jack won't mind, that he'll be glad, even.'

'She doesn't want anyone being the Daddy if you ask me,' Aunt Queenie said, and took a large drag on her fag. 'She'd see the whole thing done and gone if she could; she's very old-fashioned, your Aunt Amanda. She believes in 'love'....'

'Love?'

'Not much time for love when you're the Daddy,' she said, 'lots of the other, but actual love? Forget it. And don't you know, but she's been trying to end it all since, well since she went a bit funny, way back when her brother died. Smarter than my dad was, she is, and yet still we have the Daddy. We always will, I think.'

'What 'other' does the Daddy get?' Jamie asked, feeling his throat beginning to dry.

Aunt Queenie licked her lips, and seemed to think about something. 'Minty Hardcore,' she said finally. 'And Minty Hardcore...well she never wanted no woman, did she? It's the 'Daddy', not 'the Mummy', in't it?!'

'Aunt Amanda...well she says Minty Hardcore has to go,' he went on. 'That it's a silly idea, and that being the Daddy is all about looking after the family, and not...well she says she's a crafty little whore. She says it's about caring for the cousins, and...'

'...and not about being driven out of yer bleedin' mind with desire over Minty Hardcore?!'

Jamie nodded. 'Yeah. That's what she said. She said it's a good thing I've got a nice girl like Tiffany, so no crafty whore can tempt me. She says it's good that I believe in love.'

'Better than your Aunt Amanda have tried and failed,' Aunt Queenie sat back. 'My grandmother May thought she knew too, thought she could rule here in Barking and not give a bleedin' fig about Minty Hardcore, and credit to her she lasted a bleedin' good long time too, but she got her in the end. And she'll get you too, if you put your nose where it's not wanted. Happen that's why Amanda hides out in Bethnal Green; she thinks she's safe there or something.' her eyes narrowed and she let out a sinister little laugh, 'as if that'd make her safe from somethin' unnatural like that.'

'Do you believe in Minty Hardcore, Aunt Queenie?' he asked her.

'What do you believe?'

Jamie stared at the pictures on the mantelpiece. 'She says she's a crafty little whore; I'm never to forget that, so she says. And she's shown me things too...'

'...parlour tricks. I could win at cards like no one's business when I ran me pub, me and Albert, when we had our lock-in and the like. I could win just by lookin' through their own eyes and seeing the hand they had. We can all do that, us Woodfield girls, when we've a mind to, and some more than others.'

'Aunt Amanda says Minty Hardcore will go away if we all calm down; like when you give a pretty girl too much attention and she thinks she can pull a fast one on you, well she says Minty Hardcore is just like that; we mustn't let her pull a fast one on us.'

'Hysterical…' Aunt Queenie's eyes glazed over. 'That's what your grandmother Andrea was, you know? Absolutely bleedin' hysterical, and her a level-headed career woman working in the City as well, back when career women were something new and exciting. Reckon it drove her mad, not being able to nurse her own baby; your Uncle Phil, I mean. They say Minty Hardcore nursed him herself, on milk from her witches' tit!'

Jamie swallowed. 'Well yeah but…well not really, eh?'

Aunt Queenie nodded gravely. 'Really. And if you want my advice, Jamie Woodfield, you'll stay away. Well away. You're a nice enough lad, most of the time, and you don't want Amanda filling your head with all sorts of nonsense.'

'That's what my mum says, and she doesn't know anything.'

'Happen that she's right then. And don't worry about Jack not wanting to the Daddy either.'

'But he doesn't want to be,' Jamie protested, sipping his now cold tea. 'That's why I have to be. That's why I'm here today, visiting you; it's…well, it's what the Daddy does, isn't it?'

Aunt Queenie smiled knowingly. 'Jack doesn't have a choice in the matter; Minty Hardcore always gets her man.'

Chapter 48

Sunday 21st May 2006

When Tiffany stepped out of the salon the transformation was enough to make Jack's jaw all but hit the floor; gone were the slightly rusty red tresses and the split ends that went with such demanding home dye-jobs, and in were luscious plaited locks of pure golden blond, wisps of which hung over her heavily made up eyes like little teasers. She wore a pair of sapphire ear-rings and a matching necklace and bracelets, all this carried off to perfection by a two-piece number from the sale racks at Harvey Nicholls.

'Do I get my man?!' she asked, hands on hips.

'Wow,' Jack exhaled slowly, underneath his gentleman's umbrella. 'You look a million quid, 'tiff.'

'I hope so,' she linked her arm in his own. 'Considering it felt like it cost not far off that anyway. And it's not so much a radical transformation as a return to type, or so I like to think.'

'Where is this place then?' he asked. They were on the corner of Burlington Arcade on Piccadilly, huddled under the aforementioned umbrella against a rather heavy late spring shower.

'Well there's Turnbull & Asser,' she applied lipstick in the reflection of a nearby show window, Jack holding out the umbrella to shield her. 'Princes Charles uses them. So did your Great-Uncle Jeramiah, you know. He looked a killer in one of their suits, with his big, broad shoulders and all; your Aunt Amanda got the pictures out one time when I was 'round there with Jamie. You have shoulders just like his, you know.'

'Bet that was exciting,' Jack rolled his eyes. He was at present clad in one of David's suits, a River Island blue pinstripe number that clung nicely to his well-sculpted frame but came in a bit short at the sleeves. Still, the purpose was only to make him look smart enough to be buying a better one, 'Turnbull & Asser then?'

'No, I think Harvey & Hudson,' she set off at a determined pace. 'They're slightly more dynamic. You want to make a good impression tomorrow, don't you?'

'You bet,' he hurried after her, offering the umbrella. 'It's only part-time but it's what I want to do, y'know? Me in a suit, on Cannon Street...I'm hard just thinking about it.'

'Save it for later,' she turned and winked. 'I'm so proud of you; my Jack, doing psyche profiling for a big city firm. That's a step up from second-hand paperbacks, if ever there was one.'

'You and Jamie...it is all cool, isn't it? Still friends and all?' he followed her into Jermyn Street. 'Honestly?'

'Honestly.' She placed her hand on the front of his jacket and slowed him a little. 'Now this is where you're going to have to use that famous

Woodfield cunning and guile; we're not actually going to pay for this suit, you know.'

'I kind of thought you were going to say that...' he thrust his hands in his pockets.

She reached into her handbag and brought out a thin sheaf of cling film, inside of which was wrapped several slices of lettuce. 'Here,' she said. 'Take those out.'

'What are we going to do, trade them?!'

'Blow on them,' she said. 'Don't pull that face. Blow on them. Go on. I saw your Aunt Amanda do this once when she'd run out of cash in Tesco.'

'’tiff…it's daft!'

'Just do it,' she sidled up, slipping her fingers in-between the gaps on the buttons of his shirt. 'Just blow and think of the largest amounts you can.'

'You'll be the one doing the blowing later,' he winked, inhaling and puffing his chest up. 'And it'll be so large it'll blow your mind.'

'Promises promises,' she handed him each leaf individually. 'Fifties will do.'

After a few moments of his frantic blowing and eventual borderline alchemical transmogrification teased along by testosterone, she turned away and sighed, 'Oh look, it didn't work!' she said, and shoved the things in her handbag.

'I kind of thought it wouldn't…' he wrapped his arms around her waist. 'You really are crazy, you know?! I think being bored in Barking drove you out of your mind.'

'Crazy in love with you,' she said. They entered the shop and were greeted by a pleasant but rather effete old queen in a bow tie. Jack tried on a range of cotton shirts, and rolled his eyes more than once when the man made comments about the size of his inner thigh, all of which Tiffany found highly amusing. 'They have mother of pearl buttons,' the man explained. 'Aren't they beautiful?'

'Almost as beautiful as she is,' Jack nodded to his girlfriend, her legs crossed and the occasional shaft of sunlight illuminating her features like the searchlight of heaven itself. 'Don't you think?'

'Have you been together long?' the assistant asked.

'Not long enough,' Tiffany said. 'Let's just say I've had my eye on him for a long, long time.'

Once the shirt had been selected Jack chose an icy blue silk tie to go with it. The assistant gave them the names of several establishments that could deck them out in a reasonably good suit, and took their money without any complaints. As they left Tiffany explained that it was best to beat a hasty retreat, as the alchemised lettuce often became just that within a matter of hours, if not minutes. That was why the trick tended only to work in one place just the once, and why it wasn't exactly a foolproof way of getting rich. 'Not really of course,' she said, with a certain somewhat sly twinkle in her eye. 'I have money left over from my last modelling gig, and it's ever so modern, you know, me buying you the suit; what's that funny word they use, for men who use face creams, and talk about their feelings?!'

'Metrosexual?'

'That's it,' she nodded. 'I think you could wear that shirt to your Aunt Delia's big 'do,' she said. 'You need to get your money's worth, even if the shop isn't. Are we going to go public then?'

Jack made a face, 'If we have to.'

'Don't you love me?' they'd reached Piccadilly, and she nodded to Eros. 'Not even as he is your witness?'

'You know I do.' He slipped his hands around her waist and brought her up close, close enough for her to feel that he was 'packing it' just for looking at her. 'I just don't wanna hurt Jamie.'

'Since when have you cared so much for him?! You've barely spoken two words since you were born!'

He cocked his head, and gazed past her for a moment. 'Not strictly true…'

'Jack, you promised,' she fixed his gaze. 'He's fine, I told him a week ago today and he's cool. He has his own life now; he's met a girl at this Sight & Sound place. Louise, I think her name is…'

'Really?'

'That's what he told me. She's more on his level, if you know what I mean.'

'If you're sure…'

'I am.' She nodded confidently. 'I know Jamie better than you, and that isn't saying much. He's simple; his needs are simple, and this simple girl meets his needs, simply.'

'That's poetry.' Jack's blue eyes sparkled.

'You bring it out of me,' she smiled. 'Now, we have your shirt and tie for tomorrow, what are we going to do with the rest of our day up west?'

'Go for a meal?'

'I could show you another faux magic trick…' she purred. 'How about 'hide the sausage'? Or is that more of a game?' she shrugged, 'whatever we do, it's sure to drive me wild.'

'I do, you know,' Jack said.

'You do what?'

He glanced up at Eros, then back into her eyes. 'I do love you.'

'Oh my pet…' she reached up and tickled the nape of his neck, where his crop ended and his rather spectacular levator scapulae muscle began, causing him to shiver and retract his neck like a tortoise. 'I love you too,' she whispered, 'with all my slutty little heart.'

The Daddy Dissertation Part 8

By David Samuels

The rise and flight of Jack Woodfield

Jack and Jamie both fell for the same girl, at the same time. Her name was Tiffany Grieve, and she was around fifteen when she burst onto the scene and into their lives, sometime around late 1997, not long after their sixteenth birthday, accidentally spilling hot chocolate all over Jack's t-shirt on her first day serving behind the counter at Morelli's in the Vicarage Fields. Tiffany lived with her mother and sister on the Salisbury Road that they'd moved into only a couple of months previous, and only a couple of doors down from Heath and Sophie, and their twins Daniel and Debbie. Indeed, Tiffany's mother was one of the first on the scene when Sophie died after falling onto the train tracks leading out of Barking Underground in November 1999. The Grieves were quite private about where they'd come from and under what circumstances, but Tiffany is said to have let slip later on that they were 'from money' but that this selfsame fortune had been lost thanks to their father's drinking habits and the resulting poor judgement, and their mother was now filing for divorce and expecting only a pittance in settlement. They had relatives in the Barking area on her mother's side who were leasing the house to them for next to nothing.

Both Jack and Jamie were enchanted by this curvy, comely girl with the shoulder length rusty-red hair and the large green eyes offset perfectly by her model's cheekbones. Of course they weren't the only ones who were enchanted, but it didn't take the two of them long to beat a path to her door with the help of their many cousins, particular Aunt Delia's four lads – the modern day Woodfield boys – and before long no one else was willing to even risk asking her out on a date, although this 'don't touch' atmosphere was induced more by the heavy-handed tactics of Hayden Woodfield than by Jack and Jamie themselves.

Jack wooed Tiffany by writing her poetry and hanging around Morelli's coffee counter in his own words admittedly 'spewing' psychoanalytic ideas in order to impress her, sometimes even wearing a pair of spectacles his cousin Jessica had swiped from her father, the reviled Father Brian Woodfield. Jack talked about things on the news, about how he might help her put her modelling folio together, and about his dreams of working in the City when he'd been through university, and of the far-flung goal of a Woodfield owned and run psychoanalytic practice. He didn't stare at her chest like the other boys did, and his wardrobe consisted of more than just several pairs of trackie bottoms and Reebok tops. However, she told her sister that she found him a little too 'clinical' and some of his theories so mind-blowing that she'd end up simply having to nod and smile as though he were far less interesting than he actually was. She instead preferred Jamie bounding up to the counter with a bunch of wilting roses in his hand, talking ten to the dozen about the latest West Ham win; as a footnote – a personal author's footnote - to this it's worth adding that eight years on Tiffany ended up with Jack after all, just as he was completing the first year of his Masters at the London School of Economics, and she winning a contract to model for George at ASDA; Jamie is still selling second-hand books on the East Street market.

Jack went to college at Islington ITec for two years shortly after he'd finished school, majoring in basic psychoanalytic theory, with a little sociology thrown in for good measure. He is said at this time to have enjoyed sociology because it '…unravels all this bullshit we see from day to day'. He continued to harbour dreams of doing research for some high-brow company in an office on Cheapside or Cannon Street for a few years, completing almost a year of work experience in just such an office, albeit in the rather more modest locale of Old Street, before applying to several universities to do a degree in sociology; he was accepted to South Bank and chose to go there against his mother's wishes, Bev Woodfield being unhappy with the idea of him commuting all the way from Barking to the Elephant & Castle each day.

Never-the-less from Monday to Friday Jack made the tube journey from Barking to the Embankment, where he changed onto the Bakerloo line for Elephant & Castle. He took classes in sexuality with Professor Jeffrey Weeks, and psychoanalytic theories regarding gender under Susie Orbach, who would later return to tutor him at the LSE. It wasn't long before Jack had built up a regular little crowd around himself, some seven or eight strong but made up primarily of myself – David Samuels, co-author of this piece – and several of Jack's female admirers, as well as another friend Jack had made on his course, a rather dashing young lad from Manchester called Frank. They'd sometimes cut classes when things got a little too simplistic and head on into the West End; Tiffany would be doing a photoshoot in Knightsbridge and Jack, Frank and myself would have tea with her in the café on the top floor of Harvey Nicholls; she and Jack had remained good friends despite her at the time having thrown him over for Jamie.

Not long before beginning at South Bank, sometime around August 2001, Jack made inquiries with some of his more well-to-do relatives, i.e. 'the Hackney Woodfields', who owned properties in and around the Archway, Tottenham, and Islington areas, with a view to moving into one of them at a reduced rate. He eventually found a property he liked in the Barnsbury area of Islington, a one-bedroom flat with a large kitchen and communal garden in the basement of a two-storey property owned by the kind of city types that Jack longed to emulate. Jack moved into the flat before he even told his mother what he was up to, so that any objections she raised would therefore fall flat on their face; well, that was the theory.

In Jack's own words his mother went '…absolutely apeshit' the moment he informed her he was flying the proverbial nest. She was on the phone when he went to 'take a leak' and by the time he'd finished the first of the aunts and uncles had arrived, cousins coming along soon after. In fact, the only people who didn't raise any objection to his leaving were his Uncle Phil and Aunt Amanda, the latter of whom wrote out a cheque for his first month's rent on the spot, along with a sizeable cash donation in an envelope for '…food and anything else he might need.'. Beverly was in tears by this time, burying herself in Phil's arms as he whispered to her that everything would work out for the best. Those present shrugged their shoulders and said that Phil and Amanda obviously knew what they were doing, and after all, Islington wasn't exactly the other side of the world. Jack's cousin Jessica was said to have been inconsolable at the news, despite reassurances from Jack that she could come and stay whenever she wanted; she did just that within days of his moving there. Hayden Woodfield is said to have fled the flat on the Murphy Estate on the day of the farewell in a rare show of emotion; Jack went after him and they spent almost an hour arguing and recriminating underneath the window of Aunt Queenie's flat above the 'At Barking' bar.

When Jack had returned to the flat, and it came time to say goodbye to Jamie, the entire room fell silent, the whole flat packed to capacity. Jamie offered out his hand and said, 'Good luck 'bro.'; Jack shook it and said, 'You too, J,' and then he picked up the last of his bags and went down to where Clay was waiting in his delivery van, along with the rest of Jack's things. Beverly went into her bedroom and didn't emerge for several hours. Phil and Rose stayed with her that night.

In late 2001 Phil organised a trip to Los Angeles at considerable expense to himself and to Rose, to try and cheer everyone up in regard to Jack's departure, even though realistically he was still on their doorstep, everyone was still slightly shell-shocked and there was a general consensus of '…the lot of them having had the wind knocked out of their sails', according to various friends. At around 7am sometime during mid-October around thirty Woodfields descended on Heathrow airport with their luggage, Jack included (he was never one to turn down a free holiday), having wangled a week off university on account of his excellent opening grades. In fact the full list of Woodfields who went to Los Angeles in 2001 is as follows; Jack, Jamie, and Beverly; Phil and Rose; Casey and Tamsin, herself at the time four months pregnant; a rather reluctant Uncle Heath, along with Daniel and Debbie; Aunt Hannah, Sara, Laquisha, and Marie; Aunt Rachel, Michael, Tracy and her three-year old daughter Brittany, and her baby son Charlie, and Aunt Queenie; Father Brian, Aunt Betty, Bobby, and Jessica; Uncle Eddie, Aunt Delia, Clay, Springer, Hayden, and Nick; and Uncle Richard from Brighton, along with his 'friend', a playwright called Owen. On top of these there were the requisite boyfriends and girlfriends; Tiffany;

Sara's long-term boyfriend Ron; Michael's girlfriend, who was also Tiffany's flatmate, Elisha; Hayden and Nick's girlfriends, Sammi and Gwen, respectively; and Jamie's best friend Adam. The only person who didn't go, apparently out of choice, was Aunt Amanda; '…someone has to stay here and keep an eye on things, darling,' is said to have been her reply upon receiving the initial invitation. She stayed in Phil's flat while they were away.

Uncle Eddie got drunk on the flight over and threw up on one of the hostesses; he put it down to nerves, and in fact many of the Woodfields experienced first flight jitters, the majority of them never having even left London before the trip. Beverly had a panic attack when the first bout of turbulence hit and to calm her down she was taken up to the flight deck to meet the captain, whom she took a shine to; the feeling was mutual and they '…went to see Sunset Strip together' when he was on stop-over, and after that kept in touch for several months by postcard. By the time they landed in LA Nick was locked in the toilet throwing up after having challenged his twin Hayden to see who could drink the most miniatures, obviously having failed miserably. He stayed in his room for the first two days of the trip, something that upset Jamie a fair bit insomuch that he was probably closest to Nick out of all the cousins, in a bizarre symmetry to the way that Jack was probably closest to Hayden.

The family splintered on arrival. After unpacking at the Roosevelt Hotel on Hollywood Boulevard most of them went over the road to have their pictures taken next to various stars on the walk of fame outside Mann's Chinese Cinema; Aunt Delia's picture of her hand inserted into the frame of Bette Davis's own print sits in pride of place in the Broadway flat. Jamie and Adam got lost and were mistaken for gigolos on Sunset Boulevard. On the first proper day Uncle Phil charged a coach to take the lot of them to Universal Studios, where they got in on one of the largest family tariffs the ticket office had ever had to deal with. Aunt Queenie went on the Jurassic Park ride despite warnings that at eighty one she was far too old; as soon as they were off she was back in the queue with Uncle Phil, Jamie, and Adam to go on again. The weather was extremely hot, and there were sprinkler systems fitted into most of these queuing areas. Unaccustomed to such climates the family were soon suffering sunburn and dehydration, and Aunt Rachel almost fainted in the queue for 'Terminator 2 3D'. One of the best pictures of the Woodfields at this time is a shot taken by someone dressed as Brendan Fraser from 'The Mummy' and probably more accustomed to being photographed himself, as opposed to the other way around. Everyone is in the picture and it's enticing to examine their expressions and their general attitude at the time. Phil is dead centre in the middle and at the front, in blue shorts and a brown-ish short-sleeve shirt from Banana Republic; the entire family seems to be gravitating to him in the picture, almost as if by some sort of race memory. Phil has one arm around Jamie, who is squinting in the glare of the sun, and the other around Rose, who is smiling broadly. Even the non-family members incline to him in some way or other. Jack is off to one side as though he finds the whole thing faintly tiring, but he lolls an arm around Jessica's shoulders just for show. Jessica herself is in little more than a bikini – 'You're not wearing that out in public!' was Father Brian's reaction on seeing it – and she's clinging on to Jack for all she's worth; to anyone not in the know they'd easily be mistaken for a pair of star-crossed young lovers. Uncle Eddie looks as if he'd rather be anywhere but where he is, but Delia stands proudly ringed by her four boys, their girlfriends almost pushed out of shot. Father Brian is smiling but his arms are folded, and poor Aunt Betty is blinking, and almost facing the wrong way entirely. Casey and Tamsin are proud parents-to-be, and his brother Bobby seems happier to stand with them than with his parents. Sara has an arm each around her younger sisters Marie and Laquisha, with her lanky boyfriend Ron in the background, towering over all three of them; mum Hannah is on the left, her sister Rachel on the right, along with her children Michael and Tracy, and her little Brittany and Charlie. Lastly it's worth mentioning Uncle Heath's almost heartbroken expression; he was still grieving for his wife although it was almost two years since her death, and was drunk by almost the end of each day; Daniel and Debbie are on their knees up in front, just beneath their Uncle Phil.

That first night the youngsters went clubbing somewhere near Universal Studios and didn't return to the hotel until the early hours, whereas the 'older' generation partied more locally, with the exception of Father Brian and Betty, who were in bed by ten.

Subsequent days saw trips up to the Hollywood hills, Rodeo Drive, and out to Venice Beach in Santa Monica. There are amusing photos of Jack stripping down to his trunks and posing amidst the musclemen; his own physique was well-developed enough to earn him a round of applause from a group of girl tourists from Hong Kong, one of whom he bedded the very same night; 'Jack's about the most natural piece of meat in that steroid zoo,' Jessica is said to have told her brother Bobby. Uncle Eddie tried to emulate Jack's success and ended up being rushed to the nearest hospital when he dislocated his shoulder hanging off the monkey bars.

The rest of the trip went by relatively peacefully, the exception being Hayden getting arrested for unintentionally jaywalking and then trying to argue the toss with the policeman who eventually booked him, calling him '…a fucking cunt!' Rose felt unwell on the flight back and by the time they reached Heathrow she was running a high fever. While the rest of the family went back to Barking, Phil, Beverly and Jamie went with her to the nearest hospital. It transpired that Rose had blood poisoning, although how and why she'd got it the doctors were at a loss to say. Despite their best efforts they seemed unable to contain it and although she rallied briefly during the latter part of November, Rose eventually passed away on December 14th, 2001.

Her funeral was as big as Sophie's had been, and the song Phil chose for her to be played as the coffin rolled on its bier was 'I guess that's why they call it the blues', by Elton John. Jamie was deeply upset at the loss of a woman he'd come to regard as something of a second mother, and family members said that Phil was never the same afterwards either. He formed a closer bond with his brother Heath following Rose's death, and the pair were able to help each other along the long and oft-times painful roads of their respective losses.

The family was buoyed up by the birth of Casey and Tamsin's little girl Meggan, a couple of months after Rose's death, heralding the next in a new generation of Woodfields, following Tracy's children Brittany and Charlie. Aunt Delia is said to have rallied the family with the old adage of, 'Life goes on', and indeed it did; Jamie and Tiffany toyed with the idea of moving in together when she took a flat on the London Road, but he was reluctant to leave Uncle Phil in what he considered a 'vulnerable' state, and Tiffany ended up having one of her friends moving in with her instead. Beverly had a romance with the manager of the Spotted Dog pub and he is said to have proposed to her on one knee amidst a thunderstorm in the taxi rank on Station Parade, but she turned him down for reasons similar to those Jamie had cited in regards to moving in with Tiffany.

Jack's graduation from South Bank in 2004 with a 2:1 upper class honours in sociology was about the biggest thing that had happened to the family in ages, and academically speaking it was absolutely unprecedented. On a hot day in the middle of July an enormous number of Woodfields descended on the grounds of the Imperial War Museum in Lambeth, disposable cameras at the ready. Beverly, Phil and Aunt Amanda went with Jack to his robing, and to have his official pictures taken; Beverly burst into tears at the sight of her son in his mortar board and gown, gushing along with Frank's mother about how proud she was, about how all the years of struggle had been worth it, and how bright the future was for her wonderful son. Jack seemed rather embarrassed by this massive outpouring of emotion, but to have taken it all in his stride, to have allowed Aunt Amanda to straighten the genuine Louis Vuitton tie she'd given him for the occasion, and to have the three of them posed behind him in one of his official portraits. Tickets were strictly limited, and Beverly, Phil, and Amanda were the only family members allowed into Southwark Cathedral for the actual ceremony; the rest of the family had a picnic in the War Museum's grounds along with the families of other graduates, although rumour has it Jessica was snuck in at the last minute. During the ceremony one of the mothers is said to have hollered out, 'Hallelujah!' when her son's name was called out, and Beverly, determined to top this, jumped up and cheering and clapped and called out, 'Go on my darling!!' when it was Jack's turn. 'He's my big, blond angel,' she apparently cooed to all those around her.

They reconvened in the grounds of the War Museum where Jack patiently posed for group shots and then individual pictures with all of his uncles and aunts, and each and every cousin. Everyone seems to have been extremely proud of Jack, and for once there is a picture of Jack and Jamie together where they're actually smiling and seem pleased to be in each other's company, even if they are play-acting out a scene of mutual strangulation. Jamie never seems on this occasion at least not to have been fazed by the amount of attention lavished on Jack, as long as he was number one in their Uncle Phil's eyes.

The family went to Browns in Covent Garden for an enormous champagne slap-up meal that lasted well into the evening; various cousins and friends then accompanied Jack for a pub crawl around the immediate area that ended up with most of them spending the night sleeping in doorways or on park benches, the lucky few squeezed into the flat in Islington and enjoying the relative luxury of the two available sofas and the blow-up bed in front of the television. Jessica slept with Frank that night, and they dated for several months after.

Chapter 49

Monday 22nd May 2006

It was what Jack affectionately called 'a Kodak moment', and Jack being Jack he'd made sure that it was immortalised in just such a fashion, David two or three steps ahead of him and snapping away on a said brand disposable camera brought in a nearby Boots, snapping indeed with such conviction that passers-by mistook the suited and booted Mr. Woodfield for some kind of up and coming celebrity and stopped to take their own pictures on their mobile phones. After a couple more shots Jack held up his hand called out, 'Enough already!' He closed his umbrella and shook it dry, darting into the doorway of a nearby office and waiting for David to join him. 'Did you get me okay?' he asked. 'Did I look hunky?'

'Can't see as how I didn't,' David pocketed the camera and then went for Jack's Harvey & Hudson tie, straightening it, then stepping back and becoming unsure of his effort, going at it again with his tongue curling around the bottom left of his mouth. 'And I can't see as how you couldn't,' he added.

'Cut it out,' Jack waved him away. 'People will think we're queer.'

'Jack, I am queer.'

'Yeah well I'm not.' He scowled, then caught the slightly pained expression on his friend's face. 'Sorry matey. I'm cacking it here, you know. It's my moment, you know? Either that, or it isn't.'

'No kidding.'

'We'll go for a couple of bevies afterwards.' Jack stepped out of the doorway and set off down Cannon Street at a determined pace. 'Do you think I should ask what my chances are once the interview's over?'

'No, never do that,' David hurried after him. 'Never seem too keen. I can't see as how that's going to be a problem for you. In my experience you tend to have problems with people who are too keen for you.'

'Are you sure I look ok?' he stopped outside the office of Cornwell & Winslett. 'I haven't got snot or anything, have I? Or sleep in my eyes? How are my ears?'

'Let me look at you,' David stepped back, and he couldn't help but indulge his eyes. 'You look beautiful, Jack. I'd hire you on the spot. As your mum would say, you're every inch 'the big, blond angel'.'

'Are my teeth white? Does my breath smell?'

'Pearly; and no, it doesn't.'

'Let me check everything…' Jack flipped open his briefcase and went though, making sure he had all his references and an extra copy of his CV, just in case. 'Check, check and check. Ok, wish me luck; psyche profiling, here I come!'

'All I have,' David saw his moment and darted in for a quick peck on the cheek. 'Text me as soon as you're out.'

'Will do.'

He watched him disappear into the reception area, and then turned around and thrust his hands in his pockets. He looked up and down the length of Cannon Street, bustling as much on a Monday lunchtime as it might be on a Friday evening when everyone was fleeing the City for the weekend. He opened the umbrella, hefted up the case containing his laptop and made a left, heading for the familiar oval 'M' of the nearest McDonalds. He spent the next hour or so typing up the latest notes Jack had given him on the family history, emailing early copies as attachments through to the editors at Fortean Times, the names of course changed to 'protect the innocent'. He ordered a double cheeseburger meal and was just polishing off the last of the fries when he got a text from Jack, a simple 'where are you?' A couple of moments later Jack strode confidently into the McDonalds, beaming from ear to ear, his briefcase in one hand, his umbrella in the other, looking every bit the dapper young city gent. 'How did it go?!' David almost leapt out of his seat.

'They offered it to me on the spot,' Jack grabbed him and almost lifted him off his feet, 'on the bleeding spot, mate!!'

'I hope you said yes!!'

'Of course I bloody well did!' he wiped a fine film of rainwater off his forehead. 'Bloody fantastic, I'm telling you!!'

'What do you want to eat?!' David made for the counter. 'Then you can give me the details.'

'Get me what you had,' Jack sat back in the plastic seat and stretched his long legs, loosened his tie. 'I need a trash food rush.'

David returned a few moments later with another double cheeseburger meal and set it down before him. 'Well?!'

'A breeze!' Jack waved a hand dismissively. 'They even drew up a six month contract for me!' and here he reached into his briefcase and waved the appropriate bit of paper in David's face. 'They're willing to work around my uni hours once we start back in October, no problem. The woman who interviewed me, Jasmine, well I think she fancied me, if you want the truth. She actually leant across the desk and talked to me with her hand on her chin!'

'When do you start?'

'The week after next,' Jack squished his fries into the buns of his burger and bit deep. 'I have to email them a copy of my uni' timetable, but it's cool until October, I told them all we have are the exams anyway. She was made up. Did I tell you I think she fancied me?!'

'You're so hyper,' David beamed. 'You're almost bouncing off the ceiling!!'

''coz this is it for me!' he declared, washing down the first bite with a swig of Tango. 'This is what it's always been about, getting the suit and the job in the City; it's about as far away from Barking and that poxy East Street market as you can get! I'm made up, Davey boy!!' and in a sudden fit of excitement he drummed his fists on the hard plastic of the table, turning heads and making all of his fries dance around in their cardboard container.

'I know,' David nodded, eyes clouding over. 'I know you are.'

Jack sat back, and burped. 'What could possibly go wrong, eh?!?'

Chapter 50

Monday 22nd May 2006

Jessica Woodfield had been asking for her cousin Jack for the last hour or so, her knees drawn up to her chest and pinned there by her arms, rocking backwards and forwards slowly, to and fro, to and fro. Her bouncy blond hair was dishevelled and the black Seventies style headband she wore had slipped and was in danger of disappearing down the back of her neck. Her blue cardigan had a rip in the left sleeve and the fingers of her right hand played with the unravelling wool absent-mindedly. Her make-up was streaked all over her face like the skids a car makes after breaking sharply, and there were little finger marks forming into bruises on the tops of her breasts, just visible beneath the cream vest she wore underneath.

Father Brian Woodfield knelt on one side of her, waiting for her to speak. On the left her mother Betty gazed down at her worriedly, fiddling with the plastic beads on her necklace. In the space between them a policewoman crouched on the tips of her toes, waiting for her to speak. A policeman stood further back, gazing around at the rosaries and other religious imagery that adorned the walls and mantelpieces of the rooms above St Margaret's. 'Do you want to tell me what happened, Jessica?' the policewoman asked her, her voice soft and reassuring. 'Someone attacked you, didn't they?'

Jessica nodded, and the tears came again. 'I want Jack,' she said simply.

The policewoman looked up at Father Brian. 'Jack?'

'One of her cousins,' Betty interjected. 'They're very close.'

She looked worriedly at the marks on Jessica's breasts. 'Do you want to tell me what happened to you, Jessica?' she asked again.

'I want Jack,' she said simply, and began rocking again.

The policewoman straightened up. 'She's in shock. Do you think you can get ahold of this Jack for us?'

'I'd rather not…' Father Brian rose also, but Betty was already reaching for the phonebook. 'Betty…'

'Let's do as the constable says, dear,' Betty began dialling. 'I'll call Casey as well.'

The policewoman knelt down again. 'What do you do, Jessica?'

'She a model,' Father Brian said it as though it translated as 'prostitute'.

'A model?' the policewoman glanced at her male counterpart. 'Is that right, Jessica?' and Jessica nodded dumbly. 'What sort of model?'

'Like that awful Kate Moss,' Betty said, her hand over the receiver.

'Is that right?' the policewoman smiled. 'You're prettier than Kate Moss, Jessica.'

Jessica's eyes welled up. 'He touched me,' she said.

'Who did, Jessica?'

'The photographer…' she stopped rocking. 'He said I was cheap, and that he could touch me if he wanted; he put his hand up my skirt…' and here she broke down completely.

'I knew something like this would happen…' Father Brian sighed. 'I knew it, I knew it, and did she listen to me?!' and he turned away in disgust.

'With all due respect Mr Woodfield, now isn't really the time or place,' the policewoman said, turning to Betty. 'Any luck?'

'Her brother Casey is on his way over,' she was dialling again. 'I'm just going to…'

'I want Jack!!' Jessica snapped.

'I am dear, I am,' her mother pressed the receiver to her ear and waved for quiet.

The policewoman turned back to Jessica. 'Jessica, do you want to come into another room with me and you can tell me what happened in a bit more detail? Just you and me, and your mum and dad can wait here for your brother, and for Jack?'

Jessica nodded dumbly, and allowed herself to be led off into her bedroom, the door closed firmly behind them. Father Brian watched for a moment, and then bowed his head. 'This bloody family,' he sighed, gazing at the floor. 'There's always something, isn't there?! God, I may take your name in vain but I wish I wasn't a Woodfield sometimes!'

'Are you related to Clay Woodfield, by any chance sir?' the policeman asked, snapping to attention.

'He's my nephew,' Father Brian said.

'…'coz we're always pulling him in for selling dodgy gear of one sort or another, but off the record he's a sound bloke, your Clay; I got a microwave off him for the missus at Christmas, and she was made up!'

'Jack's on his way as well,' Betty put the phone down. 'He was in the City somewhere, Cannon Street I think he said, I couldn't really hear him. He'll be over soon enough.'

'I don't see why he has to be here,' Father Brian scowled, leaning against the mantelpiece with his arms folded. 'Isn't it bad enough Bobby prefers to live with him than with us, and I don't want to be dredging up the past but I'm afraid Jack and Jessica's little Paris escapade is still…'

'Oh do shut up, Brian dear!' Betty snapped, her easy-going façade slowly fading from view. 'Jessica is very close to Jack and she wants him here. If you want to make yourself useful go and make the officers some more tea; tea always helps.'

'That's all this family does, drink buckets and buckets of tea!' he muttered, making his way into the kitchen. 'Tamsin loses her baby? Have a cup of tea. Hayden and Nick go to prison? Have a cup of tea. Laquisha is racially abused? Have a cup of tea. Phil dies? Have a cup…'

'Oh do shut up, Brian!!' Betty finally lost it, almost throwing the receiver at him, 'for Heaven's sake!!'

Just at that moment Casey let himself in with his old house key, nodding a brief hello to the policeman, whom he recognised as a regular on the Station Parade beat. 'Mum?!' he dragged his hand back through his unkempt brown hair. 'Where's 'jess?'

'In the bedroom dear, with the nice policewoman,' she explained. 'A man...well, we don't know quite what happened yet, but she wanted Jack here so he's on his way as well.'

Casey peered into the kitchen. 'Dad?'

'Don't ask, son,' he sighed, boiling up the kettle. 'Just don't ask.'

*

Jack arrived around forty minutes after Casey; by this time Jessica and the policewoman had emerged from the bedroom, the former looking slightly more composed and a lot less tearful, whilst the latter went and conferred hurriedly with her male counterpart, making a quick call to the station on the Ripple Road with her radio. Jack was still in his interview suit as he breezed in through the living room door, his briefcase in one hand and his umbrella held tightly under the other arm. On catching sight of him Jessica cried out at the top of her voice, and all but flung herself forward, towards him. 'Oh Jack!!'

'I'm here, 'jess,' he kissed her on the cheek, hugged her tight, almost off her feet, in fact. 'Aunt Betty didn't say what happened...'

'He touched me,' she broke down again, burying her head against his shoulder. 'He said I was cheap, he put his hand up my skirt; he tried to force himself on me. I scratched him, I tried to get away...'

'Who did this?!' he looked at all of them in turn, as though they might somehow be responsible.

'Jessica's given us a very good description,' the policewoman pocketed her radio. 'Plus she seems to have 'marked' him pretty good with her nails, and we have the address of a studio as well.'

'You give me that address?' Jack whispered softly in Jessica's ear, softly, so that to the others it travelled as nothing more than a comfort. 'Promise me?' he said, gently pressing his lips to her ear. She nodded dumbly, gazing up at him, her big liquid brown eyes full of tears again. 'Sssshhhh,' he said, and bent her forward, kissing her furrowed forehead. 'I'm here now, kid. I'm here, and I love you.'

Jessica was sullen and withdrawn again by the time she arrived back at St Margaret's, Jack guiding her to the door where she stood still for a moment, vaguely disorientated, a far cry from the spirited, defiant girl who'd helped orchestrate the 'great escapade' to Paris several years previous. She spoke to Jack in the hallway and then went to the toilet to freshen up; having been examined was almost as bad as having been mauled, so she told him, and having to tell the story a third time, to a trained counsellor, had all but exhausted her. Jack slung his suit jacket down on the side of the chair and rubbed his eyes with the backs of his hands. He got his phone out and texted David, telling him not to bother saving him any dinner, and that he didn't know when he'd be back. He fully intended to stay the night, whatever the miserable old bastard glaring at him from his chair near the window said. Aunt Betty stuck her head around the kitchen door, cheery as ever. 'Cup of tea, Jack?'

'Please, Aunt Betty,' he nodded. Father Brian shifted a little in that chair of his, the light falling on the shiner he was still sporting, courtesy of Jack, who spotted it and smiled weakly at him. 'She's bearing up well,' he said. 'It seems it was an assault and not...well, you know, not a full-on...'

'Well thank Heavens,' Aunt Betty said, taking the cups off the shelf and filling them with milk and sugar.

'This would never have happened if Phil was alive,' Father Brian said sternly. 'I may not have agreed with some of the things he did, or the way he carried on with all his women and his football, but credit to him, he took care of this family. He did what he was supposed to do.'

'Do be quiet, dear,' Aunt Betty boiled the kettle and then poured the cups. 'What did Casey say, Jack? Did you see him on your way back?'

He nodded. 'He said he'd pop back later, but that he'd left the shop with someone who couldn't stay too long. Tamsin was really upset about it all when she heard.'

'Do you want something to eat, Jack?' Aunt Betty asked. 'I must say, you do look ever so handsome in your suit. Does your mother know you're here?'

'Not yet...' he scratched his crop thoughtfully. 'I'll call her shortly. I want to hang around and see what 'jess wants me to do. Can I have a sandwich or something, Aunt Betty?'

'Ham & cheese?'

'With lots of mayo, yeah, and toasted, please, if you can possibly manage it!'

'I'll bring it in, dear,' she said, as he rose out of the chair and made for Jessica's room.

''jess?' he knocked firmly. 'Can I come in, sweetheart?'

He heard something that sounded a little like an affirmative, and opened the door gingerly. The room looked more pokey and cell-shaped than ever, and she was just a little person in pink, amidst all the defiantly pink things, huddled up by the head of the bed, gazing at the black and white shot of her and Jack taken on the family's holiday to Los Angeles, she leaping onto his shoulders and he laughing out in response; happy times. 'How are you, kid?' he asked, slumping down beside her on the bed, letting the cold brick walls from the church below take the weight of his back. 'You want something to eat too? Your mum's a mean cook, you know; I'm having one of her 'Scooby Doo' sandwich specials, you know; the ones where she piles it almost to the ceiling...'

For a long time she said nothing, and then she looked up at him. 'He touched me, Jack,' she said simply.

He slung his arm around her shoulders and leant his head gently against her own. 'I know he did, kid, I know he did. But they're gonna get him.' And he closed his eyes and his nostrils flared, and his jaw jutted. 'I'm gonna get him,' he said.

'He said I was trash,' she wiped her eyes with the back of her arm. 'That my ideas of being a proper model were a joke, that the best I could hope for was to be a glamour model and that he'd show me how it was done...'

'He's a fucking cunt,' he scowled. 'You remember to give me that address, you know?'

'I think its punishment,' she looked at him through bloodshot eyes, 'for what I did in Paris.'

'How do you work that out?!' he shifted so that he could give her waist a gentle squeeze. 'I didn't think you brought into all that shit your old man spouts from the pulpit every Sunday.'

'Oh Jack, his eye is still swollen,' she giggled softly, and sniffed back the tears before they came. 'I bet he hates it that you're here. He thinks that your friend David is giving it to Bobby up the arse every night, you know!'

'David's in love with me,' he said matter-of-factly, latching onto the chance to take her mind off things. 'For which I can't entirely blame him...'

'Is he really?!'

'Yeah! He told me so; he jerks off about me all the time!'

'Oh get you!!' she slapped the back of her hand against his chest. 'You arrogant shit; you're worse than you ever were.'

'You love it,' he licked his lips. 'Good to see a smile on your face, kid,' he nudged her chin playfully with his fist. 'We'll get through this, you and me. We can get through anything, as long as we have each other.'

'God knows how,' she sighed, her head slumping down against his shoulder. She gazed around the room, and the pink seemed to wilt suddenly under the sheer oppressive weight of the Curfew Tower up above them, its long shadow a permanent feature just outside her bedroom window. 'Even Bobby gave this place up, and if Bobby gives something up well then it must be shit, can I get an Amen on that score?!'

'Amen!!'

'Don't you mind having him at your place all the time?' she looked up at him. 'Him and Daniel too, Christ I can't think of two more polar opposites...'

'Bobby sleeps on the blow-up bed,' Jack giggled, nudging her and gently sliding his fingers under her t-shirt, tickling her waist, 'and every night around midnight you'll hear his little footsteps, and he unravels the bed and attaches this little pump thing that blows it up automatically, and it's like 'sssssssssss' for about forty seconds, and me and David are in the other room pissing ourselves!! It's just so fucking funny!!'

There was a knock on the door, and a moment or so later Aunt Betty entered with a tray full of sandwiches, several cups of tea, some slices of lemon cake, and a Mars Bar for each of them. 'Here you go,' she said. 'You get stuck in. Jack, I can always make up the spare bed if you want to...or you could stay in Bobby's room, it seems only fair exchange, that is, if you're not too busy...'

'Mum, Jack hasn't said if he's...' Jessica cut in.

'I'll kip in Bobby's room,' Jack took the tray. 'I can always watch his 'Doctor Who' videos if I can't sleep, eh?!'

'Lovely!!' she slid back around the door. 'Call out if you need anything.'

'Will do, Aunt Betty!'

'Thanks mum,' Jessica called out.

'Hey it's great here,' Jack divided up the lemon cake. 'God knows why Bobby thinks it's so great on my floor, but there you go. Maybe we could swap places after all.'

'Thanks,' she said softly, rubbing his wrist with her knuckles.

'For what?'

'For staying. I know you hate Barking; I hate it too, it's so cheap and vulgar and boring...vulgar, that was the word we always used to use, wasn't it?'

'Vulgar, darling!!' Jack put on a posh voice, 'absolutely frightfully vulgar, all those chavs and their ASBOs!'

'Well you did ok in the end,' she sipped her tea. 'You got out. I'm still here. I can't even escape right.'

'Give me the word and I'll turf your brother out and you can move in...'

'...on the floor?'

'You could have David's bed.' He handed her a slice of the lemon cake and then gazed at her. 'We'll wait until they've gone to bed,' he said, nodding through the wall to the living room, 'like we used to, on holiday and stuff. Then I'll be right back in here, and I'll hold you all night long.'

'Promise not to let me go?' she said.

'I promise.'

She bit into the cake and thought for a moment. 'That'd make him happy,' she said. 'Your David I mean, if I had his bed.'

'Hey, it's my flat. You could be his fag hag.'

'I bet you've got him wrapped around your little finger...'

Jack beamed about as modestly as he could manage. 'If I think he's slipping I give him a flash of the old six-pack, and he's 'what can I do for you today, Jack??' type thing!'

'You're awful,' she jostled him in the rib. 'But I like you!' and then all of a sudden her eyes welled up again and she began to cry, dropping her slice of lemon cake onto the covers where it broke into several segments.

'Hey hey, hey,' Jack wound both his big arms around her, and kissed her hair. 'No more tears. We don't like the tears.'

'I can still feel his grubby hands crawling up my leg…' she squirmed, then found her comfort zone somewhere against his hard shoulder and settled there, closing her eyes. 'Jack?' she said.

'Yeah?'

'Don't go. Not tomorrow even. Stay with me for a bit.'

He gazed forward, at the far wall. ''jess, I've got exams coming; although I suppose I could get my notes and borrow David's laptop…'

'Please?' she gazed up at him with big brown eyes. 'I want you to stay for a bit.' And she watched his face, as he felt himself breaking under her spell. 'I miss you so much,' she went on. 'I just exist when you're not around.'

'That's not true,' he said. 'The crazy things you do…'

'…just to wind that old arsehole in there up,' she nodded through the wall now. 'I do them because I'm bored.'

'I'll have to call David later then,' he said. 'He can bring my stuff over. He loves coming here anyway.'

'He does?' she made a face. 'Is he ill?!'

'He's got this hard-on for our family,' he said coolly, reigning in the urge to tell her all about the paper he was collaborating on for Fortean Times; there were just some things he couldn't tell, not even to Jessica. 'He thinks we're all witches or something.'

'Dad always said Uncle Phil was a witch,' she shifted back slightly. 'He said he did things that were against God's law; black magic and stuff, cursing and giving people the evil eye. He said once that Uncle Phil gave a milkman who kept charging Aunt Delia over the odds the evil eye, and a week later this guy got found out having it off with a woman up George St, and the husband beat him black and blue.'

'I think that's just called being grassed up, 'jess. And no way would Uncle Phil do that. Uncle Phil wasn't evil; Not Uncle Phil's fault if a bloke couldn't keep his cock in his pants.'

'No but…well bad things happened to people who crossed us, didn't they? Or no one ever did cross us because…well, because of what they'd heard.'

'It's called 'urban myth', kiddo,' he sat back too, and scooped her crumbled lemon cake off the covers. 'David knows all about it. It's what goes on in places like Essex, where they had witchcraft and stuff for hundreds of years. People cling onto those ideas, those ways of living. Witches with ASBOS, that's what this family is.'

'Witch or not, Uncle Phil was still the Daddy,' she said.

'Yeah, I know.'

'I miss him,' she sat back. 'He was such a…presence, you know? He could really fill a room. Not many people can do that. You can, though.'

'Plenty of things I can fill,' he gave her a wicked wink. 'But I miss him too, you know, even though him and me, well we didn't always see eye to eye.'

'I'll put the TV on,' she reached over. 'We can pretend we're an old married couple in for the evening after a hard day at the office. Why are you so suited and booted today, anyway?'

'I got the job I was after,' he beamed broadly. 'Six months part-time, Cannon Street, suit, briefcase, umbrella…well, the umbrella's an optional, based on the weather, but you get the picture…'

'Oh Jack!!' she threw her arms around his neck and planted a kiss on his lips. 'I knew you'd get there one day.'

'It's for six months to begin with,' he said' I have another year at LSE, but I reckon once they see how good I am they'll offer it to me full-time, once I've completed the course, that is. It's psyche profiling for big firms, real important stuff.'

'I never doubted you for a minute.'

'I'm hanging off telling mum 'til tomorrow,' he went on, swigging his tea down. 'She'll be 'round here like a shot. Your mum hasn't told anyone what happened to you yet, has she? Apart from Casey, I mean.'

'She wants to do it tomorrow too,' she said. 'She said if she does it tonight she'll cry and you know how awful she sounds when she does that, kind of like a lame horse begging to be put out of its misery.'

He shifted his weight so that he was leaning against the wall, with Jessica fully against his chest. 'What's on the old box then?' he glanced at the TV. 'Coronation Street? I used to watch that all the time when I was little, you know. Mum loved it. I can't stand it now. Soaps are a fucking waste of time.'

'I love 'Corrie',' she took the remote off the dresser. 'But they're not half as exciting as our family, anyway; we're a soap all on our own.'

'Why do you think I left?!' he laughed, 'that and all the vulgar chavs, of course.'

'Of course, darling,' she chuckled.

'Darling darling,' he pulled her back to his chest. 'Do be a darling, darling, will you darling?!'

'Have you seen the old bat lately?' Jessica asked.

'Aunt Amanda? I never see her, 'jess. We have nothing in common. She sends me money though; I think she sends me it to keep me away. I'm not complaining. She did help me get into university though, I have to give her that.'

'Well everyone thinks she's a crazy old cow. Jamie hangs around with her all the time,' Jessica glanced up at him, as if to gauge his reaction. 'It's creepy, a lad his age and an old woman; what the hell do they talk about?!'

'Uncle Phil, I think,' Jack took the remote from her and began channel hopping. 'They both loved him so much I think they're helping each other through it the only way they know how.'

'We all loved Uncle Phil tons,' she said, 'but Jamie thinks he owned him or something. He was the Daddy for all of us.'

'Jamie's just a big kid at heart,' Jack settled on something about Channel Five about people eating themselves to death. 'I think he stayed a kid in that flat with Uncle Phil up until he died; they were so busy having fun that J forgot to grow up. He certainly forgot to learn to read.'

'Oh my god Jack, look at this fat man!!' Jessica was pointing at the screen, waving her finger. 'Look at his man-tits! Oh that is so gross!'

'Sick!!' he shielded his eyes rather theatrically.

'No one's like that in our family,' Jessica began nibbling at a corner of one of the sandwiches. 'Even the plain ones aren't fat. We don't do fatties. We don't do uglies either, really.'

'Springer's no oil painting...'

'Oh but he's sweet, bless him!' she sighed. 'It's weird, him and Clay being twins and Clay being quite handsome and all, in a greasy kind of way. Did you know about Hayden coming out for Aunt Delia's birthday?'

'Uh huh. It's gonna be a surprise.' He was grinning from ear to ear, 'can't wait to see my old mate again. I fucking miss him as much as you miss me, I reckon.'

'You miss me too though, don't you?' she almost started.

'Miss you?' he raised an eyebrow. 'Kid, you don't know the fucking half of it.'

She smiled, seemingly satisfied. 'Nick's been sent to a special prison though; they think he has mental problems. I think he told the prison doctor he was from a family of witches or something!'

'Nick doesn't really strike me as the sort,' Jack nodded. 'I think he did it because the special prison's more likely to be a soft option.' He turned his attention back to the TV a moment. 'Fuck me kid, look at that bloke's legs!'

Jessica put the sandwich aside and gazed up at him. 'Jack?'

'Yeah?'

'Do you think I'm cheap?'

'Heck no,' he didn't even take his eyes off the screen. 'You're prettier than most of the old dogs around here. You were Barking's first ever Page Three Girl!'

'I pole-danced in Paris...'

'Yeah I know,' he laughed, his eyes still transfixed on the TV screen. 'Gave me a right old boner when I saw it as well.'

'Jack!!' she slapped his chest.

'What?!'

'I was a pole-dancer!! If that isn't cheap I don't know what is.'

'It was 'the Paris escapade'!' he glanced at her. 'Don't cuss it!' and then he turned and looked at her again. 'God you knew how move,' he said, gazing off, finding the memory and playing it in his mind's eye.

'Is that your mobile?' she saw something flashing in his pocket, and moments later the ring-tune warbled out, a rather flat rendition of the Beatles' 'All you need is love'. 'Who is it?'

'It's David,' he put the phone to his ear and took the call, reminding him to bring the laptop and accompanying notes down with him tomorrow, and then he hung up. 'I'm turning it off,' he decided, doing just that. 'So you have my undivided attention.' And he pulled her closer and gazed into her eyes. 'You got lovely eyes,' he said, and he gently stroked her eyebrows with his finger. 'Do people ever tell you that?'

She smiled. 'All the time. But when you say it…'

'When I say it?' he moved his gaze down, looking at her lips now.

'When you say it…' she angled in a little closer, just as his fingers reached her neck, gently tickling that sensitive spot behind her left ear, the one that drove her absolutely crazy.

And there was a knock at the door and Aunt Betty popped her head in. 'Everything alright?!'

Jack pulled back rather hurriedly, coughed, and reached for the tray. 'Another cup of tea, Aunt Betty?' he turned and picked up his empty mug. 'Got any other cakes?' and he patted his stomach playfully. 'Me is lovin' the cake!!'

'I've made Bobby's bed up for you,' she said, taking the tray. 'I've put a dressing gown in there, and some bottled water. If there's anything else you want just let me know.'

'Oh I will!'

'Jolly good,' she closed the door, and then popped her head back in. 'How about some nacho things, with tortilla dip?'

'Yes please!!'

'Jolly good then!' and she closed the door once more.

'She's fattening you up,' Jessica said. 'She loves fattening people up. She always thought Uncle Phil was too skinny; he was here for dinner once and he just couldn't eat anymore, and when she wasn't looking he put it in his pocket!'

'I don't get fat,' Jack stroked his flat stomach proudly. 'I hardly have to do any sit-ups to make my abs show. Girlies love my abs. You could grate cheese on my abs.'

'Show me,' she said. 'I haven't seen them for ages.' And she smiled and coloured a little. 'You always had such a lovely hairy chest.'

He made to loosen his shirt out of his belt and then Aunt Betty called out from the hallway, 'Cheese dip alright Jack, instead of tortilla?!'

'Fine, Aunt Betty!!' and he turned back, but the moment, whatever it was, had clearly passed. She was glancing at the alarm clock, and then at her phone. 'Kid?' he said, embracing her around the waist, from behind.

'The police haven't rung yet…' she swallowed, and turned her head to look at him, and the colour that had flushed in her cheeks had all but faded. 'Do you think they've got him?'

'Don't worry about it. He'll get his. You keep that address in your head, okay?'

'What are you going to do?'

'You'll see. Listen,' he said, in a low, husky whisper. 'You know I love you, don't you?'

She nodded, and reached up to clasp one of his hands, and having to use both of hers to do it. 'Yeah.'

'And I'm trying to make it nice and light when all I really want to do is going out and smash someone's face in...anyone's face in, because of what happened to you.'

Jessica rested her head back on his chest, running her little fingers around the thick dark blond hair that covered his wrist where his shirt sleeve ended; his 'manly, hairy hands', she usually called them. 'Are you going to be the Daddy for me?' she asked, gazing off, out of the window.

He nodded, slowly at first, but with increasing conviction. He squeezed her waist gently. 'I'll be the Daddy for you, 'jess.'

The Daddy Dissertation Part 9

By David Samuels

The decline and demise of Phil Woodfield

Phil Woodfield passed out one Saturday morning in the Vicarage Fields shopping centre, only a few yards short of ASDA, hefty shopping bags in each hand. Milk cartons split open and eggs smashed as he went down hard, striking the side of his head and mixing in a little blood with the aforementioned items to form some kind of a macabre mess on the concourse floor. When he awoke he was in Barking hospital, and the doctors could find nothing wrong apart from the fact that he was underweight for his considerable height, that he was somewhat malnourished, and that generally he had all the physical 'stats' of a man in his early sixties, not the forty two-year old he actually was. The blood tests found no traces of any infections, no cancer cells; despite his promiscuous past pre-Rose he was clear of HIV and AIDS, and the doctors were somewhat at a loss to explain why he was, in their words, '…suddenly so frail.'

Although Phil had initially been very depressed – as one would expect – after Rose's death, that had been almost four years previous, and in that time he'd returned almost to his former self, greeting everyone in the street with a wink or a wave, taking Jamie, Hayden, Nick, Michael, and Jamie's friend Adam to almost every West Ham game, and drinking with his brother Heath and their friends in the Barking Dog every Friday night until closing time, and sometimes beyond. There were even rumours of a new girlfriend around the time of Jack's graduation, but no one ever met her, and no one of any such description was present at his funeral, although several rather formal 'suits' who refused to say who they were or where they were from were in attendance, secreted up the back near the doors, and Amanda Woodfield seemed on quite friendly terms with them.

When people began to call in on Phil they were shocked to see the change, one that seemed to have been wrought almost overnight; his hair was streaked with grey, his sideburns especially; his eyes were sunken and bloodshot, and although he'd never been meaty, a certain sort of robustness had given way to a kind of stick-thin, almost cadaverous appearance, and the West Ham strip that had once been so fetching now hung on him as though draped over a clothes-line.

Jamie coped as best he could but he broke under the pressure when his uncle woke one night screaming, and in a cold sweat; after two hours of trying to mop Phil's brow and to calm him down he called his mum and Beverly came over from the Murphy Estate in her nightgown and slippers, and against Phil's wishes she rang their brother Heath; at seven the following morning Phil was carried bodily by his younger brother the short walk from Station Parade to Beverly's flat. They put Phil in Jack's old room, and he upset Beverly by saying that he didn't want the last things he ever saw to be, '...pictures of John Lennon and Paul McCartney gazing inanely down at me.'

Aunt Amanda pooled a great deal of her savings on a private doctor, who visited the flat sometime in September 2005, performing a complete head to toe examination of Phil, blood and urine tests and all, but again he found him to be perfectly physically healthy, albeit for a man now in his mid-seventies. She also asked a friend of hers, a fortune teller on the Bethnal Green Road called 'Madame Fontana', to visit the flat and give Phil a full reading. Despite Beverly saying it was all a load of 'mumbo jumbo' she let Madame Fontana light her candles and burn her incense; 'She's stinking the place out!!', surrounding the bed with a ring of salt, and sprinkling Phil's chest with a light dusting of patchouli. The woman swayed from side to side and opened her arms wide, asking if there '...was anyone there who had any grievances with anyone here?'; for a moment there was silence, and then the candles were overturned, and the salt whipped up in a furious wind, spraying itself into Madame Fontana's eyes and causing her considerable pain.

When she'd recovered, a good several cups of tea later, she wrote down a message she'd 'received' on a scrap of paper and handed it to Beverly; 'the keys for the pillow, please' it said; I have been unable to determine either the source or the meaning of this message. Beverly showed it to Phil and he is said to have turned and buried his face in his own pillow, and stayed like that for several hours after.

In October 2005 Hayden and Nick Woodfield were working as doormen on the Legends nightclub on the London Road; their older brother Clay was dealing small time drugs inside, and there was an understanding between the brothers that anyone else attempting to do the same would be seen off sharply. Hayden clearly relished this role and was said to have been every inch 'the plastic gangster' in his long overcoat and bowtie, but Nick, a quiet, studious individual, was clearly only doing it to make ends meet whilst pursuing the acting career he'd had his heart set on for so long. When two dealers from Dagenham attempted to muscle in on Clay's patch there was a big bust-up outside the club in the early hours of a Saturday morning, wherein the two dealers were set about by Hayden rather ferociously, beaten almost unconscious by the boy, who then proceeded to slash them about the face and buttocks with his beloved Linder 9465 blade. Their 'gear' was removed and disposed of. Unfortunately one of the men pulled a gun on Hayden when his back was turned, and his life was only saved when Nick ran into the doorway of the club and picked up the baseball bat left with their coats for emergencies, and hit the man over the head with it. Someone inside the club called the police and the twins were arrested and hauled off to Barking police station, whilst the two drug dealers from Dagenham were rushed off to hospital.

Up until this point the Woodfields had never really been in trouble with the police, although Heath had been drunken and disorderly a number of times following his wife Sophie's death, and had been in more than his fair share of brawls in the Barking Dog.

There was talk that the Daddy would never have let this happen, and people began to wonder if it was time for Jack to take over, as Phil was by now bedridden and according to one family friend '...fading fast.'.

The twins were put on trial, charged with GBH and both found guilty; their mother, Jack's Aunt Delia, sobbed as they were given a year apiece in the 'Scrubs. 'Get Jack back,' she is said to have told Beverly as they left the courthouse, dabbing at the corners of her eyes with her handkerchief. 'Get Jack back.'

Of course it wasn't as simple as that. Jack had just started his sociology masters at the London School of Economics in October 2005, and found himself more than a little overwhelmed with the heavy course load, the more 'elite' atmosphere of the place, and of the more exacting standards the tutors put on his coursework, despite glowing references from South Bank. One of his tutors – Professor Claire Alexander – had recently relocated from the same university to the LSE as well, and they acclimatised in tandem, lunching together for the first several weeks as they '...felt the place out.'

As had been the case at South Bank, Jack soon found he had more than a few fledgling friends waiting for him in his classes on gender & politics, and on psychoanalysis in contemporary culture, but this time he kept himself pretty much to himself, finding the heavier workload something of a strain compared to South Bank's more relaxed attitude. The exception to this rule was a girl called Dorothy, who had come fresh from '...somewhere out west', an exotic and visually striking girl with pouting red lips, darting, cat-like eyes, and tumbling strawberry-blond hair. Jack, Dorothy, and myself formed a pretty impenetrable clique all our own as October gave way to November, the working day beginning ever earlier, with more and more hours spent in the vast, spiralling library researching the extensive public folders and journals.

By December 2005 Phil Woodfield was unable to eat and took what little nourishment the family could get down him through high protein shakes and the like, and meals mixed together in a blender. Every day Jamie would arrive at the flat moments after packing up his second-hand paperback stall on the East Street market, his face filled with a kind of uneasy optimism, asking if there had been any change for the better; when the inevitable negative reply came his face would crumple, and he'd disappear into the bedroom to sit with his Uncle Phil, usually until ten or eleven at night. He would dictate letters to be sent to Nick in Wormwood Scrubs that Phil would transcribe in order to keep his mind alert.

Jamie seems to have been unwilling or at the very least unable to accept that Phil's condition was only getting worse, and that if it continued in the fashion it already was, he would be dead before the end of the year. He was by now so skeletal that friends who hadn't seen him for any period of time would gasp visibly upon entering the sick room, and eventually Beverly had to brief people on what to expect before they went in, with their bunches of flowers and their brown paper-bags full of sweets and fruit that he could no longer eat anyway. Phil grew a beard to try and fatten his face out, and every morning Beverly trimmed it for him until Christmas Eve, when he said he didn't want it trimmed, but that he fancied looking like 'Santa Claus'; 'Jamie always thought I was Santa when he was little,' he told her with a smile. 'Perhaps now I really will be, and I'll give him the best present for Christmas ever.' When asked what that might be, he replied tearfully, 'I'll get better.' As it was he lasted only until Christmas Day; the twins found him in the sick room not long after a rather muted Christmas dinner, his West Ham season ticket and scarf clasped to his chest, as though he'd not only known it was the end, but had been 'given' time to prepare himself. The doctors were called and credit to them they were at the Murphy Estate within the hour; by then rigor mortis had already set in, and in Jamie's own tearful words, Phil was as '...cold as an ice cube.'.

Beverly couldn't stop saying how peaceful he looked, that if she nudged him hard enough he might wake up and be beam up at her, those big brown eyes wide and alert as always. Jamie said nothing while the doctors examined the body, but when they asked to allow it to be removed for a proper post mortem – this was a 'curious' condition that had led to his death, after all – he refused to let them, and even raised his fist to one of the ambulance drivers. Despite her tears his mother told him it was for the best, and that they needed to find out what had killed Phil so that they could make sure it wasn't genetic, and might not one day affect anyone else in the family; 'Tell them to check out the kiss on his arse,' Heath was overheard saying, apparently to himself, 'there's your genetics right there.' One of the ambulance drivers asked Jamie if he'd like to accompany them with Phil's body to the hospital morgue, to which he agreed. Jamie even insisted on dressing Uncle Phil himself, in his West Ham kit, but when he touched the body and found that rigor mortis was already so deep set, and that the joints were almost immovable, he broke down, slumped over the body and sobbed on his chest for almost an hour.

Whilst all this was going on Beverly and her niece Jessica were making the phone calls they'd dreaded having to make; Jack is said to have shut himself in the kitchen and made a large pot of tea, drinking most of it himself. Aunt Amanda was the next to arrive, after Heath, rather amazingly considering she lived the furthest away, and she is said to have 'wept uncontrollably' more at the sight of Jamie's grief than at the sight of Phil himself. She knelt down behind the boy and held him and they cried together. Beverly made the ambulance drivers tea and told them that this '...might take a while', that there were a lot of people who wanted to come and see Phil one more time, and to say goodbye; one of them knew Phil from the Barking Dog and agreed with her, and made the extraordinary gesture of leaving to do several more jobs elsewhere, returning to the flat in the early evening.

Aunt Queenie went in to see Phil first by prerogative of being the oldest, but Jamie refused to leave and held on to Uncle Phil's hand as each and every cousin and uncle and aunt filed into the room, usually taking one look at the body and bursting into tears, followed by a rapid shaking of the head and quick pivot out of the door, unable to cope with what they had seen. Father Brian administered the last rites a little too late admittedly, but the gesture went down well with everyone present. Beverly laid out a second Christmas dinner but the entire family just sat there and stared at it, and most of it went in the bin or in doggy bags. For once everyone seemed to have forgotten about Jack, and when he emerged from the kitchen bursting with tea and the resulting urge to relieve himself they all looked up at him expectantly. 'What?!' is said to have been his slightly astonished reaction on seeing the looks on their faces.

'It's up to you now, my sweetheart,' Beverly said, rising and taking him by the shoulders.

'Is it heck as like,' Jack replied, gazing at them one after the other, lingering on Aunt Amanda, and on Jamie, who refused to meet his eye; Jessica ran to him tearfully, and although he took her in his arms and whispered to her constantly, kissing the top of her head, he seemed unable to calm her, or to tell her what she wanted to hear. 'Look,' he told them, looking over the top of her head, his words steady. 'I'm as gutted as the rest of you, but...well, as Kid Creole said, "I'm not your daddy".'

Conclusion of family narrative

Chapter 51

Thursday 25th May 2006

A great deal of thought went into the presents Aunt Amanda brought the family for their birthdays, for Christmas, for anniversaries, engagements, and the like. For Delia's big bash this weekend – and word on the grapevine was that Bev wanted to make it a 'double celebration', for reasons known only to herself – she'd opted to go for something she knew would meet with her closest cousin's utmost approval; a piece of Seventies domestic kitsch, in the form of a table set complete with mustard serving cloth peppered with enormous brown oval patterns, matching mustard candlestick holders, and mustard and brown salt and pepper shakers. Delia had always been a great fan of everything Seventies, and the family flat on the Broadway in Barking was a veritable homage to the aforementioned era, having been effectively trapped in amber when said decade had ended and her husband, that good-for-nothing Eddie Dowden, had put his back out on his bin rounds, and refused as a result to undertake manual labour of any sort ever again, leaving them stranded in a kind of Seventies sit-com style that everyone now took as being Delia's particular brand of Woodfield peculiarity. That was doubtless part of the reason why her four boys had always been so reluctant about bringing their girlfriends back there in days gone by, or more recently even.

She wrapped the table set in her front room, the one where on warmer days and in friendlier times the window would have been wide open to the street, and neighbours passing by would have called out or stuck their head in, whiling away five minutes for a quick chat and a gossip. Sometimes kids from the council houses opposite would run past and shout out, 'Oy, you old witch!' but that had only happened once or twice, precisely because when it did she'd followed up on their taunts with a demonstration of exactly what they were talking about, and funnily enough she'd never heard a peep out of them after that.

She broke off the knots in the ribbons with her teeth and stuck a matching fancy bow dead centre of the box, then sat back and finished off her tea. There was a noise from the kitchen, the sound of a carton falling off the sideboard, and she went to investigate. The milk she thought she'd put back in the fridge had indeed somehow managed to find its way back onto the kitchen table, and from there had upturned with great gusto and left an enormous white puddle in the middle of the floor, soaking deep into the rug slung down to hide the odd stained tile or two. 'Shit', she sighed, language quite unbecoming for a lady of her years, but you didn't live in Bethnal Green all your life without picking up a little of the local lingo. She set to cleaning up the mess and when all was done and dusted went back to the front room, searching in the drawers near the TV for a collection of photographs she'd recently had developed. She soon found the one she was looking for, a sideways shot of Jamie taken in Weaver's Field a couple of weeks previous, when the weather had been better than it was now and they'd had an impromptu picnic after one of their 'lessons'; Jamie was sprawled back, his elbow resting on his knee, his right arm up and showing off the bulky leather-strapped watch she'd brought for him on the Whitechapel Road a couple of days before. 'Try and look like the Daddy,' she'd said to him, and Jamie had scowled, but Amanda had laughed and said, 'A little more benevolent, darling.' After she'd explained what 'benevolent' meant she'd taken the shot that she now set about framing, inserting the picture carefully into a silver rimmed frame she'd brought from Casey's studio the last time she'd been in Barking. When she'd finished she held it out and smiled. 'You are wonderful, Jamie Woodfield,' she said, stroking his little fuzz of hair with her thumb. She got up and made a place for the picture in-between shots of Phil and Ben. 'That's just fine,' she said to herself, and sat down, with the full intent of closing her eyes and having a bit of a nap before she went and did her shopping for the day.

There was a knock on the door around five minutes later and then the head of Mr. Shepherd the postman fought its way through the billowing curtains of the half open window, almost frightening the living bejeezus out of her. 'Ms. Woodfield?' he laughed apologetically. 'Ever so sorry; got a parcel for you?'

'A parcel?' she frowned. 'Oh of course,' and, almost slapping her bow in disbelief she shuffled around to the front door and opened it. Mr Shepherd presented her with a box that looked about big enough to hold a football; exactly what it did hold, as a matter of fact. 'For my nephew…well, my Great-Great-Nephew Jamie actually,' she smiled, plucking at the sellotape with her fingers. 'It's signed, from the West Ham team of '95. Now that may mean absolutely nothing to you or I, but take my word for it, to him it's a little like receiving the Holy Grail via Royal Mail.'

'Birthday present, is it?' Mr Shepherd raised an eyebrow, sorting through the rest of her mail.

'No…more of a general congratulation,' she said, finally winning the fight and opening the box. Although the address on the side marked it out as being the result of her winning bid on eBay some weeks previous, the contents of the box were nothing less than the head of her twin brother Ben, hale and hearty, gazing up at her with the twinkling blue eyes she'd known so well, blinking in an expression of utterly bemused innocence. 'Why am I dead?' he asked, that familiar oh so cockney lilt she hadn't heard for almost fifty years, 'why didn't you save me?! Why didn't you save me, 'sis??'

Amanda dropped the box with a start; the West Ham football inside rolled out and off down the pavement, over the kerb and into the middle of the road, where Mr Shepherd hurried to retrieve it. She braced herself against the frame of the door, feeling a tightening in her chest, and a vague feeling of breathlessness. It was more a panic attack than the symptom of anything serious, and she forced herself to control and regulate her breathing as Mr Shepherd returned, placing the ball back in the box and closing the lid over. 'There you go,' he said. 'You gave me quite a start, Ms. Woodfield. Whatever was the matter?'

'Nothing...' she forced herself to take great lungfuls of air, focusing on his cheery smile in order to sober herself up, to anchor herself to the real world. 'I had a terrible migraine earlier and I thought for a moment it was going to come back again. Sorry to have startled you so, Tony.'

'You really ought to be taking it easy,' he said, handing her a couple of brown envelope bills, and something from Richard Woodfield down in Brighton. 'You're always on the go, you are. Always on the go.'

'It's what keeps me fit,' she hefted the box under one arm and took the remaining mail with the other. 'Inactivity is the biggest killer of people my age, you know.'

'Still,' he shook his head. 'You're an old lady, if you don't mind my saying so. And yet there you are, up and down the Bethnal Green Road every day, still doing afternoons in Woolworths, why you're a credit to most of the women your age. When my old mother was your age she hardly even moved from her chair, you know?'

Amanda nodded. 'We're conditioned to be old by society, but if you're willing to stick your neck out and go against the grain...'

'...and that's what you've always done, eh Ms. Woodfield?' he nudged her arm playfully. 'Gone against the grain? I've heard some tales about you in my time, I can tell you!!'

'And one day I'll invite you in for a cup of tea and I can tell you if they're true or not,' she stepped back into the doorway. 'If you'll excuse me Tony, I really have to attend to these bills.'

'See you again soon, Ms. Woodfield,' he doffed his cap to her and clambered back on his bike, setting off at a leisurely pace up towards the Bethnal Green Road. Amanda watched him go and then slid back into her front hall, closing the door and double bolting it. She dropped the box and the letters onto the floor in front of her and let the door take her full weight as she fell against it, her face in her hands. Then she slid down, down until she felt the soft cushion of the doormat underneath.

Chapter 52

Thursday 25th May 2006

A light drizzle slanted persistently down over Station Parade as David emerged from the Underground, laden down with various items requested by Jack for his 'extended charity visit', the main bulk of which consisted of David's laptop and all of its various attachments, including printer and battery, complete with recharger, not to mention a good half ream of A4 paper. A rather bizarre late request made by text last night read; 'please bring the carrier bag with the tape tied around the top under my bed, the one that looks like it has a cushion in it. Please be careful with it'. All of this David had packed, along with a couple of extras he knew Jack would appreciate, foremost among them a couple of packs of his favourite microwaveable Sainsbury's cheeseburgers, squeezed into a carrier bag alongside a bottle of Lambrusco, of a brand partially more pricey than anything he was sure Barking might have to offer.

Making a right past the KFC he felt even more out of place than he had on his initial visit, when he'd had Jack to tell him what was what, who lived where, and even how to walk in that slightly hyper-masculine swagger and not to make eye contact with any butch young men, no matter how attractive he found them. He passed cardboard boxes selling cheap pairs of socks and underwear, the beginnings of the East Street market, and glanced up at the two windows of the Daddy flat, just above the Nationwide bank. The curtains were open but there were no signs of life. He passed the bandstand and began to navigate his way through the crowded market, past stalls selling DVDs and toiletries, fake Filas and Reebok, to a large open-sided lorry offloading cheap TV sets and microwave ovens. The first Woodfield he spotted was Jack's Uncle Heath, leaning against the post that supported the awning of his stall, countless mobile phone and Bluetooth fascias spread out before him. He imagined that Jack might end up looking like his Uncle Heath when he was about fifteen years older, a slightly tired and weather-beaten expression tarnishing those wholesome good looks. To the right and a little further down his Aunt Hannah was flogging a set of matching doormats to a discerning Asian woman with several noisy children. In the window of the Superdrug behind her he could just see Aunt Delia, the one whose big birthday bash was on for this weekend, a heavily made-up woman who might have been seventy, or even as young as fifty, it was hard to tell under so much slap, and with her hair dyed such a primary shade of peach. David hedged his bets and decided he'd have more fun asking rugged Uncle Heath where St. Margaret's was, even though he knew full well it was somewhere down the end of East Street, on the opposite side of the Broadway.

'Excuse me?' he leant over the counter, coughed. 'I don't know if you remember me, but I'm Jack's flatmate...at his graduation?'

Uncle Heath frowned, cracking his gum rather loudly. He shook his head. 'Nope.'

David swallowed. 'David? We've got your Daniel with us right now?'

'Ah!' a light seemed to go on, and he was all smiles and a big, powerful paw reached out and shook David's own offered hand with enough force to cause him to brace himself against the edge of the stall. 'How is the little shit?!'

David beamed. 'He's no trouble, Mr. Woodfield. In fact he and Bobby liven the place up a bit, and...'

'Here,' Uncle Heath reached into his money-belt and pulled out two twenty pound notes. 'For expenses incurred, and all that.'

'There's no need...'

'I insist.' Uncle Heath pressed the notes into his hand. 'Tell me him to give me a call, you know? Tell him his old dad misses him. I haven't seen him since Cardiff.'

'I will,' he nodded. 'I'm here looking for Jack, actually; I hear he's at St. Margaret's, looking after his cousin?'

'Ah yeah, shit business, that.' Heath sniffed. 'Police got the bloke but he denies it, says Jessica led him on and everything. If I ever get my hands on him...'

David could well imagine. 'It's just down there, is it?' and he nodded to the Cash Converters at the bottom end of East Street.

'Uh huh,' he nodded, offering his hand again, 'nice to meet you, David. Remember to give Daniel that message, you hear?'

'Will do, Mr Woodfield.' He set off down East Street and tried very hard not to think of what the man's reaction might be in six months' time when he saw his life, if not his name, which would have been changed, in print in a Fortean Times special edition on 'the notorious witches of London and the Home Counties'. It didn't bear thinking about, actually. Then again, he didn't even imagine that anywhere in Barking actually stocked Fortean Times to begin with, or that anyone around here would actually want to read it.

St. Margaret's was just adjacent to the primary school of the same name, and on the grounds old of the old Barking Abbey. The Woodfield family grave was just inside and to the left, a huge headstone flanked by various other, lesser erections sporting names as far back as Jacob and Jeramiah, Jason and Jeffrey. David took a couple of pictures of it on his mobile and then rang the vicarage buzzer and stepped back, moving his bags from one hand to the other in order to better distribute the weight. 'Hello?' it was a woman's voice, old, and with a West Country twang. 'Is that you, Brian?'

'Um...it's David,' he leant forward, hating these things as much as ever he had. 'Jack's expecting me. I'm his friend from university; his flatmate.'

'Oh you're the nice man who's been looking after our Bobby,' the woman said. 'Come on up, David.' And before she had properly switched the intercom off he heard her say, seemingly to herself, 'I'll put the kettle on and make us all some tea!'

He was buzzed in and made his way rather awkwardly up the stairs, faced then with a choice of four possible doors, one of which had a Dalek sticker dead centre, and the message below 'Exterminate any trespassers!'; Bobby's room, then. He was about to try the second one along when it was whipped open by a rather dotty looking woman in her early sixties, an egg whisk in one hand and a packet of Typhoo teabags in the other. 'Hello dear!' she declared, and before he could stop her he was locked into a classic aunt-style embrace, all worn nail polish and something that smelt a lot like Chanel. 'I'm Betty; Bobby and Jessica's mother. Oh, and Casey's mother too, but he moved out years ago, you know!!'

If he'd been that sort of person David would have thought something along the lines of, I don't blame him, but as it was he was blessed with an almost endless reservoir of politeness, and that, topped off with his geeky fascination for strange and eccentric families, led him to beam back at her and declare, 'I'm David, so very pleased to meet you, Mrs Woodfield!!'

'Betty, please.' She led him into the large, box-shaped living room. He was at once startled by the sight of so much religious imagery, and so much of it that awful kind of cheap, mass-produced stuff, that he almost made an audible noise. 'Would you like a cup of tea, dear?' she asked, heading off towards the kitchen, 'some lemon cake? You'll stay for dinner, of course. We love having people to dinner.'

'Of course!!' he sat down, glancing around. 'Where's Jack?'

'Oh, he took Jessica into the West End to cheer her up,' Aunt Betty called out. 'They went to see that 'Da Vinci Code' film, I think. Awful business, really.'

'It was terrible, what happened to her,' David nodded.

'I meant the film, dear,' she returned a moment or so later with a tray with the promised tea and lemon cake. 'But yes, of course that was quite awful too. And you know they caught the man who did it and he's denied it, and so now it's going to have to go to court and become all protracted and messy, and that means the upset will go on and on.'

'Yes, it can be awful,' although he had no real knowledge of the procedures involved.

Aunt Betty sat down and seemed content merely to watch him eat; Jack had warned him on the phone last night that 'fattening people up' was her main hobby, that and conserving what passed for 'green spaces' in the Barking and Dagenham area. 'How is Bobby?' she asked him. 'I've written out a cheque for you or Jack to take with you to cover his living costs. I hear he applied for a job in HMV?'

David nodded. 'Oxford Circus; he's still waiting to hear. He said he'll be back for his Aunt Delia's birthday this Saturday though.'

'Jolly good,' she nodded, 'awful business there too, with Bobby's father the other week, I mean. I hear that you're...well, you and Bobby...'

'I'm gay, yes,' he nodded, sipping his tea, unsure how this level of honesty would go down in such a religious household, although another one of Jack's handy hints had been to inform him that Betty was in no way the strict catholic that her husband, 'the Pope' was.

'I always thought Bobby was anyway,' she seemed relieved to be able to get this off her chest. 'It doesn't matter to me either way, really; we have a lovely grandchild by Casey, so I don't feel cheated or anything. You will tell Bobby that, won't you?'

'I think he knows, Betty,' David picked up his ample slice of lemon cake and took a bite. 'He's quite well adjusted, it's just he's a bit...nervous of his father.'

'His father's bark is worse than his bite,' Betty said. 'And Jack's bite was even worse, as I'm sure you know!'

'Yes, well...'

'So you live with Jack, then?' she asked, taking a sip of her own tea.

'That's right. We did sociology at South Bank together; you may remember me from the graduation...'

Aunt Betty seemed to clasp onto this comment, this allusion to a half buried mutual memory, and to rifle through her own archive for a confirmation, but came up with nothing. 'No,' she said, shaking her head. 'But it was a wonderful day!'

'We're very close,' David went on, reassuring himself it seemed more than he was informing her. 'We plan to tour Europe this summer, with our friend Dorothy.'

'Marvellous idea,' she said. 'Brian and I toured the holy cities just after we were married, you know; Rome, Lourdes...'

There came the sound of a key in the lock down below, and the sounds of urgent chatter and the occasional bout of laughter. Betty looked up at the door expectantly, and a few moments later Jack and Jessica came through, he in a casual shirt and slacks, Converse trainers, Jessica in a tight navy sweater and matching trousers, topped off with a rather fetching pair of pink pumps. 'Davey boy!!' Jack exclaimed, slapping him hard on the back. 'You made it here all by yourself! Did you bring the stuff I asked for?!'

David nodded to the collection of carrier bags and the briefcase. 'What do you think?!'

'Did you bring the laptop?'

'It's right there.'

Jack knelt down, and began rifling through the bags. 'And the other thing?'

'Of course,' David knelt down to help him sort through it. 'Although what you wanted with that old thing I'll never know.'

'Oh, you remember 'jess,' Jack looked up to the sound of Jessica clearing her throat, ''jess, you my best mate and general all-round partner in crime, David Samuels?'

'Nice to see you again,' Jessica made a comical little bow. 'Are you staying for dinner?'

'Yes he is,' her mother cut in. 'It's chicken and mushroom pie, with side salad, and lots of orange squash.'

'You should stay for the party on Saturday as well,' Jack rose, the laptop in his hands. 'I'll text my mum later and see if she can't put you up; you on for that?!'

David beamed. 'Of course!'

'Great stuff,' Jack flipped the laptop open and hit the 'on' switch. 'Are my notes still on here?'

'I updated them last night,' David leant over as the thing sprung into life, his arm gently touching Jack's hand. 'The printer's in there as well, so you can run off copies as you go along. I put the books from the library in that other bag, and I brought some nibbly bits for you as well.'

'Aw Jack!' Jessica's liquid eyes sparkled. 'He loves you!'

'Ain't that the truth,' Jack winked. 'But if you're staying here we better let those two good-for-nothings back at the flat know, and they can make their own away down for Saturday. Hey, do you think I should ask Dorothy down as well?'

'My Bobby's not a good-for-nothing, Jack Woodfield!' Aunt Betty slapped his back playfully. 'Now, Dorothy...is that your latest girlfriend?'

Jack was busy scanning through files on the laptop. 'Great stuff,' he nodded. 'Two weeks left until this fucking exam and then I'm free, 'scuse language and all, Aunt Betty.'

'She's asking about Dorothy, Jack,' Jessica nudged him in the ribs.

'Dorothy?' he raised an eyebrow, 'oh no, no. She's just a good mate, really. She proofreads my essays for me, reminds me to take my library books back on time, stuff like that. I guess she's more like a guardian angel.'

'Jack dear, I've no tomato sauce, and no vinegar either,' Aunt Betty reached for her purse and snapped the catch open. 'Be a dear and run down to the shops and get me some, would you?'

'I'll go with him,' David sprung out of his seat.

'Don't be long, lovers,' Jessica sighed, watching them go.

The sun was beginning to set as they left St. Margaret's and crossed the Broadway. The stalls on the East Street market were being folded up, awnings neatly tied into bundles of various colours, and goods heaved up into the backs of vans or stored in boxes. David sighed, looking back at the church. 'I can't look those people in the eye, you know,' he said. 'That girl thinks I don't know her from Adam, but the moment I saw her I was like, 'that's the pole-dancer!' am I right?'

Jack strode determinedly ahead, giving the odd nod to someone he knew. 'She's not 'that girl',' he said, slightly offended, 'that's my 'jess!'

David struggled to keep pace. 'I'm writing about them and all, and one day soon it's going to be out there, maybe even in book form…'

'Hey,' Jack ground to a halt just as they passed Superdrug, nodding to two stallholders who acknowledged him with a cheery wave. 'You're not having second thoughts, are you? 'coz mate, I need that money. My Aunt Amanda isn't subbing me half as much as she was at the beginning, and my mum barely makes enough to feed herself.'

'Of course not,' David shrugged. 'But don't you feel…well, even a bit guilty?'

'Why should I?' he frowned, as though the question were the dumbest thing he'd ever heard. 'They're my secrets, too. Plus the names get changed before you submit, so what's the big deal? We'll make enough to see us both right.'

'They're not stupid, Jack.'

Jack cracked a grin. 'Actually mate, most of them are. And they certainly don't buy Fortean Times or read dissertations by LSE postgraduates. They're simple people, my family. I'm the exception to the rule,' and here he blew on his knuckle and dusted his chest proudly, then grinned again. 'And anyway,' he went on, ''jess I might tell, because we're tight that way. Me and her…' and he seemed to drift off a little, before catching himself.

'Well as long as you're still cool with it.'

'I am; how else am I going to pay next year's fees?!'

David gazed down at the ground, as a Snickers wrapper blew past their feet. 'I wish I could be as detached as you; if it was my family…'

'…if it was your family you'd know exactly why I was doing it,' Jack lolled an arm around his shoulder and began to steer them up towards the Vicarage Fields, away from the blinding light of the setting sun. 'This is my compensation for being brought up by a bunch of fucking lunatics. And besides, as you said, the names get changed in the final draught. And as I said, let's face it, Fortean Times ain't exactly head of the reading material around here; not enough pictures, if you know what I mean.'

'They seem alright to me. I'd love to have a family this big, I've told you that hundreds of times.'

'Trust me,' Jack stopped a second time, turning and almost pinning him to the wall. 'You wouldn't. And when you see them on Saturday, en masse, you'll understand why. The family is the bloody first, last, and everything; it's like they aren't even aware there's a whole wide world past that dreary fucking shopping centre up there. Well not for me, I want my own life, and with your help I'm getting it.'

David let him take the lead. 'Jack?'

'Uh huh?'

'What's that old pillow for?'

Jack paused, but didn't break his stride. 'I told you not to look in that bag,' he said.

'I just…well there's a pillow mentioned in your family's history, and I was wondering…'

'It's an old hand-me-down of Aunt Queenie's,' he said dismissively. 'It's been clogging up the space under my bed for months, so I thought I'd bring it back.

Just don't worry about it.' And he turned and flashed the big, cheesy grin, like the sun itself bursting through his pearly whites, 'just chill out. After dinner we're gonna go into Jessica's room and smoke the fattest joint you ever saw. We got it while we were in Camden today; they just sell it openly on the street corners there.'

'You're going to the party with Tiffany this Saturday, aren't you?' David asked, 'even though Jamie'll be there.'

'We have to go public sometime, mate,' Jack sighed, pushing open the door to the Ripple Road entrance of the Vicarage Fields. 'It'll be cool. She says J has a new girl now anyway; Louise, I think her name was, goes with him to that college down Charing Cross Road. Apparently he's gone sweet on her. From what 'tiff says him and her have been over for a long time now.'

'Still…'

Jack stopped, just short of Argos, a bigger, cheekier grins bursting onto his face. 'Yeah, I know what you mean anyway. Reckon there'll be some fireworks this Saturday one way or the other.' And he seemed lost in thought suddenly. 'They can be like that,' he added, 'birthdays, in this family. Did I ever tell you about my sixteenth, mine and Jamie's? I mean, *really* tell you…'

Chapter 53

Friday 26th May 2006

'There'll be some fireworks if we don't find what we're looking for,' Ruth Fremantle said. 'I told them it was an archaeological investigation, but as far as windows of opportunity go, I've no idea how long that actually gives us.' She inhaled heavily on her cigarette and turned, drawing Dorothy's gaze to the tent erected around the area of grassy slope leading down to the Serpentine. 'Official documentation wasn't that hard to provide, plus some high profile people have shares and various…interests in the Hopkins Institute; even so, we should get what we're looking for and get out of here as quickly as possible.'

'What are we looking for?!' Dorothy asked, peering past her.

'Minty Hardcore's pillow.'

'Minty Hardcore's what?!'

'Her pillow,' Ruth took another drag. 'I know, I know.'

'I've never heard of Minty Hardcore's pillow. Phil never…'

'Neither had we, until Amanda Woodfield rang in this afternoon. She'd been keeping it from us for lord only knows what reason, but she seems to be in a panic; she said there was a pillow, and that it was buried in a strongbox down in front of the Serpentine on the Hyde Park Corner side, that it was one of Phil's favourite spots…'

'…one of mine too…' Dorothy gazed off into the distance. 'Sorry, I'm just absolutely knackered. I've been trolling around the West End all day with Jack and David, and with Jessica, Bobby, and Daniel Woodfield to boot.'

'I know you love this place.' Ruth nodded. 'Your idea to make our summer meetings here, remember?'

Dorothy smiled, but she was lost in thought. She glanced over at the searchlights being erected around the tent. 'A pillow in a strongbox?'

'That's right. There was no mention of it on that dissertation you…borrowed from your friend David either. From what Amanda Woodfield told me, she and Phil buried the pillow sometime in late 1981, shortly after Jack and Jamie were born; they don't even know it exists.'

'What's the significance of the pillow?'

'That's all she told me. I pressed her for details but she wasn't very forthcoming, only that we had to find the strongbox and use a blowtorch, whatever, to get it open. Jack has the keys but he doesn't know what they're for. For what it's worth she thinks it's already gone, but we're to make sure. She was very shaken up.'

Dorothy laughed a little dryly. 'Why on earth did they give him a key if they didn't want him to have it?!'

Ruth shrugged. 'Phil was sick, and his mother was calling the shots, although from what Amanda told me as far as Beverly Woodfield is concerned the key might as well have been for a piggy bank. I think someone must've whispered in her ear that it was tradition, or something.'

'Beverly Woodfield knows nothing?'

'No; she's so far up Jack's arse, if you'll pardon my English, that she can't see the wood for the trees, if you'll pardon the lukewarm pun. She's innocent.' And she coughed. 'Jack's innocent, in all the ways that truly matter. He's just about to take the classic male plunge and allow his genitals to do the thinking, is the trouble.'

Dorothy gazed up; the sky was darkening fast, and a few passers-by were forming an audience. 'What do you think the pillow is? Apart from being just a pillow, that is?'

'According to the little Amanda told me, the Daddy has the pillow, it's his by right apparently, and once he has it and he sleeps on it for one night – just one night – so she emphasised, he belongs to her.'

'He belongs to who?'

'Minty Hardcore.'

There was a cry from inside the tent, and a stout woman in black slacks and matching cardigan, her glasses on beads around her neck, came running out. 'The ground's been recently disturbed,' she said breathlessly. 'Someone's made a vague effort to cover it up, but I've an awful feeling that selfsame someone has beaten us to it.'

'Thanks Gail,' Ruth nodded. 'Keep me posted.' And the woman nodded and turned back the way she had come.

Dorothy watched her go. 'What do you think?'

'About the pillow?'

'It depends. It depends if you believe in Minty Hardcore or not.'

'And if you don't it's just an old pillow.'

'That's right; lord only knows who it actually belonged to.'

'And if you do believe?'

Ruth finished her cigarette, threw it down on the damp grass and let the last of the rainwater extinguish it. 'Then it's some kind of magical artefact that's very important in keeping Minty Hardcore's chosen bit of Essex rough in line.'

There was another shout from the tent and Gail emerged, shaking her head. 'No strongbox. Only this'; and here she held up a rolled piece of paper, bound with a black sash and with a white stamp in the centre.

'Let me see...' Ruth examined it. 'This is new; the seal...Barking Abbey?'

Dorothy shrugged. 'No connection to anything I read in David's dissertation. Barking Abbey doesn't actually exist anymore; it was dissolved hundreds of years ago.'

Ruth broke the seal and opened the letter. There, in solid and bold black handwriting was the following message; 'bad luck Amanda; bad luck Ruth;

bad luck Dorothy; bad luck poor innocent little David too. Oh, how handsome Jack is!'

'She knows.' Ruth folded up the paper. 'She knows. I think she's always known.'

Dorothy tensed up almost involuntarily. 'What do we do now then?'

'First up you need to get your friend David well away from this…'

'…that won't be easy. He's in love with Jack to a degree you wouldn't believe; it would be scary if David wasn't so placid by nature.'

'I don't care. He knows nothing of this and it's bad enough we stole his computer files. Get him out of that flat in Islington, far, far away. I don't care what you have to tell him. It shouldn't be hard, with Jack being in Barking right now…'

'Who told you that?'

'Amanda. She keeps me up to date with everything. You need to get those two no-hoper cousins out of there too, if you can; they're as innocent as David in their own way.'

'How do you figure that out? They could be up to their necks in it.'

'Oh please,' Ruth sighed. 'One's gay and the other's short and fat; this is Minty Hardcore we're talking about, remember.'

'I'm on it,' Dorothy fastened the buttons on her coat.

'Oh god.'

'What?!'

Ruth's face was drawn in realisation. 'Jack's in Barking; his favourite cousin, Jessica Woodfield, she was attacked the other day…maybe it's all been planned. Maybe none of it was coincidence?!'

'Maybe,' Dorothy opened her umbrella as the rain began again, 'maybe not. Either way, I'm on it.'

Ruth stepped forward, her hand on the girl's arm. 'Dorothy…please be careful. Even if we're wrong about all of it, and I don't think we are, just go slowly, and keep your wits about you. Minty Hardcore, well she's…'

Dorothy smiled, and her eyes flashed. 'Don't sweat it. I lost Phil to that bitch, but I'll be damned if I'm going let him down and lose Jack to her as well.'

Ruth managed a weary half smile. 'Still the love of your life, eh?'

'That's right,' she threw her a wicked wink, 'who can follow on from Phil Woodfield?! But don't worry about me, you know I can look after myself.' And she straightened a little. 'As I used to tell him when we'd had a lover's tiff, and I wanted to wind him up, Dorothy is the name of the girl who kills witches.'

The Daddy Dissertation Part 10

By David Samuels

What the Daddy does

According to the bedtime tale told by Phil Woodfield to any number of his nephews, nieces, and godchildren during his time as the Daddy, the role originated way back with Jake Woodfield's grandfather, Jaden. Jaden, according to family lore – and bear in mind this isn't common knowledge family lore – would sit under Minty Hardcore's window outside Barking Abbey and fight off all other persons who came with the intent of wooing her, so great was her beauty, and that after he'd mopped the floor with them he'd proudly roll up his sleeve, flex his mighty bicep and call up to her, 'Who's the Daddy, Minty Hardcore?!?'; to which she'd joyously holler back, 'Why you are, Jaden Woodfield!!'

That was about as much as we have of that, though. The first 'real' Daddy of the Woodfield family, one who has a role and a persona comparable to the latter-day examples, has to be Jake Woodfield; he cultivated the persona of the wild young stallion sowing his oats and marching down the middle of the road with his clan in tow, hard drinking but not a drunk, making shrewd investments with the help of those with a better knowledge of such things, and keeping his clan together in one place, making sure the name Woodfield was respected in the local community. This was around 1800, and the earliest uses of the term 'the Daddy' I can find originate in American slang around the same time, but the first time the Woodfields were actually heard to use it outside of bedtime stories is around 1834, at Jake's funeral, when his remaining sons are said to have thrown themselves on his grave crying out, 'He was the Daddy!!'

Beyond that 'Who's your Daddy' seems to have originated in the American underworld, referring to the boss of the gang, or something along similar lines, involving either the idea of a sexually aggressive older man or simply the better fighter between two men, the victor of whom taunts the loser with the admonishment, 'Who's your daddy?!'; any number of these applications applies to the Woodfield males of the 1800s in abundance. As I have said, it was a turn of phrase when Jake died; by the time Christopher was wrestling for control of the family fortune from his nephew Russell it was an actual title, albeit one without any real guidelines.

When Jacob and Jeremiah were born in 1858 there were great celebrations that the family '...would have a new Daddy', and this was the first instance of the boys being searched for Minty Hardcore's 'kiss of thanks for the thighs that thrill me so thoroughly', moments after they were delivered; in Jacob and Jeremiah's case they were the only Woodfield twins to have one identical half of the lip print each, in the likeness of a

Rorschach print. Jacob became the official Daddy simply because he seemed the more level-headed of the two, but it was common knowledge that both men divided up the duties between them; a first and a last for Woodfield twins. But what exactly did these duties entail?

May Woodfield, the mother of Jacob and Jeramiah, seems to have laid down the exact rules of what it meant to be 'the Daddy' in the Woodfield family, to have moulded the turn of phrase into something far more concrete; under May's guidance the Daddy became the man who would basically 'look out' for the entire family in almost every aspect of their lives. Woodfields had looked up to 'the Daddy' before May, but from then on they were positively encouraged to defer all decisions to him. Love matches were run by the Daddy before being cemented, and weddings were not allowed to take place without his express permission. Women who married into the family were made aware of this hierarchy — Jacob's wife Margaret is said to have found the whole idea 'quaint' — and men who married Woodfield women were left under no illusion that their brides would retain the Woodfield name or at the very least use a double-barrelled surname that accentuated the Woodfield family name above his own. Family members were encouraged to go to the Daddy with all of their problems, and he was expected to be savvy enough to sort them out; in Essex this usually meant fisticuffs. Although this may make it sound that the Woodfields of the 1900s ruled through fear and intimidation, this is far from the case; rather they were seen in something of a benevolent light, and there wasn't anyone in Barking or indeed Dagenham, East Ham and beyond who didn't seek out their help, their advice, their muscle, or anything else they had to offer.

By the 1900s the idea of 'witches' still existed in mainstream English culture but was on the wane as the ideas of the enlightenment took hold, and no one took seriously the gossip that as well as muscle, the Woodfield men also had a 'femme fatale' spirit who tipped the odds in their favour, one who was, in the words of Jeramiah Woodfield, quite willing to '…suck your cock until your eyes pop out!'; other tall tales abounded about this mysterious mistress — doubtless deferring to the idea of Minty Hardcore — that they would use her to seduce their enemies, and to dazzle their friends, to read the future for them, and to throw spells and curses of a sexual nature. How the other males in the family — and especially those who married into it — felt about the whole arrangement concerning the Daddy is unclear; no one ever contested the position of the Daddy within the family, and if any of the men who married into it ever did raise objections then they never came to anything. Only Father Billy Harkett, Felicity's husband, made any real bones about it, declaring on more than one occasion that '…no one is going to tell me what to do in my own home no matter how big his bloody cock is!', and this mostly at a time when the family was essentially 'Daddy-less'.

This era of the late nineteen hundreds typifies the image of the Daddy that is put forth today in most circles, that of Jacob or indeed Jeramiah

Woodfield, tall and almost unbelievably handsome, strutting down the Ripple Road in all their finery and topped off with a gold-tipped cane, doffing their hats to girls who dangled out their windows simply to see them pass, a fine mist of testosterone trailing in their wake like engine fuel from a plane.

The Daddy seemed at this point to have held more sway in the town than any officially elected individual, but again there were no instances of resentment or mistrust from any figures of authority.

When the Daddy eventually married great celebrations were held and the wedding was a lavish affair; both Jacob and Jeramiah's wives were celebrated beauties in their own right, but locally it was rumoured that whilst a dalliance with the Daddy might be the most exciting thing to happen to a girl, actually marrying him was another matter entirely, and they would always play 'second fiddle'; doubtless this again meant in regards to Minty Hardcore. Whereas Jake Woodfield fathered bastards left, right and centre, by the time May set the rules of the Daddy down in stone it was deemed that the Daddy should father an heir through legitimate channels, and preferably as soon as possible. Jacob lost his first son but he and Margaret soon had an heir in Gary, born in 1902; their daughters Avis and Agnes were born some years previous and despite a difficult pregnancy Margaret was forced to conceive a boy; gossips of the time whispered that Jacob couldn't give her a healthy child – both Avis and Agnes were considered 'sickly' – and that in desperation he turned to his brother Jeramiah and that it was in fact he who fathered Gary, although this has never been proved.

When Gary died in the Great War Jacob is said to have never recovered, and Margaret went mad with grief. No one was left to fill the gap despite various male cousins coming forward and offering themselves up, and so the burden fell on the two girls, Avis and Agnes to provide sons as quickly as possible; it took them almost fifteen years to produce a healthy child, and in this time May's grandson Alexander acted as something of an unofficial and unelected Daddy, approving Felicity's wedding to the deeply religious Father Billy Harkett, and even signing the papers that committed Margaret to the asylum where she eventually died. In the same vein Alexander's son Rupert is said to have taken up the role when Ben went off the rails in the company of the Kray twins in the 1950s, and when Phil was just a toddler too. Regardless of lineage everyone called Rupert 'Uncle Rupert' in the same way that everyone called Phil 'Uncle Phil' even when they were second-nephews or the like.

In regards to these statements let me elaborate; Agnes gave birth to Ben in 1935 and he was declared 'the Daddy' before he was an hour old, bearing the mark of Minty Hardcore quite clearly. However as he grew up it became quite clear that Ben was in no way fit to take on such a role; he was a simple lad, rough and attractive as a Woodfield male ought to be (although somewhat on the short side), but barely literate and far more interested in larking around with his mates on bomb sites than in guiding the family as it began to splinter from Barking and into the outlying areas of East Ham, Stepney, and Bow. His sister Amanda is said to have been fiercely protective of him, telling relatives that '…if he doesn't want to be the Daddy then just let him be!'

Rupert and Felicity are said to have kept the family going in Barking whilst Amanda headed up her own one-woman crusade to keep Ben out of trouble in Bethnal Green. When Ben died the family threw up its collective arms in despair, turning to Rupert to officially fill the void despite the protests of his wife Michele. This was 1960 and the idea of the Daddy still held a lot of weight, and the East End was still essentially a closed community. When Amanda's sister Andrea gave birth to Phil and was found to bear the clearest mark of Minty Hardcore yet seen the family went on an orgy of drunken revelry that is said to have lasted for days. Phil took the role of the Daddy – as I have previously documented – in a more jovial direction, becoming something of a raconteur and everyone's favourite uncle as opposed to the kind of 'benevolent thug', typified by the likes of Jake and Christopher; although he doled out advice and money he is said to have laughed in the faces of those cousins who asked his approval in the love matches, telling them to make their own minds up. Phil in fact seemed to break the traditional 'alpha male' image of the Daddy in other ways, being gangly and handsome in a rather more 'highbrow' sort of way, and far more fond of a laugh and a game of pool than 'a ruck', although in the tradition of all Woodfield males he had more girlfriends than could be kept count of.

To bring us almost up to date, in tandem with the role of the Daddy we have the urban myth of Minty Hardcore herself. For every male descendant of Jake's, as far as I have been able to ascertain, Minty Hardcore was very much a familiar; that is, a spirit either of a person deceased or simply a 'free-floating spirit' that attaches itself to one person or persons and performs tasks and the like in return for either sexual favours, or simple attention; many familiars are said to be bodiless – the 'free-floaters' - and to adore simply being recognised, above all else. The enemy of the familiar in this day and age would be modern psychiatry, because it dismisses them as figments of at best a warped imagination, or at worst as the result of some sort of psychotic delusion; the Hopkins Institute has a vast library on such matters and I fully intend to investigate it at a later date, and add my findings to a later draft of this work. Witch lore, especially in Essex, contains an abundance of references to these familiar creatures, all of whom have equally bizarre names; Sugar & Sacke, Sathan, Dandy, Cherrypie, Tibb, and so on and so forth. Almost all of these creatures appeared to have 'come through' in the body of an animal, most usually – clichéd as it may be – a cat. Many of the Woodfields kept – and still do – keep cats, but names such as 'Wolvie' and 'Tiggy' do not inspire me to think that these beasts might contain any vestige of supernatural force.

Nowadays you would be hard pressed to imagine Essex as the nexus of witch activity it was in the sixteenth and seventeenth centuries, but this was indeed the case; Matthew Hopkins hunted almost as many witches in Essex as he did in East Anglia, although I've yet to find any documentation to uncover whether he came across any of Jaden Woodfield's ancestors personally; the nuns who cared for his grandsons Jake and his twin Julian are said to have thought the boys descended from the numerous Essex witches of the 1600s; Julian was said to have a small but distinct sixth finger. Jake was the first to develop what has become known as Minty Hardcore's '...kiss of thanks for the thighs that thrilled me so thoroughly'. This mark, both in Jake's case and in the case of the majority of Woodfield males is a large clear red lip print located in the small over the back, over the left or right buttock. Usually only one male in each generation has this mark, although other males in the family may have something similar, something that looks like a port-wine stain, or even a nodule of flesh more in keeping with the traditional image of the 'witch's tit', a point on the body from which the traditional familiar would suckle blood in exchange for performing magical tricks. The portrait of Jake Woodfield that hangs in the British Museum – currently in the vaults undergoing restoration – shows quite clearly a human woman resting on his shoulder peering playfully at the artist, locks of strawberry blond hair falling into her eyes from underneath her brightly coloured sun bonnet; she is comely, and fine; whatever else she is, she is Minty Hardcore. Over the years the Woodfield men have been associated with so many women it is impossible to correlate this depiction of Minty Hardcore with that of any frequent female companions they may or may not have had.

Tales of Minty Hardcore as a delicious young debutante who strayed into Barking on the night before her 'stepping out', and of being flung into the care of the nuns of Barking Abbey by her father when discovered about to be deflowered by Jaden Woodfield are the most common anecdote of this familiar femme fatale, and that the kiss was the one thing she managed to bestow on Jaden of a sexual nature before she was dragged away. If these tales are to be disregarded then the only other option besides that of the familiar is the idea of her as a succubus, that is, a female sex demon who in traditional lore attacks men while they sleep in much the same way that an incubus – a male sex demon – attacks women as they sleep, for some sort of mutual sexual gratification. This is all well and good, but clearly if I am right the relationship had by the time of Jacob and Jeramiah moved to a point where it appears that she has become either dependent or fixated on the Woodfield males for her sexual satisfaction. Historically speaking stories of succubi have reared their head as long as witchcraft has been alive, and possibly before; one source indicates Lilith, Adam's first wife before Eve as the originator in some way or form of this phenomena, although there appears to be no definitive origin for them. As I have said, all definitions of a succubus are that of a female demon that attacks a man as he sleeps, seducing him almost to the point of exhaustion (that Woodfield men die relatively young is a point I shall come back to in reference in the appendix, albeit of natural causes, almost as if their bodies had simply 'worn out'); Minty Hardcore appears to be have been this and far much more. Tragic and often horrific deaths also befell women involved with the Woodfields as far back as Jake's wife Jodie and his mistress Cecilia, and continue to befall Woodfield women to this day, as well as consistent reports of 'accidents', miscarriages, and the like. This further ties in with the second option of Minty Hardcore as a succubus, jealous of the fleshly attentions only a real wife or mistress can endow; was Minty Hardcore jealous of Jake's wife Jodie, and of his mistress Cecilia in this way? There has of course been no record as far as I can tell, of a succubus actually murdering its victim's female companions. Perhaps the Woodfield male killed them himself (this seems highly unlikely in any number of cases, for any number of reasons), because they simply couldn't compare? I doubt I shall ever know. However, the fact remains that no succubus documented has been able to do the things that Minty Hardcore is alleged to have done, to last for as long as she has, and to hold the males of generations of one family in thrall the way that she has.

Or perhaps, given this abundance of contradictory and conflicting information, if I am being completely rational and allowed for one moment to voice a personal over a professional opinion, my theory is that she never existed at all. This is the line of investigation that as a sensible, level-headed human being, in the twenty first century, and as an academic, that I opt for. Jake Woodfield was a showman, and would have had his own reasons for keeping the idea of an 'evil familiar' alive, and we must – and I cannot emphasise this enough – remember that during his time this was still Essex in the early 1800s, the European Enlightenment barely taking hold of England, and doubtless meaning little to anyone who lived in an area more famous for witchcraft than it ever has been for anything else. I believe the idea of Minty Hardcore simply passed down the Woodfield line and became folklore or urban myth, and with her went the role of 'the Daddy'.

When Jack and Jamie were born in 1981, Jack bore the mark of Minty Hardcore even stronger than Phil had; so clear in fact that the doctors and nurses took photographs which they sent off to various dermatologists around the country. Now an adult, Jack physically is a throwback to the more traditional Woodfield male, strongly resembling Jeramiah Woodfield with his icy blond hair, piercing blue eyes and perfectly sculpted, Aryan features, not to mention his considerable height and poise (note to self; edit this passage later and make it slightly more academic and slightly less the summation of my own personal heart's desire), not to mention his confident, masculine attitude tempered with just a tint of metrosexual modernity. How Jack will play out the role of the Daddy in the twenty-first century remains to be seen, if indeed he deems to play it out at all. As to the family familiar, well it appear that perhaps the urban myth of Minty Hardcore may have finally met her match in the form of this modern, educated, metrosexual young man.

Chapter 54

Saturday 27th May 2006

Using Aunt Rachel's house on the Ripple Road – the undisputed childhood home of more Woodfields than any other in Barking - as the location for Aunt Delia's big birthday bash was a bit of a no-brainer, really; on top of the aforementioned, the house was bigger than either Casey or Heath's modest two-up, two-downs, and, as is worth accentuating, was far more steeped in family lore and legend than even the Daddy flat on Station Parade, itself the scene for many a birthday party, Christmas bash, and the occasional baby shower to boot. Woodfields as far back as Jacob and Jeramiah had been born in the front bedroom of the house on the Ripple Road, the bedroom that looked out over the Vicarage Fields shopping centre. 'Mad' Aunt Agnes had brought up Aunt Amanda, her twin brother Ben and their little sister Andrea in this house; Delia herself had been brought up there with her brother Brian, shortly after Agnes's death. Aunt Rachel had moved back there to care for her father Rupert sometime in the early Eighties, and the house had remained in her care and pretty much unchanged ever since.

The long hallway was this Saturday evening festooned from one end to the other with balloons of every size, shape, and colour, not to mention various random lengths of tinsel left over from the previous Christmas. More balloons and tinsel adorned the ceiling and walls of the front room, draped over the large wine cabinet and the showpiece bookcase. The back sitting room was more sedately set out, with various finger foods in glass bowls on the coffee table and perched rather precariously on the sideboards. Aunt Rachel had set out as many family photographs as possible, having spent the previous evening on her hands and knees leafing through old albums for black and white shots of Great-Uncle Alexander, Aunt Queenie in her Woman's Voluntary Service uniform during World War II, and some baby shots of Aunt Delia and Brian, two wide-eyed toddlers staring absent-mindedly away from the camera. A crowning glory shot of the entire family with Uncle Phil at the helm, taken during the Los Angeles trip of 2001, provided the centrepiece of the impromptu display.

Aunt Rachel's sister Hannah had arrived at about four in the afternoon after closing her doormat emporium early, to begin cooking the chicken and ready the salmon, shuffling through the front door with six or seven ASDA carrier bags in her hands, dumping them on the kitchen floor and demanding a cup of tea before she went on with her business. A phone call from Aunt Amanda at five assured them that Hayden had arrived from the 'Scrubs safe and sound, and was ensconced in her house in Bethnal Green until such time as the party was in full swing, whereupon the two of them would descend on the festivities in an unlicensed minicab and give Delia the best birthday present she could hope to wish for, outside of Nick's return also.

As far as music for the party went, Rachel opted for some tried and tested compilation albums that covered every decade from the Sixties onwards, sounds that would be piped rather discreetly early on in the evening but cranked up a notch once it had gotten dark outside and the East Street market was shut up for the day. At midday she had received several confirmation phone calls from old school friends of Delia's, and several more from Woodfields whose other halves could or couldn't make it for various reasons, and she was forced to run out to ASDA to buy more crisps, more ice cream, and a couple more bottles of wine, and another crate of Stella, the Woodfield male ale of choice. Her son Michael used his lunch break from the Barking Dog to help pin up the last of the birthday banners, to blow up the remaining few balloons, and by around five pm Aunt Rachel and her sister collapsed into a heap on the sofa in the sitting room, teas in hand, all but shattered and wondering how on earth they were going to get through a typical Woodfield birthday bash, the likes of which often lasted until the early hours, even for the older generation.

*

The laptop had been piquing Father Brian's curiosity for most of the afternoon, and as he picked out what to wear for his sister's birthday he strolled over to where Jack had left it on the sofa and unfastened the catch, folding open the screen and marvelling at the sheen and lustre of the highly reflective surface, a world away from their own dusty home computer screen, cordoned off on a chipped wooden desk in what should have been a broom cupboard. 'Do be careful with that, dear,' Aunt Betty called out, one eye on him and the other on fitting her earrings in the mirror that hung over the fireplace. 'It belongs to Jack's friend and he'll be very upset if you muck around with it or anything.'

'I'm just having a look...' he took his glasses from their case and put them on, then scanned the names of the various files and shortcuts on the main screen, all of them rather artfully covering a screensaver of Jack relaxing in his shorts in the back garden of the flat in Islington, something that Father Brian regarded with a faint snort of derision. 'You know, I've been thinking about getting one of these,' he said, gently prodding the inbuilt mouse with his finger. 'I think they're marvellous.'

'It's almost time, dear,' Aunt Betty stepped back from the mirror. 'We don't want to be late, do we?'

'Just a minute...' the names of one of the files on the screen had caught his attention; 'Who's the Daddy, Minty Hardcore – 1 of 10'. His finger hovered on the mouse and glided the little icon slowly towards it.

'Well I'm off.' Aunt Betty made for the stairs. 'I'll see you there then.'

'Yes yes,' he clicked on the icon and the Microsoft Word document flared into life.

*

Jamie finished wrapping Aunt Delia's present and sat back, examining his efforts. There was sellotape curling off both ends of the picture, and the white insides of the wrapping paper were visible where he hadn't managed to fold them down properly.

Uncle Phil would have been able to wrap it a treat, he thought, then smacked the top of his thigh as Aunt Amanda had told him to do if he kept on getting those, 'if Uncle Phil had only been here' type thoughts; visualise, but don't mope, is what she'd said. He did a brief visualisation of his sixteenth birthday, and then stuck the label on top of the present. Tiggy the kitten looked up at him with a puzzled expression; Jamie picked him up and talked silly kitten talk for a minute, rubbing his nose against Tiggy's own little wet button, then plopped him down in front of his biscuits and milk, and turned his phone on.

He'd considered bringing Louise from Sight & Sound this evening, to spare any blushes if people started getting the gist of things regarding him and Tiffany, but if the truth were told he was nursing hopes of a reconciliation, fuelled by the idea that Aunt Amanda would be unveiling him as the new Daddy after she'd first unveiled Hayden to a delighted Aunt Delia. Tiffany would be impressed, he knew she would. There'd been a clear signal in sleeping with him that Sunday, he'd known it. That was her way of letting him know she was still interested, even though she was going through some kind of weird personal crisis.

With that thought in mind Jamie made sure his shirt was buttoned correctly, grabbed the present, bounding down the steps to the front door and nipping out onto Station Parade, a spring in his Reeboks and the world at his feet.

*

'Do I look amazing, Jack?' Tiffany asked. She'd gone to town this evening in a way that made their visit to Mayfair the other week look like a day out in Dagenham. 'I never made this much of an effort with Jamie…'

Jack deferred the answer to Daniel, whose eyes were out on stalks as they made the short walk from the Underground, down to the Ripple Road. 'Fit as fuck, man!!' he made the appropriate 'Jafaican' hand gesture. 'Jamie will be well gutted.'

'I'm still kind of in two minds about this,' Jack chewed his lip. 'I might take J aside before the festivities begin, and have a word in his ear.'

'Oh will you relax about the Jamie thing!' Tiffany sighed. 'I think he may well be bringing this Louise with him, so it's no bad. Now Daniel, do you have our little…'

Daniel reached into the pocket of his hoodie, producing a bottle of Southern Comfort, empty of its original contents and now filled with a kind of bluish grey substance that glittered when shook, and then seemed almost to sigh, the way a flower might sigh when it unfurls for the first time. 'Got it!' he unscrewed the lid and took a whiff, and sigh was almost audible, and very, very girlish. 'It smells kind of funky though…'

'What is it?!' Jack paused to examine his reflection in the facade of the Carphone Warehouse directly under the Daddy flat; his choice of River Island short sleeved shirt accentuated his biceps and chest marvellously, and the loafers thrust him to almost 6'3. His crop was newly shawn, but he was still puzzling over whether to wear the gold 'Essex man' neck chain Tiffany had presented to him hours earlier, in the vein of his old Stone Island jacket, as something of an ironical statement. 'Gonna spike the punch bowl, Danny boy?'

Tiffany and Daniel exchanged a knowing glance. 'Yeah,' he nodded.

Jack turned back and took the bottle from him. 'What is it? Is it any good? It's not GHB or Liquid Ecstasy is it, 'coz I reckon some of the older ones might kark it if you introduce this into the mix…'

'It's just something to liven the party up a bit,' Tiffany took the bottle and handed it back to Daniel. 'You know, to give it that extra little something that other parties don't have…'

*

The party got off on a slow but steady rhythm, Aunt Delia declaring, 'Aw my gawd!' when she caught sight of the multiple banners, the balloons, and the corner of the front room partitioned off just to hold all of her presents. Uncle Eddie got a bit of a hug and a lot of a slap for all his discretion, and he even managed a blush when she squeezed his face between her hands and planted the mother of all kisses on his lips.

'Gross,' little Debbie made a face, and then went back to delving her hands in the olive bowl. 'Old people making out makes me want to barf.'

'I think it's sweet,' Jamie looked up at them, then made space on the sitting room couch as several of Aunt Delia's Superdrug co-workers planted themselves there. 'Do you think Uncle Eddie looks well?'

Debbie looked up, slowed down her relentless gum-chewing, studied him and shrugged. 'No different to me, J.'

Jamie sniffed. 'I think he looks okay. So,' and here he sat back, hands behind his head. 'Did you bring a date?'

'Oh please,' she shrugged, 'with my dad here?! I have to listen to him screwing that Carol from the market every night, but if I get fresh with a boy?! Forget it. I might as well become a nun.'

'But you're a looker, kiddo,' Jamie jostled her. 'Go for it! There'll be newbie boys here tonight, right?!'

She removed her gum in order to devour some more olives. 'We'll see. So, did you bring anyone?'

'Nah, no need,' Jamie sniffed. 'Me and Tiffany,' and he leant forward confidentially. 'Well don't say anything to anyone yet, but we're kind of talking about making it up, you know? I think she was just stressed 'coz I was so whacked out by Uncle Phil's death and all, and I was stressed 'coz she was stressed, and…'

'…but she's fucking Jack,' Debbie said matter-of-factly.

'What?!'

'What I said, J,' she popped her gum back in her mouth. 'She's fucking Jack; he's fucking her, whichever way you want to look at it. They've been at it for months. I thought you knew.' And she shrugged. 'I mean, everyone else does.' And with that said she got up off the couch and went to see if her girlfriends were on their way yet, texting frantically on her mobile with the finely honed thumb of a teenager on the rocks. Jamie simply sat there, his eyes wide, that last olive he'd eaten slowly coagulating on his tongue.

*

Aunt Amanda arrived around nine, bustling Hayden discreetly out of the minicab and into the front garden. Climie Fisher's 'Love changes everything' was blaring out through the open front windows, never-the-less almost drowned out by the tandem cocktail of incessant chatter, laughter, and occasional exclamations of surprise. 'Let me look at you, my darling' she said, pulling his hood down. He peered back at her mistrustfully, that same way he regarded everyone. He was very pretty, was Hayden; too pretty, in fact, with his large dark eyes with their smudged eyelids, his pouting perfect cupid's bow of a mouth, his nice jawline, and his hair, the same naturally dark blond as Jamie or Jack's, tousled up into something looking like a candle flame on top and swept over his ears at the sides, neatly squared off at the back, and with 'trendy' sideburns. In regards to the aforementioned, physically he was far more in the mould of Jack, with his great big barrel chest, broad swaggering shoulders, and hands the size of saucers, although whereas Jack's hands were to all intents and purposes immaculate, Hayden's knuckles were mottled and bruised, the result of countless fights, brawls, and temper tantrums, the latter wherein he'd usually turn his rage on the nearest available wall. 'You'll do,' Aunt Amanda said, wetting her thumb and smoothing down his eyebrows. 'You're still a bit of a lady-killer, Hayden Woodfield. What a pouty little mouth you have; prepare for it to be kissed many, many times.'

'Cut it out, Aunt Amanda,' he sighed, brushing her arm away. He spoke in a vague sneer, heavy on the barrow boy, the kind of accent Jack had spent the last four years trying to shed. 'You're worse than a screw!'

'Only where you're concerned,' she tweaked his cheek just that little bit harder than she tweaked anyone else's. They brushed past a couple of family friends from the Barking Dog who were smoking in the doorway and snuck inside. Aunt Rachel saw them coming and, after giving Hayden the complimentary welcome hug, hurried back to ensure that Delia was where she ought to be, and that as many of the others were there also. 'Here we go,' Aunt Amanda took him by the arm. 'Now if gets a little too much just say; you know what these family birthdays can be like…'

Someone turned the music down and then tapped Aunt Delia on the shoulder, urging her to turn herself around, at almost exactly the same time that Aunt Rachel gave Amanda the nod. With a sherry in one hand and a slice of chocolate cake in the other, Delia did as she was told and pivoted on her heel rather deftly for someone of sixty eight, her made-up eyes widening as she caught sight of her youngest twin, his hands in his pockets, blushing and half smiling. 'Hey mum,' Hayden said. 'Guess who got parole?!'

'Oh my gawd.' Her hand went to her mouth, and the tears came to her eyes. 'Oh my little buttercup!!' and she swept him up a cloud of perfume and bangles. 'When did you get out??'

'Thursday,' Hayden returned the hug. 'I've been hiding out at Aunt Amanda's ever since. Nick sends his love, mum. He's out of Grendon in about a week and they're sending him to a bail hostel in Oxford.'

'Almost all my babies are here,' Delia wiped at her eye, glancing around for her husband. 'Eddie? Eddie, look! Look who's here!!'

Uncle Eddie shuffled forward, a pint of Stella in his hand, patted on the back as he went past by cousins Michael and Sara, and by several drinking mates from the Bull pub. 'Dad!!' Hayden's eyes widened. 'You look like shit!'

'Oh love!!' Delia slapped him playfully. 'We all know that but there's no need to say it!'

Uncle Eddie wasn't laughing, however. He nodded and went to say something, then seemed to lose himself and pushed past them and out of the room, past Aunt Queenie in the hall, and out of the front door, narrowly missing cousin Casey and Tamsin as they arrived, the former hollering out, 'Not like you to leave the party so early, Uncle Eddie!!'

*

The earrings didn't match and the perfume seemed to seep out of existence the moment she sprayed it. 'Oh we're going be late,' Bev sighed, turning to Chris. 'I bet Hayden's there already. He's my godson you know, and I've probably missed his big moment.'

'Can't we be fashionably late?' he asked, adjusting his shirt. 'Or maybe we could not go at all!'

'Oh you!!' she pushed against this chest, and they fell into a fairly deep snog that Bev had to call a halt to when he hoisted her up on to the washing machine and hit the spin-dry cycle. 'We really have to be going!!' she snapped. 'Jack and Jamie are going to be there and this time you're going to meet them.'

'I know I know,' he nodded, stepping back. 'And I want to; it's just our little…announcement.'

She held up her ring finger and beamed in delight at the band thereon. 'They'll be as pleased as punch.'

He peered out of the kitchen window, the view onto the train line leading into Barking proper obscured by a fine mist of drizzle. 'I'm going for a quick walk,' he said. 'Clear my head, get rid of these nerves, back in a tick.'

'Alright sweetheart,' Bev accepted the kiss as he passed her, and went to finishing her make-up.

*

The party was in full swing by the time Uncle Richard arrived from Brighton, and the slow but persistent rain had forced those spilling out into the front garden or onto the Ripple Road back inside. All save Bobby, that is, who sat on the wall of the house with a bottle of WKD blue in his hand, his best shirt on, and a rather lost and confused expression on his face. 'That's not much of a party puss, young man,' Uncle Richard came hobbling over, his cane in one hand and Delia's present in the other. 'Has your father been berating you already?!'

'He's not even here,' Bobby sighed. 'Mum's gone home to see where he is. I'm hoping he isn't coming.'

'You have to face him some time, old fart that he is,' Uncle Richard wiped the rainwater off a patch of wall and sat down next to him. 'I heard about Jack laying him out though; best laugh I've had in ages!!'

Bobby laughed too, a little guiltily perhaps. 'I got that job in HMV, you know. The one that I emailed you, telling you I was going for? I start in a week, at Oxford Circus.'

'Splendid!!' Uncle Richard squeezed his shoulder. 'And that's the first step to finding your own place and not just sleeping on an air-bed on Jack's floor.'

'I like sleeping on Jack's floor.'

'So would I, with the aforementioned and that ever-so handsome David walking around in the buff all day,' he chuckled. 'But you need to find your own feet, Bobby Woodfield. Now, are you going to come inside and have some fun?'

Bobby thought about it, then shook his head. 'Everyone's too busy fawning all over Hayden.' And he laughed to himself. 'And you know how it is between him and me.'

Uncle Richard glanced over his shoulder. 'Well he is just out of prison, bless him. Let's hope it's tamed his wild ways. Very well then,' he plucked the bottle from Bobby's hands and took a swig, making a face moments later. 'I shall sit here with you, even if it is murder on my piles.'

*

David was at the top of the stairs, sharing a beer with Jamie's best friend Adam when someone pulled someone else into the hallway below them and said something about, '...Brian. A stroke, I think. They've rushed him to the hospital; Betty found him when she went back to see where he'd got to. Should we tell Delia?!'

''scuse me a sec,' David made his apologies to Adam and hid himself in the toilet. His first thought as he pulled the seat down and sat on it was that Father Brian had looked on the laptop, and how stupid he'd been not to have hidden his dissertation files in a separate, more discreet folder that didn't have them spread out all over that gorgeous desktop of Jack sunbathing. Then again, the stroke and the laptop might not be connected in any way, shape or form. He locked the toilet door, feeling his mouth drying and the effects of a few too many beers kicking in. It had all been going so well, and the family seemed to have accepted him wholeheartedly as Jack's best mate, although the newly feted Hayden Woodfield had looked at him when introduced as though he were something he'd just scraped off the bottom of his steel-tipped shoe.

'Shit.' David said simply, resting his head against the cistern. 'Shit on a stick.'

He flushed the toilet, unlocked the door, making a little talk with the waiting Marie. Then instead of going downstairs took a left and walked up several more stairs and opened the door to the front bedroom. The bed, the carpet, the curtains…everything was white, white and immaculate as though in preparation for the arrival of a saint or something. Many Woodfields had been born in this bed, he knew as much as he sat down on the edge of it, wincing as the springs creaked. He knew because Jack had told him, and that telling had now maybe caused someone's death.

*

Despite Tiffany's assurances Jack went to look for Jamie, to take him aside and congratulate him on his new girlfriend Louise, and then to break it to him gently about himself and Tiffany, probably amending the timescale so he didn't come off looking quite so much of a slag. But Jamie was nowhere to be found. After making the circuit of the entire house he went out into the back garden and gazed up at the sky, at the full moon, and the twinkling vista of stars behind it. 'What the fuck am I doing?!' he said to himself, shaking his head. He had to remind himself of Jessica, of what had happened to her, to make sense of the announcement he would be making in around half an hour. But he said it again anyway; 'What the fuck am I doing?!?'

'Talking to yourself, eh mate?!' said a voice from behind, 'first sign of madness, so they say.'

Jack turned, just as Hayden grabbed him around the neck in a playful headlock. They wrestled, laughing, neither one prepared to give an inch. Hayden was about the only one big enough to take Jack on, even in jest. They fell against the fence and it creaked in protest, and upstairs the back curtain twitched as someone peered out to watch them play. 'Who's the Daddy?!' Hayden grinned, securing his grip. 'Say 'Who's the Daddy!"

'Fuck you!!' Jack half laughed, and pivoted left, and the both of them went down onto the wet grass, staining their trousers, but they were laughing, and when they stopped laughing they were hugging, slapping each other on the back. 'So fucking good to see you, mate,' Jack squeezed him as hard as he could, and even planted a gentle kiss on the top of Hayden's head as he rose; the only bloke who could do that was Jack. 'God I've fucking missed you,' he went on. 'Jack, back with the lad!'

'Missed you too, you big blond tosser,' Hayden grinned, getting to his feet and dusting himself down. 'You're looking good.'

'So are you,' Jack nodded. 'Prison suits you!'

'I was runnin' the place,' Hayden waved a hand dismissively. 'They was shit scared me, all'a them plastic gangsters! poofs, the lot of them!'

Jack's face darkened. 'I could've done with you back ages ago. You won't believe the shit that's been happening.'

'Yeah? Aunt Amanda told me some…'

Jack shook his head. 'It's like…the family's falling to bits and it's up to me to save it. I feel like I have no choice; I mean, I was gonna just tell them to get on with it, but then 'jess…some bloke…' and his nostrils flared and his jaw clenched. 'I'm off for summer, from university. They need me.'

Hayden nodded. He turned back and looked at the window, where Tiffany was watching them. She blew them both a kiss, and let the curtain fall into place. 'You're the one, Jack,' he said. He put his mottled hands on Jack's shoulders. 'I'll back you up, all the way. You know it.'

Jack nodded, and they hugged, slapping each other on that back again and generally being very manly about it all. 'I know, mate,' he said. 'I know.'

*

The music of modern times gave way to a more Seventies feel as Aunt Delia found out who had control of the CD player and accosted them accordingly. Jack and Tiffany fast became the golden couple in the front room, dancing to everything from the Twist to the Conga, the latter of which resulted in a rather crowded pile-up on the stairs when it was deemed too wet for the family to attempt to conga their way down the Ripple Road and back again. Aunt Amanda impressed everyone by doing the Charleston with Delia and Aunt Queenie, but her bad hip gave her trouble and she retired to the kitchen, where Tiffany was pouring fresh drinks for the latest arrivals. 'You really ought to be taking it easy, Ms. Woodfield,' she said, setting said drinks down on a tray and hefting them up with considerable panache. 'You're always on the go, you are. Always on the go.'

'That I am,' Amanda dabbed her brow with a napkin and poured herself an orange juice. 'You haven't seen Jamie, have you Tiffany? He and I had an important announcement to make and I swear, I haven't seen him since I brought Hayden in. He didn't want to miss tonight for the world…'

'Speaking of big announcements,' Tiffany led the way back into the crowded front room. 'Jack and I are about to make one too.'

'Really?' Amanda raised an eyebrow. 'Are you sure that's not a little insensitive, given you and Jamie…'

'Oh it's not that, silly,' Tiffany laughed, handing Aunt Hannah her Bacardi and coke and joining Amanda back in the hallway. 'But don't you worry about it. You're an old lady, if you don't mind my saying so. And yet there you are, up and down the Bethnal Green Road every day, still doing afternoons in Woolworths, why you're a credit to most of the women your age. When my old mother was your age she hardly even moved from her chair, you know?'

'Oh Tiffany your mother can't be more than…' Amanda stopped suddenly. 'What did you say?'

'You've always gone against the grain haven't you, Ms. Woodfield?' Tiffany set the tray down and leant against the wall, near the telephone, her arms folded. 'I've heard some tales about you in my time, I can tell you!!'

Aunt Amanda straightened up, alert as if she'd been a flagging battery that someone had suddenly recharged. 'Where's Jamie?'

Tiffany glanced at her watch. 'Oh, about halfway down the District Line by now, I'd say; he didn't even stop to pick up a picture of his dear old Uncle Phil.'

'Who are you??' Aunt Amanda's eyes narrowed.

'Why I'm Tiffany of course,' she turned on her heel and made her way into the front room, to find Jack near the window talking anxiously with the newly returned Hayden. She turned back, adding, 'You've known me for the last six years, Ms. Woodfield.'

'Who are you?!?' Aunt Amanda shouted, grabbing her arm, almost jerking her off her feet. The music died, and those present, around twenty or thirty Woodfields plus friends and drinking partners turned and looked. 'Where's Jamie?!'

'Let go of me, you sick old woman!' Tiffany pulled away. 'Jack, she's hurting me!!'

'Aunt Amanda!!' Jack stepped forward, gently peeling Aunt Amanda's fingers from Tiffany's bare arm. 'Cool it! 'tiff, what's going on?!'

'She's not Tiffany, Jack!' Aunt Amanda made a grab for his arm next. 'She isn't Tiffany!!' and then she clocked it, their body language; she gave his own bicep, so much bigger than Jamie's, a little squeeze. 'The one that got away...' she nodded, 'how stupid of me.' And she turned on Jack. 'For once in his life Jamie actually got something ahead of you, and you couldn't bear it! Oh, you are petty and spiteful, Jack Woodfield!!'

'Me?!?' he seemed genuinely taken aback. 'You want to ask your precious Jamie the real reason he got with 'tiff here, back then!'

Tiffany pouted. 'Oh dear, she seems genuinely surprised.'

'Jamie's not the little angel you think he is, Aunt Amanda,' Jack said. 'And I'm not protecting him anymore. I've tried and fucking tried to build bridges with him, and even after Uncle Phil, well he just doesn't want to know. So I give up.' And he seemed satisfied with this, although his jowls were clenching and unclenching as though trying to force the words out. 'If he doesn't want to acknowledge he has a big brother, then fine. As far as I'm concerned, Hayden's the only brother I've got.' and he turned and nodded to Hayden, watching with by the window with folded arms.

'Mum, come away now,' Uncle Heath stepped forward, handing his can of Stella to Casey and taking hold of Aunt Amanda by the shoulders. 'You've had a bit too much to drink...'

'She isn't Tiffany!!' Aunt Amanda fought against him, a finger pointed accusingly at the aforementioned. 'She's Minty Hardcore!!'

'My god...' Tiffany shook her head sadly as they plucked her out of the room. 'She really is sick.'

*

Her make-up was fine, her hair was fine, and her outfit was fine, finally. Bev did one more twirl in front of her mirror, just as she heard the sound of the door to the flat opening, then closing, albeit closing rather slowly, almost as if someone were trying to stifle the sound. She smiled at the thought of Chris trying to sneak up on her, and how much she enjoyed being accosted by him when he did so. 'I know you're there, sweetheart!' she called out. 'Come on, we've got an engagement to announce!'

There was no reply. The light in the living room had been switched off, but the dull glow of other lights spilling in through the windows lent a kind of eerie lambency to the room, and made a vague illumination of the tall shape standing by the fireplace, hands clasped reverentially before it. 'Stop messing around, sweetheart,' Bev sighed, picking her handbag off the sofa. 'We're late enough as it is.'

The figure stepped out of what little light there was, and Bev put her hand to her mouth. It wasn't Chris; it wasn't Chris at all. It was a nun; a nun in full clerical garb, the sternest of expressions on her face, her eyes so large they almost bulged out of her face, full of reprimands yet to come, and stern commandments from various passages of the Good Book. 'Who are you?!' Bev gasped, pulling back, 'how did you get in here?!'

*

The rain had all but petered out, but Bobby and Uncle Richard were still drinking on the front wall when Hayden came out to join them, his hands in his pockets, absent-mindedly kicking at an empty can of Stella one of the party-goers had abandoned, watching it rattle along the salmon-grey brickwork of the Ripple Road. 'Your mum hasn't come back yet, has she Bobby?' he put one foot on the wall next to Bobby and glared rather menacingly down at him.

Bobby swallowed, and tried not to meet his gaze. 'It's good to see you,' he said softly.

Hayden nodded, a somewhat thin-lipped smirk spreading over his perfect cupid's bow. Then he turned. 'Hiya, Uncle Richard. You're looking pretty shit too, as it goes. Are you and my dad in some sort of club for old-aged mingers or something?!'

'Hayden.' Uncle Richard tipped his can graciously. 'Trust a bad penny...'

'Your dad's in bad shape, Bobster,' Hayden sat down beside him, and lolled an arm around his shoulder, '"leastways that's what I heard just now; better make your peace with him before he departs this mortal coil forever.'

'What do you mean?!' Bobby stood up, taking his confrontational attitude and running with it. 'Who told you that?!'

'She did.' He nodded to the window, where Tiffany was peering through the curtain at them. She blew Hayden a kiss and then let the curtain fall back into place. 'She thinks it's quite fitting the family faggots have to sit on the doorstep instead of partying with the normal folk inside.'

'Nice to see some things never change,' Uncle Richard rolled his eyes, readied himself to stand. 'And here I harboured a silly idea that prison might've made you grow up a little, young Hayden. Now why don't you clear off.'

Hayden began to laugh. And the more he laughed the darker it got, and the lights in the street seemed to suck themselves somehow into his laughter, and to illuminate him as such. Sometimes there was a nun there, the sternest nun you ever saw, hands clasped together reverentially, eyes glowering. The lights died and then there was only the nun, and Hayden was nowhere to be seen. The nun screeched, something so feral it was almost like a cat cry; 'Too many filthy poofs in this family!!' and her hand, with its gnarled fingers and its liver spots, went straight for Bobby.

*

The door to the front bedroom opened and Tiffany peered around it, satisfying herself that David was alone before stepping in and closing it firmly behind her. 'I do so love it when a plan comes together,' she said.

David looked up, deep in thought. 'Huh? Oh, hello Tiffany. Is everyone having a good time?'

'A marvellous time.' She clasped her hands before her, reverentially, 'a positively marvellous time. We're about to unveil Jack as the Daddy, just as it should be, just as it should have been from the moment Phil died.'

'What?!' Jack had made no mention of this, anything but, in fact. He met her gaze. 'Listen, that's all well and good, a grand party game even; 'pin the tail on the Daddy', but have you heard anything of Jack's Uncle Brian? I was on the stairs and I overheard someone saying…'

'Oh he's not long for this world, I think.' her face was stony. 'He read your dissertation, you naughty little boy. All those family secrets and such, and you hadn't even changed the names yet. And him with such a weak heart as well. Jack's punch may not have finished him off, but I think you certainly have.'

David stood up. 'How do you know about my dissertation? Jack and I never told…'

She took another step forward. 'It was a fun thing to do, to let Jack get his family grievances off his chest, but enough, now. I've given him some slack, now it's time to tighten the leash. I haven't come this far to be stopped by a two-bit hack like you.'

The light in the room was fading, and suddenly, very suddenly in fact, his head was spinning; it was suddenly like being drunk when everything tips sideways and up becomes indiscernible from down. He steadied himself on the wall, and she was right there, in his face, only it was an old woman's face, enshrouded in the veil of a nun, glaring up at him. 'Away from my Jack, you filthy little poof,' she spat, 'away from my family.'

*

Jack stood dead centre of the front room, his arms folded. Funnily enough it was little Debbie who stood on a chair and shouted everyone to silence. 'Got kind of an important family announcement to make!!' she rolled her eyes and clicked her gum in her mouth. 'It concerns the Daddy!!' and she turned, with a grand theatrical sweep of her arms. 'Fire away, Jack.'

There was relative silence, pricked only by Uncle Heath's protests as Aunt Amanda beat a way through to the very front, almost to the position Tiffany had now taken up as pride of place beside her man. 'Ok now,' Jack spread his arms wide. 'Most of you might never have thought you'd hear me say this, but, one psychoanalysis exam pending, I'm coming back to Barking for the summer. And I'm coming back, well…proper, like.'

'What he's trying to say is, he's going to be the Daddy,' Tiffany nodded. 'Isn't that the most wonderful news?!' she scanned their faces. 'Well I think it's wonderful, and I'm not even a Woodfield!!'

'What's going on, Jack?' cousin Michael hollered, and seconds later someone else seconded the thought.

'I'm going to solve everything,' Jack gave them his most winning smile, like the lid being lifted on the keys of a piano, turning to Tiffany, who nodded and whispered sweet encouragement. 'I'm going to deal with what happened to Jessica…'

'It's already been dealt with, my pet,' Tiffany touched his bare forearm lightly, playing with the hairs she found there. 'I forgot to tell you. It's been dealt with.'

''k,' he nodded, seeming satisfied.

'Tell them you're going to deal with Uncle Eddie's cancer too,' she whispered to him.

'Ok,' he nodded. 'And…Uncle Eddie has cancer?!'

'Just tell them, Jack.'

He cleared his throat. 'And I'm gonna take care of Uncle Eddie's cancer…' The assembled Woodfields gasped when they heard this; they had known nothing of it, least of all Aunt Delia, who almost dropped her glass. '…and Uncle Richard, well he has AIDS, but that's being dealt with as we speak…'

'Love the sinner, hate the sin,' Tiffany nodded, her hands clasped before her, like a nun might clasp them.

'Who told you about Richard?!' Aunt Amanda had to be held back by Uncle Heath and by Springer. 'Where is Jamie?!'

'I'm going to be everything Uncle Phil was, and more,' Jack climbed onto the chair provided by little Debbie, who stood on the opposite side of him to Tiffany, arms folded; Hayden soon joined them, looking every inch the plastic gangster himself. 'I'm going to look after Aunt Queenie,' Jack said. 'I'm going to settle things between Bobby and his dad; I'm going put Daniel back on track; I'm going to keep Laquisha safe from racists, and make sure none of you gets any ideas about voting BNP; in short, I'm going to do everything Uncle Phil would have done, and a shitload more besides.'

'What he said,' Debbie nodded, and to this Tiffany purred contentedly.

*

The nun came forward almost at angle, her hands emerging from the billows of her jet black robe. 'I can't have you around, can I?!' she hissed, as Bev backed away. 'Not with you being almost as big a tart…'

'I don't know what you're talking about!!' Bev backed into the kitchen, and tripped over the umbrella stand. 'You're in the wrong flat!!'

'We can't both save him,' the nun was framed in the doorway; she was the doorway. 'I can't brook your constant annoying interference.'

'Who are you?!'

'Who am I?!' the nun's face was so close she could smell the breath, the fetid breath of stained teeth. 'I'm a trap, my dear!!'

*

She was just the nun now, and Hayden was gone. Sometimes it seemed like he was standing behind her, smiling, his arms folded. 'Bobby, get in the house!!' Uncle Richard tried to push him over the wall and succeeded only in overbalancing himself, all his weight taken on his cane, which splintered in the process. 'Get in the house, now!'

Why was the Ripple Road empty, this time on a Saturday night?!? As Bobby made for the door the nun shrieked again, the awful scream of an old woman in a nightmare; her hand darted out and traversed the distance between where she was, and where he was. She caught him and he screamed, and he felt the bite of her sharp, chipped fingernails as she turned him around in her hands, like putty, and put those claws to his face. 'I only want real men,' she hissed. 'Proper Essex men, of which you, my child, I regret to say, are not one.'

*

David's phone went. It was on vibrate and it seemed to shake him out of his funk, and it even gave Tiffany pause. David answered the incoming call. It was Dorothy. 'David?!' her voice was almost audible in the still of the front bedroom. 'Christ, I've been trying to get through to you for hours, but the signal was all messed up. Listen...'

'Dorothy?' David felt scared, as scared as he'd been as a child when he would be sent to bed for some minor misdemeanour or other, to lie there in his room all alone, and imagine someone watching him at the window. 'Dorothy, something's wrong.'

'You bet it is. Now listen to me. Wherever you are, get out. Go somewhere public, somewhere where there are a lot of people; text me when you get there, and wait for me to come and get you. She can't do anything if there are lots of people around, Phil always told me that; she can't do anything if there are people who don't believe. She...' and then the signal began to break up.

'Dorothy?!' David shook the phone, 'Dorothy?!'

'Interfering old cow,' Tiffany knocked the mobile out of his hand. 'I have to admit though, I never saw her coming. Phil was clever, almost as clever as that sly old Aunt Amanda; running to the Hopkins Institute for help after Rose died...'

'You're scaring me, Tiffany,' David fell back, back onto the bed. She stepped on his mobile, her heel going straight through the screen.

'Quite fitting,' she stood over him, and he was swallowed in her shadow. 'You're so fascinated by this family, it's fitting you should end up on this bed. But you know too much, and I'm afraid that little laptop of yours will have to be disposed of too. We can't have people reading about the Woodfields as though they were some sort of exhibition; we can't have them reading about me.'

'Tiffany, please...'

'Jack doesn't need you anymore.' She was older, older and almost a pillar of black now. 'Not now that Hayden is back, Hayden is his best friend; Hayden always was. And Hayden doesn't think filthy thoughts about him like you do, all the time you lusting after my beautiful Jack...'

David wept. 'I'm sorry...'

'May God have mercy on you,' the nun hissed as she crossed herself. 'You are an abomination.'

*

'Does anyone here have a problem with this??' Jack looked at the lot of them, at the faces of his aunts and uncles, his cousins, friends and their friends. 'Because I can do it, you know. I've been having...lessons.' And here he turned to Tiffany, who made a demure bow. She sidled closer and clung to him, running her hands up and down his big, hairy arms. 'Are you ok?' he said, spotting what no one else had, a fine film of sweat on her brow. 'You look a little...'

'It takes concentration...' she said softly.

'What does?'

'Never you mind,' and she seemed to regain her composure a little. 'Isn't he every inch what a proper Daddy should be?!' she purred, 'tall and handsome and so, so in control. Doesn't he remind you of Jeramiah, with his blue eyes and his broad shoulders?!' and here she rustled Jack's crop lovingly. 'He'll make Phil proud. Things have been allowed to get out of hand. Jack will take control; Jack is ever so manly.'

'Who's the Daddy?!' Hayden called out, knocking a plume of balloons out of the way with the back of his hand. 'Who's the Daddy?!'

'Who's the Daddy!!' little Debbie thrust her fist up. 'Who's the Daddy?!?'

There was silence, but it was Uncle Heath, much to Amanda's astonishment, who took up the call. 'Who's the Daddy?!' he said, his can of Stella raised in a toast. 'Who's the Daddy?!?'

*

Bev whimpered; she whimpered like when she'd been six or seven and her Aunt Amanda told her fairy tales at bedtime, tales of Minty Hardcore, and how she seduced their Great-Great-Uncle Jaden, that awful tale of that mean old nun and the awful things she'd done in the name of liking men like Jaden. She opened her eyes one last time and the nun's face was still there. It was the only thing she saw, it was that close, and it made her stop whimpering finally, and start screaming.

*

Tiffany flung her arms around Jack's neck. 'Kiss me, Jack!!' she commanded, as all around them the chants grew louder, their sources ever more diverse. 'Kiss me!'

'We've done it, babe,' he lifted her off her feet, as Laquisha shook a champagne bottle and blew the cork off, burying them in bubbly. 'I did it all for you, 'tiff. I just wanted to make you happy.'

'I am happy, my pet,' she purred in his ear. 'The happiest I've been in…well, since nineteen eighty one, at least.'

Jack pulled back slightly. 'Huh?'

'Nothing,' her left leg arched as his arms went around her waist, up and down her back. 'Kiss me, and be my big strong Daddy.'

Jack did as he was told, and then pulled back. 'I love you, 'tiff,' he whispered, and just for a moment he thought of Jamie, and his happiness discoloured, albeit briefly. 'I love you,' he said again, to make it go away.

'And I love you, my pet,' Minty Hardcore declared, over the cheers and the cries, her fingers on the firm line of his jaw, directing his lips back toward her own. 'With all my slutty little heart.'

To be continued.

Made in the USA
Charleston, SC
22 September 2013